PHILIPPA GREGORY

THE LITTLE HOUSE

A NOVEL

HarperCollins*Publishers*

HarperCollins books may be purchased for educational, business, or sales promotional use. For information please write: Special Markets Department, HarperCollins Publishers, Inc., 10 East 53rd Street, New York, NY 10022.

FIRST EDITION

Designed by Christine Weathersbee

Library of Congress Cataloging-in-Publication Data

Gregory, Philippa.
    The little house : a novel / Philippa Gregory.
      p.   cm.
    ISBN 0-06-017670-9
    I. Title.
PR6057.R386L58   1996
823'.914—dc20   96-24337

96 97 98 99 00 ❖/HC 10 9 8 7 6 5 4 3 2 1

THE LITTLE HOUSE

✷— One —✷

On Sunday morning, on almost every Sunday morning, Ruth and Patrick Cleary drove from their smart Bristol flat to Patrick's parents' farmhouse outside Bath. They had only been married for four years and Ruth would have preferred to linger in bed, but this Sunday, as almost every Sunday, they had been invited for lunch. Patrick always enjoyed returning to his home. It had once been a dairy farm, and Patrick's father had sold off the land, only retaining a circle of fields around the house, a little wood, and the winding drive. The house itself was lovely: an eighteenth-century manor farm of yellow Bath stone. While never being so vulgar as to lie, the Clearys liked to suggest that their family had lived there since the farmhouse had been built. Patrick's father was fond of claiming that he came from Somerset yeoman stock. But it was not true. It had been a clever purchase in the mid-1960s, and the profit, as house prices had risen and land prices had rocketed, would make a small fortune should they ever wish to sell.

Patrick's mother opened the door as they came up the path. She was always there when they arrived, ready to fling open the door in welcome. Once Ruth teased Patrick, saying that his mother spent her life crouched in front of the brass letterbox, peeping out so that she could throw open the door as her son arrived, wrap him in her arms, and say, "Welcome home, darling." Patrick had looked offended, and had not laughed.

1

"Welcome home, darling," his mother said.

Patrick kissed her, and then she put out her arms to Ruth and kissed Ruth's cheek. "Hello, dearest, how pale you look. Have you been working too hard?"

Ruth was surprised to find that immediately she felt exhausted. "No," she said.

"Freddie, they're here!" Ruth's mother called into the house, and Patrick's father appeared in the hall.

"Hello, old boy," he said lovingly to Patrick. He dropped an arm briefly on Patrick's shoulder and then turned to Ruth and kissed her. "Looking lovely, my dear. Patrick—saw you on television last night, the piece on the commuters. Jolly good. They used a bit of it on *News at Ten*. Good show."

Patrick grimaced. "It didn't come out how I wanted," he said. "I had a new film crew and they all had their own ideas. I might be the reporter, but none of them want to listen to me."

"Too many chiefs and not enough Indians," Frederick pronounced.

Ruth looked at him. He often said a sentence, like a little motto, that she had never heard before and that made no sense to her whatsoever. They were a playful family, sometimes quoting family jokes or phrases of Patrick's babytalk that had survived for years. No one ever explained the jokes to Ruth; she was supposed to laugh at them and enjoy them, as if they were self-explanatory.

"That's shoptalk," Patrick's mother said firmly. "Not now. I want my assistant in the kitchen!"

It was one of the Sunday rituals that Patrick helped his mother in the kitchen while Ruth and Frederick chatted in the drawing room. Ruth had tried to join the two in the kitchen once or twice and had glimpsed Patrick's indispensable help. He was perched on one of the kitchen stools, listening to Elizabeth and picking nuts from a bowl of nibbles she had placed before him. When Ruth had interrupted them, they had looked up like two unfriendly children and fallen silent. It was Elizabeth's private time with her son; she did not want Ruth. Ruth was sent back into the sitting room with the decanter of sherry and instructions to keep Frederick entertained. She learned that she must wait for Patrick to put his head around the door and say, "Luncheon is served, ladies and gents." Then Frederick could stop making awkward conversation with her and say, "I could eat a horse! *Is* it horse again?"

Elizabeth served roast pork with cracklings, applesauce, roast potatoes, boiled potatoes, peas and carrots. Ruth wanted only a little. In Bristol in the canteen of the radio station where she worked as a journalist, she was always hungry. But there was something about the dining room at the farmhouse that made her throat close up. Patrick's father poured red wine and Ruth would drink two or three glasses, but she could not make herself eat.

Patrick ate a good lunch, his plate always favored with the crunchiest potatoes and the best cuts of meat, and always had seconds.

"You'll get fat," his father warned him. "Look at me, never gained a pound till I retired from the army and had your mother's home cooking every day."

"He burns it all up," Elizabeth defended her son. "His job is all nerves. He burns it all up with nervous energy."

They both looked at Ruth, and she managed a small uncomfortable smile. She did not know whether to agree that he would get fat, which would imply an unwifely lack of admiration, or agree that he lived on his nerves, which would indicate that she was not protecting him from stress.

"It's been a devil of a week," Patrick agreed. "But I *think* I may be getting somewhere at last."

There was a little murmur of interest. Ruth looked surprised. She did not know that Patrick had any news from work. She wondered guiltily if her own work, which was demanding and absorbing, had made her neglect his ambition. "I didn't know," she said.

He smiled his wide, handsome smile at her. "I thought I'd wait to tell you until it was shaping up," he said.

"No point in counting chickens," his father agreed. "Spill the beans, old boy."

"There's talk of a new unit, to do specialist local film documentaries," Patrick said. "It'll be headed by a news producer.

The best news producer we've got." He paused, and smiled his professionally modest smile. "Looks like I'm in line for the job."

"Good show."

"Wonderful," Patrick's mother said.

"What would you do?" Ruth asked.

"Regular hours!" Patrick replied with a little chuckle. "That's the main thing! I'd still do reports to camera but I wouldn't be on call all the time, and I'd not be running around out of hours. I'd have more control. It's an opportunity for me."

"Is this a bubble-size celebration?" Patrick's father demanded of Ruth.

She looked at him blankly. She simply had no idea what he meant.

"Champagne, darling," Patrick prompted. "Do wake up!"

"I suppose it must be." Ruth stretched her mouth in a smile, trying to be bright and excited. "How wonderful!"

Patrick's father was already on his way to the kitchen. Elizabeth fetched the special champagne glasses from the sideboard.

"He's got a bottle already chilled," she said to Patrick. Ruth understood that this was significant.

"Oh ho!" Patrick said as his father came back into the room. "Chilled already?"

His father gave him a roguish wink and expertly opened the bottle. The champagne splashed into the glasses. Ruth said, "Only a little please," but no one heard her. She raised her full glass in a toast to Patrick's success. It was a very dry wine. Ruth knew that dry champagne was the right taste; only inexperienced, ill-educated people liked sweet champagne. If she continued to make herself drink it, then one day she too would like dry champagne and then she would have an educated palate. It was a question of endurance. Ruth took another sip.

"Now I wonder why you were keeping a bottle of champagne on ice?" Patrick prompted his father.

"I have some grounds for celebration—but only if you two are absolutely happy about it. Your mother and I have a little proposition to put to you."

Ruth tried to look intelligent and interested but the taste of the wine was bitter in her mouth.

"It's Manor Cottage," Frederick said. "On the market at last. Old Miss Fisher died last week and, as you can imagine, I was onto her lawyer pretty quick. She left her estate to some damn-fool charity . . . cats or orphans or something . . ." He broke off, suddenly embarrassed, remembering his daughter-in-law. "Beg pardon, Ruth. No offense."

Ruth experienced the usual stab of pain at the thought of her lost parents, and smiled her usual bright smile. "It doesn't matter," she said. "It doesn't matter at all."

"Well, anyway," said Frederick, "the house will be sold at once. I've waited for years to get my hands on it. And now, with you getting into more regular hours, it's ideal."

"And the land?" Patrick asked.

"The garden, and the field, and that copse that joins our bit of wood. It rounds off our land to perfection."

"Pricy?" Patrick asked.

Frederick laid his finger along his nose to indicate inside knowledge. "Her lawyer is the executor. And the charity won't be putting it up for auction. They'll want a quick, simple sale. The lawyer will take the first reasonable offer."

"Who's the lawyer?" Patrick asked.

Frederick grinned—this was the punch line. "*My* lawyer," he said. "As it happens. By happy coincidence. Simon Sylvester."

Patrick chuckled. "We could sell our flat tomorrow."

"We should make a handsome profit on it," his father concurred. "You could stay here while the cottage is being done up. Couldn't be better."

"If Ruth agrees," Elizabeth reminded them.

Both men turned at once to her. "I don't quite . . ." Ruth said helplessly.

"Manor Cottage is on the market at last," Patrick said. "Come on, darling, the little house at the end of the drive. The one I've always had my eye on."

Ruth looked from one bright impatient face to another. "You want to buy it?"

"Yes, darling. Yes. Wake up!"

"And sell our flat?"

They nodded.

Ruth could feel that she was being slow, and worse than that, unwilling.

"But how would I get to work? And we like our flat."

"It was only ever a temporary base," Frederick said. "Just a little nest for you two young lovebirds."

Ruth looked at him, puzzled.

"A good investment is only worth having if you're ready to capitalize," he said firmly. "When the time is right."

"But how would I get to work?"

Elizabeth smiled at her. "You won't work forever, dearest. You might find that when you have a family-sized house in the country you feel like giving up work altogether. You might have something else to keep you busy!"

Ruth looked blankly to Patrick.

"We might start a family," he translated.

Frederick gave a shout of laughter. "Her face! Dear Ruth! Have you never thought about it? We could be talking Chinese!"

Ruth felt her face stiff with stupidity. "We hadn't planned . . ." she said.

"Well, we couldn't really, could we?" Patrick confirmed. "Not while we were living in town in a poky little flat, and my hours were all over the place, and you were working so hard. But promotion, and Manor Cottage, well, it all comes together, doesn't it?"

"I've always lived in town," Ruth said. "And my job means everything to me. I'm the only woman news producer on the station—it's a real responsibility, and this week I broke a national story—" she glanced at Patrick. "We scooped you," she reminded him.

He shrugged. "Radio is always quicker than telly."

"We were going to travel . . ." she reminded him. It was an old promise. Ruth was an American child—her father a concert pianist from Boston, her mother an Englishwoman. They had died in the quick brutality of a road accident on a winter visit to England when Ruth was only seven years old. Her mother's English family had taken the orphaned girl in, and she had never seen her home again. When Ruth and Patrick had first met, he had found the brief outline of this story almost unbearably moving and had promised Ruth that they would go back to Boston one day, and find her house. Who knew—her childhood toys, her books, her parents' things might even be in storage somewhere, or forgotten in an attic. And part of the chasm of need that Ruth carried with her always might be filled.

"We still can," he said quickly.

"We'll finish this bottle and then we'll all go down and look at Manor Cottage," Frederick said firmly. "Take my word for it, Ruth, you'll fall for it. It's a little peach. Bags of potential."

"She's not to be bullied," Elizabeth said firmly. "We might think it paradise to have the two of you on our doorstep, but if Ruth doesn't want to live so close to us, she is allowed to say no."

"Oh, it's not that!" Ruth said quickly, fearful of giving offense.

"It's just the surprise of it," Patrick answered for her. "I should have warned her that you've had your eye on that for years and you *always* get your own way."

"Amen to that!" Frederick said. The father and son clinked glasses.

"But I like our flat," Ruth said.

❦

Ruth borrowed a pair of Elizabeth's Wellington boots for the walk, and her waterproof jacket and her headscarf. She had not come prepared, because the afterlunch walk was always Frederick's time alone with Patrick. Usually Elizabeth and Ruth cleared the lunch table, stacking the plates in the dishwasher, and then sat in the living room with the Sunday papers to read and Mozart on the hi-fi. Ruth had once gone with the men on their walk, but after a few yards she had realized her mistake. They strode along with their hands buried deep in their pockets, shoulder to shoulder in a silent enjoyable communion. She had delayed them at stiles and gates because they had felt bound to hold her hand as she clambered over them, or warn her about mud in gateways. They had kept stopping to ask if they were going too fast for her or if she was tired. Their very generosity to her and concern for her had told her that she was a stranger, and unwelcome. They wasted no politeness on each other. With each other they shared a happy, wordless camaraderie.

The next Sunday Frederick announced: "Time for my constitutional," and then he had turned to Ruth: "Will you come with us again, Ruth? It looks like rain."

As she had hesitated, Elizabeth said firmly, "You two run along! I won't have my daughter-in-law dragged around the countryside in the rain! Ruth will stay here with me and we can be cozy. We'll kick our shoes off and gossip."

After that, the two men always walked alone after lunch and Ruth and Elizabeth waited for them to return. There was no kicking off of shoes, and no gossip. Elizabeth was a naturally formal woman, and they had no friends in common. Ruth always asked after Miriam, Patrick's elder sister, who was teaching in Canada. Miriam was always well. Elizabeth asked after Ruth's work, which was filled with drama and small triumphs that never sounded interesting when retold, and asked after Ruth's aunt, who had brought her up after the death of her parents. Ruth always said that she was well, but in truth they had lost contact except for Christmas cards and the occasional phone call. Then there was nothing more to say. The two women leafed through the newspapers together until they heard the dog scrabbling at the backdoor and Elizabeth rose to let him in and put the kettle on for tea.

Ruth knew that Manor Cottage mattered very much to everyone when she was invited on the walk, especially when Elizabeth walked too.

They went across the fields, the men helping the women over the stiles. They could see the Manor Cottage roof from two fields away, nestling in a little valley. The footpath from the farmhouse led to the back gate and into the garden. The drive to the farmhouse ran past the front door. There was a stream that ran through the garden.

"Might get a trout or two," Frederick observed.

"As long as it's not damp," Elizabeth said.

Frederick had brought the key. He opened the front door and stepped back. "Better carry her over the threshold," he said to Patrick. "Just for luck."

It would have been awkward and ungracious to refuse. Ruth let Patrick pick her up and step over the threshold with her and then put her down gently in the little hall and kiss her, as if it were their new house, and they were newlyweds, moving in.

The old lady's rickety furniture was still in the house and it smelled very faintly of damp and cats' pee. Ruth, with a strong sense of her alien childhood, recognized at once the flavor of a house that the English would call full of character, and that her father would have called dirty.

"Soon air out," Frederick said firmly. "Here, take a look."

He opened the door on the sitting room, which ran the length of the cottage. At the rear of the cottage were old-fashioned French windows leading to a muddy garden, desolate under the November sky. "Pretty as a picture in summer," he said. "We'd lend you Stephens. He could come over and do the hard digging on Tuesdays. Mow the lawn for you, trim the hedges. You'd probably enjoy doing the light stuff yourself."

"So relaxing," Elizabeth said, with a nod to Ruth. "And very therapeutic for Patrick!"

They turned and went into the opposite room. It was a small dark dining room, which led to the kitchen at the back overlooking the back garden. The backdoor was half off its hinges, and damp had seeped into the walls. There was a large old-fashioned china sink, with ominous brown stains around the drain hole, and an enormous ash-filled, grease-stained coal-burning range. "Oh, you'll have such fun with this!" Elizabeth exclaimed. "Ruth, how I envy you! It's the sweetest little room, and you can do so much with it. I can just imagine a real farm-house kitchen—all pine and stencils!"

A laurel bush slapped waxy green leaves against the kitchen window and dripped water mournfully on the panes. Ruth gave a little shiver against the cold.

"Upstairs is very neat," Frederick observed, shepherding them out of the kitchen through the dining room and back into the hall. "Pop on up, Ruth. Go on, Patrick."

Ruth unwillingly led the way upstairs. The others followed behind her, commenting on the soundness of the stairs and the attractive banister. Ruth hesitated on the landing.

"This is so lovely," Elizabeth said, throwing open a door. "The master bedroom, Ruth. See the view!"

The bedroom faced south, down the valley. It was a pretty view of the fields and in the distance a road and the village.

"Sunny all the day long," Frederick said.

"And here are two other bedrooms and a bathroom," Elizabeth said, gesturing to the other doors. She led Ruth to see each of them. "And this *has* to be a nursery!" she exclaimed. The pretty little room faced over the garden. In the cold autumn light it looked gray and dreary. "Roses at the window all the summer long," Elizabeth said. "Look! I think you can just see our house!"

Ruth obediently looked. "Yes."

She turned and led the way downstairs. While the others returned for a second look at the damp kitchen, Ruth went outside and waited in the cold front garden. When they emerged, all smiling at some remark, they looked at her expectantly, as if they were waiting for some pronouncement that would make them all happy, as if she should say that she had passed an exam, or that she had won the lottery. They turned bright, hopeful faces on her, and Ruth had nothing to offer them. She felt her shoulders lift in a little shrug. She did not know what they expected her to say.

"You *do* love it, don't you, darling?" Patrick asked.

"It's very pretty," she said.

It was the right thing to say. They looked pleased. Frederick closed the front door and locked it with the care of a house-holder. "Ideal," he pronounced.

Patrick slipped his arm around her waist. "We could go ahead, then," he said encouragingly. "Put the flat on the market, make an offer on this place, move house."

Ruth hesitated. "I don't think I want . . . "

"Now, stop it, Patrick," Elizabeth said reasonably. "You've only just seen it. There's lots to take into account. You have to have a survey done, and you have to have your own flat valued.

Ruth needs time to get adjusted to the idea; it's a bigger change for her than anyone!" She smiled at Ruth conspiratorially: the two women in league together. "You can't rush us and make a decision all in one afternoon! I won't allow it!"

Patrick threw her a mock salute. "All right! All right!"

"It's a business decision," Frederick supplemented. "Not simply somewhere to live. You and Ruth might have fallen in love with it, but you have to be sure it's a good investment too." He smiled fondly at Ruth and tapped her on the nose with the house key before putting it into his pocket. "Now don't turn those big eyes on me and tell me you have to have it, little Ruth. I agree, it looks like an excellent bargain for the two of you, but I shall let my head rule my heart on this one."

"Hark at him!" Elizabeth exclaimed. She slipped her hand in Ruth's arm and led her around the corner of the house to the back garden. "He's determined to have the place, and he makes it sound like it is us who are rushing him. Come and see the garden! It's just bliss in summer. A real old-fashioned cottage garden. You can't plant borders like this in less than twenty years. They just have to mature."

Ruth trailed after Elizabeth to the back garden and obediently admired the decaying, dripping wallflowers and the seedpods of stocks. At the back of the flower bed were the tall dead spines of delphiniums and before them were bloated pods of last season's love-in-the-mist. The lawn was soggy with moss; the crazy-paved pathway was slick with lichen and overgrown with weeds.

"Best way to see it," Frederick said. He picked a stick and switched at a nettle head. "See a property in the worst light and you know it. There's no nasty shocks hidden away. You know what you're getting. If you love it like this, little Ruth, then you'll adore it in summer."

"I don't think I could really . . ." Ruth started.

"Good gracious, look at the time!" Elizabeth exclaimed. "I thought I was missing my cup of tea. It's half past four already. Frederick, you're very naughty to drag us down here. Ruth and I are faint for tea!"

Frederick looked at his watch and exclaimed in surprise. They turned and left the garden. Ruth plucked at Patrick's sleeve as he went past her. "I can't get to work from here," she said swiftly. "It'd take me hours to get in. And what about when I have to work late? And I like our flat."

"Hush," he said. "Let them have their little plans. It doesn't do any harm, does it? We'll talk about it later. Not now."

"Here, Patrick!" his father called. "D'you think this is a legal right of way? Can you remember, when you were a boy, was there a footpath here?"

Patrick gave her a swift, encouraging smile and joined his parents.

Ruth was quiet at tea, and when they finally pulled away from Manor Farm with a homemade quiche and an apple crumble in the usual Sunday box of home-cooked food on the backseat, she still said nothing.

They were in an awkward situation. Like many wealthy parents, Frederick and Elizabeth had given the newlyweds a home as their wedding present. Ruth and Patrick had chosen the flat, but Frederick and Elizabeth had bought it for them. Ruth dimly knew that shares had been sold, and sacrifices made, so that she and Patrick should start their married life in a flat that they could never have afforded, not even on their joint salaries. House prices might be falling after the manic boom of the mid-eighties, but a flat in Clifton would always have been beyond their means. Her gratitude and her sense of guilt showed itself in her sporadic attempts at good housekeeping, and her frenzied efforts to make the place look attractive when Frederick and Elizabeth were due to visit.

She had no investment of her own to balance against their generosity. Her parents had been classical musicians—poorly paid and with no savings. They had left her nothing, not even a home; their furniture had not been worth shipping to the little girl left in England. Patrick's family were her only family, the flat was her first home since she had been a child.

Frederick had never delivered the deeds of the flat to Patrick.

No one ever mentioned this: Patrick never asked for them, Frederick never volunteered them. The deeds had stayed with Frederick, and were still in his name. And now he wanted to sell the flat, and buy somewhere else.

"I've loved that cottage ever since I was a boy," Patrick volunteered, breaking the silence. They were driving down the long sweeping road toward Bristol, the road lined with gray concrete council housing. "I've always wanted to live there. It's such luck that it should come up now, just when we can take it."

"How d'you mean?" Ruth asked.

"Well, with my promotion coming up, and better hours for me. More money too. It's as if it was meant. Absolutely meant," Patrick repeated. "And d'you know I think we'll make a killing on the flat. We've put a lot of work in, we'll see a return for it. House prices are recovering all the time."

Ruth tried to speak. She felt so tired, after a day of well-meaning kindness, that she could hardly protest. "I don't see how it would work," she said. "I can't work a late shift and drive in and back from there. If I get called in on a story it's too far to go; it'd take me too long."

"Oh, rubbish!" Patrick said bracingly. "When d'you ever get a big story? It's a piddling little job, not half what you could do, and you know it! A girl with your brains and your ability should be streets ahead. You'll never get anywhere on Radio Westerly, Ruth, it's small-time radio! You've got to move on, darling. They don't appreciate you there."

Ruth hesitated. That part at least was true. "I've been looking . . ."

"Leave first, and then look," Patrick counseled. "You look for a job now and any employer can see what you're doing, and how much you're being paid, and you're typecast at once. Give yourself a break and then start applying and they have to see you fresh. I'll help you put a demo tape together, and a CV. And we could see what openings there are in Bath. That'd be closer to home for you."

"Home?"

"The cottage, darling. The cottage. You could work in Bath very easily from there. It's the obvious place for us."

Ruth could feel a dark shadow of a headache sitting between her eyebrows on the bridge of her nose. "Hang on a minute," she said. "I haven't said I want to move."

"Neither have I," Patrick said surprisingly. They were at the center of Bristol. He hesitated at a junction and then put the car into gear and drove up toward Park Street. The great white sweep of the council chamber looked out over a triangle of well-mowed grass. Bristol Cathedral glowed in pale stone, sparkled with glass. "I would miss our little flat," he said. "It was our first home, after all. We've had some very good times there."

He was speaking as if they were in the grip of some force of nature that would, resistlessly, sell their flat, which Ruth loved, and place her in the countryside, which she disliked.

"Whether I change my job or not, I don't want to live in the back of beyond," she said firmly. "It's OK for you, Patrick, it's your family home and I know you love it. But I like living in town, and I like our flat."

"Sure," Patrick said warmly. "We're just playing around with ideas; just castles in the air, darling."

On Monday morning Ruth was slow to wake. Patrick was showered and dressed before she even sat up in bed.

"Shall I bring you a cup of coffee in bed?" he asked pleasantly.

"No, I'll come down and be with you," she said hastily getting out of bed and reaching for her dressing gown.

"I can't stay long," he said. "I'm seeing Ian South this morning, about the job."

"Oh."

"And I'll ring the estate agent, shall I? See what sort of value they'd put on this place? So we know where we are?"

"Patrick, I really don't want to move. . . ."

He shooed her out of the room and down the hallway to the kitchen ahead of him. "Come on, darling, I can't be late this morning."

Ruth spooned coffee and switched on the filter machine.

"Instant will do," Patrick said. "I really have to rush."

"Patrick, we must talk about this. I don't want to sell the flat. I don't want to move house. I want to stay here."

"*I* want to stay here too," he said at once, as if it were Ruth's plan that they move. "But if something better comes up we would be stupid not to consider it. I'm not instructing an estate agent to sell, darling. Just getting an idea of the value."

"Surely we don't want to live down the lane from your parents," Ruth said. She poured boiling water and added milk and passed Patrick his coffee. "Toast?"

He shook his head. "No time." He stopped abruptly as a thought suddenly struck him. "You don't imagine that they would interfere, do you?"

"Of course not!" Ruth said quickly. "But we would be very much on their doorstep."

"All the better for us," Patrick said cheerfully. "Built-in baby-sitters."

There was a short silence while Ruth absorbed this leap. "We hadn't even thought about a family," she said. "We've never talked about it."

Patrick put down his coffee cup and turned to go, but he swung back as a thought suddenly struck him. "I say, Ruth, you're not opposed to it, are you? I mean, you do *want* to have children one day, don't you?"

"Of course," she said hastily. "But not . . ."

"Well, that's all right then." Patrick gave his most dazzling smile. "Phew! I suddenly had the most horrid thought that you were going to say that you didn't want children, like some ghastly hard-bitten career journalist. Like an awful American career woman with huge shoulder pads!" He laughed at the thought. "I'm really looking forward to it. You'd be so gorgeous with a baby."

Ruth had a brief seductive vision of herself in a *broderie anglais* nightgown with a fair-headed, round-faced, smiling baby nestled against her. "Yes, but not for a while." She trailed behind him as he went out to the hall. Patrick shrugged himself into his cream-colored raincoat.

"Not till we've got the cottage fixed up as we want it and everything, of course," he said. "Look, darling, I have to run. We'll talk about it tonight. Don't worry about dinner, I'll take you out. We'll go to the trattoria and eat spaghetti and make plans!"

"I'm working till six," Ruth said.

"I'll book a table for eight," Patrick said, dropped a hasty kiss askew her mouth, and went out, banging the door behind him.

Ruth stood on her own in the hall and then shivered a little at the cold draft from the door. It was raining again; it seemed as if it had been raining for weeks.

The letter flap clicked and a handful of letters dropped to the doormat. Four manila envelopes, all bills. Ruth saw that the gas bill showed red print and realized that once again she was late in paying. She would have to write a check this morning and mail it on her way to work or Patrick would be upset. She picked up the letters and put them on the kitchen counter, and went upstairs for her bath.

⁂

*T*he newsroom was unusually subdued when Ruth came in, shook her wet coat, and hung it up on the coatstand. The duty producer glanced up. "I was just typing the handover note," he said. "You'll be short-staffed today, but there's nothing much on. A fire, but it's all over now, and there's a line on the missing girl."

"Is David playing hooky?" she asked. "Where is he?"

The duty producer tipped his head toward the closed door of the news editor's office. "Getting his cards," he said in an undertone. "Bloody disgrace."

"What's the matter?"

"Cutbacks is what," he said, typing rapidly with two fingers. "Not making enough money, not selling enough soap powder, who's the first to go? Editorial staff! After all, any fool can do it, can't they? And all anyone wants is the music anyway. Next thing we know it'll be twenty-four-hour music with not even a DJ—music and adverts, that's all they want."

"Terry, stop it!" Ruth said. "Tell me what's going on!"

He pulled the paper irritably out of the typewriter and thrust it into her hands. "There's your handover note. I'm off shift.

I'm going out to buy a newspaper and look for a job. The writing's on the wall for us. They're cutting back the newsroom staff: they want to lose three posts. David's in there now getting the treatment. There are two other posts to go and no one knows who's for the chop. It's all right for you, Ruth, with your glamour-boy husband bringing in a fortune. If I lose my job I don't know what we'll do."

"I don't exactly work for pocket money, you know," Ruth said crossly. "It's not a hobby."

"OK," he said. "Sorry. We're all in the same boat. But I'm sick of this place, I can tell you. I'm off shift now and I'm not coming back till Wednesday—*if* I've still got a job then." He strode over to the coatrack and took his jacket down. "*And* it's still bloody raining," he said angrily, and stormed out of the newsroom, banging the door behind him.

Ruth looked over to the copy taker and raised her eyebrows. The girl nodded. "He's been like that all morning," she said resignedly.

"Oh." Ruth took the handover note to the desk and started reading through it. The door behind her opened and David came out, the news editor, James Peart, with him. "Think it over," James was saying. "I promise you we'll use you as much as we possibly can. And there are other outlets, remember." He noticed Ruth at her desk. "Ruth, when you've got the eleven o'clock bulletin out of the way, could you come and see me?"

"Me?" Ruth asked.

He nodded. "Yes," he said, and went back into his office and closed the door.

There was a brief, shocked silence. Ruth turned to her oldest friend. "What did he say to you?" she asked David.

"Blah blah, excellent work, blah blah, frontiers of journalism, blah blah, first-class references, blah blah, a month's pay in lieu of notice and if nothing else turns up why don't you freelance for us?"

"Freelance?"

"The new slimline Radio Westerly," David said bitterly. "As few people as possible on the staff, and the journalists all freelance, paying their own tax and their own insurance and their own phone bills. Simple but brilliant." He paused as a thought struck him. "Did he say you were to see him?"

"After the eleven o'clock," Ruth said glumly. "D'you think that means that I'm out too?"

David shrugged. "Well, I doubt it means you've won the Sony Award for investigative journalism. D'you want to meet me for a drink after work? Drown our sorrows?"

"Yes," Ruth said gratefully. "But perhaps I won't have sorrows to drown."

"Then you can drown mine," David said generously. "I'd hate to be selfish with them."

Ruth rewrote the bulletin, one eye on the clock. At the desk behind her David made telephone calls to the police, the fire station, and the ambulance, checking for fresh news. He sounded genuinely interested; he always did. She remembered him from journalism college: when everyone else would groan at a news-gathering exercise, David would dive into little shops, greet shop assistants with enthusiasm, and plunge into the minutiae of local gossip.

"Anything new?" she threw over her shoulder.

"They're mopping up after the fire," he said. "There's an update on the conditions from the hospital. Nothing too exciting."

She took the slip of copy paper he handed to her, and went into the soundproofed peace of the little news studio. The door closed with a soft hiss behind her, Ruth pulled out the chair and sat before the desk to read through the bulletin in a murmured whisper, marking on her copy the words she wanted to emphasize, and practicing the pronunciation of difficult words. There had been an earthquake in the Ural Mountains. "Ural Mountains," Ruth whispered. "Ural."

At two minutes to eleven the disc jockey's voice cut into her rehearsal. "News coming up! Are you there and conscious, Ruth?"

"Ready to go," Ruth said.

"Thank the Lord for a happy voice from the newsroom. What's up with you guys today?"

"Nothing," Ruth said frostily, instantly loyal to her colleagues.

"We hear of massive cutbacks, and journalists out on the streets," the DJ said cheerfully.

"Do you?"

"So who's got the push?"

"I'm busy now," she said tightly. "I'll pop down and spread gloom and anxiety in a minute. Right now I'm trying to read a news bulletin."

He switched his talkback button off. Ruth had a reputation for a quick mind and a frank turn of phrase at the radio station. Her headphones were filled with the sound of the record—the Carpenters. "We've only just begun. . . ." Ruth felt her temper subside and she smiled. She liked romantic music.

Then the disc jockey said with his carefully learned mid-Atlantic accent: "Eleven o'clock, time for Radio Westerly news with Ruth Cleary!"

He announced her name as if there should have been a drum-roll underneath it. Ruth grinned and then straightened her face and assumed her solemn news-reading voice. She read first the national news, managing the Ural Mountains without a hitch, and then the local news. At the end of the bulletin she read the local weather report and handed back to the DJ. She gathered the papers of the bulletin and sat for one short moment in the quiet, gathering her reserves together. If David had been sacked then it was unlikely that they would be keeping her on. They had joined at the same time from the same college course, but David was probably the better journalist. Ruth straightened her back, opened the swing door, and emerged into the noise of the newsroom. She passed the script of the bulletin to the copy girl for filing and tapped on the news editor's door.

James Peart looked so guilty she knew at once that he would make her redundant. He did.

"This is a horrible job," James said miserably. "David and you, and one other. It's a foul thing to have to do. But I have suggested to David that he look at freelancing and I was going to suggest to you that you look at putting together some light documentary programs. We might have a slot for some local pieces: family interest, animals, children, local history, that sort of thing in the afternoon show. Nothing too ambitious, bread-

and-butter stuff. But it's the sort of thing you do rather well, Ruth. If you can't find full-time work, you could do that for us. We'd lend you the recording equipment, and you could come in and use the studio. And you'd get paid a fee and expenses, of course." He broke off. "I know it's not much but it would keep your hand in while you're looking round."

"Bread-and-butter?" Ruth asked. "Sounds more like slop."

James grimaced. "Don't shoot the messenger, Ruth," he said.

"Who shall I shoot then?" she said. "Who's responsible for putting me, and David, and someone else out of a job?"

He shrugged. "Market forces?" he offered.

"This is rubbish," she said firmly. "Why didn't you tell them that you couldn't run the newsroom understaffed?"

"Because my job's on the line too," he said frankly. "I did tell them that we should keep the staff, but if I make too many waves then I'm out as well. I can't lose my job for a principle, Ruth."

"So I lose mine for the lack of one?"

He said nothing.

"We should have had a union," she said stubbornly.

"Yes," he said. "Or better contracts, or better management, or more profits. But those days are gone, Ruth. I'm sorry."

She was silent.

"Look, there's nothing I can do but offer you freelance work," he said. "I'll do my best to use everything you do. You're a good journalist, Ruth, you'll make it. If not here, then London. And I'll give you good references. The best."

Ruth nodded. "Thanks," she said shortly.

"Maybe Patrick knows of something in television," James suggested. "He might be able to slot you in somewhere. That's where the money is, not radio."

"He might," Ruth said. Patrick had never, in the whole length of their relationship, expressed any admiration for Ruth's work. He thought radio journalism was parochial and uninteresting.

James got up and held out his hand. "You'll work till the end of the week, and then take a month's salary," he said. "I do wish you luck, Ruth. I really wish this hadn't happened. If things look up at all then you'll be the first person I'd want to see back on the staff."

Ruth nodded. "Thank you," she said.

"If there's anything at all I can do to help . . ." he said, showing her toward the door.

Ruth thought of her inability to pay the bills on time and run the flat as it should be run, of Patrick's legitimate desire for a meal when he came home after working all day. Of Patrick's pay rise and the ascendancy of his career. Maybe a period of freelance work would be good for them both.

"I'll be fine," she said. "Don't worry. It looks like it's all falling into place."

She rang to leave a message for Patrick that she would be home late, but would meet him at the restaurant, and she ran through the rain to the pub. Although it was barely opening time, David was sitting up at the bar and was smiling and lightly drunk.

"Flying start," he said genially. "I took the sensible course of a vodka tea."

"Gin and tonic," Ruth said, hitching herself up onto the barstool. "Double."

"You got the push too?"

"I did."

"What did he suggest? Freelancing for *Panorama*? Career opportunities on *News at Ten*? Or you could go back to the States and run CNN?"

"It's odd," Ruth said with mock thoughtfulness. "He didn't mention any of them. Probably thought they were beneath me."

David made a face. "Poor bastard's doing his best," he said. "He promised me if I went freelance they'd use my pieces, and I could come into studio to edit for free."

Ruth nodded. "He offered me the same. Suggested I do local bread-and-butter stuff for the afternoon program."

"It's a great business the media!" David said with sudden assumed cheeriness. "You're never out of work. You're either resting or freelancing. But you're never unemployed."

"Or taking time out to start a family," Ruth said. She screwed her face up at him in an awful simper. "I think the first few years are so precious! And I can always come back into it when the baby starts school."

"Boarding school," David supplemented. "Stay home with him until he sets off for boarding school. Just take eleven years off. What's that, after all? It'll pass in a flash."

"No child of mine is boarding! I think a mother should stay home until the children are grown," Ruth said earnestly. "University age at least."

"First job," David corrected her. "Give them a stable start. You can come back to work twenty-one years from now."

"Oh, but the grandchildren will need me!" Ruth exclaimed.

"Ah, yes, the magic years. So you could come back to work when you're . . . perhaps . . . sixty?"

Ruth looked thoughtful. "I'd like to do a couple more months before I retire," she said. "I really am a career girl, you know."

They broke off and smiled at each other. "You're a mate," David said. "And you're a good journalist too. They're mad getting rid of you. You're worth two or three of some of them."

"Last in, first out," Ruth said. "You're better than them too."

He shrugged. "So what will you do?"

Ruth hesitated. "The forces are massing a bit," she said hesitantly. She was not sure how much to tell David. Her powerful instinctive loyalty to Patrick usually kept her silent. "Patrick's parents have a cottage near them that has come up for sale. Patrick's always wanted it. He's getting promoted, which is more money and better hours. And we have been married four, nearly five years. There is a kind of inevitability about what happens next."

David had never learned tact. "What d'you mean: what happens next? D'you mean a baby?"

Ruth hesitated. "Eventually, yes, of course," she said. "But not right now. I wanted to work up a bit, you know. I did want to work for the BBC. I even thought about television."

"You always said you were going to travel," he reminded her. "Research your roots. Go back to America and find your missing millionaire relations."

"If I'm freelance that'll be easier."

"Not with a baby," David reminded her.

Ruth was silent.

"I suppose there *is* such a thing as contraception," David said lightly. "A woman's right to choose and all that. We are in the nineties. Or did I miss something?"

"Swing back to family values," Ruth said briskly. "Women in the home and crime off the streets."

He chuckled and was about to cap the joke but stopped himself. "No, hang on a minute," he said. "I don't get this. I never thought you were the maternal type, Ruth. You don't really want a baby, do you?"

Ruth was about to agree with him, but again her loyalty to Patrick silenced her. She nodded to the barman to give them another round of drinks and busied herself paying him. "You don't understand," she said. "Patrick's got this very established conventional sort of family, and he's a very conventional sort of man. . . ." She looked to see if David was nodding in agreement. He was not.

"They're very influential," she said weakly. "It's very difficult to argue with them. And of course they want us to move house, and of course, sooner or later, they'll expect a baby."

"Come on," David said irritably. "It'll be you that expects it, and you that gives birth. If you don't want to have a baby, you must just say no."

Ruth was silent. David realized he had been too abrupt. "Can't you just say no?"

She turned to look at him. "Come on, David," she said. "You know my background. You were with me at college. I never had any family life worth a damn. When I met Patrick and he took me home, I suddenly saw somewhere I could belong. And they took me in, and now they're my family. I don't want to spoil that. We see them practically every Sunday. . . ."

"D'you know what I do on Sunday mornings?" David suddenly asked. "I don't get up till eleven. I take the papers back to bed with me and read all the trivial bits—the travel sections and the style sections and the magazines. When the pubs open I walk across the park to The Fountain and I have a drink with some people there. Then I take away a curry back home, and I read all the papers, and watch the telly. Then if I feel energetic I go for a jog. And if I feel lazy I do nothing. And in the evening I go round to see someone I like, or people come round and see me. I can't imagine having to be polite all day to someone's mum and dad."

"They're *my* mum and dad," she said.

He shook his head. "No, they're not."

He saw, as she turned away from him, that he had gone too far. "Sorry," he said. He shifted his barstool closer and put his hand on her knee. "Tell you what, come back to my flat with me," he said. "I'll read last Sunday's papers to you."

Ruth gave him a wan smile, picked up his hand, and dropped it lightly in his lap. "Married woman," she said. "As you well know."

"Wasted on matrimony," he said. "That sexy smile of yours. I should have taken my chance with you when I had it, when you were young and stupid, before you found Prince Charming and got stuck in the castle."

"Don't be silly," she said. "I'm very happy."

David bit back the response. "Well, we both are!" he said lapsing into irony again. "What with our vivid emotional lives and our glittering careers! Speaking of which—what about our glittering careers? What will you do?"

"I'll look round," she said. "And I will do some local pieces for James. I can keep my hand in and they won't look bad on a CV. What about you?"

"I need a job," David said. "I can freelance for a week or so, but when the money runs out I need a paycheck. I'll be sweeping the streets, I reckon."

Ruth giggled suddenly, her face brightening. "Walking them more like," she said. "A tart like you. You could pop down to the docks."

David smiled back at her. "I try to keep my self-respect," he said primly. "But if you know any rich old women I could be tempted. What about your mother-in-law? Would she fancy a fling with a young gigolo? Is she the toyboy type?"

Ruth snorted into her drink. "Absolutely," she said. "You could pop out on Sunday afternoons and rendezvous in that bloody cottage!"

ℝ *Two* ℝ

Ruth was late at the restaurant, and her high spirits evaporated when she saw Patrick's sulky face over the large menu.

"Sorry, sorry, sorry," she said as she slipped onto the bench seat opposite him. "I went out for a drink with David from work and I didn't watch the time."

Patrick's bright blue eyes widened in surprise. "Well, thanks very much," he said. "I hurried here to be with you and then I sit here on my own while you go boozing with some guy from work."

"He's just been made redundant," Ruth said. "And I was too."

Patrick, who had been about to continue his complaint, was abruptly silenced. "What?"

"I've been made redundant," Ruth said. "Me and David and someone else. We're all out at the end of the week with a month's pay in hand. They offered us freelance work."

Patrick's face was radiant. "Well, what a coincidence!" he said. "Aren't things just working out for us?"

"Not exactly," Ruth said rather tartly, fired by David and by two double gins. "I wanted to keep my job; and if I left it I wanted to go somewhere better. I didn't want to get the sack and have a baby as second best."

Patrick quickly summoned the waiter. "D'you want spaghetti, darling? And salad?"

"Yes."

25

Patrick ordered and poured Ruth a glass of wine. "You're upset," he said soothingly. "Poor darling. How disappointing. Don't feel too bad about it. We'll look round. We'll find you another job. There must be people who would snap you up. You're so bright and a damn fine journalist."

Ruth's mouth quivered. "I *liked* it there!" she said miserably. "And I was doing some really good stories. I even scooped your lot a couple of times."

"You're an excellent journalist," he said. "That's why I'm so confident you'll find work at once somewhere else . . . if you want it."

As Ruth lifted her head to protest, he held up his hand. "Not another word!" he said. "You've had a shock. We won't talk plans tonight. Not a word about jobs or flats or cottages. Not a word! Let me tell you about the interview I did with Clark today— you'll die."

Patrick told Ruth a story and she laughed politely. Their food came and Patrick continued to lay himself out to please her. He was witty and he could be charming. Ruth, enjoying the mixture of red wine and gin, found herself laughing at his stories and capping them with stories of her own. It was midnight before they left the restaurant, and Patrick put his arm around her as they walked home together.

"I love you," he said softly in her ear as they opened the front door and went into the warm hall.

They went upstairs together and Ruth turned to embrace him in the bedroom. Patrick held her close and kissed her with warm, seductive kisses. It was so unusual for them to make love during the week that Ruth was slow to respond. She stayed in his arms, content to be kissed, her eyes closed.

"Into bed with you, Mrs. Cleary," Patrick said and gave her a little push toward the bed. Ruth lay back and stretched luxuriously. Patrick dropped his head and nudged sexily at her breasts, his hands pushing up her skirt until he found the waistband of her tights.

"Patrick!" Ruth said. She half sat up. "Perhaps I had better go to the bathroom!" she said. She meant that she needed to put in her diaphragm, their only contraception.

"I want you," he said urgently. "I want you right now."

Ruth gasped with surprised delight at his urgency. He was stripping down her tights and panties, and kicking off his own shoes. Ruth giggled drunkenly, delightedly.

"I *have* to go," she protested.

Patrick shucked off his trousers and pants in one swift movement and swarmed up over her, kissing her neck and her ears. His hand reached behind her back and undid her bra, slid his hand under the lace and caressed her breast. Ruth felt her desire rising, felt herself careless, sexy, urgent.

"Come on, Ruth," he whispered. "Like when we were first lovers. Let's take a chance. Let's take a sexy chance, Ruth. I want to be right inside you with nothing between us. Come on, darling, I want to."

His fingers stroked insistently between her legs. Ruth, drunk on wine and drunk with desire, protested inarticulately but could not bring herself to stop. In a small sober part of her mind she was watching him, calculating the days from her last period, fearing the sudden rush of his desire, terrified of pregnancy.

He rolled on top of her, moving steadily and deliciously, Ruth opened her legs and felt her desire rise and rise to match his, but then her caution chilled her. "Patrick, we shouldn't . . ." she started to say.

With a sudden delighted groan he came inside her.

⁂

*R*uth's routine changed little after her week's notice expired and she became freelance. She left home at the usual time and she came home, if anything, later than usual. It was as if she were afraid that any slackening would prompt Patrick to exploit her unemployment.

"You could take it easy," he said on the first Monday.

"Better not," Ruth said. "I want to show them I'm serious about getting work."

Patrick had not pursued his theme—that Ruth could rest, or could tidy the flat, or could visit his mother and see the cottage. He had kissed her and left for work. He was in less of a hurry now in the mornings. He strolled to his car and let the engine warm and the light frost melt from the windshield before he drove away. He no longer had to be in at the television newsroom first; he now had status. He had a parking slot of his own outside the building and a secretary who had to be in before him to open his mail. Patrick's stock had risen dramatically, and his timekeeping could decline. Some mornings in November it was Ruth who was up first and Patrick who lured her back to bed. On at least two mornings they made love without contraception. Patrick had been urgent and seductive and Ruth could not refuse him. She was flattered by his desire and enchanted by its sudden urgency. One morning she was half asleep as he slid inside her and she woke too slowly to resist. One morning she acquiesced with a sleepy smile. Escaping pregnancy the first time, she was becoming reckless.

In mid-December she felt nauseated in the mornings and felt tired at work. She was trying to persuade the afternoon show producer to commission a series on local Bristol history.

"Something about industry," she suggested. "From shipbuilding to building Concorde at Filton airfield. We could call it *Bristol Fashion*."

"Sounds a bit earnest," he criticized.

"It could be fun," she said. "Some old historical journals. I could read them. And some old people talking about working on the docks and in the aircraft industry before the war. There's loads of stuff at the museum."

He cocked an eyebrow at her. "Are you sure? Oh, well, maybe. See what you can dig up. But nothing too dreary, Ruth. Nothing too historical. Bright and snappy. You know the kind of thing."

She closed his office door quietly behind her and went to the ladies' room. She ran the cold-water tap and splashed cold water on her face and rinsed her mouth.

One of the newsroom copy takers, combing her hair before the mirror, glanced around. "Are you all right, Ruth? You look as white as a sheet."

"I feel funny," Ruth said.

The woman looked at her a little closer. "How funny?"

"I feel really sick, and dreadfully tired."

The woman gave her a smiling look, full of meaning. "Not up the spout, are you?"

Ruth shot her a sudden wide-eyed look. "No! I can't possibly be."

"Not overdue?"

"I don't know . . . I'd have to look. . . . I'm a bit scatty about it. . . ."

The woman, with two children of her own at school, shrugged her shoulders. "Maybe it's just something you ate," she said.

"Probably," Ruth said hastily. "Probably that's all."

The woman went out, leaving Ruth alone. She looked at herself in the mirror. Her fringed pale face, her large dark eyes. She looked scared, she looked sickly. Ruth shook her head. She could not see herself as a woman who might be pregnant. She had an image of herself as a girl too young, too unready for a woman's task of pregnancy.

"It's something I ate," Ruth said to her reflection. "It's bound to be."

◈

$\mathcal{S}$he bought a pregnancy test kit on the way home from work and locked herself in the bathroom with it. There were two little test tubes and a collecting jar for urine and immensely complicated instructions. Ruth sat on the edge of the bathtub and read them with a sense of growing panic. It seemed to her that since she could not understand the instructions for a pregnancy test then she must, therefore, be totally unfit to be pregnant. She hid the test, tucking it behind the toilet cleaner, secure in the knowledge that Patrick would never have anything to do with cleaning the toilet, and brushed her teeth, splashed water on her face, and pinned on a bright smile for Patrick's arrival home from work.

She woke in the night, in the shadowy bedroom, and found that she was holding her breath, as if she were waiting for something. When she saw the gray-orange of the sky through the crack in the curtains she knew it was morning, and she could do the test. She slipped out of bed, careful not to wake

Patrick, and went to the bathroom. She locked the door behind her and took the pregnancy test from its hiding place. She lifted her nightgown and peed in the toilet, clumsily thrusting the collecting jar into the stream of urine for a sample. Then she poured urine and test powder into the little test tube, corked it, shook it, wrapped herself in a bath towel for warmth, and waited.

She had to wait ten minutes before the test was completed. Ruth made herself look away from the tube, fearful that the strength of her wishing would make the results go wrong. She was longing with all her heart for the liquid to stay its innocent pale, pale blue. She did not want to be pregnant, she did not want to have conceived a child. She turned her mind away from Patrick's new insistent lovemaking. She had thought their marriage had taken a sudden turn for the better; she had seen it as a renewal of desire. She had explained his new demanding sexiness as being a relief from the stress of his job as a reporter, a celebration of his new status as a manager. She did not want to think that he had been aiming for this very dawn, for Ruth sitting on the cold floor of the bathroom waiting for the result of a pregnancy test to tell her that she was no longer a free woman with a multitude of choices before her.

She glanced at her watch: eleven minutes had gone by. She looked at the test tube. In the bottom of the tube it had formed a sediment: a bright, strong dark blue. It was unmistakably a positive test. She screwed up her eyes—it made no difference. She took it closer to the light over the mirror. It was the bright blue that meant pregnancy. Ruth folded up the instructions and put the test pack away behind the toilet cleaner again. She was supposed to retest within a week, but she knew she would not bother to do it. She had known this yesterday morning, when the woman in the ladies' room had asked her if she was up the spout. She had recognized the information as soon as it was spoken. She was pregnant. Patrick and his parents had got what they wanted.

$\mathcal{S}$he did not tell Patrick of her pregnancy until Boxing Day morning, when he was hung over from his father's best Armagnac, which they had drunk on Christmas afternoon, and liverish with the richness of his mother's Christmas cooking. Some resilient piece of spite made her withhold the information from the assembled family on Christmas Day. She knew that they would have fallen on her with delight; she knew they would have said it was the best Christmas present they had ever had. Ruth did not want them unwrapping her feelings. She did not want them counting on their fingers and predicting the birth. She did not want her own small disaster of an unplanned pregnancy being joyously engulfed by the whole Christmas myth of baby Jesus and the speech of the Queen, who was not her queen, and carols, which were not her carols.

Spitefully, Ruth kept the precious news to herself, refused to spread exuberant delight. Throughout Christmas lunch, when they had skirted around the subject of the cottage and the proposed sale of the flat now that Ruth had nothing to keep her in Bristol, she refused to give them the gilt on the gingerbread of their plans. She ate only a little and drank only one glass of champagne. When the men drank Armagnac and snoozed before the television in the afternoon, Ruth defiantly walked in the cold countryside on her own.

"Pop down and see the cottage," Elizabeth recommended. "Get a feel for it without the men breathing down your neck. It's you that needs to fall in love with it, not them."

Ruth nodded distantly at Elizabeth's conspiratorial whisper. She knew that she could tell Elizabeth that she was pregnant and be rewarded with absolute discreet delight. Elizabeth would tell no one until Ruth gave permission. Elizabeth was always ready to bond with Ruth in an alliance of women against men, but Ruth would not join in. She hugged the small embryo to herself as she hugged the secret. She would not crown their day. The baby was a mistake, but it was her private mistake. She would not have it converted into a Cleary celebration.

Patrick emerged blearily from under the bedcovers. "God, I feel dreadful," he said. He sat up in bed, his eyes half closed. "Could you get me an Alka-Seltzer?" he asked. "Too much brandy and too much cake."

Ruth went down to the kitchen and fetched him a glass of water and two tablets. As they foamed she waited, only at the exact nauseating moment of his first sip did she say, "I'm pregnant."

There was a silence. "What?" Patrick said, turning toward her.

"I'm pregnant," Ruth repeated.

He reached forward but then recoiled as his head thudded. "Oh! Damn! Ruth, what a time to tell me! Darling!"

She sat out of arm's reach on the window seat.

"Come here!" he said.

She went, slowly, to the bed. Patrick drew her down and wrapped his arms around her. "That's wonderful news," he said. "D'you know you couldn't have given me a better Christmas present! When did you know?"

"Three weeks ago," Ruth said unhelpfully. "Then I went to the doctor to make sure. It's true. I'm due in the middle of August."

"I must phone Mother," Patrick said. "Oh, I *wish* you'd told me yesterday. We could have had a real party."

Ruth disengaged herself from the embrace, which was starting to feel heavy. "I didn't want a real party," she said.

He tried to twinkle at her. "Are you feeling shy, darling?"

"No."

"Then . . . ?"

"I didn't particularly want a baby," she said. "I didn't plan to get pregnant. It's an accident. So I don't feel like celebrating."

Patrick's indulgent gleam died and was instantly replaced by an expression of tenderness and concern. Gingerly he got out of bed and put his arm around her shoulders, turning her face in to the warmth of his chest. "Don't," he said softly, his breath sour on her cheek. "Don't talk like that, darling. It just happened, that's all. It just happened because that's how it was meant to be. Everything has come right for us, and when you get used to the idea I know you'll be really, really happy. *I'm* really happy," he said emphatically, as if all she needed to do was to imitate him. "I'm just delighted, darling. Don't upset yourself."

Ruth felt a sudden bitterness at the ease with which Patrick greeted the news. Of course he would be happy—it would not be Patrick whose life would totally change. It would not be Patrick who would leave the work he loved, and who would now never travel, and never see his childhood home. For a moment she felt filled with anger, but his arms came around her and his hands stroked her back. Ruth's face was pressed into the warm, soft skin of his chest and held like a little girl's. She could feel herself starting to cry, wetly, emotionally, weakly.

"There!" Patrick said, his voice warm with love and triumph. "You're bound to feel all jumbled up, my darling. It's well known. It's your hormones. Of course you don't know how you feel yet. There! There!"

She's very wound up at the moment," he whispered to his mother on the telephone. Ruth was taking an afternoon nap after a celebration lunch in the pub. "I didn't dare call you earlier. She didn't want you to know."

Elizabeth's face was radiant. She nodded confirmation to Frederick as he registered the news and stood close to Elizabeth to overhear their conversation. "Wait a moment," Elizabeth said. "Your father wants a word."

"Do I hear right? A happy event?" Frederick exclaimed.

Patrick chuckled. "I have to *whisper*!" he said. "She's asleep and she swore me to secrecy."

"Wonderful!" Frederick said. "Clever girl! And congratulations, old man!"

There was a brief satisfied silence.

"Bring her over," Frederick said. "We'll crack a bottle on the baby's head. Can't celebrate over the phone."

"I can't," Patrick said again. "I tell you, I am sworn to utter secrecy. She doesn't want anyone to know yet. She's all of a state. A bit weepy, a bit unsure. I don't want to rush her."

"Oh, don't talk to me about weepy!" Frederick said comfortably. "Your mother cried every day for nine months. I thought she was miserable, but then she told me she was crying for happiness." He gave a slow, rich, satisfied chuckle. "Women!" he said.

Patrick beamed into the phone. He very much wanted to be with his father. "I'll come see you this evening," he said. "I'll make some excuse. I won't bring her, we'll have our celebration drink, and next time we come she can tell you herself, and you can both be absolutely amazed."

"I'll put a bottle on ice," his father said. "At once."

"Patrick?" his mother asked as she came back on the phone. "Ruth is quite all right is she?"

"It's all a bit much for her, that's all," Patrick said. "And you know how much her job meant to her. It's a big shock."

"But she *does* want the baby?" Elizabeth confirmed. "She is happy about it?"

"She's over the moon," Patrick said firmly. "She's happier than she knows."

⁂

*A*s Ruth's pregnancy progressed, she found that Patrick's determination to move from the flat was too powerful to resist. In any case, the flat belonged to his father, and his father wished to sell. There was little Ruth could do but mourn their decision and pack as slowly and unwillingly as possible. Most days she did not go into the radio station, taking calls and preparing work at home. On those days the estate agent might telephone and send potential buyers to look at the flat. Ruth would show them around without enthusiasm. She did not actively draw their attention to the defects—the smallness of the spare bedroom, the inconvenience of the best bathroom's being *en suite* with their bedroom—but she did nothing to enhance their view of the flat.

It could not work. They were selling at a time of rising prices and rising expectations, and there were many people prepared to buy. Indeed, by playing one couple off against another Patrick and Frederick managed to get more than the asking price and a couple of months' delay before they had to move out.

"But the cottage isn't even bought yet," Ruth said. "Where are we going to live?"

"Why, here of course," Elizabeth exclaimed. She reached across the Sunday lunch table and patted Ruth's unresponsive hand. "It's not ideal, my dear, I know. I'm sure you would rather be nest building. But it's the way it has worked out. And at least you can leave the cooking and housework to me and just do as much radio work as you want. As you get more tired you might find that a bit of a boon, you know."

"And she'll eat properly during the day," Patrick said, smiling lovingly at Ruth. "When I'm not there to keep an eye on her, and when she doesn't have a canteen to serve up lunch, she just snacks. The doctor has told her, but she just nibbles like a little mouse."

"I don't feel like eating," Ruth said. The tide of their goodwill was irresistible. "And I'm gaining weight fast enough." Against the waistband of her skirt her expanding belly was gently pressing. At night she would scratch the tight skin of her stomach until she scored it with red marks from her fingernails. It felt as if the baby were stretching and stretching her body, her very life. Soon she would be four months into the pregnancy and would have to wear nothing but maternity clothes. Already the rhythm of trips to the prenatal clinic was becoming more and more important. Her conversations with Patrick were dominated by discussions about her blood pressure, the tests they wanted their baby to have, or, as now, her food. Even her work had taken second place. Only the project about the early industry of Bristol was still interesting. Ruth was reading local history for the first time, and looking at the buildings around her, the beautiful grand buildings of Bristol built on slave-trade money.

"Don't nag her, Patrick," Elizabeth said. "No one knows better than Ruth what she wants to eat and what she doesn't want."

Ruth shot Elizabeth a brief grateful look.

"And you will be absolutely free to come and go as you wish while you stay here," Elizabeth said. "So don't be afraid that I will be fussing over you all the time. But a little later on you might be glad of the chance to rest."

"I do get tired now," Ruth admitted. "Especially in the after-noon."

"I think I slept every afternoon as soon as Patrick was con-ceived," Elizabeth remembered. "Didn't I, Frederick? We were in South Africa then. Frederick was on attachment. All that won-derful sunshine and I used to creep into a darkened room and sleep and sleep."

"You were in Africa? I never knew."

"Training," Frederick said. "I used to go all over the world training chaps. Sometimes I could take Elizabeth, sometimes they were places where I was better off alone."

"You were working for the South African government?" Ruth asked.

Frederick smiled at her. "It was a wonderful country in those days. The blacks had their place, the whites had theirs. Every-one was suited."

"Except the black homelands were half desert, and the white areas were the towns and the goldmines," Ruth said.

Frederick looked quite amazed: it was the first time Ruth had ever contradicted him. "I say," he said. "You're becoming a bit of a Red in your condition."

"Oh, Ruth's full of it," Patrick volunteered, taking the sting from the conversation. "She's researching for a program on early Bristol industry, and she's gone back and back. I told her she'll be at the Garden of Eden soon. She's got her nose in these books from morning till night."

"Clever girl," Elizabeth said. "You'll need a little study when you move in. I could convert the small bedroom for you to work."

"Thank you," Ruth said. "But I will have finished quite soon."

"And anyway, she should be putting her feet up," Patrick said. "She's been reading far too much, and spending half the day in the library."

"And what about you, old boy?" Frederick asked. "How's the new post?"

Patrick smiled his charming smile. "Can't complain," he said, and started to tell them about his secretary, and his office, his reserved car space and his management-training course. Ruth watched him. She felt as if she were a long way away from him. She watched him smiling and talking: a favorite child of applauding parents, and as she watched them their faces blurred and their voices seemed to come from far away. Even Patrick, beloved, attractive Patrick, seemed a little man with a little voice crowing over little triumphs.

✑— Three —✑

Ruth and Elizabeth were to go down to the cottage together, to measure for curtains and carpets, and discuss color schemes. The builders had all but finished, the new kitchen had been built, the new bath plumbed-in. Elizabeth had tirelessly supervised the workmen, ascertaining Ruth's wishes and chivying them to do the work right. Nothing would have been done without her, nothing could have been finished as quickly without her. Patrick, absorbed in setting up the documentary unit at work, had been no help to Ruth at all. Without her mother-in-law she would have been exhausted every day by a thousand trivial decisions.

Ruth had planned to walk down to the cottage in the morning, when she felt at her best. But Elizabeth had been busy all morning and the time had slipped away. It was not until after lunch that she said, "I'm so sorry to have kept you waiting. Shall we go down to the cottage now? Or do you want your nap?"

"We'll go," Ruth decided. In her fifth month of pregnancy she felt absurdly heavy and tired, and the midafternoon was always the worst time.

"Shall I drive us down?" Elizabeth offered.

"I can walk." Ruth heaved herself out of the low armchair and went out into the hall. She bent uncomfortably to tie the laces of her walking boots. Elizabeth, waiting beside her, seemed as lithe and quick as a young girl.

Tammy, the dog, ran ahead of them, through Elizabeth's rose garden to the garden gate and then down across the fields. Ruth walked slowly, feeling the warmth of the April sunlight on her face. She felt better.

"I should walk every day," she said. "This is wonderful!"

"As long as you don't overdo it," Elizabeth warned. "What did the doctor say yesterday?"

"He said everything was fine. Nothing to worry about."

"Did he check your weight?"

"Yes—it's OK."

"He didn't think you were overweight?"

"He said it didn't matter."

"And did you tell him how tired you're feeling?"

"He said it was normal."

Elizabeth pursed her lips and said nothing.

"I'm fine," Ruth repeated.

Elizabeth smiled at her. "I know you are," she said. "And I'm just fussing over you. But I hate to see you so pale and so tired. In my day they used to give us iron tablets. You look so anemic."

"I'll eat cabbage," Ruth offered. She climbed awkwardly over the stile into the next field.

"Careful," Elizabeth warned.

The two women walked for a little while in silence. In the hedge the lambs'-tails on willows bobbed. Ruth remembered the springs of her American childhood, more dramatic, more necessary, after longer and sharper winters.

"I forgot to tell you," Elizabeth said. "Patrick rang this morning while you were in the bath. He said he has to go up to London this afternoon for a meeting and it'll probably go on late. He said he'd stay up there."

Ruth felt a pang of intense disappointment. "Overnight?" She hated being in Patrick's parents' house without him. She felt always as if she were some unwanted refugee billeted on kindly but unwilling hosts.

"Possibly Tuesday as well," Elizabeth said. "You can have a nice early night and a lie-in without him waking you in the morning."

"I'll ring him when we get home," Ruth said.

"He's out of touch," she said. "In a meeting, and then on the train to London."

"I wish I'd spoken to him," Ruth said wistfully.

Elizabeth opened the gate to the garden of the cottage and patted Ruth on the shoulder as she went through. "Now then," she said briskly. "You can live without him for one night."

"Didn't he ask to speak to me?"

"I said you were in the bath."

"I would have got out of the bath, if you had called me."

"I wouldn't dream of disturbing you," Elizabeth declared. "Not for a little message that I can take for you, darling. If you want a long chat with him you can save it all up until he comes home the day after tomorrow."

Ruth nodded.

"There's nothing wrong, is there? Nothing that you need him for?"

"No," Ruth said shortly.

Elizabeth had the front-door key; she opened the door and stepped back to let Ruth go in. "Don't cling, dear," she said gently. "Men hate women who cling. Especially now."

Ruth turned abruptly from her mother-in-law and went into the sitting room. Elizabeth was undoubtedly right, which made her advice the more galling. There was still a large patch of damp beside the French windows, which not even the summer sunshine had dried out.

"Now," Elizabeth said, throwing off her light jacket with energy. "You sit down on that little stool and I'll rush round and take all the measurements you want."

From the pocket of the jacket she pulled a notebook and pen and a measuring tape. Ruth sulkily took the notebook while Elizabeth strode around the room calling out the measurements of the walls and the window frames.

"Fitted carpets, I think, don't you?" she threw over her shoulder. "So much warmer. And good thick curtains for the winter, and some lighter ones for summer. Perhaps a pale yellow weave for summer, to match the primrose walls."

"I thought we'd paper it. I want the paper we had in the hall at the flat," Ruth said.

"Oh, darling!" Elizabeth exclaimed. "Not William Morris willow again, surely!"

"Didn't you like it?"

"I loved it," Elizabeth said. "But don't you remember what Patrick said? He said he kept seeing faces in it. You don't want it in your sitting room, with Patrick seeing faces peeping through the leaves at him every evening."

Ruth reluctantly chuckled. "I'll have it in the hall then," she said.

"And this room primrose yellow," Elizabeth said firmly. "I have some curtain material that will just do these windows, and the French windows too. Old gold they are. Quite lovely."

Ruth nodded. She knew they would be lovely. Elizabeth's taste was infallible, and she had trunks of beautiful materials saved from her travels around the world. "But we shouldn't be taking your things, we should be buying new."

Elizabeth, on her knees before the French windows, scratching critically at the damp plaster, looked up, and smiled radiantly. "Of course you should have my old things!" she said. "I can't wait to see my curtains up at your windows and the two of you—no, the three of you—happy and settled here." She looked back at the damp plaster. "I shall get someone out to see to this at once," she said. "Mr. Willis warned me it might be a specialist job."

They moved to the kitchen, the dining room, and then to the three upstairs bedrooms. Elizabeth carried around the little stool from the sitting room, and insisted on Ruth's sitting in the middle of each room, while she bustled with the tape measure, calling out numbers.

Empty of furniture, but with new kitchen units in pale pine and with a remodeled bathroom upstairs, the cottage did look pretty. Ruth felt her spirits rising. "If they hurry up with the decorating we should get in before the baby's born."

Elizabeth, stretching across the bedroom window, nodded. "I'm determined to see that you are," she said. "Cream cotton at all the upstairs windows, I think, and then it matches whatever-color walls you choose. But that nice Berber-weave carpet I told you about all through the top floor."

"In the flat we had varnished boards," Ruth said. "I liked them."

"Weren't they wonderful?" Elizabeth reminisced. "Georgian pine. And you did have them beautifully done." She recalled herself to the present. "So we'll have the biscuit-color Berber carpet all around the upstairs floor, and pastel walls. We can choose the colors at home. I've got the charts."

"All right," Ruth said, surrendering her vision of clean waxed floorboards without an argument. She felt suddenly very weary. "The sooner we choose it and order it the sooner the house is ready, I suppose."

"You leave it to me!" Elizabeth said with determination. "I'll have it ready by August, don't fret. In fact I'll leave you to have your rest when we get home, and I'll zip into Bath and come back with some fabric samples. You can choose them this evening and we can order them tomorrow. I'll order the carpets at the same time."

"And tiles or vinyl for the kitchen," Ruth said wearily. "I haven't chosen them yet. Patrick was going to take me into town tonight."

"Would you trust me to choose it for you?" Elizabeth offered. "I can look when I'm ordering the carpets. They've got a wonderful selection there."

Ruth got up from the stool. Her back ached and there was a new nagging ache in the very bones of her pelvis. The walk home over two hilly fields seemed a long, long way.

Elizabeth broke off, instantly attentive. "Shall I fetch the car, darling?" she asked gently. "Have you overdone it a bit?"

"I can walk," Ruth said.

"Or I could run home and fetch the car for you," Elizabeth repeated. "I could be back in a moment. You perch on your little stool and I'll have you home in a flash."

Ruth resisted for no more than a moment. "Thank you," she said gratefully. "I'd like that."

Elizabeth threw her a swift smile and slipped down the stairs. Ruth heard the front door bang and her quick footsteps on the path. She sat on her own in the quiet cottage and felt the friendly silence gather around her. "It'll be all right when we're in here," she said to herself, hearing her voice in the emptiness of the house. "As long as we get in here in time for the baby. The last thing that matters is the wallpaper."

Elizabeth, half running across the fields, fueled with energy and a sense of purpose, reached the house and picked up the ringing telephone. It was the builder, calling about Manor Farm cottage and the damp around the French windows.

"Yes," Elizabeth said. "My cottage. You must get that damp problem cured at once, Mr. Willis. My cottage must be ready by August. I have promised my son and daughter-in-law that I'll have it ready for them by then."

*I*t was not ready by August. The damp under the French windows was caused by a faulty drain. The flagstones of the path outside had to be cut back and a little gravel-filled trench inserted. None of it seemed very complicated to Ruth, and she wished they would hurry the work; but in the final month of her pregnancy she found a calmness and a serenity she had not known before.

"The work will be finished this week," Elizabeth said worriedly. "But then that room will have to dry out and be decorated. I've got the curtains ready to hang, and the carpet fitters will come in at a moment's notice, but if Junior is born on time he'll just have to come home to Patrick's old nursery here."

"It doesn't matter," Ruth said calmly.

"Bit of a treat really," Patrick said. He was eating a late supper. Frederick had already gone up to bed. Elizabeth and Ruth had waited up for Patrick, who had been delayed at work by someone's farewell party. Elizabeth had made him an omelette and he ate it, watched by the two women. "I like to think of him in my nursery."

"But I wanted to make the cottage ready for you," Elizabeth pursued. "I *am* disappointed."

"It doesn't matter," Ruth repeated. She had a curious floating feeling, as if everything was bound to be all right. She smiled at

Elizabeth. "I'll be five days in hospital anyway; maybe it will be finished in time."

Elizabeth shook her head disapprovingly. "In my day they kept you in for a fortnight," she said. "Especially a new mother who was completely inexperienced."

"We'll have to start somewhere," Patrick said cheerfully. "And we've done the classes, or at least Ruth has. I'll have on-the-job training."

"If you so much as touch a nappy I'll be amazed," Elizabeth said.

"He certainly will," Ruth replied. "He's promised."

Patrick grinned at the two of them. "I am a new man," he pronounced, slightly tipsy from the drinks at work and the wine with his supper. "I'll do it all. Anyway, even if I miss the nappy stage I've already bought him a fishing rod. I'll teach him fishing."

"And what if it's a girl?" Elizabeth challenged.

"Then I'll teach her too," Patrick said. "There will be no sexism in my household."

Ruth got to her feet; the distant floaty feeling had become stronger. "I have to go to bed," she said. "I'm half asleep here already."

Patrick pushed his plate to one side and was about to leave the table to go upstairs with Ruth.

"I was just making coffee," Elizabeth remarked. "I thought I'd have a coffee and a cognac before bed."

"Oh, all right," Patrick said agreeably. "I'll stay down and have one with you. All right, Ruth?"

She nodded and bent carefully to kiss his cheek.

"I won't disturb you when I come up," he promised. "I'll creep in beside you. And I'll be up early in the morning too. I'll slip out without waking you."

"I won't see you till tomorrow night then," Ruth said. Despite herself her voice was slightly forlorn.

"Unless tomorrow is the big day and he has to come dashing home," Elizabeth said cheerfully. "Patrick, you must leave a number where we can reach you all day, remember."

"I will," he said. "I'll write it down now."

"On the pad beside the telephone in the sitting room," Elizabeth instructed.

"Night, darling," Patrick said cheerfully and went to write his telephone number down as his mother had told him to do.

uth lay in her bed. The floating feeling grew stronger as she closed her eyes. The sounds of the countryside in summer breathed in through the half-open windows. They still sounded strange and ominous to Ruth, who was used to the comforting sounds of a city at night. She flinched when she heard the sudden whoop of an owl, and the occasional bark from a fox, trotting down the dark paths under the large white moon.

Ruth slept. Inside her body the baby turned and settled.

Between two and three in the morning, she woke in a pool of wetness, a powerful vise closed on her stomach. "Oh, my God!" she said. "Patrick, wake up, the baby's coming."

He took a moment to hear her, and then he leaped from the bed, as nervous as a father in a comedy film. "Now?" he demanded. "Are you sure? Now? Should we go to the hospital? Should we telephone? Oh, my God! We're low on petrol."

Ruth hardly heard him; she was timing her contractions.

"I'll get Mother," Patrick said at last and fled from the bedroom and down the corridor.

As soon as Elizabeth appeared in the doorway in her cream corduroy dressing gown, she took complete charge. She sent Patrick to get dressed in the bathroom and helped Ruth change from her nightgown into a pair of trousers and a baggy top.

"Everything ready in your suitcase?" she confirmed.

"Yes," Ruth said.

"I'll phone the hospital and tell them you're on your way," Elizabeth said.

"No petrol!" Patrick exclaimed, coming in the door, his sweater askew and his hair unbrushed. "God! I'm a fool! I'm low on petrol!"

"You can take your father's car. Get it out of the garage and bring it round to the front door," Elizabeth said calmly. "And don't speed. This is a first baby; you have plenty of time."

Patrick shot one anxious look at Ruth and dived from the room.

"The suitcase," Elizabeth reminded him.

"Suitcase," he repeated, grabbing it and running down the stairs.

The two women exchanged one smiling look. On impulse Elizabeth bent down and kissed Ruth's hot forehead. "Good luck," she said. "It's not that bad, really. Don't be frightened. And there's a beautiful baby at the end of it."

She helped Ruth to her feet and down the stairs. At the front door the Rover was waiting, Patrick standing at the passenger door. Ruth checked as a pain caught her, and Elizabeth held her arm, and then guided her into the car.

"Drive carefully," she said to Patrick. "I mean it. You have plenty of time."

"Yes, yes," he said. "I'll call you."

She stepped back from the car and waved until it was out of sight. "Dear little Ruth," she said lovingly. "At last."

She closed the front door and went up the stairs to her bedroom. Frederick was still asleep. Nothing ever woke him. Elizabeth tapped him gently on the shoulder. "They've gone to the hospital," she said softly, thinking that the news might penetrate his dreams. "Dear little Ruth has gone to have our baby."

⚜

*T*he childbirth course Ruth had completed, and which Patrick had attended twice, had laid great emphasis on the bonding nature of birth for the couple. There had been exercises of hand-holding and back rubbing, and little questionnaires to discover each other's preferences and fears about the birth. Patrick, who was not innately a sensual man, had been embarrassed when he was asked to massage Ruth's neck and shoulders in a roomful of people. His touch was light, diffident. The teacher, a willowy ex-hippie, had suggested that he grasp Ruth's hand, arm, shoulder, until he could feel the bones, and massage deeply, to get in touch with the core of Ruth's inner being.

"As if you were making love," she urged them. "Deep, sensual touching."

Patrick, horribly embarrassed, had made gentle patting gestures. Next week there was an urgent meeting at work and he missed the class altogether.

Ruth conscientiously brought home notes and diagrams, and discussed the concept of active birth. She and Patrick were sitting on the sofa while Elizabeth and Frederick watched television. Ruth kept her voice low but Elizabeth, overhearing, had laughed and remarked: "I only hope he doesn't disappoint you by dropping down in a dead faint. He's always been dreadfully squeamish."

"In our day fathers were completely banned," Frederick said. He turned to Elizabeth. "You wouldn't have wanted me there, would you?"

"Certainly not!" she said. "I gave birth to two children in two different countries, and never had a class in my life."

"I want to have a completely natural childbirth," Ruth said firmly. "I want to do it all by breathing. That's what the classes are for. And I am counting on Patrick to help me."

"I'm sure it will be fine," Elizabeth reassured her. "And, Patrick, you know all about it, do you?"

"Not a thing!" Patrick said with his charming smile. "But Ruth has given me a book. I'll bone up on it before the day. I just can't get on with the class, and a roomful of people watching me."

"I should think not!" Frederick said. "It's a private business, I should have thought."

"And it's more difficult for me," Patrick said, warming to his theme. "Everyone knows me, they've all seen me on the telly. I could just see them watching me trying to massage Ruth and dying to rush home and telephone their friends and say, 'We saw that Patrick Cleary give his wife a massage.'"

"I'm sure they wouldn't," Ruth said. "They're all much too interested in their own wives and babies. That's what they're there for, not to see you."

"Don't you believe it," said Frederick. "Fame has its disadvantages too."

"But I'll read the book," Patrick promised. "I'll know all about it by the time it happens."

But Patrick had not read the book. It was in his briefcase on a journey to and from London. But he had bought a newspaper, to look for news stories for the documentary unit, and then there were notes to make, and things to think about, and anyway the journey was quite short. The book, still unread, was in his pocket as he helped Ruth into the maternity unit of the hospital.

As soon as the nurse admitted Ruth it was apparent that something was wrong. She called the resident and there was a rapid undertone consultation. Then he turned to them. "I'm afraid we'll have to do a section," he said. "Your baby is breached and his pulse rate is too high. He's rather stressed. I think we want him out of there." He glanced at Ruth. "It'll have to be full anesthesia. We don't have time to wait for Pethedine to work."

The words were unfamiliar to Patrick, he did not know what was going on, but Ruth's distress was unmistakable. "Now wait a minute . . ." he said.

"We can't really," the doctor said. "We can't wait at all. Do I have your permission?"

Ruth's eyes filled with tears and then she drew in a sharp breath of pain. "Oh, yes," she said. "I suppose so . . . Oh, Patrick!"

"Permission for what?" Patrick asked. "What's going on?"

The resident took him by the arm and explained in a quick undertone that the baby was in distress and that they wanted to do a cesarean section at once. Patrick, out of his depth, appealed to the doctor, "But they'll both be OK, won't they? They'll both be all right?"

The doctor patted him reassuringly on the back. "Right as rain," he said cheerily. "And no waiting about. I'll zip her down to surgery and in quarter of an hour you'll have your son in your arms. OK?"

"Oh, fine," Patrick said, reassured. He looked back at Ruth

lying on the high hospital bed. She had turned to face the wall; there were tears pouring down her cheeks. She would not look at him.

Patrick patted her back. "It'll all be over in a minute."

"I didn't want it to be over in a minute," Ruth said, muffled. "I wanted a natural birth."

The nurse moved swiftly forward and put an injection in Ruth's limp arm. "That's the pre-med," she said cheerfully. "You'll feel better now, and when you wake up you'll have a lovely baby. Won't that be wonderful? You go to sleep like a good girl now. You won't feel a thing."

Patrick stood back and watched Ruth's dark eyelashes flutter and finally close. "But I wanted to feel . . ." she said sleepily.

They took the bed and wheeled it past him. "What do I do?" he asked.

The nurse glanced at him briefly. "There's nothing for you to do," she said. "You can watch the operation if you like . . . or I'll bring the baby out to you when it's delivered."

"I'll wait outside," Patrick said hastily. "You can bring him out."

They went through the double swinging doors at the end of the brightly lit corridor. Patrick suddenly felt bereft and very much alone. He felt suddenly afraid for Ruth, so little and pale in the high-wheeled bed, with her eyelids red from crying.

He had not kissed her, he suddenly remembered. He had not wished her well. If something went wrong . . . he shied away from the thought, but then it recurred: *if* something went wrong then she would die without his even holding her hand. She would die all on her own, and he had not even said, "Good luck," as they took her away from him. He had not kissed her last night, he had not kissed her this morning, in the sudden panic of waking. Come to think of it, he could not remember the last time he had taken her in his arms and held her.

The book in his pocket nudged his hip. He hadn't gone to her prenatal classes, he hadn't even read her little book. Only two nights ago she had asked him to read a deep-breathing exercise to her when they were in bed, and he had fallen asleep by the third sentence. He had woken in the early hours of the morning with the corner of the book digging into his shoulder, and he had felt irritated with her for being so demanding, for making such absurd requests when everyone knew, when his mother assured him, that having a baby was as natural as shelling peas, that there was nothing to worry about.

And there were other causes for guilt. He had moved her out of the flat she loved and taken her away from Bristol and her friends and her job. He hadn't even got her little house ready for her on time. He hadn't chosen wallpaper or carpets or curtains with her. He had left it to his mother, when he knew Ruth wanted him to make their home with her. He felt deeply, miserably, guilty.

The uncomfortable feeling lasted for several minutes, and then he saw a pay phone and went over to telephone his mother.

She answered on the first ring; she had been lying awake in bed, as he knew she would. "How are things?" she asked quickly.

"Not well," he said.

"Oh! My dear!"

"She's got to have a cesarean section, she's having it now."

"Shall I come down?"

"I don't know . . . I'm waiting in the corridor . . . I feel at a bit of a loose end . . . It's all a bit bleak."

"I'll come at once," Elizabeth said briskly. "And don't worry, darling, she'll be as right as rain."

Elizabeth leaped from her bed and pulled on her clothes. She shook Frederick's shoulder. He opened one sleepy eye. "Ruth's gone to have her baby. I'm going down there," she said. There was no need for him to know more. Elizabeth never lied but she was often sparing with information. "I'll telephone you with any news."

"What's the time?"

"Three in the morning. Go back to sleep, darling, there's nothing you can do. I'll call you when I know more."

He nodded and rolled over. Elizabeth sped downstairs and put the kettle on. While it came to the boil she made sandwiches with cold lamb from last night's joint, and prepared a thermos of strong coffee. She put everything in a wicker basket and left the house, closing the front door quietly behind her.

*t was a wonderful warm midsummer night; the stars were very bright and close and a harvest moon broad and yellow leaning on the horizon. Elizabeth started her little car and drove down the lane to the hospital at Bath, and to her son.

His face lit up when he saw her. He was sitting on a chair outside the operating theater, very much alone, looking awkward with his sweater askew over his shirt collar. He looked very young.

"No news yet?" she asked.

"They're operating," he said. "It's taking longer than they said it would. But a nurse came out just now and said it was quite routine. She said there was nothing to worry about."

"I brought you some coffee," she said. "And a sandwich."

"I couldn't eat a thing," he said fretfully. "I keep thinking about her. . . . I didn't even kiss her goodnight, she was asleep by the time I got to bed last night, and I didn't kiss her before she went in."

Elizabeth nodded and poured him a cup of coffee and added plenty of brown sugar. He took the cup and wrapped his hands around it.

"I didn't go to her classes either," he said. "Or read her book."

"Well, they didn't do much good," Elizabeth said. "As things have turned out."

He brightened at that. "No," he said. "All those breathing exercises and in the end it's full anesthetic."

Elizabeth nodded and offered him a sandwich. He bit into it, and she watched the color come back into his cheeks.

"I suppose she'll be all right?" he said. "They said it was quite routine."

"Of course she will be," Elizabeth said. "Some women *choose* to have a cesarean birth. It's much easier for the baby, and no pain at all for the mother. She'll be fine."

Patrick finished his cup of coffee and handed it back to his mother just as the theater doors opened. A nurse in a green gown, wearing a ballooning paper hat over her hair and a white paper mask over her nose and mouth, came through the door with a small bundle in a blanket.

"Mr. Cleary?" she asked.

Patrick got to his feet. "Yes?"

"This is your son," she said. "And your wife is fine."

She held the baby out to him and Patrick rubbed his hands on his trousers and reached out. He was awkward with the baby; she had to close his hands around the little bundle. "Hold him close," she urged. "He won't bite!"

Patrick found himself looking into the tiny puckered face of his sleeping son. His mouth was pursed in mild surprise, his eyelids traced with blue. He had a tiny wisp of dark hair on the top of his head and tiny hands clenched into tiny bony fists.

"Is he all right?" Patrick asked. "Quite all right?"

"He's perfect," she assured him. "Seven pounds three ounces. They're just stitching your wife up now and then you can see her in Recovery."

Elizabeth was at Patrick's shoulder looking into the baby's face. "He's the very image of you," she said tenderly. "Oh, what a poppet."

The baby stirred and Patrick nervously tightened his grip.

"May I?" Elizabeth asked. Gently she took the baby and settled him against her shoulder. The damp little head nodded against her firm touch.

"Shall I take you in to see your wife?" the nurse asked. "She'll be coming round in a little while."

"You go, Patrick," Elizabeth said. "I'll look after Cleary Junior here."

Patrick smiled weakly at her and followed the nurse. He still could not take in the fact that his baby had been born. "Right," he said. "Right."

Elizabeth had already turned away. She was walking slowly down the length of the corridor, swaying her hips slightly as she walked, rocking the baby with the steady, easy rhythm of her pace. "And what shall we call you?" she asked the little sleeping head. She put her lips to his ear. It was perfectly formed, like a whorled shell, surprisingly cool. Elizabeth inhaled the addictive scent of newborn baby. "Little love," she whispered. "My little love."

It was nearly midday before Ruth woke from her sleep and nearly two o'clock before the baby was brought to her. He was no longer the scented damp bundle that Elizabeth had walked in the corridor. He was washed and dried and powdered and dressed in his little cotton sleep suit. He was not like a newborn baby at all.

"Here he is," the nurse said, wheeling him into the private room in the little Perspex crib.

Ruth looked at him doubtfully. There was no reason to believe that he was her baby at all; there was nothing to connect him and her except the paper bracelet around his left wrist, which said, "Cleary 14.8.95." "Is it mine?" she asked baldly.

The nurse smiled. "Of course it's yours," she said. "We don't get them mixed up. He's lovely, don't you think?"

Ruth nodded. Tears suddenly coming into her eyes. "Yes," she said weakly. She supposed the baby was lovely. But he looked very remote and very isolated in his little plastic box. He looked to her as if he had been assembled in the little box like a puzzle toy, as if he were the property of the hospital and not her baby at all.

"Now what's the matter?" the nurse asked.

"I bought that suit for him," Ruth said tearfully. "I bought it."

"I know you did, dear. We found it in your case and we put it on him as soon as he had his bath. Just as you would have wanted it done."

Ruth nodded. It was pointless to explain the sense of strangeness and alienation. But she felt as if the little suit had been bought for another baby, not this one. The little suit had been bought for the baby that she had felt inside her, that had walked with her, and slept with her, and been with her for nine long months. It was for the imaginary baby, who had an imaginary birth, where Ruth had breathed away all the pains, where Patrick had massaged her back and held her hand and talked to her engagingly and charmingly through the hours of her labor, and where, after he had been triumphantly born, everyone had praised her for doing so well.

"You want to breast-feed him, don't you?"

Ruth looked at the sleeping baby without much enthusiasm. "Yes, I did."

"Well, I'll leave him here with you, and when he wakes up you can ring your bell and I'll come and help you get comfy. After a cesarean you need a bit of help."

"All right," Ruth said.

The nurse gave her a kind smile and left the room. Ruth lay back and looked at the ceiling. Unstoppably the tears filled her eyes and ran out under her eyelids, hot and salty. Beside her, in his goldfish-bowl crib, the baby slept.

In half an hour the nurse came back. She had hoped that Ruth would have broken the hospital rules and put the baby in bed beside her, but they were as far apart as ever.

"Now," she said brightly. "Let's wake this young man up and give him a feed."

He was not ready to wake. His delicate eyelids remained stubbornly closed. He did not turn his head to Ruth even when she undid the buttons of her nightgown and pressed her nipple to his cheek.

"He's sleepy," the nurse said. "He must have got some of your anesthetic. We'll give him a little tickle. Wake him up a bit."

She slipped his little feet out of the sleep suit and tickled his toes. The baby hardly stirred.

"Come along now, come along," the nurse said encouragingly.

She took him from Ruth and gave him a little gentle jiggle. The baby opened his eyes—they were very dark blue—and then opened his mouth in a wail of protest.

"That's better," she said. Quickly and efficiently she swooped down on Ruth, propped the little head on Ruth's arm, patted his cheek, turned his face, and pressed Ruth's nipple into his mouth.

He would not suck. Four, five times, they repeated the

procedure. He would not latch onto the nipple. Ruth felt herself blushing scarlet with embarrassment and felt the ridiculous easy tears coming again. "He doesn't want to," she said. She felt her breasts were disgusting, that the baby was making a wise choice in his rejection.

"He will," the nurse reassured her. "We just have to keep at it. But he will, I promise you."

The baby had dozed off again. His head lolled away from her.

"He just doesn't want to," Ruth said.

"We'll give it another try later on," the nurse said reassuringly. "Shall I leave him in with you for now? Have a little cuddle."

"I thought he had to go into his cot?"

She smiled. "We could break the rules just this once."

Ruth held him out. "It hurts on my scar," she said. "Better put him back."

ᘒᴥ Four ᴥᘒ

Patrick came at visiting time at four in the afternoon with a big bouquet of flowers. He kissed Ruth and looked into the crib.

"How is he?"

"He won't feed," Ruth said miserably. "We can't make him feed."

"Isn't that bad? Won't he get hungry?"

"I don't know. The nurse said he was sleepy from my anesthetic."

"Did she seem worried?"

"How should I know?" Ruth exclaimed.

Patrick saw that she was near to tears. "Here," he said. "Look at your lovely flowers. And dozens of bouquets at home—it looks like a florist's shop. They sent some from my work, and my secretary told Radio Westerly and they sent some."

Ruth blinked. "From Westerly?"

"Yes. A big bunch of red roses."

"That was nice."

"And your little chum."

"Who?"

"That David."

"Oh," she said. It seemed like years since she had last seen David.

"And how are you, darling?"

"I'm fine," she said. "My stitches hurt."

"Mother said they would. She said that we would all have to look after you especially well when you come home."

Ruth nodded.

"She said she would come down later if that was all right with you. She didn't want to crowd us this afternoon. But she and the old man will come down this evening if you're not too tired."

"Perhaps tomorrow?" Ruth suggested.

"They're very keen to see the grandson," Patrick prompted. "Dad especially."

"All right, then."

"They asked me what we would be calling him. I said that we'd probably stick with Thomas James."

Ruth glanced toward the crib. She had imagined Thomas James as a fair-haired boy, not this dark-headed little thing. "I never thought he'd be so small," she said.

"Tiny, isn't he?" Patrick said. "Shall I pick him up?"

"Better let him sleep," Ruth said.

They both gazed at the sleeping baby. "Tiny hands," Patrick said again.

"I never thought of him like this," Ruth said.

"I never really imagined him at all. I always kind of jumped ahead. I thought about teaching him how to fish, and taking him to cricket and things like that. I never thought of a tiny baby."

"No."

They were silent.

"He is all right, isn't he?" Patrick asked. "I mean he seems terribly quiet. I thought they cried all the time."

"How should I know?" Ruth exclaimed again.

"Of course, of course," Patrick said soothingly. "Don't get upset, darling. Mother will be down this evening and she'll know."

Ruth nodded and lay back on her pillows. She looked very small and wan. Her dark hair was limp and dirty, her cheeks sallow. There were dark shadows under her eyes.

"You look all in," Patrick said. "Shall I go and leave you to have a sleep?"

Ruth nodded. He could see she was near to tears again.

"Everything all right?" he asked.

"Yes," she whispered.

"See you tonight then." He bent over the bed and kissed her gently. She did not respond, she did not even turn her face to him. She let him touch her cheek as if she were sulking after some injury. He had a flash of irritation, that he should be behaving so beautifully, with such patience and forbearance, and she should be so limp. In the films he had seen of such situations as these, the young mothers had sat up in bed in pretty beribboned bed jackets, and smiled adoringly at their husbands and gazed devotedly at their babies. Patrick was too intelligent to mistake Hollywood images for reality, but he had expected something more than Ruth's resentful apathy.

He straightened up and turned to the crib. "See you later, Thomas James," he said quietly, and went from the room.

Ruth slept for only half an hour. At five o'clock the nurse woke her with dinner. Ruth, hungry and chilled, was confronted with a tray of grapefruit juice, Spam salad with sliced white bread and butter, followed by violently green Jell-O. As she drew the unappetizing dishes toward her, the baby stirred in his crib and cried.

Ruth's stitches were still too painful to let her move. Shifting the tray and picking up the baby was an impossibility. She dropped a forkful of icy limp salad and rang the bell for the nurse. No one came. The baby's cries went up a notch in volume. He went red in the face, and his little fists flailed against the air.

"Hush, hush," Ruth said. She rang the bell again. "Someone will come in a minute," she said.

It was incredible that a baby so small could make so much noise, and that the noise should be so unbearably penetrating. Ruth could feel her own tension rising as the baby's cries grew louder and more and more desperate.

"Oh, please!" she cried out. "Please don't cry like that. Someone will come soon! Someone will come soon! Surely someone will come!"

He responded at once to the panic in her voice, and his cry became a scream, an urgent, irresistible shriek.

The door opened and Elizabeth peeped in. She took in the scene in one rapid glance and moved forward. She put down the basket she was carrying, picked up the baby, and put him firmly against her shoulder, resting her cheek on his hot little head. His agonized cries checked at once at the new sensation of being picked up and firmly held.

"There, there," Elizabeth said gently. "Master Cleary! What a state you're in."

She looked over his head to Ruth, tearstained in the bed. "Don't worry, darling," she said gently. "The first days are always the worst. You finish your dinner and I'll walk him till you're ready to feed him."

"It's disgusting," Ruth whispered. "I can't eat it."

"I brought you a quiche and one of my little apple pies," Elizabeth offered. "I didn't know what the food would be like in here, and after I had Patrick I was simply starving."

"Oh! That would be lovely."

Holding the baby against her neck with one casual hand, Elizabeth whipped a red-and-white-checked cloth off the top of the basket with the other, and spread it on Ruth's counterpane, followed by the quiche in its own little china dish. It was still warm from the oven, the middle moist and savory, the pastry crisp. Ruth took the miniature silver picnic cutlery from the basket and ate every crumb, while Elizabeth wandered around the room humming lullabies in the baby's ear. She smiled when she saw the empty plate.

"Apple pie?"

"Please."

Elizabeth produced a little individual apple pie and a small cup of thick cream. Ruth ate. The apple was tart and sharp, the pastry sweet.

"Better now?" Elizabeth asked.

Ruth sighed. "Thank you. I was really hungry, and *so* miserable."

"The quicker we get you home and into a routine the better," Elizabeth said. "D'you think you could feed him now? I think he's awake and hungry."

"I'll try," Ruth said uncertainly.

Elizabeth passed the little bundle to her. As Ruth leaned forward to take him, her stitches pulled and she cried out with pain. At the sharp sound of her voice and the loss of the rocking and humming, Thomas opened his eyes in alarm and shrieked.

"There," Elizabeth said, hurrying forward. "Now tuck him in tight to you." Expertly she pressed the baby against Ruth. "I'll pop a pillow under here to hold him close. You lie back and make yourself comfortable." She arranged the baby, head toward Ruth, but Thomas cried and cried. Ruth, half-naked, pushed her breast toward his face, but he would not feed.

"It's no good!" Ruth was near tears. "He just won't! I can't make him! And he'll be getting so hungry!"

"Why not give him a bottle just for now?" Elizabeth suggested. "And feed him yourself later on when you feel better?"

"Because they say you *have* to feed at once, as soon after the birth as possible," Ruth said over a storm of Thomas's cries. The baby, more and more distressed, was kicking against her and crying. "If he doesn't take to it now he'll never learn."

"But a bottle . . . "

"No!" Ruth cried out, her voice drowned out by Thomas's anguished wails.

The door opened and the nurse came in. "I'm sorry I couldn't get down before," she said. "Are you all right in here?"

"I think the baby should have a bottle," Elizabeth said smoothly. "He's not taking to the breast."

The nurse responded at once to Elizabeth's calm authority. "Certainly, but I thought . . ."

Ruth lay back on her pillows, the baby's insistent cry half deafening her.

"Shall I take him?" Elizabeth asked.

"Take him," Ruth whispered.

"And give him a bottle, get him fed, darling, and settled?"

Miserably Ruth nodded. "All right! All right!" she said with weak anger. "Just do what you want!"

Elizabeth took the baby from her. "You have a nice rest," she said. "I'll get him sorted out."

The nurse stepped back. "Aren't you lucky to have your mum to help you?"

"Yes," Ruth said quietly, thinking of her own mother, so long dead, and distant and unhelpfully gone.

*T*hree weeks later Ruth and Thomas came home. Ruth had been proved right in one respect. Thomas, offered the bottle by Elizabeth and then dandled on Frederick's knee, never breast-fed. Despite Ruth's intentions, despite all the books, the good advice, and her resolutions, her baby had been born by cesarean section and was fed from the start on formula milk. He was a potent symbol of her failure to complete successfully the job she had not wanted to take on. Ruth had not expected to be a good mother; but she had set herself the task of learning how to do it. Conscientious and intelligent, she had done her absolute best to master theories of childbirth and childrearing. But Thomas was a law to himself. She felt that he had been born without her—simply taken from her unconscious body. She felt that he preferred to feed without her. Anyone could hold him while he had his bottle. He appeared to have no preferences. Anyone could comfort him when he cried. As long as he was picked up and walked, he would stop crying. But Ruth, exhausted and still in pain from the operation, was the only one who could not easily pick him up and walk with him.

It was Elizabeth who cared for him most of the time. It was Elizabeth who knew the knack of wrapping him tightly in his white wool shawl, his little arms crisscrossed over his stomach, so he slept. It was Elizabeth who could hold him casually in the crook of her arm while she cooked one-handed, and it was Elizabeth's serene face that his deep blue eyes watched, intently gazing at her as she worked, and her smile that he saw when she glanced down at him.

While Ruth slept upstairs in the spare bedroom of the farmhouse, Elizabeth rocked Thomas in Patrick's old baby carriage in the warm midsummer sun of the walled garden. While Ruth rested, it was Elizabeth who loaded Thomas into her car in his expensive reclining baby seat and drove to the shops. Elizabeth was never daunted at the prospect of taking Thomas with her. "I'm glad to help," she told Patrick. "Besides, it makes me feel young again."

The health visitor came in the first week that Thomas and Ruth were home. "Aren't you lucky to have a live-in nanny!" she exclaimed facetiously to Ruth, but in her notes she scribbled a memo that mother and child did not seem to have bonded, and that mother seemed depressed. On her second visit she found Ruth surrounded by suitcases and languidly packing while Elizabeth was changing Thomas's diaper in the nursery.

"We're moving to our house," Ruth said. "The builders have finished at last. I'm just packing the last of my clothes."

The health visitor nodded. "You'll miss having your family around you," she said diplomatically, thinking that at last mother and baby would have some privacy. "Is your new house far away? I shall have to have the address. Is it still in my area?"

"Oh yes, it's just at the end of the drive," Ruth said. "The little cottage on the right, Manor Farm Cottage. We're within walking distance."

"Oh," the health visitor hesitated. "Nice to have your family nearby, especially when you've got a new baby, isn't it?"

Ruth's pale face was expressionless. "Yes," she said.

❧

They moved on the third week in September. Elizabeth had organized the arrival of their furniture from the store, and placed it where she thought best. Elizabeth had hung the curtains, which she had ordered, and they looked very well. She and Patrick went down to the cottage with the suitcases and unpacked the clothes and hung them in the new fitted wardrobe in the bedroom. Patrick had planned to make up the bed and prepare Thomas's crib, but the new telephone rang just as they arrived in the house, with a crisis at work, and he stood in the hall, taking notes on the little French writing desk, which Elizabeth had put there, while his mother got the bedrooms ready and made the crib in the nursery with freshly ironed warm sheets.

The gardener had started work a month ago, and the grass was cut and the flower beds nearest the house were tidy. Elizabeth picked a couple of roses and put them in a little vase by the double bed. The cottage was as lovely as she had planned.

Patrick put the telephone down. "I *am* sorry," he said. "I didn't mean you to do all this. I promised Ruth I would do it."

"You know I enjoy it," she said easily. "And anyway, I don't like to see a man making beds. Men always look so forlorn doing housework."

"You spoil us," Patrick said, his mind on his work.

"Will you go up to the house and fetch Ruth?"

"I should really go in to work. There's a bit of a flap on—a rumor that some Japanese high-tech company is coming in to Bristol. We had half a documentary about their work practices in the can, but if the rumor's confirmed we should really edit it and run it as it is. I need to get in and see what's going on."

Elizabeth was about to offer to fetch Ruth for him, but she hesitated. "I think you should make the time to bring her and Thomas down here, all the same," she said. "I'm sure she's feeling a bit neglected."

He nodded. "Oh, all right. Look. Run me back home and I'll dash in, pick her up, whiz them down here, and settle them in, and then I'll go in to the studio."

Elizabeth led the way to her car, and they drove the mile and a half up to the farmhouse.

Ruth was rocking Thomas's pram in the garden, her face incongruously grim in the late-summer sunshine, with the roses still in lingering bloom behind her. "Ssssh," she said peremptorily. "He's only this minute gone off. I've been rocking and rocking and rocking. I must have been here for an hour."

"I was going to take you both down to the cottage. It's all ready," Patrick whispered.

Ruth looked despairing. "Well, I'm not waking him up. He's only just gone. I can't bear to wake him."

"Oh, come on," Patrick said. "He'll probably drop off again if we just transfer him into his car bed."

Ruth thought for a moment. "We could walk down, and push the pram down with us."

Patrick instinctively shrank from the thought of walking down the road, even his own parents' private drive, pushing a pram. There was something so trammeled and domestic about the image. There was something very poverty-stricken about it too, as if they could not afford a car.

"No," he said quickly. "Anyway, I don't have the time. I have to go in to work. I wanted to drop the two of you off."

"Not work again . . ."

"It's a crisis. . . ."

"It's always a crisis. . . ."

"Why don't the two of you go?" Elizabeth interposed. "And leave Thomas here. Ruth can settle in, have a little wander around, have a bit of peace and quiet. I'll keep Thomas here until you want him brought down. You can phone me when you're ready. The phone's working."

"That's very kind of you," Ruth said, "but . . ."

"It's no trouble to me at all," Elizabeth assured her. "I have nothing to do this afternoon except a spot of shopping, and Thomas can come with me. He loves the supermarket. I'll wait till he wakes and then take him out."

Ruth hesitated, tempted by the thought of an afternoon in her new house.

"If I get away early I'll come home in time for tea," Patrick offered. "We could have a bit of time together before we collect Thomas."

Elizabeth nodded encouragingly. "Enjoy your new house together," she said. "Thomas can stay with me as long as you like. I can even give him his bottle and bathe him here."

Ruth looked directly at Patrick. "But I thought we were moving into our house, all together, this afternoon." She let the demand hang in the air.

Elizabeth smiled faintly and moved discreetly out of earshot. Patrick slipped his arm around Ruth's waist and led her away from the pram. "Why don't you go down to our little house, run yourself a bath, have a little rest, and I'll bring home a pizza or a curry or something and we'll have dinner, just the two of us, and christen that bedroom?"

Ruth hesitated. She and Patrick had not made love since the birth of Thomas. She felt a half-forgotten desire stir inside her. Then she remembered the pain of her stitches, and the disagreeable fatness of her belly. "I can't," she said coldly. "It's too soon."

"Then we'll have a gentle snog," Patrick said agreeably. "Come on, Ruth, let's take advantage of a good offer. Let's have our first night on our own and fetch Thomas tomorrow. Mother will have him overnight for us; he's got his cot here and all the things he needs. And they love to have him. Why not?"

"All right," Ruth said, seduced despite herself. "All right."

⁂

*R*uth had longed to be in her own house, and to settle into a routine with her own baby. But nothing was as she had planned. Thomas did not seem to like his new nursery. He would not settle in his crib. Every evening, as Patrick returned Ruth's cooling dinner to the warming oven, Ruth went back upstairs, rocked Thomas to sleep, and put him into his crib. They rarely ate dinner together; one parent was always rocking the baby.

During the day, Thomas slept well. Ruth could put him in the pram and wheel it out into the little back garden.

"That's when you should sleep," Elizabeth reminded her. "Sleep when the baby sleeps, catch forty winks."

But Ruth could never sleep during Thomas's daytime naps. She was always listening for his cry, she was always alert.

"Leave him to cry," Elizabeth said robustly. "If he's safe in his cot or in his pram he'll just drop off again."

Ruth shot her a reproachful glance. "I wouldn't dream of it," she said.

"But if you're overtired and need the sleep . . ." Elizabeth said gently.

"She's determined," Patrick said. "It's in the book."

"Oh, the book," Elizabeth said and exchanged a small hidden smile with Patrick.

Ruth stuck to the book, which said that the baby should be fed on demand and never left to cry, even though it meant that she could never settle to anything during the day, and never slept at night for more than a couple of hours at a time. She saw many dawns break at the nursery window before Thomas finally dozed off to sleep and she could creep back into bed beside Patrick's somnolent warmth. Then it seemed to be only moments before the alarm clock rang out, and Patrick yawned noisily, stretched, and got out of bed.

"Be quiet!" Ruth whispered at him. She was near to tears. "He's only just gone off to sleep. For Christ's sake, Patrick, do you have to make so much noise?"

Patrick, who had done nothing more than rattle the clothes hangers in the wardrobe while taking his shirt, spun around, shocked at the tone of her voice. Ruth had never spoken to him like that before.

"What?"

"I said, for Christ's sake do you have to make so much noise? I've been up all night with him. He's only this minute gone off."

"No, you weren't," Patrick said reasonably. "I heard him cry out at about four, and I listened for him. I was going to get up, but he went back to sleep again."

"He was awake at one, for an hour, and then again at three. He *didn't* go back to sleep at four, it was you that went back to sleep at four. *He* woke up and I had to change him and give him another bottle, and I was up with him till six, and I can't *bear* him to wake again."

Patrick looked skeptical. "I'm sure I would have woken if you had been up that often," he said. "You probably dreamed it."

Ruth gave a little shriek and clapped her hand over her mouth. Above her own gagging hand, her eyes glared at Patrick. "I couldn't have dreamed it." She was near to tears. "How could I have dreamed anything? I've been awake nearly all night! There was no time to dream anything, because I've hardly ever slept!"

Patrick pulled on his shirt and then crossed the room and sat on the edge of the bed, touching her gently on the shoulder. "Calm down, darling," he said. "Calm down. I'm sorry. I didn't know you'd had a bad night. Shall I call Mother?"

"I don't *want* your mother," Ruth said fretfully. "I want you to be quiet in the mornings so you don't wake him again. I want you to get up without waking *me*. And I want *you* to come home early so you have him this afternoon and I can sleep then."

Patrick got up and briskly pulled on his trousers. He hated demanding women, having had no experience of them. "No can do, I'm afraid. I've got a meeting at six. I was going to be late home anyway. I'll call Mother as I go out. You get your head down and get some sleep. She'll be down straightaway and she can get Thomas up and dressed and take him up home for the day."

"I don't want your mother," Ruth insisted. "I want you to look after Thomas. Not her. He's your son, not hers."

Patrick smoothed the lapels of his jacket down over his chest and glanced at the pleasing reflection in the mirror. "I can't be in two places at once," he said. "Be reasonable, Ruth. I'm doing my best, and I'm working all the hours God sends to make a go of this documentary unit. If I get the pay rise I've been promised we could get some help, perhaps a girl to come in and look after Thomas a couple of mornings a week."

"I don't want a girl," Ruth said. "I want *us* to look after our son. Not a girl, not your mother: you and me."

Patrick said nothing. The silence seemed to be on his side.

"So I'll call Mother, shall I?" he asked, as if she had not spoken.

The temptation of a morning's sleep was too much for Ruth.

"All right," she said ungraciously. "I suppose so."

∽ Five ∽

*I*t's Ruth," Patrick said without preamble when his mother answered the phone. "She's not up to managing Thomas this morning, and I have to go to work. Can you have him?"

"Of course," Elizabeth said easily. "You know how I love him."

"Weren't you doing something today? Isn't it your day at the church for flowers or something?" Patrick asked with belated politeness.

"Yes, but Thomas can come too. He's so good. He's no trouble at all."

Patrick felt himself relax. The sense of permanent crisis that eddied around the little house was stilled by his mother's calm competence. "I wish you could teach Ruth how to handle him," he said suddenly. "We don't seem to be getting on at all."

There was a diplomatic silence from his mother.

"She can't seem to settle him at night, and then she's tired out all the day. She wanted me to come home early from work and I simply can't." Patrick realized he was sounding aggrieved and at once adjusted his tone. "I suppose we're beginners at this," he said, the good humor back in his voice. "Apprentices."

"There's nothing wrong, is there?" Elizabeth asked. "Apart from her being tired?"

"What d'you mean?"

"I don't know. I just wondered if she was perhaps a little depressed. Baby blues or something?"

Patrick thought for a moment. If he had been honest he would have known that Ruth had been unhappy from the moment the pregnancy had been confirmed, from the moment she gave up her job. She had been unhappy at the move to the little house so far from her hometown, she had been unhappy at living so close to his parents. And now she was unhappy with being left alone all day, every day, with a new restless baby.

"She seems to be making very heavy weather of it all," he said eventually. "I don't know if she's depressed. She's certainly making a meal of it."

"I'll come down at once," Elizabeth said. "See what I can do."

"Thank you," Patrick said with real gratitude. Then he put the receiver down, picked up his car keys, and drove to work with the sense of having done all that a man could be expected to do for his wife and child.

Elizabeth tapped on the front door very gently, and when there was no reply let herself in with her own key. In the kitchen Patrick's morning cup of coffee was cooling on the table. Someone had forgotten to switch on the dishwasher the night before and the plates were still dirty. The kitchen curtains were closed, and the room looked shadowy and hung over. Elizabeth drew the curtains back and fastened them with their tiebacks. She moved around, easily, confidently, clearing up and wiping the worktops, admiring the color scheme, which she had chosen. The sitting room was reasonably tidy, but it had the neglected appearance of a room that was seldom used. Elizabeth picked up the evening paper and put it in the log basket for lighting the fire, put the *Radio Times* tidily beside the television. She plumped up the cushions on the sofa and moved the coffee table into place. There were no flowers in the room, just a dying African violet in a pot with browning leaves and dry petals. Elizabeth frowned slightly, fetched a glass of water and dribbled it onto the thirsty soil.

She heard a movement and a little cry from the nursery

upstairs and went soft-footed up the stairs. The Berber-twist carpet she had chosen went well with the William Morris wallpaper, which Ruth had insisted on using. Elizabeth took it all in with the pleasure of a house owner.

The cry from the nursery grew louder as Thomas woke.

"Coming! I'm coming!" There was an exasperated yell from the bedroom, and then the bedroom door was flung open and mother- and daughter-in-law suddenly faced each other.

Ruth was in a dingy maternity nightgown, her body, still fat with the weight of pregnancy, only partly masked by its folds. Her feet were bare, her hair limp, her face a mask of tiredness, dark shadows deeply etched under her eyes. She looked exhausted and unhappy. Elizabeth was trim in gray wool slacks with a pale cashmere sweater. She had a light-colored scarf pinned at her neck with a small expensive brooch; she wore the lightest of makeup. Her perfume, as usual, was Chanel No. 15.

"Oh," Ruth said blankly.

"Patrick phoned me to come. He said you wanted to sleep."

The wails from the nursery grew louder. Both women checked a move to go, deferring to each other with careful courtesy.

"I was up all night," Ruth said. To her own ears she sounded as if she were making excuses to a strict teacher.

"Of course, my dear, and I love to have him."

"I wanted Patrick to come home early. . . ."

"Well, men have to work." Elizabeth stated an inarguable fact. "And I'm just up the road doing nothing. Let me get him up and give him his bottle and get him dressed, and I'll take him up to the farm with me. And when you've had a good sleep, and a bath" (and washed your hair, she mentally added) "then you can come up to the farm and fetch him, or I'll bring him back."

"I don't like to impose," Ruth said awkwardly.

"Nonsense. If it were your mother within walking distance, she would be caring for you both."

At the mention of her absent mother Ruth's face changed at once. Her eyes filled with ready tears. "Yes," she said miserably.

"So let me. At least Thomas has one granny. And Frederick

can take him out for a walk in the pram this afternoon. The exercise and the fresh air will do them both good."

Ruth nodded.

Elizabeth turned for the nursery and went in. The room smelled sickly sweet from the bin of dirty diapers. Thomas, rosy-cheeked and bawling, was kicking in his crib. His diaper, sleep suit, even his bedding were soaked through with urine.

"What a little terror!" Elizabeth exclaimed. She took a towel from the changing table and wrapped him as she picked him up. Thomas, feeling the security of being held firmly and confidently, settled down to a little whimper of hunger. Elizabeth held him close to her neck, and he snuffled against her warm skin and familiar perfume.

"You go back to sleep," Elizabeth said kindly to Ruth. "You look all in. Shall I bring you up a cup of tea and some breakfast?"

"No!" Ruth said, repelled at the thought of Elizabeth in her bedroom. "I'll get something, it's all right."

"I'll sort out this young man and take him up to the house, then," Elizabeth said. "He can come into the garden while I pick some flowers and then we'll go down to the church. It's my day for the flowers."

"Oh no!" Ruth suddenly remembered. "It's clinic day. He has to go to be weighed."

Elizabeth smiled. "They surely can't think he needs weighing every week," she said. "He eats like a horse."

"He *has* to go," Ruth said. "They fill in his weight chart to make sure he gains steadily. He has to go every week."

Elizabeth suppressed her opinion of clinics and weight charts when anyone holding this armful of wet kicking baby could know that they had a perfectly fit child in their arms. "I'll take him, then," she said.

"I have to," Ruth said. She was looking increasingly anxious. "I have to go with him."

"Nonsense," Elizabeth said firmly. "What do they do—weigh him? and write up his chart? I can take him on my way in to church."

The thought of someone dropping in to the baby clinic while

en route to somewhere else quite stunned Ruth. To her it was a target to aim for all morning. The clinic, with the other screaming babies and the frighteningly competent staff, the brisk unfriendliness of the nurse, and the cliquish circle of other mothers, was a place she dreaded. Thomas had to be weighed naked, so she had the task of undressing him and then dressing him again, while the other mothers watched her incompetent fumblings. He screamed all the time as she struggled with the intricate fastenings, and she thought that the staff despised her for her inability to care for her child. Other mothers had toddlers in tow as well, and they managed to control both babies and small children while Ruth was obviously defeated by just one.

"It's awfully hard," she said. "You have to undress him to be weighed, and they fill in the card, and then you have to dress him again."

"I should think I could manage that," Elizabeth said.

Ruth looked at her curiously. Elizabeth was smiling gently, humorously, as if the task were genuinely an easy one. It was obvious to Ruth that Elizabeth found the nightmarishly difficult task of caring for Thomas natural and enjoyable. She felt her throat tighten; she turned to go to her bedroom before Elizabeth saw her cry. "All right then," she said.

"Will you come to the house when you are ready?" Elizabeth asked the closing door.

"Yes," Ruth said, her voice muffled. The door clicked shut.

Elizabeth faced the closed door, Thomas snug against her shoulder. "I'll look after him till you come then," she said, contentedly.

❦

*T*he clinic was held in the health center in the Babies Room. When Elizabeth tapped on the door and walked in with Thomas strapped into his plastic carrier, the noise hit her like a wall of sound. Half a dozen babies were crying and the mothers were shouting comments and gossip over the noise. The health visitor on duty and the one clinic clerk wore expressions of stolid patience. Elizabeth went up to the desk.

"Thomas James Cleary," she said.

The clerk found the form. "Undress over there," she said. "The health visitor will call you."

Elizabeth looked at the cold plastic changing mat on the high narrow shelf with disfavor. Instead she sat on one of the low chairs and undressed Thomas on her knee, wrapping him in a shawl when he was naked.

"Thomas Cleary," the health visitor said. "Oh! It's Thomas's grandma, isn't it?"

Elizabeth rose. "Yes," she said. "I am Mrs. Cleary."

"Mother not well?" the health visitor asked as they watched the red arrow of the scales tip over at sixteen pounds.

"Overtired," Elizabeth said.

The health visitor nodded. "Moved into her new house, then? I should have called in, really. Doing all right is she?"

Elizabeth allowed a shadow of doubt. "It's very hard work," she said. "Coping with everything. Especially with a first child."

The health visitor passed the form to the clinic clerk, who entered the weight carefully in the appropriate column. Elizabeth, who had raised two healthy children without benefit of scales or health visitors, tried to look appropriately respectful. Unseen, the health visitor flipped through her notes. She remembered Ruth when she found the note she had written about the mother and baby failing to bond, and now here was the grandmother turning up at the clinic.

"Let's have a little sitdown and a chat," she invited.

Elizabeth sat in the chair and started to put a new diaper on Thomas. The health visitor noted her easy competence with him. "None of my mothers can do that," she said. "They all dress them on changing mats."

"We didn't have changing mats in my day," Elizabeth said. "I always feel safer with him on my knee."

"Is Mother all right?"

Elizabeth hesitated. "She's very overtired."

"Bit depressed?" the health visitor offered.

Elizabeth shrugged. "I try not to interfere. I'm only here today because my son asked me to have Thomas for the morning."

"And do you have him often?"

"Whenever I am asked."

The health visitor felt a certain unease at Elizabeth's patrician reserve. She was not confiding. It was hard to know how to ask the next question.

"Are mother and baby on good terms?" she asked clumsily. "Getting to know each other? Lots of play and tickling?"

Elizabeth shot her a guarded look, which spoke volumes. "I think so."

The health visitor looked at her notes. Thomas was well-dressed and clean; he was gaining weight; there was no reason to fear that there might be anything wrong at home. But she remembered Ruth's sleepy uninterest in the baby at the farmhouse and how every time she had come the baby had been with his grandmother. Now the grandmother was bringing him to the clinic. When Ruth had come she had looked stressed and anxious, roughly pulling the baby's clothes over his head, bundling him into his baby carriage. She had forgotten to bring a spare diaper on one visit and she had been near tears. The child should not be at risk, with this extended family around him, and yet . . . and yet . . .

"D'you think it's a bit too much for her?" she asked. "New baby, new house, and her husband must work all hours, doesn't he?"

Elizabeth warmed at the mention of Patrick's fame. "He's terribly busy."

"Does Mother need a bit more support perhaps?"

"Well, we do all we can," Elizabeth said, a slight edge to her voice. "Every time I'm asked I have Thomas for her. She knows she only has to pick up the phone."

"So what's the problem?" the health visitor asked boldly.

Elizabeth slid her a swift sideways glance as she straightened Thomas's tiny socks. "Not the maternal type," she whispered. It was like admitting a crime.

"Not?"

"Not."

The two women sat in conspiratorial silence for a moment. "I thought not," the health visitor said. "She just didn't seem to take to him."

"He was a cesarean, and she couldn't feed him. She didn't stick at it so it never happened, and now she just seems quite incapable of getting up to him in the night or waking up in the morning."

"Is she depressed?"

Elizabeth checked an impatient response. "I don't know," she said carefully. "I wouldn't know. We've never had any depression in our family, or anything like that."

"Perhaps the doctor should see her, have a word."

Elizabeth shrugged. "We can always care for Thomas," she said. "I'm free all day, and he can come with me for all my little chores. We're going to do the church flowers now, I've got a carful of Michaelmas daisies."

"Lovely," the health visitor said. "Will you make an appointment for your daughter to see the doctor then?"

Elizabeth hesitated. "She's my daughter-*in-law*," she emphasized. "It makes it a little difficult."

The health visitor nodded, thinking. "What about her mother?"

"Both her parents are dead," Elizabeth said. "And there's no family to speak of. She's very alone in the world. It's a mercy we are there to care for her."

The health visitor hesitated. Her first impression of a young mother struggling to cope with a new baby and to deal with continual interference was changing. In the light of Elizabeth's discreet emphasis, she thought now that Ruth was sliding into depression despite the help of her family.

"Could your son bring her in to see the doctor?"

Elizabeth shook her head. "It would look so strange. She would wonder what was going on."

"I know," the health visitor said. "Tell her that the doctor wants to see her and Baby for an eight-week check. Absolutely routine, and I'll see that Dr. MacFadden knows that we are concerned."

"I'm not *concerned*," Elizabeth said carefully. "Not exactly *concerned*."

"Well, I am," the health visitor said baldly. "And I want her to see the doctor."

*R*uth ate breakfast cereal on her own in the quiet kitchen. Elizabeth had been right in seeing the potential of the cottage. In the autumn morning sunshine the little house glowed. Ruth looked around the new kitchen fittings and the bright pale walls as if they were the walls of a prison. She ate spoonful after spoonful of muesli and tasted nothing. She drank a cup of instant coffee, then she put her head down on the kitchen table and crouched quite still.

She nearly dozed off, sliding from despair into sleep, but she roused herself and went up the stairs, her bare feet warmed by the thick carpet that Elizabeth had chosen. Their bedroom was untidy with cast-off clothes. Ruth walked to the bed, seeing neither the mess nor the pretty view from the bedroom window, which looked over the little garden up the hill to the farmhouse. She climbed into bed and pulled the duvet over her shoulders and closed her eyes. She was asleep in moments.

It was three o'clock in the afternoon when she jerked awake with a gasp of terror. There had been a dream in which Thomas had been missing. She had been looking for him and looking for him. She had been searching the path all the way from the little house to Manor Farm House, and everywhere she looked she could hear his cry, just ahead of her. At Manor Farm, Elizabeth had been in the garden, pruning shears in hand. She had paused in pruning the roses and asked Ruth what was wrong. Ruth had been weeping with distress, but when Elizabeth asked her what she was searching for, she could not remember Thomas's name. She knew she was looking for her baby, but the name had completely gone. She just stared at Elizabeth, speechless with anxiety, knowing that Thomas was missing and she could not remember how to call him back to her.

Ruth gave a little gasp at the shock of the dream and then looked around her bedroom in surprise. The light was wrong for early morning, Patrick was not there, then slowly she remembered that Elizabeth was caring for Thomas, and that she had promised to fetch him from the farmhouse.

"Oh, no," she said softly and jumped out of bed, reaching for the bedside telephone. She dialed the number from memory and waited anxiously.

"Manor Farm." It was Frederick's voice.

"Oh! It's me!" Ruth said. "I overslept, I'm so sorry. I'll come up straightaway."

"Hold tight," he said. Elizabeth had told him that the health visitor thought that Ruth was depressed. He was not surprised, believing that all women were prone to anger and tears and unexplained grief. "Steady the Buffs."

"But I said I would come up. . . . I thought I'd be with you before lunch. . . ."

"So when you weren't I took him out for a little walk, he had his sleep, and now he's out shopping with Elizabeth," Frederick said. "Nothing to worry about at all."

Ruth found that she was gasping with anxiety. "I just feel so awful. . . ."

"Steady the Buffs," he repeated. "We've had a lovely day with him. Elizabeth adores him. We'll pop him down to you when they come home. No trouble at all."

"Thank you," Ruth said weakly. "I was so tired I just slept and slept. . . ."

"Good thing too," he said kindly. "Best medicine in all the world."

"Thank you," Ruth said again. She could feel her eyes watering at the kindness in his tone. "I'll wait for them to come home."

"You do that," Frederick said, and put down the telephone.

As he did so, Elizabeth's car drew up outside the front door, and he went out to help her with the shopping.

"Ruth called," he said. "Apparently she's only just woken."

Elizabeth paused, about to lift Thomas from his seat. "Shall I take Thomas down there? How did she sound?"

Frederick hesitated. "A bit fraught," he said.

Elizabeth unbuckled Thomas from his car seat. "I'll take him down later," she said. "At bedtime. There's simply no point in Ruth having him if she can't cope."

Frederick held out his arms for his grandson. "Hello, young chap," he said lovingly. "Here for the duration, eh?"

*R*uth made the appointment to see the doctor, thinking that it was a routine checkup for Thomas, as the health visitor had advised. Elizabeth insisted that Patrick drive Ruth to the health center and go in with her. After a cursory look at Thomas, Dr. MacFadden suggested that Patrick take Thomas outside—"while I have a word with Mum."

Ruth flinched slightly at being called "Mum," but she let Patrick and Thomas go.

Dr. MacFadden glanced at his notes. He was a young man, newly married and childless. He had endured sleepless nights himself when he was a young doctor on attachment to a busy hospital, but he did not think that dreary blending of night and day, that sea of fatigue in which all colors became gray and all emotions melted into weariness, was similar to the experience of caring for a small sleepless baby. After all, one was work and directed to a goal while the other was part of a natural process. He knew that women with new babies were always tired. He did not think of them as being sick with lack of sleep. He looked for another cause for Ruth's white face and dark-ringed eyes.

"And how are you?" he asked gently.

Ruth felt her face quiver. "I'm fine," she said stubbornly. "Tired."

He glanced down at his notes. He had not seen her during pregnancy, she had gone to the hospital for her prenatal care. He had seen her and Thomas only once before, at their six-week checkup, and had thought then that she looked ill and depressed.

"Feeling a bit down?" he suggested.

"A bit," Ruth said unwillingly.

"Are you sleeping all right?"

She looked at him as if he were insane. "Sleeping?" she repeated. "I never sleep. It feels as if I just never sleep at all."

"Baby keeping you up all night?"

"I never get more than a couple of hours together."

"A lively one," Dr. MacFadden said cheerfully. "Does Father take a turn with you?"

"No," Ruth said. "He's very busy at work. . . ."

He nodded. "Are you a bit weepy?"

She turned her face away. "I'm miserable," she said flatly.

"I think we can do something to help with that," he said. "I expect you feel a bit distant from the baby, do you? It's perfectly normal."

Ruth turned her face back to him, questioning. "Is it? I just keep thinking how *unnatural* it is."

"No, no, lots of mothers can't bond with their babies straightaway. It takes a bit of time."

"He just seems . . ." Ruth broke off at the impossibility of explaining how Thomas—who had been born on his own and preferred to feed without her, and who now crowed and gurgled at the sight of his grandmother or his grandfather, or his father, without apparent preference—seemed so utterly independent of her and remote from her. "It's as if he weren't my baby at all," she said very quietly. "As if he belonged to someone else but I'm . . ." she paused, "I'm stuck with him."

Dr. MacFadden nodded as if none of this was so very dreadful. "I expect you resent having to care for him?"

Ruth nodded. "Sometimes," she whispered. "At the start of the day when Patrick goes, and Thomas is awake and I look ahead and it just goes on and on forever. I never know whether he'll go to sleep or not. And if he *does* sleep during the day I can't rest. I'm always listening for him to wake up. And sometimes he only sleeps for a few moments anyway, so just when I've gone back to bed and I'm dozing off he wakes up and I have to get up again, and then he cries and cries and cries," her voice rose. "And there are times when I could just *murder* him!" She clapped her hand to her mouth and looked aghast. "I didn't mean that. I didn't mean to say that. I'd never hurt him. Never!"

"A lot of mothers feel like this," Dr. MacFadden said gently, retaining a sympathetic smile and holding his voice steady. "It's perfectly normal, and it's very good to acknowledge it. You'd be surprised how many mothers I see who feel just as you do, and when they've had a bit of sleep and a bit of help they bring up perfectly happy children."

"I wouldn't hurt him. . . ." Ruth repeated.

Dr. MacFadden nodded and wrote a note. It said: "? baby

at risk?" "I'm sure you wouldn't," he said. "But you're obviously a bit overwrought just now. Have you ever shaken him or smacked him at all?"

"No! No, of course not."

"That's good," he said soothingly. "No baby was ever hurt by a thought, you know."

Ruth nodded. "I wouldn't hurt him," she said. She sounded less and less certain.

"No," he said. "Now I'm going to write you a prescription that will help you feel more relaxed, and will make things a bit easier. I want you to take one in the morning and two at night, and come back and see me in a week."

"What are they?"

"Amitriptyline," he said. "Just to get you on your feet, to help you through a difficult patch. All right?"

"Yes," Ruth said.

"Start with two at night, and then one every morning, for a week," he said. "And come back and see me next week."

Ruth nodded and rose slowly from her chair.

"I'll have a word with Dad about getting you some more help," Dr. MacFadden said. "Sometimes us men can be a bit insensitive. We don't always understand or make allowances. And a new baby in the house is a bit like a bomb going off, you have to take time to let the dust settle."

Ruth nodded, still saying nothing, and went out to the waiting room. Thomas was asleep in his baby carrier, Patrick was leafing through a magazine. Ruth thought it was obvious to any casual observer that this was an easy baby to manage. Anything that was going wrong between her and Thomas must be her fault. Ruth sat down and looked at Thomas's rosy, angelic sleeping face. Dr. MacFadden nodded to Patrick from the door of his office and Patrick went reluctantly in.

"She's under a lot of strain," the doctor said frankly. "I'm glad we spotted it now. I'll have the health visitor pop in every week, and I've put her on Amitriptyline to try and make life a little easier. Do you have help at home?"

"My mother lives just up the road," Patrick said. "She'll have Thomas any time we want, but she doesn't want to interfere."

The young doctor shook his head. "Don't worry about interfering just now," he said. "What Mum needs is as much help as she can get. Tell your mother not to be shy about chipping in. All help gratefully received. Mum needs a proper break and a couple of nights' sleep."

Patrick nodded, only partly convinced. "I don't see why she can't cope," he said, and then corrected himself. "I'm concerned of course. . . ."

"Some women have the knack and others have to learn it," Dr. MacFadden said airily. "This mum is taking it hard. She'll settle down in a little while, if we give her the help now. Can you get home a bit more? Give her a bit more support?"

Patrick shook his head, refusing. "I'll try," he said.

"Sounds like the best bet is Grandma then," the doctor said. "And thank heavens you've got a good grandma on the spot."

✂— Six —✂

The pills were innocuous-looking, friendly little pebbles. Ruth took two at bedtime and within moments felt a dreamy sense of release and calmness, as if she had just gulped down a schooner of sherry. She chuckled at the thought of it, and Patrick, getting undressed for bed, stared at the unfamiliar sound of Ruth's sexy giggle.

"Are you all right?"

"Happy pills," Ruth said. "Now I know I'm a depressed housewife."

"Well, I haven't seen you smile in months," Patrick commented. He got into bed beside her and pulled the covers over on his side.

"I feel better," she said. "And your mother is coming early in the morning so I don't have to get up. Heaven."

"How would you ever have managed without her?"

Ruth felt as if she were floating in a warm bath. "How would you?" she retorted, but her tongue felt slow, and nothing could threaten her good humor. "I don't see you ironing your own shirts."

"Well, you should be doing them really," Patrick pointed out. "It's not as if you're working now."

Ruth chuckled again. "I'll swap you," she said. "Eight hours a day, and half of those in meetings or chatting to people, against twenty-four hours a day on call with Thomas."

Patrick turned over and turned off the light. "Well, you've got tomorrow morning off," he said, "and every morning that you want, so you've not got much to complain about."

The pleasant drunken feeling was growing stronger. "I'll complain if I want," Ruth said stubbornly, and then giggled at her own intransigence. "I bloody will if I bloody want to," she said.

She slept for only an hour before Thomas's loud wail echoed through the house. She got up and staggered down the stairs to where the bottles were ready in the fridge. She ran the hot tap and shook the bottle under the stream of hot water until the milk was warmed through, then she trudged up the stairs again to the nursery.

Thomas was thrashing in his crib, arms and legs flailing, desperate with hunger and distress.

Ruth did not feel her usual tide of panic at his cries. "Oh, hush," she said calmly. She picked him up: he was wet. "Oh, never mind," she said. She wrapped him in a blanket and sat with him in the rocking chair. The rocking rhythm soothed them both. Ruth hummed quietly to Thomas. He sucked greedily and then more and more slowly, then his eyes closed and his head lolled away from the bottle. Ruth took it from his mouth and transferred him gently to her shoulder. She patted his back. Thomas burped richly but did not wake. Slowly, carefully, she transferred him back into his crib, putting him down as if he were a basket of fragile eggs, taking her hands away only when his full weight was on the mattress, first one hand, and then another.

Only then did she remember that she had not changed his diaper. "Oh, damn," she said carelessly. "Never mind." She left him, wrapped in the damp blanket, and went back to her bed and fell asleep.

Two hours later Thomas woke again. Ruth, dreaming of some strange street far away from Thomas and Patrick, with white clapboard houses and wide fresh lawns, got out of bed unwillingly. It was colder now: the little house had lost its overnight heat. Through the landing window a white moon sailed in a yellow aura of frosty clouds. Ruth trailed downstairs again, warmed a bottle, and trudged back up the stairs.

Thomas was wet through, sodden diaper, sleep suit, blanket. Even his bedding was wet, his little duvet and his sheets. Ruth put him down on the cold changing mat and stripped off his clothes. He kicked and screamed in distress as she pulled the snaps apart and tore off the disposable diaper. His bottom was bright pink as if he had been scalded. She wiped it quickly with the cold, wet baby wipes and patted it dry and then smeared on some cream. He wriggled and she could not fasten the diaper properly. In the end she got it on his writhing body, and pushed his hands and feet into the arm and leg holes of the sleep suit. She did up the snaps and found they were wrongly fastened when she had two extra at the top.

There was nothing she could do to the crib bedding, she thought. She settled back into the rocking chair. Thomas was too distressed to take his bottle. "Hush," Ruth said tiredly. She gave him a little shake to make him stop crying. "Be quiet, Thomas, your bottle is here."

It seemed to work. The baby clutched at her with frightened hands and latched onto the bottle. Ruth rocked in the chair, enjoying the silence after the painful crying. "Hush," she said.

When Thomas fell asleep again, she remembered that the crib was damp. She took a clean blanket and wrapped it around him, leaving the wet duvet spread out on the landing to dry.

In the bedroom Patrick had moved diagonally across the bed; there was no room for Ruth. She slipped in beside him and pushed him gently. He did not move. Ruth curled up in the small space available and went instantly to sleep.

Thomas slept for an hour and a half and then woke, thirsty, irritable, and sweating in the tight swaddling of the blanket. Ruth went downstairs to the kitchen again, heated up a bottle, and trudged back up. Thomas was damp with sweat, his dark hair stuck to his head, his neck and face moist. He cried desperately, irritable with the heat. Ruth lifted him up and unwrapped him. The chill air of the cold room hit him and he started to shiver. His loud, angry cries turned to despairing wails of discomfort. She cuddled him up to her warmth and pushed the bottle into his mouth. Thomas whimpered but then started to suck, and went quickly to sleep.

This time she could not get him to go back into his crib. Every time she put him gently on the damp mattress he turned and cried again, and she had to pick him up, offer him his bottle, and rock him to sleep once more. Four or five times Ruth rocked him to sleep and then gently, carefully, put him down in his cot, and four or five times he started awake, and had to be picked up and rocked again.

It was half past five before Ruth got back to bed. This time Patrick had moved over, taking the duvet with him, and there was a wide space of cold sheet. Ruth got in beside him and gently tugged a corner of duvet to cover her. She lay wakeful, her feet were cold, she was certain Thomas would wake again and cry. She lay, waiting for him to cry, knowing that she would have to get up, staring blankly at the ceiling. She knew she should sleep, she knew that she was tired. But she could not make herself sleep. She was certain that the moment she fell asleep Thomas would wake, and she thought she could not bear to be woken again. It was almost better to be awake, to stay awake all night, if needs be, than to suffer that terrible disappointment of being dragged from warmth and dreams.

At half past six Ruth took her pill and at once felt the easy floating sense of release, and fell asleep. She did not even wake when Patrick's alarm clock went off, and he got out of bed at half past seven. He went downstairs and made himself a cup of coffee. At a quarter to eight his mother's car drew up outside and she came quietly up the path. He opened the front door to her.

"They're both of them sound asleep," he said. "I don't know what we're making such a fuss about."

"You go off to work," his mother said. "Have you had breakfast?"

"I had a cup of coffee, I didn't want anything else."

She shook her head. "D'you have time for a boiled egg?" she asked. "I can have it on the table with some toast in five minutes?"

He hesitated. "All right."

Elizabeth moved quickly around the kitchen while Patrick sat at the table, waiting for his breakfast. Within the promised time it was before him: lightly boiled egg, lightly browned toast, and a fresh pot of tea.

"Does she seem better?" Elizabeth asked.

"The pills certainly seem to be doing her some good," he said. "She was quite cheerful last night, and she was only up once in the night."

"They'll soon settle down," Elizabeth said. "I was very tense with Miriam. First babies are always difficult."

"Well, bless you for coming in." Patrick wiped his mouth on a piece of paper towel. Elizabeth made a mental note to buy some linen napkins. "I don't know what we'd have done without you. The doctor practically prescribed you."

"You know how much I love Thomas," Elizabeth said lightly. "I'd have him all day every day if it was any help."

Patrick gave her a kiss on her cheek, and went to the door. "When the Sleeping Princess awakes, you might tell her that I'll be home late tonight," he said. "I've a late meeting at work and a working dinner after. Tell her not to wait up."

Elizabeth nodded. "Then I'll have Thomas for another spell this afternoon, if you're not coming home," she said. "I don't think Ruth can manage all day without a break."

"Bless you," Patrick said absently, and left.

Elizabeth waited a few minutes as the noise of his car died away, and then tidied up the kitchen. She unpacked the dishwasher and loaded it with Patrick's breakfast things. She threw the egg shells in the flip-top bin and caught sight of the rubbish from last night's dinner. The packet from a frozen pie, the empty bag of frozen chips, and an empty bag of frozen peas. Elizabeth frowned and then rearranged her face into an expression of determined neutrality. She reminded herself that there was no innate virtue in homemade food. Patrick had never tasted a frozen ingredient until he had left home, but it was not fair to expect Ruth to show the same dedication to high domestic standards as Elizabeth. "A different generation," she said quietly to herself.

She opened the fridge door to see what was for dinner. The fridge was virtually empty except for a pint of milk, a box of eggs (which should be kept in the larder and not in the fridge), and cheese. The cheese was out of date.

A little cry from upstairs prevented her from exploring the larder cupboard. She hurried up the stairs and picked Thomas up just as Ruth's bedroom door opened.

"Oh! Is it morning already?"

Elizabeth took in the untidy nursery, the discarded sleep suit, the row of empty bottles, and the stained duvet drying on the banister.

"Yes, dear, but it's still quite early. I'll take care of Thomas, you go back to bed."

"I didn't realize you were here." Ruth's speech was slow, slightly slurred.

"I'll take over now," Elizabeth said reassuringly. "You can leave it all to me."

"I didn't hear Patrick get up."

"He'd have crept out. We were trying to get you some more sleep."

"I couldn't sleep," Ruth said. "When I got back to bed and it was light, I couldn't sleep for ages."

"I'll get this young man a bottle and you go back to bed," Elizabeth said. "When shall I bring him home? Lunchtime?"

"Yes, please," Ruth said slowly.

"Patrick said to tell you that he would be home late tonight; he's out to dinner. He said not to wait up."

Ruth's shoulders, her whole body, slumped. "He's out all evening?"

"Shall I come round? Or would you like to come up to the farm for dinner?"

Ruth shook her head slowly. "No, no," she said. "I'll be all right here."

Elizabeth scanned her with a keen glance. "I'll bring Thomas back at midday, and I'll pop down again in the middle of the afternoon, to see if you want a hand," she said. "It's no fun trying to cope on your own."

"No," Ruth said dully. She did not even look at Thomas in his grandmother's arms. She turned and went back into her bedroom, as if she did not want to see him, to see them together. The little bottle of pills was beside her bed. She knew she had to take one in the morning. She took one and let it rest on her tongue. It tasted strange: it spread a numb tingling through her mouth, it had an acrid bitter taste, a powerful taste. She swallowed it and felt the ease and relief seep through her. Thomas, Elizabeth, even Patrick seemed a long way away and no longer her responsibility. She closed her eyes and slid into sleep.

*E*lizabeth gave Thomas a little of his bottle and then took him downstairs to the kitchen, She made up a couple of spoonfuls of baby rice with the warmed milk and spooned them competently into Thomas's milky smile. She took him back upstairs to the bathroom and stripped off his damp nightwear. His bottom was sore, the skin was puckered and nearly blistered. Elizabeth folded her mouth in a hard line. She laid him on his back on his changing mat while she ran a bath for him, and after his bath let him kick free of his clothes and diaper, so that the air could get to his sore skin. The marks were fading quickly, but Elizabeth still looked grim. Leaving him safe on his mat, on the floor, she went into the nursery. The mattress was still damp and was starting to smell. The bedding had obviously been wet all night. Elizabeth stripped the bed, wiped the mattress cover with disinfectant, took the mattress to the utility room to dry, and piled the damp clothes and duvet in the laundry basket.

She went back to Thomas and dressed him in his day clothes, tickling and stroking him, playing peekaboo over the towel. Then she put him into his baby carrier, bundled all the washing into a large bag, and drove baby and laundry up the drive to the big house.

Frederick was waiting for them. "How's the young Master Thomas?" he asked, coming down the shallow flight of steps and opening the rear door of the car.

Elizabeth made a small grimace, but did not say a word until they were in the house with the door shut. Not even the blackbird on the lawn should hear her criticizing her daughter-in-law. "His crib was soaked, his bedding flung all round the house. He has a nappy rash. It looks to me as if she just shut the door on him and didn't go to him all night."

Frederick had Thomas on his knee, gently bouncing him up and down, holding his little clenched hands. "I thought she was up all hours with him?"

"There's no evidence of it, except for half a dozen dirty bottles. She clearly isn't changing his nappy or changing his bedding," Elizabeth said. "Patrick said that she was up only once in the night, but she looked like death this morning. They had frozen food for dinner last night—I saw the packets, and Patrick was dashing out of the house this morning with nothing but a cup of coffee inside him."

"It won't do," Frederick said firmly. He turned his attention to Thomas. "It won't do, will it?" he demanded. "Won't do at all. Someone will have to take your mummy in hand. And *we* know the woman to do it!"

"No, no," Elizabeth said, smiling. "I can't go barging in there and take over, much as I long to. The sitting room! And the state of the kitchen already! But it's Ruth's home and she must have it as she likes."

"But what does Thomas like?" Frederick asked the baby's bright face. "Thomas doesn't want a damp cot, does he? Perhaps he'd better come here for a few days."

"I can hardly suggest . . ." Elizabeth said.

Frederick looked up. "If she can't cope with the baby, if she's not getting up to him in the night, and if he's being neglected, then it's your duty," he said bluntly. "No suggest, no ifs and buts. If the child needs care and he's not getting it, then you tell Patrick that Thomas is to come here until Ruth pulls herself together."

"She looks awfully ill."

"What does the doctor say?"

"Overtired, that she needs more support."

"Well, give her more support," Frederick ordered. "*We* don't mind having Master Cleary to stay, do we? And Master Cleary won't be going into a damp bed with Granny to look after him, will he?"

"Oh, *don't* call me Granny," Elizabeth exclaimed. "You sound just like that dreadful health visitor."

Frederick chuckled. "Granny Cleary did a spell and they all lived happily ever after," he said to Thomas. "Happily ever after."

***

The phone woke Ruth at eleven in the morning.

"Did you think I was dead?" David asked.

"Oh, my God!" Ruth said delightedly, incredulously. "No! I thought I was. Dead and gone to hell."

"I sent you flowers."

"I know. I kept it. A little violet in a pot."

"And I thought about you a lot. But I didn't know whether I should call or not. They said you had a rough time. I didn't want to intrude."

Ruth gave a little breathless chuckle. "Oh, if you *knew* how lovely it is to hear your voice! Someone who isn't completely obsessed with babies! I expect you even read a book or a newspaper sometimes!"

"Man of the world," David said promptly. "Urbane, elegant, unemployed."

"Still no work?"

"Freelance, I call it. You got out while the going was good."

"I didn't exactly get out," Ruth reminded him.

"Well, after your departure and mine there were three other people laid off, and a whole load of journalists sacked off the evening paper too. Bristol is knee-deep in unemployed hacks, all falling over each other trying to get to a story first."

"Are you doing shifts at Westerly?"

"I am the midnight man," David said impressively. "Nine till midnight most nights. None of the staff want to work those hours, but it keeps a bit of money coming in, and I can steal pens and paper, and watch telly in the warmth for free. These things matter when you're a bum."

"What about features?"

"I am a creative powerhouse," he said with mock dignity. "I generate a feature a minute. And I sell quite a few. But it's a brutish and short existence. You are well out of it. What's it like being a professional wife and mother?"

Ruth tried to say something lighthearted in reply. She found her throat too tight to speak. "I . . ."

"Too blissful for words?"

Soundlessly she shook her head.

"Are you OK?" David asked, suddenly serious. "I didn't mean to be cheap. Are you OK, Ruth?"

"Yes," she said very quietly. "It's just that . . . Oh, David, I didn't know . . ."

"Know what?"

"I didn't know what it was like," she said eventually. "I am so tired all the time, and it's so lonely. Thomas is lovely, of course, but there's so much *washing* to do. And I spend my days wiping down work surfaces so they're clean enough. And at night . . ." she broke off.

"What about night?"

"He just never sleeps," she said in a little strained voice. "It doesn't sound like much when it's someone else's baby, everyone says that babies don't sleep . . . but when it's your own . . . David, I just doze and wake, and doze, and get up again, all night long."

"It sounds like hell."

"Oh, no," Ruth said quickly. "Because the house is so nice, and Thomas is so lovely, and Patrick helps all that he can . . . it's just . . ."

"Can I come round and see you?" David asked. "One afternoon, this afternoon?"

"Oh, yes," Ruth said, thinking of the long afternoon and evening ahead of her. "Oh, that would be lovely. But—you mustn't mind . . ."

"Mind what?"

"I don't look the same at all," Ruth confessed. "I'm miles overweight. I look dreadful."

"I won't mind," David said reassuringly. "The more of you the better as far as I'm concerned."

⚭— Seven —⚭

hen she opened the door to him he nearly recoiled in shock. She was overweight, as she had warned him, but it was her face that shocked him. She was white, an almost candlewax white. Her eyes were ringed with shadows, black as mascara, and her face was hard and sharp, with lines of fatigue and sadness that he had never seen before.

He stepped forward and put his arms around her and held her close. She didn't feel the same: she was carrying more weight and her breasts were bigger. He sensed the extra weight—she was softer, whereas before she had been light to the touch. He thought she might be breast-feeding the baby and felt himself shrink back, for fear of hurting her or even touching her in some way that was now no longer allowed. Her hair, which had been so smooth and glossy, was tired and lank, and she smelled different: of indoors, of baby talcum powder, of small rooms.

"So this is the palace," he said with forced brightness. "And where is His Highness the baby?"

"In the sitting room," she said. She led the way in. There was a small log fire burning in the grate. On a towel before the fire Thomas was kicking his legs and looking at the ceiling.

David regarded him from a cautious distance. "He looks nice," he said. "Here," he dived in his pocket. "I brought this for him. I didn't quite know what he would like."

It was a small yellow plastic duck.

Ruth felt her eyes fill with tears. "Thank you," she said. "Oh, David! Thank you!"

"Here!" he reached out for her but then remembered the embarrassment of the doorstep embrace. "Don't cry. What's the matter?"

She sank onto the sofa and pulled a handkerchief out of the pocket of her baggy maternity jeans. She still was not slim enough to fit her ordinary clothes, and her maternity clothes were worn and shabby. "I'm sorry," she said miserably. "It's nothing. It's everything. Sorry."

He waited for a moment, looking at Thomas, who stared with unfocused blue eyes at the space before him.

"Is it Patrick?" David asked.

Ruth shook her head and crushed her handkerchief back into her pocket again. "There's nothing *wrong*," she said. "It's just that I'm so tired, and everything seems such an effort, and the least thing makes me cry."

David felt completely lost with this new, weepy Ruth.

"Is this—er—what-d'you-call-it?—postpartum depression?" he asked.

"*I* don't know," she said abruptly. "No. I told you. I'm just tired."

"Well, can't someone else have him at night?" David glanced down again at Thomas, who looked completely innocent of any desire to disturb anyone.

"Well, Patrick can't, he's working too hard. And his grand-mother could, but I don't like to ask her."

"But you need help," David said reasonably.

"Oh, stop!" she said with a sudden flare of temper. "Don't come in here with a load of questions and solutions, David. I'm perfectly all right except for the fact that I'm running all the time on a couple of hours' sleep. If you were as tired as me you'd hang yourself."

"OK," he said quickly. "OK. I won't say another word."

She gave him a brief watery grin. "And they do help out," she said, "Patrick's family. She started coming in in the mornings so that I can sleep. And I've seen the doctor. So I'm OK. Really."

David nodded, still unconvinced.

"Tell me the gossip," Ruth commanded, trying to distract them both. She went down on the floor and waved a rattle in front of Thomas. He put his hands up to reach for it, and she waved it again.

David dredged up some small scandals from work and then, warming to the theme, told Ruth how the station had been restructured and how the few competent journalists left were running around and working twice as hard, and all applying for other jobs.

"It sounds like chaos," she said.

"It is. And the place is always packed with people freelancing or coming in to sell ideas or tapes. James couldn't bring himself to sack anyone outright, so everyone who should have been sent home is now working there for free. The telephone bill must have doubled, and of course we're all selling pieces all around the country so the studios are always booked. I doubt they've saved any money at all."

Ruth nodded. "Patrick's place is cutting back too," she said. "He's really worried. They've only had the new documentary unit up and running for a few months and they're already reconsidering."

David nodded, suppressing his prejudiced belief that Patrick's egotistical direction of the unit was the greatest problem it faced.

"D'you want a cup of tea?" Ruth asked.

David nodded.

At once she looked strained.

"What's the matter? Shall I make it for you?"

"I know it sounds silly," she said. "But since he's happy here I don't really want to disturb him. If I pick him up and he starts crying it's really difficult to make him stop. I know it sounds stupid . . ."

"Not stupid to me," David said stoutly. "I don't want him to start crying. Shall I make the tea while you watch him?"

She hesitated. "I know it's crazy," she said in a sudden rush. "And everyone else just picks him up and lugs him about. My mother-in-law takes him to the shops with her, and out in the car, and everywhere she goes. But I just can't face it . . . I just

95

can't face him crying and crying, and I don't know how to make him stop."

David patted her hand feebly. "I bet everyone feels like that."

She looked at him, scanning his face to see if he was sincere. "D'you think so?"

"Lots of them," David said. "But people don't talk about it."

She turned her head away from him and looked at the fire. "Sometimes I'm not sure if I love him at all," she said very quietly. "I don't enjoy being with him much, and I'm so tired. . . ."

She fell silent.

"I'll make the tea," he repeated. "Would you like that?"

"Yes," she said. "Everything is in the cupboard above the kettle. The milk is in the fridge."

David nodded and went to the kitchen. When Ruth heard him filling the kettle and switching it on, she quietly took the bottle of pills from her pocket and took one. Within moments she could feel her anxiety melting away. She leaned over Thomas and smiled down at him. She blew into his little face and watched him pucker in surprise at the sensation. When David came in with the tea she was rosy and smiling.

"I can't stay long," he said. "I've got a shift." He handed her a mug.

"What's going to happen about your work?" she asked.

He was pleased to see her taking an interest and looking more like the old Ruth. "I'll get somewhere," he said. "I've got an interview in London next week. Something will come up, and I'm staying in practice and my voice is heard. Something'll come up."

"I hope so," she said. "Don't go missing on me, will you? Don't go without giving me your address. I don't want to lose touch."

He nodded, getting to his feet. He thought that in all the years that he had known her Ruth had never invited his attention. He had always been pursuing her, and she had always been casually indifferent as to whether he was there or not. Now it seemed that she needed him, and he was guiltily aware that this tearful, plump, white-faced housewife was not the woman he had desired.

"Of course," he said. "Give me a ring when you're free and we'll go out to lunch."

"Yes," she said, but she knew that she would not dare to ask Elizabeth to baby-sit while she went out to lunch with a man. Patrick obviously would not baby-sit under those circumstances, and naturally enough, with a mother-in-law next door, Ruth had no other baby-sitters. "It's a bit tricky to get out while Thomas is so young," she said. The Amitriptyline had steadied her: she did not feel like crying, she managed a smile. "In a couple of years I'll be out dancing every night."

He patted her on the shoulder in farewell. He did not want a closer embrace. "I'll see myself out," he said. "You stay there with him. He's a lovely baby."

"I know he's lovely," she said. She sounded uncertain. "I know he is."

David let himself out and closed the front door behind him. The air was sharp and cold. He felt a sense of release and an elated awareness of his own youth and freedom. He was deeply glad that he was not Ruth, trapped in the little house, waiting for Patrick to come home, seeing no one but the baby. He was even glad that he was not Patrick, coming home every night to a plump, white-faced woman who cried for nothing, and a baby that never slept. He went quickly down the garden path, as if he were afraid that Ruth might call him back and he would see her crying again.

As he was unlocking the door of his car, an Austin Rover pulled in and parked in front of him. The woman driver, an elegant, attractive woman, gave him a friendly smile.

"Are you going? Have I left you enough space?" she asked.

The mother-in-law, David thought. And me creeping off like a clandestine lover. "That's fine," he said boldly. "I've just been visiting Ruth Cleary. "

"Oh! I'm Mrs. Cleary," the woman sounded convincingly surprised, as if it had not occurred to her that he might have come from the cottage. "How nice for Ruth to have some company."

"I'm David Harrison. I used to work with her, at Radio Westerly."

"I'm sure she misses her work a lot," Elizabeth said. "She'll have enjoyed hearing about it. Are you still working there?"

"Yes," David said. "She seemed a bit tired."

Elizabeth smiled. "A new baby can be absolutely exhausting," she said. "I've brought her down some supper, and I'll take Thomas back home with me to give her a little break."

David brightened. "I'm sure that's a good idea," he said. "She doesn't seem to be getting much sleep."

Elizabeth's charming smile never wavered. "Actually," she said, lowering her voice, "I've been rather worried about her. I was afraid she was getting depressed."

"She seemed very weepy," David said.

Elizabeth nodded. "Exactly," she said. "And she's on anti-depressants, but they don't seem to do her much good."

"Ruth is taking antidepressants?" He was shocked.

Elizabeth nodded sadly. "It's her choice. And I can hardly inter-fere."

David shook his head incredulously. "I don't believe it!"

"I'm afraid she's very low."

"I wouldn't have thought she was the type. . . ." David was adjusting his view of Ruth from the confident, bright jour-nalist, the quickest, most able worker in the newsroom, to the sad housewife on happy pills. "They can be addictive, can't they?"

"The doctor prescribed it," Elizabeth said doubtfully. "He must be aware of the situation."

"But Ruth!"

"I know, it hardly seems possible, does it? She's just finding motherhood terribly hard going."

David thought for a moment. "Is it the baby? Is there any-thing wrong with him?"

"No, that's the absurd thing. He's an absolute peach. He sleeps well and he eats well and he's no trouble at all. I think she may be one of those women that simply never take to motherhood."

"Well, it's not as if she planned it . . ." David said indiscreetly.

Elizabeth's face gave nothing away as she registered this cru-cial piece of information. "No," she said. "But she was quite happy about it, wasn't she?"

David grimaced. "I never thought so. It couldn't have come at a worse time, and she's a natural journalist. . . ."

Elizabeth nodded. "Oh."

"Is there anything I can do?" David asked.

Elizabeth hesitated for a moment "How kind of you to offer," she said coolly. "But I'm sure we can manage."

David heard the snub, and opened the door of his car.

"It's been so nice meeting you," Elizabeth said. Her smile was warm. "I hope to see you again."

"Thank you, Mrs. Cleary," David said. "I'd like to keep in touch with Ruth—and with Patrick too, of course."

"Oh, but you must!" she said earnestly. "Poor Ruth needs all the support she can get."

David blinked. He had never thought of Ruth as "poor Ruth" before. "Thank you very much, Mrs. Cleary."

"Call me Elizabeth! Please!"

"Well, thank you, Elizabeth. Good-bye."

Elizabeth watched him pull away and then went into the cottage.

There was no one in the sitting room but there were wails of distress coming from the upstairs bathroom. The sitting room smelled of vomit.

"Oh, dear," Elizabeth said softly, and went up the stairs.

Ruth was trying to undress Thomas, who was liberally covered in regurgitated milk. Ruth's hair and shoulder and the front of her shirt and trousers were sodden.

"He just threw up!" she said desperately. "He was drinking well, a whole bottle, and then the whole lot suddenly came up. Is he ill?"

"No," Elizabeth said reassuringly. "He's fine. He just probably overdid it a bit."

In her haste Ruth had not undone all the buttons on Thomas's shirt. Pulling it over his head, she had got his head stuck. He was shrieking piercingly from inside the garment.

"Oh, God!" Ruth cried above the noise.

"Shall I?" Elizabeth asked.

Ruth shot a desperate look at her.

"You go and get changed out of those dirty clothes," Elizabeth commanded kindly. "And leave Master Thomas here to me. I'll bathe him and change him and take him up to the farm. When you're ready there's supper for you downstairs in the warming oven. Patrick can collect Thomas on his way home. You have a quiet evening on your own for a change." She moved forward and took Thomas—vomit and all—onto her lap.

Ruth hesitated, glancing at Elizabeth's immaculate slacks and cashmere sweater. "Are you sure you don't mind?"

"Mind?" Elizabeth laughed. "Ruth dearest, I have nothing else to do and it is my greatest treat. He'll be fine once he's clean and dry again, and his grandfather will play with him all evening. Just relax and leave it to me."

She slid her fingers inside the narrow neckband of the shirt and undid the buttons. Thomas, suddenly released, came out red-faced and tearful.

Ruth slipped from the bathroom as Elizabeth stripped off the rest of the wet, foul-smelling clothes, wrapped Thomas in a warm towel, and started to run a bath.

When he was washed and changed and sweet-smelling and sweet-tempered, she put him in her car and drove up to the farm. Frederick looked up as she carried the baby seat into the drawing room.

"Hello, my dear! Hello, Master Thomas? All right?"

"She was practically in hysterics because he had brought up his feed," Elizabeth said. "She really can't cope at all."

Frederick unbuckled Thomas from his baby seat. "Well, that's no good," he said, speaking half to the baby.

"She'd had a friend call for tea," Elizabeth said. "David Harrison from Radio Westerly. Very charming, rather attractive."

Frederick turned his attention to his wife and raised his eyebrows. "Not quite the thing, is it?"

"I'm sure there's no harm in it," Elizabeth said. "And she's terribly lonely."

"Better mention it to Patrick all the same."

"I don't like to tell tales. . . ."

Frederick turned back to Thomas. "Us chaps must stick together," he informed him. "*I* shall tell Patrick."

*R*uth was asleep when Patrick came in, and he did not disturb her. But in the night she woke, half listening even in sleep for a cry from the nursery. The house was silent; Patrick was breathing noisily at her side. The pillow and his hair smelled slightly of cigar smoke. Ruth moved away. She glanced at the illuminated dial of her bedside clock. It was four in the morning. Thomas had never slept through till four in the morning before. She lay back smiling. Perhaps everything was working out at last. Thomas sleeping through the night, David calling to see her, perhaps life was returning to normal. She closed her eyes and dozed off again.

She woke with a start. It was half past four. Thomas still had made no sound. A superstitious fear made her sit suddenly upright. She thought of crib death, suffocation, kidnapping, any one of the fears that new mothers carry with them all the time, wherever they are. She slipped out of bed and tiptoed along the dark landing. She listened at the door of Thomas's room. She could not hear him. Usually in sleep he made little snuffling noises, or stirred. She could hear nothing.

Careful not to wake him, she gently touched the door, pushing it open one silent millimeter at a time. The carpet under the door made a soft hushing noise as the foot of the door brushed against the new pile; but still Thomas did not wake.

She crept forward so that she could see over the side of the crib. His little duvet was folded at the foot of the bed. Thomas was not there. The cot was empty.

Ruth screamed. "Thomas!" and scrabbled for the light switch. Frantically she looked around the room as if he could have crawled out of bed and hidden. The nursery was empty. She ran across the landing to the bedroom. Patrick was sitting up in bed, bleary-eyed.

"What the . . ."

"Thomas! It's Thomas! He's gone! Oh, God, Patrick! He's gone!"

"No . . ." Patrick shook his head.

Ruth was unstoppable. "Christ, someone has taken him! Patrick, get up, call the police! He's gone. I just woke up and thought he was quiet and went to his room and his cot is empty!"

She could feel hot tears pouring down her cheeks and hear her voice getting louder and higher in panic. "I thought it was funny that he hadn't cried but then I went . . . "

"Ruth, get a grip!" Patrick shouted over the tide of her hysteria. "He's quite all right. He's at home. He's with Mother. I left him up there! We thought you'd like the break."

Ruth was screaming but the words slowly penetrated. She fell silent, she stared at Patrick, but oddly the tears did not stop, they still poured down her cheeks. "He's where? Where?"

"He's at home," Patrick said. "With Mother. In my old nursery, in my old cot. Safe and sound."

Ruth whimpered, a soft animal sound. "I thought he'd been taken. . . ."

"I know. I should have woken you and told you. But you were asleep and I thought you needed your sleep."

"I thought he was gone."

"I'm sorry. We thought it was the best thing to do."

Ruth's dark eyes were huge. "It's worse than that," she said.

"Shush," Patrick got out of bed and put his hands on her shoulders, drawing her back to bed. "Settle down, Ruth, I'll make you a cup of tea. Have one of your pills."

"I thought he was gone," she said again.

Patrick looked around for Ruth's bottle of Amitriptyline and shook two of the little pills into his hand. "Take this," he said. "Calm down, Ruth."

He offered her a glass of water and her teeth clanked on the glass; her hands were trembling so much she nearly spilled it. She took the pills and sipped the water. He thought that she looked old and haggard. He had never seen her less attractive. He had a headache from the wine at his dinner and he was deeply tired. He had a weary sense of one crisis following another, and everything left to him.

"Come on, darling," he said. "Lie down. Go to sleep again. It's all right now."

She looked at him with her enormous tragic eyes. "It's worse than that," she repeated.

"Worse than what?"

"Worse than thinking he was gone."

"Shush, shush," he said. He slipped into bed beside her and drew the covers up.

Ruth felt the pills beginning to weave their sleepy magic around her. Already her terror felt as if it had happened to someone else, as if it were another woman who had woken in the night to find her baby's crib empty, and her baby stolen away.

"It's worse than that. . . ."

"What is worse?" he asked wearily.

"I was glad," Ruth said with bleak simplicity. "I thought, Oh, good, he's gone, and at last I'll be able to get some sleep." She smiled her misty, uncertain smile at Patrick, her eyes unfocused. "I told you it was worse," she said. "I thought he was kidnapped and I thought, At least I'll be able to get some sleep now. That's really bad, isn't it?"

"Shush," Patrick said automatically. "Not to worry, shush, Ruth."

Ruth nodded, her eyes slowly closed, she slept.

For more than an hour Patrick lay, with his head thudding and his eyes open, looking at the darkness and hearing over and over again in his mind Ruth's slurred confession, and wondering what it meant.

❦

*P*atrick left for work at the usual time, leaving Ruth asleep and a note for her on the pillow. It said:

THOMAS IS WITH MOTHER AT THE FARM. PHONE THEM WHEN YOU ARE READY TO HAVE HIM BACK. MOTHER SAYS SHE CAN HAVE HIM ALL DAY IF YOU WOULD LIKE A REST. I WILL BE HOME AT THE USUAL TIME, AND I WILL SHOP FOR SUPPER. TAKE IT EASY, DARLING. SEE YOU AT 6.

He had written it in black felt tip, in printed capital letters, as if he could not trust her to read script.

❦

*B*ut Patrick did not go to work; he drove up to the farm and let himself in with his front-door key. His mother was in the kitchen in her embroidered pale-blue silk housecoat. Thomas was sitting, padded with a pillow, in Patrick's old wooden high chair, watching her with quiet approval. Elizabeth was making toast for herself and baby rice for Thomas.

"Good morning, darling," she said over her shoulder as Patrick came in. "Come for breakfast?" Then she saw his face, and turned quickly around. "What's wrong?"

"Ruth," Patrick said the one word as if it would explain everything.

"Sit down," she said automatically. "I'll make you some breakfast. Tea? A couple of boiled eggs?"

"Yes, please," he said. "I have to phone work. I have to tell them I'll be late."

She heard him go into the hall and telephone his office. Swiftly and efficiently she put on the kettle, set a couple of eggs to boil, and sliced bread for toast. Then she sat before Thomas and spooned baby rice and milk for him. When Patrick came back into the kitchen it smelled warm with the familiar smell of breakfast. His son turned a wobbly head and looked at him.

"Where's Dad?"

"He went out with his gun to get some rabbits, early," his mother said. "He should be back soon. D'you want to talk to him?"

"To you both," Patrick said.

She nodded and wiped Thomas's face with a square of soft gauze. She set the table before Patrick and poured his tea. The last of the sand fell silently through the egg timer, and she brought two eggs out of the saucepan. She put them in the egg cups of his childhood, a set of little friendly faced china animals. Patrick managed a wan smile.

"Thomas will enjoy these when he's a little older," she said. "He likes it here."

"Sleeps well in my cot?" Patrick asked.

"He only woke once," she said. "And then he went straight down again."

Patrick nodded and ate his toast and boiled eggs. She watched him chewing and carefully swallowing, and she felt her throat tighten in sympathy.

"You never really let go," she said looking from her son to her grandson. "You never stop loving if you are a mother."

Patrick glanced up at her, and she was shocked at the strain in his face. "Really?" he said doubtfully.

She nodded and put her hand gently on his shoulder. "Well, *I* never will."

The backdoor opened, and they heard Frederick ordering the dog to his basket, shucking off his boots, racking his gun, and locking the case. He padded into the kitchen in his shooting breeches and thick socks. "Hello, old man," he said. "Come for a bite to eat?"

Patrick nodded. "Did you get anything?"

"Couple of rabbits. We'll have pie tonight, shall we, my dear?"

"If you skin them," Elizabeth said.

Frederick chuckled. "I will."

"Do you want any breakfast?"

"I'll take a cup of tea," he said. "I went out with a roll of bread and cheese. I did very well, thank you, my dear."

Elizabeth poured the tea. "Patrick wants to talk with us," she said.

Thomas let out a little squeak and Elizabeth drew up her chair beside him and gave him a wooden honey scoop to hold, her eyes on her son.

"Trouble?" Frederick asked.

Patrick nodded. "It's Ruth," he said. He paused, hardly knowing what to say. "She woke in the night and went to look for Thomas. I didn't wake her when I got in; I thought I should leave her to sleep." He looked at his mother. "She was sound asleep; I thought I should leave her."

"Quite right," Elizabeth said briskly. "She was desperately tired yesterday."

"So when she woke she didn't know where Thomas was."

"She must have known," Frederick interrupted. "She knew he was with us. If he wasn't at your home, then clearly he was still with us."

"She panicked," Patrick said. "I woke up to hear her screaming like an express train in the nursery. She thought he was kidnapped. She was screaming and crying. She couldn't even hear me when I told her that everything was all right."

Frederick exchanged a glance with Elizabeth.

"Poor dear," Elizabeth said.

"I had to shout her down," Patrick said. "She wouldn't hear me, she went on screaming and screaming. When she was finally quiet I gave her two of her pills and she went all soft and sleepy. But she kept saying there was something worse, there was something worse."

Thomas reached for the honey scoop where Elizabeth had placed it on the wooden table of the high chair. Elizabeth guided his little hand to it.

"She was half asleep but I think she meant it," Patrick said. "She said that she wished that he had been kidnapped so that she wouldn't have to look after him anymore. So that she could get some sleep."

Elizabeth drew in her breath sharply. Frederick rose to his feet and stood, looking out the kitchen window, his back to the room.

"I see," he said quietly.

"I didn't know how seriously I should take it. . . ." Patrick began. "I thought I should talk it over with you."

Elizabeth nodded. "Quite right," she said. She glanced at Frederick's back. "Do you think she meant it, Patrick?"

Patrick shrugged. "I can't tell," he said. "We should perhaps talk to the doctor, but I didn't want to take this any further without talking it over."

Elizabeth hesitated, glanced toward Frederick again. "Did she ever want him?" she asked. "Did she ever want to be a mother?"

Patrick shook his head in silence.

Frederick turned back from the window. "I think we have a serious problem," he said. "And we've both seen it coming, Patrick. Your mother has been worried sick about Ruth's care for the baby. When she collects him in the morning he's been neglected all night. When she returns him in the afternoon, Ruth never seems to want him back. Frankly I think she's rejected him. This comes as no surprise to me at all."

Patrick looked at his mother. "You never said . . . "

She shook her head. "How could I? It's not my place to criticize my daughter-in-law. And besides I kept hoping that she would get better. She started on the pills and I thought she would be less depressed. I made sure she could sleep during the day. I thought that things would improve. Short of taking Thomas away from her all day and all night I didn't see how I could do more."

There was a brief silence.

"She needs help," Patrick said. "Do I start with the GP?"

Elizabeth said nothing.

"He's not been up to much so far," Frederick said. "Antidepressants indeed!"

Both men turned to Elizabeth. Still she said nothing.

"I think we need something a bit more decisive," Frederick went on. "Get this sorted out once and for all. We've been worried sick, Patrick, I can tell you. We knew she wasn't pulling her weight, but we didn't know what more we could do."

Patrick shrugged. "But I don't know what to do," he said. "I suppose she should see a therapist. Get some help. I could ask the doctor, and the health visitor was good, wasn't she?"

Elizabeth slowly shook her head. "I'm not sure that we want the health center to know all about this."

"Why not?" Patrick asked.

"If we call them in—the doctor and the health visitor and the social workers, all of them—we can't control what happens. What if they say that Ruth has to go to hospital for a couple of months? What if they say she has to have treatment?"

"We could manage," Frederick said easily.

"Yes, but what if they won't let us manage? What if they say she has to take him with her? Or what if they say that he has to be put into care, that we're too old to have him? Once you call these people in, they can do what they want. What if they say Ruth has been neglecting him or abusing him and they take him away from us?"

The two men looked blankly horrified. "They couldn't say that!" Frederick exclaimed.

"The authorities these days have tremendous powers," Elizabeth reminded him. "If they think that Ruth has endangered Thomas, they can take him right away from us all and we might never see him again. Once you ask them in, you give them the power to do what they want."

"But they couldn't think that Ruth . . ." Patrick broke off.

Elizabeth looked steadily at him. "She has neglected him since the day he was born," she said calmly. "From the first days in the hospital when she wouldn't feed him, till now when she says she wishes he was kidnapped. She never wanted him, did she? He was conceived by accident."

Patrick nodded. "It was my fault," he confessed. "I wanted a baby."

"Nothing wrong in that," Frederick said stoutly.

"Nothing at all," Elizabeth said. "It's not you in the wrong, Patrick, it's her. She should have learned to love him. If the health visitor knew the half of it, I think she'd call in social services, and once they start, anything can happen."

Frederick looked absolutely stunned. "I've had no experience of this sort of thing . . . are you sure you're right?"

"How should we have any experience?" Elizabeth demanded, an edge of disdain in her voice. "No one in our family has ever been mentally ill. No one has ever needed health visitors and doctors and drugs and psychiatric treatment."

Patrick looked at her as if he were a naughty little boy but she might give him a note to excuse him from detention. "This is awful," he said.

Her face softened. "It's not your fault," she said gently. "It's not your fault, darling, I know how hard you've tried. And it's not little Thomas's fault either—a sweeter, easier baby never lived." She glanced out the kitchen window across the fields to where the roof of the little house was just visible. "It's Ruth," she said simply. "She's just not up to it."

Patrick breathed slowly out and put his head in his hands. Frederick looked at his wife's stern, beautiful face. "You're right," he said unwillingly. "What d'you suggest, my dear?

"I think Thomas and Patrick should move in here, so that we can look after them. Patrick can have some regular meals and regular hours for a change, and Thomas can be properly cared for. This running up and down from one house to another is no good for him at all."

Frederick nodded.

"And Ruth can come and live here or stay with her aunt. She needs a complete break."

"She hardly ever speaks to her," Patrick protested.

"Are there no American relatives at all? Where she could go for a long visit?" Elizabeth asked.

"No, she's almost completely alone in the world."

Elizabeth nodded. "Then it's up to us," she said. "We're her only family; no one is even going to inquire. We could send her to a convalescent home to have a good rest, get away from it all. Or she can stay on her own in the cottage. And when she feels strong enough she can come back, and take up her life with Patrick and Thomas again."

Thomas knocked the honey scoop to the floor. Elizabeth bent down and picked it up, rinsed it under the tap, and handed it back to him.

"It's a nightmare," Patrick said unbelievingly. "I would never have dreamed this could happen to us."

Elizabeth put her hand gently on the nape of his neck. The skin was as soft under her fingers as it had been when he had been just a little boy, bent over his homework. She felt a great rush of tenderness to him, and to his little son.

"You come home, darling," she said gently. "You and Thomas come home and leave it to Mother. I'll sort it all out for you."

⌒ Eight ⌒

*I*n the little house Ruth stirred and woke. The brilliant autumn sun was streaming in the window, the white light blindingly bright in the white bedroom. On her pillow was Patrick's note written in large printed capitals. Ruth read it carefully, smiled at the instruction to take it easy—touched by his consideration. Her bottle of pills was at her bedside. She knew she had to take one in the morning but she thought she had forgotten to take one at bedtime. She took two, letting the warm sleepy drunkenness spread through her. She had forgotten the empty crib and her panic of the night before. She had a vague, distant memory of some awful fright—like the shadow of a nightmare.

She lay back on the pillows. The little digital clock said 10:32. Ruth closed her eyes and slept again.

She woke at one o'clock with an anxious start. She had been dreaming that Thomas was crying, but then she saw Patrick's note again and realized that the house was empty. She read it, as if for the first time, and took her morning pill. She felt as if she were floating. Slowly, luxuriously, she got out of bed and went, a little unsteadily, to the bathroom. The walls undulated comfortably around her. She ran a bath and poured a long stream of bath oil into the hot water. She slipped off her nightgown and sank into the hot, scented water. She lay back and closed her eyes. Far away she heard the telephone ring but she could not be bothered to answer it. She thought for a brief moment that it might be Elizabeth, that something might be wrong with Thomas.

"No point asking me," she said into the steam-filled room. "I'm the last person to ask. I haven't a clue."

When the water grew cold, she heaved herself out of the bath, wrapped herself in a large towel, and lay on the bed. She felt too deliciously idle to move. When the telephone rang on the bedside table beside her, she could hardly be bothered to pick it up.

"Ruth?" It was David.

"Oh, hello."

"You sound funny."

"I've just woken up."

"But it's half past two!"

"I know. Bliss, isn't it?"

"Where's Thomas?"

For a moment Ruth could not remember. "Oh, he's with Elizabeth," she said. "She knows how to look after him."

"I'm just down the road from you," David said. "I had to cover a council meeting in Bath. I've done my report and I'm on my way home. I wondered if you'd like to come out for a drink."

"All right," Ruth said.

"I'm at the Green Man, on the Radstock Road, very close,"

"I know it," she said. "I'll come at once."

"See you in a minute then."

The phone clicked and he was gone. Slowly and thoughtfully Ruth began to dress. Choosing her clothes seemed a tremendously difficult task. She tried and discarded three or four skirts before pulling on a pair of black leggings and a black embroidered smock top. Most of her clothes were still too tight at the waistband, but she had a superstitious fear of buying anything the next size up. She thought that if she went into a bigger size she would never be thin again. In the meantime she had a wardrobe full of smart clothes, all the wrong size, and an increasingly shabby selection of maternity clothes, which she was tired of seeing. She brushed her hair and peered at her pale face in the mirror. "Oh, well," she said. "It's only David."

The loss of her looks, of her slim, sharp figure seemed unimportant. Ruth was cocooned in a warm, drugged haze, far away from everything. As she turned to leave she remembered that she usually took her morning Amitriptyline as she dressed. She took one, and then, guiltily, took another. She slipped the bottle into her pocket, to take one later. The feeling of drunken sensual relaxation was too enjoyable. She did not want it to wear off.

She drove unsteadily to the pub. The road seemed distant and far away, the car sluggish. She felt as if she were driving some immensely slow ocean liner on a great sea. When she came to the pub, she missed the wide turning into the parking lot and had to reverse back up the road. A van, rounding the corner, pulled out around the wildly zigzagging car and hooted loudly. Ruth waved pleasantly at the driver.

When she walked into the pub she could not at first see David. It was as if he materializd out of darkness. She blinked and smiled at him.

"Hi," he said. "What d'you want?"

"I'll have a gin and tonic," she said.

He glanced at her, and then gave the order to the barman. Ruth went to a seat in the corner and sat down, with her back to the window.

"Are you OK?" he asked, as he brought the drinks over and sat opposite her.

"Perfectly," she said. Her lips felt thick and unwilling; she took her time over the word, and said it with care.

He looked at her narrowly. "Have you been boozing?" he asked. "On the cooking sherry, Ruth? Housewife's temptation, you know."

She shook her head. "No," she said. "Just sleeping. I'm addicted to sleep. I could sleep forever, I think."

"Are you taking drugs?" he asked blankly.

She widened her eyes to emphasize her innocence. He saw that the pupils were dilated. Her dark eyes were all black. "Of course not," she said. "We don't get an awful lot of dealers up at Manor Farm, you know."

"I meant antidepressants."

She sipped her drink and turned her face away from him.

"Why on earth should you think I'm taking antidepressants?"

He thought of admitting that Elizabeth had told him, but shrank from the appearance of a conspiracy against her. "I thought you were a bit down. If you've been to the doctor, it's the obvious conclusion."

"Not me," she said firmly.

He sighed. He did not think she had ever lied to him before. At college together, at long boring events when they had waited together for an interview, she had never avoided a question or glossed an answer. It was not that they had sworn mutual honesty, it was the comfortable consequence of having nothing to hide. There was nothing in his life that he was ashamed of, there was nothing that Ruth could not tell him. He had thought that her baby would make a difference to their relationship. But he could never have predicted this.

"Jesus, Ruth . . ." he said unhappily.

Ruth turned to look at him. He seemed very distant; his distress was very unimportant.

"Oh, what does it matter?" she said idly. She took another gulp. "What does it matter either way?"

"It matters to me," he said. "I don't mind what you take or what you do. You know that. I've never tried to muscle in on your life, or tell you what I think. But you've always told me what you were feeling about things, and I've always been frank with you. It's strange—you being so distant. It feels awful. It feels like hell."

She nodded. "I do feel distant," she said, her speech slightly slurred. "I *like* feeling distant," she said. "D'you know I think this is how Patrick feels all the time. I think Amitriptyline just makes women feel like men. It fits you for a man's world. I love Patrick, and I love Thomas, and I'd lay down my life for them. But if you asked me whether I'd rather go home and care for them, or go to work right now, I'd far rather go and do the job I'm good at with people who like me for what I am and not because I'm married to them, or gave birth to them . . . or married their son," she added.

"But that's because you miss your work," David suggested.

She shook her head. "It's the pills," she said. "It's how men are all the time. Most men would rather go to work than spend time at home, you know that. Men are detached and distant. Even Patrick is. Amitriptyline just makes us equal. I feel detached and distant too."

"*I'm* not detached," he said passionately. "It's not true of all men."

"You're not now," she said, as if it hardly mattered to her. "But once you're married and the novelty has worn off, you will be."

He downed his pint. "It's a dismal, dismal prospect," he said fiercely.

"Isn't it?" she said calmly. "Get us another drink; do." She handed him a five-pound note. David took it and went up to the bar. As the barman fetched their drinks, he watched her in the smoked mirror behind the bottles. She took something from her pocket and put it in her mouth.

"You've just taken one," he said flatly as he came back and put her drink before her. "I saw you."

She gave him her familiar mischievous smile. "Oh, sod off, David," she said. "I've seen you pissed often enough. I am taking Amitriptyline and it makes me feel equal to Patrick. It makes me feel relaxed with Thomas, and then I can look after him better, and I don't mind when Patrick works all hours. It makes me unwind. You should be pleased for me."

"It doesn't seem right," he said stubbornly. "Your life should be better for you. You shouldn't need it."

"Well, it isn't, and I do," she said easily. "It's just while Thomas is so small. When he's a bit older, and sleeping through the night, when Patrick's job is more secure . . . oh, lots of things will change. This is just a rough patch I have to get through somehow."

He nodded. Her speech was getting worse; she sounded drunk.

"I'm sure you shouldn't be mixing them with gin," he said.

She chuckled. "You're an old woman," she said. "Now shut up and tell me the gossip. What story were you covering, and how much did you have to do? Is the Bath studio still in the bottom of the council cellar? Is the mad caretaker still there who won't let you in unless you show your driving license?"

David nodded. "Yes, *she's* still there. I've been there three times in the last fortnight and she pretends not to recognize me. I say, 'Hello, Mrs. Armitage,' and she says, 'Name?' just like that, and I have to sign in. It was a vote about selling a school playing field to a supermarket. I did a nice package for Westerly and I've sold it."

She smiled. She felt as if he were far away, a charming, once-beloved friend. "And what were you doing before—on the other three times in the studio?"

"Planning inquiry—a new bypass. And a Farmers Union meeting. Ruth—"

Her eyelids were drooping. "Yes?"

"You look half asleep."

"It's the baby," she said drowsily. "Every time I fall asleep he wakes up. I think he knows it. When he's up at the farm he sleeps all the time. But when he's with me he does it in half-hour shifts."

"It's not the baby," he said. "You're completely out of it."

She giggled sleepily. "I wish I was," she said. "Completely out of it. Completely. Out. It."

Her head was dropping toward the table.

"Ruth . . ." he said urgently.

"Your round," she said. She folded her arms on the table, and to his horror she slumped lower and lower until her head was resting on her forearms. "Nighty night," she said. Her smile, half hidden by the sleeve of her smock, was her old mischievous smile. "Sorry, David, I'm a complete goner."

He went to shake her but she was already asleep. For a moment he looked at her with tenderness, and then he realized that she was stranded in the pub with him, with no way of getting home.

"Ruth!" he said urgently, and shook her shoulder.

She slumped to one side. She was clearly not going to wake. He glanced uncomfortably to the bar; the barman was watching him.

It suddenly occurred to David that she might be seriously ill.

He did not know how many Amitriptylines she had taken, or if she had taken more than the three gins he had seen her drink. "Christ!" he said.

He shook her again, more urgently. She was completely limp. He let her fall gently toward the table and went up to the bar. There was nothing to do but face the music.

"Watch her," he said flatly to the barman. "I'm getting my car up to the door and I'll drive her home."

"Pissed?" the barman asked.

"She's ill," David said loftily. "She's on antibiotics and she shouldn't have mixed them with drinks. I'll take her home."

The barman raised an eyebrow. "She won't remember a thing then," he said suggestively.

"Christ," David said again miserably, and went out to fetch his car.

The barman had to help him lift Ruth into the front seat. Her legs had completely gone. David thought that in all their times of comradely drinking he had never seen her completely out of control. He missed, with a brief passionate pang of nostalgia, Ruth's giggly drunkenness, he remembered her howling with laughter and clinging to his arm.

"Christ," he said again and started the car.

He knew he had to take her home, and he dreaded meeting Patrick. He drove to the cottage in a mood of stoical dread, but when he drew up outside the little house and saw the drive empty of cars and the door shut he realized that it would be worse than that—he would have to take her to her mother-in-law's house.

"This is a fucking nightmare," he said precisely to the windshield. He shook her gently. "Ruth, Ruth!"

Her head dropped back, her jaw dropped open. Again he was afraid. He thought that for all he knew she might be sliding into a coma caused by a drug overdose. He thought of Elizabeth's air of calm competence and he felt a great longing to hand over the whole problem to her. Besides, she was baby-sitting Thomas, and she would have to know that Ruth could not collect him. He gritted his teeth and turned down the drive toward Manor Farm.

It was worse than he could have predicted, for when Elizabeth opened the dark front door he saw Patrick in the hall behind her.

"I'm dreadfully sorry," he said. "Ruth is with me, and I think she's ill."

Patrick exclaimed and came quickly past his mother out to the car.

"We were at the Green Man," David said to Elizabeth. Her steady gaze never wavered. "She had three gins, and I know she took at least one Amitriptyline. I think she'd had some before she came out. I'm afraid she's ill. Perhaps you should call a doctor." He spoke precisely; he felt quite sick with embarrassment.

Patrick came up the shallow steps with Ruth in his arms. David shrank back.

"Put her in the yellow bedroom. I'll come up in a moment."

Patrick nodded grimly and climbed the stairs. He ignored David completely.

Elizabeth's face was full of sympathy. "Thank you for bringing her home," she said. "We've been worried. We didn't know where she'd gone or what she was doing."

"She was quite safe," David said awkwardly.

Elizabeth came out with him to his car. "Does she often drink to excess?" she asked gently.

"Never!" David exclaimed.

"You've never seen her drunk before?"

"Well . . . we've been friends a long time," he said. "We were at college together. We all used to drink then . . . and in the old days, when we were working, we might have a drink after work, we used to drink a bit then . . . but everyone did . . . after work you know . . . after a tough day. . . ." He sounded as if he were making excuses.

She nodded gravely. "So this is nothing new."

"I'm terribly sorry," David said. "But it's not how it looks."

Her silence was worse than an interrogation.

"We're just friends," David said. "Very good friends. I'm very fond of her. But that's all. She's always been in love, madly in love, with Patrick."

Elizabeth nodded. "Is she still?"

David was about to swear that nothing had changed, but

then he remembered Ruth in the pub saying that men were like women on Amitriptyline—cut off from life, insensate.

"I don't know," he said honestly. "She's not like herself at all."

Elizabeth lowered her voice; David leaned closer to hear.

"We are thinking that she needs a complete rest," she said. "A complete break."

David felt an intense sense of relief that someone else would deal with the problem.

"Do you think that would be a good idea?" Elizabeth asked him. Her anxious scrutiny of his face assured him that his opinion was of material importance. "Do you think that would be the best thing for her?"

"Yes," David said. "Yes, I think so. She can't go on like this."

Elizabeth nodded. "I'll see if I can find somewhere that she can go, and get her booked in at once then," she said. "But if she calls you—or writes—" she paused.

David waited.

"You wouldn't take her away, or visit without telling us, would you? Even if she asked you. If she has a drink problem or a drug problem she must stick it out. You will help her stay there, won't you? Even if she calls you and wants to leave?"

"Jesus," David said miserably.

Elizabeth touched his hand. "I am sorry to have to ask for your help," she said. "But you are her only friend. If she were to turn to you we have to know that you would do the best for her—which isn't always the easiest thing to do."

David nodded. "If she calls me, or writes, I'll let you know," he said. "I wouldn't want to interrupt her treatment. She has to get well again."

Elizabeth nodded. "That's what we all want."

He swung into the car seat and then hesitated. "But if she gets better, and wants to go back to work, or—I don't know—change everything—I'd always be on her side."

Elizabeth's smile was understanding. "You're *her* friend," she said. "I understand that. And she comes first for you. That's as it should be."

David nodded and she stood back and let him slam the door. She waved as he drove away, and he glanced in his rearview mirror at the elegant figure receding into the distance. He thought she was a beautiful and intelligent woman, he thought she would care for Ruth and manage the whole family with skill and sensitivity. He had another contradictory feeling—which he ignored—that he had betrayed Ruth, and betrayed their long friendship, and that he should have done anything with her but drive her home to that woman.

Frederick was consulting Sylvesters, his lawyers.

"Small problem," he said in his usual shorthand. "Just a brief inquiry."

"Yes, Colonel Cleary," Simon Sylvester said.

"Domestic sort of thing." Frederick cleared his throat. "Daughter-in-law. Not up to caring for the new baby. Rather a poor show."

Simon Sylvester drew a notepad toward him and scribbled the Cleary name on top.

"Drinking," Frederick said shortly. "And drugs. We're concerned for her, of course, but mainly for the well-being of the child. Any idea where we stand?"

Simon Sylvester thought quickly. "The child's well-being comes under the Children Act, so any action would have to ensure that his interests are paramount."

Frederick nodded. "Goes without saying," he said. "Where do we stand with the mother?"

"In what way?" Simon Sylvester asked cautiously.

"Getting her sorted out," Frederick said with frank brutality. "Locked up, dried out, that sort of thing."

"If she's a danger to herself and to others, you can get her committed under the Mental-Health Act," Sylvester said. "But it's rather drastic."

"How d'you do it?"

"You have to have a warrant from her doctor and next of kin to say that she must be hospitalized. You can keep her inside for a period of assessment, and that can be renewed or challenged."

"One relation and a doctor?" Frederick confirmed. "And how long does she get locked up for?"

"Twenty-eight days," Sylvester said. "Renewable. That's for assessment. It's a rather drastic piece of legislation, actually. There's no appeal. No way out. If you can get her GP to say she needs treatment, she can be inside for six months."

"And the child? Would they want to take him into care?"

"I think he would stay with the father. Father can cope, can he?"

"We can cope." Frederick said.

"Then you want a residence order. Father goes before a magistrate and explains the situation. Magistrate rules where the child is to live."

"There'd be no problem with that," Frederick said.

His lawyer smiled. Frederick Cleary was a magistrate himself and on first-name terms with every member of the bench in the county.

"Thanks for your advice," he said. "Very useful. I may call again."

"It's a measure of the last resort," his lawyer cautioned him. "I imagine that she would resent it very bitterly. It would be hard to restore a proper family atmosphere after such an action."

Frederick nodded. "Point taken," he said briskly. "But I like to know what I've got up my sleeve."

Dr. MacFadden came as soon as Elizabeth called him and examined Ruth as she lay asleep in the yellow bedroom. When he came downstairs, Elizabeth, Frederick, and Patrick were all waiting to see him in the hall.

"She can sleep it off," he said. "She'll probably sleep the rest of today and wake up tomorrow with a headache. No harm done."

"Not this time," Elizabeth said. "Fortunately she was with a friend who brought her home to us. If she had been at home with the baby, or tried to drive somewhere, it could have been very serious."

Dr. MacFadden nodded. He was fighting with a sense of guilt. He thought he should have spotted that Ruth was unstable enough to overdose. He had a strong sense that Ruth had let him down by misusing the medicine he had given her.

"The thing is," Frederick said firmly, "that the time has come for a more permanent solution. We can't go on like this."

Dr. MacFadden responded at once to the voice of authority. "Yes," he said.

"We're thinking of sending her on a little holiday," Frederick said. "Give her a complete break, away from it all. How does that sound to you?"

"Good idea," the doctor said. "A very good idea."

"That's agreed then," said Frederick. "We want no repetition of this."

"Where will you go?" Dr. MacFadden asked Patrick.

"She'll go alone," Elizabeth said smoothly. "My son cannot leave his work at the moment. I shall care for Thomas while she's away."

"Oh. Fine."

Dr. MacFadden headed for the door. Frederick went with him to his car. "The thing is," Frederick said confidentially, "that I'm not sure she's entirely well. We might have to consider some sort of mental treatment. She's a bit unstable, there's a family history—very artistic people—and she's completely failed to care for the baby, and now drinking and taking drugs . . ."

Dr. MacFadden's sense that Ruth had been irresponsible with her prescription gave him a sense of grievance, and he liked and respected Frederick and Elizabeth. "Whatever you want . . ."

"Hope we won't have to call on you," Frederick said.

Uncertainly Dr. MacFadden nodded. He did not know quite what Frederick meant. "Anything I can do . . ."

"Hope it won't be necessary," Frederick said. He stood back from the car as the doctor drove away.

❧

*E*lizabeth made them a lunch of salad and omelettes, denoting a sense of urgency. Patrick pushed the food around his plate and ate little. His mother watched him even while she rocked Thomas with her foot resting against his little bouncing chair.

"I think we had better make up our minds that something

needs to be done," Frederick said, when they had finished eating. "We can't have a repetition of this."

Elizabeth nodded, watching Patrick.

"What can we do?" he asked his father. "What can we do?"

"I think she needs to go away, a complete break, and get dried out," his father said frankly. "She's no good to anyone if she's drinking and taking drugs like this."

"She's not an alcoholic . . ." Patrick demurred.

"Of course not," Elizabeth agreed with him. "But she needs help."

"Where could she go?"

"Celia Fine's daughter went to a marvelous man in Sussex," Elizabeth said. "I'll call her and get the number."

"Celia's daughter was on heroin!" Patrick exclaimed.

Elizabeth shrugged. "Well, she's a starting point."

"The thing is that I think we might be overreacting," Patrick said. "Ruth's been through a rough time and I haven't been really aware . . . if I can get home more, and we keep an eye on her . . . "

Both his parents were silent.

"I don't think we can take the risk," Elizabeth said. "Not with a new baby."

"Let's bite the bullet and get it sorted out," Frederick said. "Once and for all."

Patrick was nearly convinced. He looked at his mother. "I wish I knew I was doing the right thing."

She put out her hand and touched his fingers. "I know," she said. "Leave it to me."

As the doctor had predicted, Ruth slept all afternoon and all night. When she woke in the morning her mouth was dry and tasted foul, her head thudded. She did not at first recognize the room, and then she could not remember how she had got to the farm. She could remember nothing of the previous day at all. She did feel anxious about Thomas; she could not remember when she had last seen him.

The door opened and Elizabeth came in with a beautifully laid breakfast tray.

"Oh, you're awake!" she said with evident pleasure. "I am glad. And how are you feeling?"

"Fine," Ruth said. "Well—headachy and foul. But fine. But I can't remember coming here. And where's Thomas?"

Elizabeth put the tray on Ruth's knees, anchoring her to the bed. "We have Thomas," she said. "I collected him the day before yesterday—d'you remember? And he stayed overnight last night, and the night before."

"Is he all right?"

"Of course."

Ruth shook her head. At once the pain in her head and neck thudded. She closed her eyes for a moment. "I don't remember," she said.

"You're not very well," Elizabeth said gently. "You're not very well at all, Ruth. Better take two of your pills."

Ruth looked at her. The light seemed very bright. Elizabeth's shirt in cream and her gray tailored skirt seemed to shimmer with excess light. The bottle of pills was on the breakfast tray. Ruth took two.

"What's happened?" Ruth asked.

"We think you have a problem caring for Thomas."

"I'm fine," Ruth said. Her voice was thin and faraway.

"You know you're not," Elizabeth said calmly. "There's a doctor coming in half an hour to see you, and if he thinks he can help you then we want you to go with him, to his center, where he can treat you."

"What for?"

"Depression," Elizabeth said.

"I'm not depressed," Ruth said. "I'm just tired. I never sleep. There's nothing wrong but that."

Elizabeth smiled. "So go with this doctor and have a good long rest. You've been through so much, Ruth. You need a rest."

"But what about Thomas?"

"He can stay here with us."

"What does Patrick say?"

"He agrees."

Ruth lay back on the pillows. "Where *is* Patrick?" she asked at length.

"He's dressing Thomas in the nursery. He'll come and see you in a minute, when you're freshened up."

"How long do I have to go away for?"

Elizabeth did not show that she had heard the defeated acquiescence in Ruth's voice. "Not long," she said reassuringly. "And you can come home whenever you wish. But we all want to see you rested and well again."

"What *did* happen yesterday? How did I get here?"

"You took too many of your pills, and you met David at the pub, and you drank too much. You passed out and he brought you here. You left the keys in your car and it was stolen overnight. We had to put you to bed. You slept all afternoon and all night."

Ruth felt a deep corrosive sense of humiliation. "David brought me?"

"He had to carry you out of the pub."

"And Patrick was here?"

"He had come for Thomas. None of us knew where you were. You just walked out of the house; you left it unlocked."

Ruth dropped her head, her hair tumbled forward hiding the deep red of her cheeks. "My car . . ."

"We've reported it missing. It may just have been taken by joyriders, it may turn up." Elizabeth hesitated. "It won't be insured since you left the keys in it. I'm afraid you may have lost it."

Ruth pushed the tray to one side, Elizabeth put the bottle of pills on the bedside table, and took the tray away. "Be brave, darling," she said gently. "A Dr. Fairley is coming at ten. If he thinks he can help you, he has a wonderful house in Sussex where they can give you lots of rest, and make you well again. You can come back to Patrick and Thomas and make a fresh start."

Ruth turned her head away.

"Unless you'd rather not . . ." Elizabeth suggested.

Ruth turned back. "Rather not what?"

"Unless you'd rather start again somewhere else?" Elizabeth said gently. "Your career is so promising . . . you could start a new life. . . ."

"Move away?"

"If you wanted."

"With Patrick and Thomas?"

Elizabeth met her eyes. The two women looked at each other. Elizabeth was serene and powerful, Ruth looked sick. "No, Patrick and Thomas will stay here," Elizabeth said firmly.

Ruth nodded. "I see."

She said nothing more. It was as if Elizabeth's calm assurance had set the tone of the whole day. Ruth hardly said a word to Patrick when he came in to see her, and answered the doctor in monosyllables. She did not ask for Thomas, who was, in any case, out for a long walk with his grandfather. Dr. Fairley had come in his large comfortable car, and offered to drive her to Springfield Hall at once. Patrick produced a suitcase already packed, and put it in the trunk. Elizabeth gave Dr. Fairley an envelope containing a check with the fees for the first month. Ruth, wrapped in one of Elizabeth's pale camel-hair coats, walked to the car and got in. She saw her feet going down the steps but she had no awareness of the hardness of the paving stones.

"See you soon, darling," Patrick said, bending down to the car. "I'll come down and see you at the weekend. And you can phone me."

"Will you be at home?" she asked, meaning the little house.

"Yes, I'll stay here," he said, meaning the farmhouse. "It'll be easier, and I'll see more of Thomas."

She nodded.

"When you're better I'll bring him down to see you," Patrick promised. "And soon you'll be home."

"I don't know what's wrong with me," Ruth said dully.

"Dr. Fairley can deal with all of that," Patrick said reassuringly.

"But if I don't know what's wrong with me," Ruth's brain was working slowly but stubbornly, through the haze of hangover and Amitriptyline, "if I don't know what's wrong, then how can I know when it's better?"

Patrick leaned forward and kissed her cheek. "Trust Dr. Fairley," he urged. "He's had a lot of experience. Mother says he's the best in his field. Mother and Father are paying a packet for you to stay there. He'll make you well again."

"But how will I know?" Ruth asked stubbornly. "How will I know that I'm better?"

Patrick smiled his handsome smile. "When you're my lovely girl again," he said.

The doctor got into the car beside Ruth, and started the engine. Patrick stepped back and carefully shut the door. "I'll call tonight," he said. "And every night. See you at the week-end!"

Ruth stared past him, unseeing.

The doctor put the car in gear and they moved smoothly off, down the drive. Ruth could just see, at the side of the house, Frederick pushing the pram around and around the garden, rocking Thomas to sleep and waiting for her to be gone. They had not wanted her to see her baby, in case she made a scene. Ruth lay back against the comfortable headrest and closed her eyes. She would never have been able to make a scene in Elizabeth's house, she thought.

"All right?" Dr. Fairley asked. He glanced sideways at her and saw that her eyes were shut but that tears were trickling from under her closed eyelids and running down her cheeks.

"How would I know?" she asked. "How can I tell?"

∽ Nine ∽

At nine weeks, Thomas was too young to cry for his mother, but Elizabeth thought that he had noticed her absence. He was placid and happy, quick to laugh or coo with pleasure, but his brightest vitality seemed to drain away during the month that his mother was away.

Elizabeth tried to ignore it, and she never mentioned it to either Frederick or Patrick. But she could not deny that—though he slept through the night, and ate well—Thomas was quieter and less joyful than when his mother had been, however incompetently, taking care of him. Elizabeth found herself strangely offended by his loyalty. She would have preferred him to turn to her completely. She had thought that he would forget Ruth as soon as he ceased to see her. But there was something loving and stubborn about little Thomas, and Elizabeth could see that when a door opened and he turned his head to the noise, a light died from his face when someone else came in, when it was not his mother.

Elizabeth loyally mentioned Ruth once or twice a day, and showed Thomas her photograph. Patrick telephoned her every evening at seven o'clock, and drove cross-country to Sussex every Saturday morning to spend the day with her.

He came back from these trips tired and silent, and his father made a habit of sitting with him late on Saturday night, with a bottle of malt whisky and a jug of still spring water between the two of them in companionable silence.

On Sunday morning they all went to church and came back to Elizabeth's Sunday roast, then in the afternoon they took Thomas for a walk. Elizabeth had bought a backpack for Thomas; Patrick would put it on, and Elizabeth would lift Thomas onto his father's back. With the dog at their heels they would walk across the fields and up to the hills, Frederick, Elizabeth, Patrick, and little Thomas, his head bobbing with every step.

He often fell asleep on these walks, and would sometimes sleep all the way home, not stirring even when the pack was carefully set down on the sofa while Elizabeth made tea. Then they would read the Sunday papers—the *Sunday Telegraph* for Frederick, who mistrusted the sports coverage in any other paper, and the *Sunday Times* for Elizabeth and Patrick.

When Thomas had slept for an hour, Elizabeth would wake him for his supper. He was no longer given jars of baby food or powdered mixes. Elizabeth had painstakingly cooked, pureed, and frozen a wide selection of adult meals to make tiny dinners just for him. Patrick always bathed him on Sunday night, and put him to bed. When Patrick came downstairs, leaving Thomas asleep, Elizabeth would have a large gin and tonic ready for him, in a crystal goblet packed with sliced lime and ice.

They were a deeply contented unit. Patrick felt as if he had never left home but had somehow been miraculously joined by the next son and heir. He enjoyed being a father to Thomas in a way that he had not experienced when Ruth had been there. Under her care Thomas had been a problem, his sleeping—or lack of it—was a continual unspoken area of conflict between them. His clothes, his feeding, his diaper changes were all areas where Ruth silently and resentfully pressed Patrick to do more, and which Patrick silently and skillfully avoided.

But with Elizabeth running the nursery Patrick need do no more on a weekday than kiss his son's milky face at breakfast time in the morning as he left for work, and play with him for half an hour before bed in the evening. He never saw Thomas except washed and clean and ready for play. He never wiped his face, sponged his hands, changed his diaper, or struggled to get his vest over his little head. It was the fatherhood that Frederick had enjoyed: in which a father returns from the outside world at predictable intervals, volunteers a period of enjoyable and bonding play, and disappears again when the chores of babyhood are to be done. Father and child meet only at their best moments. The tantrums, the washing, the feeding, all take place miraculously out of sight. It was the fatherhood enjoyed by men who employ either professional nannies or devoted wives. It was not the way fatherhood was usually practiced in the 1990s, when men and women are working toward equality of work and mutuality of experience. Patrick much preferred it.

He liked the way Thomas's little face lit up when he came into the room. He liked the way his presence was a treat and not a duty. He liked the way he could open the front door and hear his mother say to his son, in the tones of absolute delight, "Here's Daddy home!" and Thomas, cued by her enthusiasm, would kick his feet and wave his hands and beam.

They all spoke of Ruth with tenderness and concern, but within a fortnight there was an unavoidable sense that this lifestyle—this comfortable, affectionate, orderly lifestyle—was better than anything any of them had experienced before. Patrick went to work in the morning with a well-cooked breakfast inside him, and a sense of order and solid well-being. He came home at night knowing that no domestic crisis would have broken out, and that his home would be tranquil and welcoming. His work became easier, no longer interrupted by desperate phone calls from home, and his attitude to his staff became more relaxed and tolerant. The documentary unit produced a couple of good ideas and one very good film, which was short-listed for a minor award. Patrick's style—confident, well-dressed, and relaxed—fostered the impression that he was a brilliant young man, doing well in a competitive business.

He had never looked more handsome. His clear, regular features were enhanced by the immaculate cleanness of his shirts and the pressing of his suits. His shoes shone with polish and loving attention. Even his briefcase was polished.

Frederick enjoyed the company of his grandson. He developed his own little rituals with him: taking him for a walk in the afternoon, rocking him to sleep in his pram. Frederick played with him for an hour in the morning, while Elizabeth prepared lunch and supervised the work of the daily cleaning woman. Thomas was settled and quiet with his grandfather. Sometimes Elizabeth would put her head around the door and see Frederick solemnly reading paragraphs from the *Telegraph* while Thomas lay in his bouncy chair, his wide, serious eyes fixed on his grandfather, as if the English touring cricket team was the most entrancing story.

"This is the life," Frederick said to her one lunchtime, as they had a glass of sherry before eating. Thomas had eaten earlier and was asleep in his pram in the conservatory.

"Don't get too attached to it," Elizabeth warned. "It will all change when Ruth comes home."

"Yes," Frederick said thoughtfully. "It seems almost a shame. I can hardly bear to think of Thomas leaving us. He's so happy here, and Patrick looks so much better too."

Elizabeth nodded. "I'm afraid we have no choice really," she said. "It's not as if she left him; it's not as if there was a problem with the marriage. She just couldn't cope with a new baby. It's not as if they were separated or divorced."

Frederick nodded. "I suppose everything *was* all right for them," he said. "It was just Ruth getting overtired? It couldn't have been something more?"

Elizabeth gave a small shrug. "He's never said anything to me," she said. "But if they were having difficulties I wouldn't be surprised. Patrick's not a man to wait for a woman forever. And Ruth was seeing that other young man—from the radio station."

Frederick shook his head. "It doesn't seem right," he said, dissatisfied. "We're all so happy now, and she could come home at any moment, and we'll be back to square one again."

"No," Elizabeth agreed. "I don't think Thomas should go back to her until she's completely better. Even if she comes home, I don't think Thomas and Patrick should go back to the little house until we are all confident that she's completely well again."

There was a brief silence.

"Patrick doesn't seem to see much of a change in her," Frederick volunteered. "He said she hardly spoke to him last time he was there. Didn't look at the flowers we sent. Hadn't read her book. Very quiet."

"Maybe it'll be longer than a month then."

"Maybe." He hesitated, finding the truth. "I can't say I'll be sorry."

Elizabeth shot him a small half-hidden smile.

*t Springfield House in Sussex Ruth's days passed in structured activities. She was called at eight o'clock and she showered and was down to breakfast at nine. She was making a tapestry and she worked on the large frame from half past nine until eleven. At eleven they all stopped for coffee, and her group— five men and five women—went to the meeting room for their session of group therapy. Ruth said nothing during the first four meetings. She barely listened. There was a young woman addicted to drugs, and one in deep depression; there was a woman recovering from alcoholism and one woman being treated for anorexia. The men Ruth had not observed at all. She sat in the circle on the soft, comfortable chairs and observed her feet. They were not allowed to wear shoes in the group-therapy room. Ruth had a pair of pink socks; she moved her toes gently inside them and felt the soft wool caress her insteps. As much as possible she made herself deaf to the low-toned murmur of the group.

The walls of the room were an encouraging yellow-tinged cream. There was a large reproduction of an Impressionist picture hung on one wall, and a large picture window overlooking the well-kept garden. Ruth looked at the picture, at the millions of little dots of paints, at the illusion of solid flesh and sunlit river water. She did not want to see the garden in its cold, sodden bareness. It reminded her of home, of the little house set amid the cold fields and the drive leading up to the farm.

She missed Thomas and she put the pain away from her mind every waking moment. She thought of her cesarean scar and the strange loss in her belly after he had been born. She thought of the sense of weightlessness and the loss of the curve of her stomach. She felt that she had lost him at birth, when someone had put her to sleep and taken him from her, and that she had been a fool to let them do that—to steal her baby away from her own body. And now she had let it happen again. She had put herself to sleep and let them steal her baby from her.

She could think of nothing to do but to stay asleep. She turned her head to study the picture again. She admired the bright sugar-almond pink of her socks. She decided that she would not think about Thomas, who was too young to think about her. She would not miss Thomas, who would be cooing in his grandmother's arms. She would not acknowledge this dreadful pain—a pain as deep and as agonized as an amputation. She would not ever think of the little house, the boredom and claustrophobia of her relationship with Patrick, the wet fields and the dominating, imposing presence of the farm, and the gradual, irresistible theft of her baby.

After lunch they lay down on their beds, or chatted in the common room. Ruth liked an afternoon rest. She lay on her bed, watching the ceiling, not thinking about Thomas, not thinking about Patrick, not thinking about the little house.

Sometimes people walked past her door. Sometimes one of the other women from her group came in and tried to talk to her. Ruth turned a blank, pale face to their inquiries.

"I'm sorry. I'm very tired," she said politely. And they would go away.

Someone raised his voice in the group, Ruth turned her attention to the picture, trying to block out the sound. Then Agnes, the recovering alcoholic, suddenly turned on her. "Why d'you never talk?" she asked abruptly.

Ruth slowly turned her blank, uninterested gaze.

"Why d'you never talk?" Agnes demanded. "You've sat in that same seat for three days, looking at nothing and saying nothing. In recreation time you lie on your bed. You're like a sleepwalker. You're half dead."

Ruth looked toward the group leader, George. He was a young man in a crisp white jacket, the duty nurse. She expected him to tell Agnes that Ruth must be left alone. He said nothing.

"I want an answer!" Agnes said.

Ruth looked to George, the nurse. Still he said nothing.

"Say something!" Agnes pressed. "Say anything! You sit like you're dumb, like you're deaf and dumb."

George nodded, waiting like the rest of the group.

"I've got nothing to say," Ruth said unwillingly.

Agnes leaped to her feet and came toward her. Ruth recoiled. "Why not?" she demanded. "Why nothing?"

Ruth shook her head.

George leaned forward; the whole of the group were watching this exchange. Agnes looked around. "Isn't she half dead?" she demanded.

A couple of the men nodded, and one of the women. Ruth felt anger flare inside her.

"Do I have to listen to this?" she asked George. She expected him to take her part, to tell Agnes to sit down.

He smiled gently, saying nothing.

Ruth looked into Agnes's angry face. She was flushed, her face shiny with sweat. Her black curly hair was greasy and uncombed. Ruth pulled her feet up, out of Agnes's way; she sat holding her toes.

"I want you to answer me," Agnes said determinedly. "You say nothing and you do nothing. I want you to tell me what it is that is keeping you so quiet."

"Nothing," Ruth said unwillingly. Against her pulled-up legs she could feel her heart pounding. "It's nothing. I'm sorry."

"Sorry for what?" one of the women said.

"Nothing," Ruth said. "I just want to be left alone."

"But I don't want to leave you alone," Agnes said. "Why do you never speak to anyone?"

Ruth looked to George again. He was leaning forward, waiting for her answer.

"I'm not well," Ruth said.

"Why do you cut yourself off?" Agnes demanded.

"I'm overtired," Ruth said. "I need to sleep . . ."

"You've been sleeping ever since you got here!" Agnes exclaimed. Other people nodded. It was like a steady, insistent tow, bringing Ruth out of the depths of her despair into a bright, interrogating light. "Why d'you never say anything? Why do you even try not to listen?"

"I don't . . ." Ruth said desperately.

"You do," one of the men said. His voice was gentle. Ruth

turned to him, hoping he would rescue her from this attack. "You do try not to listen, and you look at the picture any time someone raises their voice."

"It's just . . ." Ruth started and then broke off.

They were all waiting. She looked up at the picture and then out the window over the wet fields. The view reminded her, inescapably, of the little house and the dreadful, dreadful loss of Thomas. She could feel panic building inside her at the thought of his absence, and then she found it bursting out of her mouth, in a high childlike voice, which she did not even recognize.

"I miss my mother!" she suddenly exploded in a voice that was not her own but a child's voice ringing with grief. "I miss my mummy! She's dead and I can't bear it! And I don't know what will happen to me! And I miss her! And I miss her! And I miss her!"

She was screaming as she cried, and she felt her face hot and wet with an unstoppable stream of tears. No one moved toward her, no one enfolded her in their arms, no one even touched her. Ruth hugged herself while the dreadful racking sobs went on, and rocked her own body back and forth, and felt the horror of being a little girl, weeping in deep grief, with no one at hand. Only when the hoarse, horrified sobs quieted, George the nurse crossed the floor toward her and put his arms around her and drew her head onto his shoulder as if she were a very small girl.

"I see you miss her," he said gently. Ruth could hear his voice coming from deep in his chest. "I think that was the most awful thing to happen to a little girl."

Ruth felt her energy stream through her, from her toes to the very top of the head, as if her tears had somehow burst through a blockage that had cut her in half, kept her half dead, half cold, half turned to stone for all her life since the death of her mother. "It was," she said with certainty. "And everyone told me not to mind, and that everything would be all right."

George pulled back so he could see her face. For the first time since she had been in the group she looked directly at him, her cheeks were flushed, her eyes were red-rimmed but bright. She looked alive for the first time since he had seen her. "*Was* every-thing all right?" he asked.

Ruth drew a breath that seemed to resonate through her very bones. "No," she said with a simple certainty. "I did mind, though I never told anyone how much. And everything was not all right. And everything has been wrong ever since."

❧

*T*hat afternoon Ruth slept without dreaming, a deep, easy sleep as if she had been at hard manual work all day. When she woke it was time for tea, and she went down to the refectory and saw Agnes and one of the men from the group at a table together. When they saw her they turned and smiled, and Ruth took her tea tray over to their table and joined them. Nobody said very much, but Ruth knew that she was among people who had witnessed her deep and agonized grief, and had not turned away.

❧

*T*hat evening Patrick telephoned from work to speak to his mother.

"There's a new producer here, at a bit of a loose end," he said. "I was wondering if we could stretch to another place at dinner?"

"Of course," Elizabeth said agreeably. In the background Patrick could hear his son cooing.

"I can hear Thomas," he said with pleasure.

"Yes, he's just finishing his tea," his mother said. "Of course you can bring someone home, darling."

"About eight o'clock then," Patrick said. "She's new to the area so I'll drive her out and home again after dinner."

Elizabeth noted in silence that he had asked if he could invite a guest before explaining that it was a woman. "Of course," Elizabeth said.

"About eight then," Patrick said again.

Elizabeth put down the telephone and turned back to Thomas's tea. Frederick was proffering a spoonful of strained blackberries at arm's length. Thomas waved sticky hands. His face, his hair, his arms to his elbows were plastered in dark juice.

"A guest for dinner," Elizabeth said neutrally.

"That'll be nice," Frederick said. "Anyone we know?"

"A lady producer," Elizabeth said, her tone carefully level.

"Oh," Frederick said.

There was a brief silence. Thomas reached out, took the spoon, and put it to his cheek, his nose, and finally his mouth.

"I wonder if that's quite cricket?" Frederick said thoughtfully. "With Ruth in a convalescent home, and all. You know if she were in hospital with a broken leg we'd be visiting her every day, and there would be no guests at dinner."

Elizabeth rinsed a warm washcloth at the sink to wipe Thomas's face and hands. "Exactly," she said.

Frederick waited for an explanation.

"If she were in hospital with a broken leg, then we would know that she was happily married to Patrick, and a good wife and mother, and that she had suffered an unfortunate accident and was coming home soon."

She wiped Thomas's mouth with careful efficiency, undid the straps on the high chair, and lifted him out.

"Instead she had a breakdown and could not cope with motherhood or married life, and we don't know if she will ever come home, or what sort of state she'll be in when she does come home."

"Still married," Frederick said softly.

"I don't see Patrick as tied to a sick woman for the rest of his life," Elizabeth said. She held Thomas against her shoulder and patted him gently on the back, waiting for him to burp. "I don't see that he should sacrifice his life, with all his prospects, just because she can't cope."

Frederick nodded, unconvinced.

"Besides," Elizabeth said, "what matters most is Thomas, and making sure that Thomas is safe and happy."

Frederick nodded. "Here with us," he said.

"Yes."

*D*espite Elizabeth's welcome and Frederick's unfailing courtesy, the evening did not go well. The visiting producer, Emma, had thought that when Patrick invited her to dinner he would be taking her to a restaurant, and she had worn a rather low-cut black dress. In the sitting room, on the chintz-covered sofa, she looked overdressed and tarty. Elizabeth, sitting beside her in a smart woolen suit with her pearls, could not put her at ease.

"Do you all live together?" Emma asked curiously.

"My daughter, Miriam, lives in Canada," Elizabeth said, carefully misunderstanding. "She's got the travel bug. She's just like her father. She did two years voluntary service in Africa and now she teaches disadvantaged children in Canada. She's just outside Toronto. Patrick has his own house, just down the drive. He's staying at home while his wife is away."

At dinner Emma announced that she was a strict vegetarian. Elizabeth's smile never wavered. She left Frederick carving the joint of beef and went to the kitchen, reappearing with a vegetable quiche and a green salad.

"I would have said," Emma remarked. "But I thought Patrick was taking me out for dinner."

"I do admire you," Elizabeth replied. "I couldn't bear to give up meat."

Emma did not want any dessert. Emma took tea instead of coffee after dinner. She did not drink brandy or port, which she was offered. She asked for another gin and tonic instead, which was usually served only as an apéritif.

"Of course," Frederick said pleasantly. "Will you have it with your cup of tea or after?"

Fortunately, Patrick had a report from his documentary unit on television that evening, and so they watched it in silence.

"Excellent," Frederick said as he switched off the set at the end of the program, and after they had admired Patrick's large billing as executive producer.

"I thought you went rather soft on the police," Emma remarked. "Someone should have put the civil-liberties angle."

"It wasn't that sort of program," Patrick explained.

"I understand that—that's my problem with it," Emma

insisted. "It's soft-focus news. I think you'd get more viewers if you were harder."

Elizabeth and Frederick exchanged a brief look. They had never heard Patrick contradicted by Ruth; it was a strange and unpleasant experience to have this badly dressed stranger take him to task in their own drawing room.

"It seemed right at the time." Patrick did not reveal that hers was exactly the same comment made by the Head of News. "The right tone for the piece."

"But all your pieces have this tone," she said. "Kind of daytime television, comfy viewing. I thought you'd go for more bite."

"Maybe," Patrick said equably. "Look! Is that the time? Would you like a nightcap, Mother? Emma? Father?"

"Not for me," she said briskly. "I'll call a cab."

"I'll drive you back," Patrick said, getting to his feet. He had rather assumed that he would run her back to her hotel in Bristol, and that she would invite him up to her room for a nightcap and that they would have sex.

"Not all the way to Bristol at this time of night!" she said. "I made a note of the number."

Briskly she went out to the hall and telephoned for a taxi. Frederick and Elizabeth tidied the cups and glasses and went into the kitchen and tactfully closed the door.

"I was rather looking forward to driving you back to Bristol," Patrick said engagingly. He smiled his charming television smile.

"I was rather looking forward to a quiet restaurant and walking back to my hotel," she said smartly.

"Sorry." Until now it had not occurred to him that he was being snubbed, that she had disliked spending the evening with his parents. He was so accustomed to Ruth's complaisance that this woman's rejection of him, of his parents, even of his mother's cooking did not make sense. He thought he was bestowing on her a great privilege—inviting her to his home. "Perhaps we got off to a bad start . . . you see . . ." he paused and played for her sympathy . . . "my mother is caring for my son, so I like to be here in the evening, in case he wakes. My wife is away, she's ill, and my son needs me. He's only a baby."

"I know, I've heard all about it."

Patrick uncomfortably wondered what exactly she might have heard. "She's in a convalescent home, a sort of health farm. She's unstable."

"I have children too," Emma said surprisingly.

"You do?"

"Yes. Two, actually. At home. I'm divorced. Their father has them when I have to go away."

"I had no idea. . . ."

"I never discuss them at work," she said smartly. "People patronize a woman if they know she's a mother and managing on her own."

Patrick felt obscurely that his sympathy card had been soundly trumped. He managed a game smile. "It's hard work bringing them up on your own. I'm only just learning the ropes."

"I'd certainly like the live-in staff you have," Emma said acidly. "Does your mother get up to him at night, as well as having him all day?"

"He goes through the night now," Patrick lied. "Thank God!"

Emma raised her arched eyebrows.

Patrick heard the taxi draw up outside and went to the door. He slipped Emma's coat around her shoulders and just brushed the bare nape of her neck.

"See you tomorrow," he said softly. "And maybe we'll find that quiet restaurant later in the week."

"Maybe," she said. "But perhaps you had better stay at home with your mother."

❦

Ruth slowly started to talk in the group. She told them of the death of her mother and father and how her aunt had tried to protect her from grief, from the bereavement itself. They had buried her parents without telling her, she had never been able to say good-bye; and whenever her aunt, or her husband, Ruth's Uncle Stephen, had found the little girl in tears, at bedtime, or bathtime, or walking slowly home from school, they had said bracingly to her, "Don't cry now! What have you got to cry about?" And Ruth—not understanding that they were thinking of the orphanage where she could have gone, if they had not agreed to take her—could only look at them and wonder if they had forgotten already.

She told the group about the long years of loneliness and silent grief, that she had been teased for talking "funny" at school, and for not knowing the English children's stories. She told them that in the end she had decided to erase her American childhood from her mind, smooth out the American twang from her speech, pass as an English girl in an English home. Not until she met Patrick—and especially Patrick's family—had she found a complete solution to the emptiness, and to the question of where she belonged. Elizabeth and Frederick and the beautiful house, the warmth of their welcome, and the ease with which they called her daughter made her feel as if she were not lonely and sad and missing her parents, and a foreigner in a strange country, but were instead pampered and loved and wanted.

She tried to describe the farmhouse and Elizabeth's hospitality and her kindness, but the people in the group did not smile and nod as if they understood.

"It's like a perfect house," she said. "A perfect house, and they are just perfect parents."

There was a brief silence. Ruth wondered why she sounded so unconvincing. Then Agnes spoke.

"I think they've done you over," she said.

"What?"

"I think they've done you over."

Ruth checked her reply, swallowed the words, started again, almost choked. "What d'you mean?"

"I think they saw you coming," Agnes said. "Lonely, all on your own, no parents, and no guardians who cared that much for you, and I think they thought they could make you fit in. You'd spent all your childhood trying to fit in. You would learn to fit with them. They wanted you because you wouldn't rock the boat. They could keep their darling son, and you wouldn't be able to take him away. You didn't have anywhere to take him away to."

Ruth was about to exclaim that Agnes was talking complete

nonsense, but she saw that other people were nodding, as if they agreed.

"It's not like that at all," she said swiftly. "They're very loving people. They are wonderful in-laws! Why, when I was so tired with Thomas, Elizabeth would have him all day, every day. She's got him now so Patrick can go to work. She's been completely wonderful. She's been like a mother to me."

Agnes shook her head stubbornly. "Or else she liked you because she knew you'd never have the balls to take Patrick away from her, and then she took your son from you."

The enormity of the lie filled Ruth's head like a rushing wind. "That's a dreadful thing to say! That's a wicked thing to say! She loves me, and of course she loves her son and her grandson, and she would do anything to make us all happy. Anything!"

"Yes," Agnes said. "But what if what makes Patrick happy and Thomas happy is to get rid of you?"

Ruth went white and turned to George. "Tell her to shut up," she said sharply.

George leaned forward. "Why is it such a bad suggestion?" he asked. "If it's not true, it doesn't matter what she says. Does it?"

Agnes looked triumphant, like a bully in a playground. "They've done you over," she said again. "And they've nearly won. They got you into such a state that you were hardly there at all. You've lost your baby and you've lost your husband and you're in the loony bin. You're a loony, and they did it to you. Don't tell me that they love you."

"No!" Ruth screamed. She jumped and ran at Agnes to push her ugly gloating face away. George moved like lightning and grabbed her from behind. He wrestled her to the ground and held her still. Ruth wriggled and swore, words that she had never used. Words that Elizabeth had never heard.

"No physical contact," George said in her ear. He sounded perfectly calm. "Those are the rules. No physical contact."

"I'll kill her!" Ruth gasped. "I'll kill the bitch!"

"No physical contact," George said again.

In the distance, Ruth heard a bell ring and heard the noise of running feet. Then George's weight was lifted from her and she lunged toward Agnes again. At once she was enveloped in a tight fold of material, like a white sheet. She bucked and struggled, but they had her fast. They slung her, like a rolled carpet, onto a trolley and wheeled her out of the room, to her bedroom. They humped her onto the bed without unwrapping her; if anything the bindings were pulled tighter. All Ruth could see was the ceiling, and all she could feel was the firm, gentle handling. "I'll kill her," she said again.

"No physical contact," one of the nurses said. "Now you have a little sleep, and next time you see her, you tell her what you think of her."

There was a slight prick in the skin of her inner arm and then Ruth felt the delicious languor spreading all over her. "It's not true, what she said," she whispered.

"Well, you tell her that," the nurse recommended. "No point in killing her. But you could tell her that she's wrong."

"She is wrong," Ruth asserted. "They love me like a daughter. I know they do."

"Good," the nurse said soothingly.

Ruth started to drift into sleep. "They do . . . they do . . ." she whispered. "I know they do."

⁂

*W*hen she woke it was early evening. She stirred and found that someone had undone her bindings and she was free to get up. She stumbled to the bathroom, her feet were still cramped, and then she went cautiously to the dayroom. Half a dozen people were watching television. It was Thursday evening; they were watching *Top of the Pops*. Ruth blinked at the strange lunatic costumes and joyless erratic dancing on the program, and the orderly silence of the inmates.

One of the men from her group glanced around and saw her. "OK now?" he asked.

Ruth nodded, feeling embarrassed.

"You're doing really well," he said.

She puzzled over that for a moment. He spoke as if her grief and her rage were somehow signs of material progress.

"Are you being funny?"

He shook his head with a smile and then turned back to the television screen. "It's bottling it all up that is crazy," he said. "Letting it out is sane."

"Do you mean . . ." she started.

He shook his head again. "Don't ask me, I'm a schizophrenic," he said cheerfully. "I'm as crazy as you can get."

Ruth took the chair beside him. "Have you been here long?"

He nodded without taking his eyes from the screen. "Long and often. In and out. I go out when I get straight, and then I come back in again when I start flying, or hearing voices, or chatting to God."

"You do that?"

He nodded. "That's the best times."

"I've always been frightened of mad people," Ruth observed.

He was not interested.

"I've always been frightened of people who talk in the street. They always seem to come and talk to me."

"Well, I wouldn't," he said with sudden energy. "I wouldn't talk to you because you're always trying to be nice. I'd rather talk to someone who was really there. Real and nasty. Someone who had a bit of substance. Not a pink jelly."

Ruth recoiled at the unexpected attack. "I'm not a pink jelly!"

He clicked his tongue as if he had been guilty of some minor social solecism. "Tell me in group," he said; and he watched the television, and would not speak to her again.

✎ Ten ✎

On Monday morning Patrick went in late to work. He wanted to telephone Ruth's convalescent home, and he did not want the call overheard.

Elizabeth, leisurely polishing the banister in the hall, while Frederick rocked Thomas's pram in the garden, was able to hear most of the conversation without appearing to listen.

"Dr. Fairley? It's Patrick Cleary."

Dr. Fairley drew Ruth's notes toward him. "Ah, Mr. Cleary. Good to hear from you. Your wife is making excellent progress," he said.

"She would not speak to me on the telephone, and she did not want to see me this weekend. I thought something must be wrong."

"No," Dr. Fairley said calmly. "She is getting in touch with her feelings. We have to be patient with her. She is experiencing anger and grief. She is doing very well."

"Anger?" Patrick asked blankly. "What does she have to be angry about?"

Dr. Fairley hesitated. "This is therapeutic work," he said tactfully. "Sometimes a patient goes back almost to babyhood. Sometimes it is recent or recurrent grief. But your wife is confronting her difficulties well and is making good progress."

"What d'you mean—therapeutic work?" Patrick demanded. "What has she got to be angry about? She's had everything she wanted all her life, and especially since we were married. If she says that she's been badly treated it's just not true."

"I do not attend her group sessions," Dr. Fairley said gently. "So I do not know the details. Even if I did, then the confidentiality of the patient would mean that I could not discuss such things with you. But I can say—in the broadest of terms—that she is getting in touch with her feelings, and expressing them."

"When I phoned the other night they said she could not come to the telephone because she was 'in treatment,'" Patrick said, his voice very tight.

Dr. Fairley turned back a page and sighed a small silent sigh. "Yes, that was the case. She was under restraint," he said gently.

"Under restraint?" Patrick demanded.

"Yes."

"You had her in a padded cell? In some kind of straitjacket?"

"Please, Mr. Cleary, don't distress yourself with these anxieties," Dr. Fairley said gently. "There was an incident in her group between herself and another patient, and she was sedated and returned to her bedroom. She woke at—let me see—just after seven o'clock and watched television with the other patients. She behaved perfectly normally at supper, and took part in all the activities the following day."

"Are you telling me that she was fighting with someone, that you knocked her out, and then she got up and watched television?"

"Yes, that is what seems to have taken place. As I say, I am not her group leader, so I was not there myself."

"Is she mad?" Patrick demanded, outraged.

"No, most certainly not."

"Then what is going on?"

Dr. Fairley sighed gently. "Mr. Cleary, you must be patient with her, and even with yourself. She was deeply wounded as a child by the death of her parents, and she has to come to terms with that loss and with her grief and anger. Her inability to care for her own son no doubt springs from that early trauma, and of course, on top of that, she feels the natural anxiety of the young and inexperienced mother. She is doing wonderfully well in coming to terms with all of this, and she is making good progress."

Patrick was silent for a moment, trying to take it all in. "When will she come home?" he asked.

Dr. Fairley thought of Ruth as he had seen her that morning. Her step was more confident; she had acknowledged him in the corridor. "I think she should be the one to decide," he said. "But I would think within a fortnight. Then I would recommend a therapist near to you, so that she can go on with her therapeutic work. But she will know what she needs. She will be the best person to decide."

"Even though she's the mad one?" Patrick asked rudely. "Are the lunatics running the asylum?"

Dr. Fairley observed the rise of his own temper until he had it under control and out of his voice. "Your wife is not mad, Mr. Cleary," he said politely. "She was a sad and angry little girl and she has had difficulties in adult life. But she is as sane as I am, or as you are. And indeed there are many therapeutic communities that are self-run."

Patrick bit back a retort. "I'll visit her on Sunday unless I hear to the contrary," he said shortly.

"I will give her your message," Dr. Fairley said with courtesy. He put down the receiver. "And she is certainly more pleasant than you," he said roundly to the absent Patrick. "Better mannered, less selfish, more loving, and generally a nicer person to be with. She is growing to be an honest and mature woman while you are just a bossy little boy!" Then, with his temper relieved, Dr. Fairley pulled on his jacket and went to do his rounds.

Patrick sat in silence for a moment, and then the sitting-room door opened and his mother brought in a tray with freshly made coffee.

"Thank you," he said heavily.

She poured him a cup in silence and handed it to him. "Bad news?"

He made a face. "I can hardly tell. The doctor says that he thinks she'll be home within a fortnight. But after that she'll need to see some local chap." He looked at his mother in bewilderment. "She was violent," he said wonderingly. "She attacked a patient and had to be sedated, and tied up, or something."

Elizabeth sank to the sofa. "Oh! my dear!"

"I can't imagine it!" Patrick said. "Little Ruth! Why, until we had Thomas, I don't think I ever heard her say a cross word. She never once even raised her voice to me. What can have happened?"

"Didn't he explain?"

Patrick shrugged. "He said he was bound by patient confidentiality—but he didn't seem too concerned. He made me feel as if I were making a bit of a fuss over nothing."

Elizabeth nodded. "I suppose he sees worse every day," she said, "in his work. It must be dreadful."

"But Ruth . . ."

"Did he say what we should do when she comes home?" Elizabeth demanded.

Patrick shook his head. "I didn't ask . . . what d'you mean . . . what we should do?"

Elizabeth's look was open and concerned. "To protect Thomas," she said.

Patrick was astounded. "Protect him?"

"If she is violent, and she is with Thomas, on her own . . ."

Patrick gave an abrupt exclamation, put down his cup of coffee and went to the window. In the garden outside Frederick was rocking the pram, the rhythm of the movements slowing as Thomas fell asleep, and then stilled. Frederick bent down and carefully put on the brake, adjusted the hood of the pram against the bright wintry sunlight, and checked that Thomas's little hands were warm in their knitted mittens. He turned and came toward the house.

"She can never be alone with Thomas," Patrick said as if the words were forced out of him. "I'll have to check with Dr. Fairley and make sure they are aware . . . but for our own peace of mind we'll have to watch her all the time."

Elizabeth nodded, her face full of pity. "Oh, Patrick," she said softly.

He turned to her and managed a little smile. "I'm all right," he said. "Thank God I've got you and the old man."

She nodded. "You'll always have us," she assured him. "For you and little Thomas. We'll always be here for you both."

*I*n the group session Ruth and Agnes sat facing each other, as wary as fighting cocks. George said his usual gentle introduction, "Who would like to start?" and Ruth said quickly, "I would."

"Last time I was carried out of here," she said bitterly. "George, you held me, and you called some other nurses, and you carried me out and stuffed me full of some drugs."

George nodded.

"I was angry," Ruth said. She was breathless with nerves at speaking to the whole group, but she was determined to finish. "I was angry but I wasn't mad. I'm not insane. There was no need to take me out like that. It frightened me."

"Um . . . I don't believe that." It was the man from the television room.

Ruth turned to him.

"I don't believe you were frightened," he said. "You didn't look frightened. But you looked really mad."

"I'm not mad," Ruth said quickly.

"Slip of the tongue," he said easily. "Freudian slip. You looked angry. I'm just saying I don't believe you were frightened."

Ruth took a breath. "Yes," she said. "I was angry."

The man smiled at her. "Well, that's what I thought," he said.

"Ruth, we have a no-physical-violence rule for group work and all our therapeutic work, you know that," George said gently. "You can embrace someone or hold their hand, but you must not hit or threaten them with any physical violence at all. You agreed to that when you started with this group, and you have to hold to that agreement."

He paused, waiting for Ruth's reply.

She nodded.

"I have to know that you agree."

"I nodded."

"I have to hear you *say* that you agree that there will be no physical violence to yourself or to others."

"I agree to no physical violence to myself or to others," Ruth said sullenly.

"OK," George said. He settled back in his seat and smiled at her. "Now, go on with what you were saying."

Ruth felt temporarily deflated. "I was saying I was angry," she repeated.

George nodded. "Was there any special reason?"

"I was really angry with Agnes."

"Then tell her," George advised.

Ruth turned to Agnes. "I was really angry with you."

It was a bad day for Agnes. She was shrouded in a huge man's cardigan. The leather patches on the elbows were down at her wrists. She was folded up in her chair, her knees under her chin, her face moody.

"Oh, yes," she said without interest.

"You said some things about my family that are unforgivable," Ruth said, "and untrue. You said that they had done me over. I don't begin to know what you mean. But I do know that they have loved me and cared for me, they took me into their family when I never had anyone to care for me before. They bought us our first flat, and I loved it there and I was really happy there. Then when we had our baby they bought us a beautiful cottage in the country. My mother-in-law is wonderful with the baby. They have both been wonderful to me."

Agnes nodded listlessly.

"It is not how you said," Ruth said urgently. She badly wanted Agnes to respond. "What you said wasn't true. They have been wonderful to me, and I really appreciate it."

"OK," Agnes said wearily. "OK."

"They love me," Ruth said. "They do all they can for me. Why, at this very moment they are looking after Thomas so I can be here!"

Agnes shrugged and looked away.

"To suggest anything else is a lie," Ruth said forcibly. "Elizabeth loves me as if I were her own daughter, and she adores Thomas. She furnished our house for us, with her own lovely things. She thinks about us all the time. She's a wonderful woman."

"They bought your house and she furnished it?" the man from the television room asked Ruth.

"Yes! Yes! Why on earth not?"

He smiled his shy smile at her. "It's just a bit odd," he said quietly. "Usually people choose their own houses and furniture."

Ruth looked at him with dislike. "I was pregnant," she said. "And ill. She did everything for me; she was quite wonderful."

"So is it her house or yours?"

"Mine!" Ruth exclaimed. "Of course it's mine!"

He nodded as if in agreement. "You pay the mortgage?" he suggested.

Ruth suddenly flushed and turned to George the nurse. "Do you want the details of my bank account?" she asked. "Is this what we're supposed to be doing here? Discussing my personal finances?"

"You wanted to go first," one of the women said sulkily. "So get on with it."

"I just wanted to say one thing to Agnes!" Ruth protested.

"Well, now someone has asked you something," the woman said. "So do you pay the mortgage on your house or not? Let's just get on with it!"

"But what has that got to do with anything?"

George smiled his patient smile. "Perhaps nothing," he said equably. "But is there a reason why you don't want to tell us?"

"There's no reason," Ruth said, "because there's no mortgage. They bought the house and gave it to us outright." She threw an angry look at the quiet man. "I hope you're satisfied," she said.

He nodded and would have stopped, but George intervened. "What were you thinking about, Peter," he asked gently, "when you asked about the mortgage?"

The man spoke to him alone. "I was just thinking that maybe they *hadn't* given Ruth her home at all, but just let her live in one of their houses, and then furnished it how they liked. I just wondered how much it is her house, and how much it belongs to her husband's parents."

George nodded. "I was wondering that too," he said companionably. He turned back to Ruth. "I think we were all wondering that," he said gently.

Ruth slumped back in her seat. "I'm tired of this," she said. She felt a small pleasure at refusing to speak to them. "I'm tired. I've said all I had to say."

The thin woman leaned forward. "So answer the question,

and let's move on," she said. "Is it her house—your mother-in-law's house—or is it yours?"

"Of course it's mine," Ruth said. "I live there, don't I?"

"But she owns it?"

"Yes."

"And she furnished it?"

"Yes."

"And you have no lease and you pay no rent?"

Ruth shrugged. "Yes. So what?"

The thin woman shrugged back, mirroring Ruth's weary contempt. "Then it's not your house," she said. "And actually you've got no rights at all. You're not even a tenant. You're a squatter. They can evict you any time they like."

"I'm their daughter-in-law, for God's sake!" Ruth suddenly yelled.

The woman nodded. "All that means is that you are married to her son," she said. "You haven't got a home or a family at all."

Ruth gasped at that as if she had been hit. She turned to George and he saw her face was white. "That's a dreadful thing to say," she whispered. He saw her face crumple like a little child's. "That's a dreadful thing to say to someone—that they have no home or family."

He nodded, his face was tender. "It is a dreadful thing," he said, repeating the words she had used. "And especially hard for you, Ruth."

She nodded. He could see that her eyes were filling with tears, her face looked stricken. He thought it was how she would have looked when she learned she had lost both parents and her home. And now she had learned that she had not been able to replace them.

"It's a dreadful thing to say to *anyone*," she said, still pushing the truth away.

"But worse for you," he suggested again. "Because you know what that loss is like."

"I can hardly remember. . . ."

He shook his head. "I think you know what that loss is like," he said again, and watched in pity as her expression dissolved and she turned in her chair, buried her face in the soft back, and wept. "I can't remember," she insisted. "I was too young to remember."

His face was tender with pity. "I think you *do* remember, Ruth."

They all heard the catch in her throat, and then the deeper grief as she wept. George stepped across the circle and held her in his arms. His embrace was comforting, professionally sexless. Ruth—far away in memories, deep in grief—felt only the relief of arms around her, holding her.

⁂

*I*n the farmhouse Thomas stirred in his pram. He opened his eyes and saw the comforting canopy of the pram and the little dancing toys that Elizabeth had strung from one handle of the hood to the other. He made a shape with his mouth and moved his lips. A sound was coming, slowly, he could make a sound. "Ma," he said. "Ma."

⁂

*T*hat evening Ruth sat between Agnes and Peter when they ate their supper in companionable silence. When she turned toward her room, Peter said quietly: "You did well today," and Agnes looked up and smiled.

"It's hard," Agnes said. "But Pete's right. You did do well today. In the end."

Ruth was aching with tiredness. "I've never felt so bad in my life," she said.

Agnes nodded. "Oh, yes," she said. "You've got to get all the bad stuff out before you feel better. Don't you feel better at all?"

Ruth paused and thought. Somewhere there was a sense that a lie had been challenged, that a truth had been told. She thought of the pleasure she used to have as a journalist on the rare occasions when she had caught someone out in a deception. She felt as if she liked knowing the truth, and that for most of her marriage with Patrick she had been lying about herself, and that others had been lying too.

"Yes," she said honestly. "I do feel better. I'll do some more tomorrow."

"Good," Pete said.

***

*A*nother woman started the session the next day. Ruth watched and listened as another person's pain unfolded before her, and saw how George and the group gently encouraged her to speak. She was the daughter of a wealthy family; she was addicted to drugs. She trembled with desire for the comfort of drugs as she spoke of the damage they had done to her. Ruth thought of her own longing for the easy sleep given to her by Amitriptyline and shivered. When the other woman dissolved into tears and then wrapped her arms around her own thin body, shivered a little, and said, "I'm done," Ruth spoke.

"You were right yesterday," she said to them generally. "The little house is not my home, it belongs to Frederick and Elizabeth." She took a breath. "And Patrick is my husband, but he was their son before he ever met me, and he is more their son than he is my husband." She looked around. "I'm not doing this very well," she said with a new humility. "I don't know how to be honest about this."

"You're being honest," George said.

"He's theirs," Ruth said. "He likes being in their house best. He likes being with them more than he likes being with me." It was a sharp, bitter truth she was telling. "It's her. She makes him comfortable in a way that I don't know how to. It's not just cooking and furniture. He acts like he belongs there. At our home he acts like he is on a visit." She thought for a moment. "A working visit," she said. "It's not a very nice place to stay."

She choked on the words for a moment, recognizing the little house in that damning phrase. "They don't love me particularly," she said. She had a strange sense like diving into completely unknown deep water, which might wash her in any direction at all. "They love me because Patrick brought me to them and said he wanted me. If he had brought someone else it would have been her. Up to a point, it could have been anyone.

156

If we were to separate," her voice shook slightly, "if he found someone else, they would like her just as much. They hardly see me. In all the time I have known them, they only really saw me when I was pregnant. They cared for me then because it was important that Patrick's child was well. It wasn't me they cared about. It never has been."

She could hear the words spilling out as if it were someone else talking from far away, saying things that turned her life completely upside down, or like a negative instead of a print, when everything that should be white is black, and everything that should be black is white. But she recognized what the voice was saying, and there was a clear, clean honesty at last in what the voice was describing. And everything that had puzzled Ruth and hurt her in the past—Patrick's "helping" in his mother's kitchen before Sunday lunch, Patrick's private walk with his father after lunch—all made sense now. These were the techniques they were forced to use to share the joy of their son's presence, and divide the task of entertaining his wife. Each of them wanted time alone with him, each of them had to pay for the pleasure by spending time alone with her.

"I am a real burden to them," she said brutally. "What they want is Patrick—and now Thomas too. But they had to have me. They found all sorts of ways of managing me. But I never really fitted in."

There was a silence.

"And is this a new way?" Peter asked.

George shot him a bright, acute look.

"What d'you mean?"

"Is this a new way to manage you? Put you in a loony bin?"

She recoiled. "They didn't do it," she said positively.

Peter raised an eyebrow. "Who pays?"

"You always ask that!" she said impatiently. "Who pays! Who pays! There are other things more important than money, you know! It doesn't always matter who pays!"

He nodded. "But it tells you a lot," he observed. "Who is paying for you to be here?"

"Who's paying for you?" she retorted like a child.

"My company," he said easily. "They know that the way they

work drove me crazy. They know that if they had worked well I wouldn't have had a breakdown. They know they did it. So they're putting it right. Is that what's happening for you?"

Ruth was about to deny it but she paused. She thought of the little house, which she had never wanted, and the baby, which she had conceived and carried against her will. She thought of the remorseless good nature of Elizabeth and Frederick and their view of life, which accepted no argument, or even dissent. She thought that she could never have fitted into the mold of their daughter-in-law, that in the end something would have had to crack. The distance between the flat in Bristol and the farmhouse outside Bath had preserved their mutual privacy, but once Ruth was on the doorstep she was bound to be scrutinized, and once she was scrutinized they would have to see that she did not do things as Elizabeth did them, and that if they were not done as Elizabeth did them then they would be bound to be wrong. And anyone persisting in being wrong would be crazy to behave in such a way— crazy, mad, insane.

"Yes," Ruth said quietly. "They did it to me. They didn't mean to do it to me, and there was the birth, and being really tired, and all the hormones jumbled up as well, and Thomas not sleeping—but yes, living next door to them has driven me completely insane, and now they are trying to put it right."

"So you're a loony, in the loony bin," Peter said cheerfully.

The rest of the group smiled. It was like some form of initiation. "Yes," Ruth said, joining at last. "I am a loony in a loony bin, and I am going to get sane and get out."

❧

*P*atrick arrived at the clinic on Saturday night looking tired. Ruth normally met him at the door and they went to her bedroom. This Saturday she was not waiting at the door, and he had to make his own way down the hall to her room. A woman came out of a door and stared at him without smiling. Patrick recoiled. He was accustomed to the curious gaze of the audience upon a minor celebrity, but there was nothing of that pleading half-smile from the woman. She gazed at him in quite a different manner. As if he were not important, as if she did not like him.

"Evening," Patrick said pleasantly. He could not comprehend dislike at all.

She looked through him and beyond him. She did not want to see him, and by very little effort she could make him transparent.

"Evening," Patrick said again, but with less certainty, and dived into the relative safety of Ruth's bedroom.

He was surprised to find it was empty. At other visits Ruth had waited for him at the front door, and when he was ready to go he had left her lying, weeping silently, on the bed. He had thought that there was nowhere else to be but waiting at the door for him, or lying on the bed and grieving for his absence. He had not seen the dayroom, or the group room, or the garden, or Ruth's handicrafts room. He sat in the chair, waiting for her, and then he strolled around the room, looking at the bed, the wardrobe, the chest of drawers, the curtained window. He glanced at himself in the mirror and smoothed his hair. His good-looking reflection reminded him of the woman who had looked through him in the corridor. "Barmy cow," he said. He showed his even teeth in his charming smile. "Barmy cow," he said again.

"Oh, I don't know," Ruth said, coming in behind him.

He whirled around. "Hello, darling!" he said. "Feeling better?"

"Much worse," she said precisely. "How is Thomas?"

"He's fine. Completely fine. Mother said to tell you that she thinks he's cutting a tooth. But he's completely fine. Everything under control."

Ruth closed her eyes briefly at the thought of her son cutting a tooth, and her not knowing.

"And how are *you?*" said Patrick, putting emphasis on the "you" and making his voice warm.

"Worse, as I said. But *how* are *you?*" Ruth inquired in an exact parody.

Patrick hesitated. He was not sure how to deal with Ruth, who looked the same, rather better actually: the same dark-eyed, petite, kissable little thing, still a little plump, but now unrecognizably difficult. She was tense, he decided. He would reassure her. "I'm fine. Missing you all the time."

"Eating well?" Ruth asked. There was something not quite caring about her tone.

Patrick made a little downturned mouth. "Home cooking," he said dismissively.

"Sleeping well? No crying babies at night?"

He scanned her face. "Thomas is sleeping quite well," he said. "And Mother gets up to him. You knew that."

"Oh, yes," Ruth said viciously. "I know that your mother gets up to see to my baby. I know that I left him with her, not with you—his own father. I know that the last trump wouldn't wake you after one of her dinners and a couple of your father's best bottles of claret and a couple of nightcaps."

He recoiled. "Steady on," he said.

"You sound just like your father addressing the natives in Poona," she said mercilessly. "You're something like a hundred years out of date. Both of you."

"Ruth . . ."

"Patrick . . ." she mimicked his reproachful tone.

"I don't know what's wrong with you. . . ." he started.

"If you don't know what's wrong with me then why did you put me away?" she demanded.

"I hardly put you away," he said, stung. "You were knocking back pills and boozing on top of it. You weren't fit to care for Thomas. It's all very well to get self-righteous about it now, Ruth, but you were a danger to Thomas and to yourself. What did you expect us to do?"

She was instantly deflated. "Oh."

"'Oh,' what? Mother was worried sick that you would hurt yourself, or hurt Thomas. They couldn't keep supervising you and him at long distance. I couldn't be home all the time. What did you want us to do? Are you saying you shouldn't have come here? Are you saying you want to come home?"

Ruth put her hands out, as if to halt him. "Patrick . . ."

"It's all very well sitting here and thinking about everything and blaming us, but we're just doing the best we can under a completely impossible situation. People at work keep asking me how you are and I keep saying that you're fine. People in the village keep asking why you're not looking after Thomas, and Mother keeps having to say that you're resting. You've put us in an impossible situation, and now you're trying to blame us."

She was white-faced. "I'm sorry," she said weakly. "I know a lot of it was my fault."

"I'd have thought all of it was your fault," Patrick said powerfully. "Your choice, all along the line."

"I didn't want to move out of Bristol. . . ." Ruth started.

"Oh, you can keep harking back forever," Patrick said impatiently.

"I didn't want to live there, right next door to them. . . ."

"It was an excellent choice of house, a wonderful investment, and we would have been mad to turn it down."

"But it's not *my* house. . . ."

"Why not?"

"Elizabeth decorated it, she chose almost everything. . . ."

Patrick turned toward the door and then spun around. "Mother did everything she could to make you comfortable and to spare you worry, and now you're making her out to be some sort of harridan," he said. "It's so unfair, Ruth. You're being so unfair to everyone. She did everything she could to make it easy for you and now you're accusing her of interfering."

Ruth's lips were white. "I'm not," she said weakly.

"Well, it sounds like that."

"I just thought . . . I've been thinking and thinking, Patrick."

"Well, stop thinking disloyal and unfair thoughts and start thinking how you're going to pull yourself together and come home," he said brusquely. "Your child is being cared for by my mother, your house is being run by her. She's looking after me, and she's doing all her own usual work. And you're in here—at *their* expense, I might remind you, because we could never afford the bills—you're in here, and all you're doing is lying around on your bed imagining how badly you've been treated."

"I'm not! I'm not!" Ruth cried. She pitched forward into his arms, and Patrick felt his satisfaction mix with desire at the warm, desperate closeness of her. "I'm sorry, Patrick, you don't

161

know what it's like here. We chew over everything, over and over, and at the end you don't know what to think."

He stroked her hair and stepped to one side a little, pressing her slight body closer to his. He glanced at the bed and wondered if the door was shut whether anyone would come in. It was not as if it were a hospital, after all. It was a private nursing home and his parents were footing the bill and it was his own wife. . . .

Ruth was sobbing, her body shaking with grief. He patted her back. "There," he said, absentmindedly. If the door had a bolt on it he had a good mind to shut it and to have Ruth on her little narrow hospital bed. Female despair had always stimulated Patrick, and it had been a long time since he and Ruth had made love. Emma's rejection had shaken him; he wanted Ruth's grateful response.

"There," he said again. Ruth was still crying.

Patrick reached behind him and flicked the door shut with his spare hand. Ruth looked up, her face tearstained and sore.

"The doors have to stay open," she said.

"Not during visiting time, surely. . . ."

She shook her head. "All the time."

"I thought we might be together. Ruth, together."

She shook her head. "The doors have to stay open."

He felt sexually frustrated and angry with her. "For God's sake, Ruth, I'm paying for this!"

She stepped back from him; her face was still young and blotched with her tears but she looked different, she looked wiser, and she looked at him as the woman in the corridor had looked, as if she were not arrested by his handsome face but as if she could see into his very soul—and it was completely transparent, there was nothing there at all. She looked as if she could see completely through him. "No," she said slowly. "No, Patrick. I think *I* am the one who is paying. You are benefiting."

✃— *Eleven* —✃

*T*homas was in his crib. Slowly into his line of vision his clenched fist swam forward, and then backward again. He observed it with careful concentration. Just when he was starting to make the connection between the sensation of movement and the phenomenon of vision, he was completely surprised by another hand, which approached from the other side.

He opened his mouth in amazement. "Ma," he said. "Ma-ma."

"He's saying 'grandma,'" Elizabeth said with wonderment. "Frederick—come and listen! Thomas is saying 'grandma.'"

Her smiling face swam into Thomas's line of vision. "What a clever boy!" she said. "What a clever boy."

Somewhere in Thomas's memory cells was the fading image of another face. It was not smiling, it was pale and tired-looking, but she smelled right, and she was infinitely dearer. His lip trembled. "Ma-ma," he said. But they would not hear him.

✦

*R*uth was getting ready to leave the convalescent home, having her farewell interview with Dr. Fairley.

"So tell me," he said agreeably. "What differences have you been able to make in your life since being with us?"

Ruth looked across his desk. "I've stopped using tranx," she said, and then she corrected herself with a rueful grin at him. "Tranquilizers, I should say."

"Yes," he said. "I'm glad of that. They seem like they're helping but they don't get you very far."

She shook her head. "No," she said shortly. "I should never have been offered them, and I should never have used them."

He nodded. "You could still consult the doctor for other illnesses," he said. "He might be a very good GP for broken legs. Postpartum depression is very hard to treat."

"Yes," Ruth said. "And he was under pressure from my family, I'm sure."

"Ah, your family . . ."

Ruth smiled. "I've thought a lot about them too, these last few weeks."

"Yes?"

"They're not all bad," she said. "I wanted more from them than they could ever have given. Patrick's not a bad man—he's vain and he's been spoiled, but I love him, and he's the father of my child, and I've got every reason in the world to go home and to try and make it work with him."

"Oh," Dr. Fairley said, neutrally.

Ruth nodded. "I'll see what we can do," she said. "He's very attractive, and he's brilliant at his job. In many ways I'm lucky to have him. I don't think he's God's gift to women anymore, but I do know that many women would want to be in my position. And I want to make it work. We've got a lot going for us—a lovely home, a wonderful baby, plenty of money, and he's got a great career—we should be able to make it work. I'm going to try."

Dr. Fairley, thinking of the several difficult phone calls with Patrick, nodded and reserved his opinion.

"His parents adore him," Ruth said simply. "And of course they will never love me like that. It was unfair to them and unfair to myself to hope for more. I was playing happy families in my head. I wanted them to fill all the spaces of my childhood—I know that now, but I didn't know it then. I wanted my own parents back so badly. . . ."

She broke off and reached for a tissue from the box on his desk, wiped her eyes and blew her nose, without apology for the show of emotion. "They're good people, and they love

Patrick and they love Thomas and they love me too—up to a point—I'm going to go back and accept that limitation." She gave him a little brave smile. "And in time, when they see that I care for Patrick and I care for Thomas, they'll respect me," she said. "They'll see that I'm a good wife, and a good mother, and they'll respect that."

"Good," Dr. Fairley said with careful neutrality.

Ruth nodded. He let a little silence fall on her good intentions.

"And what about you," he said. "As an individual?"

She spread her fingers out on her lap. "I'll look after Thomas while he's little, and I'll do some freelance work," she said. "I might write, if I can't get back into radio work. I might write magazine articles; I could do that. And when Thomas is older and goes to school, then I'll go back to radio work again."

He nodded. "And how will you keep from being depressed, at home on your own with a small demanding baby?" he asked.

She smiled her urchin smile. "I shall see the consultant that you have referred me to," she said, ticking off the tasks on her fingers. "I shall *not* ever take tranx or uppers or downers or anything again. I shall make a relationship with Patrick that is a real relationship between adults based on love and self-respect. I shall learn to enjoy being with Thomas. I shall ask Elizabeth for advice and help but I shall stop her invading my life, and I shall try to become friends with Frederick, and to see him as a real person, and to make him see me as a real person and not just as an adjunct of Patrick. I shall see my friends from Radio Westerly, and I shall find friends in the village, women who have babies like Thomas, and I shall spend time with them and talk about babies and child care with them."

He nodded again. "That all sounds very practical and workable," he said. "And how will you know that it is working for you? How will other people know?"

She nodded at the lesson that George and the others in her group had taught her. "Oh, yes! I will know that I am OK because I will not feel the need of any kind of drug, and I will not be sleepy all the time. I will enjoy things like food and talk and jokes. I will feel joy and sadness. And I will start to love

Thomas." She suddenly looked up, and her eyes were filled with unshed tears. "I want to love Thomas," she said suddenly. "I feel as if I have only given birth to him now, as if all the days before were just part of a hard pregnancy. I'm ready to love him now, and I want to see him and hold him and smell him and bathe him and kiss him."

Dr. Fairley smiled for the first time since she had come into the room. "I think you will make an excellent mother," he said. "Thomas is a lucky boy to have such a loving mother, who has come through so much to be with him."

She nodded. "I have," she said simply. "And I want to be his mother now, and I never did before."

"I think you have worked very hard," he said. "You've come through a great shadow on your life, and you will never be so alone and so unhappy again."

She looked at him with hope. "Can you promise that?"

He nodded. "Yes, not because I'm a magician, but because the loss of a parent for a little child is perhaps one of the worse things that can happen. And you were never allowed to acknowledge that loss until now. You've faced it now and started to deal with it, and it's unlikely that you will ever have to face anything worse."

She nodded. "I feel as if I've been crying nonstop ever since I arrived."

"Maybe you will cry some more," he suggested. "And there is nothing wrong with crying."

She reached for the tissues again. "I cry all the time."

He smiled gently. "Newly exposed emotions can be very sensitive," he said. "When I first did my therapy I went around weeping for months. I felt completely out of control and completely wonderful. Everyone else thought I was miserable, but it was a different feeling from sadness."

She was silent for a moment.

"Anything else?" he asked, trying to read her face and the relaxed set of her shoulders.

She looked up and he saw she was smiling through her tears. "No," she said. "I think I've finished. But I do thank you for having me here, and for all that you and everyone has done for me."

He made a little gesture with his hands. "It is my job," he said. "And you have a right to the best treatment we can do." He hesitated. "If you ever need us, we will still be here," he said. "Don't feel that this was like school that you have to leave and can never go back."

"I don't think I'll need to come back," she said. "Things are going to be different at home. I'm going to be straight and honest and adult with them, and things will be very different."

Dr. Fairley thought of the remorseless niceness of Elizabeth, and of Patrick's little-boy charm. "I wish you the very best of luck," he said simply.

❧

*P*atrick came to collect Ruth and was relieved to find her waiting in the hall with her small suitcase at her feet. There was no one to see her off. When she saw the car draw up outside, she got up and carried her suitcase down the shallow flight of steps. Patrick took it from her, feeling that she should not be carrying heavy weights, that she was ill. He put it in the trunk and held the car door for her. Ruth got in and he slammed the door carefully. He remembered bringing her home from the hospital when Thomas was born and felt the same irritable concern, as if Ruth had just played a masterstroke, which would ensure that all the attention was focused on her instead of him.

"Thank God I don't have to spend another minute in that place," he said abruptly as they drove through the tall gates.

"Yes," Ruth said neutrally. "How are things at home?"

"Fine."

"And Thomas?"

"Fine."

"What's he doing?"

"How d'you mean: 'what's he doing?'"

"I mean, how does he look, what is he eating, how is he behaving?"

"He looks just the same," Patrick said. He did not mean to be unhelpful, but the differences in Thomas's development were too slight to be noticed by him. "Mother will tell you," he said.

"Was it a tooth coming through?"

"No, he was just a bit pink-cheeked and restless."

Ruth nodded and looked out the window. The easy tears threatened to come at the thought of Thomas's being pink-cheeked and restless and her not there to comfort him.

"So that's that, is it?" Patrick asked after a while.

"What is?"

"You don't have to go back again?"

She shook her head. "I'll see a therapist in Bath for a while," she said. "But I don't plan to go back to Dr. Fairley."

"Does he say you're completely OK?"

Ruth threw him a swift smile. "I don't think he quite deals in those sorts of judgments," she said, amused. "I don't think he would recognize the concept of completely OK."

"Well, he says you're normal?"

"I was always normal."

"Well, you're better then?"

"Better than normal?"

Patrick clicked his tongue. "Look, Ruth, it's been a long worrying time for me, and I had to go in to work at seven this morning to get something out of the way so I could collect you today. I've driven two hours here and I'm driving two hours back, and I'm not in the mood for clever games. I'm asking you if you're OK now. Can you tell me that?"

Ruth belatedly remembered her resolution to be straight and clear with Patrick and his family. "I'm sorry," she said. "What was wrong with me was a form of postpartum depression, which took me back to the loss of my parents." She could feel the tears coming and she swallowed and took a deep breath. "I have spent a lot of time grieving for them, and now I feel ready to take up my life again. I am really sorry that things went so bad with Thomas, and I want to start all over again with him. And I'm really pleased that, however bad it's been, it's happened now, and it's over and done with now. He and I can start our relationship again and he's still only three months old. Agnes says . . ."

"Who's Agnes?"

"One of the patients—Agnes says that her children were really wonderful from about six months, so I want . . ."

"I hardly think her opinions would be very helpful."

Ruth recoiled. "What?"

"Well, what's wrong with her?"

"Nothing, nothing's wrong with her."

"What was she in there for?"

"She has an addiction. But . . ."

Patrick snorted. "Well, I hardly think we need take some druggie's opinion on child care, need we?"

Ruth paused for a moment before carefully replying. "She is a rather wonderful person, who is very brave, and who was very kind to me. I liked her a lot, and I'm going to stay in touch with her."

"In touch with her?"

"Yes."

"You mean write to her?"

"Yes, and when she comes out I'll visit her and I'll ask her to visit us. I want her to see Thomas, and I want to meet her children."

Patrick shook his head, but said nothing.

"You don't approve," Ruth said flatly.

He shook his head again; he was smiling.

"You don't want me to see her?"

Patrick was imperturbable. He watched the road with his level blue eyes.

"Patrick, please speak to me," Ruth said, trying to keep her rising temper out of her voice. "Agnes is a friend of mine. Of course I shall want to see her, and of course I shall write to her."

"Fine," Patrick said flatly. "Fine. Whatever you like, Ruth, and I hope it makes you happy and helps you, and makes her happy and helps her. *I* don't want to meet her, and I won't meet her. And I don't want her to see Thomas either. But you have every right to do whatever you like, pursue your new friends and life."

Ruth felt an uneasy sensation of tumbling, as if her return to her stable marriage and life were a mirage, and that she had never been more insecure. "It's not a new life," she said. "My life is with you and Thomas. I'm coming home to my old life, that's what I want. But Agnes was a good friend to me, and I want to stay in touch with her. That's all." Her voice was plaintive and she checked herself. "Come on, Patrick. We're not even home yet. I don't want to quarrel with you."

He shook his head. "Of course not," he said. "There's no quarrel. I said that you can have the friends that you want. But I don't have to meet them, do I?"

"No."

"And my family certainly won't meet them," he said. He leaned forward and switched on the radio, drowning out any further conversation. "D'you mind if I catch the news?"

❧

*E*lizabeth was listening for the car, waiting for the scrunch of the wheels on the gravel. She had kept Thomas from his morning sleep so that he would be certain to be asleep when his mother came home, to give them all time to assess Ruth before she saw her son. She saw Patrick's car from the nursery window; in the antique wooden crib below the window Thomas was soundly asleep. She closed the nursery door behind her and ran down the stairs to open the front door as Patrick drew up and Ruth got out.

Elizabeth noticed at once that they had been listening to the radio rather than talking together, that Patrick looked strained and sulky. Then she looked at her daughter-in-law. Ruth was looking wonderfully well. The tired, strained look had quite gone from her face, her eyes were bright again, her hair clean, her face young and optimistic. It was how she had looked when Patrick first brought her home and Elizabeth had realized, with a feeling of dread, that this would be the girl who would be her daughter-in-law, that this was the one he would marry.

"Darling!" she exclaimed and hurried down the steps and put her arms around Ruth and held her tight.

Ruth had lost weight in the four weeks she had been away from home; Elizabeth could feel the bones in her shoulders and her hips as they embraced.

"It's so good to have you home," she said. "It's wonderful. Come in, I've got lunch ready for you."

"Where's Thomas?" Ruth said as she went into the hall.

"Upstairs having a sleep. I've just this minute put him down."

Ruth started for the stairs and did not see the swift exchange of looks between Patrick and his mother.

"I'll come up too," Patrick said and followed Ruth up the stairs.

She tiptoed into the nursery and leaned over the side of the crib. Thomas was asleep on his back, his eyelashes curled on his pink plump cheeks. His downy hair was close around his perfectly round skull; his mouth was a tiny rosebud. One hand was outflung above his head, the fingers curled into the palm. The other was thrown sideways as if the baby were quite abandoned into sleep. Ruth drank in the sight of him, as if she had been thirsty for him for months. "Oh, God, he's so lovely," she whispered.

Patrick leaned against the doorpost.

Ruth reached down and put her finger on the little wrist. There was a small line where the plump arm met the plump hand; Ruth stroked it. Thomas stirred slightly in his sleep and turned his head. Ruth bent low over the cot and inhaled the warm scent of his breath. He smelled of warm skin, of baby shampoo, and of milk.

"Let's go down," Patrick said. "Mother won't want him woken up if she's just put him down."

"You can go," Ruth whispered.

He did not move.

Ruth leaned into the cot and let her lips and nose brush Thomas's fine hair, inhaling the scent of him, sensing the warm sweetness of him. She felt like some animal—a mother lion—reclaiming a lost cub. She wanted to strip him of his little romper suit and sniff him all over, she wanted to lick him, she wanted his naked warm skin against her own. With a sharp pang she realized that she had lost her chance to breast-feed him, and that only now was she ready for that intimacy.

"Come on," Patrick said from the doorway.

171

Ruth glanced behind her. "You go on down," she said. She had forgotten he was there. "I just want to see him for a moment. I'll be down in a minute."

"I'll wait," Patrick said.

"No, go on," she said.

He did not move. Ruth kissed Thomas gently on his warm rounded skull but she felt Patrick's scrutiny on her back. She straightened up and tiptoed toward the door. "He's so vulnerable," she said. "I had forgotten all about that. When I was ill I felt as if he were a little monster, draining the life out of me. Now that I can see him properly I can see what a delicate little thing he is. Completely defenseless."

She slipped her hand in his arm and leaned against him. "I'm so glad to be home," she said. "Thank you for being so patient, darling, you've been wonderful. I'm so glad to be home."

Patrick kissed the top of her head and led the way from the nursery and down the stairs.

Elizabeth and Frederick were waiting for them in the sitting room with the decanter of sherry and glasses. There was a jug of fresh orange juice on the tray as well. Frederick came forward and kissed Ruth with a word of greeting.

"Sherry, darling? Orange juice, Ruth?" Elizabeth asked.

Ruth hesitated. "I can drink sherry," she said awkwardly.

Elizabeth shot a quick look at Patrick.

"We thought you'd have to be on the wagon," he said. "We assumed you'd prefer juice."

"I'd like an orange juice," Ruth said. "But I can drink alcohol if I want."

Frederick poured the drinks with care and handed Ruth her juice and then sherry to Elizabeth and Patrick. "Never does to mix them," he observed to nobody in particular. "Drugs and drink, never do mix."

"I'm not taking any drugs," Ruth said.

Again Elizabeth and Patrick exchanged that swift intimate glance.

"I thought you'd be on something, until you get to see the Bath therapist," Patrick said.

Ruth shook her head. "The whole point of going there was to

get off the drugs," she said. "And it was only Amitriptyline, I wasn't a complete crackhead. And now I'm clean."

Elizabeth's face was a study of polite interest. "I'm very glad to hear it," she said, ignoring the drug jargon as she would have ignored a swear word.

Frederick glanced uncomfortably at her, uncertain as to how they should handle this glimpse into a world they could usually ignore.

"I wanted to say something to you, to you all," Ruth started. She was reminded with a surprising rush of nostalgia how she would sometimes start talking in her group. She looked at the anxious faces around her—Frederick's distinguished craggy scowl, Patrick's handsome half-smile, Elizabeth's unaffected charm. "I wanted to say that things were very bad for me from the moment Thomas was born—even before. And I'm really sorry that they turned out like that. I've thought through what was wrong and it will never be that bad again. I want to start afresh with you." She looked at Patrick and then she looked from him to his mother and his father. "I want you to give me another chance," she said. "You've been generous and kind and helpful to me and now I want to come to you as an equal and start again."

There was a silence. Frederick cleared his throat. "Fair enough," he said. "Everyone has a right to one mistake."

Ruth's face lightened with sudden joy. "Frederick, you're *so* straight!" she exclaimed with pleasure. "Thank you."

Elizabeth recoiled slightly at Ruth's easy use of his Christian name. "Of course, my dear," she said. "You know we wanted to help you with Thomas and we've been glad to do everything we can. I'm so pleased that you are home and completely cured."

Ruth hesitated at the word "cured" with its implication of illness and a suffering patient, but she let it go. She was learning quickly that the outside world had retained its own codes and language even while she had been changing.

"I'll be a good mother to Thomas, and a good wife to Patrick," she promised. "And a good daughter-in-law to you." She looked from Frederick to Elizabeth.

"Well, I'll drink to that," Frederick said, robustly closing the conversation. He raised his glass. "Here's to little Ruth coming home and looking like a pretty girl again."

The others raised their glasses to her, and Ruth—blushing slightly and smiling at the compliment—did not detect that she had been silenced.

"Lunch is served," Elizabeth said, seeing Frederick had finished his sherry. "Only a casserole, I'm afraid. I didn't know how long the journey would take you."

"Lovely," Ruth said.

They ate in the dining room. The weather had turned wintry, and halfway through the meal Elizabeth put on the lights. The sky outside the windows was dark and brooding, and there was a sudden scud of rain on the panes.

"I wanted to walk home," Ruth said in disappointment. "We'll have to drive."

A sharp look of complicity passed between Elizabeth and her son. But neither of them spoke.

"When will Thomas wake?" Ruth asked. "I so want to see him."

Elizabeth glanced at her little gold watch. "In about half an hour," she said. "If he doesn't wake, you can pick him up. He sleeps for about an hour and a half morning and afternoon now. Any more than that and he doesn't go off at night."

"You'll have to take me through his day," Ruth said. "I'm completely out of practice. And Patrick said you thought he might have had a tooth coming! I couldn't believe it."

"It was a false alarm," Elizabeth said. "I don't know how I came to mistake it. But one little cheek was scarlet and so hot! It must have been a little fever he had. It was all over within the day."

"Did you call the doctor?"

Elizabeth smiled. "There was no need. I just gave him plenty to drink and kept an extra-special eye on him."

Ruth nodded. "And what's his weight?"

Elizabeth was vague. "Oh! I haven't taken him to the clinic," she said. "Not since you went away."

"But you're supposed to!" Ruth exclaimed. "Every week!"

Elizabeth's smile was a little fixed. "They only weigh them and measure them," she said. "I could see myself that he was thriving."

"But they're supposed to see him. . . ."

"It's not so important after six weeks," Elizabeth said soothingly. "I'd have taken him if he'd gone off his food or anything. But he was obviously so well. . . ."

"I took him *every* week," Ruth exclaimed.

Elizabeth had flushed slightly; she glanced at Patrick.

"Well, Mother didn't," he said flatly. "You can start again, now that you're back."

Ruth looked from one to another, trying to read their expressions. "I don't understand why not?" she said, looking at Elizabeth. "Why didn't you take him?"

"I think I have explained," Elizabeth said. Her voice was slightly higher with irritation.

"I don't understand," Ruth said again stubbornly.

"I was embarrassed," Elizabeth said, forced into honesty. "I thought they would ask where his mother was, and I didn't want to say that she was mentally ill, that she was in a home. I thought it would go down in his records if I said that, and he would be branded, for the rest of his life, as a boy whose mother was mad."

Ruth gasped. Frederick turned his attention to the rim of his water glass, and examined it minutely.

"They wouldn't write such a thing," Ruth stammered. "And I was not mad . . . and in any case, it's *in* the notes, in my notes. I had postpartum depression, there's nothing shameful in it. . . ."

"It's in *your* notes," Elizabeth said. "But I saw no reason for it to be in Thomas's notes too. I saw no reason for him to have that mark against him. I didn't want them to know unless it was absolutely essential. And it was not absolutely essential. I didn't want the nurse to know, or the health visitor, or any passing social worker. I believe that private things should be kept private."

"So where does everyone think I have been?" Ruth demanded.

"On holiday," Elizabeth replied concisely. "Brighton. A health farm."

Ruth gasped. "But surely no one would believe such nonsense! I'm not the sort of woman who goes for a month to a health farm!"

Elizabeth shrugged and glanced at Patrick, handing the whole difficult conversation over to him.

"What did you want us to say?" he asked. "With my position, the press would have been onto me, wanting to know about you, and about Thomas. The social workers might have wanted to take Thomas into care. We had to think all this through, and we did the best we could. It's a bit rich coming back, all full of good intentions, and then telling us we've done everything wrong."

Ruth recoiled at once from his anger. "Yes, I'm sorry. I didn't mean to be critical."

"Well, you were critical," Patrick said. "And to Mother who has worked to make Thomas happy night and day since you went off, and keep the family together."

Ruth nodded. "I'm sorry," she said again.

"And it's all very well saying it should all have been done differently," Patrick continued, his voice rising. "But we might as well say that you shouldn't have given in to it. If you felt ill you should have told us. Taking handfuls of Amitriptyline and going out and getting drunk wasn't quite the way to cope with it."

Ruth could feel her heart beating faster, and tears coming to her eyes. She had forgotten about the pub, about her car abandoned in the parking lot, about being drunk and drugged in front of her in-laws. She looked down at her hands clenched tight in her lap and felt her cheeks burn.

"If there's going to be any criticism . . ." Patrick started ominously.

"Steady the Buffs," Frederick said simply. "Water under the bridge, I think. Spilt milk." He looked at Elizabeth. "What about some coffee, darling?"

She rose automatically and started clearing the plates. Ruth got up too. "Let me help."

"Certainly not," Elizabeth said coldly. She cleared the plates in silence and took them to the kitchen. Ruth sat at the table like a naughty child, her eyes downcast.

"You'll never believe the weather we've had," Frederick said kindly. "I think it's rained every day since the middle of November. All my late roses were completely washed out, and the river has flooded further down the valley."

Ruth took a sip of water. "Really?"

"The lane was running with water last Wednesday," Frederick said. "I warned them, when they wanted to build that new estate on the lower levels—you can work with Nature but you can't beat her. They bricked in the riverbank, and now it's completely overflowed and there will be water all through the ground floors of those new houses if it doesn't stop raining soon."

"What a shame," Ruth said automatically. She pressed her lips together to restrain the sobs, holding in her anger and her pain.

Elizabeth came in with the coffee and put a cup precisely before each of them, cream and brown sugar in the center of the table.

"Yes, you can work with Nature but she always gets her own way in the end," Frederick said into the continuing frosty silence. "Still, it's a black cloud that has no silver lining—the floods have done my willow trees no end of good. You should take a stroll down and see them, my dear. They're very pretty, standing in the water. When the light is right you can see their reflection—rather picturesque." He nodded at Patrick. "You might take a snap of it. It might look rather well."

"Coffee?" Elizabeth asked distantly.

Mutely Ruth passed her cup and held it while Elizabeth poured with a steady hand.

"I'm sorry, Elizabeth," she said in a little voice.

Elizabeth hesitated. "I would much rather you called me Mother, as you did before," she said. "Or does that have to change too?"

~ *Twelve* ~

There was a little cry from the nursery. Ruth leaped to her feet. "I'll go!" Patrick wearily put down his cup and followed her. When he got to the nursery she was lifting Thomas from his cot, her hand under his firm little head, her arm around his compact body.

"Oh, Thomas!" she said. The ready tears were pouring down her face as she held his head to her cheek and inhaled the scent of him. His cry stilled as he was picked up, and he sensed the new feeling of being held by his mother, and the smell of her, and the gentle brush of her hair against his head.

"My baby," she said.

Patrick softened at the sight of them, at the tenderness in Ruth's face, at the tiny movement as Thomas snuggled closer into her arms. In his first spontaneous gesture since she had come home, he stepped toward her and put his arms around them both. Ruth leaned back against him and tipped her head back against his shoulder. Patrick bent down and kissed her cheek, salty-tasting from her tears.

"I love him," she said. "I really love him, Patrick, whatever it looked like when I was ill. The love was all there, just waiting to come out."

"I know," he said. "I'm glad you're back."

They heard Elizabeth coming up the stairs, and Patrick immediately released her and stepped away.

179

"I just wanted to make sure you had everything you need," Elizabeth said pleasantly. "Patrick knows where everything is, I think. There are his clean nappies there, and a clean romper suit there," she gestured to the chest of drawers. "He's generally wet through and needs to be changed at once."

Ruth looked around for a changing mat to put him down. There was none.

"Oh! Of course!" Elizabeth exclaimed. "I sit on the chair and change him on my knee. I'm so old-fashioned!"

Ruth smiled in relief at the warmer tone. "I've never learned to do it," she said. "I'll have to put him on the floor."

"Oh no!" Elizabeth said. "Too drafty with this miserable weather. Give him here, and I'll get him dressed in a moment and bring him down to you." She took Thomas from his mother's arms and sat on the rocking chair in the corner of the nursery. Competently, she stripped him of his damp romper suit, and unpinned the cloth diaper. Ruth did not leave, as she had been told to do, but stayed to watch.

"A cloth nappy?"

"I can't bear the disposable kind," Elizabeth said. "I think it's so unhygienic!"

"Unhygienic?" Ruth protested. "I don't know anyone who uses real nappies these days!"

Elizabeth, with the baby securely on her lap, looked up and laughed. "I just do it the way I always have done," she said. "In the old days we put the nappies in to soak and washed them through at the end of the day, and the baby had clean, warm, dry cloth nappies every time he needed them. You never run out when the shops are shut, you're not putting chemicals against the baby's skin, and you're not polluting the environment with all that paper waste!"

She wrapped the clean diaper around Thomas and pinned it skillfully with one pin at the front, and then tied a waterproof cover on top. Before he could protest, she had pulled a clean romper suit over his head and thrust his little hands and legs into the holes and fastened him up.

"There!" she said with satisfaction. "Now you're ready to go to your mummy." She handed Thomas back to Ruth and busied herself with picking up the wet suit and clearing away the wet diaper. Ruth took Thomas back into her arms but he smelled different. There was the pleasing aroma of clean diaper and ironed laundry, but he smelled slightly of Elizabeth's washing powder, and his head and hands smelled pleasantly of Elizabeth's perfume. By taking him and changing his clothes, she had somehow made him her baby again; Ruth felt like an intruder.

She turned and went slowly downstairs with Thomas held to her shoulder. "That's a sight for sore eyes!" Frederick exclaimed, and drew her into the sitting room. "Let's hope he's not forgotten you!"

For a moment Ruth looked stricken, and then she cuddled Thomas a little closer. "Well, we'll just have to start from the beginning again," she said. She sat on the chair and laid the baby along her knees so that she could look into his open clear face. "Hello, Thomas," she said lovingly. "Hello."

Elizabeth came in and smiled at the two of them. "I think we should light the fire, Frederick," she said. "It's so dark and cold."

Frederick stepped forward and bent over the grate and started to lay the fire with kindling and small pieces of coal.

"Perhaps you should have a rest, Ruth?" Elizabeth offered. "I can have Thomas if you would like a lie-down. You'll find all your things in your bedroom."

Ruth glanced at Patrick, who had followed his mother into the room. "I thought we'd be getting home," she said uncertainly.

His quick glance to his mother should have warned her, but Ruth had spent four weeks with people who were committed to clarity and frankness, and she had lost the skill of decoding silences. "I want to take Thomas home," she said, after a moment.

Elizabeth said nothing; she waited for Patrick to speak.

"I thought we'd stay here for a while," he said. "The heating has been off at home, and the place needs to be warmed through and aired before we can take Thomas back, anyway. And there's nothing to eat in the house. We've been living here. I just shut up the cottage."

"I've kept an eye on it, don't fret," Frederick assured her. "When I take Thomas out on a walk we often stroll down that way. It's safe and sound."

"Well, I'll go down there now and put the heating on," Ruth said. She still had not understood. "It should be warmed up by this evening. We can go home at Thomas's bedtime."

Patrick cleared his throat. "I thought we'd stay here for a while," he said again.

Ruth looked from Patrick to Elizabeth to Frederick as she realized a decision had been made. "How long for?" she asked simply.

"A couple of weeks."

"Weeks?"

"Yes."

Ruth had the strange sense of the ground falling away underneath her feet again. "What d'you mean, Patrick? Why can't we go home?"

At the sound of the alarm in her voice Thomas's face puckered up and he let out a little wail. Elizabeth started forward at his cry and then checked the movement. Deliberately, she went and sat in a chair at the fireside and looked at the flames, which were curling around the kindling in the cold grate. Frederick sat back on his heels and looked at the fire.

"Don't upset Thomas," Patrick said. "Let's leave it for now."

Ruth took a breath. "I won't upset Thomas," she said quietly. "I want to go to our home. Is there something wrong, something you're not telling me?"

Patrick glanced at his mother.

"We were just thinking what was best for you, Ruth," she said gently. "You've only come out of hospital this morning. You don't want to overdo things in your first week."

"We thought you'd want a bit of help," Patrick agreed. "And Thomas is used to being here. A bit of continuity is what he needs, and I would feel much happier at going off to work and leaving you if I knew you were here."

Ruth nodded slowly. "I see that," she said. "But I am quite better now. I wasn't in hospital because I had a broken leg, or a physical illness. I don't need to rest. I was unhappy, but I understand it now. I feel quite different."

"Well, you may feel different, but we feel the same," Patrick said bluntly. "We saw that you couldn't cope with Thomas, and it got worse and worse and none of us knew what to do. We don't want that happening again."

"Neither do I," Ruth said quickly. "It won't."

"So it would suit everyone if we stayed here for a while, until we see how things are going. To reassure ourselves." He glanced at Elizabeth for confirmation. She made an infinitesimal nod. "Keep things under control," he said.

Ruth thought of the lessons of her group. "And how will we know that everything is all right?" she asked.

Patrick glanced at his mother. "We'll know," she said with a little smile. "We'll all know that things have turned out perfectly, Ruth. We'll just know it."

"Then how will we know if things are *not* going well?" Ruth persisted.

"Oh, I hope that won't arise!"

"But if it does arise?"

"If you are ill again?"

Ruth shook her head. "I won't be ill again. But how will we know that things are not going well enough for us to go back to the little house? Who is to decide? And on what basis?"

Elizabeth shrugged. "I don't even want to think about it," she said. "You tell me that you're well now, and that's enough for me, Ruth dear. You'll be the one that decides. Let's take it one day at a time and see how it goes."

Ruth paused for a moment, and then the warmth of Thomas against her shoulder gave her renewed strength. "The thing is," she said slowly, "that I don't want to live here. I know you've been wonderful"—she looked from Frederick to Elizabeth—"but we have our own home and our own lives to lead, and I want to go to our own home, and start again."

"And so you shall!" Elizabeth said firmly. "As soon as you are completely well, you'll start life again in your new home, and we'll be the first to congratulate you."

Ruth hesitated, looking from Elizabeth's smiling face to Patrick's determined one. "I really have to make this clear. I am not living here permanently."

"Of course not," Elizabeth said pleasantly. "You have your own life to lead—why, we've even replaced your car!"

"My car?"

Frederick rose from his place before the fire. "Your old car never turned up, I'm afraid. Whoever took it from the pub parking lot probably had it resprayed and resold within the week. And your insurance didn't cover you for theft when the keys were left in it."

Ruth flushed scarlet with shame at the memory.

"Bought you another," Frederick said gruffly. "Little runabout. Welcome-home present. Show of support."

"Because we know you need your freedom," Elizabeth supplemented sweetly.

Ruth felt the easy tears rise into her eyes again. "You're so good to me!" The words were wrenched out of her by their simple generosity. "Thank you."

Elizabeth came forward and took Thomas from her. "We just want you to be happy," she said gently. "Let's all be happy, now."

<hr />

*R*uth bathed Thomas in the yellow bathroom that night and Elizabeth tidied the linen cupboard on the landing outside the bathroom so that she could listen at the door and make sure that Thomas was safe.

When Ruth came down with Thomas all pink and smiling and clean, his grandfather held him while Ruth made his bottle, and then handed him back with a goodnight kiss.

"He likes to be rocked while he has his bottle, and then when he has finished his bottle, you put him up on your shoulder and rock him like that," Elizabeth instructed. "You'll feel him go all limp and his breathing deepen when he has fallen asleep, and then you can put him in his cot. I leave the night-light on, and he has his duvet cover just up to his tummy."

Ruth nodded and took her son up the stairs to the nursery.

"You go," Elizabeth said in an undertone to Frederick. "You can read the newspaper in our bedroom and just keep an ear open. Just in case."

He nodded obediently, and folded his paper under his arm and followed Ruth and his grandson up the stairs.

"She's bound to notice after a while," Patrick said to his mother. He followed her out into the kitchen and poured them both a gin and tonic while she sliced vegetables for the evening meal.

"I think we can be tactful," she said. "There are three of us; we can take it in turns. I think we can always have someone within earshot."

"We won't go back to the little house until I am confident that Thomas is safe with her," Patrick said firmly. "Whether she likes it or not."

She glanced at her son. "That must be your first duty," she said. "Your first duty must be to our boy."

Ruth's days took on a new routine, living at the farmhouse with Patrick and his parents. If Thomas woke in the night she went to him and rocked him to sleep again. Then he would often sleep until eight o'clock, so Patrick got up and left for work without disturbing her. Elizabeth and Frederick were always up from seven, Elizabeth to cook Patrick's breakfast and see him off to work, Frederick to eat breakfast and go out for his morning stroll with the dog around the fields.

When Thomas woke, he and Ruth would go downstairs for breakfast, Ruth in her dressing gown and Thomas in his sleep suit. Elizabeth would have Ruth's toast and coffee ready, and she would feed Thomas while Ruth ate, and then take him upstairs to dress him while Ruth had a shower.

If the day was sunny and bright, Ruth would wrap Thomas warmly and put him in the pram for Frederick to push him a little way down the lane until he fell asleep. Then he would come home and draw the pram into the house, through the French windows of his gunroom, where Thomas could sleep undisturbed by the noise of housework in the rest of the house. Frederick would potter at his workbench or his desk, tying flies for the fishing season, or writing letters while Thomas slept in his pram in the corner of the room.

Ruth had nothing to do. Elizabeth would not accept any help in the house; she said she had her own way of doing things and there were no chores to do. Instead, Ruth started walking down the lane to her own house, the little house, vacuuming and dusting the cold rooms, cleaning the windows, and tidying the cupboards, and then locking it all up and walking back to the farmhouse in time for lunch.

Ruth always picked Thomas up after his morning sleep, changed his diaper and played with him before lunch. Obediently, she dressed him in the bulky cloth diapers that Elizabeth preferred, and fed him with Elizabeth's freshly pureed dinners. In the afternoon Ruth would play with Thomas in the living room, or in her own bedroom. She did not notice that someone was always with them. If they were in the living room together, playing on the mat before the fire, then Frederick would be in his chair, behind the *Daily Telegraph*. If they were in her bedroom or in the nursery, then Elizabeth would be cleaning the bath, or doing the flowers on the landing, or dusting the picture frames. Ruth, absorbed in finding a new and valuable intimacy with her baby, simply did not notice that she was constantly supervised.

Patrick, secure in the knowledge that his child was safe, came home in time for dinner at seven-thirty, sometimes only just in time to kiss Thomas goodnight.

"You hardly see him," Ruth complained.

"I see him at the weekends," he said. "And besides, when you were away I saw him all the time. He needs his mother now."

Elizabeth cooked an impressive dinner every night, with either a starter, entrée, and cheeseboard, or with a main course and a homemade pudding. After dinner they watched television in the sitting room, the nine o'clock news followed by whatever program was on BBC1 or BBC2. If Frederick wanted to watch something different, he went to his gunroom. If Patrick wanted to watch either of the independent channels, he went upstairs to their bedroom and watched it on the small television up there. It was an unwritten and unchallenged rule that they watched only the BBC in the sitting room. The only time the rule was broken was when one of Patrick's documentaries was on, and then it was watched and videotaped in solemn silence. Some evenings Patrick took Ruth out for a drink, once to the cinema. But Patrick's work was still so demanding that during the week he preferred to go to bed early, and he slept heavily.

At the weekend Patrick and Ruth took Thomas to the park, or out for a walk, or for a stroll around the city center, window-shopping. On Saturday night they generally left him with Elizabeth and went out for dinner. On Sunday morning they slept in, and Elizabeth had him all to herself until eleven o'clock, when they all went to church. After Sunday lunch they went for a walk. It was all as it had been when Patrick and Ruth used to visit on Sundays, except now the visit had been prolonged indefinitely, and sometimes Ruth feared that she would never get home.

On Thursday afternoon, in the second week, Elizabeth had Thomas all afternoon when Ruth went in to see the Bath therapist—a woman called Clare Leesome. She had consulting rooms on the ground floor of her house, a solid Victorian house, on the outskirts of Bath. Ruth rang the doorbell and Clare showed her into a room furnished with soft chairs and large floor cushions. Clare Leesome sat on one chair, Ruth sat on another. The house was very quiet. Clare asked Ruth a few questions and then sat very still, letting her slowly reveal more and more. She started with the clinic, and the discovery of her grief at her parents' death. Clare Leesome nodded; she took no notes. Ruth cried as she spoke of the death of her mother, and the therapist watched her cry as if tears were a sign of health, an appropriate expression, and not a symptom of illness that should be apologetically mopped up. They agreed that they would meet weekly for Ruth to talk through the loss of her parents. It was to be an open-ended arrangement, to last as long as Ruth wished.

"I don't want to be one of these people with an analyst for the rest of my life," Ruth said.

Clare smiled. "No," she said. "I don't work like that either. But you have been through a difficult time; there are bound to be things that will come up for you that you will want to talk over."

"And will I be happy?" Ruth demanded. "Will I stop crying and crying and feel steadily happy?"

"If your life gives you cause to feel happy," Clare replied. "I am not a magician. If you have a sad and troublesome daily life, then you will feel sad and troubled. But if you have a happy and fulfilling life, then you will feel happy and fulfilled. All we can do is to make sure that you feel the emotion that is relevant— so that you're not unhappy when everything is going well. It will be up to you—when you are in touch with your feelings and can make the judgments—to decide whether your life needs to change or not."

❦

Ruth telephoned David at Radio Westerly at the end of the second week. For some reason, which she did not choose to examine, she used the telephone in the little house, when she was visiting one morning.

"Hello."

"Ruth! God! How wonderful to hear from you! Are you out?"

"No, I drove my motorbike and jumped over the wire, what d'you think?"

"I think you're out."

"I am."

"And—are you all right?"

"Yes. Look, I'm so sorry that you were stuck in the middle. I can hardly remember the pub, but they tell me you had to bring me home. I imagine it was dreadful."

He chuckled. "God, Ruth, you will never know. They were all frightfully British and restrained about it. I should think Patrick wanted to murder me."

"How awful. I *am* sorry, David."

"Think nothing of it," he said grandly. "I only wish I had known what to do. I did feel that I had abandoned you, and then I heard you'd gone off for a—er—a rest."

"You did the right thing," she assured him. "And they found me an excellent residential therapy center. I wasn't locked up screaming, you know. It was an excellent place and I'm really well now."

"Want to come and get drunk then?" he offered mischievously.

She giggled. "Sounds good to me."

"Lunch?"

"Elizabeth baby-sits for me on Thursdays. I go into Bath to see a therapist. I could have lunch with you first."

"Twelve o'clock at the Black Bull?"

"OK," she said. "If there's any problem you can phone me. I'll give you the number."

"I've got the number."

There was a little pause. "I'm not at home. We're at Patrick's parents' house."

He was instantly alert. "Oh. Why's that?"

"They wanted us to stay until we are all settled down again. I think they wanted to know I was going to be all right."

"So when do you go back home?"

"It was supposed to be this weekend. But Patrick has to go away overnight, and they don't want me on my own in the little house, so it'll be the middle of next week."

He thought for a moment. "I'll see you for lunch, anyway." He thought about wishing her luck. For an odd superstitious moment he had a sense of her as facing obstacles that were almost too great for her. "Without fail," he said, as if he could will her through the days so that he could see that she was safe and well. "Is Thomas OK?"

"He's fine."

"And Patrick?"

"Fine."

"See you on Thursday then," he said.

When the phone clicked and she was gone, he felt as if he had lost her to the Cleary family all over again.

❧

The decision that Ruth should stay at the farmhouse while Patrick was away was made almost by default. Ruth had thought that they would move out on Friday, but then the meeting in London came up, and Patrick would not be home until Sunday. He said he could not face the packing and the disruption and the moving of all Thomas's toys and things when he had just got home; he said he would do it in the following week. Thus the third week of the visit started.

"I could move us," Ruth said brightly at dinner on Tuesday night. "You don't need to do anything, Patrick. I could do it all."

"I want to help," Patrick said. "I just can't do it for a couple of days. There's no problem, is there? We can move into the little house at the weekend."

"I just feel that we're rather in the way. . . ." Ruth started.

"Oh, no," Elizabeth said swiftly. "You know we love having you here. Don't feel that, Ruth! We'll be quite lost without you."

"Give it another week," Frederick advised. "Then you can go back in time for Christmas."

"Thomas's first Christmas," Elizabeth said, smiling. "What are you going to get him?"

"Is he too small for one of those bouncy things?" Patrick asked. "Those bouncy things that you hang on doorways?"

"I always worry that they'll collapse!" Elizabeth said.

"Not if its properly hung," Frederick advised. "I could put you up a good solid butcher's hook in the kitchen ceiling, if you wanted. Screw it into the beams. He'd have to bring the whole house down with him to get it down."

"Chap at work says his daughter spends half the day in hers," Patrick said. "He says she loves it."

"But when shall we go home?" Ruth asked abruptly.

Patrick leaned over and patted her hand. "It's lovely to see you so well and anxious to get back," he said affectionately. "But I don't want to rush back."

"And you're more than welcome here, Ruth," Elizabeth said. "I should hate to see you getting overtired again."

"I wasn't overtired," Ruth said carefully. "I was depressed. I was suffering from the mental illness of depression. But now I have recovered, and I am continuing with therapy to make sure that I stay well. We'll have to go back sooner or later; I'd like to get back and get on with our lives."

There was a brief silence. "What does your therapist say?" Patrick asked.

"Nothing . . ." Ruth replied, surprised. "That is, I haven't asked her. She hasn't said anything about where we live. It hasn't come up."

"She doesn't know that you want to move back to living on your own, without any support?" Patrick asked heavily.

Ruth was lost for words. "No," she said. "We've not discussed it."

"Perhaps you should see what she thinks," Elizabeth said gently, a glance at Patrick. "When you go on Thursday. Talk it over with her."

"Two heads are better than one," Frederick added. "Ask the experts."

"It's not really anything to do with her," Ruth said. "We talk about my feelings, not my living accommodation."

"But she'd have an opinion," Patrick urged. "Ask her what she thinks. Then we'll have something to go on."

Ruth felt absurdly blocked, as if she had been driven into a cul-de-sac. "All right," she said grudgingly. "I'll ask her on Thursday afternoon."

❧

On Wednesday morning Patrick telephoned Clare Leesome and left a message on her answering machine. On Wednesday afternoon she called him back. When she said her name he got up and shut the door to his office, with elaborate caution. "Thank you for calling back," he said.

"Certainly."

"It's about my wife, Ruth Cleary."

"Yes?"

"As you may know, we're living at home with my parents. When she went into the clinic it was the only way we could manage with the baby, and it seemed a good thing that she should have the continued support when she came out."

Clare Leesome wondered at the smoothness of Patrick's sentences, and thought it was a prepared speech.

"She now wants to move back into our own house, and we have suggested that she take your advice."

"Oh," Clare said unhelpfully.

"Our feeling is that she needs the support of our family," Patrick said confidingly. "The baby is a very active, wakeful child, and with her history . . ." he trailed off but she did not interrupt him. "She was violent in the clinic with another patient, and she was short-tempered with Thomas. . . ." Still Clare Leesome held her irritating silence. "We feel that she should stay living with my family until we can be sure that she has completely recovered."

There was a complete and unhelpful silence.

"I wanted your advice," Patrick said.

"Concerning what?" Clare asked, as if Patrick's lengthy pre-amble had never been said.

Patrick curbed his temper. "I wanted you to advise me that we are doing the right thing in keeping her at home with all of us," he said.

She said nothing for a moment. "I'm not sure," she said eventually. "I don't have enough facts to make a judgment."

"The facts are as I have described them," Patrick said tightly. "And she has this history of not being able to care for Thomas. . . ."

"I wouldn't call it a history exactly," Clare said thoughtfully. "I'd call it an episode."

"Well, what more do you need to know? History, episode, the facts are that she was incapable of caring for a newborn baby on her own."

"Oh, yes," Clare said pleasantly. "As are most people . . ."

"So I want to know that you agree that it is best for her to live with my family until we are sure she is better."

"As I say," Clare repeated, "I couldn't judge."

"Surely you must have an opinion!"

Clare noted Patrick's rising tone. "It depends on so many things," she said. "Her relationship with you, with your mother, with your father. The family dynamic. Her contact with the child, issues about privacy, issues about sharing. I cannot say what Ruth thinks. I think, if it were me, I would rather live in my own house."

Patrick wanted to shout at her. He held the telephone away

from his ear for a few moments and took a couple of deep breaths. "But we are talking about a disturbed woman," he said.

"Oh, no," Clare said briskly. "If you mean psychotic—she's certainly not that!"

"I don't know the jargon!"

"No," Clare agreed.

"I'm saying she's unstable!"

"If you mean neurotic—she's not that either."

"She needs help," Patrick insisted.

"I think she is getting help," Clare said mildly. "Regular therapeutic help."

"She needs more than that," Patrick said. "She needs supervision. I want you to tell her that she would be best looked after at home with our family."

"No," Clare said decidedly. "I cannot tell her any such thing."

"But I just explained . . ."

"You explained why *you* think she should be looked after at home by your family. But I don't have enough facts to judge." She paused for a moment. "Indeed, on what I have seen of your wife, and on what you have told me, I think she would do better to live in her own house."

Patrick felt his temper flare. "I have told you she would do better where she is! But you won't listen!"

There was a complete silence.

"I'm sorry," Patrick said. "I'm under terrible stress. I must ask you to overlook that. I can't tell you how worried and unhappy I have been about her . . . and it has been months of worry."

"Of course," Clare said pleasantly.

"I just want to know that she and the baby are safe," Patrick said in his gentlest, most engaging voice, "while I am at work and cannot keep an eye on them."

"I am certain that she is perfectly safe with the baby," Clare said. "I am convinced that she can look after him perfectly well. And if there were to be any trouble at all, then you would have plenty of warning, and time to devise strategies for coping with any emerging problem."

"I would feel easier if she were being cared for by my mother," Patrick said.

Clare nodded. "Perhaps you would," she said. "But that is not the issue, as I understand it."

"I would prefer it if she stayed with my parents," Patrick said again, as if emphasis could achieve his wishes.

"I think you should follow her preference in this," Clare said levelly. "Has she said what she would like to do?"

"No," Patrick lied quickly. "No. Not at all."

Clare heard the lie at once. "Then I suggest you ask her," she said simply.

"Will you advise her to stay with my parents, if she asks you tomorrow?"

"No," Clare said firmly. "I will advise her to do what she wants to do. I think her best interests lie in determining her own life."

"Thank you for talking to me then, Ms. Leesome," Patrick said. He emphasized the 'Ms.' slightly; it made him feel better. It named her as an eccentric, as a feminist, as a troublemaker. "I assume that this conversation has all been in confidence?"

"Very well," she said.

"Thank you," Patrick said. "Good-bye." He waited until he heard the click of the telephone before he crashed the handset down into the receiver. "Snotty bitch," he said aloud. "Snotty know-all bitch."

ᴥ Thirteen ᴥ

David was late at the Black Bull pub, and when he arrived Ruth was sitting at a corner table with a mineral water before her. He waved to her, bought himself a pint of lager, and then threaded his way through the tables, which were busy with shoppers and businessmen eating sandwiches.

"You look fabulous!" he said. "I can't tell you how good it is to see you." He sat down beside her and scanned her face. "Lost weight," he commented. "Pink cheeks, bright eyes—looks like a good place, your clinic."

"Health farm," Ruth said promptly. "Cold showers and cucumber face masks. Actually, that's what they're telling everyone."

David looked puzzled. "What?"

"Patrick's family—well, his mother mostly—when anyone asked after me she told them I had gone to a health farm to recuperate from the effort of childbirth. Just as well for her that I've come back looking well."

"Why does she tell people that?"

Ruth giggled, and it was her old reckless giggle. "The *shame,* darling! She seems to think that I was completely bonkers and we must make sure the neighbors don't know."

David nodded. "The stigma of mental illness," he said pompously. "I shall do a program on it."

"It's a real problem for her," Ruth said more seriously. "And it's funny because she was the one to see that things were going badly, and she did the most to help. But when it comes to naming names she'd rather look the other way. According to her I was overtired, and now I am nicely rested."

David nodded. "She was really concerned about you when I met her."

Ruth nodded. "She is nice," she said. "And she's all-of-a-piece, you know? In the way that modern women aren't. She knows her job—which is home and support and child care where necessary—and she does it really well. She has no ideas about feminism or freedom or career or any of that stuff. And it makes her very powerful. The home is completely hers, and it is run without a hitch. She aims at perfection and she gets very close."

David nodded. "The sort of woman a successful man needs to have behind him. Would she marry me?"

She took a sip and shook her head. "Oh, no! Women like her are very careful with their choices. They know that they are choosing a career as well as a husband. They choose a successful man, and then they get behind him. I can't see you getting the gold-spoon treatment in the same way."

"And what about her husband? Your father-in-law?"

Ruth smiled. "He's rather a sweetie," she said. "He's very quiet compared to her. But he's solid, you know? He's dependable. I could tell you what he thinks about every single thing. You know where you are with him."

"And where are you with him?"

A shadow crossed her face. "Well, I was Patrick's girlfriend, which made me a pretty young thing..." Almost unconsciously she had mimicked Frederick's staccato speech. David grinned hearing it. "And then I was his wife, so I became the daughter-in-law, outside comment, above reproach. And then I had Thomas, so I was a lovely girl, and a wonderful mother. And then I had my breakdown, so I was a jolly poor show. And now I'm better, and I think I'm becoming a plucky little thing."

David laughed aloud. "A plucky little thing?"

She grinned at him. "Yes. But you can see why I like him so much. You don't have to do much to earn his approval. You just have to stay inside a boundary of good behavior—and it's quite a wide boundary."

"But what if you crossed it?" David asked curiously. "What if you did drugs, or had an affair, or abandoned the baby and Patrick. What would happen then?"

"Oh I'd drop off the edge of the world!" she said gaily. "I'd become a *jolly* poor show, and he'd never talk about me ever again."

David nodded. "Wow," he said. "It's a world I know nothing about. My family don't have that sort of confidence." He thought for a moment and then he smiled. "And we bear grudges," he said. "Nobody drops out of our world for bad behavior; we resurrect them every Christmas and have the quarrel all over again."

She chuckled. A waiter came to the table and they ordered two rounds of sandwiches.

"So what are you doing today, without Thomas and all?" David asked.

"I see a therapist on Thursdays," Ruth said. He liked how she told him without hesitation. She had caught none of her mother-in-law's shame. "She's just round the corner from here."

"What d'you do?"

"Nothing really. From the outside it looks completely boring. I talk, and she listens, and every now and then she says something. And it's completely illuminating, and I see things in a quite different way."

He shifted uneasily. "I'd hate you to change."

She shook her head. "I'm changing already," she said. "There were always two of me—the confident one at work, and the dependent baby me at home."

"I didn't know that," he said. "I only knew the one at work. I like her."

"You may not have seen the baby one, but you saw the consequences," she said swiftly. "You saw how I wouldn't stand up to Patrick, how whatever he wanted—we did. You saw me lose my job without a fight and move house and even have Thomas because that was what Patrick wanted."

David felt a quiver of apprehension at her plain speaking. "Are you saying you didn't want any of that?"

"You know I didn't," she said simply.

"How could he make you do it?"

She shrugged. "I couldn't bear to contradict him, I suppose," she said. "I wanted him to love me more than anything else. I couldn't ever make myself stand up to him." She glanced at him and laughed aloud. "You look astounded," she said.

He took a gulp of beer. "I *am* astounded! I did see a lot of that, and I couldn't quite understand how at work you could be so—I don't know—assertive—"

"Bossy," she interpolated.

"Bossy," he agreed. "Bossy in the newsroom, and then rush home at six o'clock frightened that you'd be late in cooking supper for him."

She nodded. "I think a lot of women are like that anyway," she said fairly. "And I did think he was rather a catch, you know. I did think I was lucky to get him, and that I'd better make an effort to hold on to him. And also . . . I was completely besotted with him. I would have done anything for him. I felt completely grateful and delighted that he loved me. And I loved it when he was pleased with me." She stopped and gave a little laugh. "It sounds absurd now," she said. "But I felt like I was a not very attractive kid, and that if I tried really hard, he might let me tag along."

David made a face of distaste, and took another swallow of beer. "I see," he said.

She nodded. "A bit pitiful, wasn't it? If I'd had parents who loved me I'd never have been so dependent. Or if I'd been older when I first met him . . ." she shrugged. "Anyway, that's how it was. I met him when I was very young and very alone, and very impressionable. And when he loved me I was tremendously grateful."

"And now?" David asked.

To his relief she looked suddenly radiant. "Now we start all over again!" she said. "Now we have to make a marriage between equals, rather than between the wonderful Patrick and the little drip: me. It's a real opportunity. It's a real challenge!"

He took up his sandwich and bit into it. "I thought you might leave him," he said bluntly.

She shook her head. She was very certain. "No," she said. "Because none of it is his fault. I love him, and he's my husband, and the father of my son . . . and he's done nothing wrong. He accepted the relationship I offered, and when it all went wrong for me he did the very best he could to get it right again. You can't fault him."

David thought for a moment of Patrick's charming selfishness. "I wouldn't call him exactly faultless. It suited him too," he observed.

She was eating, and she nodded with her mouth full. She swallowed and said, "Yes, but he didn't force me into anything. He made it clear it was what he wanted, and then I went along with everything. As soon as I have the strength to make my own choices, we'll have to share the decision making. We'll be equal."

David was quiet for a moment—wondering how far he could go. Then he decided to speak out. "No, you won't," he said finally. "You'll never be equal."

"Why not?"

"Because the setup is weighted against you. He's got a good career and you have a baby. He earns money, and gives you some of it. He controls an office with a budget and half a dozen staff, and you control a little house. He's a man, and you're a woman, and most of all—when you count his family on your doorstep—there are three of them and only one of you."

He was afraid that he had said too much because the brightness had drained from her face, and she pushed her plate to one side. She nodded.

"I'm sorry," he said. "I'm a big mouth. Sorry, Ruth. I spoke out of turn."

She put her hand out to him and touched the back of his hand. "It's OK," she said. "It's OK. And anyway . . . you're right." She took her glass and sipped her water. "I'll have to take it slowly," she said thoughtfully. "And I have to get it right this time."

*A*nd what did Ms. Leesome have to say today?" Patrick demanded at dinner that night.

"Why d'you call her that?" Ruth asked.

"What?"

"*Ms.* Leesome. She's single. You can call her Miss. Or you can call her Clare."

"I thought that was how she was to be addressed."

"Absolute nonsense," Frederick said loyally from the foot of the table. "Much better to do it as they do in France. If you're under thirty, you're *Mademoiselle*; if you're over, you're *Madame*. Then everyone knows where they are. I can't bear this *Ms. Ms.* business."

"It *is* a very ugly sound," Elizabeth agreed. "Like the word *miserable*. Patrick used to say it when he was ill, when he was a little boy. He used to say: 'I feel a bit mis.'"

Ruth smiled. "Did he?"

"All right," Patrick said. "How was Miss, Mrs., or Clare Leesome today?"

"She was fine," Ruth said. "I did ask her about whether we should stay here, and she said it was completely my decision. I asked her whether she thought I would be OK on my own with Thomas while you were out at work, and she said that only I could be the judge of that and that it must be our decision: yours and mine."

"Oh," Patrick said. "Did she express no opinion at all?"

"She said it should be our own decision," Ruth said.

"And so it should," Frederick said fairly. "Provided the medics are happy, you two can do as you wish." He nodded kindly at Ruth. "But you're always welcome here, my dear, for as long as you like."

"I would rather stay a little longer," Patrick said thoughtfully. "I've got rather a busy time coming up, and the little house is so cold and dark in winter."

"Certainly," his mother said. "Ruth, do keep us company for another week or two, and you and I can go down and get your house ready for you to move back. You could go back over Christmas, when Patrick has some time off."

"But it's only December eighth now," Ruth protested. "And

we were supposed to go home last weekend."

"Let me sort out the Christmas holiday time," Patrick offered. "I'll take some extra days off and we can go down to the house together, get everything ready, and move together over the Christmas holiday."

"There's hardly anything to do," Ruth protested.

"Oh, there's all Thomas's toys, and most of his clothes. There's all Patrick's clothes and books and a lot of your things," Elizabeth protested. "And I think the chimneys need sweeping, and it would be nice to have the windows cleaned outside and in before you go back. Why don't we take the opportunity for a little spring cleaning, and then you can go back and make a fresh start?"

"I just thought we could put the heating on, and go back," Ruth protested.

Frederick smiled at her and put his warm hand over her own. "I think you're outnumbered," he said gently. "Retreat gracefully, that's my advice, little Ruth! Live to fight another day."

For a moment she did not think of the kindness of his advice or the roguish smile on his face. She thought of her situation as she had described it to David, and his certainty that she would never win against the Cleary family because it would always be three against one.

"I'll retreat then," she said with a weak smile. "But we are agreed—aren't we—that we'll be home for Christmas?"

"It's a promise," Patrick said easily, and smiled at his mother.

❧

They were not. When Ruth and Elizabeth left Thomas with Frederick and went down the drive to the little house to put on the heating and check that the chimneys had been properly swept, the place was icy cold, the heating had not come on. There was a problem with the thermostat. Elizabeth telephoned the heating contractor, while Ruth prowled unhappily around the cold bedrooms, but it was the week before Christmas and he was very busy.

"You would have spent Christmas Day with us anyway,"

Elizabeth said consolingly as Ruth came slowly downstairs. "So it's only an extra couple of nights."

Ruth looked so disappointed Elizabeth was afraid she might cry. "Don't look so desolate, darling!"

"But I wanted to put up decorations in my own home. I wanted Thomas in his nursery on Christmas morning!"

Elizabeth's smile was understanding. "Of course," she said. "And it's such a shame that it hasn't worked out like that. But perhaps you'll do our decorations at home? I have a wonderful box of things, some bells and scarves from India, and some from Africa. I have a whole box of Victorian decorations from my mother. You might like to look through them, and you can pick out what you like and take them home with you for next year. This year you can be with us, and next year we can come to you. You've got a lot of Christmases ahead of you, Ruth dear. It's not just this one."

"I wanted to spend Christmas here," Ruth said stubbornly.

Elizabeth nodded. "Next year," she assured her. "And anyway, you wouldn't have anything prepared for this year, surely?"

Ruth did not understand her. "Prepared?"

"Your Christmas pudding? Your Christmas cake? Your dried flowers?"

Ruth looked completely blank.

"Don't you make your own?" Elizabeth asked.

Ruth thought back to all the Christmases she had spent with the Cleary family since her marriage. The pudding was the pinnacle of a delicious dinner. She had never thought whether it was homemade or bought, she merely registered that it tasted better than anything she had ever had before.

"I make it in September," Elizabeth said. "So that it has time to mature. And I make my Christmas cake in November, and ice it in December. And when my hydrangeas flower in summer, I pick them and dry them for the Christmas decorations. When the holly berries come out in November, I put bags over them to stop the birds' getting them so they are fresh and red for the table decorations and the hall. I buy a crate of Cox's Pippins in October, when they're just in season, and store them in the spare garage and then polish them and put them in the apple pyramid in the hall in the middle of December. And I freeze a summer fruit pudding in July for us to have on Boxing Day. Surely you remember!"

"I remember," Ruth said awkwardly. "I just didn't realize that you planned so far ahead."

Elizabeth laughed gently. "How else could everything be ready for the day?" she asked. "It's no good dashing around a week before, hoping to get things in time. There are seasons to good housekeeping. You have to think about autumn in midsummer, and you have to think about Christmas in mid-autumn."

Ruth felt hopelessly superficial. "I haven't even bought presents yet," she said.

Elizabeth laughed, ushered Ruth out of the hall, and closed the front door behind them. "Then thank heavens you don't have to worry about the house as well as everything else," she said. "I'll have Thomas every afternoon this week and you can go into Bath and shop. I hope it's not too crowded."

Ruth watched Elizabeth drop the key to the front door of the little house in her camel-hair-coat pocket. "When did the heating man say he could come?"

Elizabeth made a face. "You know what they're like," she said. "Not until after the New Year holiday. I think everything just shuts down between Christmas Day and New Year's Day. Still, you can go home the first week in January, and then you can start afresh in the New Year."

Ruth turned and trudged up the lane to the farmhouse. Elizabeth followed her, a little way behind. She nodded to the Labrador, who ran between the two of them and stopped to sniff at a gatepost. "So that's all right," she said quietly. "We've got another month."

☙

Ruth and Patrick were in bed, Thomas asleep in the nursery next door, Elizabeth and Frederick in the bedroom further down the landing. Ruth had been with Clare Leesome in the afternoon, and she was alert and excited. Patrick had been up early, and had spent an arduous day in the editing room with a producer who had misunderstood what was wanted from the very first day of filming. Huge reels of film would be wasted; some parts would have to be reshot. The documentary was way over budget, and Patrick was so confused between the initial brief, the producer's interpretation, and his own second thoughts that he felt quite incapable of patching together a film that would make any sense at all.

He spent a long time in the bathroom, sitting on the toilet and reading *Broadcast* magazine. He did not acknowledge it, even to himself, but he was rather hoping that Ruth would be asleep by the time he finally emerged. He undressed and put on some pajamas. Before they had moved into the farmhouse Patrick had generally slept naked, or wearing only a pair of boxer shorts. But under his mother's roof he wore crisp cotton pajamas, which he changed twice a week and which she washed and ironed. He came to bed smelling pleasantly of fabric conditioner and clean cotton, but Ruth missed the caress of bare skin and the natural scent of his body. On the infrequent occasions that they had made love since her return from the clinic, she found herself irritated by the pajamas. Patrick's fumbling with the trousers and his laziness in leaving on the jacket were a powerful antidote to sexual desire.

Patrick looked at himself in the bathroom mirror. He had put on weight since living back at home, and his jawline was fatter than it used to be. He stretched up his chin and watched the skin recede. He looked at himself critically. He feared he was losing his looks and that his young, glossy handsomeness would not develop into his father's craggy, attractive face, but would blur into plumpness and indistinction.

"I should get fit," he said thoughtfully to himself. "Do some training, join a gym."

He did not mean it. The hours that he worked and the demands of his home life made any extra activity too much of an effort to be pleasurable. He shook his head at his reflection. "No time," he said. "Never a damn moment."

He shook his head again, feeling harassed and unfairly treated. He splashed water on his face and brushed his teeth and rubbed his face briskly in the warm towel. The touch of the fleecy cotton on his skin cheered him at once. At least he was now living in a well-run home, he thought. The towels in the Bristol flat had been unreliably supplied, and often he had to use a damp one.

He went quietly across the landing, noting the line of light under his parents' bedroom door, and thought of them placidly reading their books in their big double bed. He had a vague sense that marriage should be like that: secure, mutually dependent, at peace.

Ruth was waiting for him, sitting up in bed, turning the pages of a magazine.

"You've been ages," she said with a smile. "I nearly came to find you."

"I thought you'd be asleep," he said. He turned back the duvet and got in beside her. At once she held out her arms and he slid into her embrace. The thought of making love to her surfaced in his mind and he instantaneously dismissed it. He would have to get up early in the morning, and he needed his sleep. If Thomas happened to wake then, Ruth might expect him to go to the nursery. After lovemaking Ruth generally went to the bathroom, and that would disturb his parents, and—more than anything else—Patrick was rarely aroused under his mother's roof. There was something deeply inhibiting about the family home. His mother changed their sheets twice a week, and would know if they had made love. He could not bear the thought of their hearing the squeaking of the bed, or Ruth's breathy cries or, worst of all, his own groan at climax. The thought of his parents' hearing his lovemaking, or even worse, deliberately listening and then perhaps exchanging a smile, froze his desire before he was even conscious of it.

"Let's have a cuddle," Ruth said invitingly.

Patrick stretched out and put out the bedroom light and cuddled her up against his shoulder as he lay on his back. There then ensued a dance as formal as if it had been choreographed. Ruth wriggled up the line of his body to kiss his neck, just below his ear, and spread her thigh across his groin, pressing against his penis. Patrick wriggled up also, to tuck her down to his shoulder again, pushing her down in the bed, so she was not sprawled across him. She raised herself up a little and reached across to kiss him on the lips; he felt her breasts press against his pajama jacket, warm and heavy against his chest. He kissed her with tenderness and then took her head in his hands and firmly placed it on his shoulder.

"I love sleeping cuddled up with you," he said, and then pushed her gently so she rolled over on her side and he cuddled up behind her.

Ruth moved slightly backward, so that her buttocks were pressing against his penis. Despite himself, Patrick found that he was getting aroused. Ruth moved a little away, and then back again. Patrick put his hand down and held her hipbone to push her gently away.

"Enough of that!" he said, in a warm, caressing tone. "I have to sleep." As soon as he spoke he knew he had made a mistake in making his refusal explicit. She moved away from him at once, rolled onto her front, and raised her head so she could see his face in the half-light from the window.

"It's been ages," she said.

He sighed. He hated any analysis of personal life, and since she had been seeing Clare Leesome her desire to talk and talk and talk was even worse.

"I'm just very tired tonight," he said. "And you must be exhausted too. Was the traffic terrible coming out of Bath? It's late-night shopping now, isn't it?"

She would not be diverted.

"We haven't made love for ten days," she said. "And before that, it was a fortnight."

He forced himself to chuckle in a soft, confident tone, and drew her back toward him. "I know," he said. "It's difficult at the moment. I'm incredibly busy at work and I feel really stressed, Ruthie darling. Wait till my Christmas days off and we'll make up for lost time."

"You can't," she said flatly. "You can't ever make up for lost time."

He thought how much he hated these conversations, which could go from the most basic practicalities—such as the last date that they had made love—to the most fanciful of philosophies—such as whether you can make up for lost time.

"I know," he said. "And it's as bad for me as it is for you. Let's sleep now, and have an early night tomorrow. Mother can baby-sit and we can go out for something to eat. How would that be?"

He stroked her hair, willing her to feel sleepy.

"It's being here that puts you off, isn't it?" she asked. "In your parents' house?" She had a strong sense of how his mother's care, his mother's roof, made him regress to the little spoiled boy he must have been.

"Not at all," he said firmly. "I've told you what it is, and it's very simple and very boring. It's being overworked, darling. Nothing complicated and psychological at all. Now can we go to sleep?"

She was silent for a little while, and he thought that he had got away with it. But then he knew by the tautness in her body that she was crying, and keeping her tears silent.

For a moment he thought he would take her in his arms and kiss the tears off her silly pretty face. But he knew that if he held her he would want to make love to her, and the thought of his parents awake, and hearing everything, was too much for him. He pretended to hear nothing, to know nothing, and shut his eyes, and waited for sleep.

ᢒ— *Fourteen* —ᢒ

*C*hristmas Day was organized into a state of domestic perfection by Elizabeth. They woke in time for church, and as Ruth went downstairs, carrying Thomas dressed in his smart new navy sweater-and-trouser set, she smelled the warm, appetizing scent of cooking turkey from the kitchen. Frederick drove them all to church, and they sat near the crèche so that Thomas could see the stable scene with his wide, interested eyes.

When they came home Frederick produced a bottle of champagne and they opened their Christmas presents. Frederick and Elizabeth had been generous to Ruth. They had bought her an expensive set of bath oils, gels, and shampoo, and a wide-cut swing jacket in a soft russet tweed. Ruth felt its soft warmth as she spread it out.

"If you don't like it, I can take it back," Elizabeth said, watching her face. "But I thought it was such a lovely color! And such wonderful material."

"I love it," Ruth said honestly.

Patrick had bought her a watercolor painting of Princes' Crescent, where they used to live. When he saw her face as she recognized the clean curved line of the building, he thought he had been rather tactless. For a moment she looked as if she might weep.

"I thought it would remind us . . ." he said weakly.

She glanced up at him with a speaking look. "I don't ever

209

forget. It was our first home. . . ." The fact that the little house at the end of the drive had never been a proper home, and was even now cold and empty, did not need saying.

"And what has Thomas got from Mummy and Daddy?" Elizabeth asked brightly.

They could not persuade him to pull at the paper, so Patrick and Ruth unwrapped the big box. They had bought him a baby bouncer. Frederick let out a little cheer. "You know, it crossed my mind that you might get him that. I put up a hook in the kitchen last night. We can try him out in it now."

"Last night!" Patrick exclaimed.

"While I was stuffing the turkey," Elizabeth said, smiling. "So don't blame *me* if there's plaster in the chestnut stuffing!"

They took the harness and the elasticized strap through to the kitchen and adjusted it carefully. Then Ruth put Thomas into the seat and clapped her hands in delight as he put his toes cautiously down to the ground, and then ecstatically kicked off, again and again. "He loves it!" she said.

"He can watch me serve lunch," Elizabeth said.

"Can I do anything?" Ruth asked, knowing what the answer would be.

"You go and have another glass of champagne with Frederick," Elizabeth said warmly. "Patrick can help me, and Thomas can tell us what to do."

Ruth smiled, and she and Frederick left the kitchen. At the doorway she glanced back. Patrick, his mother, and his child made a pretty picture of domestic contentment. There was a unity about the three of them, as if they were parents and child, as if Thomas belonged to them alone. As if she and Frederick were visitors to this family, welcomed in the drawing room, but banned from the intimacy of the kitchen and the natural love that flowed between the other three.

In the drawing room Frederick poured her another glass of champagne. "You have no objection to us going back to the little house, have you?" she asked frankly. It was rare that they were alone together, and even rarer that they should speak of matters of importance.

He bent over and fiddled with the neck of the bottle. "I know Mother was worried that you wouldn't be able to cope," he said.

"She must see that I can manage now."

He did not meet her eyes. "And Patrick wanted to know that you were all right during the day, when he couldn't be with you."

She nodded. "But I am fine."

He looked her in the face for the first time. "I've no ax to grind," he said simply. "If you are well and Thomas is well and Patrick is happy, then anything else is your own business. And it shouldn't be me that you're speaking to. . . ."

She thought he was giving her some kind of clue. She waited.

He nodded in the direction of the kitchen. "Patrick. Your husband. It's his job to provide you with a home, and his job to see that you're happily settled in it." He paused for a powerful moment. "And his job to make sure that you get on with your own lives."

After Christmas lunch, following the annual tradition, they telephoned Miriam in Canada. The phone rang for a while at the other end, and when it was answered it was a man's voice. He called Miriam to the phone.

"Hello, darling," Elizabeth said. "Who was that?"

She listened intently. "Oh. So how long has he been living with you? Two months! Why didn't you . . . ?"

Ruth could hear the tantalizing sound of speech but not distinguish the words. She thought she had never seen Elizabeth so rattled.

"I'm not prying!" Elizabeth exclaimed. "I'm trying to wish you a Happy Christmas, darling!"

The telephone squawked indignantly. Ruth realized she was grinning and straightened her face.

"I am absolutely not trying to interfere. . . ." Elizabeth said. She broke off and held the telephone away. Even Ruth, on the other side of the room, could hear Miriam's anger.

Elizabeth exchanged a look with Frederick. "She really is quite impossible," she said. She put the telephone back to her ear. "Your father wants to say hello." Elizabeth beckoned to Frederick.

"Hello, Mimi," he said affectionately. "Happy Christmas."

Ruth watched Elizabeth following the one-sided conversation. Frederick told his daughter that they had been to church and eaten Christmas dinner; he told her that they were missing her. Ruth noticed that there was no mention of Patrick and Ruth's living at the farmhouse, and that the reference to Thomas did not mention his mother's health.

"She wants to talk to you." Frederick passed the receiver to Patrick.

"Did she say who he was?" Elizabeth whispered.

Frederick shook his head. "I wasn't going to ask," he replied. "She'll tell us soon enough, if she wants to."

"It's been two months and she's never so much as mentioned a boyfriend," Elizabeth exclaimed.

Frederick smiled and patted her hand. "She's thirty-six," he said. "I don't think she'd call him a boyfriend. And she can run her own life."

"I just like to know!"

He smiled. "I know you do. But that little bird has definitely fled the nest. She'll tell you when she's ready."

Patrick, finishing his conversation with his sister, said, "Goodbye, Happy Christmas," in his most charming voice, and put down the phone.

"That's done," he said.

"Fancy Miriam living with a man," Elizabeth said to her son: her younger child, her favorite.

Patrick chuckled. "Brave man," he said.

"But fancy her never saying!" Elizabeth wondered. "She must know that I would want to know. It's so eccentric of her to try and cut us off like this."

Patrick shrugged. Ruth had a sense of quite scandalous nosiness. "Surely she's had boyfriends before," she said.

"Never one that passed muster," Frederick said tactfully.

"Completely awful people," Elizabeth said roundly. "One

young man who lived in a tent and traveled around the country trying to stop people building bypasses."

"An ecologist," Frederick supplemented.

"Shall I phone back?" Elizabeth hesitated. "Now she's had a chance to cool down. So we can have a proper chat?"

"Leave it," Frederick counseled her. "She'll tell us all we need to know in her own time."

They went through to the drawing room, and when Thomas became fretful and sleepy Patrick took him upstairs to his crib. Elizabeth sat on the sofa and looked at the gardening book that Ruth and Patrick had given her. Ruth sat in domestic peace and silence and felt the afternoon stretch unendingly before her.

"Let's go for a walk," she suggested.

Patrick, who had been settling down for a doze, was reluctant.

"Do you good," said his father unsympathetically. "Work some of that weight off your middle!"

"And there's Christmas cake for tea, remember!" Elizabeth warned. "Go on, both of you! I'll wake Thomas when he's had his nap."

It was sunny and cold. Patrick walked briskly down the drive. "I'm glad you suggested a walk," he said. "I was ready to drop off! Where shall we go?"

"Let's go to our house," Ruth said.

For a moment he looked as if he might refuse.

"I really want to," Ruth prompted.

"All right," he said reluctantly. "It just seems a bit odd."

They walked in step for a few paces. "It *is* odd," Ruth said. "It's not odd going to look at it, it's odd that we don't live in it."

"Mmmm," said Patrick discouragingly. "Doesn't Thomas love his bouncy thing!"

"Yes," Ruth said. "But we don't have a hook for it in our house, and they have a hook in the farmhouse."

"We can put up a hook!" Patrick said bracingly. "There's no problem with that!"

Ruth hesitated. The wine she had drunk at lunchtime, and Miriam's open defiance of her mother, made her feel reckless. She felt ready to force the issue. "Or we could not bother," she

213

said. "We could stay in the farmhouse forever and never live in our own house."

He checked. "What?"

"You obviously don't want to go, and your mother obviously wants us to stay there. Shall we decide now that we all live together, and you and I never have a home of our own again?"

"No," Patrick said instantly. "No one lives like that. It would look so odd . . . and it's not . . . like Argentinean peasants or something."

"It is odd," Ruth agreed, stretching her strides to keep pace with his.

"And I like our house," Patrick said as the trim front garden came into view around the curve of the drive. "I like living here."

"Yes," said Ruth.

"The stay in the farmhouse has just dragged on a bit," Patrick said thoughtfully. "First you being ill, and then I was worried about you, and then I really wanted to move at Christmas, but the heating was off . . . it's just been one thing after another."

"I can't make us move," Ruth said simply. They had reached the garden gate, and she swung around to face him. Her face was flushed from the walk, her eyes bright and clear. He felt a sudden straightforward desire for her. In that moment he stopped seeing her as a sick woman, as a mad woman. Suddenly he saw her for what she was, young, sexual, desirable. "I can't make us move," Ruth said again. "It has to be your decision. I've done all I can, and I can't make it happen. If you don't put your foot down, we're going to be there forever."

She turned from him and went to the front door. "I don't have a key," Patrick said.

She took it out of her pocket and opened the door. "No," she said. "This is your mother's key. You have to decide, Patrick, whether this is their house or ours. You have to decide whether we will live here or not."

He stepped into the hall. The dry, dusty smell of an unused house was like a reproach.

Ruth went ahead of him into the sitting room. "Let's have a drink," she said. "A Christmas drink in our own home."

He smiled, attracted by the clandestine sense of an assignation. "I'll see what we have."

Ruth struck a match and put it to the kindling in the grate. At once the firelight made the room look warm and friendly. She drew the curtains against the red setting sun.

Patrick came back with a bottle of port and a couple of glasses. "The cupboard's a bit bare," he said. "This is all I could find."

Ruth smiled at him, her face lit by firelight, the room warming up. There was an intimacy about being alone in their house, like a newly married couple when the last of the wedding guests have finally gone, and the bawdy jokes are over, and there is silence.

"It's silly," Patrick remarked. "I'd forgotten what a nice house this is."

He poured the wine and looked around. "We'll move back, shall we? As soon as the heating is fixed?"

Ruth raised her glass to him. "And start again," she said as if it were a toast. "I'm sorry that it went wrong before, Patrick. I am quite different now."

He sat beside her on the sofa and kissed her gently. "It's been a tough year," he said. "And I wasn't all the help I should have been. We'll do better next year."

She turned to him and Patrick put down his glass and kissed her again. With a sense of delightful discovery Patrick slid his hands under her blouse and felt her warm, soft skin. Ruth sighed with relief and welcomed Patrick into her body.

⁂

*E*lizabeth knew.

As they came in the door, pink-cheeked and breathless from walking quickly home up the darkening drive, she took one swift look from one to another and knew that they had been to their own house and made love.

Ruth saw the glance and had an immediate impression of Elizabeth's disapproval. For a moment she thought that the older woman was shocked at her son's sexuality—sneaking out in the afternoon like a teenager—but then she had a sense of something deeper and more serious, something like envy, something like a challenge.

"You were a long time," Elizabeth said. "I'm surprised you could see your way home."

Patrick looked embarrassed. "It's only dusk," he said.

"We went to our house," Ruth said. She looked Elizabeth in the eye. "We lit the fire in the sitting room and had a glass of port to celebrate Christmas. It was lovely."

Elizabeth smiled but she looked strained. "I'm surprised the chimney drew," she said. "It's been cold for so long."

They went into the sitting room. Thomas was on his play mat on the carpet; when he saw his mother he crowed with delight, and his arms and legs waved. Ruth picked him up and turned to her mother-in-law, with her son's head against her cheek.

"We've missed it," she said firmly. "We'll move back next week, as soon as the heating is fixed."

Elizabeth slid a conspiratorial glance at Patrick, but he did not see. He was looking at his wife and son. "I'll go over tomorrow and put up a hook for his bouncer," he said.

❧

On Boxing Day it somehow turned into a family walk. They all went to the little house together. Elizabeth and Frederick walked down the drive with them, Ruth pushing Thomas in his pram. "We'll bring Thomas away when he's had enough," Frederick said.

"It's too cold for him down there without heating," Elizabeth remarked. "Heaven knows how we managed in the old days. The only warm rooms ever were the kitchen and the drawing room. The stairs and the hall were drafty and cold, and the bedrooms were like ice."

Frederick nodded. "I used to have chilblains every winter when I was a child," he said. "And chapped hands. You hardly ever hear about chilblains now."

Patrick was half listening. "It would make quite a nice little film," he said thoughtfully. "The medical side of recent progress.

People not getting chilblains anymore because the houses are warmer, but getting more asthma."

Elizabeth laughed and slipped her hand in her son's arm. "Fleas," she said. "If you dare to mention them. Now that we have centrally heated houses fleas don't die off in winter. The vet was telling me they breed all the year round. It's a real problem. There's a mini epidemic."

"And house mites," Frederick said cheerfully, coming up on the other side of Elizabeth. "That's the cause of your extra asthma if you ask me. Not enough fresh air."

Ruth, lagging behind, pushing the pram, saw the three of them, walking in step in the happy unity that seemed so easy for them to achieve. But it was Elizabeth and not Patrick who glanced back toward her and called, "What about you, Ruth? Are you one of the post–central heating children? Or was your home cold?"

Ruth shook her head. Her aunt's house had never been a home, and she could scarcely remember her childhood home. But then she had a sudden sharp recollection of her home in the States, before the death of her parents. They had rented a small white clapboard house, cool in summer and snug in winter. When Ruth was in bed at night, she could hear the comforting gabble from her parents' television downstairs. The warmth from the boiler in the cellar spread through the house. In autumn her father used to put up storm windows and go up on the roof to check the shingles. Her mother used to make him wear thick working gloves. "Your hands!" she would exclaim. Ruth remembered her father's hands, long-fingered, soft, with the power to wring music from wood. "I don't remember," she said shortly.

They reached the gate. Frederick paused to help her with the pram, while Elizabeth and Patrick opened the front door and went in together.

The sitting room was musty and dark, with the curtains still closed. The little fire had burned out in the grate. Ruth had not drunk all her port yesterday, and there was a sour, stale smell from the dregs in the glass. The cushions on the floor and the pushed-back sofa showed very clearly to Elizabeth's quick assessing gaze that they had made love on the floor. Ruth felt deeply uncomfortable, as if they had been detected in some secret assignment. The room did not look intimate and seductive as it had looked the day before; it looked sordid.

Elizabeth went over and threw back the curtains. The harsh winter sunlight showed the dust and the red stain inside the wine glasses. Without a word of criticism or condemnation Elizabeth unlocked the sash window and threw it up. The clean winter air flooded in. Ruth picked up the dirty glasses and the bottle and took them to the kitchen. As she left the room she saw Elizabeth stooping to pick up the cushions from the floor, brush them off, and replace them on the sofa. Ruth had a moment of cringing embarrassment that one of them would be stained, that Elizabeth would take off the cover of the cushion for washing; all in that remorselessly civilized way.

In the kitchen Frederick was unpacking the tool kit while Patrick tapped the plasterboard ceiling, looking for the joists.

"Mind you don't hit a cable," Frederick said. "Hang on a minute. I've got one of those cable detectors in here."

"You've got a tool library in there," Patrick said, smiling. "Is there any DIY gadget you haven't got?"

"I like a good tool kit," Frederick said. "And your mother likes things just so at home. It's very satisfying to do a good job."

"Aha," Patrick said as the hollow sound of his tapping changed. "I think it's here."

"Tap again?" Frederick said, listening. "Yes. That sounds like it. Now where d'you want the bouncer, Ruth?"

Ruth gestured to a space between the kitchen table and the backdoor. "There?"

"Oh, no," Elizabeth said. "He'll reach up and pull off the tablecloth."

Ruth hesitated. She had never thought of putting a tablecloth on the kitchen table, which was scrubbed pine.

"It should be here," Elizabeth said, gesturing closer to the backdoor. "And then in summer you can have the door open, and he can bounce in the sunshine."

Elizabeth was right. Ruth found a smile. "Oh, yes," she said, trying to sound pleased.

"Shall I have a look at the central heating while I'm here?" Frederick asked. "I might be able to get it going."

"It's under guarantee," Elizabeth warned. "Don't just thump it with a spanner."

Frederick raised his eyebrows to Patrick in a mutual silent complaint about the unreasonable and suspicious nature of women. "I'll just look," he said, and went to the utility room. A few moments later they heard the boiler click and then flare.

"Extraordinary thing," Frederick said, coming out of the utility room. "The clock was disconnected. Can't think how it could have happened. The boiler wasn't firing because it was disconnected from the clock."

"Must have been loose when they put it in," Patrick said. He drilled the hole for the bouncer hook, and plaster dust filled the air.

"I suppose so . . ." Frederick said. "But I can't see why it would suddenly come out. You'd expect it to flicker on and off. . . ."

"Oh!" said Elizabeth, waving her hand before her face in protest at the dust. "Let's get Thomas out of here! Shall we go upstairs and make the beds, Ruth?"

"I'll go," Ruth said. "You play with Thomas in the sitting room." She felt she could not bear to have Elizabeth turning over the cold sheets, just as she had turned over the sofa cushions.

"All right." Elizabeth lifted Thomas out of the pram and smiled at his welcoming gurgle. "We'll be happy enough! Call me if you want a hand."

"Yes," Ruth said.

There was a companionable male muttering from the kitchen as the men hung the baby bouncer, and then Thomas's delighted giggle from the sitting room as Elizabeth tickled the small outspread palms of his hands. Ruth, going up the stairs alone to the cold bedrooms, felt left out and lonely, but did not know how she could join in.

She made the beds quietly, finding that she was listening to the sounds of the others down below. When the men finished in the kitchen, they joined Elizabeth and the baby in the sitting room. She could hear them chatting, Elizabeth advising Patrick not to order more logs or coal until prices came down in the summer. "We have plenty," she said. "I ordered extra because I guessed you might run out. Father will bring a trailer load down for you later in the week."

Ruth thumped the pillows into place, and shook the duvet.

"I'd offer you a cup of coffee," Patrick said. "But we haven't got anything in at all."

"I cleared it all out when Ruth had her breakdown," Elizabeth said. "Better than letting it go to waste. But I kept a complete list of what was in the larder so I can replace it for you to the last tin of beans!"

"We can go shopping. . . ." Patrick said.

"Not today you can't," Elizabeth reminded him. "Boxing Day. I shouldn't think Sainsburys will be open till Tuesday. I can go in then."

"So you're with us for a few more days?" Frederick asked.

"It looks like it," Patrick said. "We'll leave the heating on and come down and air the place. But I don't want to run up the drive every time I want a cup of tea."

Ruth slammed the bedroom door and came noisily down the stairs. They all looked up at her and smiled. "Can't you lend us some basics?" she asked Elizabeth. "A loaf from the freezer? A small jar of coffee? A couple of tea bags? A pint of milk?"

"We don't want to put Mother to any trouble," Patrick intervened.

"Of course not," Ruth said determinedly. "But you're so well organized, Elizabeth, I just assumed you'd have plenty in the house. Don't you have anything to spare?"

Elizabeth hesitated. "I always have a loaf in the freezer. . . ."

"My dear, you know you keep in enough to feed an army!" Frederick exclaimed. "Let's all go home for lunch and then you two can take your pick of the larder and bring down whatever you want."

"And anything you haven't got I can pick up at the garage shop," Ruth said pleasantly.

"Of course," Elizabeth replied. "I hope you won't catch me out. I think I can give you everything you need. If you're sure you want to go now. It seems rather a rush. . . ."

Ruth nodded, meeting her eyes. "We were only waiting for the central heating to be mended," she said levelly. "And it's on now. We can move back in."

~ *Fifteen* ~

hat evening Ruth and Patrick curled up before a log fire in their own sitting room after a supper of curried turkey and rice. Elizabeth had given them slices from the Christmas turkey for their supper and Ruth had driven down to the garage shop for a tin of curry powder. Upstairs, Thomas slept in his own crib in his own nursery again.

Frederick had given Patrick a bottle of claret to celebrate their first night back in the little house, and they drank the bright red wine and put the glasses down on the wooden floor, and cracked nuts with a sense of behaving naturally in private at last.

"I'm glad we came home," Patrick said. "I thought at the last moment we were going to get stuck until the shops opened on Tuesday."

Ruth nodded. "It's always one thing or another," she said. "Elizabeth didn't want us to leave."

Patrick nodded. "You can see why," he said fairly. "She's so close to Thomas you would think he was her own son."

"No, I wouldn't," Ruth contradicted. "I would never think that Thomas was anyone's son but yours and mine."

Patrick gave her his charming smile and pulled her against him. "Manner of speech," he said against her hair.

"Not my speech," Ruth said stubbornly as his kisses moved from her warm, smooth head to the line of her neck. She turned her face to him and opened her mouth as he kissed her.

221

"Bedtime," Patrick said suddenly. "In our own bed at last, thank God."

They went upstairs with their fingers interlinked and made love, in their own bed, with no one but a passing owl to hear.

⁓

The end of Patrick's holiday time was like the end of a small reserve of peace. His alarm clock went off early, by accident, and woke Thomas. Instead of the enjoyable well-organized breakfast Ruth had planned, she had to warm Thomas's early morning bottle and then change his diaper halfway through his feed. Thomas—who liked to have his bottle undisturbed—took noisy exception to this, and his complaint soured his temper for the rest of the morning. Ruth could not put him down and make Patrick's breakfast as she had wished, but had to wedge him under her arm while she filled the kettle and tried to make tea one-handed.

Their early start did not give them more time, it merely increased the confusion. Patrick could not find his cuff links—which he had left up at the farm—and so had to change his shirt for one with buttons at the cuff. It was a pale blue, which meant that he had to choose another tie as well, and the blue tie that matched had been left up at the farmhouse. "For heaven's sake, as though it mattered!" Ruth snapped. Thomas dropped his bottle and let out a pitiful deprived wail.

"Just *leave* breakfast!" Patrick ordered. "I'll get a cup of coffee at work. I never said I wanted a cooked breakfast in the first place!"

"But Elizabeth always—" Ruth bit the sentence off.

Patrick came toward her and quietly took Thomas from her. "Make yourself a cup of tea," he said gently. "I'll hold him while you drink it. Mother gets everything ready the night before, and she gets up at the crack of dawn to get everything done. There's no need to try and be like her. We live here now."

There was a brief silence. Ruth blinked. "I don't think I'll ever learn to do it like her," she said.

"I know," Patrick said frankly. "And there's no point in us

trying to be like them. We'll have to do things our way. I was a fool to wake him this morning anyway. If he'd stayed asleep we would have had loads of time."

Ruth poured boiling water onto two tea bags in mugs, added milk, and flipped the wet bags into the bin. "It's not the same."

"I married you," Patrick replied stoutly. "I could have chosen to stay at home and have real tea in a bone-china cup and a cooked breakfast every day of my life."

"But don't you want both?" Ruth asked.

She saw it—the little flicker of greed that crossed his face, and his instantly smoothing it away. The momentary acknowledgment that yes, indeed, he did want someone to mother his child, and to be his lover, and to cook for him and care for him to the standard of his mother's house.

"No," Patrick said, as if he meant it.

Ruth smiled. "Good," she said, as if she believed it.

❧

*I*t seemed to take all morning to get Thomas dressed, and then she had to entertain him in one room after another, as she tried to get the household chores done. He had learned now to reach for something and grasp at it, and his favorite game was to be propped by pillows and offered one object after another to hold and then negligently drop. In the bathroom, while she dutifully cleaned the toilet, the sink, and the bath, Ruth passed him toothbrushes, washcloths, and a box of dental floss. Thomas accepted them with pleasure and dropped them all, and looked around for something more. Ruth handed him the little duck from his bath toys, and his sponge. She was leaning over the bath, rinsing the suds away with the shower attachment, when she heard a muffled ominous choke.

She spun around. Thomas had crammed most of the sponge into his mouth but was quite incapable of getting it out again. Yellow sponge bulged from his lips, his eyes were staring, his face flushed as he struggled for air.

"My God!" Ruth said and flew at him. She pulled the sponge

from his mouth and Thomas whooped for breath, and then smiled. The incident had not disturbed him at all.

"I could have killed him," Ruth said. "Oh, God."

She snatched him up and held him tight, and they walked downstairs together. Ruth saw her hand on the banister and it trembled so much that she could hardly feel the wood beneath her fingertips. She took Thomas into the sitting room and laid him on his back on the sofa, so that she could look into his inquiring face.

"Oh, God, Thomas," she said. A sense of her passionate love for him set her trembling again. She took in his clear skin and his wide, innocent eyes. You could still see a little pulse in the top of his head; even his skull was vulnerable. "Such a little cough!" she said marveling at the softness of it. "What if I hadn't heard?"

Behind her, the front door opened suddenly. "Hello!" Elizabeth called. "Anyone at home?"

"In here," Ruth said. She had a sudden instinct to hide Thomas, as if Elizabeth would know, just by looking at him, that Ruth could have suffocated him.

"I was just passing—" Elizabeth stopped dead. "Good Lord, Ruth, you're white as a sheet! What's wrong?" At once she looked at Thomas with an expression like terror on her face. She went straight past Ruth and picked him up. Thomas crowed with delight at her touch, and she turned with him in her arms, as if she were rescuing him. "What happened?" she demanded tightly.

"It was nothing," Ruth said.

"Nothing?"

Ruth faced her mother-in-law and felt tears coming.

"Did he fall down the stairs?" Elizabeth demanded.

"No," Ruth said in a low, shaky voice. "He choked."

"What on?"

"His bath sponge." Ruth swallowed down her tears. "I didn't think," she said. "I gave him his sponge to look at and when I turned round he had crammed it all in his mouth. I just pulled it out."

"All of it?"

Ruth gasped at a new fear. "I didn't look. I didn't think to look in his mouth. Could he have swallowed some? Could it be stuck in his throat?"

"Look at the sponge!" Elizabeth snapped. "Fetch it now!"

Ruth ran up the stairs and came down with Thomas's sponge. It was cut in the shape of a little boat. It was complete and intact. The yellow keel made of sponge, the orange superstructure, and the little green sponge funnel on top.

Elizabeth looked it all over carefully. "Thank God for that," she said, her voice carefully controlled. "Why weren't you watching him?"

Ruth answered Elizabeth as if the older woman had every right to cross-question her. She felt so miserably guilty that the hostile interrogation was almost a pleasure. "I was cleaning the bath," she said. "I was just giving him things to look at."

"You have to have a little box," Elizabeth said with weary patience. She put Thomas against her shoulder and stroked his back in gentle circular motions. "A little box with his toys for the day. You swap them around every night so he has different ones every day. You take the box around with you, wherever you go in the house, and when you need a moment to do something, you give him something from the box."

"Oh," Ruth said numbly. "I didn't know."

It was as if there were too much to learn. Ruth would never grasp it all in time.

Elizabeth nodded, with her lips pressed together. "He's nearly asleep," she said. It was true. Thomas, inhaling the familiar scent of his grandmother and held firmly in her arms, with his back patted and her voice in his ear, was drifting off into sleep.

Without asking, Elizabeth went out into the kitchen and put Thomas in his pram. "He'll sleep now, and you can get your chores done and then supervise him properly when he wakes up," she said. She glanced out the French windows to the little garden, where the winter sun was bright. "He can go out," she decided, opened the doors and trundled the pram into the garden.

"Thank you," Ruth said.

Elizabeth tucked the blankets closely around him, then put

the waterproof cover on top, and pulled up the hood against the cold air.

"Actually, I was just calling in to see if you wanted any shopping," she said.

Ruth shook her head. "I'll go later. I'll take Thomas this afternoon."

"I'll have Thomas while you shop," Elizabeth offered. "It's hard work doing it all with a baby as well."

Ruth flared briefly. "I can do it," she said. "I am perfectly capable of shopping and caring for my baby at the same time."

Elizabeth raised an eyebrow. "I'm glad to hear it," she said. "You know where I am if you change your mind. We're both in this afternoon. It will be no trouble if you want to drop him off on your way out."

Ruth nodded. "Thank you," she felt forced to say.

Elizabeth slid past her and out into the hall. "I shan't say anything to Patrick," she promised. At once Ruth's mistake seemed infinitely worse if it had to be concealed from her husband. "He'd only worry."

"Thank you," Ruth said again. "I'll probably tell him myself, anyway."

Elizabeth nodded. "As you wish," she said. "I'm sure he'll be sympathetic. We're all aware how hard you are trying. . . ."

"It was an accident," Ruth said defensively. "It must happen thousands of times a day."

Elizabeth smiled coldly. "Perhaps," she said. "It never happened to either of my children."

⁂

Ruth took Thomas with her to the shop, but Elizabeth had been right—it was a struggle to cope with shopping and a baby as well. For the first half hour everything went well. Ruth parked in the mother-and-baby space, and put Thomas in the reclining seat on the top of the cart, and he observed with interest the bright lights of the ceiling and his mother's head coming and going. But after a while he became bored and started to cry.

Ruth was only halfway around the store. She had bought vegetables and fruit and some cheese, but the aisles of cleaning powders and detergents and nursery goods were ahead of her, as well as the bakery and the delicatessen sections.

"Shush, shush," she said putting her cheek beside Thomas's hot face. "Soon be finished."

Thomas got a handful of hair and pulled.

"Ow!" Ruth said and unwound the determined little fingers. At once he yelled louder, his hands reaching out to grasp her again.

"Shush!" Ruth said less tenderly. She turned the heavy cart and started to push it down the detergent aisle. Thomas's wails grew louder and louder, his face was scarlet, he squeezed real hot tears from screwed-up eyes. A woman glanced sharply at Ruth, as if she were doing something wrong, something to make the baby cry.

Ruth tried to smile unconcernedly, and leaned forward and patted the baby's cheek. "Not long now," she tried to say.

Thomas was straining against the safety harness, his little legs kicking irritably. His cry now had a desperate urgent quality as if he were in dreadful danger. The nagging, demanding shriek filled the store, and pulled at Ruth's nerves. She felt every wail as if it were a physical pain.

She abandoned the rest of the shopping list and abruptly headed the cart to the checkout. A man went past her and looked at her irritably—as if she were disturbing the peace of his afternoon on purpose. Ruth felt enormously, absurdly angry with him, and envious of his carefree stride and his half-empty cart. Thomas gave one last huge wriggle and then vomited up his entire lunch and his afterlunch bottle over the seat and over the shopping in the cart.

"Oh, God," Ruth said.

Thomas screamed. Ruth unbuckled him and snatched him up. He was sobbing convulsively, drenched in sour-smelling vomit.

With one spare hand Ruth pushed the shopping cart to the checkout. Thomas wept gently against her neck as Ruth bent deep into the cart to pull out the shopping and stack it on the belt. Some of it was sprayed with Thomas's vomit. The cashier did not hide her distaste, holding the packages with a finger and thumb and wrinkling her nose. She pressed the intercom and asked for someone to come and clean the moving belt, which was now sticky from Thomas's vomit. There was no one to pack. Ruth crammed the shopping into bags, working one-handed with Thomas held against her neck, her shirt and jumper getting steadily wetter with his tears and saliva.

"Sixty-eight pounds, ten," the girl said brightly.

Ruth handed over her card, and then awkwardly signed one-handed. The girl gave her the receipt and the card without a smile, as if it were all Ruth's fault. Her look was disdainful, but also pitying.

Grimly Ruth pushed the cart to the car, strapped Thomas into his baby seat, and unpacked the shopping into the trunk. She pushed the cart with unnecessary force into the line of waiting carts, and drove away.

Thomas fell asleep at once, exhausted by his crying and vomiting. When they got home Ruth did not have the heart to wake him. She lifted him gently out of the car seat, and laid him in his crib. He lay sprawled, with his arms spread wide and his little hands open. His hair was plastered to his little head with sweat; his clothes were saturated with vomit. Ruth smiled at him with immense tenderness. "Oh, darling, darling boy," she said gently. "I'm so sorry. We'll do it better next time."

She put up the side of the crib and went downstairs to unpack the shopping. Almost at once the telephone rang.

"Is that Mrs. Cleary?"

"Yes."

"This is Saver Store. We have your handbag here, Mrs. Cleary."

"Oh, my God!" Ruth said. She had no recollection of her handbag at all. Then she remembered. She had put it on the roof of the car while loading Thomas and the shopping, and then driven off.

"We found it in the car park."

"Thank you," Ruth said. "Can I collect it tomorrow?"

"I'm afraid we are not allowed to keep lost property of value overnight," the man said firmly. "We will have to take it to the police station and you will have to apply and collect it from there."

"But you know it's mine!" Ruth said irritably.

"Yes, indeed, Mrs. Cleary. And if you wish to collect it before four P.M. you can do so, provided you have some means of identity."

Ruth glanced at the clock on the microwave. "It's three-thirty now!" she said.

There was an unhelpful silence.

"Oh, all right," Ruth said. "I'm coming straightaway."

She hung up and then dialed Elizabeth's number. "I'm so sorry," she said without preamble. "But I've left my handbag at Saver Store, and I have to collect it before four or they pass it on to the police. Thomas has just fallen asleep. Could you possibly pop down and watch him for me for three quarters of an hour? Just so I can go down and fetch it now?"

"Of course," Elizabeth said pleasantly. She glanced at Frederick, who was pouring tea. "I can come at once."

Ruth slung the last of the frozen food into the freezer and pulled on her jacket. As she heard Elizabeth's car pull up she went down the path to greet her. "Thank you," she said.

"It's no trouble at all," Elizabeth said nicely. "But what a nuisance for you! Has Thomas slept long? Do you want me to wake him?"

"He's fine, he's just gone off," Ruth said. "If you would just listen for him in case he wakes. I'll probably be back before he has even stirred."

Elizabeth nodded and went into the house. Ruth got into her car and drove back to the shop.

Alone in the house Elizabeth looked around the sitting room. The fire was not laid and the cold ashes and coals in the grate looked unwelcoming and frowsy. She rolled up some newspaper kindling, and laid a little fire and put a match to it. At once the room looked warmer and cheerful. She straightened the cushions on the sofa and drew the curtains. One of the hooks had come undone at the top and the fabric was falling awkwardly. Elizabeth fetched a chair from the kitchen and rehooked the curtain.

She returned the chair to its place by the kitchen table and looked around. The dirty dishes from Ruth's and Thomas's lunch were sitting on top of the dishwasher, which had just finished its cycle. Elizabeth's critical gaze took in everything: the stain on the new worktop, the spattered range, the kitchen curtains not tied back with their coordinating loops but left to hang. She glanced into the larder. Thomas was being fed factory-made baby food again; she looked at the rows and rows of expensive jars and frowned at the waste of money. The freezer door was not properly shut. Elizabeth got down on her knees and had to rearrange the boxes to make it fit. Almost unconsciously she moved boxes around until all the meat was together on a meat shelf, and all the vegetables, arranged in order of their sell-by dates, were stacked on the vegetable shelf.

The house was silent.

Elizabeth thought she would check on Thomas and went soft-footed up the stairs to his bedroom. She acknowledged to herself that she need not see him. He would cry out when he woke and she could go to him then, but Elizabeth loved to watch Thomas asleep, she liked to sit in the chair in his nursery and sew, or write letters while he slept. She felt that his sweet, peaceful sleep and her patient watching cast a spell around the two of them.

She opened his bedroom door and, smiling, approached the crib.

Thomas, his face stained with tears and his clothes thick with dried vomit, lay on his back, his face pink and his head sweating from the heat of his outdoor clothes.

"Oh, my God," Elizabeth said. For a moment she thought that he was desperately ill. She picked him up and he stirred and opened his eyes and smiled to see her, then dropped his head down to her shoulder and dozed off again.

He smelled awful. His diaper was dirty and his clothes were impregnated with vomit. He was still sweaty.

Elizabeth's face was like stone. She marched him out of the house and down the garden path and into her car. She strapped him carefully into the baby seat and drove back up the drive to the farmhouse. She unstrapped him and carried him in.

"Look," she said savagely to Frederick. "Look at him!"

He came out of the sitting room, folding his paper. "Brought the little chap back?" he started, but then he saw her face. "What is it?"

"Look at him," she said through her teeth. "I found him like this in his cot. God knows how long he's been there. He's obviously been sick all over himself and been left to cry. She didn't even take his coat off after they had been shopping. She just slung him in his cot and left him."

Frederick's face was shocked. "What did she say?"

"Nothing! She told me not to disturb him; she said he'd just gone to sleep. I should think she *didn't* want me to disturb him. I should think she was praying that I would just sit downstairs and wait for her to come back!"

Frederick looked grave. "There may be an explanation," he said carefully. "Things do happen, my dear. Maybe the telephone rang and she was called away. . . ."

"I have just found my grandson, dirty, sick, and neglected, in his crib," Elizabeth said with emphasis. "There is no excuse for that."

She turned and went upstairs to the nursery, which had once been Patrick's and now had Thomas's name on a little china nameplate on the door. She sat in the low nursing chair and gently and efficiently stripped off his outdoor suit, and then his little shirt and his trousers. Thomas stirred but hardly woke. She undid his diaper and cleaned him and put on a fresh cloth diaper from the pile that was waiting. She wrapped him in a little blanket and laid him in his crib to finish his sleep. Thomas, dreaming of the fascinating lights of the store and his mother's face swimming in and out of his vision, stretched out again and sank into sleep.

Elizabeth came downstairs and took Thomas's dirty clothes into the kitchen. The weatherproof suit, which was the worst, she laid to one side, and handwashed the rest.

Frederick came in and made her a pot of tea in silence. "Will you speak to Patrick?"

She nodded. "They will have to come back here."

He hesitated. "It's no way for a young couple to live," he said. "They need a bit of privacy."

"So that she can neglect our grandson and we not know?"

"I think we should listen to her version. She certainly loves him. I don't think she'd neglect him willfully."

Elizabeth wrung out the little shirt and trousers and changed the water in the sink. She watched the suds swirl down the drain and then turned and faced her husband. "Are you saying we should do nothing?" she demanded. "Not warn Patrick, cover up for her, keep it a secret?"

Frederick thought for a moment and then he shook his head. "Of course not," he said. "The baby comes first. But I am sorry she hasn't made a better go of it."

"We all are," Elizabeth said smartly.

❦

*P*atrick, seated in the editing studio with a producer, trying to find cuts in a program that was ten minutes too long, was irritated by the note his secretary brought in, which read: "Your mother rang and said to tell you that you should urgently phone home. At once."

"Sorry. Just a minute," Patrick said. He understood that home did not mean the little house, but the farmhouse. He picked up the studio phone and dialed the number. "It's me," he said shortly.

The producer watched his face change. He looked shocked, and then incredulous. "All right," he said. "I'll come at once."

"Trouble?" the producer asked.

Patrick switched on his charming smile. "I am so sorry," he said. "I was enjoying this and it's a good piece. There's a family crisis at home: my son is sick. I have to go. Can you finish it without me and bike a copy over to my house for me to see tonight? I'll phone you first thing in the morning."

"All right," the producer said. "I hope your son is OK."

Patrick's smile wavered slightly. "Oh, sure," he said. "It's probably nothing."

He drove home badly, overtaking and cutting in. Partly he was anxious to get home, but also he felt a mixture of rage and distress and, oddly, embarrassment. He felt that Ruth's inability to cope with Thomas reflected badly on him. He felt that his parents deserved a better daughter-in-law, that he should have chosen a better partner. The closeness and sympathy of the days since Christmas dissolved under the acid of his realization that Ruth would never be able to cope.

His mother opened the door to his step on the threshold. "Patrick," she said, and drew him into an embrace, which was consoling and powerful and reassuring.

She led him into the kitchen. Thomas was sitting in his old high chair in his accustomed place by the table. Frederick was opposite, out of reach of the flying spoon that Thomas waved as he waited to be fed. Elizabeth sat down before him and spooned food into his open mouth.

"What's the problem?" Patrick asked, leaning against the door. "He looks well enough."

Elizabeth glanced at Frederick and said nothing. Frederick spoke for them both.

"Ruth took him shopping this afternoon and apparently left her purse in the shop, or something. She phoned Mother and asked her to go down and hold the fort while she drove back to the shop. When Mother got there she found Thomas in his outdoor clothes in his cot. He'd been sick and he was dirty. Mother brought him up here at the double, and here we are. And now she's AWOL. She should have been home by now but she's not reported in. It's a bad business, Patrick."

Patrick straightened up and turned a little away. He looked out the kitchen window so they could not see his face. Elizabeth and Frederick exchanged a look.

"He had cried himself to sleep," she said. "He was in a dreadful state. And his clothes must have been on him for a while; they were drying out. There's his weatherproof suit. I kept it for you to see."

Patrick glanced down at the garment, which was drying with large blotches of white stains of vomit. He turned back to the two of them. "What shall I do?" he asked like a man who has run out of answers. "What shall I do?"

*R*uth was delayed at the store because the security officer who had spoken to her on the telephone could not at first be found. Then, when he came, she had to produce satisfactory proof of identity and fill in a claim form before she could receive her handbag. Then she had to count the money in her purse and confirm that nothing was missing on an itemized receipt. Nothing could be hurried, everything had to be done in order. Ruth bit back her temper and checked her watch. It was five o'clock before she left the shop, and then she was caught in the rush-hour traffic. It was a quarter to six by the time she got home, and she felt flustered and apologetic. She expected to see Patrick's car in the drive alongside Elizabeth's but neither was there, and the house was in darkness.

Inside, the little fire in the sitting room had died away to pale embers, hardly lighting the darkened room. The house was silent except for the soft occasional click of the pipes.

Ruth snapped on the lights in the hall and on the stairs and experienced blinding rage. Elizabeth had *not* come and baby-sat, as had been agreed. Elizabeth had taken Thomas. Even now, Ruth knew, Thomas would be sitting in his high chair in the farmhouse kitchen, eating one of Elizabeth's home-cooked dinners. From the absence of Patrick's car Ruth guessed, rightly, that Patrick would be there too. At half past six exactly Frederick would pour a gin and tonic for each of them, and Elizabeth would take Thomas upstairs for his bath, and Patrick would be invited to sit in the bathroom and watch his son.

The farmhouse, the family, the order, and the serenity seemed infinitely more solid and more attractive than Ruth's house. Elizabeth's mothering of Thomas was more assured, her cooking was better. Ruth opened the sitting-room curtains and looked up the drive toward the farmhouse. There were no headlights coming down the drive as Patrick and Thomas came home to her. Ruth knew that if she did not go and fetch them, or telephone them at once, then Elizabeth would bathe Thomas and put him to bed in Patrick's old nursery, and then come downstairs to cook Patrick's supper.

Ruth picked up the telephone and dialed the farmhouse.

Patrick answered. "Where are you?"

Ruth recoiled from the hostility in his voice. "Home, of course. What's the matter?"

"I'll come straight down," he said, and hung up without explanation.

Ruth replaced the receiver on the hook and wandered through to the kitchen. Automatically, she filled the kettle with water and switched it on. She wondered if Elizabeth had complained at being left with Thomas for twice the length of time that Ruth had promised. But it was so unlike Elizabeth to complain that Ruth was certain it could not be that.

She heard Patrick's car in the drive, and his key in the lock. She went out into the hall to meet him. "Where's Thomas?"

"At home."

"Why didn't you bring him?"

He stepped into the light and she saw his face. She had never seen him look like that before: he looked exhausted, drained, and gray. "He's staying there for tonight," he said baldly. "I needed to talk to you alone."

Ruth thought at once that he had been sacked, or wanted to confess an affair, or some scandalous difficulty at work. "What's the matter?"

Patrick went into the kitchen and sat at the table. Ruth sat opposite him. In the silence the kettle boiled, and switched itself off.

"Tell me about Thomas today," Patrick said quietly. "How was he?"

"He was fine! He was fine! Patrick—please tell me what's going on."

"I need to know this first," he said. "What did you do this afternoon?"

"We went shopping," Ruth said. "Then when we came home the shop rang and said I had left my handbag there, so I phoned your mother, and drove down and picked it up, and she took him up to the farmhouse—without telling me," Ruth added.

Patrick nodded. "When did you put him in his cot?"

"When we came back from the shops. He fell asleep in the car so I just put him in." Ruth stretched across the table and held his hands. "Patrick, stop this. Tell me what is the matter."

His hands, under her own, were like ice. "The matter is this: that Mother found him in his crib, covered in vomit, sweating from the heat, having cried himself to sleep," he said dully. "And she says that this morning you let him choke on a sponge."

Ruth gasped. "It was an accident!" she said, outraged. "And she said she wouldn't tell you!"

Patrick gave her a sharp accusing stare.

"I was going to tell you," Ruth said quickly. "It was just an accident. And this afternoon wasn't like that. He was sick in the shop. I just put him in his crib."

There was a silence.

"Patrick!" Ruth said. "I just told you! He was sick in the shop and he fell asleep in the car, so I just put him in his crib and let him sleep."

He did not meet her eyes.

"So it's OK," Ruth said.

Still he said nothing.

"She's making a fuss about nothing," Ruth said stoutly.

Patrick got up from the table as if he had heard enough. "I don't agree," he said levelly. "She is very concerned that you left him in his crib like that, and so is the old man. And so am I."

Ruth got up too. "But this is absurd!" she said. She put her hand on Patrick's arm. "There's nothing wrong! We had a completely awful day, but there's nothing really wrong! It was just one of those days—you know—where everything goes wrong, and you feel like throwing him out the window, you know what it's like!"

Patrick suddenly turned on her. "No, I don't know!" he exploded. "I don't know about days when my son chokes and nearly suffocates in the morning and is then abandoned to be sick in his cot all afternoon and his mother wants to throw him out the window. I don't know about days like that!"

Ruth fell back, shaking her head. "It wasn't like that . . ." she said.

"Thomas will sleep at the farmhouse tonight." Patrick gave the order with a strange tone in his voice, as if it were not his decision but some new immutable law. "And tomorrow you and I will go up there and decide with Mother and Father what to do. We don't think you can be left on your own with him, Ruth."

"You mean she doesn't."

The spite in her voice repelled him. "If you mean my mother, then you are right," he said. "My mother does not think you are fit to be in sole charge of my son. And neither does my father. And neither do I."

"How dare you!" Ruth cried. "He is *my* son as much as yours, he is *my* son, and I love him, and I care for him, and I would never hurt a hair of his head, and you may not say such a thing! Ever! Ever! Ever!"

"You just said you felt like throwing him out the window!"

"Everybody does!" Ruth screamed. "It's called real life! Everybody feels like that sometimes. It doesn't mean I don't love him!"

Patrick turned and went for the front door and Ruth flung herself on him and pulled at his arm and his shoulder, to turn him to face her.

"You can't do this!" she said. "You can't take him away from me like that!"

His face was bleak. He looked at her and Ruth shrank back from the coldness in his eyes. "Yes, we can," he said.

"Patrick," she whispered. "Please don't—please don't be like this."

He shook his head. "It's you," he said. "Not me."

He opened the door.

"Where are you going?" she asked. Her voice sounded little and thin against the great dark of the country winter night outside.

"I'm going up to the farm," he said. "I'm sleeping there tonight. I'll come down and pick you up in the morning."

She would have stopped him but he turned quickly and went down the path, got into his car, backed it carefully into their drive, and drove off.

In his rearview mirror he could see the bright oblong of the doorway spilling light into the garden, and Ruth's silhouette, clinging to the doorpost, as if her legs were giving way underneath her.

237

⌒ *Sixteen* ⌒

*R*uth did not sleep that night, she sat in the window seat of the sitting room, wrapped in her duvet, with her head leaning against the icy glass, looking out at the night sky and waiting for the first signs of light. She thought that she had never in her life been in a worse situation—not in depression, and not in recovery. Every other situation had been created by her accident or by her own folly. For the first time in her life Ruth realized that she had enemies.

She wept a little—that Patrick should leave her so abruptly, that he should have sided with his parents against her, without even considering her version of events. But as the sky grew even darker and the wind came up she moved from self-pity into a cold determination. She realized that she had lost Patrick, and lost her marriage. Now she had to fight for her child.

In the farmhouse Patrick got up at two in the morning, after restless sleep with anxious dreams, poured himself a large brandy, and took it back to bed with him. Frederick woke at five, in the solid winter darkness, as black as midnight, sighed at the grief of the day ahead, and went downstairs to make a pot of strong tea.

Only Elizabeth and Thomas, with clear consciences, slept well. Thomas did not wake until half past seven, and Elizabeth laid him on her bed with his morning bottle while she washed and dressed.

At nine o'clock prompt, Frederick telephoned his solicitor, Simon Sylvester. The call was as brief as Frederick's distress and distaste could make it. Simon Sylvester advised him that the first step in taking a child from its mother was to get a residence order with Patrick and his parents nominated as guardians. Subsequently there would have to be social-worker reports.

"It would help your case no end if the mother was committed," Simon Sylvester said cheerfully. "Especially with a record of drinking and drugs. Is she likely to put up a fight?"

"No," Frederick said, thinking of Ruth's vulnerable desperation. "No fight in her at all."

"Parents? Family?"

"No one. The family are American, and the parents are dead."

"Then she can go inside on your say-so: you're the nearest of kin. She can be locked up by this afternoon and you and your son named as guardians this evening," Simon said. "If you've given up on her, that is. If you're throwing her overboard."

Frederick heard the abrupt dismissal of Ruth without flinching. "Be on standby then," he said. "I'll call you at midday."

At half past nine, Patrick, looking hollow-eyed and gray-skinned, went down the drive to fetch Ruth.

She was waiting, at the sitting-room window bay. For a moment he thought that perhaps she had not gone to bed at all, but had stood there, waiting and hoping for him all night.

When she came out of the house, slammed the front door behind her, and got in the car, he saw that she was alert and wakeful. She had showered and washed her hair, she had changed into a dark cashmere polo-neck sweater, and black jeans. She looked slim, desirable, and challenging.

He drove in silence and she sat beside him in silence. They were both waiting for the other to speak and assessing, by the thousand small signs that intimate couples know, how long the quarrel might extend, how angry it might be, whether there might be a meeting of the eyes, an understanding, a meeting of the fingertips, a reconciling kiss.

Ruth hunched her right shoulder and looked out the side window. Patrick drove, never taking his eyes off the road, as if it were not his own drive, which he knew well enough to walk in the dark.

When they got out of the car at the farmhouse, the front door opened.

"Dear Ruth," Elizabeth said gently. "Come in."

Ruth followed her into the drawing room, where the fire was lit and the silver coffeepot was on the polished table. Ruth read the signs with a quick glance. This was a best-china occasion; it was intensely serious. Then she saw Thomas in his bouncy cradle-seat.

She did not rush to him and snatch him up. She sat down quietly on the floor beside him, and held up his little duck so he could take it from her and drop it, and have it offered again. There was something very composed about Ruth's gentle play with her son. His eyes went from the toy to her serene face with pleasure.

Elizabeth's silver coffee service and little enameled spoons seemed suddenly to strike a false note, as Ruth sat cross-legged on the floor, playing quietly with her son as if they were alone together.

Frederick came in. "Ruth," he nodded to her, hardly smiling.

"Coffee?" Elizabeth asked.

It seemed that no one wanted coffee.

For a moment no one spoke. It had not been planned in detail. Frederick and Elizabeth and Patrick had merely agreed that some decision must be made, since matters with Thomas could not go on. But they had not descended to conspire against Ruth, and Frederick's consultation with his lawyer was a secret known only to him. Only he knew that the papers to commit Ruth, without her consent, to a mental hospital were being drawn up. Only he knew that Thomas could be a ward of court tonight.

"What's this all about?" Ruth asked. She addressed Elizabeth directly and without hesitation. "I had an accident with Thomas yesterday morning when he put his sponge in his mouth, and yesterday afternoon I put him into his crib when he had been sick while we were out shopping. He was never left alone, he was never in any danger. When I had to go out, I telephoned you."

Elizabeth inclined her head but said nothing.

"I am caring for him perfectly well," Ruth went on, her voice controlled and tight. "There is no need for concern."

Still Elizabeth said nothing.

"We are concerned, Ruth," Frederick said bluntly. "These things—whether they are exactly as you describe or not—these things have all happened on the first day that Patrick goes back to work and leaves you alone in the little house. If you are not coping with Thomas, Ruth, we will have to insist that you let us help."

Ruth shot a look at Patrick. He folded his arms and leaned back.

"How help?"

"I'll come down in the morning and take him out for his constitutional in his pram. Or if rain stops play, I'll rock him in the hall or wherever, while you do your chores. Elizabeth will come down in the afternoon to give you a break. Patrick will be home at six every evening. So you have some support."

Ruth hesitated. "Is this an offer, or is it an order?"

Frederick cleared his throat. Elizabeth was looking at her well-polished tan shoes. Patrick's eyes were on his father's face. Thomas cooed softly and Ruth offered him another toy.

"You can take it as you wish," Frederick said. "It's a description of what is going to happen."

"Forever?"

"Until we are sure that you are well enough to care for him on your own."

Ruth nodded. "And how will you know I am well?" she asked.

Frederick hesitated and looked at Elizabeth. "We'll all know," she said again. "You'll be our darling happy girl again, and you'll thank us for standing by you now."

Ruth made a little face, as if the prospect of thanking Elizabeth was rather more than she could stomach.

"And if I refuse?" she asked.

Patrick stole a quick look at his wife. There was a hardness and a maturity about her that he had never seen before. A sharp brilliance in her look, as if she would face the worst truths in the world, and look them in the eye. She was many miles away now from the grateful ingenue he had married. There was something adult about her now, and rock hard. He was not sure if he liked her, but there was something undeniably erotic in the way she just nodded and moved coldly and intellectually to the next question. He nodded. She was outmanning the men. She had not come as a bereaved mother to weep and call for the return of her baby. She had come out as a lioness to fight until the death.

"I hope you will see that this is for the best," Frederick said, avoiding the challenge.

She smiled, a scornful, bitter smile, very beautiful on her face. "But if I do *not* see that? If I refuse?"

Frederick nodded, accepting her challenge and showing his hand with all the deceptive honesty of the skilled poker player. "Then we keep Thomas here and you are welcome to live here with us again, or visit constantly."

She looked to Patrick again but he was looking at the fire.

"I could take Thomas right away," she said thoughtfully.

Frederick shook his head. "We would not permit that," he said. "Thomas stays here, either with us or with you with our supervision." He hesitated. "Besides," he said. "You have nowhere to go, and no money. You have no friends who would take you in, and no family. It would not be fair to you or Thomas, and it's not necessary, Ruth."

She shot a look at him. "Not necessary to be free?"

"This is a brief difficult phase in a long, long life," Frederick said. He spoke solemnly, as if he were weighing her down with the wisdom of his experience. "In months, maybe in weeks, we will have half-forgotten this, and by next year we will hardly remember it at all. Lots of families have difficulties in adjusting to a new baby. There is no reason why our family should be any different. Let us help you, Ruth, and take it in the spirit in which it is meant—because we love our son, and we love our grandson, and we love you."

There was a silence. Thomas was bored and started to cry in a fretful, inconsequential way. Ruth lifted him out of his bouncy cradle-seat and sat him on her lap. "Nearly time for his nap," she said.

"He can go upstairs," Elizabeth said. "I'll make his bottle."

Ruth nodded, and rocked him gently, held firmly under her cheek against the comforting sound of her beating heart. Thomas's downy little head was warm under her chin.

"I have no choice," Ruth observed.

Her father-in-law nodded. "That is correct," he said gently. "You have no choice now. But the situation could change completely in a matter of weeks, and then you will be free to do whatever you and Patrick think right."

Ruth nodded. "You force me to agree," she said simply.

Elizabeth came back into the room with the bottle in her hand. "You agree?"

"Yes." Ruth nodded dismissively toward Frederick. "He can come down in the morning and you can come down in the afternoon. The rest of the time Thomas is left with me."

Patrick suddenly realized that he had been sitting with his arms crossed and his shoulders hunched for what felt like all the morning. He released his grip and felt his muscles relax.

"Well done, darling," he said gently. "And thank you."

Ruth looked at him with large dark eyes, which told him nothing. "I'll put him to sleep in the nursery here," she said. "I'll bring the pram up and you can wheel him down when he wakes. I want him brought down to me straightaway, as soon as he wakes."

"I'll do that for you," Frederick said quietly. He had to suppress a sense of triumph. It had been a long time since he had been faced with a situation of outright and damaging conflict. It had been something of a diplomatic pleasure as well as a duty to bring Ruth into line.

"I'll drive you home," Patrick offered. "Dad can come too and collect the pram. That'll save you the walk."

Again she gave him the dark, unfriendly stare. "All right," she said. "When he's asleep."

⁂

That day Ruth did as they wanted. Frederick pushed the pram down the drive as soon as Thomas had woken, and Ruth greeted them at the garden gate, drew the pram into the house, played with Thomas, and then gave him his lunch. After lunch, which he ate with relish—it was one of the brighter-colored jars—Ruth took him upstairs to change his diaper and changed all his clothes as well. His morning clothes smelled of Elizabeth's perfume.

At about three o'clock, when Thomas started getting tired again, Ruth put him in his pram and rocked him until his eyelids slowly closed and his one waving foot fell back into the pram. Then she tucked him up and put the pram in the back garden, and started to wash the kitchen floor.

Glancing out the French windows, she saw Elizabeth, who had entered the garden by the bottom gate, bending over the pram, and gently rocking it with the handle. Ruth opened the backdoor.

"I should like you to tell me when you arrive," she said abruptly. "Don't go straight to the pram like that. He might have been just dozing off and you would have wakened him."

Elizabeth straightened up and nodded. "I'm sorry," she apologized. "I will in future."

She came into the kitchen, glancing around. "Would you like to go out?" she asked. "Or have a rest? I can finish the chores while Thomas is sleeping."

"I'm in the middle of washing my kitchen floor. I hardly want to leave it and go out. Would you mind sitting in the sitting room?"

Elizabeth nodded, saying nothing, and went quietly through. Ruth mopped with silent resentment, wrung out the mop, poured away the dirty water, and put the mop and bucket away in the cupboard under the stairs.

She put her head around the sitting-room door. "I need to do some shopping," she said abruptly. "I'll be about an hour."

Elizabeth was sitting on the sofa, looking at the *Guardian* newspaper. "Of course," she said pleasantly. "If he wakes I'll bring him in and play with him here."

"He is not to be taken out of this house," Ruth said flatly. "When I come back, he is to be here."

"Of course." Elizabeth gave her daughter-in-law a tentative

smile. "Of course, Ruth. We're all working together on this."

Ruth's face was like a wall. "That's not how I see it," she said. "You are not to give him his tea, you are not to bathe him. I will do that when I come home."

"I will change his nappy," Elizabeth stipulated.

Ruth hesitated. "All right," she said and turned and went out the door.

Elizabeth sat completely still until she heard the car drive away, and then she went through to the kitchen and glanced out the window at the pram. As the noise of the engine died away down the lane she gave a little sigh, and her shoulders relaxed, as if a burden had slid away. She drew the curtains into the proper tiebacks. "Poor, dear, unhappy Ruth," she said softly. "Such a shame . . ."

Then she went out into the garden to see Thomas.

❧

Ruth was back precisely within the hour, and she unloaded the shopping from the car and left the front door open for Elizabeth to leave.

"I will see you tomorrow," Elizabeth said on the doorstep.

Ruth nodded, and shut the door in her face.

Elizabeth gathered the collar of her coat about her ears, and ran down the path to her car. As she drove away from the little house she was smiling.

Thomas was fretful at dinnertime and would not eat. He kicked out as he went into his high chair, and his bowl of dinner went flying, landing with a splash of bright tomato red all over the newly washed floor.

Ruth had to heat another bowl of dinner to give to him, and then leave him, squirming crossly in his high chair, starting to cry, as she cleared up the kitchen floor. Just as she thrust the last red-stained lump of kitchen towel in the bin, Thomas's dinner bowl—which should have been fixed with a suction cup on the tray of his high chair—came unstuck and flew across the kitchen to land on the floor again.

"Oh no!" Ruth said. For a moment she thought she would not

be able to hold back the tears, but then her face hardened. It was no longer a question of having a bad evening, or washing the floor twice. It was a question of keeping custody of her child, and the danger of Patrick's family's labeling her as insane. In the face of that nightmare Ruth felt she could not afford easy, small emotions. She was facing the worst thing that could possibly happen to her; the spilling of Thomas's dinner was nothing.

She scooped him out of his chair and, leaving the sticky mess on the kitchen floor, took him up the stairs, and laid him gently on his changing mat to get him undressed for his bath.

Thomas, enjoying the change of scene, was all smiles. His face, striped liberally with red tomato sauce, was radiant. When Ruth tickled his bare tummy and gently blew, he gurgled with laughter, and Ruth found herself making soft airplane-bombing noises and zooming down to kiss the round of his fat, warm stomach.

She lifted her head when she heard the front door open. Patrick was home. She heard him put down his briefcase, go into the kitchen, exclaim at the state of the floor, and then come up the stairs. Ruth stripped off Thomas's dirty diaper and left it on the changing mat, and carried Thomas, wrapped in a warm towel, to the bathroom.

"Hello," Patrick said cautiously.

"Hello," she said.

"How are things?" he asked.

"Fine."

Ruth ran the bath and then put Thomas carefully in it, one hand behind his back, one in a firm grip on his arm.

"Anything I can do?" Patrick asked. In the farmhouse he was required to sit on the chair in the bathroom, drink a gin and tonic, and smile occasionally at his son.

"Yes," Ruth said pleasantly. "Can you clean up the changing table, there's a dirty nappy there, and then wash the kitchen floor and clean up the kitchen, and then peel some potatoes for supper, and put them on. Make Thomas's bottles and bring them up."

Patrick blinked. "The kitchen floor looks like a butcher's shop," he remarked.

"Doesn't it?" Ruth agreed. "I've washed it twice already today. That's just one effort. Hurry up, Patrick, or we'll never get supper on."

"I'll have to change," he said.

She nodded. Slowly, he went to the bedroom to change into jeans and a sweatshirt. With his two parents on call and Ruth at home all day, he did not see why he should have to wash the kitchen floor on his arrival home after a long day at work. He slipped his feet into comfortable moccasins, and went downstairs.

The kitchen was most unappealing. From the bathroom upstairs he could hear Ruth playing with Thomas, the noise of splashing, and Thomas's delighted giggles. Patrick sighed heavily and fetched the mop.

He had barely finished before Ruth called down the stairs, "He's ready for his bottle!"

"Coming!" Patrick shouted back.

He made up the feed and carried it up the stairs. Thomas was pink and sweet-smelling from his bath. His pajamas were a soft white cotton all-in-one sleep suit, which encased his plump little feet and his round, compact body. When he saw his father bringing the bottle, he beamed, stretched out his hand, and babbled.

"He's saying hello!" Ruth exclaimed.

Ruth settled herself in the nursing chair and held Thomas on her lap. Patrick handed her the bottle and drew the curtains against the dark winter night. "Goodnight, son!" he said cheerfully, and went to the door.

"Nappy," Ruth reminded him. "You've forgotten the dirty nappy."

With a half-suppressed sigh Patrick folded up the disgusting little package and took it downstairs. Ruth cuddled Thomas close and rocked him.

⁂

*P*atrick felt at a disadvantage through the evening. He was expecting Ruth to reproach him for not standing up for her against his parents, but she cooked lamb chops and served them at the table as if she were a perfectly contented wife and mother. The potatoes were disagreeably spotty where Patrick had missed the eyes and markings, and rather hard. Ruth ate them without comment. Patrick left some of his on the side of his plate, with a slightly martyred air, but then absentmindedly ate them up.

He glanced at the clock on the microwave. "I have to see the nine o'clock news," he said, and got up from the table.

"OK," Ruth said obligingly. "We can stack the dishwasher later."

Patrick said nothing. He had rather thought that Ruth would clear up the kitchen while he watched the news and then bring him a cup of coffee when she had finished. Ruth looked at him as if she could not see these half-formed thoughts behind his eyes.

"Oh, let's do it now," he said.

They cleared the table in silence, and Ruth wiped down the worktops and put the breakfast things ready. Then they went through to the sitting room. It was nearly time for the ten o'clock news. Ruth shucked off her shoes and curled up in an armchair to watch. "Be a darling, and make me a cup of tea," she asked. "I'll watch the news and then I'm up to bed. It's been a long horrible day."

He paused at the doorway. "I'm sorry about this morning," he said awkwardly. "It'll all be all right soon."

She had her head turned toward the television screen, and she did not turn back to look at him. "Yes," she said shortly.

They went to bed together. Patrick expected her to turn on her side and present him with her smooth pale back. But when he put out the light he felt her arms come around him with surprising strength.

He was going to hold her, to pat her back in a consoling manner. But she reared up over him and put her mouth down to his and kissed him, penetratingly, hard.

Patrick felt pierced by lust. He pulled her toward him, and she came astride him at once, her arms wound tightly around his neck, her body hard and heavy along him. As she kissed him he felt her teeth graze his lips, and he groaned with sudden, surprising desire.

Ruth slipped a quick cunning hand down his body and found

and grasped his penis. Tumbling deep into desire, Patrick had a sense of adultery, of forbidden pleasure. In the years of their marriage Ruth had never assertively taken the initiative. She had often invited, but she had never forced the issue. This hot, angry sexual woman on top of him was a woman he did not recognize, but he knew, as he instinctively thrust upward, that she was what he wanted.

Ruth's silky nightgown rode up over her thighs, over her back. "Oh, God!" Patrick said at the touch of her skin. She lowered herself on him with a gasp and then moved, rocking him faster and faster. Patrick, in a blur of sensation, just followed the rapid, demanding movements of her hips, felt himself drawn in, demanded, and finally consumed. She moved her weight so the bone inside the flesh pressed the flesh tantalizingly, delightfully, irresistibly together.

They lay still for a moment, and then, without a word, Ruth rolled off him. Patrick was still far from thought, whirling in a powerful sexual daze.

"Ruth?" he whispered after a little while.

She did not reply, and he thought she had fallen asleep. He stretched out a hand to caress her, but she rolled away, and all he touched was the warm sheet where she had been. He had a sudden urgent curiosity to know where this wild desire had suddenly come from. How his girl-wife, his orphaned, patronized bride, had suddenly fixed on her own womanhood and her own sensuality, and had found the courage to take him and show him a passion that he had never known before and that was light-years from their usual quiet domestic couplings.

"Ruth?"

On her side, eyes open, Ruth heard him whisper her name, but she lay still. She felt a fierce, wild joy. She had taken Patrick as her mate, at last, after years of waiting for his passion and waiting for her own. She had won him to her, and she would keep him. Not any longer by trying to please him, but by determinedly and excitingly pleasing herself.

She waited until she heard the quiet rhythm of his sleeping breath, and then she rolled onto her back and stretched with pleasure. "At least that's one thing she can't do," she said softly.

ᐒ Seventeen ᐒ

$\mathscr{F}$rederick walked down the drive to Ruth's house. The day was bitterly cold, the sky heavy and gray. "Looks like snow," Frederick said to himself.

He rang the doorbell, and Ruth answered. Thomas was already in his pram, well wrapped-up. "I'll only take him for a short walk, twenty minutes or so," Frederick said. "It's freezing."

Ruth nodded without smiling. He had never seen her before without that slightly nervous, slightly deferential smile. It was an unnerving change; she looked suddenly older, more powerful. For the first time in his life Frederick thought that she was a beautiful young woman.

"When you come back you can bring him in," she said. "If he's asleep, the pram can go in the hall. I'm doing the bedrooms."

Frederick touched his cap to her in the courteous way he always treated her. She looked at him ironically, but said nothing. "If you want to go out," he offered, "I can stay with him all the morning."

She shook her head. "You said an hour," she said. "An hour in the morning and two in the afternoon. This is not at my request, nor my convenience. This is what you insist on doing. If you want to change it, then you can go home and I will have him all to myself this morning."

"We'll stick to our agreement then," Frederick said. He turned the pram around and went up the drive toward the farmhouse.

251

Ruth could see the puffs of air from his breath as he walked. The pram wheels made dark lines in the whiteness of the frost. She shut the door.

Frederick walked for ten minutes away from the house and then back again. Thomas, rosy-cheeked in the cold air, did not sleep.

"He's still awake," Frederick said. "Shall I rock him in the kitchen or the hall?"

"He can come out and play," Ruth said.

"I can keep him amused while you do your chores," Frederick offered.

She gave him a cold look. "Of course. You have forty minutes yet." She shut the sitting-room door on them both, and Frederick heard her go up the stairs.

Thomas was overtired by lunchtime and would eat only breakfast cereal; the soothing milky taste was what he wanted. Ruth gave him his bottle in his pram and wheeled him out into the garden. The clouds were clearing and the sun was coming out; the garden was a monochrome of black shadows and blinding white frost on the grass. Ruth rocked Thomas until he turned his head from his bottle and fell asleep, and then she quietly took the bottle from the pram.

Promptly at five to three Elizabeth drove down and parked her car. She walked around to the back garden and saw the pram. She leaned in and put her finger down inside Thomas's little mitten, and touched his cheek to see that he was warm enough. The backdoor to the kitchen opened.

"I have asked you to come to the front door," Ruth said. "I asked you yesterday not to disturb him when he is sleeping."

Elizabeth straightened up, but she did not look at all reproved. "I was checking whether he was warm enough," she said. "He's fine."

"I know," Ruth said. "I checked him myself five minutes ago."

Elizabeth laughed her easy laugh. "Well, we're both happy then," she said.

Ruth stepped back as her mother-in-law came in the house. "Now," Elizabeth offered, "is there anything I can do for you? You know I hate to sit and do nothing."

Ruth shook her head, her face blank. "No," she said. "Nothing."

"Well, I'll have the pleasure of reading the newspaper until Thomas wakes," Elizabeth said. "And then I will change him and play with him until five o'clock. Are you going out?"

A swift expression of deep unhappiness crossed Ruth's face. "If I have to."

Elizabeth's smile never wavered. "Why, you must do whatever you would like to do," she said. "Thomas and I will not be in your way. You could rest, or read, or make some phone calls, or cook supper—whatever you would normally do, Ruth!"

There was a short silence. There had been no normality since the arrival of Thomas.

"I'll go for a walk," Ruth said.

"Wrap up warm!" Elizabeth called.

The front door slammed.

Elizabeth went out to the kitchen and peeped through the window to see the pram. Thomas was still asleep. Elizabeth opened the larder door and checked the contents. Absentmindedly she opened the freezer door. Someone had disarranged the order of the meat and the vegetables. She reorganized them so that they were in the right places. She glanced around the kitchen. The floor tiles, which she had chosen to reflect light in the rather dark backroom, were cloudy. Ruth had not dried them properly, Elizabeth thought. She stacked the kitchen chairs on the table, put the rubbish bin outside, and fetched the mop.

It took a little longer than she had expected. There had been a hardened lump of red baby food on the floor near the stove, which Ruth had obviously been too idle to get down and scrub. Elizabeth went on her knees to it and got it clean again. Then she restored the kitchen to order and glanced at the clock. Ruth had been gone only twenty minutes; there was still plenty of time. Elizabeth had telephoned Patrick at work that morning to confirm that the new arrangements were working well. Patrick—who had sounded remarkably relaxed, even happy—had said that things were fine at home. But he had mentioned that there seemed to be a lot of chores to do in the evening, peeling the potatoes, for instance. Elizabeth took the bag of potatoes to the sink and peeled and sliced them, and left them in a saucepan of salted water.

She inspected the bag of potatoes with distaste. She believed that food should not be stored in polyethylene, and always emptied her own potatoes into an earthenware crock. In the absence of anything better, she found an old wickerwork basket, which had once held a large flower display, given for Thomas's birth, and put the potatoes in that.

Then she cleaned the sink, gave the windowsill a quick wipe, and tied back the curtains properly—they had once again been left hanging loose.

A little cry from the garden summoned her. She went out and brought him indoors, decanted him from the pram, changed his diaper with quiet efficiency, and brought him downstairs again to play on the floor before the fire.

The front door slammed. Ruth looked around the door at the picture of her mother-in-law, the flickering fire, the contented baby. "I think I'll have a bath," she said, and went upstairs.

She did not come down until two minutes before Elizabeth was due to leave, at 4:58 exactly. Elizabeth rose to her feet and put on her coat as Ruth came in the room.

"Did you enjoy your walk?"

"No," Ruth said succinctly.

"You'll want me earlier tomorrow," Elizabeth reminded her. "You see your therapist tomorrow, don't you?"

"Yes."

"I'll come at one then, shall I? And don't feel you have to hurry back. I can perfectly well give him his tea."

"You are not to feed him or to bathe him or to take him out of this house," Ruth said levelly. "The agreement was that Frederick comes down in the morning and you come down in the afternoon. There were no extensions. And he is to stay here."

Elizabeth looked at the wallpaper above Ruth's bowed head. "I see no reason for any of us to be rude," she remarked.

There was a complete silence. Elizabeth savored the sense of moral victory. In a moment the girl would lift her head and apologize.

But Ruth met her eyes. "I see every reason to be rude," she

said. "You have come between me and my husband and between me and my child. You are destroying my happiness and my life."

"Oh, Ruth!" Elizabeth cried. She reached out her hand but Ruth stood motionless, unresponsive. "I am trying very, very hard to do the very best for you, and for Patrick, and for Thomas." She looked imploringly into the young determined face. "Whatever else you think, you cannot say that I am not trying to make you and Patrick happy together." Her gesture took in the comfortable sitting room, furnished in the colors she had chosen, the fire she had lit, the curtains she had hemmed. "All I have ever wanted has been your happiness," she said gently.

Ruth's expression did not change. "It's past five."

Elizabeth turned away from the flinty look in Ruth's face. "I'll come tomorrow at one," she said simply, and let herself out.

As soon as the door shut, Ruth shuddered, and pitched herself down on the floor beside Thomas. He half rolled onto his side to see her and reached out a plump little hand to her cheek. Ruth lay, smiling into his little face, enjoying his small caress.

"Ma-" Thomas said, enjoying the sound.

Ruth hardly dared breathe.

"Ma-" Thomas said again.

"Yes," Ruth said firmly. "I am."

❦

The next day Elizabeth was on time, as always, but Thomas was not ready for her. He had eaten well at lunchtime, and Ruth had not been able to hurry him. When Elizabeth walked into the kitchen without knocking, Ruth was on her hands and knees picking up dropped food from the floor beneath the high chair and Thomas was spooning a jar of apple puree into his face and around his smiling mouth.

"How lovely to see him eating so well," Elizabeth said. She picked up the jar and checked the ingredients. There was no added sweetener, which was the only thing in its favor, she thought. "You run along," she went on. "I'll clear up here."

Ruth hesitated. It was clearly nonsensical to tell Elizabeth not to change Thomas's clothes when his shirt was liberally smeared with dinner and his hair full of apple puree.

"Go on," Elizabeth urged. "I can cope."

Ruth went out into the hall and put on her old black reefer jacket. Elizabeth noted that the new coat—the Christmas present—had not appeared. "Anything you would like me to do for supper?" Elizabeth asked brightly. "Then you can be back late; you don't want to have to rush."

"It will take me half an hour to get to Bath, an hour's appointment, half an hour home again, and maybe ten minutes for delays," Ruth said. "I'll be home by half past three. I don't need any help." She paused. "And I would rather you did not peel potatoes. Patrick does them when he comes in."

Elizabeth gave a small sigh, and then picked up Thomas. "Let's go and wave good-bye to Mummy," she said cheerfully, and took him to the sitting-room window.

As Ruth's car drove away, Elizabeth looked around the room. The grate had not been cleaned, it was filled with ashes. There was a cup of coffee left on the floor by one of the chairs. The sofa cushions had been put on back to front, there were newspapers on the floor beside Patrick's chair, and the room needed dusting. "Lots to do!" she said happily to Thomas. "I don't know what kind of state your mummy would get into if I wasn't here."

She climbed up the stairs with him against her shoulder. There were wet and soiled clothes in the nursery laundry bag. Elizabeth stripped Thomas, changed his diaper, and put the dirty clothes in the bag. Then she dressed him in the clothes that were her favorites—a strong bright blue for a boy—and took him, and the laundry bag, downstairs again. She just had the washing in, and was tying back the curtains in the kitchen windows, when the telephone rang.

"Hello, Mother," Patrick said. "How are things?"

"Fairly well," she said cautiously. "She's not getting the laundry done, and the house needs a bit of attention, but she seems to have been all right with Thomas today. He was having lunch when I arrived—just jars, of course."

"I was calling to say I have to be late," Patrick said. "I can't get home before half past seven."

"What would you like us to do?"

He hesitated. "I'm not sure. Ideally, I'd like you to have Thomas for the evening, really. His dinnertime and then bathtime and bedtime are a lot for Ruth to manage on her own."

"Of course we can," she said sweetly. "I'll take him home now, and Ruth can come up for dinner. You could both come. We'll put Thomas to bed in the nursery, and Frederick can bring him down in the morning."

Again Patrick hesitated. "Don't you think she would resent it? How is she with you?"

Elizabeth laughed her assured happy laugh. "Oh, my dear! She's in such a rage with us that none of us can do anything right. But it is the right thing for Thomas and that must be the only thing we are thinking of. I'll take him up to the farmhouse now, shall I?"

"Leave her a note," Patrick reminded her. "Tell her that I called and said I would be late, and that I'll come and collect her at seven-thirty, and we'll come on to dinner with you. But we'll bring Thomas back. We can take him home in his carry cot."

"Oh, don't take him out in the cold night air!"

"No," Patrick said firmly. "I know that she won't want him to stay at the farm without us. He'll come home with us. It won't hurt the once."

"I'll make a steak and Guinness pie," his mother promised. "And I guarantee—no black-eyed potatoes!"

"You must teach me how to cook," Patrick said, smiling. "I blame you for spoiling me."

Elizabeth went around the house, checking that everything was right for Ruth's return. She laid the fire in the sitting room and whisked a duster around the more obvious surfaces. She grimaced at the little room. "Well, Thomas," she confided. "It's not how *we* would like it, but I suppose it will have to do until I can come down with Mrs. M. and do a thoroughly good clean."

Then she bundled Thomas into his outdoor things, strapped him in his car seat, and carried seat and baby to the car, slamming the front door behind her.

*R*uth sat in the waiting room at the therapist's house, staring blankly before her. There had been a long break over the Christmas holiday and this was her first visit since then. A very great deal seemed to have happened. Ruth felt that she could not even be sure that Clare Leesome would recognize her. She felt completely changed, as if overnight she had ceased to be a vulnerable young woman and had found inside her someone hard and cold and determined.

Clare looked reassuringly the same. She was wearing a long dark skirt and a deep red soft sweater. "Hello, Ruth," she said.

Ruth sat in the chair opposite her.

"And how are things?" Clare asked.

Ruth looked around the room, absorbing the sense of enclosed safety. It struck her that Elizabeth had never been here, never dusted the mantelpiece, never rearranged the books on the desk. The room was a refuge from Elizabeth and from the whole Cleary family.

"They are as bad as they can be," she said eventually.

Clare waited.

"Thomas had an accident, he choked on a sponge, and then he was sick out shopping and I put him in his cot without changing him because he was asleep. Patrick's mother told Patrick about the accident and that I left him to be sick—and they have insisted that Frederick visits in the morning, and Elizabeth comes in the afternoon." Ruth's composed bitter voice suddenly shook. "They don't trust me with him."

Clare nodded gravely. "How very, very dreadful for you," she said. It was the trigger for Ruth's grief. Ruth choked and then burst into tears. Through her sobs, Clare could hear her voice, as pained as a child, telling of her outrage, her loss, and her terror that they would take Thomas away from her forever.

Clare let her weep until Ruth sat up and pushed her hair away from her flushed face.

"I hadn't cried," she said. "I have been so angry."

Clare nodded. "I think anyone would feel sad and angry," she said. "You are in a very unfair situation. It is perfectly reasonable to be very unhappy and very angry."

Ruth nodded. "I don't know what to do," she said. Her voice

was still thin; she looked at Clare like a bewildered child.

"Wipe your face," Clare said gently.

Ruth looked around. There was a box of tissues on the desk. Clare did not pass them to her but gestured that she should go and fetch them. Ruth got up and walked slowly to the desk, fetched the tissues, and sat down again. She wiped her face; she felt the peace of the room penetrate her.

"I feel better now," she said, and her voice was steady again.

"What are you doing?" Clare asked.

"I am going along with it," Ruth said. "I let them come for their visits and then they go again. I've stopped running around Patrick so much and he is having to do more chores. He's not being treated like he's doing me a favor coming home anymore."

Clare smiled. "And how does he like that?" she asked.

Ruth had a sudden recollection of the surprise of her passion in bed with him. "He doesn't like the washing up," she said. "But there are compensations."

Clare, reading the inward smile, let that comment go. "And do they say when they will trust you again?"

Ruth shook her head. "Elizabeth says she will 'just know.' So I feel like I am on probation all the time."

Clare nodded. "And, of course, no one can survive that sort of inspection," she said. "People make mistakes all the time."

"Yes," Ruth said eagerly. "Of course I make mistakes with him. But I would never hurt him on purpose."

Clare paused. "But what is the grain of truth in what they are saying?" she asked. "Would you hurt him by accident? Are you careless? Do you wish you did not have to care for him all the time?"

Ruth sat silent, thinking deeply. She summoned a picture of Thomas, his bright eyes and his smiling face, the dimples of his knuckles and his knees. The plump firmness of his little feet and the perfect straightness of his toes. "Sometimes I don't want to care for him," she said honestly. "When I'm tired or hungry, and I have to see to him first before I can do anything for myself. When he comes first all the time. Sometimes I wish someone would take him away—just for an hour, so I can get something done without always waiting for him to wake up.

And then at other times it is perfectly all right." She paused. "I made a mistake with the sponge," she said. "It didn't matter. And putting him into his cot to sleep when he had been upset and sick was the right thing to do. Elizabeth made it seem awful, but she wasn't there, and she doesn't know what he was like. He had just that moment fallen asleep and I couldn't face waking him up again."

Clare waited in case there was anything more. But Ruth just looked up at her and smiled, an innocent, heartfelt smile. "I love him so much," she said simply. "I would lay my life down for him—in an instant, without even thinking about it. To suggest that I would hurt him on purpose is quite impossible."

Clare smiled back. "I think you should know that I believe that you are a very good mother," she said gently. "I think you are learning all the time how to care for Thomas, and that you are an excellent mother."

It was like a benediction. Ruth leaned back in her seat and closed her eyes. "Thank you," she breathed.

Clare nodded. "Is there anything more?" she asked.

Ruth shook her head, satisfied. "I'll hang on," she said. "I have nothing to hide. They'll see how good I am with him. They will see it."

Clare thought for a moment. "And even if they do not see," she emphasized, thinking of Patrick's careful manipulative phone call, and wondering what his mother and father were hoping and fearing and engineering, "even if they do not see, then if you are mothering Thomas to the best of your ability and keeping him safe, then no one can take him away from you."

Ruth looked at her for a moment, not as a patient in need of help but as a woman looks at another woman when she has finally understood the odds that are stacked against her. "If they really want to take him away from me, they'll do it," she said. "You don't know what they're like. They know lawyers and doctors, they even have judges as personal friends. If they want something they get it. I just have to hang on and hope that they will be satisfied with this."

*T*he traffic was bad on the return journey and Ruth did not get back to the little house until the early winter dark had fallen. She looked for the light from the windows as she turned in to the drive, but they were dark. Only the porch light was on, to light her way to the closed front door. She felt a sensation of growing terror. They had done it. They had done what she had feared they might do. They had taken Thomas. The house was deserted, and her child was gone. She turned the car carelessly in the driveway and scraped the fender. There was an expensive sound of crumpling metal and the screech of paint against the gatepost. Ruth tore open the driver's door and ran up the front path to the house.

She fumbled with the keys and flung the door open, but she knew before she stepped into the dark and silent hall that the house was empty. Thomas was not there.

For a dreadful moment she was certain that he had been injured: some accident, and Elizabeth had rushed him in her car to the hospital. "Oh, God," Ruth moaned, envisaging too clearly his face crumpled by some dreadful fall, his hair matted with blood, a twisted limb, a broken arm . . . "Oh, God."

She turned and ran from the house, out to the car again, and tore the car door open. She reversed back out into the lane, still on the same steering lock so she hit the gatepost again. This time she did not even hear the noise or feel the impact. She slammed on her headlights and stepped hard on the accelerator and stormed up the drive to the farmhouse. Frederick would know what had happened, and where they were.

In the gravel turning circle she braked and a spray of sharp gravel flew up from her wheels. There were two cars parked outside the house: Frederick's and Elizabeth's. Ruth's mind was working furiously. If Elizabeth's car was here, then she was probably here, Thomas was probably here—unless they had gone to the hospital in an ambulance.

Ruth ran across the gravel to the front door, pushed it open without knocking, and went into the hall. The sitting-room door opened.

"I thought I heard your car," Frederick said calmly. "How nice—"

She pushed him in the chest, hard and angrily, forcing him

back. She brushed past him and saw, at the fireside, Thomas, lying on his back on Patrick's old nursery play mat with Patrick's old nursery toys around him.

For a moment she simply stared at him, as if she could not believe that the horror story of her imagining was not real, as if she could not believe that this was truly her son, and his grandmother on her knees on the floor beside him, showing him things, and tickling his palms to make him laugh.

"What the hell are you doing?" Ruth cried harshly.

Elizabeth looked up. "What's the matter?"

"What the hell, what the bloody hell are you doing with my son?"

Ruth strode across the room and snatched up Thomas. He was startled and let out a little cry. Frederick at once stepped forward and then waited, very alert.

"Ruth," Elizabeth said soothingly, "Ruth, calm down."

"I told you," Ruth gabbled, spitting in her anger. "I told you he was not to be taken out of my house. I ordered you to leave him there!"

Elizabeth stretched out her hand. "I know, I know you did."

"I thought he was *dead*!" Ruth screamed at her. "I got home, I thought he was dead! I came up here to see what had happened, what dreadful, dreadful thing had happened, and here you are, having tea, playing on the floor. . . ." Ruth suddenly collapsed into sobs. Frederick instantly moved forward, and took Thomas from her. The baby let out another wail and Frederick slipped from the room with him. Ruth's knees gave way beneath her and she slumped to the floor.

"Hush, Ruth," Elizabeth said gently. "Calm down, dear."

Ruth's harsh sobs were turning into rasping breaths. She could not breathe, she could not get air. Elizabeth stood behind her, listening to her laboring for oxygen. Frederick came back into the room, without Thomas, and silently held up a key to show that Thomas was safely locked in the nursery. Elizabeth nodded and mimed a telephone, and mouthed the word "doctor." He nodded at once and withdrew.

"Shhh, Ruth, ssshhh," Elizabeth said. "Breathe, dear, don't get in such a state."

Ruth did not even hear her. She was struggling in a battle against her closing throat and her constricting chest; her harsh rasping gasps filled the pretty room.

Elizabeth could hear Frederick's low, urgent voice in the hall but Ruth heard nothing, fighting in a world of growing darkness and growing panic and growing pain.

"Drink this," Frederick said firmly. He put a cold glass in her hand and held it to her lips. Ruth gagged on the brandy and spat most of it back. Frederick held it to her mouth again and she choked and swallowed, and choked again. He knelt down beside her and gently cupped his hands over her mouth and nose. "Breathe gently," he said. "You'll be all right, breathe gently."

Slowly Ruth's breathing steadied as she stopped hyperventilating. Frederick gave her another swallow of brandy, then he helped her onto the sofa, lifted her legs up. Elizabeth propped a pillow behind her head. "There," she said, and her voice was full of pity.

"The doctor is coming to see you," Frederick said gently to Ruth. Her skin was pale and thick, like wax, he thought. "Just lie here. Have another sip of brandy."

Elizabeth slipped from the room and out to the hall, waiting for the sound of the doctor's car. She did not want to be near Ruth. She could hardly bear to see that ugly distorted face. Ruth did not fit in the pretty room, in the ordered life. Elizabeth heard Frederick's soothing murmur and the more distant whimper from the nursery, where Thomas was locked in, safely away from the anger and the tears. Then she heard the sound of the doctor's car.

She opened the front door as he was coming up the steps. "She had some kind of hysterical fit," she said softly. "She took it into her head that Thomas was dead and she came racing up here screaming and crying. Then she had a fit. Frederick is with her; she's on the sofa."

He nodded, briefly pressed her hand, and went into the sitting room.

Frederick was sitting in the chair at Ruth's head, talking to her gently, very softly, giving her little sips from the glass of brandy. Dr. MacFadden took in the scene and came toward Ruth.

"Hello," he said gently.

Vaguely she looked up at him.

"D'you know who I am?" he asked.

She looked blank. It felt as if his voice were coming from a long way away, as if it could be nothing to do with her, as if she had tumbled down a long slope into a place where nothing mattered very much anymore.

"I'm tired," she said. Her voice rasped, her throat was sore from screaming and that dreadful struggle for air.

"Would you like to sleep?" he asked. "Shall we get you into bed, and I could give you an injection and you could get some rest? You look all in."

She nodded. William MacFadden tipped his head to Frederick and the two men supported her and took her from the room. Elizabeth led the way upstairs and into the guest bedroom. The bed was made up; Elizabeth twitched off the covers.

"Just slip her shoes off and get her in," the doctor advised gently.

They laid her back on the bed as if she were a corpse, with a detached respect. Elizabeth took off the shoes and noticed the run in Ruth's tights. She pulled the cover over her.

"My bag," William MacFadden said quietly to Frederick, and then turned back to the bed. "Can you hear me, Ruth? Can you hear me?"

She turned her head on the pillow and looked at him. He thought he had never seen such a weary, tragic face. "Yes," she said softly.

"I'm going to give you an injection so you get a good night's sleep," he said, speaking clearly and strongly. "In the morning I'll come and see how you are. You'll stay here for tonight."

Her mouth formed a word. "Thomas."

He turned to Elizabeth. "What's she saying?"

Ruth tried again: "Thomas."

"I don't know," Elizabeth said.

Frederick came in with the bag and William took out an injection, wiped Ruth's bare vulnerable inside arm with antiseptic, and injected Valium into a pale blue vein.

"Thomas," Ruth whispered. "I want Thomas." And then she was asleep.

⌒ Eighteen ⌒

Patrick came home at half past seven and opened the front door with a cheerful call. "I saw the little house was in darkness, so I guessed you were all up here."

His mother shook her head, and Patrick instantly caught her gravity. "What is it?"

"It's Ruth, she had some kind of hysterical fit," she said. "She came up here, thinking Thomas was dead. I don't know exactly what she thought. We called the doctor and he sedated her, and now she is asleep upstairs. He's coming to see her again tomorrow."

He looked aghast. "What on earth was wrong?"

Elizabeth shrugged. "She went to see her therapist and then she stormed back in this terrible state."

He looked from her to his father. "I am sorry," he said helplessly. "I am sorry. You've both tried so hard . . . I am sorry."

"All part of the job," Frederick said with gruff sympathy. "And Thomas is all right."

"He's in his cot asleep," Elizabeth said. "D'you want to see him?"

Patrick nodded. "I'll go up," he said.

"Stiff gin and tonic when you come down, old man," his father said. "Doubles tonight. Bring the color back into our cheeks."

"Supper in half an hour," Elizabeth said, going toward the kitchen.

Patrick mounted the stairs slowly and opened the door to his old nursery. His mother had redecorated it for Thomas in the same wallpaper and colors that he remembered from his earliest childhood. The wallpaper was a cream background with small Winnie the Pooh bears floating, holding on to balloons, and smaller Piglets floating beside them. There was a frieze picture of more characters from the stories. The room was warm, with yellow linen curtains drawn against the dark night. It smelled faintly of clean laundry, baby powder, and, as he approached the crib, the warm, sweet smell of sleeping baby.

Patrick paused, looking down at the shadowy face of his son. A sense of great despair and unhappiness swept over him as he looked at those upcurved, untroubled eyelids and the little pout of the mouth.

"I don't know what to do," Patrick confided to the still room. "I don't know what to do for the best."

Before he went downstairs he glanced in at Ruth. She was sweating from the bedclothes piled on top of her clothes. She was lying on her back and breathing noisily, through her mouth. Hesitantly, he took off the blankets and left her with just a sheet and a counterpane. He touched her as he might touch an infected animal, warily and with distaste. The slim, demanding, erotic woman of just two nights before seemed like a dream. Ruth was sick again, he thought, and he hated sickly women.

They ate in silence. No one was very hungry. Patrick drank a good deal of red wine, and when Elizabeth went to bed early, the two men had a whisky together. Patrick slept in his old single bedroom. He did not share the guest bed with Ruth; he felt that it would be like sleeping next to a corpse.

❧

The click of the automatic central heating switching on jolted Ruth into wakefulness, and she lay for a moment in complete confusion. Her throat was sore and her mouth dry and foul; she was fully dressed and in a room she did not at once recognize. She sat up, swallowed, and then remembered that Thomas was all right, and that she had been so very afraid for him, so painfully, agonizingly, afraid.

She swung off the bed and went tiptoeing out of her room to the nursery. Thomas was in the crib, still sleeping. She could see the gentle rise and fall of his chest, and hear his soft breath and his little occasional snuffle. One hand opened, in a dream, and closed again. She watched him for several minutes, drinking in the reassurance that he was clean, dry, well, at peace, and then she turned and went back to her bedroom.

She had no clean clothes, she had no toiletries, she could not brush her hair or clean her teeth. She felt dirty and at a disadvantage, but she splashed water on her face and combed her hair with her fingers. The smooth bob fell into place but hung very limp and plain. She rubbed her teeth with a wet finger and rinsed her mouth. Then she went downstairs.

Frederick was in the kitchen in his dressing gown, sitting at the kitchen table with a pot of tea and his newspaper. He rose when he saw her, and she saw a swift uneasy look cross his face.

"I'm all right," she said abruptly.

He nodded and sat down again. "Would you like a cup of tea?"

She took a cup and saucer from the cupboard. "Yes, please."

There was an awkward silence.

"I'll make up a bottle for Thomas," Ruth said. "He'll probably wake soon."

"I can do it," Frederick offered.

"I will." Ruth turned her back to him and busied herself with measuring scoops and boiled water from the kettle.

"The doctor is coming back to see you this morning," Frederick remarked.

Ruth kept her face turned away. She had only the dimmest memory of yesterday evening. At Frederick's prompting she recalled the face of William MacFadden and her slide into silence and sleep.

"All right," she said. She glanced at Frederick. "I was frightened yesterday because the house was in darkness. Elizabeth promised me that they would be there when I came home. I had no idea what was going on."

267

"I left a note," Elizabeth said abruptly from the doorway. She was in her dressing gown, but her hair was smooth and her face was wide awake, her eyes clear. Beside her Ruth felt frowsy and unkempt. "Patrick rang to tell me that he would be home late, and that I was to bring Thomas here so that the evening would not be too much for you." She stepped forward and rested her well-manicured hand on Frederick's shoulder. "Did you not see my note? On the hall table?"

Ruth shook her head. "I didn't see it." She thought for a moment. "There was nothing on the hall table," she said certainly. "There was no note there, nothing."

Elizabeth met her gaze but did not reply.

There was a distant wail from upstairs as Thomas woke for his early morning feed. Both women reached for the bottle but Elizabeth let Ruth take it. She stepped back as the younger woman went out and nodded to Frederick. "Stay within earshot," she said softly.

He nodded, and followed Ruth up the stairs to the nursery. Briskly, Elizabeth began to lay the dining-room table for breakfast.

❧

*W*illiam MacFadden came to visit during his break from morning surgery, at eleven o'clock. Patrick had fetched Ruth's clothes from the little house, and she was dressed in a clean shirt and blue jeans. She looked young and pretty and well.

"You look a lot better," he said approvingly.

Patrick took Thomas from her and went to the bedroom door. "I'll be in the nursery if you need me," he said.

Ruth let them go. "I'm better," she said to William. "I'm fine."

"No aftereffects?"

She shook her head.

"I wonder if you should go on a course of mild sedatives," William suggested. "You do seem a little high-strung, something to make you a little more relaxed?"

Ruth looked at him. "No," she said shortly. "I've had enough of your pills."

He felt that she was blaming him, and disliked her for it. "It was a nasty panic attack you had," he said smoothly. "Distressing."

"My baby had disappeared from his home," Ruth said bitingly. "I had no idea where he was or what was happening. Of course I was afraid."

"You must have known he would be safe with your mother-in-law. . . ." Dr. MacFadden interrupted.

Ruth shot him a hard look. "No, I did not," she said.

He raised his eyebrows as if he did not want to comment, or even consider what she said.

"Is there anything I can do for you? Would you like to see me at the surgery? You could have an evening appointment so we are not at all rushed? I could refer you to a therapist?"

"No, thank you," Ruth said.

He paused for a moment longer, but the list of patients who needed to see him was on his mind, and he did not know what should be done for Ruth.

"Very well, then," he said. "I'll see myself out."

Elizabeth and Frederick were waiting for him in the hall.

"How is she?" Elizabeth asked.

"Irritable," he replied. "But she is in control of herself."

Frederick walked with him to the car. "Should we have her committed?" he asked frankly. "Get this sorted out once and for all?"

Dr. MacFadden recoiled. "She's not psychotic!"

"I don't know what she is!" Frederick gestured to Ruth's new car. The front fender, which had suffered a double blow, was crumpled beyond repair. "That's the second car she's gone through in as many months. She can't seem to manage."

"Is she at risk?"

The two men looked at the car.

"Obviously," Frederick said.

Dr. MacFadden took a deep breath. "If you want her committed for an assessment of her mental health, then I would sign the forms," he promised.

"Good man," Frederick said quietly. "I think we'd all be happier."

*U*pstairs Ruth went to find Patrick. "I should like to go home now," she said.

Patrick was dressing Thomas and had one hand inexpertly laid on Thomas's stomach while spreading cream on his bottom with the other.

"Oh!" he said.

Ruth nodded. "As soon as Thomas is dressed. I have a whole load of things I want to get done today."

"I rather thought we'd stay here, till you're completely better."

"There's nothing in the least wrong with me," Ruth said simply. "I came home last night to a dark house and my baby missing and I was terribly upset. If he had been there, as he should have been, then everything would have been all right. If you want to make sure that I am not upset, then you should let me look after my own baby."

"Hush . . ." Patrick said, glancing at the open door.

"Elizabeth had no right to take him out of the house without my permission," Ruth said as clearly as before. "And she has no right to tidy my deep freeze, or peel potatoes, or tie back my bloody kitchen curtains!"

"Everything all right up there?" Frederick called up the stairs. "Time for a cup of coffee?"

"We're just going!" Ruth called back. "I'll have coffee at home, thank you."

She stepped forward and slipped Thomas's vest over his head, and pulled his shirt on top. Thomas let out a wail of protest while she captured each foot, put on his socks and his felt slippers. She picked him up and carried him downstairs.

"If you're sure . . . ," Elizabeth said. She glanced at Patrick, coming down the stairs behind Ruth. He shrugged.

"Frederick will pop down at midday," Elizabeth suggested. "And I'll come down this afternoon."

"On one condition," Ruth specified. They were all wary of her.

"What is that?" Frederick asked.

"That Thomas is never, never to be taken out of my house, without my express permission."

270

Elizabeth prompted Patrick with a glance.

"But, Ruth, that was my idea, not Mother's," he said. "I rang and said I would be late. It was my idea that we should all come up here for dinner, to save you the bother of coping with Thomas on your own and cooking dinner."

"I am a wife and mother," Ruth said, laying claim to titles she would have despised a year earlier. "I am a wife and mother and I have a job to do. I have to care for Thomas and I have to manage our house. If I can't do it, I'll get help. I'll hire help. But I won't have people continually interfering. Thomas is to stay at home."

There was a silence; they all looked down the stairs toward Frederick. "For a trial period of one week," he said carefully. "And if there is another upset, or any cause for concern at all, then we will reconsider."

Ruth, holding Thomas under her chin, met his gaze. "What d'you mean?"

"If there is another upset, then you will have to seek treatment," Frederick said frankly.

For a moment he thought she had not heard him, her face was so blank. "Treatment?" she said. "I'm not ill."

"That is not for you to judge," Frederick said simply. "You are not qualified to judge. Neither am I; none of us are. But if things do not get better we'll call in the experts."

"You want me to go back to Springfield House?" she asked incredulously.

Frederick shook his head. "A closed hospital," he said quietly.

Ruth's breath came out in a little hiss. "You're planning to have me committed," she said slowly. "You're planning to call me a loony and send me to a loony bin."

Elizabeth and Patrick recoiled at the words but Frederick never wavered. "If that's how you want to describe it," he said steadily. "I have the power to do it, Ruth. Any close family member, with a doctor's agreement, can do it."

She nodded, saying nothing. Her eyes met his, but he saw from the dark dilation of her pupils that she saw nothing. "I know," she said softly. "I know you have the power."

They were all silent for a moment, as if they were all aghast at how far they had come.

271

"I don't want to do it," Frederick said gently.

She nodded again. "I believe you," she said. "I believe that you would do it very reluctantly and sadly."

"I will only do it if it is my duty: to keep Thomas safe, and to keep you safe."

She focused her shocked eyes on his face. "And those are your only criteria?" She glanced toward Elizabeth. "Thomas's safety? Not what anyone else says about me? Not whether I'm good enough—or not?"

"No," he said steadily. "Your safety and Thomas's safety are the only criteria."

She breathed out again, and came slowly down the stairs. "Very well," she said. "I understand what I am facing."

Slowly she walked past him to the front door. He opened the door for her and she walked past him, without a word of thanks, without turning her head. Patrick followed her and got into his car, while Ruth put Thomas into the baby seat in her car.

"What was this?" Frederick asked, pointing to the crumpled fender.

For a moment she looked blank, then she said abruptly: "It doesn't matter. It doesn't matter at all," and she got in the car, started the engine, and drove steadily away.

Elizabeth caught a glimpse of her son's set face as he too drove past. He raised a hand to them, and followed Ruth's car down the drive.

❦

*I*n the little house things were incongruously normal. The heating was on and the house, thanks to Elizabeth's tidying, looked smart and welcoming. Ruth was taking off Thomas's coat in the hall when Patrick came in.

"There's no note," she said abruptly.

Patrick looked at the hall table, where his mother said she had left a note for Ruth. It was empty.

"There must be," he said.

Ruth looked at him but said nothing. "Are you going to work now?"

"If you can manage." Patrick glanced at his watch. "I won't be late tonight, especially if I can get in now."

"I can manage."

He paused at the front door. "Are you sure?" he asked.

She nodded, her face blank. "Your father is supervising me this morning, and she's coming this afternoon, and you'll be home by six. I won't ever have more than an hour on my own with my son, if that's what you want."

"You know it's not what we want!" he exclaimed, but broke off. "We'll talk tonight," he promised, hoping that they would not have to talk. "We'll have a good long talk tonight."

He kissed her gently on the side of her face. To his surprise she turned and kissed him back, on the mouth. He tasted the slightly sweet warmth of her breath. There was a promise in the kiss; Patrick felt desire.

"It's not me that needs to get back to normality," Ruth said quietly. "Think about it, Patrick. It might be the rest of you."

When Elizabeth came down at two o'clock she rang the front doorbell, as she had been told to do. Ruth, who had dropped the latch to prevent Elizabeth's walking in, took her time opening the door, and when she saw Elizabeth she turned and went back to the kitchen, where Thomas was sitting in his high chair, watching his mother, and hammering a spoon on the tray.

"As you know, there was no note," Ruth said over her shoulder. She was frying chopped meat on the stove. Elizabeth watched as the little droplets of hot grease spattered on the range and Ruth did not wipe them up.

"I beg your pardon?"

"There was no note to tell me where Thomas was. You said you had left a note but you did not."

Elizabeth suppressed a small sigh, put down her handbag and went back out to the hall. In a few minutes she came back in holding a folded sheet of paper. "It had fallen down behind the hall table," she said. "But I am surprised you did not see it on the floor."

Ruth peremptorily took it and read it. It was very clear and very reassuring. She handed it back to Elizabeth without comment.

"Has he had a sleep today?" Elizabeth asked.

"No," Ruth said. She took the frying pan over to the sink and drained the fat off the meat, letting it run down the drain. Elizabeth bit her lip on the advice that Ruth would get blocked drains if she poured melted fat down them.

"I will sponge his face and hands and change him and give him a rock in the garden then," Elizabeth offered. "It's quite warm in the sun."

Ruth nodded. "I'm going down to the village to get some tomato puree," she said. "Remember that he is to be here when I come back. Whatever Patrick says. Whatever anyone says."

Elizabeth nodded, and lifted Thomas out of his high chair. Ruth had again not fastened his safety straps.

⌇~ Nineteen ~⌇

*T*he following day was Saturday, and Patrick did not go in
to work. They had a cautious weekend together. Patrick
suggested Sunday lunch at the farm, but Ruth gave him a look
that was a clear refusal. Instead, he took Thomas up to the
farmhouse after lunch and brought him back in the evening.
Ruth slept away the afternoon.

When the routine of the week started again, nothing
changed. Elizabeth and Ruth spoke less and less at arrival and
departure, but Elizabeth did not touch things in Ruth's kitchen,
or do her chores. Ruth waited, without much hope, for someone, Frederick or Patrick, to acknowledge that the house was
well run, that the child was well and happy, and that she no
longer need be supervised.

When Thursday came, and Ruth had an appointment with her
therapist, she found that Patrick had taken the afternoon off work
and was going to drive her in to Bath and back out again in the
evening. "Or we could stop for a drink if you like," he suggested.

"Why?"

"Because of last week," he said shortly.

"I was upset last week because Elizabeth took Thomas out of
the house without my permission and without telling me
where they had gone," Ruth repeated steadily.

"She left a note," he said.

"She *says* she left a note."

He looked at her with open dislike. "I hardly think my mother is likely to lie," he said.

Ruth got into Patrick's car and slammed the door. "Oh, don't you," she said under her breath.

Her session with Clare Leesome was uneasy. Toward the end, Clare asked her: "Are you feeling angry, Ruth?" and saw from the swift, direct look that Ruth was too furious to speak; even to her.

"Not particularly," Ruth said unhelpfully.

At the end of the session Ruth said, "I don't think I will come again. I think I should finish now."

Clare's face showed nothing but interest and concern. "Do you think so?" she asked.

"Yes," Ruth said. "As long as I am coming here, then they have something on me. It reminds them that I was ill. They say 'visiting your therapist' as if I was completely mad. They can use it against me."

Clare nodded. "You could see me and not tell them," she suggested.

Ruth thought for a moment and shook her head. "She would find out," she said. "She reads my diary, she would check the odometer on the car, she knows everything."

Clare privately thought that it was unlikely that anyone would go that far, but she said nothing. "I think your main concern should be whether you feel you have finished working with me," she said gently. "Not what anyone else may think about you."

Ruth stood up. "Nothing matters more than that I keep Thomas," she said flatly. "Seeing you is jeopardizing that. So I'm going to stop seeing you. If things ever get better, I may telephone and ask to come back." She picked up her handbag. "Thank you," she said shortly. "You've been very helpful."

"I cannot ask you to stay," Clare said quickly. "But it is not a choice between seeing me and keeping Thomas. Anyone would understand that it is a sign of good health for you to work through your feelings with a therapist. No one would take a child away from a mother who was a progressing patient."

Ruth shook her head, and went to the door. "They will if they want to," she said flatly. "So thank you. Good-bye."

I 've stopped seeing my therapist," Ruth said baldly, when they got home. Thomas was in his high chair eating squares of toasted cheese. Elizabeth poured Patrick a cup of tea.

Elizabeth and Patrick exchanged a swift alarmed look.

"Why?" Patrick asked.

"Because I don't need a therapist anymore. I am completely cured of depression," Ruth said briskly.

Elizabeth hesitated. "But you are still—sometimes—very unhappy, Ruth," she said cautiously.

"Oh, yes," Ruth said with open dislike. "I'm very, very unhappy, and I am very angry with the situation that you, the three of you, have put me in. But none of that needs therapy. What is needed is that the situation change."

Elizabeth turned and unfastened the curtains from the tie-backs and drew them against the darkening sky.

"It will change," Patrick said reassuringly. "Everything will change as soon as you are completely relaxed and on top of things."

"And when do you think that will be?" Ruth challenged him, but she was looking at Elizabeth. "Next month? February?"

"Oh, for sure," Patrick said. "February."

B ut February came and went and still Frederick arrived for an hour every morning and Elizabeth for two hours every afternoon. It was very cold and misty, and they played with Thomas in the sitting room while Ruth tidied the rest of the house, or did the ironing, or cooked Patrick's supper. There was not enough for her to do to fill three hours every day. Elizabeth suggested that she make matching cushion covers for the sofa, and promised her some wonderful material, and the loan of her sewing machine. Ruth looked blank. "We have cushions already," she said.

Ruth's antagonism solidified and settled in the four weeks in which it became apparent that nothing would ever change.

Thomas had been adopted into his grandparents' routine, and Ruth had to go along with the rhythm of their lives, however empty and truncated it left her own.

As the weather improved in March, Frederick took Thomas for longer walks up the drive. One day they were caught by a sudden shower of rain and he took shelter in the farmhouse, telephoned Ruth to say that they were in the dry, and he would bring Thomas back as soon as the shower lifted. Thomas stayed for lunch at the farmhouse that day, and Elizabeth brought him back in the afternoon. Frederick's hour in the morning imperceptibly extended to two, and Elizabeth lingered on in the afternoons. Ruth found that she was gradually excluded from Thomas's play times and wakeful times. He woke her in the early mornings, at about seven o'clock, and she had the task of trying to dress a protesting and growing baby, and feed him his breakfast. But when he had eaten and was sponged clean and all smiles, it was Frederick who took him out for a walk and pointed out catkins and the early snowdrops. When Frederick brought him home he was either asleep or grouchy and hungry and Ruth had the task of feeding him, changing his diaper, and laying him down for his nap. When Elizabeth arrived, he was generally still in the garden sleeping, and when he woke he was all smiles. Elizabeth had the relaxed afternoon playtime; when she left at between four and five o'clock, he was starting to get tired and hungry again. From five till bath time was his worst period of the day. Hungry but refusing to eat; tired, but it was too early for his bath and bed. The two or three hours until Patrick came home were the most onerous and least satisfactory of the day, and Ruth coped with them alone and unaided, after a boring, lonely day on her own.

"If she would only ask for help," Elizabeth sighed to Frederick. She had telephoned to check the arrangements for tomorrow and had heard Thomas wailing lustily in the background and banging his spoon on his plate. "I can manage that baby with one hand tied behind my back."

"She only has him for a couple of hours," Frederick said. "You would have thought she could have managed that."

Elizabeth did not explain that Ruth's couple of hours were

always the busiest and most stressful hours of the day. She just smiled. "I would have hoped so," she said.

During the days Ruth did not have enough to do. She wrote a couple of proposals for programs for Radio Westerly, but they rejected one without even discussing it, and the other she lost heart in, and threw away. She started to practice cookery and bought herself a couple of books of menus. When the weather grew warmer in March, she tried to take an interest in the garden.

But always, over her shoulder, was the knowledge that her mother-in-law knew far better what should be done. Elizabeth would pop into the kitchen while Ruth was kneading pastry, with flour spilled on the floor and smeared against her sweater where she had leaned against the worktop, and she would smile and say, "Gracious! What are you making! Enough to feed an army?" and go back to Thomas, leaving Ruth to realize that she had got the quantities wrong, and that the huge lump of pastry would go to waste.

When Ruth was weeding on her hands and knees on the damp lawn, Thomas sleeping in his pram beside her, Elizabeth arrived through the back gate, leaned over the pram to see her grandson, and then turned to Ruth.

"Those aren't weeds, darling," she said helpfully. "They're dwarf asters. You'd better put them back in again."

Ruth looked at the huge pile of plants she had spent an hour digging up.

"Oh, dear," said Elizabeth. "And those are daffodil bulbs, which shouldn't have been disturbed. I don't think you'll get a lot to flower now."

"I'll put them back," Ruth said grimly.

"Let me help. Thomas is still asleep," Elizabeth offered. "I'll get some gloves."

"I'll do it," Ruth said.

Elizabeth laughed. "You do like to learn the hard way!" she exclaimed and went inside the house, leaving Ruth to the cold soil and the muddy lawn, and the pile of wilting plants. Ruth could see the kitchen curtains move as Elizabeth tied them back in the right way.

Ruth no longer protested at Elizabeth's tidying of her house. It was easier to find things in the freezer when they were all on labeled shelves. It was more convenient with small things at the front of the larder. The curtains did look prettier tied back. The only habit Elizabeth still maintained that Ruth still hated was the casual way that she entered the house through the garden gate, checked on the baby, and then came in through the backdoor with a casual "Hello!"

If Ruth locked the backdoor—which meant locking the pram outside—Elizabeth checked Thomas in the pram and then strolled around to the front door and tried it. If it was locked, she might ring the bell or she might open it with her own key. She had no sense at all that the little house was not her own property, that she should await an invitation to enter. When Ruth complained to Patrick, he merely shrugged and said, "Well, they *do* own it legally, darling." When she asked Elizabeth to use the front door, and to leave the pram in the back garden alone, Elizabeth just laughed and said, "But I do so love to see him asleep."

Ruth did not complain to Frederick. In the months that passed between his warning that he would take Thomas away from her, she took great care not to offend Frederick, and to deny Elizabeth nothing. She never forgot that she was living at home, and caring for her son, with their permission.

⤞⤝

In March and April the daffodils came out. As Elizabeth had predicted, Ruth had spoiled the show in the back garden, but the ones at the farmhouse were superb. Elizabeth brought armfuls down every day and filled the little house with them. She walked across the fields on every fine day, and came in the back gate. Ruth would watch her from one of the bedroom windows, her light step, her carefree proprietorial glance at their fields, at their hedges, at their drive, and then at their little house. Ruth's hands would tighten as she watched Elizabeth come into the garden, and then, every time, every single time, Elizabeth would lean over the pram, rocking the handle slightly with her hand, and whisper to Thomas as he lay asleep.

One time Ruth ran downstairs and flung open the kitchen door as Elizabeth turned to the house. "I've asked you a thousand times to leave the pram alone!" she snapped.

Elizabeth was quite unmoved. "I just like to say hello," she said.

"Why do you have to speak to him?" Ruth demanded. "You do it every time."

Elizabeth walked past her, fetched a vase, and filled it with water for the flowers. "I just say hello," she said pleasantly. It was as if she did not care what her daughter-in-law thought, as if Ruth's anger and resentment were as much a part of an otherwise agreeable world as clouds and late frosts.

"The grass will need cutting as soon as the daffodils have died back," Elizabeth said. "And the daffodils will need a little feed. I'll ask Frederick to bring down the mower, and I have some fertilizer ready to do our daffodils."

"We can buy our own mower," Ruth said at once.

Elizabeth laughed again. "Don't be so absurd!" she said. "We hardly use it, it's just a little electric mower for the front lawn around the roses, but it will do your patch of lawn. Frederick can mow it for you when he comes down."

"I will do it," Ruth said stubbornly.

Elizabeth turned. "Are you quite well, Ruth?" she asked with concern. "You seem rather irritable. Should you have a little rest this afternoon?"

Ruth looked from her mother-in-law's radiant face to the bright yellow trumpets of the daffodils and back to Elizabeth's unwavering smile. "I'm going shopping," she said sulkily.

"Don't hurry back!" Elizabeth called. "We'll be fine!"

❧

Frederick brought down the mower in his car the next day. "This is not to be used until I've put a trip switch on the cable," he said. "I had no idea that I'd ever used it without one. With a trip switch, if you slice the cable by accident, then the power cuts out and you don't get a shock."

"Would it be a bad shock?" Ruth asked.

"Oh! Quite lethal!" Frederick said cheerfully. "You'd get the full two hundred and forty volts! That'd make your hair stand on end! A number of people die every year. But the trip switch will do it. I'll pop into Bath and buy one this afternoon when Elizabeth is with you."

"She doesn't have to come down," Ruth said. "You could go to Bath together."

He looked away. "It's how she likes it," he said briefly. "We're in a nice routine now."

"But when will it change?" Ruth pressed him. "You can't want to come down every morning and afternoon, and all through the summer as well! When will it change?"

He picked up the mower and went toward the little shed at the side of the garden. "When he goes to school, I suppose," he threw over his shoulder. "When he's off our hands, a bit."

"School?" Ruth repeated blankly.

Thomas, who had been kicking his feet in his pram, struggled to sit up and gave a little shout. Frederick instantly came out of the garden shed and took hold of the pram. "We'll go up the lane and see if we can see some birds' nests," he promised. He reached behind the baby and propped him up, so that he could see the passing scenery. He tipped his hat to Ruth. "See you later, my dear," he said.

"Do you and Patrick and Elizabeth think that we are going on like this forever?" Ruth demanded. "Until Thomas is old enough to go to school? For four years?"

Frederick maneuvered the pram out through the back gate and gave her a smile. "Why not?" he asked. "It suits us all so very well."

Ruth put a hand out to delay him. "Am I never to have my baby to myself?"

His smile was kind. "Steady the Buffs," he said comfortably. "Let's not get dramatic. We're doing very nicely as we are."

Ruth's hand dropped from his sleeve, and she stepped back and watched him go up the drive, pushing Thomas's pram, and chatting to him. She thought that she would stand thus, by the garden gate, watching her son taken away from her, every day for four years. Then, when he was old enough to go to school, it would not be the school of her choice; and she would not be waiting for him at the school gate every afternoon. He would be sent to a school that Patrick and his parents preferred, and several times a week they would collect him. Most likely, it would be Patrick's old school, where his mother and father were still friends with the staff. When Thomas was seven—or at the very latest eleven years old—they would send him to boarding school, Patrick's old school, and she would not see him at all, from one holiday to another. He would never be her little boy, just as he had never been her baby.

Up the lane, every now and then Frederick would stop the pram and hold a leaf for Thomas to see, or incline the pram so that the baby could peep into the hedge. Ruth felt as if they might never come back to her, as if Thomas was slowly, slowly going away, and that nothing she could do, neither rage nor docility, would regain him. As Frederick said, it was a routine that suited them all very well. Ruth could see that nothing would change it.

She turned away from the garden gate and went into the garden. In one corner was the new garden shed, where Patrick kept his new tool kit—a moving-in present from his father. She took out a large reel of extension cable, and took it to the kitchen. Carefully, she took the screwdriver and removed the set of sockets from the end of it, leaving the cables bare. Two cables she wrapped in insulating tape. One—the brown live-power cable—she held with the pliers and cut and stripped the insulation away to expose a good length of copper wires. Then she put the cable and the tool box out of sight, in the cupboard under the stairs.

When Frederick brought Thomas home she smiled and thanked him for taking Thomas for his walk, lifted the baby from the pram, and showed Frederick out of the house. She gave Thomas his lunch and laid him down to sleep—not in his pram, but in his cot. Thomas watched the mobile hanging from his nursery ceiling, and fell asleep.

When his eyes closed and his breathing was steady and regular, she went down to the garden, plugged in Frederick's mower, and mowed two and a half rows, taking great care with the cable. She stopped mowing the grass at the point where the pram was usually left for Thomas's afternoon nap, and then she unplugged the mower and took it back to the shed. She wheeled the empty pram out into the garden, placing it where the cut grass abruptly ended, and bundled the blankets, so it looked as if a baby were asleep inside.

Ruth stepped back to admire the illusion of a sleeping baby in the pram, then she went back into the house and fetched the extension cable from under the stairs. She took the stripped live wire, twisted it around the shiny chrome frame of the pram, and then spooled the cable out, running it back toward the house, in through the backdoor, and plugged it into the socket at the kitchen worktop, but left it switched off. She went back out to the garden and looked again at the pram. The cable was almost completely hidden by the long uncut grass and by the drooping leaves of the dying daffodils. Ruth picked up handfuls of leaves and mown grass and scattered them along the line of the cable until it could not be seen from any angle.

She went to the garden shed and unwound the bright orange cable of the electric mower. She took down a pair of garden shears from the hook Frederick had made for them. Two yards from the end of the cable of the mower she snipped it cleanly in half and examined the cut. It was a good clean cut, as a mower running at full speed would make.

She left it in the shed and went back out to the garden, checking the run of the cable once again, and the connection with the pram. She went into the house and switched on. She realized she was holding her breath, waiting for something to happen, as if she would be able to see the lethal 240 volts snaking down the cable to the pram. She took up Frederick's gift to Patrick of the live-wire tester and went out to the pram. Half thinking that none of this was real, and certain that none of it would work, she laid the metal end of the little screwdriver on the pram. At once the red bulb in the handle lit up. The pram was live.

Ruth went back to the house and flicked off the switch. It was five minutes to two. Elizabeth would arrive at any moment.

"It's up to her," Ruth said. Her mouth was curiously stiff, as if her body, like her consciousness, was slowly solidifying, freezing into horror at what she was doing. "It's not up to me, it's completely up to her."

The garden gate banged. Through the window Ruth saw Elizabeth walk in the garden gate without invitation, as she always did, looking around her with pleasure, as she always did, at her garden and her house. She strolled up to the pram, put both hands on the pram handle, and leaned in, as she had been asked—so many times—not to do.

"There you are, then," Ruth remarked inconsequentially, and switched on.

There was a sudden movement as Elizabeth was flung several feet backward from the pram. Her legs kicked, her arms flailed, and then she was still: completely still.

With dreamlike slowness Ruth unplugged the extension cable and wound it up toward the pram. The live wire had seared a small dark mark on the metal. Ruth rubbed it with her finger. It hardly showed. She took the cable to the garden shed, and tried to rewire the set of sockets on the end. Her hands were useless: they were trembling too much, and her fingers were slack and uncontrollable. She pushed the wires into the sockets and left them till later. She took the electric mower out of the shed and put it precisely at the end of the cut grass, where the pram had been. She wheeled the pram into the house. There were a few tiny grass clippings that had come in on the wheels. Ruth got down on her hands and knees and cleaned the wheels of the pram, and wiped the floor from hall to backdoor, to catch every single spot of green.

She went back out to the garden. Elizabeth was lying where she had fallen; Ruth did not even look at her. She put the severed mower cable under the still blade of the mower, and ran the rest of the cable into the house and plugged it in.

She looked around the kitchen. Everything was back in its place, where it should be. Only then did she walk cautiously out to the garden and look into Elizabeth's face, as she lay on her back in the grass.

Elizabeth gazed up at Ruth's. Ruth recoiled with an

exclamation of horror. Elizabeth had seen this, had seen all of it, had lain there, watching. Ruth fell back, but Elizabeth did not rise up from the grass and come, accusingly, after her. She lay as she had fallen, her hands clenched as they had been wrenched from the pram handle, her palms scalded. Ruth stepped a little closer again. Elizabeth's open eyes were sightless. The woman was dead. Ruth stared down into Elizabeth's blanched face as if, at the end, there might have been some reconciliation. She paused for no more than a moment, then she screamed, as loudly as she could, and raced back into the house. She snatched up the phone and telephoned 999. The operator was calm, Ruth babbled about an accident, her mother-in-law cutting the grass, and managed to give the address. Then she telephoned Frederick at the farmhouse. The phone rang and rang before he answered.

"Ruth!" he said. "I was just getting the car out to go to Bath. . . ."

"Come at once! Oh, come at once!" She was weeping, hysterical.

"Is it Thomas? What have you done?"

At that one question Ruth felt a leap of extraordinary, liberating joy. Frederick's first thought had been that she might have hurt her child. "No! No!" she said, her voice high and light. "It's Mother! It's Mother!"

He slammed down the phone and she pictured him running to the car. In moments he was pulling up at the front door and running up the path.

"She got the mower out before I could stop her!" Ruth exclaimed. "I was upstairs and I came running downstairs as soon as I heard the noise of the mower. But when I got out there it was—"

She broke off, Frederick brushed past her into the garden, flung himself down beside his dead wife. Ruth, very still, watched from the kitchen window as he gathered her into his arms and held her very close. Then Ruth sighed and turned away. Very carefully and tidily, she started to tie back the kitchen curtains as they ought to be.

*T*here had to be an inquest. Ruth gave her evidence in a thin, shocked voice, and Frederick and Patrick sat on either side of her and held her hand.

The funeral was a few days later, the village church filled with mourners and bright with spring flowers, as Elizabeth would have wanted. The arrangements were not quite as she would have done them, but Ruth was learning from one of the flower rota ladies how they should be done.

The lunch was provided by a catering company, although Ruth had wanted to do it all herself. She had supervised the layout of the buffet, and it was Ruth who had insisted that they change the paper napkins for proper linen ones.

When everyone had gone home, Ruth and Patrick did not want to leave Frederick alone in the echoing house. "We'll stay tonight," Ruth decided. "I'll make a quiche and salad, and we'll all have an early night."

Next morning Elizabeth's cleaning lady, Mrs. M., came in as usual, and had to come to Ruth for instructions. Together they cleared and cleaned the dining room of the remains of the buffet, and dusted and vacuumed the drawing room. Together they put fresh sheets on the upstairs beds, while Thomas struggled along the floor, practicing crawling. Ruth sent Patrick down to the little house to pack their clothes for a stay of several days. "We can't leave your father on his own," she said. "And I have so much to do here."

When Patrick came back there was a light lunch on the table, and Ruth and Frederick were having a glass of sherry while Mrs. M. fed Thomas in the kitchen.

"I should go in to work this afternoon," Patrick said hesitantly. "Unless you need me here?"

Ruth shook her head. "Will you be home at six?" she asked.

Patrick nodded.

"Dinner at eight then," she said.

Patrick kissed her cheek and felt her breath warm against his ear.

He came home on time and heard Thomas splashing in the bath while his grandfather supervised. Ruth came out of the kitchen wearing his mother's apron, carrying two glasses of gin and tonic with ice and lime.

"Will you take one up to Frederick?" she asked. "He's standing in for you!"

Patrick took the two iced glasses without a word. This was a new Ruth; he did not want to comment until he had the measure of her.

"I'll come up in a moment," she promised. "I just have to turn the joint. We're having roast beef tonight."

Frederick and Patrick together persuaded Thomas out of the bath and into his pajamas, then Ruth appeared with his nighttime bottle and rocked him to sleep. When she came down again, it was ten to eight and dinner was ready. Frederick carved the meat. It was perfectly done.

~ *Twenty* ~

They agreed to stay for a fortnight, until Frederick should be able to cope on his own. But when Patrick mentioned at breakfast one morning that they should return to the little house, Ruth shrugged.

"It seems so convenient," she said. "If Father wants us, that is?"

Frederick smiled, spooning homemade marmalade onto his plate. "No doubt about that," he said. "But I'll understand if you want to get back. I'll have to adapt, that's all."

"No, why?" Ruth interrupted charmingly. "There's so much to do here, Patrick, you don't know the half of it. There's the garden to see to, and the house, and the baking, and the flowers. I don't think I can possibly manage it, coming up every day."

"I don't mind at all," Patrick said uncertainly. "I thought you'd want to go home, that's all, to our house."

She poured him another cup of fresh coffee. "I never really liked it," she said dismissively.

"It is a bit cramped," Frederick acknowledged.

"And I can't possibly run two houses. . . ."

"Do you want to stay here?" Patrick demanded.

She slid him a look from under half-closed eyelids. "If Father wants us," she said. "I should have thought it was the ideal solution."

"But what about . . ." Patrick broke off. "You know, not crowding each other—a bit of privacy."

"I had a thought about that," Frederick said. "It struck me that Ruth might be thinking along these lines, and I was wondering about moving into your old bedroom, Patrick, at the end of the corridor. You two could have the master bedroom with the bathroom beside it, make a little suite for yourself in there."

"Yes," Ruth said simply. "That's what I thought too. I know an architect who can come and have a look at it, whenever we like. And we need to redecorate upstairs anyway; it really is getting rather shabby. We could do it all at once."

"Not more decorating," Patrick groaned in mock horror.

Ruth did not even smile. "I know exactly what I want," she said. "I know exactly how I want everything done, and I have a box of the most beautiful curtain material just crying out to be used."

METAPHYSICS
AND
OPPRESSION

STUDIES IN CONTINENTAL THOUGHT

John Sallis, general editor

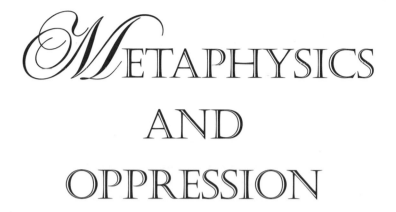

METAPHYSICS AND OPPRESSION

Heidegger's Challenge to Western Philosophy

John McCumber

INDIANA UNIVERSITY PRESS   BLOOMINGTON & INDIANAPOLIS

THIS BOOK IS A PUBLICATION OF

INDIANA UNIVERSITY PRESS
601 NORTH MORTON STREET
BLOOMINGTON, INDIANA 47404-3797 USA

WWW.INDIANA.EDU/~IUPRESS

TELEPHONE ORDERS 800-842-6796
FAX ORDERS 812-855-7931
E-MAIL ORDERS IUPORDER@INDIANA.EDU

LIBRARY OF CONGRESS CATALOGING-IN-PUBLICATION DATA

MCCUMBER, JOHN.
METAPHYSICS AND OPPRESSION : HEIDIGGER'S CHALLENGE TO
WESTERN PHILOSOPHY / JOHN MCCUMBER.
P.   CM. — (STUDIES IN CONTINENTAL THOUGHT)
INCLUDES BIBLIOGRAPHICAL REFERENCES (P.) AND INDEX.
ISBN 0-253-33473-X (ALK. PAPER). — ISBN 0-253-21316-9
(PBK. : ALK. PAPER)
1. HEIDEGGER, MARTIN, 1889-1976. 2. METAPHYSICS—HISTORY.
3. POLITICAL PERSECUTION—HISTORY. I. TITLE. II. SERIES.
B3279.H49M3754   1999
193—DC21   98-45926

1 2 3 4 5   04 03 02 01 00 99

UNOKATESTVÉREMNEK *Jánka Schwarznák*

ABBAN A REMÉNYBEN, HOGY TALÁN EGYSZER
TALÁKOZNI FOGUNK.

CONTENTS

CONTENTS

ACKNOWLEDGMENTS

Every great teacher is a great student, for teaching is merely the last touch on study. It has been my good fortune to have studied with three great teachers/students of Heidegger: Stephen Erickson, Graeme Nicholson, and Reiner Schürmann. They are as different from each other as philosophers can be. Yet each makes Heidegger a central point of philosophical reference, and each makes freedom a *Leitmotif* of his thought. It is simply impossible to study with these teachers and remain content with any of the caricatures of Heidegger current in today's academic world—or with the caricatures of freedom that dominate the so-called real world. For their most basic lesson, to me, is that philosophy is the committed struggle of a human individual and must renew itself, every day, from the ground up.

In addition, this book has incurred many other debts. I can mention only a few of them here: T. David Brent, Walter Brogan, Tina Chanter, Rebecca Comay, Janet Rabinowitch, Jeff Rice and Great Expectations Bookstore, and the Unicorn Historical Perspectives Working Group. I had two departmental chairs during the writing of this book, and am deeply indebted to them: Géza von Molnár and Kenneth Seeskin. I owe a very special debt, in this matter as in many others, to John Sallis.

My thanks to you all on behalf of this book—and my apologies to you all for its inadequacies.

PROEM

I never met my cousin Janka Schwarz, never even saw her picture. She lived in the city of Arad, in Romania, and I knew her only from the letters which she sent a couple of times a year to her American relatives. My Uncle Bob would read them ceremoniously at Eisner family gatherings. "Now, I've had a letter from Janka," he would say, and we would all gather round while he extricated it from the inside left breast pocket of the blue suit he always wore for Serious Occasions. Then he would intone the letter while everyone from his elder brother, my grandfather, to the youngest grandchild listened solemnly. When Uncle Bob finished there were no comments; we would sit in silence as the letter went back into the breast pocket. Then the Serious Occasion was over and we kids would run along and play.

What letters they were! Never long, translated into English by a friend of hers, they still managed fairly to sing with life. And *of* life: of births and growing children, new and unseen cousins whom she welcomed one by one into the world and then accompanied, as best she could, in her imagination. She wrote of our occasional bereavements, for which the letters would console us—reminding us, for example, that no matter what happens the stars are full of music; we need only listen to hear. She wrote about the novels she read, and about the deathless poetry of changing seasons. Every fall she wrote about the children going off to school and about unpacking winter clothes. She was always somehow the first to notice the spring warmth creeping across the prairies—our American prairies, never her own Central European ones. While I was still a child I realized that Janka never wrote about herself. She was living far away from her own life, in her picture of ours.

Her own life, I learned growing older, was grim indeed. Culturally Hungarian, she had the misfortune after the war to find herself and her city,

X

Arad, on the wrong side of a *boundary*—in Ceausescu's Romania, where Hungarians were a disadvantaged minority. Jewish, she refused to convert to the new religion, Communism—just as her ancestors (unlike mine) had refused conversion to Christianity. Her refusal was not in the name of religious Judaism but was—like herself—entirely secular: in the name of nothing more than Janka Schwarz, who would be at the *disposition* of nothing larger than herself. The result, as my grandfather once summed it up sadly, was that "if a chicken comes into Arad, Janka doesn't get it."

Finally, as a woman, Janka was unable to take action to improve her situation: she was allowed no *initiative* over her world. Her only hope was an entirely passive one: that we, her rich American relatives, would buy her way out of Romania. It was a hope she rejected. In spite of our frequent offers, she preferred to stay in Arad. In Arad, her husband had lived. From Arad, they had been shipped in the trains. To Arad, only she had returned.

Eventually, still older, very old indeed, I understood: Why trade her memories of her own family (which she never mentioned) and her dreams of ours (which she spun incessantly) for a reality she knew she could never understand? What could we ever have been to her, once she was among us, but a different sort of prison?

In her three oppressions, Cousin Janka was of course not alone. Indeed, we are all with her to some extent. For I have come to believe that what she was enduring were nothing less than fundamental structures of the West itself. These structures were first codified (defined and legitimated) in Aristotle's metaphysics. Though they have come under increasing stress, particularly in the modern world, they have never since been openly challenged or even stated. Their codification consists, briefly—its whole story is the West's whole story—in the view that the universe consists in part, and should consist entirely, of entities that (a) have determinate and inviolable *boundaries;* (b) exhibit within those boundaries a structure of domination in which a single part (traditionally called the Form) *disposes* of the whole; and (c) do not accord to any component within those boundaries the *initiative* to affect anything outside them.

So with Janka. Caught within the boundaries of Romania, outside those of her own Hungary, she was bereft of serious legal protection. Unconverted to Communism, the all-disposing form of a totalitarian society, she was dismissed as a retrograde social phenomenon. Psychologically unable to emigrate to the world outside, she was able to affect one distant part of that world—including a small boy—only through the momentous quiet of her letters.

This book argues that these three fundamental structures of oppression—boundary, disposition, and initiative—are not based only on the passions of nationalism and religion which Communism appropriated. They are not grounded merely in human genetic endowments or modern economic forces. They are deeply *philosophical* in nature and cannot be wisely combated unless this is understood.

The pages of this book contain no life-giving fantasies of family life, no sublime appeals to star music. But they do attempt to understand the oppressions of Janka Schwartz: to mark their philosophical codification and lay bare their structures; to show that much modern philosophy attempts, unknowingly, to criticize them; and to convert its unknown critique into a conscious challenge.

So, Janka, this book is for you.

ABBREVIATIONS

Adk	Heidegger, "Andenken"
AGS	Heidegger, "From a Dialogue on Language"
AT	Charles Adam and Paul Tannery, eds. *Oeuvres de Descartes*
Cats	Aristotle, *Categories.*
DD	Heidegger, "The Thing"
de An.	Aristotle, *de Anima*
de Corp.	Hobbes, *de Corpore*
EE	Aquinas, *On Being and Essence*
EN	Aristotle, *Nicomachean Ethics*
Essay	Locke, *An Essay concerning Human Understanding*
Gen. An.	Aristotle, *On the Generation of Animals*
KG	Aquinas, *On Kingship or the Governance of Rulers*
Lev.	Hobbes, *Leviathan*
Loemker	Leroy Loemker, ed. *Gottfried Wilhelm Leibniz: Philosophical Papers and Letters*
LT	Douglass, *The Life and Times of Frederick Douglass*
LU	Weltfish, *The Lost Universe*
Metaph.	Aristotle, *Metaphysics*
Oec.	Aristotle, *Economics*
PDM	Habermas, *The Philosophical Discourse of Modernity*
Pol.	Aristotle, *Politics*
PP	Descartes, *The Principles of Philosophy*

SS	Beauvoir, *The Second Sex*
ST	Aquinas, *Summa Theologiae*
SZ	Heidegger, *Being and Time*
T1, T2	Locke, *First* and *Second Treatises of Government*
Tr.	Hume, *A Treatise of Human Nature*
UKW	Heidegger, "The Origin of the Work of Art"
WHD	Heidegger, *What Is Called Thinking?*

METAPHYSICS
AND
OPPRESSION

INTRODUCTION: TWO HEIDEGGERS AND THEIR CHALLENGE

THE CHALLENGE AND THE STRATEGIES

Martin Heidegger: only Ludwig Wittgenstein can compete with him as the greatest philosopher of the twentieth century. Martin Heidegger: life-long Nazi.

The gap is too great for the mind to span, and the topic is urgent. That a Nazi can be a great philosopher is no trivial possibility. We are challenged to comprehend it, and the tradition gives us only a few strategies in terms of which to do so.

One such strategy requires us to take one of the two characterizations as basic, reducing the other to mere appearance, even delusion—to what Hegel would call *Schein*. Thus Victor Farias can, indeed must, write a book maintaining that Heidegger was not a great thinker at all but a mere peasant anti-Semite from Germany's sullen backwaters.[1] And Joseph Kockelmans can, must, write:

> If it had not been for Heidegger's involvement with National Socialism during the period in which he was rector of the University of Freiburg . . . probably nobody would have expected that in a treatise on his philosophy

a chapter on his political philosophy would be mandatory. . . . [Heidegger's] behavior was indeed unacceptable on several accounts. Yet it is impossible to defend the thesis that this behavior merely made manifest a political philosophy that had always been there and always would remain there.[2]

It is not my intention to equate Kockelmans's honest argumentation with Farias's diatribe.[3] I wish merely to point out that the two men's responses engage some of the most basic premises of our civilization. For in terms of a certain very ancient and influential strategy of thought, one of Heidegger's identities—thinker or Nazi—must constitute his "essential" nature, while the other is a mere "accident," a *Schein.* True to these ancient parameters, Farias and Kockelmans respectively take one of the two incompatible characterizations and make it basic, which requires dismissing the other. But the response fails, because neither "great philosopher" nor "committed Nazi" is a mere accident to be dismissed. Both of them define the person who bears them. This means that we also cannot invoke another ancient gesture, that of relegation to mutual indifference. We cannot say that in one part of his life Heidegger was a great philosopher while in some other respect he was a Nazi, the way table sugar is both white and sweet. Heidegger *was* a great philosopher—and, in some horrid sense, he *was* a committed Nazi. Both conditions go to his core if he has one, and neither can be argued away.

My discussion so far follows the four "rules" which Jean-François Lyotard has proposed for the investigation of the Heidegger "dossier."[4] First, according to Lyotard, the importance of Heidegger's thought in general must be admitted. He was no second-rate hack eager to be used, of whom the Nazis found plenty when they came to power.[5] Moreover, Heidegger's association with Nazism must be seen as "deliberate, profound, and . . . persistent"; it was not a naive flirtation. Neither Heidegger himself, then, nor his Nazi affiliation can simply be dismissed before the discussion begins.

Once we have seen this, the "Heidegger problem" can be recognized *as* a problem. When it is, two further "rules" come into play. On the one hand, neither of the two sides can be played down in favor of the other (this is the rule that Farias and Kockelmans break). On the other, they also cannot be left in mutual indifference, "simply acknowledging the coexistence of the two faces of Heidegger, one venerable, the other ignoble." This second pair of rules thus formulates what we already know: that there must be no *reduction* of either side of Heidegger's thought to mere *Schein,* and no *indifference:* the necessity of each side to the other must be recognized.

Lyotard himself observes these rules by beginning, as do several of his *confrères* in the "poststructuralist" tradition,[6] from structuralism. He begins, that is, from the replacement of the "author" by the "text." Instead of seeking and criticizing the shaping force of a single authorial personality over the development of an entire *oeuvre,* he seeks to trace the welter of complicities and incapacities which, in various texts, constitute the unstable "interface" between Heideggerean thinking and Nazism. Hence for Lyotard such key Heideggerean terms as *Volk, Arbeit, Führung,* and especially *Entscheidung* and *Entschlossenheit* are "words that, while creating enormous confusion in the context of the thirties, are very useful to Heidegger's 'hard thought.'"[7] For Jacques Derrida, taking a similar approach, the distance between *Being and Time* and the "Rectoral Address" is marked by a "sudden inflammation and inflation of the concept of *Geist.*"[8] For Philippe Lacoue-Labarthe, the slippage goes back to Pericles' invocation, in his Funeral Address, of *euteleia,* the "economy of means which was taken up into the philosophical economy of final causes."[9]

Working not on the level of the author but on the levels of the text, these and other thinkers have been able to find a multitude of gestures, themes, and concepts which allow for a slippage between the "good" Heidegger and the "bad" one. This is an extraordinarily fruitful approach, and I return to it later—but only briefly, for the problem as I seek to pose it here resides precisely on the level poststructuralism tends to occlude. This is the level of the overall unity and direction of Heidegger's various texts. When we ask about the basic unity and direction of Heidegger's later thought, what appears is less a slippage from philosophy to Nazism than the yawning of a rather difficult chasm.

It is Jürgen Habermas who pursues this level of investigation most responsibly and thoroughly, though not all the way to the end.[10] Habermas's basic strategy in reconciling the two Heideggers is developmental, and this once again answers to one of the most ancient maxims of the West: nothing can have contradictory properties in the same respect, and anything which exhibits such properties must be undergoing change (*alloiôsis*). And so Habermas constructs a story according to which Heidegger started out (in *Being and Time*) as an important philosopher but betrayed his philosophical contributions and finished as a contemptible apologist, first for Nazism and later for himself.

Unlike the strategies of Farias and Kockelmans, Habermas's treatment follows Lyotard's four rules: it takes both Heideggers seriously and seeks to understand the necessity of each to the other, thus avoiding both reduction and indifference. But Habermas's developmental thesis is nonetheless ultimately untenable. I have argued at length elsewhere[11] that *Being and Time,* for all its achievements, is no innocent piece of philosophy. Though it may not actually encourage Nazism, it clearly leaves Heidegger open to it. For in *Being and Time,* intelligibility is subject to world: I can understand nothing that is not within the horizons of my world. Escape from this world is achievable not through critical reason but only in a mute and mystified "resolve" (*Entschlossenheit*).

In Heidegger's later writings, by contrast, intelligibility is no longer delimited by world but is the surge into world of the radically new (and

3

therefore of the radically foreign). These writings can in fact be seen as one of philosophy's few antidotes, if not to Nazism itself at least to the cultural closure and chauvinism that were and are its most fertile soil. Not that those later writings can be happily acquitted of Nazi complicities either; as will be seen, a sort of dogmatic irrationalism, if not proto-Nazism, runs through them. As in the earlier works, it runs together with philosophical greatness.

Habermas misses the greatness in the later Heidegger because he has been betrayed by his selective and philosophically biased choice of texts. That makes his reading not so much wrong as partial. To show this, I will list seven theses Habermas advances concerning the later Heidegger, all of which seem to me to be false. Having argued that Habermas is in fact wrong on these points, I will then try to show why he is also right and what that teaches us about Heidegger's thought.

According to Habermas:

1. The later Heidegger has no "systematic" account of language but simply makes global assertions about it, such as that it is the "house of being" (*PDM*, p. 193/163).

2. These views of language hypostasize the "world-disclosing" function of language, in which a language can inform us about its users, at the expense of truth-telling, in which language informs us about the world (*PDM*, p. 183/154).

3. Because of this, truth claims in the ordinary sense—claims which transcend the local conditions of those making them—have no place in Heidegger's thought (*PDM*, p. 182/154).

4. Hence Heidegger makes no effort to provide a rational grounding for the various assertions he himself makes (*PDM*, p. 181/152; also cf. p. 163/136).

5. This means, on one side of the "ontological difference," that beings can be interpreted in any way whatsoever (*PDM*, p. 183/154).

6. On the other side of the ontological difference, Being itself, articulated in poetry and metaphysics, is undialectical: "das schlechthin Unmittelbare" (*PDM*, p. 181/153).

7. And yet, amid all this irrationalism, Heidegger continues to understand both philosophy and human Being itself as theoretical in character. Remaining committed to pure theory, Heidegger's thought is—laudably enough, in Heidegger's own view—socially and ethically irresponsible (*PDM*, pp. 179f/150f, 185/156).

Heidegger's work is thus, for Habermas, philosophy degree zero. Unlike the Pragmatists and Michel Foucault, for example, who moderate the vaunted "rigor" of their philosophical predecessors in favor of making philosophy more useful to people, Heidegger destroys all rigor while continuing to maintain that philosophy itself is purely theoretical.[12]

The references in Habermas's four main articles on Heidegger show that he bases his account of Heidegger's thought on the following works: *Being and Time; Was ist Metaphysik?* with its introduction and afterword; *Nietzsche; Das Rekorat;* other speeches from the Nazi time, as anthologized by Guido Schneeburger;[13] *Grundbegriffen der Metaphysik;* "Platons Lehre von der Wahrheit"; "Brief über den 'Humanismus'"; "Vom Wesen der Wahrheit"; *Einführung in die metaphysik; Heraklit; Hölderlins Hymne "der Ister";* "Die Überwindung der Metaphysik." Absent from this list are some formidable works: the books *Erläuterungen zu Hölderlins Dichtung, Die Frage nach dem Ding, Holzwege, Der Satz vom Grund, Unterwegs zur Sprache, Was Heißt Denken?;* most of the essays in *Vorträge und Aufsätze;* and others. Remarkably, Habermas has omitted from his account of Heidegger *all* of the interpretations of philosophers and poets which Heidegger published after his Nazi engagement, except for the Nietzsche and Heraclitus volumes: the bulk, then, of Heidegger's later publication.[14] Habermas ignores these works to such an extent that he can write that in 1929 Heidegger broke with academic philosophy "in order thenceforth to philosophize in . . . immediate confrontation with problems of the time perceived as urgent."[15] This is a remarkable way to characterize an *oeuvre* which consists largely of detached, even apparently escapist, meditations on long-dead thinkers and poets.

Dealing as they do with specific texts, Heidegger's essays on poetry and the history of philosophy are as close as he comes to concreteness in his thought. Ignoring them while excoriating Heidegger for leaving behind all concrete matters after the *Kehre* is, to say the least, dangerous. Perhaps attention to these other works would reveal a different perspective on Heidegger—or even a different Heidegger.

Granting that Habermas is basically right about the texts he does discuss (I will come back to this), we seem to be left with two possibilities. Either the rest of Heidegger's later work confirms what Habermas says about him, in which case my claim that Habermas has missed any greatness in Heidegger's later thought is mistaken. Or it does not, in which case Heidegger's later thought bifurcates oddly between philosophical greatness and obscurantist drivel. In either case, what is needed is an investigation into Heidegger's more concrete works to see what sorts of things they are and what sorts of rigor they contain.

HEIDEGGER THE GOOD

Habermas's reason for excluding Heidegger's later interpretations of poetry and philosophy is obvious. They contain, at least on the surface, nothing relating to Heidegger's views on society and modernity, the topics of Habermas's interest. They seem to be mere exercises in textual interpretation, relevant, if to anything, to our understanding of poetry and of the history of metaphysics. But the view that poetry and metaphysics are irrelevant to political philosophy is itself burdened with a number of unexplored presuppositions (some of which this book intends to explode). As long as they are unexplored, these presuppositions can only constitute a philosophical bias.

Biases often have respectable origins. This one, for example, was shared by no less a thinker than Immanuel Kant, who cut metaphysics out of science by relegating it to an unknowable "supersensible" realm. But what if Kant was wrong? What if metaphysics lies not *beyond* the sensible realm but *beneath* it—like bones beneath skin? What if the "empirical realm" these bones underlie shapes our political and social practices? What if society's metaphysical skeleton has become, over millennia, unbearably arthritic? If all that is the case, it may be that the only way to free the skeleton up, to "cut it appropriately at the joints" as Plato recommended, is to use the demarcative scalpels of the poet. And if *that* is the case, not only metaphysics but poetry as well has direct relevance to political and social thought.

As I have argued elsewhere,[16] Heidegger's later thought seeks to clarify and advance the emergence of meaning into language.[17] This emergence is an historical process in which names receive new meanings, i.e., come to play different roles in opening up nature so that mortals may dwell within it. Because the emergence of meaning is given historically (or, in more Heideggerean terms, is an historical giving), Heidegger's later thought is *essentially* dialogical: "every thinker," he writes, "remains constantly in dialogue with those who have gone before and, perhaps more so and in a yet more hidden way, with those who will come after."[18] Because the emergence of new meaning is what enables mortals to dwell, such dialogue is for Heidegger the *Grundgeschehen,* the basic event, of human existence itself: "dialogue and its unity bear our Dasein."[19]

The "dialogues" of Heidegger's later thought stand under the following standards:

A. *All* the historical stages in the emergence of a meaning (or all the stages, i.e., words, in a poem) must be presented: "Every word must be laid on the scale." Every word of an interpreted text must be considered in the interpretation, and every word of Heidegger's own interpretation must be weighed by the reader:

> even the most inconspicuous word . . . is a word of [poetic] greeting. It speaks in remembrance and thinks the past foreignness and the coming at-homeness back into its own primordial belonging-together.[20]

B. The different stages of an historical development or a poetic naming must be accurately presented. If no nineteenth-century German ever wrote the poems of Hölderlin nor any ancient Greek the work of Parmenides—if, like the poems of Ossian, their works were shown to have been products of later fraud—then Heidegger's entire philosophical meditation would be falsified. The same would hold for any of the other thinkers Heidegger discusses.[21]

C. These stages of emergence must be construable as, in one of Heidegger's most important terms, "hints."[22] In order to be accomplished in "hints," the move from one stage to another cannot be fully transparent to reason. If it were, we would have a "middle term" or concept, not a hint; we would have a traditional development of the *logos* rather than a Heideggerean play of revelation and concealment.

D. On the other hand, the stages of emergence cannot fall apart completely; each must be shown to add to the gathering emergence of a single, radically new, meaningful name. Referring to the pathways of poetic wandering, Heidegger writes:

> Such ways do not end in that they just break off. The ways end in that they rest—and this because they gather themselves in the singing of completion. The singing, however, lingers in a continual wandering and traveling, which continuously measures its steps in the meter of the versification, in the measure of poetic saga.[23]

The aim of Heidegger's later concrete works, in fact, is not merely to capture or reflect upon the process of emergence of meaning that is carried out, for example, in a poem of Hölderlin, but actually to carry that process forward.[24]

In sum, as I have put it elsewhere:

> That thinking is "in accord with the topic" of Appropriation which presents all stages in the gathering of new meaning into language as an authentic name; which shows that they cannot be reduced to stages in a transparent development of thought, but nonetheless contribute successively to the gathering emergence of that name; and which presents this via a dialogue with history, not as resulting from the artful subjectivity of a single thinker.[25]

This process of emergence of new meaning via "hints" is basic to Heideggerean thinking. For it is, he tells us, nothing less than Appropriation—the way to language—itself.[26] Nor is it confined to the later Heidegger. The notion of Being as the gradual emergence of radically new meaning dates all the way back to *Being and Time*'s original definition of a phenomenon as that which shows itself in itself, i.e., which has a structure that progressively reveals that unique structure itself. And the theme is carried forward in Heidegger's later works in the concept of "way."[27]

That impeaches the fourth of Habermas's seven critical points. For none of it is irrationalistic in Habermas's sense, according to which something is "rational" if it can be criticized.[28] We can certainly argue and come to agreement over whether Heidegger has accurately transcribed the thinkers and poets with whom he deals; over whether the transitions he uncovers in history or in a poem can be conceptually understood or not; over whether a particular stage actually contributes to the overall development; and over whether the final meaning resulting from all this is truly new or not. To be sure, Heidegger's tracing of the emergence of meaning is not what Habermas would call a process of "reflection," which aims at clarification of what is already there implicitly. Heidegger's thought does not seek full clarity, and it aims to end, precisely, in something truly new, i.e., something which is not there before Heidegger's own thought "produces" it. Habermas is not wrong to call Heidegger's later thinking a "devotional narrative presentation" of Appropriation.[29] But it does have standards, and it can be criticized.

Among these standards (*ad* Habermas's points 2 and 3) is, we have seen, that of propositional truth. Heidegger's thinking in fact does not supplant but incorporates and presupposes a correspondence theory of truth. Similarly, his thought does not precede all argumentation or dispense with it but presupposes and uses it; his interpretations contain, on every page, very traditional forms of inference and explication.

Moreover (*ad* 5), Heidegger's way of handling a text locates it in the context of the historical emergence of some single name. This Heideggerean context may indeed seem radically different from contexts in which that text has been understood before. But it does not follow that the text (or, more generally, a being) may be interpreted in any way whatsoever; the story must be complete, "hintful," and give birth to new meaning at its end. Appropriation, or Being, is in this undialectical, because its transitions are not determinate, i.e., transparent, negations. But (*ad* 6) it is not "immediate." It is, rather, what we may call a process of less-than-transparent mediation, what Heidegger first calls a "phenomenon" and later a "way."

Finally (*ad* 7), this is not merely a "theoretical" undertaking, for the creation of new meaning is not simply the contemplation of meaning already there. As essays such as "Bauen Wohnen Denken," ". . . dichterisch wohnet der Mensch," and "The Origin of the Work of Art"[30] make clear, Heideggerean disclosure is a sort of social practice in which faithful attention to the basic words of the past seeks to open up new futures.

I conclude that (*ad* 1) if the later Heidegger never engages in a systematic account of language—or, indeed, "account of" anything—his later essays provide material for such an account. Though they deal primarily with language as disclosure of world, that is because that is how and where, for Heidegger, new meaning emerges. To disclose a world is part of constituting it *as* a world, and language attains radical newness in constituting world. Heidegger's essays, then, do not deny the truth-telling capacities of language; they are just looking at a different kind of linguistic phenomenon. It is a phenomenon Habermas himself never investigates: the manifold emergence of meaning itself, the origin of what Habermas calls the life-world.[31]

HEIDEGGER THE BAD

Nonetheless, Habermas is also right about Heidegger.[32] Many of Heidegger's texts, especially those which Habermas consults, are indeed replete with dogmatic assertions about science, "the essence of technology," and the depredations of the modern age.[33] Much of this is clearly warmed-over cant from the European right wing. Worse, Heidegger is truly unable to distinguish Eisenhower's America from Stalinist Russia.[34] Worst of all, ineffably worst, he cannot distinguish what the Germans did to the Jews from what the Allies did to the Germans—or even, according to reports, from what agribusiness does to the land.[35] There are, then, two very different strains in Heidegger, and we do seem to have two Heideggers—not Early and Late but Good and Bad. How can both be the same person?

The modern age presents an inconceivable variety of projects, many working at cross-purposes to one another and, often enough, to their own deeper rationales.[36] A concretely intelligent critique of them would have to include, as Habermas demands, careful and detailed analyses of science, politics, and everyday life. Heidegger engages in none of them. It seems, as Habermas has argued, that mere *Weltanschauung,* the reduction of philosophy to uncritically developed ideology, has taken over his thought. If so, then no *philosophical* account of the two Heideggers is possible. We are left with a philosopher who had some excellent things to say about history, language, and meaning but who simply could not keep quiet when tempted, beyond his capacities, to offer general diagnoses of the time. We are back at the strategy of relegation to mutual indifference: in respect of some things Heidegger was a great thinker and in respect of others, a Nazi fool.

But that strategy was unacceptable. Must we leave it there? According to Habermas, Heidegger uncritically adopts a *Weltanschauung* approach to philosophy during his openly Nazi period, in 1933–1934. But this view requires us to attribute to Heidegger a rather tortured development. For he had given a highly critical account of the concept of *Weltanschauung* in the 1927 lectures published as *Basic Problems of Phenomenology.* And he reiterated his critique in *Beiträge zur Philosophie* of 1939.[37] So in order to accept Habermas's account, we would have to accept that Heidegger was vehemently critical of *Weltanschauung* philosophy in 1927, embraced it in 1933–1934, and criticized it again in 1939. Such an evolution is not impossible, but it is unlikely. Habermas's view, therefore, is also unlikely. And this renews my basic question. Is there something in Heidegger's thought which would enable us to explain *philosophically* the disparity between what I claim to have found in Heidegger's later writings on poetry and the history of metaphysics and what Habermas finds in the others?

If we read him as I have suggested, Heidegger (among other things) uncovers and exemplifies a certain sort of phenomenon which I have called the "emergence of meaning." As Heidegger practices it, it is a socially relevant dialogical process based on a certain sort of remembering—one which re-presents the emergence of meaning through history in the interests of furthering it. This is, clearly, radically different from most of what goes on not merely in philosophy but also in the contemporary world in general. If what Heidegger does is to be styled "remembering," then it may seem that everything else must, if radically different from it, be some sort of forgetting. This presents us not merely with a constant theme in Heidegger—that the modern age has "forgotten" Being—but with a problem to which *Being and Time*, quoting Augustine, alludes obliquely. How, Augustine asks, can I remember forgetting?[38]

Augustine suggests that we can remember forgetting if what is in our own mind at the time of our effort is not forgetting itself but an image or perhaps a sign of it. For a sign or image can be detached from its referent and used to signify it in its absence. Whether, in such a case, I am "remembering" forgetting itself or only its image or sign is open to question for Augustine. In any case, his answer will not work for Heidegger. That is because Heidegger's thought, as I have noted, is not merely supposed to reason *about* the emergence of meaning. It is actually to carry this emergence forward—or, as I present matters in chapter 10, to put it "into play." A Heideggerean essay does not merely trace the emergence of some meaning but is *part* of that path of emergence itself—a point Heidegger makes by continually referring to his later writings as themselves "ways" or "paths" and by giving his books titles such as *Wegmarken, Holzwege*, and *Unterwegs zur Sprache*. That is why Heidegger cannot "give an account of" language or of anything else; in Reginald Lilly's terms, his aim is not to justify a set of assertions about Being but "to 'make' Being *become* a phenomenon."[39]

Because Heidegger's later writings are not a set of assertions and inferences about Appropriation but instances of it, they do not keep the distance that language normally maintains between sign and signified, concept and object, state of affairs and description. Since this distance is still, in spite of the best efforts of numerous philosophers, not well understood, discourse which presupposes it remains on a certain level unclear. It is perhaps Heidegger's avoidance of this conceptually hazy distance which leads him to the single statement which most exercises Habermas: that his way of thinking is "*strenger als das begriffliche* (more rigorous than the conceptual variety)."[40]

It follows that Heidegger's procedures do not ultimately allow him to signify something in its absence. His own unique thought *is* what it *is about*.

Appropriation is not something outside Heidegger's texts which he has to argue for but the very way the texts themselves work.[41] And so: how indeed can Heidegger remember forgetting? In order for him to treat of forgetting, forgetting itself, not some sign or image of it, must be installed in his texts. His writings about the "forgetting of Being" must be instances of such forgetting, just as his writings about Appropriation are instances of that.

Heidegger's word for this forgetting and for its manifold consequences is *Gestell,* which I "translate" as "Gestell." It is clear even before one understands the nature of the Gestell in any detail that Heidegger will not be able to articulate its nature by means of his own thought. For the capture and carrying forward of the emergence of meaning in various single words cannot present the manifold phenomena of a civilization that denies precisely this. For him to talk in *his* way about the Gestell would require the Gestell itself to be installed right in his own language. He can, in other words, speak *from* its standpoint but not *about* that standpoint from his own.

The radical disparity between the kind of emergence of meaning that Heidegger himself practices and (almost) everything else that goes on in the modern world ought of itself to give Heidegger's thought critical potential as against the rest of modernity. In fact, it now seems that the disparity between his own thinking and the rest of modernity may be so great that Heidegger cannot intelligently discuss modernity at all. Yet, if the critical potential of his thought is to be realized, it seems that he must try to talk about the present age in some way and to some extent. The only resource he has in this is to exploit the very disparity that causes the problem and to erect a critique of modernity upon a *radical negation of his own basic idea*—that of "way." Heidegger's diagnoses of the modern world, though familiar and unempirical, are not in their entirety mere right-wing ranting. They are predicated on the single insight that the modern world denies the complex gathering of meaning into single names that he has uncovered. More broadly, the modern world exhibits no "ways."

What is the negation of a Heideggerean way? Such a way progresses via hints, which connect its stages in ways that cannot themselves be fully articulated. One could deny this in several ways. One could ignore the gradual emergence of a term through a manifold of stages, so that the meaning of a term would be a single static unit—a Platonic move, perhaps, but one which the modern world, dedicated to change and transformation, obviously does not make. Or one could admit the transitions through multiplicity but deny unity, so that the process of transition, instead of exhibiting the emergence of a single being (name), becomes a movement from one being to another. This sort of movement from one being to another, as opposed to allowing and experiencing the inner complexity of a single being to unfold itself, is another standard theme in Heidegger, dating back to the analysis of "curiosity" in *Being and Time* and of *Irren* in "Vom Wesen der Wahrheit."[42] It plays a pivotal role in "Die Frage nach der Technik," where, after a typical Heideggerean recapitulation of the history of *technê*, the subject of the Gestell is introduced via a play upon *fördern,* "to further," and *fordern,* "to command." The Gestell is then that which commands a furthering quality of human activity, i.e., that it be and be seen only as a movement from one thing to another. All such activity, for Heidegger, is predicated upon a forgetting of Being.[43]

Thus for Heidegger it is not Being which is the other of (his) thought; Being is the element of thought, the gathering multiplicity of meaning which thought traverses. The true other to thought in Heidegger is the Gestell, which denies unity to the gathering power of hints. Any overall account of the modern era will have to be in large part an account of the Gestell; and this is, strictly speaking, impossible for Heidegger. When he gives it, he is trying to remember forgetting without using a "sign" for it.

Heidegger's introduction of the term *Gestell* is thus an attempt to show, not discuss, the forgetting of Being in modern society. But he cannot show it in any specific way. For Heidegger apparently views *all* meaning as originating in the kind of emergence which he uncovers; in spite of his pluralization and denial of origins, Appropriation remains for him the only manner in which new meaning emerges, the "way to language."[44] So he can only view movement from being to being, conceptualizable transition, as a loss of all meaning whatsoever—a kind of meaninglessness. And it is, of course, impossible to distinguish different sorts of meaninglessness from one another, for any such distinction would give them meaning of a sort. Thus the Gestell is, in the familiar phrase of another well-known Swabian, the "night in which all cows are black."

Habermas's criticism now turns out to be misdirected. It is not Being but the Gestell which is wholly immediate; which reveals only itself and hides—indeed, consumes—everything else, cutting off truth in all senses; which can yield no "systematic" account of language, whose true powers it denies; whose supposedly transparent justifications always break down at some point; which attacks beings from any and all directions; and which, for its own comfort, relegates philosophy to the status of "theory." What Habermas's critique of Heidegger really shows, then, is that at certain points in certain texts, Heidegger's own thought takes on characteristics of the Gestell itself. And these texts—the ones Habermas reads—are the points at which Heidegger abandons his own ways of thinking and tries to "treat" the Gestell. Paradoxically, Heidegger remains true to himself in this abandonment; the Gestell itself, not an image or sign, is installed in these texts.

Abandoning his thoughtful pathways to err in a night of demonic cows, Heidegger cannot distinguish the wandering of a rootless American, hitting the road and feeling great about it, from the wretched march of a Russian through the Gulag or the mad flight of a Sudeten German from the Red Army: all are movements from being to being. When it comes to the Jews of Europe, shipped in cattle cars to extermination, Heidegger has nothing whatever to say. And says it in the most obscene ways.

Turning to less outrageous sins: the emergence of meaning, I have suggested, is a dialogical practice. It is a local and partial one. It is inconsistent with this to ignore, as Heidegger does, the true plurality sources of meaning. For meaning emerges not merely along the multiplicity of hintful paths that Heidegger follows but from the will of human beings: from agreement and convention, from the arbitrary stipulations of logicians, from discussion and communicative action, and sometimes even from the consolidating gestures of Hegelian dialectic. All of these and many more are differentiations within the Gestell which Heidegger is unable to recognize. When he attempts, as he does in many of the texts on which Habermas bases his interpretation, to give global accounts of modernity rather than simply practice his own way of thinking, Heidegger forgets to remember.

The manifold pathways of Appropriation and the demanding meaninglessness of the Gestell relate to each other, oddly enough, much as do the "two Heideggers." Neither can be ignored. Neither can be given the status of a mere "accident," or *Schein,* while the other is the essence or underlying reality. Neither is possible without the other, but neither can be understood in terms of the other. And there is no larger category—say, philosopher-Nazi or Appropriation-Gestell—which can embrace both.

It is then impossible to bring either Heidegger's thought or his personality together into what we would consider a "rational" whole. And yet each side of the personality—the philosopher and the Nazi—is an inescapable part of the "whole" that was Martin Heidegger, just as Appropriation and Gestell are both essential to his thought. Heidegger is what he is for us today not because of either of his personalities alone but because of the unspannable gap between them. His thought is what it is because of the equally unfathomable struggle of Appropriation and Gestell. To understand these gaps and struggles without resorting to the concepts of harmony and indifference, essence and accident, and temporal development that are basic to Western metaphysics: *that* is the challenge Heidegger throws down to us.

SCOPE AND METHODS OF THIS BOOK

Heidegger's thought is a challenge to oppression.

The view that Martin Heidegger, lifelong Nazi and abstruse opponent of metaphysical errancy, actually formulated the twentieth century's most important challenge to oppression takes some arguing. In the course of this argument I claim that what Heidegger's thought preeminently challenges is not really the Gestell, but a very ancient parameter so deeply embedded in our life and thought as to remain invisible to us. I call this parameter "ousia."

As a parameter,[45] ousia functions at once like a concept and like a set of instructions. Fronting referentially onto the world and pragmatically onto our behavior, it both mirrors the beheld and structures the beholder. In its "mirroring" or referential function, ousia denotes a certain structure. According to the reading of Aristotle that I present in chapters 1 and 2, something is an ousia if

1. it is securely and determinately bounded;

2. one unitary component within its boundaries—what Aristotle calls the "form"—generates and/or orders everything else within these boundaries;

3. only this governing unit affects the world outside these boundaries.

I call these traits "boundary," "disposition," and "initiative" respectively.

In its pragmatic or properly "parametric" function, ousia is deployed in three ways:

I. *Referentially:* anything which meets conditions 1-3 is an ousia.

II. *Hermeneutically:* anything which approximates conditions 1-3 should be interpreted as if they held.

III. *Practically:* everything human not coming under conditions 1-3 should be remade to conform to them as far as possible.

It is this deployment of ousia that I call "metaphysics." Its oppressive character should be obvious. Heidegger "challenges" it by putting forth an alternative ontological model, one on which at least some beings are generated and shaped not by form but by—nothing at all. Instead of the plenitude of a determinate form, they contain at their core—like Heidegger himself—nothing but an active, shaping gap. I have coined the term "diakena" to denote such active gaps.

The Greek word *kenos* means "empty." When the word is substantivized in the neuter as *kenon,* it means "emptiness." *Kenon* is Aristotle's word in *Physics* IV for the "void" whose existence he denies. Aristotle's argumentation there is not directed against "diakena" in my Heideggerean sense, whose existence he never seems even to suspect. For the Aristotelian void, like vacuums since, is not only abhorrent but also merely passive: being a nothing, it can do nothing. Heidegger's crucial discovery, if we may call it that, is that even nothings can be dynamic, shaping forces.

I seek to capture this active side of the diakena with the prefix "dia." As a prefix, *dia* basically means "through," but it can also connote an active *passage* through. Logos, for example, means "word"; an active passage through words is a *dialogos,* a dialogue. *Noêsis* is reason; *dianoia* is the running through of an argument. A diakenon thus relates to Aristotle's passive *kenon* rather as a dialogue relates to a word. It is an active gathering by emptiness (or by emptinesses; since one nothing has in itself no characteristics by which be distinguished from other nothings, the division of diakena into singular and plural is often questionable).

As I use the term in this book, then, a diakenon is an emptiness which gathers a being or beings around itself.[46] That a set of beings or of aspects of one being is diakenically gathered is evident when

A. none of them is adequately understood apart from the others;

B. none grounds or explains the others;

C. no yet more basic phenomenon can ground, i.e., explain, all of them together.

No indifference, then, no reduction, and no sublation. As with the two Heideggers, or with Appropriation and Gestell.

This characterization of ousia and diakena is cryptic. Further clarification is the task of the entire book. As will become evident, ousia cannot be understood apart from its history—and neither can Heidegger's challenge to it. Narrating selected portions of this history will occupy the first two parts of this book.

First "codified" (defined and legitimated) by Aristotle, ousia was entitled to structure our lives parametrically because—as Aristotle's metaphysics had it—ousia structured the natural order, to which we in turn belonged. Ousia then received an exemplary "consolidation" in Thomas Aquinas: it was underwritten not merely by nature but by an omnipotent God. But the consolidation did not last. With the rise of modern science, ousia was "evicted" from nature, and that left its role in structuring the human world increasingly suspect until, with the Empiricists, it became altogether indefensible. At that point ousia went wholly underground; it continued to function, but in an entirely invisible way.

Hegel, that least understood of thinkers, made attempts to show ousia out of the human realm as well. His strategy was to mount a dialectical "story" of the conversion of ousiodic structure into one of reciprocity. This story led to the nineteenth century's most powerful challenges to ousia— in Marx, Nietzsche, and Freud. It would take me too far afield to recount all that here; I hope to do it elsewhere.[47] In any case, it was left to Heidegger to mount a final attack. In this he both failed and succeeded: succeeded because he was able to find ways to bring diakena to the codifying powers of language; failed in that he did not know he was contesting ousia at all but thought his "enemy" was presence.

In addition to tracing this internal, philosophical history of ousia and diakena, I seek also to indicate how ousia is basic to much (though hardly all) of Western civilization. Its bounded and disposed units, I suspect, are to us Westerners what hexagonal cells are to honeybees: they are what we so busily build. To suggest this basicness—for space will not permit me to argue it—I discuss a number of social "engines." Such an "engine" is a discourse, institution, or mechanism which gets people to live and act in accordance with an ontological structure, ousiodic or not. When an engine is ousiodic, it aims at getting people to live within fixed boundaries, in accordance with dispositive factors which generate or order what happens within these boundaries, and to forgo affecting the world outside these boundaries. The engines I discuss—discursive and nondiscursive—are only a few of the simpler ones. They include dwellings, such as the House of Pansa at Pompeii and the Pawnee earth lodge; institutions, such as colonialism, slavery, and the Roman Empire; and discourses, such as those of V. Y. Mudimbe on colonialism, Frederick Douglass on slavery, and Simone de Beauvoir on marriage. In every case, my discussion seeks to show how much more research needs to be done into the often highly complex ways in which ousia structures our lives, our societies, and our selves.

There is another sense in which this book is incomplete: chronologically. It does not carry its history down to the time of its writing. Between myself, its author, and Heidegger, the most recent thinker it discusses, there stand, for one thing, the profound achievements (and profounder failures) of "analytical" philosophy. In a line of more direct historical succession stands a variety of developments in post-Heideggerean "continental" philosophy. Four continental thinkers are particularly crucial to the present undertaking because I have borrowed heavily from them—not merely in the sense that I have taken over a number of their doctrines but in the deeper sense that they have actually taught me how to think. From Jacques Derrida I have learned how to get beneath the surface of philosophical texts to see them as interplays of insight and exclusion. From Michel Foucault I have learned to enter into a sort of "descriptive proximity" in which beings can be seen to constitute themselves ousiodically *and* to subvert themselves diakenically. From Jürgen Habermas I have learned the only way to tell a Grand Story in the postmodern world: as much as possible to allow other discourses (in this case, texts from the history of philosophy) to converge into a story of their own rather than forcing one on them. And from Richard Rorty I have learned the importance not merely of destabilizing or defending the old philosophical and cultural vocabulary but of proposing new and concrete terms in which to discuss it and other things ("ousiodic," "diakenic," "parametric"). Space does not permit the kind of discussion these four thinkers deserve, and I am reserving it to a subsequent work entitled *The Great Demarcation*.

Even that book, however, will not complete the task I have set myself. For it will only point to a deeper problem. That is the problem of making knowledge, and with it philosophy, properly responsible to time. Ousiodic views of time and thence of logos and knowledge need to be criticized from the standpoint not merely of the diakena but of the diakena brought together with the Hegelian "death of ousia." While I am unable to exclude time completely here, especially in the case of Heidegger, I reserve this task for yet another book, entitled *The Capture of Time.*

It should be obvious that this book is not a conventional history of philosophy. It does not take as its theme the views of a single philosopher or text but seeks to tie thinkers from disparate periods together into a single persuasive narrative. It is not necessary to this end to resolve along the way all the traditional textual problems with which so much contemporary scholarship, particularly in the Anglo-Saxon lands, is occupied. As any reader convinced by my first book, *Poetic Interaction,* will know, the contradictions and lacunae which infest the texts of the philosophical tradition are often part of the philosophical work these texts perform. Not all of them need to be removed, and not all of the secondary literature which discusses them needs to be discussed in turn. In general, I attempt in this book to achieve what J. L. Ackrill set as his task with regard to Aristotle: "to expound, with the aid of quotation and paraphrase, a continuous chunk of text which develops ideas basic to . . . philosophy and [which] will provide a starting-point for the discussion of many problems."[48] The differences are that in my case the "continuity" of the texts I treat are in part established by my treatment of them itself, and the problems to whose discussion my treatment leads are not merely philosophical in nature.

This book is also unlike a traditional history of philosophy in that it centers not on a doctrine or problem but on a parameter, on a philosophical gesture which *hermeneutically* structures other discourses and *practically* structures nondiscursive practices. The resulting history is "philosophical" in that it embodies critical perspectives which, though various in the different thinkers it treats, share a basic philosophical commitment. This commitment is not to truth (though questions of truth emerge at times) but to lucidity: the capacity of philosophers to understand and state what they themselves are doing. In particular, the complicities of ousia with oppression are not in themselves objects of criticism—for here, beneath the moon, oppression is sometimes necessary. What can always be criticized in a philosophy, however, is its lack of lucidity, the failure of a philosophical system or approach to say how it is structured and why. In respect of ousia, this failure is shared by every philosopher I discuss.

A few words are presumably in order about how I intend and do not intend that this book be judged. It is useless to tell me that ousia as I discuss it is either a Procrustean bed to which I reduce the panoply of the West or that it is too empty and flexible to be informative. It should by turns appear as both, but finally it should be neither.

As to the accusation that ousia is the instrument or result of my own reductive Procrusteanism, I can say, that ousia is not the only basic parameter of Western ontology. In particular, my discussion of Aristotle is at some pains to distinguish ousia from another parameter, which I call "substance"; in my discussions of later thinkers, the competition between these two different ways of viewing Being become thematic, with substance recurrently occluding—but never quite displacing—the parametric functioning of ousia. Moreover, the nature of ousia changes in each thinker and period I discuss (and in many more that I do not discuss). I try to recognize these changes. The simplicity of the parameter of ousia is also balanced by the complexity of ways in which it is put into practice; the engines I discuss, important though they are, are only a few simple ones and are far from being the entire history of the West. There is plenty of room for materialist, economic, social, or Darwinian explanation if one wishes to pursue it. It might be worth considering, however, that our civilization may indeed be governed by just a few relatively simple structural paradigms and that their paucity and simplicity are part of what has enabled the West to reproduce itself over millennia and expand to global domination.

As against the charge that ousia is too empty and flexible to explain much, I can hope that it takes on flesh and detail when I discuss individual thinkers. And after discussing Heidegger's great alternative to it—the diakena—it will be evident that the emptiness and generality of ousia are deceptive: it actually contains very substantial commitments of very important kinds.

Finally, I do not wish this book to be judged by the number of true sentences that it establishes or contains; by the number of people, especially older ones, whom it may outrage; or by the number of people, especially younger ones, whom it may inspire. All these criteria are quite valid: but my own are very different. This book has succeeded if it opens up unsuspected dynamics in the various texts and phenomena it discusses, ties them together in a narrative which is not only coherent but diverse and so is what I call Noble,[49] and lays bare the pattern and trajectory of basic principles that structure *our* lives.

PART ONE

THE CODIFICATION AND CONSOLIDATION OF OUSIA (ARISTOTLE AND AQUINAS)

1

ARISTOTLE'S CONCEPT OF OUSIA

Ousiodic structure is of unfathomably ancient date, and the word "ousia" existed as a term of art well before Aristotle.[1] But it was he who, knowingly or not, first *codified* ousia in my sense: *defined* it ontologically as a concept and *legitimated* it metaphysically as a parameter. The narrative I construct here, therefore, begins with him.

Ousia functions throughout the Aristotelian corpus as part of a larger conceptual economy including, among many other terms, "substance," "essence," "form," and "matter." This chapter explores certain aspects of ousia's relation to these terms, tracing something of its *conceptual* articulation in Aristotle. This articulation, as conceptual, aims to tell us what sorts of things can count as ousiai, what not, and why. But, as I suggested in the introduction, ousia is not merely a concept, not merely a device by which the mind captures or mirrors reality accurately. It also has powers *hermeneutically* to structure discourse on specific types of being, because beings to which the concept of ousiodic structure does not apply can often be interpreted as if it did. And it functions *practically* to structure the practices and makeup of the human world: individuals and societies which do not meet ousiodic criteria should be remodeled where and as possible to do so.

The hermeneutic and practical functions of ousia tell us what to do with something once its status with respect to the concept of ousia has been determined. They embody what could be regarded as a set of directives for us—directives which tend to be dismissed by philosophers as the "practical implications" of the concept of ousia. But the dismissal is misleading; almost all concepts structure our behavior to some extent (if only because we use them in communication), and any hard and fast distinction between a "concept" on one hand and its "practical implications" on the other is questionable at best. We rarely mirror the beheld without directing the beholder. Both functions are often, if not always, exercised by a single being which I call a *parameter*.

Though concepts generally exist only as facets of parameters, they serve special functions and can be abstracted from them; otherwise philosophers could not talk about "concepts" at all, let alone exclusively. This, I take it, is what Aristotle is doing in his *Metaphysics:* giving an abstract account of what it is to be an ousia which passes over ousia's parametric functions—functions on which this account is nevertheless deeply dependent. My discussion of Aristotle in this chapter therefore requires a good deal of abstract argument. This is not only unavoidable but one of the unpalatable messages of this book: that in the West, where the political rests upon the metaphysical, the most concrete struggles presuppose the most abstract arguments.

Three "traits" of the concept of ousia as I develop it out of a number of Aristotle's writings also play important parametric roles in Aristotle's other writings and later developments. As in the introduction, I call these traits "boundary," "disposition," and "initiative." "Boundary" means that a thing has (or can hermeneutically be interpreted as having, or in practice ought to have) definite spatial limits marking a continuous space beyond which no part or quality of the thing is. "Disposition" (*diathesis*), in *Metaphysics* V.18, refers to the passing arrangement of the parts of a thing. As I use the term in this book, it refers to the fact that one aspect of a thing—for Aristotle its form or essence—generates its parts out of matter, orders them, and maintains them in that order (or can be interpreted as doing so, or ought to do so).[2] "Initiative" means that a thing affects the world beyond its boundaries via the movement of its form or essence beyond those boundaries into that world (or can be interpreted as doing so, or ought to do so).

These three traits of ousia are not identified as such by Aristotle, and it takes some digging to lay them bare. But they can be shown to provide the hermeneutical basis for certain of his other discourses, such as psychology, biology, ethics, economics, and political philosophy. This chapter, then, discusses the concept of ousia as sketched in the central books of Aristotle's *Metaphysics.* Chapter 2 discusses its hermeneutical role in structuring more concrete discourses in *De Anima,* the *Nicomachean Ethics, Economics,* and *Politics.* Its practical functions are also adumbrated there. Following the discussion of Aquinas in chapter 3, chapter 4 seeks to enlarge upon this adumbration in an historically suggestive way.

But there is a problem in getting under way: Aristotle's writings on metaphysics, or "first philosophy," are tantalizingly difficult to interpret. Unlike the texts of, say, Hegel, which usually appear to make no sense at all, those of Aristotle often seem to have meanings which, though presently quite unclear, are just around the intellectual corner and could be grasped with just a bit more effort. The effort rarely succeeds, and that has given rise to several famous *cris de coeur*. One, which deserves to be quoted extensively, is from Montgomery Furth:

> The various outcroppings [of Aristotle's views on substance] that do occur in his text as received, are surrounded and separated by sizable stretches of other material that is older, or representative of other standpoints, or concerned with other topics, or otherwise off our reservation. When to this is added the pervasive general difficulty of his written record—overpacked, sometimes concise to the point of being cryptic, sometimes patently confused, sometimes palpably inconsistent—it becomes quite obvious that . . . there is no possible way to make it all fit. . . . Beyond this there are a number of important directions not completely worked out: there are concepts and issues that can be seen on [Aristotle's] own principles to be critically significant and requiring detailed analysis and discussion, which in the extant corpus are simply not squarely addressed, and where the relevant points of theory must be pieced together from scattered remarks, or inferred from patterns of practice, or supplied by "deduction" from interpretive hypothesis.[3]

Terence Irwin is yet more plaintive:

> Characteristics of animals, senses of words, varieties of political systems all move him to full and precise description; but on the most important issues of all his remarks are often brief, inexplicit, and inconclusive. Some of the best informed students of Aristotle recognize the frustration that many readers must feel in trying to fix his view on some fundamental issues. Perhaps his sketchiness about first principles reflects his awareness of the obscurity and difficulty of the questions they raise, and the tentativeness of his answers.[4]

And Hermann Bonitz, whom Irwin quotes, is even more trenchant:

> Is enim ut est diligentissimus in cognoscendis rebus singularibus . . . ut est acutus et ingeniosus in redigendas his singularis rebus ad summas, quas distinxit, omnium entium categorias; ita quum de iaciendis altissimis doctrinae fundamentis et de confirmandis interque se conciliandis principiis agitur, plurimum relinquit dubitationis.[5]

In addition to the genetic and textual problems noted by Furth, Bonitz and Irwin point to a remarkable *pattern* in Aristotle's writings (a pattern which is also evidenced by Furth's whole strategy of turning for metaphysical illumination to Aristotle's biological writings).[6] For it happens that Aristotle's concrete analyses are, in general, notably clearer and better worked out than the more general views on which they are based. That is good news for the next chapter but bodes ill for the present one.

How ambitious need we be? Is it certain that this pattern is a perverse lapse in Aristotle or a loss of confidence on his part? What if the unclarities, inconsistencies, and lacunae in his writings on basic principles were not mere defects to be removed by modern logic but part of the very way his philosophy is supposed to work? What if, in short, the point of "First Philosophy" is not so much to provide a true and precise account of the basic structures of reality as to furnish a set of very general pointers, an abstract parametric basis for further and more concrete investigation?[7]

If Aristotle saw his basic principles less as faithful accounts of reality than as directives for understanding and coping with a variety of more concrete topics and issues, he would have good reason to leave these basic principles "sketchy." The Constitution of the United States is an analogy. Like Aristotle's metaphysical texts, it is notably full of omissions and unclarities. But these, however frustrating, are part of its strength: by not spelling its directives out in rigid detail, the Constitution leaves future generations enhanced scope for realizing them—and so, like Aristotle's thought, has survived longer than much clearer and more detailed efforts.[8]

Boundary, disposition, and initiative are nowhere identified by Aristotle as basic traits of being; they lurk, like gold or sharks, in the depths of his texts. My aim here is to discuss his account of ousia in just enough detail to force them to the surface. From this perspective, clarity means reading Aristotle so that his texts most clearly delineate these traits. It does not mean seeking the precise meaning of "ousia" in all its logical ramifications; many passages can be left in the obscurity to which Aristotle himself consigned them. Certain topics which are central to more traditional scholarly investigations are thus of small import, as is much of the voluminous secondary literature (though I thankfully take what guidance I can). I explain the more tendentious of my exegetical decisions, but in general my account is to be judged *narratively,* by the clarity and importance—the illuminating power—of the parameter that emerges from them. Such a judgment, of course, can be issued only at the end of the entire book.

Finally, my interest in parametric structuring also means that my account is geared to ousia as form in matter; Aristotle's account of immaterial substances, which many have credibly seen as the crux of his entire ontology,[9] is largely ignored.

SUBSTANCE

Aristotle's most extended grapple with the nature of ousiodic structure occurs in certain passages of his *Metaphysics,* in particular the treatise on ousia that stretches through Books VII-IX. I translate its opening words as follows:

> Being is said in many ways, as we have enumerated previously in our considerations on the different senses of words. For in one sense it means what a thing is, a "this"; and in other senses it means quality or quantity or any of the other categories thus predicated. But, even though "being" has all these senses, it is obvious that the first of them is "being" in the sense of the "what-it-is," i.e., which signifies ousia.

"Ousia" is thus the primary or basic *significatum* of the word "being." When we say *what* a thing is we state not its size, its color, or the disposition of its parts but its basic nature, as in "this is a horse." This kind of predication is prior to predication in other categories, such as quality, quantity, and position; so much, we are told, is "obvious." Some things remain, however, less than obvious. What is ousia?

The *Categories,* if that is the "previous enumeration" referred to in this quote,[10] have already told us that an ousia is a *tode ti,* a this-something or (as I call it) a "substance." Various qualities come to inhere (*eggígnesthai*) in a substance, but it does not itself come to inhere in anything else (*Cats.* 1a22f). For a quality to come to inhere in a substance means for it to be incapable of existing apart from that "in" which it is (ibid.), which presents us with a first difficulty in understanding Aristotle's metaphysics. For his treatment of the nature of qualities and of their inherence in substances is elliptical enough to leave it open whether the qualities in question are truly individual or more general. Is the paleness of Socrates unique to him, as J. L. Ackrill thought?[11] Or is it a complexion he can share with Callias, as G. E. L. Owen argued?[12]

If the former, then substances have inviolable boundaries: nothing "present in" Socrates can ever be anywhere except in Socrates. If the latter, qualities can exist in more than one substance and perhaps can even migrate from one to another. In either case, however, substances have boundaries. That is implicit in the most extended characterization of them in the *Categories,* at 4a10-13: "But what is most characteristic of substance appears to be this: that, although it remains one and the same in number, it is capable of receiving contraries." If a substance is a "receiver" (*dektikon*) of qualities, it presumably receives them from somewhere, which suggests that they do exist beyond its boundaries; in any case, it is into these boundaries that it must receive them.[13] This naturally raises the question of *how* the reception comes about. When a fire warms water, does heat not leave the one to be "received" by the other? How does it do so?

That is not an issue in the *Categories.* The passage just quoted, for example, aims to show that the reception of a quality comes about through a change in the receiving substance itself (cf. *Cats.* 4a29f); at least one of Aristotle's examples there, that of someone standing up, is hard to assimilate to the idea of reception of a quality from some other thing (where was "standing" before Theaetetus "received" it?). The discussion of "affection" in *Categories* 9a28–10a10, for another example, is limited to (a) the power, noted but not explained, of a quality to produce a perception, and (b) the power of some qualities of a substance to produce changes in other qualities *of that same substance* (as when embarrassment leads to blushing). Accounts of how one substance can effect changes in a different substance are missing, as in the brief discussion of affection in *Categories* 9. In sum, as Furth puts it, "There is evidence [in the *Categories*] of a notable concern not to get involved in 'causes.'"[14]

What we do find in the *Categories* are terse and minimal germs of what we are looking for: the ousiodic traits of boundary, disposition, and initiative. "Boundary" here just means that, as has been seen, a quality is either received into a given substance or remains outside it (or perhaps both). This will remain central to Aristotle's later, more sophisticated articulation of the concept of ousia, as to later substance-ontologies in general. "Disposition" is conceived simply as inherence: all the other properties of a substance exist only because they inhere in its underlying nature (*Cats.* 5 2b38). This nature is not, as in the later *Metaphysics*, a determinate form. Indeed, as Furth has argued, it is not excluded here that the substrate can be a "bare particular," a substrate and nothing more—without even the basic properties that define a "substantial kind" for it.[15] But a bare particular, having no determinate nature, cannot affect its properties in any determinate way. The generation and arrangement of the parts and properties of a substance is thus not yet an issue for Aristotle, which means that the substrate here in the *Categories* is inert. Qualities of a substance are given being by the substrate in which they inhere; but they are not generated or ordered by that underlying unity, as they will be in later and richer versions of ousia.

What I call "initiative" is here conceived in the barest possible way. A substance, in virtue of its substrate, exists independently of other things. When a substance "receives" a new quality, whether from another substance or not, it can only happen via a change within the substance itself; and it must be a change which, like everything in this substance, is somehow caused or supported by its substrate. The *Categories'* treatment of change is thus not only meager but negative. Focused on the "reception" of qualities, it has no account of how they are "sent," of what the *Metaphysics* later calls "active potency," the positive ability of one ousia to produce changes in another ousia.

To be a thing, according to the *Categories*, is thus to possess boundaries and to consist within them of a substrate and properties which come to inhere in it. Disposition remains merely passive, while initiative is viewed only negatively. The *Categories* presents us, then, not with Aristotle's full concept of ousia but with a related concept (and parameter) which I call "substance." I refer to the early ontology of Aristotle's *Categories* as an ontology of substance and to the account in the *Metaphysics* as an ontology of ousia.[16]

The concept of substance is not abandoned altogether in Aristotle's later ontology; the demand that the primary beings be basic substrates (which Irwin calls the "subject-criterion") continues to exist alongside the demand that such beings have essences (the "essence-criterion").[17] Philosophy after Aristotle, as will be seen, not only uses the concept of substance but persistently confuses it with ousia, usually to the advantage of substance, which comes at times wholly to elide ousia and its richer versions of disposition and initiative.

OUSIA

A being which sets a standard for itself is an ousia. The beginning of my narrative of ousia is a remodeling of an older Aristotelian account of what it is to be a thing (an account which remodels even older Platonic and Presocratic accounts).[18] In the passage quoted from the *Metaphysics* we saw that ousia is a "what-it-is" or a "this"—which does not get us obviously beyond the *Categories*. But there is more. Ousiai alone, and nothing in the other categories, exist *kath' autá*, or (literally) "according to themselves." Unlike a substance, which consisted of a substrate and properties, an ousia seems thus to have an oddly reflexive structure. It does not *merely* exist (the way a heap of grain exists) but exists *in virtue of* its accordance with something: with itself.[19] And this means that an ousia is in a peculiar way distanced from self: it sets a standard according to which it exists, and this standard is itself. The idea of an immanent standard according to which one exists is foreign to Aristotle's substance ontology, for it suggests that something which fails to live up to its own immanent standard is somehow less of a being than something which does.[20]

What the *Categories* articulated in terms of "coming to inhere" is now discussed in terms of "separation" (*Metaph.* VII.1 1028a20-25). This is another of Aristotle's tantalizingly imprecise notions, but it seems that an ousia is in at least two ways "separate."[21] First, nothing in the other categories can be "separated" (*chôrízesthai*) from ousia. An ousia can walk or not walk, can separate itself from the activity of walking; but walking has to be the movement *of* something, on which it is dependent and from which it is inseparable. This something will itself ultimately be an ousia, so that when we say "it walks," we have implicitly said "an ousia walks."[22] Instances of all the other Aristotelian categories are similarly inseparable from ousia; it alone is separable from them. It seems to follow, though it is not stated explicitly here, that ousiai are separable from each other as well.[23] For if to be inseparable from an ousia is the prerogative of things in the other categories, then no ousia is inseparable from another ousia.[24] But if ousiai are separable from each other while things in the other categories are inseparable from them, then no non-ousia is inseparable from two different ousiai, for they could be separated from each other and then it would be separated from itself. Hence any non-ousia is either inside or outside some single ousia, and we may conclude that ousiai, like substances, have determinate boundaries.

The trait of boundary thus survives the move from substance to ousia. But other things do not. The properties an individual ousia exhibits are not, in contrast to those of a substance, democratically arranged; some are more "proper" or basic than others. These are the properties which constitute it as an ousia: its "what," the standard it sets for itself. Not only is ousia basic to all other kinds of thing, then, but any individual ousia has within itself a (still more) basic nature, its "what." Such a standard cannot be supplied by an inert substrate. The effort to articulate what can supply it and what sort of "standard" it can be propels Aristotle's ontology from substance to ousia.[25]

The first stage of this propulsion can be seen by noting that the primacy of ousia is not only ontological but also includes, among other things, priority in *logos* and in cognition.[26] Ousia is prior in logos because, as we saw at the beginning, it is the primary *significatum* of "being." This turns out to mean, here, that in the spoken or written logos of a thing—its definition or the statement of its rational structure—the definition of its ousia must be contained. Hence we can have the logos of an ousia without the full logos of the thing, but we cannot have a logos of a thing without having, as part of it at least, the logos of its ousia. This would not have been the case for substances, which (to recall Furth's point) *could* be bare particulars and hence would have no logos because they would lack any qualities for a logos to capture.

In addition to being "logically" prior in this sense, ousia also has a form of cognitive priority. For we think we know a thing best when we know its ousia, rather than when we know its other characteristics. Knowledge of these other characteristics is not separable, then, from knowledge of ousia, while knowledge of ousia can be had without knowledge of other characteristics. This, too, differs from the substance ontology of the *Categories*. For if the substrate there is a bare particular, there is nothing in it to be known, and the qualities which come to inhere in it are not said to be necessary to knowing it.

Both substances and ousiai have determinate boundaries, then, and because of that have unity. But a substance consists merely of a perhaps bare substrate and properties, while ousia is a rational, cognizable, and hence determinate aspect of a thing. Where a substantial substrate passively underlies its properties, an ousiodic form will actively appropriate and arrange them. Where a substrate merely receives properties from outside, the form of an ousia will be able actively to transgress its boundaries in an outward direction, implanting itself elsewhere in the cosmos.[27]

ESSENCE

Ousia as immanent standard is essence. Of the four ways in which Aristotle says people use "ousia"—to signify essence, universal, genus, or substrate (*Metaph.* VII.1 1028b33-35)—the best one turns out to be that which signifies essence (*to ti ên einai*). This is only to be expected, because when (in *Metaph.* VII.4) Aristotle takes up the question of ousia as essence, the first thing we are told about the latter notion is that it is "what [a thing] is said to be according to itself," *kath' auto.* If, then, an ousia is something which exists "in accordance with itself," i.e., in accordance with a certain standard which it itself *is,* then its essence is that standard as linguistically expressible: as logos. The essence thus manifests what I have called the "logical" priority of ousia. It is that in a thing which is most basic and can be put into words, the *primum significatum* referred to earlier, the point at which being and language first meet.

Metaphysics VII.4 argues that this standard must be defined without reference to anything yet more basic in the thing. The essence of Mozart, for example, is not to be a musician, because musicianhood is merely a specific way of being a human; Mozart can engage in specifically musical activity only in virtue of his more general capacities as a rational animal. Since nothing can be a "musician" without already being human, to define "human" in terms of "musician" would be not only incorrect but circular. Whatever is true of a thing "according to itself," then, must not include what I will call "relegated properties" (often called *propria*), those taken from other categories which presuppose the essence and would make its logos circular.

In addition to excluding terms for relegated properties, the formula for an essence must meet certain other constraints. Aristotle mentions here two further ways in which something can be predicated *not* according to itself. One is when we predicate something wholly extraneous or "accidental" to the essence, such as "pale" of a human being. Paleness, here, is not only not part of the essence; it is also not derivative from it the way "musician" is: when we say "pale," we have not implicitly said "human," because not all pale things are human. Rather, it is added wholly *ab extra* and may be taken away—for example, by later experience, as soon as we see that not all pale things are human beings, that not all humans are pale, or that some pale humans cease to be pale while remaining human. Such accidental properties are excluded from the essence while remaining within the boundaries of the thing whose accidents they are. I call this "immanent exclusion."

That a thing has accidents shows—though Aristotle once again does not make it explicit—that it has definite boundaries. For since the accidents of a thing are entirely adventitious to it, they cannot be assigned to this thing (rather than to another) in virtue of its essence: Socrates is not pale because he is a man, or even because he is Socrates. The only thing which makes paleness a quality of Socrates must then be that paleness is a characteristic of his matter, i.e., is within the spatial boundaries of his body. I call properties which are not within those confines—which do not belong to Socrates at all—"externally excluded" from him.

The second way a predication may fail to be "in accordance with self" is when the formula of an essence leaves out something that is needed, as if one tries to formulate the essence of "pale cloak" and defines only "pale." And so we arrive at the view that the logos for the essence of a thing must contain a set of predicates such that none is relegated; each is needed; and no necessary one is missing. Such a formula is a "definition" (*horizmos*), and the essence of a thing is its definable self. This means that the essence is a unity: heaps cannot be defined, and a heap of words, such as the dictionary, is not a definition of the word "dictionary." This unity means that none of the predicates contained in the definition of a thing's essence can apply to that thing unless they all do: if only some apply, then the thing is of another, more generic kind and has another definition.[28]

Strictly speaking, only ousiai have essences, because it is ousiai alone that can be accounted for using only ultimate terms. The definition of any other sort of being must make reference not only to that being itself (be it a color, size, or whatever) but also to the fact that it inheres in an ousia. Hence "definition is the formula of the essence and essences belong to ousiai either alone or chiefly and primarily and in the unqualified sense."[29]

There are, then, three ways in which a property can be attributed to a thing. Either it is one of the properties which constitute the thing's essence (as rational is constitutive of human); or it is a relegated property obtaining in virtue of this essence (as one is musical in virtue of being human); or it is a merely accidental property (such as paleness). The predications we make conform to this trilevel structure. The expressible nature of a thing, its essence, thus resides *in the thing* as its logos or the recipe for what it is to be that thing. As Daniel Graham notes, this reverses the direction of argument in the *Categories*, where the ontology was reached via an account of predication: "Here, language is not a model for metaphysics. Metaphysics autonomously determines a restructuring of language."[30]

But there is a problem. The essence of a thing is that subset of its properties expressed in the predicates included in its definition. It is, therefore, within the thing but not the whole of it. And yet, *Metaphysics* VII.6 tells us in its opening words that a thing is not other than its essence, either: for a thing is presumably not other than its own ousia, and its ousia is the same as its essence. So the thing should be the same as its essence. Only so, in fact, can its existence in virtue of its essential structure be existence "according to self." The essence of a thing must, in short, *be* that thing. But how can a thing be the same as a particular subset of its properties? How can a whole equal one of its aspects?

It cannot. Aristotle is quite clear here that an accidental unity, such as a pale human, is not the same thing as its own essence. If it were, the essence of human being and that of pale human being would be the same. So would the essence of human being and that of musical human being; and "pale" and "musical" themselves would coincide.[31] Only beings with no accidental properties at all, such as Platonic Forms, could be the same as their essences. For each such Form possesses only that set of properties designated by its definition: it has just those properties that are necessary to its being the Form that it is, and no others, certainly not accidental ones. A Platonic Form, then, is the same as its essence (*Metaph.* VII.6 103b14-18). Or would be, if such Forms existed: Plato's separation of forms from their instances fails, for Aristotle, on numerous grounds.[32]

We are left with the view that what Plato attributes unconditionally to Forms, Aristotle attributes with reservations to individual sensory objects: they "are" their essences. Just what these reservations are has for millennia been the subject of an enormous literature.[33] In spite of appearances, to say that a thing "is" or "is the same as" its essence is not to make an identity claim; for, as has been seen, a thing has properties which its essence does not. Nor, for that reason and others,[34] is it to say that the properties of a thing come to inhere in its essence as in a substrate. It seems more promising to associate the locution with the trilevel logos that the concept of essence posits within a thing. The thing then "is" its essence in that any of its properties is either part of this essence, derivable from it, or merely accidental to the thing.

But if Aristotle means to say this or anything similar, an apparent identity claim is an odd way to do it. As will be seen in the next chapter, a thing (such as a moral agent) "is" its essence in that it *can be considered* as equivalent to this essence (as the moral agent can be considered as "in the strictest sense" his reason—his own human essence).[35] This suggests that the apparent identity statement should be seen as belonging not to the conceptual articulation of ousia but to its parametric functioning. So viewed, it tells us what to do once we have established that a thing confronting us is an ousia. In particular, it tells us that any property which is not part of the essence of that thing is to be either relegated to derivative status or immanently excluded as accidental. Relegated predicates, as specifications of the essence, can always be brought in if particular circumstances require. Since they follow from the more general formula for essence, we know what they are: their nature is fully specified by, though not in, the essence. And accidents, though within the boundaries of the thing in question, are excluded from its identity. In this combination of relegation and exclusion, we see two enrichments of the basic trait of disposition: any property of an ousia is either wholly dependent upon its essence or not part of its identity.

FORM

Essence in transit is form. The essence, that within a thing which is ultimate and definable, can be further clarified by what *Metaphysics* VII.10-12 tells us about definition. A definition is a linguistic whole, and so has parts (which I call "essential predicates"). A thing is also a whole and also has parts; and there is, VII.10 tells us in its opening words, an isomorphism between the relation of the parts of the definition to the definition and the parts of the thing to the thing.

This seems obviously wrong, because things do not obviously resemble definitions. But Aristotle quickly qualifies it: the isomorphism in question does not apply to all the thing's parts. Some parts of a thing are "material," others "formal." The matter of a thing is part of that thing only in a qualified sense. Similarly for the "material parts" of a thing, which are composed of form (*eidos*) and matter. The strictest "parts" of a thing are just the properties designated by its essential predicates. These are aspects of the other side of the composite, the form. Just as the predicates essential to a thing must be present in the definition of its essence, so the properties necessary to its being what it is must be present in its essence itself. Definitions are constructed so that there is, for any thing, a one-to-one correspondence of such predicates to such properties. In this sense, the isomorphism holds.

The thing's "material" parts are those into which it passes away.[36] So anything which remains after the thing ceases to be (as body parts remain, for a while, after a person has died) is a material part. Opposed to this are the parts, or properties, which do not pass away, at least not in this sense: what I call the thing's "ousiodic form."

"Ousiodic form" is my version of the traditional phrase "substantial form," which the medievals introduced because Aristotle recurrently uses "form" (*eidos*) to refer both to the essence as intelligible and, more widely, to any determinate, i.e., cognizable, property of a thing: the sense in which, for example sense perception is the reception of the "sensible form" of a thing into the organ of perception.[37] Aristotle's justification for this equivocal use of "form" is presumably that "form" in its wider sense, like "being" itself, is transcategorial (cf. *Metaph.* VII.9 1034b8f; XII.4 1070b16-22). Qualities, quantities, relations, and the like can also be determinately cognizable, i.e., can also be forms. But the primary sense, as always, would be the ousiodic sense: form as a determinacy which is not simply to be perceived in a thing but exercises disposition and initiative over it.

This hardly exhausts the difficulties with Aristotle's treatment of form. Aristotle himself notes that the nature of form is the "most perplexing" of the three candidates for ousia (form, matter, and the composite). Commentators can only agree; as G. E. M. Anscombe and Peter Geach put it, "There is hardly a statement about form in the *Metaphysics* that is not contradicted, at least verbally, by some other statement."[38] Relieving all this distress is hardly in order here (especially when a voluminous and burgeoning literature has conspicuously failed to do so).[39] What I can reasonably hope to do is just to displace a couple of the more obvious problems in favor of a deeper one which plagues not only Aristotle but metaphysics after him as well. I call it the problem of the "migration of form."

To formulate this problem in a preliminary way: it seems that what I call initiative, the movement of a form across the boundaries of an entity in which it has come to be, is at odds with both boundary and disposition. For what good are boundaries that are porous? And if forms from outside can enter into me, they affect me—so what happens to the disposition of my form over my body? This issue, which I will spell out a bit more at the end of this chapter, is a major, if largely buried, concern of Western philosophy; it will be seen to trouble Descartes's account of the mind, Hobbes's of the sovereign state, and Locke's of property ownership.

We can approach the problem as it affects Aristotle's views on form by considering the relation of (ousiodic) form and essence. If the essence of a thing is that within it which can be defined and if the formal parts of a thing are parts of its definition, then the form of a thing ought to be its essence, as it is often taken to be.[40] But there ought also to be a difference between the two; for if form and essence were identical, why would Aristotle have two separate locutions for them?[41]

The following general consideration may prove illuminating. At *Metaphysics* VII.4-6, the "essence" of a thing is what that thing "really" is: its true identity.[42] Our modern ideas about the uniqueness of individuals make it sound odd to go on and say that this identity of mine can be shared by others. Odder still, indeed strangely threatening even to the Greeks, would be the claim that what makes me me, my ultimate identity, can actually leave me and "migrate" to other individuals.[43] But that is precisely what Aristotle wants to say happens, certainly in at least two very special cases: generation and perception.[44] This problem of the "migration of form" illuminates, I think, two others: Aristotle's use of "essence" and "form" and his insistence that the latter must somehow be both unique to me and shared by others—both particular and universal.

It is noteworthy that with VII.7 the *Metaphysics* passes from a discussion of essence as constituting the identities of individuals to essence as transiting between individuals. The two perspectives are not merely disparate, as Furth notes,[45] but opposed; for it is not only unsettling but paradoxical to talk about the identity of a thing, what it "really" is, moving from it to another thing.[46] While Aristotle can hardly be said to shrink from admitting and investigating just this paradox, it is also clearly advantageous for him to have two different ways of referring to what, he wants ultimately to show, is the same thing. Because of later developments in my narrative, it is also advantageous for us; and I use "form" and "essence" as follows.

"Essence" refers to form considered simply as reposing within the thing of which it is the form; "form" (or, when necessary, "ousiodic form") refers to the essence as something which has arrived in this being from other beings and/or which will pass on out of it—especially into offspring or a knower.[47]

This view, like its rivals, cannot be shown to make perfect sense of Aristotle or to capture the intentions of his impossibly convoluted texts.[48] But it accords, generally, with Aristotle's usage. Though an exhaustive canvass would be out of place here, it seems that the word *eidos* is used by Aristotle mainly in contexts which either explicitly or implicitly trade on the idea of the migration of a thing's form to another thing. Hence, of the four main senses of *eidos* given in Bonitz's *Index aristotelicus,* all but one—the one in which Aristotle uses *eidos* in Plato's sense, when discussing him—do so trade.[49] In accordance with this, Bostock glosses *eidos* in the wide sense as "any characteristic that may be acquired or lost in a change," and in the narrow sense as "that kind of form that is acquired in . . . a substantial change."[50] Similarly, Irwin's examples show that Aristotle's clearest references to particular forms are in connection with reproduction.[51] And finally, Aristotle says that individuals, insofar as they have matter, are not definable or knowable:

> there is neither definition nor demonstration about sensible individual ousiai, because they have matter whose nature is such that they are capable of being or not being.[52]

Cognition, as discussed in the next chapter, is a case of the transit of form; matter, which does not transit, cannot be known.

Essences which have made a transit—forms in the sense of species—are as a result in more than one thing at once, and so are what Aristotle calls "universals" (cf. *Metaph.* VII.13 1038b10-12). This brings up another perplexing Aristotelian knot: what, in form as Aristotle conceives it, is supposed to be particular and what universal? At *Metaphysics* VII.15, Aristotle suggests that if definition is of the essence as *form,* it is of a universal,[53] and commentators such as Daniel Graham have argued that form (and essence) must be universal for Aristotle.[54] But Aristotle also refers to the form of a thing as being particular, i.e., as the principle of unity of that individual thing—most obviously in identifying the soul of a living thing with its form—and many commentators have found particular forms in Aristotle.[55] Is form, then, universal or particular, or neither or both?

Here again, the migration of form can shed some light. A "universal," for Aristotle, is in many places at once; as Irwin argues, it necessarily has a plurality of instances.[56] And, as Irwin also notes, universals can come into and go out of existence: if everything were healthy, as the *Categories* has it (*Cats.* 14a6-110), then sickness—a universal—would not exist. But if such is the case, it seems that sickness for Aristotle can first exist without being a universal, then become one. For suppose that everything is healthy and that one thing gets sick. At this point, since plural instantiations are required for universality, sickness can only be a particular quality of the infected being, like the unique complexion of a human being. If this being then infects another, sickness has plural instantiations and so becomes a universal. Universality and particularity, then, are not as mutually exclusive for Aristotle as is often thought. The only way for him to maintain *that* would require him to claim that just one being could not become sick, that sickness, as a universal, could enter the cosmos only by two or more beings getting sick simultaneously. If, in accordance with Aristotle's wide use of the term "form," we call sickness a form, then it seems that form itself can be either universal or particular, as Aristotle implies in *On the Heavens:* "any shape or form has, or may have, more than one particular instance."[57]

My suggestion is not that form for Aristotle is neither individual nor universal, like a medieval common nature, but is a more Hegelian one, that it is dynamically both: it can pass over from the one to the other. Universality is something that particulars *achieve.* They achieve it by the transit of form from one thing to another.[58]

With respect to ousiodic forms, this thought experiment is not only imaginary but counterfactual. There never was for Aristotle just one human being; the human species, like other species, has always been a universal. But that, for him, is a separate issue; there is nothing inherent in the nature of form itself that prohibits there from having been just one human being.[59] So if some counterfactual Aristotelian Adam *had* passed his uniquely human form along to a proto-Hellenic Eve, then ousiodic form too would move from particular to universal. The upshot is that ousiodic form itself is universal—has a plurality of instances at all times—not simply in virtue of its being form but in virtue of the passage of the human form from parent to child in reproduction; in virtue, then, of what I call the "transit of form," which proves to underlie the question of the universality and particularity of form as it did the relation of the locutions "form" and "essence."

To state the results of the foregoing as baldly as possible: Aristotle claims, in *Metaphysics* VII. 4-6, that the true identity of a thing is its essence. When he comes on this basis to confront the problem that *Categories* so carefully excluded—that of how things "send" properties to and "receive" them from one another—it is in a highly acute form, for among the qualities thus sent and received, it appears, are those which constitute a thing's essence or identity. Aristotle buys some conceptual space by giving a different name to essence-in-transit, calling it "form" (a term which in its wider sense applies to any non-material feature which can move from one entity to others). And then he stumbles across the fact that form so considered must oscillate between the universal and the particular: operating on its own matter, it is the unique identity of an individual; transiting from one area of matter to another, it gets universalized.

Behind two of the many obvious problems with Aristotelian metaphysics there thus lies, if I am right, not a coherent doctrine but a further problem: the problem of how form can transgress boundary. This problem is inherent in the concept of ousiodic structure in both its Aristotelian and later versions. I will discuss its Aristotelian version in more detail later in this chapter. But first, I have to show how the concept of ousiodic form as essence-in-transit enriches Aristotle's concept of disposition.

The disposition of essence over nonessential properties consisted, we saw, in the fact that any nonessential property of a thing could either be derived from its essence or excluded from the thing's identity. Both cases presupposed that such nonessential properties were already present, that the essence of a (material) thing stood, from the start, in relation to something nonessential in that thing. This was, in fact, suggested by the definition of essence as "what a thing is said to be according to itself," which implied that it is possible to speak of a thing not "in accordance with itself"; and it was appealed to in Aristotle's critique of the Platonic forms, mentioned earlier.

The perspective of form allows a deeper question to be asked—that of how form comes to be in a particular expanse of matter at all, rather than of what sorts of relation it has to other properties once it is there. The answer to this question, the disposition of form over matter, is correspondingly more basic than the disposition of essence over nonessential properties. Form, unlike essence, is portrayed as actively unifying matter, with the form itself and with other matter. As Haring puts it,

> Form, the primary intelligible reality, determines the whole individual. Thereby, it governs also the material parts of the whole. Severed from the whole, the parts lose their roles, that is, their power qua parts, and often even their structure. A finger severed from body is removed from the aegis of soul, and is a finger in name only.[60]

The power of the sapling to bring nutrients in the soil together within its own body so as to constitute leaves, branches, roots, bark, and so on, each in its proper place, exemplifies this unifying activity of form. It is the power of the form at any given time to *order* the parts of the thing.

There is more. The formal parts of a thing—the properties not indirectly but actually referred to in its definition—are prior to the thing itself, which they constitute by their unity. The material parts, by contrast, are posterior to the unity which they compose (*Metaph.* VII.10 1035b2–26). The tree would not have leaves and bark were it not a tree; and it was a tree, i.e., had that form, before growth had produced its branches and bark.[61] The matter which the form unifies, then, is not merely brought together with other matter and arranged, as if the growing tree found roots and branches in the soil and grafted them onto itself. Rather the form of a natural composite actually *generates* its parts from other matter.[62] The disposition of an ousiodic form over its matter consists, then, in the capacity of the form first to generate the thing's material parts and then to order them and maintain them in order. Considered in terms of this enriched account of disposition—almost the richest of all—the being of a thing consists in the generation and subsequent ordering of its material parts by its form. Those properties of its parts and of the whole which can be accounted for by the action of the form in this way are what I call "relegated" properties; those which cannot are immanently excluded as merely "accidental."

The cause, or *archê*, of the generation and ordering of the material parts of a thing must, since it imparts unity, be a unit. But it cannot be any of the thing's parts, formal or material. For the parts of a thing, as *Metaph.* V.25 tells us,[63] are that into which the whole is divided and so cannot preexist the whole. A part of a thing, in other words, cannot generate all its parts, because it cannot generate itself. Nor can it order them; for then the question would arise of how the single part comes together with the other parts so as to make them cohere with each other, and we would face a regress (*Metaph.* VII.17, 1041b1-33). Nor can the unifying aspect be composed of such parts, for the same reasons. So the unifying element must be the whole of the thing's essence, which thus does not simply lie inert in the matter, as the canonical discussions in *Metaphysics* I and *Physics* I so misleadingly suggest form does,[64] but is a unifying activity over that of which it is the essence.[65]

Ousia gains parametric status for Aristotle from the cooperation of this enriched concept of disposition with the cognitive or explanatory function of form. Any form, ousiodic or not, can migrate from one expanse of matter to another and can be known to do so. So it can be known independently of any particular expanse of matter that it may be in. All we need do to gain knowledge of forms (in the broad sense) is look at what two material things have in common. As Haring puts it,

> The step from individual to species is the step from form-in-*this*-matter to form as having a typical effect in a typical domain. What drops out of account is the individual matter.[66]

In this way, form-in-transit can give rise to a "universal" in the more usual contemporary sense. This is what makes form the "primary intelligible reality" and gives it an explanatory role.[67] Since it is in the interests of rational beings such as ourselves to have the world be explainable, it is in our interests to have it be as "formal" as possible. In particular, the greater the disposition of the ousiodic form over its matter, the more intelligible the composite will be. This, as will be seen in chapter 2, is part of what gives ousia its parametric status for Aristotle: any being should be first approached as having a form disposing its matter. If that fails, and to the extent possible, we should bring it into that condition.[68]

In summary, I take the ousiodic "form" of a thing to be a unitary active principle which, arriving in an expanse of matter, shapes this matter into parts of a living body and then maintains these parts in their proper functioning order. Because form can move from one expanse of matter to another, it can also be known apart from the unique features of any expanse of matter. Considered on its own in this way, form is what we would call universal and therefore intelligible. As Joseph Owens puts it,

> the Aristotelian form is one with the thing, but not *entirely* so. It is the thing expressed according to the form, but not according to the matter. Yet that suffices for the thing known and the principle of knowability to be one.[69]

MATTER

That which submits to form is matter. Form makes matter a "this." In itself, matter is not a "this," or indeed an anything. Hence the negativity of Aristotle's most attentive definition, in *Metaphysics*. VII.3, of matter:

> By matter I mean that which in itself is neither a particular thing nor of a certain quantity nor assigned to any other of the categories by which being is determined. (1029a19-21)

Matter is thus somehow outside the determinations of being, and Aristotle goes on to say that it is neither positive nor negative with respect to the categories; quantity, quality, and the rest can no more be asserted of it than they can be denied.[70]

The reason matter escapes the categories is that matter is other than *all* predicates. Consider the famous "stripping-away" argument of *Metaphysics* VII.3.[71] It seems, writes Aristotle, to be matter, rather than essence, of which all things are predicated. For if I can say "this human is musical" and predicate musicality of some human, I can as well say "this is a human." In the latter predication, the essence—and hence the form—is given by the predicate; so what it is predicated of, the "this," must be matter. But what we have when *all* form is imaginatively stripped away from the subject and located in the predicate is not really predication at all. For with all predicates stripped away from a particular quantity of matter (including, of course, those denoting quantity, size, and shape), there is no way whatsoever to identify the subject of the predication; there is nothing definite enough to be separate from anything else, no "this."[72] Indeed, it is extremely doubtful that Aristotle thinks that any such thing as truly propertyless matter, or prime matter, can ever actually exist; matter is always found under some form.[73] As V. C. Chappell puts it,

> Matter is by nature a kind of abstraction. It can be distinguished in thought . . . but it cannot in fact exist apart from some thing or other whose matter it is. . . . Though we may take no notice of the thing that is constituted or composed by matter in a given instance, its existence is assured. *By its very nature, matter cannot be free.*[74]

In my terms, Aristotle here is subsuming the substantialistic concept of a substrate under the ousiodic rubric of matter and form. For when we do have the attribution of an essence to some underlying substrate, we learn, it is because the matter of that substrate already contains some form (in the broad sense of determinate properties). Hence, as Aristotle points out in discussing actuality and potentiality, no "active potency" can take effect except in matter which has the properties which render it capable of receiving this form. You cannot make saw (or a human) out of wool.[75] So we can say "this is a casket" (or "this is a human being") and be predicating the form of the particular informed matter in which it has come to be, such as wood (or bones and flesh).

According to *Metaphysics* VIII.4, then, there are different kinds of "proper" or "proximate" matter. Indeed, a thing may have several levels of matter within it, with different degrees of determinacy or form. Human matter, which for Aristotle is originally the menstrual fluid, has, for example, a form more complex than the elemental earth and water which it contains. These elements, in turn, are more complex than the "elementary qualities" (hot, cold, dry, moist) out of which they are formed.[76] What we are to pay attention to in giving an account of a being is its "proximate" matter, the matter which is able to receive its ousiodic form. This matter may be highly formed indeed, so much so as to be "identical" to the form—except that the form exists actually and the proximate matter exists potentially, i.e., is potentially exactly what the form is actually (*Metaph.* VIII.6 1045b18-20).

That only certain sorts of matter can receive any particular form and thus are "hypothetically" necessary for it[77] means that matter constrains the forms which it can receive, and in this it functions as a sort of principle or *archê* (*Metaph.* IX.1 1046a22-25). But only to an extent, for the form of an ousia imposes its own limits:

> while the growth of fires goes on without limit as long as there is a supply of fuel, in the case of all complex wholes formed in the course of nature there is a limit or ratio which determines their size and increase, and limit and ratio are marks of soul but not of fire, and belong to the side of formulable essence rather than to that of matter. (*De An.* II.4 416a17-19)

Fire is an element, not an ousia, for Aristotle; its growth is limited only by the amount of flammable material available. In ousiai, this limiting role of matter is reduced. While a natural form requires a sufficient amount of the proper kind of matter—oak trees will not grow in the sea—what *primarily* limits the growth of an ousia is its own nature, which is such as to be able to control only a certain amount of certain kinds of matter. Thus fire can burn down an entire supermarket; but I cannot eat one, because of the kind of form that I have.

Form sets boundaries to matter. Boundary has not been explicitly discussed by Aristotle previously. The point of view of essence, I suggested, shows (but does not say) that things have definite boundaries; what distinguishes the accidents of one thing from those of another thing can only be that they are located within its boundaries, for they are not caused by the essence of that thing. In the discussion of form, boundary is also left implicit; it is what a form must transgress in order to move from one thing to another, but it is not discussed in its own right. Now we see where boundaries come from: in an ousia, boundary is an effect of form.

Aristotle's treatment of matter also, and fatefully, enriches the trait of disposition. Form, I argued, exercises disposition over matter in that it transforms it into material parts, then maintains these parts in their proper functioning order. But matter is not, as it will be in later philosophy, wholly passive in this. In addition to constraining the form which requires it, matter also, as Mary Louise Gill has shown, opposes and "subverts" it. This is because, of its own accord, the more determinate matter of a particular ousia has a natural tendency to resolve itself back into the elements from which it is formed.[78] As Gill puts it,

> When the elements have been worked up into a higher object . . . the potentiality *to be* the higher object, though now realized, still determines the matter accidentally. On the other hand, the potentiality *not to be* that higher construct but to be some simpler stuff instead is a potentiality that determines the very nature of the material genus, because the properties that constitute the genus can specify the nature of a simpler body. *The elements thus achieve their fullest being when they are separate in a state of uncombined simplicity.* To put the point metaphorically, the elements do not "strive" upward toward complexity but downwards toward simplicity.[79]

Hence matter is not merely too "mushy" to provide the boundaries of ousiai, as the stripping-away argument suggested. Rather it actually "tends to reject the higher form."[80] Some sort of active principle is needed to keep this from happening, and this active principle, Gill argues, is the "immanent form"—in a living thing, its soul. Aristotle writes:

> We must ask what is the force that holds together the earth and the fire [in a living thing] which tend to travel in contrary directions; if there is no counteracting force, they will be torn asunder; if there is, this must be the soul and the cause of nutrition and growth. (*De An.* II.4 416a6–8)

Now we see the full force of the problem of form's migration for Aristotle. For the "identity" of an ousia is not merely a set of properties which allow us to recognize the thing on different occasions and to distinguish it from other things. It is that in the thing which holds it together. To think of it as leaving the thing and migrating elsewhere is not just odd but paradoxical; and not just paradoxical but, in some cases at least, downright scary.

Form is thus needed to explain the fact that matter comes in the determinate, enduring packets which we call "bodies." The substance ontology which began this chapter simply assumed the existence of bodies,[81] as do the modern substance ontologies of Descartes and Hobbes, which I discuss later. In general, as the history of Western metaphysics progresses, matter loses its Aristotelian capacity to resist form and becomes increasingly docile. For Aquinas, as will be seen, this docility is still enough of an oddity to require nothing less than the direct action of God to produce it. For the moderns, it is taken for granted. At all stages, to recur to Chappell: *"By its very nature, matter cannot be free."*

Finally, though matter always exists together with some form, in itself it escapes all predicates and so is unknowable according to itself (*agnostós kath' hautên; Metaph.* VII.11 1037a27f; also 1036a9). It renders the composite to some degree unknowable, as we have seen, and itself can be known only indirectly, through whatever constraints it places on the composite's form (*Metaph.* VII.8 1034a7f, VIII.3 1044a10–12).

INITIATIVE

My account of the concept of ousia in Aristotle uncovered a problem with the migration of form. The problem is nowhere explicitly identified by Aristotle; but some of his texts have hinted at it, and my subsequent narrative amply confirms its existence. It shows up on too many levels and in too many ways to be susceptible of complete treatment at a general level, and detailed understanding of it will have to await subsequent chapters. But for the moment, it can be understood a bit more by considering some of Aristotle's views on "active potency."

Active potency is the capacity of a thing to cause changes in another thing or in the thing itself *qua* other.[82] In accordance with Aristotle's general doctrine of causality, the changes any being causes in another being consist in the imparting of a determinate quality already actual in the agent to that other being: "the actually existing is always produced from the potentially existing by an actually existing, e.g., man from man, musician from musician."[83] Such change is what Gill calls an "imposition of form."[84] As the wording indicates, it is, in a sense, nonnatural; it is the complement of nature (*physis*), which is the capacity to cause change in oneself *qua* oneself. In Aristotle's words:

> I mean by potency not only that definite kind which is said to be a principle of change in another thing or in the thing itself regarded as other, but in general every principle of movement or of rest. For nature also is in the same genus as potency—not however in something else but in the thing itself *qua* itself.[85]

Nature and active potency, then, are both traced back to the activity of form in matter. When something happens by nature, a form acts "from within" on matter whose boundaries it determines and whose content it generates and/or orders. When the form "human being" dominates the ethical "matter" of my own life (which is seen in the next chapter to be my desires), so that I can deliberate in a rational way, I am not exercising active potency over that ethical "matter"; I am operating in accordance with nature. If I happen to be a doctor and the sick person I happen to be curing is myself, then I am causing changes in myself *qua* other, via the activity of my capacity to heal.

In the case of active potency, a form introduces itself into matter beyond its boundaries. Active potency is thus the way an ousia makes itself felt in its absence.[86] It is realized by a quality passing from one thing to another; in other words, by a transgression of the boundaries of the two things. When the quality which leaves a thing is part of its essence, the transgression is what I call "initiative." A stallion is exercising initiative when it begets a colt because its ousiodic from is passing along into the world outside. If the colt then snuggles for warmth against its sleeping father, the stallion is not exercising initiative, for "warm" is not part of the essence of horse; it is a relegated property which a horse has in virtue of being a living thing. Even less initiative is involved if the colt finds a rock still warm from the sun and snuggles against it, for hot is not even a relegated property of stone but a mere accident. Nondeliberate actions of human beings are similar: the person who thoughtlessly bumps another person is not exercising initiative, for the action is not the effect of her form, her reasoning capacity. Her behavior is "accidental."

Active potency as Aristotle conceives it is in tension with both boundary and disposition. For the transit of any form from one entity to another transgresses the boundaries of both, and porous boundaries are not boundaries. Moreover, active potency impeaches the disposition of a thing's essence over its matter. For when a thing is affected from without, its matter receives properties which come not from its own form but from outside. Worse, the transgression is for Aristotle always reciprocal; any agent is affected by, as well as affecting, that on which it acts—as when a knife used for cutting eventually becomes dull.[87] The exercise of an active potency thus impairs not only the boundaries but the disposition of *both* patient and agent. It would be better for Aristotle, one suspects, if active potency did not exist. Though Aristotle does not say this in so many words, it is suggested by his general characterization of it as, so to speak, "nonnatural." In general, actuality—the full presence of form in its matter—is prior to and (as Aristotle does say explicitly) better than even active potency for good (*Metaph.* IX.8 1049b5f; cf. *Metaph.* IX.8-9). Aristotle also makes this point more specifically: activity which does not leave the actor to produce an independent product (*praxis*) is superior to production (*poiêsis*), which does (*Metaph.* IX.8 1050a 23-1050b1).

In general, as I show in the next chapter, more concrete Aristotelian discourses seek to limit active potency to only a sort of necessary minimum, to cases in which the form which leaves the individual to migrate into the outside world is its ousiodic form. Initiative thus gains normative status: we should try to limit our effects on the outside world to just those caused by our ousiodic forms.

Even that, however, tends to be problematic. The begetting of offspring is a case of it; but it is only a *pis aller,* a second-best solution to the problem of immortality. Far better would be for the form of a living thing to remain permanently within its boundaries, i.e., for the living individual to be immortal. Because that is not possible, living things produce offspring, thus assuring themselves of generic, if not individual, immortality. Aristotle writes:

> Since . . . no living thing is able to partake in what is eternal and divine by uninterrupted continuance (for nothing perishable can ever remain one and the same), it tries to achieve that end in the only way possible to it, and success is possible in varying degrees; so it remains not indeed as the self-same individual but continues its existence in something *like* itself—not numerically but specifically one.[88]

It is unsurprising, then, that the highest being in Aristotle's cosmos, the Prime Mover, is not an efficient but a final cause—for that is the only way in which it can cause something without changing itself (*Metaph.* XII.7 1072a23-27).

This problem of the migration of form—due, I suggest, to the fact that it both transgresses the boundaries of the agent and patient and impeaches the disposition of their forms—remains in later philosophy. It resides in the fact that boundary and disposition, on the one hand, and initiative, on the other, are intrinsically at odds with one another. The only way to render boundaries and disposition absolute is, as with the Prime Mover, to deny initiative.

In the narrative I have given of it here, Aristotle's *concept* of ousia has emerged via the progressive enrichment of three basic traits: boundary, disposition, and initiative. Aristotle does not center his own discussion of ousia on these traits, but I hope to have shown that they are at work in its depths.

Substances already exhibited boundaries which, though not explicitly discussed, were that into which contraries were "received"; similarly, ousiai were said (if unclearly) to be, if not "bounded," "separate," not least from each other. In the section entitled "Essence," boundary was still not mentioned; but it was implied by the existence of accidents. Boundaries were then (in "Form") shown, but not said, to be transgressed in generation and cognition, and finally in "Matter" they were openly said to be established by ousiodic form.

Disposition began as the passive underlying of a substance's many qualities by its single substrate. In "Ousia" this was enriched so that the unity of a thing sets a standard for it in some obscure way. In "Essence" this turned out to mean that any property not belonging to the essence is either relegated to derivative status or excluded as accidental. Such exclusion is not effected by the boundaries of the thing, because what is excluded from a thing as accidental to it remains within its boundaries. It is, however, excluded from the thing's essence, and so from the thing itself insofar as it "is" its essence. In "Form," disposing activity was exercised not over properties but over matter. The form of a thing is what unifies it, and this turned out to mean that the form generates the thing's material parts (out of appropriate matter) and orders them. In "Matter," this activity turned out to include keeping the thing's body from flying apart into its constituent elements.

Initiative, for substances, was abstract and negative; it lay in the fact that any change occurring in a substance has to involve its basic nature, since the qualities (etc.) involved in such change were supported by the substrate. Its paradoxical status was first indicated, I suggested, by Aristotle's use of the two terms "essence" and "form" for what really was the same thing. The universality and particularity of form were then seen to be two aspects of its transitive character. In "Initiative," active potency was the capacity of a thing to affect what is (or is considered to be) outside its boundaries. As a transgression of boundaries, active potency is already outside nature. Since its exercise reacts upon the actor, it constitutes an impeachment not only of boundary but of disposition as well. This impeachment will remain problematical, not only in more concrete Aristotelian discourses but also in later philosophy.

Any ousia exhibits a hierarchy within itself. Most basic, or (we might say) at its top, is its essence, a complex but unified activity whose different aspects—the being's formal parts—are always found together in anything of that particular species. This is the "standard" that the thing sets for itself, so that when it exists according to its essence it exists "according to itself." One step down are what I called "relegated" properties. These are properties which have secondary status because they are specifications of the primary ones, as "musician" is a specification of "rational animal": music is the rational way of dealing with the structure of sound.

Another step downward brings us to the "material parts." These parts, because they can only be formed from certain sorts of matter, are not parts of the essence; since they contain matter, they are only incompletely knowable. Yet they are, like heart and lungs, necessary for the maintenance and welfare of the being itself. They are disposed by the essence: generated, ordered, and maintained in that order by it.

A further step down are the wholly accidental characteristics, which the thing has simply because of the kind of matter that it contains: properties such as the color of eyes, which do not derive from the essence and do not normally contribute to the welfare or maintenance of the thing. Some of these, such as the tan of one's skin or the absence of a finger, may result from the accidental impingements of other things. Though these are, as accidents of the thing, found within its boundaries,[89] they are excluded from the thing's basic identity and could be changed without affecting this identity.

Finally, beneath all these—beneath essence and Being themselves; sullen and posterior, unknown and unknowable; communicating its unknowability upward almost to the level of essence itself; seeking resolution downward into its own elemental nature; abasing the pristine universality of the form into the random and defective uniqueness of the individual; supporting all characteristics, exhibiting none; lurking in the lowest depths; the shrouded Alpha from which all things come, and the dark Omega into which they must return—roils the ancestress of the id and of the proletariat, of body and *différance* and of all that is colonized or seeks liberation: matter.

With this concept of ousia begins not merely the history of metaphysics but that of the West itself. For the idea that reality is, or ought to be, composed of entities within whose determinate boundaries one aspect is dispositive, initiatory, and generally "equal" to the whole was not easily done away with by philosophers once Aristotle had codified it. In spite of ancient and recurring occlusion by the related parameter of substance, occlusion which had already begun in the Hellenistic world, ousia provides the Western structures of self, household, and empire. In defiance of later attacks, beginning with what is called "modernity" and carried into a final challenge by Heidegger, it remains basic to our lives today. It is what we understand, seek, and make. It structures our sciences and societies, our loves and lovers. It is what we "really" are; it is our essence.

2

OUSIA AS PARAMETER IN ARISTOTLE

Chapter 1's digging should have made plausible that any ousia, for Aristotle, exhibits the three traits of boundary, disposition, and initiative in some way and to some degree. These three traits thus constitute a concept of ousia which, if not Aristotle's explicit formulation, is nonetheless a product of his work. But this "concept" turns out to have a rather problematic status. Though it is articulated in a discourse on the nature of the thing in general and tells us what (in Aristotle's view) it is to be such a thing, Aristotle makes quite plain that some things are qualities, quantities, relations, etc., rather than ousiai. Indeed, it is notably unclear just what the concept of ousia is supposed to refer to. This is what Montgomery Furth calls the "population problem," and he argues that it is not the job of metaphysics to solve it: Aristotle lays out the criteria for being a "substance" in such a way as to leave it for empirical investigation which beings it applies to.[1]

It seems from this that ousiodic structure does not exhibit itself directly in our experience. If it did, it would be immediately evident which things are ousiai, and further investigation would be unnecessary. We would also know immediately from seeing a thing which of its characteristics belong to its material parts and which to its essence or form, since such a distinction is basic to being an ousia at all. But we do not; as I noted in the preceding chapter, Aristotle writes that it is sometimes hard to tell which of a thing's properties are formal and which material, since both kinds of properties may always be found together.[2]

What "ousia" does do is guide our investigative behavior. It licenses a particular sort of reflection upon sensory experience, which Aristotle calls "induction" (*epagôgê*).[3] Such reflection compares things with one another and with themselves over time, seeing which properties they retain for the entire span of their existence and which they have in common with others of their kind. Once we have isolated these properties, we must (as I noted in chapter 1) go on to find that subset of them which is basic to the rest. Only then do we finally have the formula for the essence of the thing. As Terence Irwin puts it,

> If something's being F explains its being G and the converse is not true, then F is the basic subject and therefore the substance. . . . Aristotle, therefore . . . shows . . . that intuitive tests may not pick out basic subjects, and that commonsense subjects may not be substances.[4]

It is one thing to perceive that an approaching thing is a human being;[5] knowing that "humanity" is her *ousiodic* nature and knowing what "humanity" is are other things, and they take a good deal of reflection.[6]

The concept of ousia can thus be applied *descriptively* to entities only as the result of a reflective practice which it *parametrically* licenses and structures. This leads to at least three sorts of questions. First, what is it in our sensory experience that incites such reflection? If we do not directly sense ousia as such, what is it in the things that we do sense which leads us to reflect upon them in such a way that we become aware of their essential properties? How, in other words, does ousia find what I call "empirical purchase"? Second, how does the parameter of ousia structure other, more concrete Aristotelian discourses? And finally, with what nontheoretical practices is ousia bound up? What kinds of work does it perform and license us to perform? What kinds of activity does it trigger? What social structures can it sanction?

In this chapter I suggest an answer to the first sort of questions. But my main purpose is to broach the second question by pointing out a few of the many ways in which the metaphysical parameter of ousia structures other types of Aristotelian discourse. Once that has been done, we can at least begin to see how ousia structures nontheoretical practices.

The parametric functioning of ousia turns out to have three sorts of justification. First, as I noted in chapter 1, form is what is intelligible; to have a "theory" about something means having knowledge of its form or essence. The more characteristics of the thing derive from its form (including especially behavioral characteristics), the closer our knowledge of its form comes to being knowledge of the thing as a whole. Hence to understand something in an Aristotelian way means to approach it as having within it a single, unified, intelligible principle which, in my terms, bounds and disposes its matter. In this way, ousia provides what I call a *hermeneutical* basis for more concrete investigations.

Second, to talk about a thing, for Aristotle, *is* to talk about ousia: the metaphysical articulation of ousia is the discourse of the thing in general. Discussions of other types of thing, then, can only concern (a) specific types of ousia and (b) their qualities, quantities, relations, etc. Since human beings, households, and states are specific types of thing, they are structured as the thing in general is for Aristotle: as ousiai with boundary, disposition, and initiative. This type of structuring can be captured syllogistically ("all changeable ousiai have a structure of form and matter; x is a changeable ousia; therefore x has a structure of form and matter"), and I call it *argumentative*.

Finally, ousia provides a series of analogies, in which various specimens of ousiodic structure can be understood by being likened to one other, more familiar instances of it—particularly, as will be seen, to the household.

As the quotes from Irwin and Bonitz with which I opened chapter 1 suggest, the doctrines of Aristotle's more concrete discourses are for the most part rather clearer than those of his metaphysics.[7] This chapter requires less digging, then, as it comes to discuss more concrete Aristotelian discourses.[8] We also know now what we are looking for, and I can be extremely selective, confining myself to just a few basic traits of Aristotle's treatments of human individuals, households, and states.

COGNITION

In Aristotle's account of cognition, the soul functions as an ousia, exhibiting various types of boundary, disposition, and initiative. The cognitive "faculties" of sensation (*aisthêsis*), imagination (*phantasia*), and thought (*nous*) are in fact so structured that each level serves as matter for the next and so is bounded and disposed by it. Initiative, as always, remains problematic.

The beginning of Book II of *De Anima* contains the following:

> We are in the habit of recognizing, as one genus of what is, ousia, and that in several senses, (a) in the sense of matter or that which in itself is not "a this," and (b) in the sense of form or essence, which is precisely that in virtue of which a thing is called "a this," and thirdly (c) in the sense of what is compounded of both. . . . Among ousiai are by general consent reckoned bodies, especially natural bodies, for they are the principles of all other bodies. Of natural bodies some have life in them, others not; by life we mean self-nutrition and growth and decay. It follows that

48

every natural body which has life in it is an ousia in the sense of a composite. Given that there are bodies having life . . . the soul cannot be a body; for the body is the subject or matter, not what is attributed to it. Hence the soul must be an ousia in the sense of the form of a natural body having life potentially within it.[9]

This passage presents an argument which can be loosely summarized as follows: all ousiai contain matter and form; natural bodies are ousiai and so contain matter and form. Some natural bodies are alive, and in these we find (matter and) form as an active principle of nutrition and growth. Soul must occupy the place of this principle and so is "the form of a natural body having life potentially within it." (This sort of "argumentative" parametric justification will be seen again. Every time Aristotle characterizes the object of an investigation as an ousia, he goes on to approach it in terms of the binary couple of form and matter.)

Since cognition is an activity of soul, ousiodic structure must apply to it too. Aristotle's account begins with sensation, which in *De Anima* II is the reception into a sensory organ of the sensible form (i.e., some determinate quality) of a thing. Crossing the boundary of a sensory organ, the form is received into it as a signet ring's shape is received into wax: "without matter."[10] Just what Aristotle means by the "reception of form without matter" has inspired a fair amount of scholarly activity, largely concerned with whether and how such reception may be or be reduced to physiological processes.[11] The fact of the controversy should not surprise us, for the reception of form into a sensory organ is clearly a transgression of the boundary of the perceiving body, and if I am right it *should* be problematic for Aristotle. Its resolution need not detain us, for merely recognizing it means recognizing that the knowing soul has boundaries.[12]

Noteworthy at this point is the way Aristotle associates the reception of form with change (*kinêsis*).[13] Consider the following passages:

Color sets in movement (*kinei*) what is transparent, e.g., the air, and the sensory organ is moved (*kineisthai*) by that, it being continuous [between the two]. (*De An.* II.7 419a13-15)

What has the power of producing sound is what has the power of setting in movement (*kinêtikon*) a single mass of air which is continuous from the moving body up to the organ of hearing. The organ of hearing is physically united with air, and because it is in air, the air inside is moved (*kineitai*) concurrently with the air outside. (*De An.* II.8 420a2-5)

Smell and touch (and therefore taste) are also said to function through a medium, like sight and sound, and so presumably have the same "kinetic" dimension.[14]

Sensation is thus produced by a change or "motion" spreading along a medium from object to sensory organ. This begins to sound like the situation in Aristotle's other special case of the transmission of form, generation.

For what is stored in the semen, as Furth notes, is not the form itself, but a patterned set of, precisely, "motions" (*kinêseis*) or concoctings which, passing into the matter supplied by the mother, "'shape' and 'set' that matter in stages as the development advances."[15] What Furth denies for generation:

> The genetic material carries specific form, not by containing little whole animals or parts of animals, but as *information* that under the proper circumstances can proceed to direct the stepwise construction of co-specific offspring.[16]

is just what Aristotle denies for vision:

> Color . . . is not an efflux (*aporriais*) of anything to anything. (*De An.* II.10 422a14f)

In both cases, Aristotle is evidently trying to show how form can "pass" from being A to being B without ever actually leaving A. His answer is that while still within A, the form resolves itself into *kinêseis* which travel to B, where it is then reconstituted from them.[17] This appeal to *kinêsis* as that which can transgress boundaries, however it is to be understood more closely, seems to be one of Aristotle's solutions to the problem of the migration of form which I introduced in chapter 1. Aristotle may first have formulated it with respect to generation and then carried it over to cognition, or the other way around. Either way, the tactic is a good example of what I call "parametric structuring," which is not merely a deductive relation in which one discourse furnishes premises for another but a whole family of relations—analogies, homologies, metaphors, presumptions, common strategies, shared gestures—by which one discourse affects the shape and content of another.

Once lodged in a sensory organ, the *kinêsis* becomes an object of the imagination (*phantasia*), the faculty intermediate between sense and reason—and becomes subject to disposition by the soul.[18] For objects of imagination are not merely within the perceiving body, as are sensed forms, but are to some degree under "our" control:

> [imagining] is up to us when we wish (for it is possible to produce [*poiêsasthai*] something before our eyes, as those do who set things out in mnemonic systems and form images of them). . . .[19]

What we sense, though received within our corporeal boundaries, is not at our disposition; we cannot choose what we see or hear. But in imagination the soul both generates its images ("produces something") and orders them ("when we wish"). It has, then, disposition over them, but in a highly imperfect way. For the soul's "generation" of images is really a regeneration of them; it cannot call up an image of something that it has never sensed.[20] And the order it gives to images is merely the more or less arbitrary sequence in which it calls them up, whenever it "wishes."[21]

In imagination, then, sensible forms which have transgressed the boundaries of the body are (re)generated and ordered by the soul. Boundary, already introduced in sensation, is in imagination supplemented by disposition.

De Anima II.1 argued that the distinction into matter and form could be found in the composite animal because it was part of the nature of ousia. *De Anima* III.5 introduces its famously incomprehensible distinction between "productive" and "receptive" intellect (*nous*) by restating this:

> Since in every class of things, as in nature as a whole, we find two factors involved, (1) a matter which is potentially all the particulars included in the class, and (2) a cause which is productive in the sense that it makes them all . . . these distinct elements must also be found within the soul. (*De An.* III.5 430a10-14)

Like the sensory organs, the "passive" intellect, which here plays the role of "matter" and "potentiality," "receives" forms. But it receives them from the imagination, not from outside the ensouled body:

> The thinking part of the soul must be, while impassable (*apathes*), capable of receiving the form of an object. . . . To the thinking soul images serve as if they were objects of perception (*aisthêmata*). . . . (*De An.* III. 4 429a 14-16, III.7 431a14f)

> But between the two cases there is a difference; the objects that excite the sensory powers to activity, the seen, the heard, etc. are outside. The ground of this difference is that what actual sensation apprehends is individuals, while what knowledge apprehends is universals, and these are in a sense within the soul. That is why a man can exercise his knowledge when he wishes, but his sensation does not depend on himself—a sensible object must be there. (*De An.* II.5 417b18-23)

The objects of intellect are within it only "in a sense" because its boundaries are not spatial but generic; it is "unmixed" with the body and "separable" from it, and has no bodily organ.[22] One motivation for this appears to be that, on the one hand, mind is "impassable" (or "incapable of being affected," *apathes*) and so must have boundaries. On the other hand, it must be able to "receive" anything whatsoever, for there can be nothing which we cannot cognize.[23] In other words, intellect cannot have boundaries at all in any ordinary sense, for everything would be able to transgress them and they would not be boundaries. In order to exist at all, it seems, the boundaries must be generic; intellect is a different *kind* of thing from anything else, and only as such can it be called the "place of forms."[24]

We can expect, then, that this particular case of the transgression of boundary—one in which objects of cognition move from the imagination to the intellect—will be even more problematic than usual for Aristotle.[25] Essential to it is the abstraction of universal forms (*noêta*) from their "partial and inadequate" presentations in the *phantasmata*.[26] As with the ingestion of matter in nutrition, the materials received by the intellect cannot be left as they are. Apples must be broken down into nutrients the body can use, and the *phantasmata* must undergo a much greater change: they must be converted into abstract concepts. When that has happened, the receptive intellect not only receives intelligible objects from the imagination but actually "becomes" them in turn; they are merely (so to speak) configurations it assumes.[27]

If the receptive intellect "receives" and "becomes" its objects, it is the productive intellect which "makes" them and uses them the way an art uses its materials (*De An.* III.5 430a10-17). It is, then, the originary source (*archê*) to the matter (*hylê*) of the passive intellect (*De An.* III.5 43a19). Generating the objects of intellect (and exercising in this one kind of disposition over them), it plays a role analogous to that of the soul itself in imagination: where "we" produce (*poiein*) images "before our eyes," productive intellect "makes" (*poiein* again) universals in the receptive intellect. As with the perceptual faculty, Aristotle is clearly trying here to give an account of the intellect which locates in it the traits of boundary and disposition. In both cases, boundary and disposition enter on different levels. Boundary is introduced first, in sensation and passive intellect respectively. Generation (or regeneration) of what has thus crossed the relevant boundary is then the job of "us" or of the active intellect.

Aristotle's account of the intellect has legendary difficulties. If I am right, his attempt to locate boundary and disposition within the intellect is the source of at least two of them. Because intellect must have boundaries yet be completely open, its boundaries must be of a unique kind, generic rather than spatial. Intellect then becomes something mysteriously immaterial. And in order to locate disposition within the intellect, it must be divided into one aspect which "receives" and "becomes" intellectual objects (matter) and another which "makes" and "uses" them (form). Both moves have led to frequent and prolonged confessions of commentatorial bafflement, which I will not rehearse here.

The intellect not only generates its objects but orders them in ways which, though complex, are comparatively understandable. The simplest formed matter of knowledge, the "indivisible object of thought" which productive intellect generates, is "the definition in the sense of the constitutive essence" of an object (*De An.* II.6, 430a26, 430b 27f). As the *Posterior Analytics* argues, definition is itself for Aristotle a kind of ordering, in terms of genus and difference.[28] Putting those simple objects together so as to formulate a judgment is also an ordering, for it is a unification: "In each and every case, that which makes (*poioun*) one is mind" (*De An.* III.6 430b5). Similarly for building an inference out of judgments: syllogisms begin with the definition of an ousia, a procedure which reveals its essence. Their purpose is to show what other attributes inhere in a thing in virtue of that essential nature.[29] Where the disposition of imagination over its images was arbitrary ("whenever we wish"), that of intellect over intelligibles is thus rationally ordered.

Finally, since forms exist in matter, the intellect also "thinks the forms in the images," i.e., carries out the kind of reflection I discussed: it knows Callias's essence as humanity and knows what humanity is (*De An.* III.7 431b2). But the image here has lost any capacity to call itself up unbidden, it is merely something that the mind thinks together with the essence in question (*De An.* III.8 432a8f, 12-14). And this gives us a clue to a further problem. I have argued that the sensory and intellectual components of cognition are each given, separately, an ousiodic structure of boundary and disposition. But how do these "quasi-ousiai" relate to one another in the knowing soul?

It is important here to realize that, as Deborah Modrak points out, "intellect" (*nous*) is given a broader sense in the *De Anima* than in other Aristotelian writings, where it tends to mean just the cognition of first principles.[30] That it can here cognize the form in the thing by way of the *phantasma* or image of this thing brings it into a relation not only to the imagination but to the sensory organs themselves. As Modrak writes, "If thinking is not possible without *phantasmal*, and *phantasmata* consist in sensible qualities originating from perceptions, then thinking would require use of the organs making up the perceptual system."[31] In order to make use of the sensory organs, intellect must order them in certain ways. It must generate not only the universals resident within its passive component but the appropriate image in the imagination, and that presupposes the correct functioning of the sensory organs from which this image was produced. The intellect is in this sense the dispositive form of the knowing soul as a whole, the "form of forms" (where passive intellect was merely the "place" of them). As Kathleen Wilkes puts it, in the *De Anima* "we have a monarchy: reason, in man, is at the top of the pyramid in capacities."[32]

To know a thing is thus to know its form as its constitutive essence.[33] As we saw in chapter 1, we do not know things insofar as they contain matter, so to know the individual thing itself is to know the form in it. To cognize an essential form as operating in a particular quantity of matter is to know this form as essence, and since a thing "is" its essence, it is to know the thing itself as ousia. Thus, when I know my friend, it is as an instance of the form "human being." Whatever in my experiences of her does not contribute to or manifest this form is not strictly an object of my knowledge. In a sense, then, I cannot really know my friend, because as a material being she is partly unintelligible.[34]

The parameter of ousia, applying as it does to everything natural, structures Aristotle's views on knowledge and the knowing soul. But this parametric use of ousia leads to a problem. Given his problems with the migration of form, it seems that the highest form of knowledge ought to be knowledge which in no way transgresses the boundaries of the knower—self-knowledge. Aristotle seems to accept this, for, as we have seen, he strives to maintain in *De Anima* that the intellect (both receptive and productive) is "in a sense" identical with its objects. And indeed, the highest and best knowledge, that of the Prime Mover, is self-knowledge, *noêsis noêseôs* (*Metaph.* XII.9 1074b24–34). We humans approximate this sort of knowledge in *theôria*, the contemplation of eternal truth (*EN* X.7). But finite creatures that we are, we must contemplate forms that are in matter, and we do this better—get a better image—if the matter is not our own. So we seek to cognize, for example, the ordered movement of the heavenly bodies or the virtuous actions of our friends (*EN* IX.9 1069b34seqq). At this point, theoria becomes the apprehension of a perfection (a form) which is outside ourselves.

The problem is that such cognition must proceed by way of sense; and sense, as we have seen, is the transgression by a sensible form (essential or not) of the boundary of a thing—of two things, in fact, the knower and the known object. Sensation is, therefore, the exercise of an active potency in the object: its power to cause changes (*kinêseis*) in its environment (e. g., if it is colored, to change the ambient light) and eventually in the sensory organ of the perceiver.[35] But the sensible form which passes from an object to a soul, like any form, cannot change—and so cannot be changed by the passage. As Aristotle puts it in *De Interpretatione,* the things in my soul are said to be "likenesses" of the things outside my soul (1 16a7seq). In terms of his later hylomorphism, they are not "likenesses" of things outside but are formally identical with them. In *De Anima,* this leads to the puzzling claim that as regards their "proper objects" (e.g., for vision, colors), the senses are infallible. Mistakes come in only when we attribute the "objects" we sense to things outside us, when we think that the pale form we see is Coriscus.[36]

The claim is puzzling because, as the discussion of the senses at *Metaphysics* IV.5 implicitly concedes,[37] such is not empirically the case. A sensible property, such as a color, can be distorted by the medium through which it passes before reaching the eye, and it can also be altered by the constitution of the eye itself, so that we can be deceived about the true color of a thing. Further, things which are far away look small to us, and sound faint. The heat that I feel from a fire at a distance of ten feet warms me; that which I feel at two inches burns me. In short, experience teaches that sensible qualities are sometimes changed and are always diminished by traversing a medium. At *Metaphysics* IV.5, as opposed to *De Anima,* the discussion is much more commonsensical: we do in fact act as if the information from our senses is reliable, and to ask why we are justified in this is to ask an unreasonable question (*Metaph.* IV.6 1011a8–13).

I will not go further into how the infallibility of the senses can be made plausible, for once again I want to displace the question rather than solve it. In this regard it is important to note that perception of sensory qualities, even if infallible, does not work out to knowledge of a thing.[38] Coriscus is not merely a heap of sensory qualities; he exists in virtue of the hierarchy I traced in the preceding chapter, comprising essential, derivative, and accidental properties (along with his unknowable matter). If knowledge is the transmission of form, then the relational structure of Coriscus's properties must somehow be transmitted along with the properties themselves. How?

What if there were another sort of "form," a determinate quality which could exist not merely as similar but as identical in both the object known and in the knowing soul? What if it were, moreover, a quality which applied to all the relations of other qualities and complexes of qualities among themselves?

Such a quality, it seems, is connectedness (along with its opposite, separateness). Whatever relations one quality of a thing might have to others or to the whole thing itself—essentiality, derivativeness, accidentality—all are forms of connection (or separation). The truthful cognition *of a thing* for Aristotle does not in the final instance consist in the reception of its individual sensible properties into my soul but in the apprehension of their connection with each other. And connection is not affected by the size or the specific qualities of what it connects; if the cloud I see looks smaller than a dime, I can still truthfully perceive the connection between it and its color or between it and another cloud. If the cloud's whiteness has been distorted by the intervening medium or even by my eyes, that is no matter insofar as my cognitive business is not to perceive the whiteness at all but to connect whatever whiteness that I see with the object's other perceived properties. The proper objects of my perception are thus, in a practical sense, unimportant. Sitting across from Coriscus in a gloomy room, I may not perceive *his* pallor exactly right, even though my sight gives me an infallible experience of the pallor that arrives in them. But what is important is that I connect pallor of some type with Coriscus. Which, I take it, is the final point of the discussion in the *Metaphysics:* no matter what they think they perceive, no one in Libya starts out for the theater in Athens.

The connection of sensible properties is expressed in a positive judgment, their separation in a negative one. When the separations and connections in my mind are identical to those existing in the objects I perceive, I have attained "truth."[39] Aristotle attains, with this, the philosophical tradition's dominant concept of truth as at once the correspondence of things in the mind (judgments) with things outside the mind and the single excellence proper to cognition.

The appropriate question here, posed most relentlessly by Nietzsche, is: why should truth be so important? As Aristotle himself recognizes (*On Dreams* 460b3-9), we often make do with workable lies. We treat things that are very different (e.g., snowflakes, the leaves on a tree) as if they were identical. If we know that Corscus's pallor is the symptom of a fatal disease, we may deny, even to ourselves, that he is pale. Why should truth as correspondence rather than some more pragmatic notion (in the spirit of *Metaphysics* IV.5) be the sole criterion of excellence in knowledge?

The answer, I suggest, is that truth as Aristotle defines it turns out to be the minimal transgression of the boundaries of a thing by its properties—one in which the properties move but do not change. It is *because* the transgression is minimal that truth is not only a good thing but the only goal of cognition. In virtue of this last feature, Aristotle's concept of truth has had important parametric consequences in structuring our views of knowledge and science.[40]

The parameter of ousia has structured Aristotle's account of cognition in several ways. It has told him to construe the knowing soul as itself an ousia, a composite of form and matter exhibiting the three traits of boundary, disposition, and initiative. The exhibition is complex: the perceptual faculty in general and the intellect, each showing ousiodic structure, are "nested" within the cognitive structure of the soul as a whole, in which intellect as a whole plays the role of form.

The object known is also structured as an ousia. Because the forms which upon reflection are discovered to constitute the object's essence are those actually disposing and bounding it as its essence, to know them is to know the object—for, as the locution I discussed in the preceding chapter has it, the known object "is" its essence. The more definite its boundaries, and the more effective the disposition of the form over its matter and parts, the more knowable it is.

Cognition itself, finally, is presented as a process in which a sensible form, arriving from an external thing, moves from residence in a sensory organ to identity with the receptive intellect. (As when, in a Roman house, a visitor is ushered from the *prothyrium,* or entranceway, where the boundary of the house is transgressed, through the *atrium* to the *tablinum,* where the master sits.) As it is progressively interiorized, the form comes more fully under the disposition of the soul until it is at last a universal which is "identical" with it.[41] The relation between perception and its object is treated as a case of initiative, the problematic nature of which leads Aristotle to define truth in terms of separation and combination, two "forms" which can always pass unchanged from an object into the soul of a knower.

BIOLOGY

The quote from *De Anima* which opened the preceding section applied not just to the cognitive faculties but to ensouled things in general.[42] Because living bodies are composite ousiai, they must contain form and matter; the form is the soul, which not only maintains the body in its active organization but also generates its parts and boundaries. In *Generation of Animals* II.1, Aristotle explains the process of fetation, the coming-to-be of an animal organism, as the operation of the animal's form, stored as "motions" (*kinêseis*) in the semen, upon the matter supplied by the menstrual blood (*katamênia*). In this process, which Furth describes as "the laying down of structures in temporal succession of which each is a basis for the next,"[43] the parts of the fetus are condensed by turns out of the basic human material (*Gen. An.* II.4 739b2123). They do not fashion each other (e.g., the heart does not, through some efficient causal chain, form the liver), because

> in things formed by nature or by human art (*technê*), that which is *poten-tially* comes about by virtue of that which is in actuality, so that the form or shape of what comes to be would have to be contained in what shapes it: as if the heart had the form of the liver.[44]

The ultimate agent in this process is said to be not the semen itself but that which made it: the father, and most strictly his form, which is actually what is passed as potentiality to the offspring.[45] Hence the form of a living thing generates its parts. A living thing also has a boundary—its skin—formed on it like scum on a boiled liquid. It is a continuous membrane which is fissured only (and expectably) where matter must be discharged or taken in and at the nails.[46] Finally, the most basic and distinctive way an animal alters its surroundings is by locomotion—by pursuing and avoiding other things. Such initiative is exercised through the heart, which forms an unmoved center in the animal, against and around which its various bones move.[47] In this the heart operates as what might be called the "organ of appetite" (*orexis*). It is by appetite, which is part of its essence, that the animal takes the initiative to alter its surroundings (*De An.* III.9, 10).

Like his account of knowledge, Aristotle's account of the living thing in general is structured by his account of ousia, with its three traits of boundary, disposition, and initiative. However, not everything is an ousia, a point which, as I have noted, is in one sense obvious and unproblematic for Aristotle; ousia is one among several categories, and some things are qualities, quantities, and so on. Though things in other categories are not themselves ousiai, they exist and are intelligible, as we saw, only through their relation to ousia.

In the biological realm, things are different—and more problematic for the descriptive status of ousia. For not everything that manifests itself in a living thing can be referred to the activity of its form. In particular, Aristotle writes that individuals can transgress (*parekbainein*) the form of their species in three ways (I have added the emphases in the following quote):

> The first beginning of such transgression is when a female is formed instead of a male. This is, on the one hand, necessary for nature, because genera . . . have to be preserved; and it does happen that the male [form] may not *dominate* [the menstrual matter], and so it is inevitable that there should come to be female offspring among living things. . . . If the seminal fluid is well-concocted, the movement derived from the male will make the shape after its own pattern. . . . So if this movement gains *mastery* it will make a male and not a female, and a male which takes after its father, not after its mother; if however it fails to *dominate* in respect of

> some potentiality, then it makes something deficient in regard to that potentiality. . . . Now everything, when it departs from type, passes not into any casual thing but into its own opposite; thus, applying this to the principle of generation, that which does not get *mastered* must of necessity depart from type and become the opposite, in whatever respect the generating and moving agent has failed to gain *mastery*.[48]

Aristotle's account of generation is famously sexist, because it makes the mother into a mere vehicle for the paternal form.[49] But the female for him is not only passive; she is a "transgression." Such transgressions do not stop with females. Monsters are the same sort of thing, but unnecessary in that they do not contribute to reproduction.[50] And indeed, "anyone who does not resemble his parents is already, in a sense, a monster; for in such creatures nature has in some way transgressed the genus" (*Gen. An.* IV.3 767b7f).

Aristotle's biological deployment of the parameter of ousia thus leads to a world in which females, monsters, and children who do not resemble their parents (or fathers?) are not *results* predicted by his theory of generation but transgressions, anomalies to be explained. They are anomalies of an odd type, for they are more numerous than the "normal" phenomena: females are half the population, and we must add to them "monsters" and sons who do not resemble their parents. Most cases of generation, then, are anomalous to Aristotle's account of it. This is treated by Aristotle not as a problem for his theory (and still less as a problem for his metaphysics of ousia) but as a failure of form itself. And in this failure we encounter a crucial aspect of form, one that has been hidden in the texts I have discussed: its relation to matter is one of domination (as indicated by the italics in the above quote). Form, it turns out, is more than a shaping force and much more than the inert form of artifacts like spheres and tables. Its relation to matter is a battle for "mastery" and "domination."

A new vocabulary, a language of domination, thus breaks forth in Aristotle's biology at the precise moment when the parametric status of ousia—its ability to structure biological discourse—is threatened by the massively anomalous world to which it leads. Such domination was hinted at in *De Anima* II.4, where Aristotle quoted without criticism Anaxagoras's assimilation of *gnôrizein* to *krátein*, of "cognizing" to "dominating" (*De An.* III.4 429a19f). As I argued in chapter 1 (following Gill), it was already present, beneath the surface, in the *Metaphysics* itself. For the matter of a thing tends to resolve itself into its own elemental nature and must be restrained by something immaterial: the form of the thing. Aristotle's biology of domination is prepared by his metaphysics of ousia. As the quote I adduced from *De Anima* there puts it,

> We must ask what is the force that holds together the earth and fire [in the bodies of living things], which tend to travel in contrary directions; if there is no counteracting force, they will be torn asunder; if there is, this must be the soul.[51]

That the domination of matter by form is not a mere localized accretion to Aristotle's metaphysics and epistemology is also shown by the fact that it explains what I call the "empirical purchase" of ousia: what it is in our sensory experience that incites the process of reflection which I referred to in the previous section, by which we come to know a thing as an ousia. For it follows from the above quote that anything which is not a mere heap, which is not "torn asunder" by its own elemental tensions but coheres over time, must have within it a "counteracting force" which resists its dissolution. A plant shows itself to cohere in that it has definite boundaries which increase in an ordered way as it grows and which it maintains in the face of various sorts of insult; the wind, for example, does not easily carry away its parts as it would the individual grains in a pile of wheat.[52] An animal coheres in that it moves or rests as a unit without something else pushing it. None of these things would happen if there were not, for Aristotle, some sort of central, unifying principle—an essence—which keeps the matter in a thing from falling back to its own elemental nature.

Boundary, disposition, and initiative, when they maintain themselves over time, are thus the sensory manifestations of ousia; it is they which incite us to the kind of reflection by which we learn the nature of a thing's essence. In Aristotle's phrase, a natural thing is an ousia if it possesses a source of motion or rest within itself:[53] if it moves and rests without being impelled from outside or maintains its boundaries without flying apart into its elements. It follows that we must watch something for a while in order to tell whether or not it is an ousia. A snapshot of it—or a view of knowledge which, like Descartes's, assimilates knowledge to what we would call snapshots—will not be able to tell the ousiai from the heaps. Something is recognizable as a living thing—indeed, as an ousia that exists by nature—in virtue of its being known to have had a certain sort of past.

As I argue in subsequent chapters, the empirical purchase of Aristotle's concept of ousia is obscured whenever philosophers (preeminently those we call "medieval") take the paradigm of how form comes to be in matter to be its reception not by the elements but by what comes to be called "prime matter." For prime matter is pure potentiality, as inert and unresisting to form as a substantial substrate is to its properties. Ousia is also obscured as long as philosophers (preeminently those we call "modern") persist in conflating ousia with substance, in taking the dynamic domination of matter by form for the inert repose of a property in a substrate.

From its Aristotelian inception, metaphysics has thus been concerned, perhaps chiefly, with domination. In order to understand this, we must first seek to understand better the dominance which the parameter of ousia has over the thought of Aristotle. We saw that when it led to a theory of generation in massive disaccord with the facts, it was not refuted (the way a scientific theory would be if it encountered enough anomalies). Instead it maintained itself as the cognitive paradigm by asserting that those cases which would be counterexamples to it, were it a scientific theory, are in fact merely defective or incomplete examples of its operation, "deficient" beings such as women. The power of ousia to maintain itself in the face of such massive disaccord with the facts remains to be explained.

ETHICS

Women and monsters, having been born the way they are, cannot change. But sometimes the gap between ousia and one of its defective instances can be narrowed, even closed, by upgrading the instance. This is crucially true of men and brings us to Aristotle's ethics.

In structuring Aristotle's ethics, his account of truly human (male, Greek, freeborn) life and action, ousia moves beyond the purely theoretical realm. For it now shapes a discourse which, in turn, is meant to shape our lives: "We are inquiring not in order to know what virtue is but in order to become good" (*EN* II.2 1103b27-29). Because it aims to make people good, ethics stands under a constraint lacking in the purely theoretical investigations I have discussed so far: it should be as independent as possible from (sectarian) metaphysical considerations and should appeal instead to common knowledge, drawing its truth "from the facts."[54]

But if the *Nicomachean Ethics* hides the parametric functioning of ousia under a veneer of good sense, it does not eliminate it.[55] As in the preceding paragraph quote shows, ethics for Aristotle is about how to achieve a purpose, becoming good; and form as telos structures the *Nicomachean Ethics'* entire account of human life and flourishing. Beginning with the words "Every art and every inquiry, and similarly every action and pursuit, is thought to aim at some good" (*EN* I.1 1094a1), Book I quickly becomes a quest for the *human* good. This is sought in terms of the specific "work" (*ergon*) humans as such perform,[56] and this turns out to be the exercise of the rational principle—which, we saw in *De Anima,* is the ousiodic form of the human being.[57] The exercise of reason, then, is the "human good," the telos at which we should aim. A good person will be one in whom reason, the human form, is actively at work and for whom such activity is happiness itself, the goal of life.

True to the metaphysical account of form in matter, the rational principle of Book I is, immediately upon its introduction, said to be—like the intellect in *De Anima*—double in nature: "one part [of the soul] has such a principle in the sense of being obedient to one, the other in the sense of possessing one and exercising thought."[58] The former principle—desire—plays, I suggest, the role of "ethical matter" in the *Nicomachean Ethics'* account of the structure of the moral agent; the latter, "active reason," plays the role of ousiodic form.

One place to see this is in the moral hierarchy that, at the beginning of

EN VII.1, spans the realm between gods and beasts. The human extremes of this hierarchy are the "good," or "virtuous," man and the "unhindered," or truly evil, man. The middle states are the more important for current purposes because they mark the line between the good and the bad: the "continent" man is the lowest form of good man, while the "incontinent" man is the highest form of bad man. Most important, however, are the Greek terms Aristotle employs for these two states, respectively *enkratês* and *akratês:* the man "in" dominance and the man "without" it. The same Greek word, *krâtein,* was used in Aristotle's discussion of females and monsters, where it explicitly referred to the capacity of form to shape the matter of the fetus.

It is not the whole "man" who has mastery here but his reason: "the continent and the incontinent man are so called because in them reason dominates or does not, *reason considered as being the man himself . . .* " (*EN* 1168b31–1169a1, italics added). The echoes of *Metaphysics* VII.6, as well of *De Anima's* discussion of imagination, are clear: reason is the essence of man; like all things, men "are" their essence. So each man "is" his reason. If reason is not in control of our lives, then "we" are not in control of our lives; but if reason dominates, then "we" dominate. The metaphysical statement that the thing in general "is" its essence is thus, in the human realm anyway, a *moral* claim. It is the domination of reason over desire which makes one's reason the same as oneself. Where it is not present it should be installed.

I will dodge the enormous literature generated by Aristotle's treatment of incontinence in *EN* VII,[59] confining myself here to the general sketch of the ethical domination of reason given in *EN* I.13. The soul, like the body of which it is the form, is complex. In addition to the nonrational "vegetative" soul, which handles nutrition and growth, it contains another part "which is by nature opposed to reason, fights against it, and resists it"—as matter does form (*EN* 1102b16f). In spite of its antagonism to reason, this part—which, as noted, is desire—is also, in a passive sense, rational. For it is able to recognize reason and obey it.[60] When it does, we have the highest level of the moral hierarchy, the virtuous man, in whom desire "speaks with the same voice" (*homophônei*) as reason. When desire opposes reason and the man nonetheless acts as his reason advises, he is "continent." When the man follows his desires though reason tells him not to, he is "incontinent." And when his reason chimes in with desire, telling him that whatever he happens to want is what in fact he should do, then he is "unhindered" (*akolastos*) in his evil.

To put this rough Aristotelian sketch into my terms, the incontinent man is in something like the following situation. He is led by his desires, which can move body parts independently of reason (as desires do in animals).[61] Though within the incontinent man these desires tend to be for external objects, such as food and drink.[62] Because they are provoked by and push the incontinent man toward external objects, his moral *boundaries* are continually transgressed. Because his desires resist and oppose reason (in what

Gill might call "tension and commotion"), the *disposition* of reason over his acts is impaired. And because desire, not reason, governs his interaction with the world beyond his skin, the *initiative* for his acts belongs to desire, not to his ousiodic form. To be unethical is thus to violate boundary, disposition, and initiative all at once.

It is clear that desire, in this, plays the ethical role of matter, which, in Jonathan Lear's phrase, needs to be "organized" by reason.[63] The good man, having achieved such organization, possesses boundary, disposition, and initiative in plenary human form. His ultimate desire is not for external objects but for the activity of his own rational principle—of what he himself most is—and so his actions are not determined from outside.[64] The boundary of his body is in good order, as witness his relative imperviousness to eros (*EN* 1156b2, 1167a3-12, 1171b29f) and his attention to diet.[65] His desires, unlike even the continent man's, are at the disposition of his reason to the point of "homophony."

Aristotle's sketch of the moral hierarchy thus outlines his view of the right relation between reason and desire, which in turn is a main theme of the *Ethics* as a whole. The accounts of the voluntary and involuntary in Book III, of deliberative excellence in Book VI, of akrasia and pleasure in Book VII, and of friendship in Books VIII and IX—as well as other discussions—are all deeply indebted to it, in ways which I am tempted to go into here. I will resist the temptation, for enough has been said to show that from the ethical perspective, as from the biological one, the human individual has for Aristotle an ousiodic structure. The human form establishes boundaries biologically in the fetus and secures them ethically in the adult male. It exercises disposition over human matter, both the bodily organs that come to be through the activity of the form and the "ethical matter" represented by the desires and organized by reason. Finally, it possesses initiative as regards the outside world, in that the good human being does as reason directs. When this does not in fact hold—as it usually does not in ethical life, for most people are governed by desire (*EN* I.5 1095b14-22)—we are dealing not with a truly human being but with a defective one. Once again the parametric structuring of ousia leads Aristotle to see certain pervasive phenomena of reality—the majority of people who are less than good—as anomalies to be explained. Once again, they are explained as failures of reality, not of his theory.

HOUSEHOLD

The Greek word *oikonomia* means, literally, household management; Greek "economic" theory, to the extent that there is such a thing,[66] is the study of the household. This study ought to have a crucial role in Aristotelian philosophy, the basic program of which is summed up at *Metaphysics* VII.3:

> Just as in conduct our task is to start from what is good for each and make what is without qualification good good for each, so it is our task to start from what is more knowable to oneself and make what is knowable by nature knowable to oneself. (*Metaph.* VII.3 1029b7-9)

The home one grows up in is one's most "familiar" community,[67] and so it is unsurprising that Aristotle's *Politics* should start with an investigation of the household, as the community most knowable to us. But the treatment covers just a few chapters and is oddly off kilter: most of it is devoted to the justice of slavery and to the acquisition (not the administration) of possessions.[68] I will, therefore, supplement my consideration of some of the *Politics* with Book I of the Pseudo-Aristotelian *Oeconomica.*[69]

That work begins in what we have seen to be good Aristotelian fashion, with an argumentative invocation of the general nature of ousia: "that for the sake of which each thing is and comes to be is in fact the ousia of that thing" (*Oec.* I.1 1343a13f). As with human life and flourishing in the *Nicomachean Ethics,* we can understand the household by seeing what its telos is. Shortly after, at the beginning of the second chapter, we find that the household is divided into two parts: human beings and property (*Oec.*I.2 1343a18f). As with other investigations, then, the identification of the household as an ousia leads to a separation of two components, one of which (though this is not stated) assumes the role of matter, the other that of form.

But it is not only inanimate objects which function as "matter" in the household. The *Oeconomica,* like the *Politics,* explicitly views slaves as one type of possession.[70] Moreover, in the biological sphere we found a trio of anomalies: women, monsters, and anyone who did not take after his parents. They were said to result from the inability of matter to "dominate" form, and hence their biology was, so to speak, overly conditioned by its matter. In the *Politics,* Aristotle formulates an analogical triad regarding social status: "For the slave has no deliberative faculty at all; the woman has, but it is without authority; and the child has, but it is immature."[71] The analogy, I suggest, is precise. Woman, of course, is explicitly included on both sides. The slave, lacking the actively rational part of the human mind, is biologically a sort of monster:[72] his mind has what I have called "ethical matter," passive reason or desire, but not the ethical "form" of active reason. Similarly for children: even boys do not ethically take after their fathers because, unlike them, they still "live at the beck and call of appetite" (*EN* III. 112 1119b5).

Desire—the "matter" of ethical life—thus excessively conditions the behavior of women, children, and slaves. Since they cannot acquire active reason,[73] they cannot exhibit ousiodic structure within themselves. What they must do—for their own good—is participate in reason in the only way open to them, by adhering to a structure in which a single active reason informs not merely its owner's life but several others' lives as well.[74] This arrangement is the household, with a mature male at its head. The art of household management is the art by which the head rules the three other kinds of people, who in turn order and use the house's inanimate possessions (*Pol.* I.3 1253b1-4; I.4 1253b33). The result, as William Booth puts it, is a paragon of disposition:

> Every particular item of property has its own function, inseparable from the article itself. And thus, every item has its place, both in terms of its use and even its location in the home. . . . The natural order of the household, visible to all its members, means that each person has his position within it, as does each piece of property.[75]

The household thus disposed has definite boundaries. They are not only physical (its walls) but include limits on the possessions within them; we should own only as many things as are necessary or useful and not more (*Pol.* I.8 11256b30-39). Going beyond this requires retail trade with outsiders and should—like all transgressions of boundary—be minimized.[76] In accordance with the ousiodic trait of initiative, the art of acquiring such possessions is exercised by the *pater.*[77]

While the man is allowed to transgress the boundaries of the household—most importantly to engage not in retail trade but in public life and politics (concerning which women are simply not mentioned), the woman maintains the internal order of the household:

> For providence made man stronger and woman weaker, so that he in virtue of his manly prowess may be more ready to defend the home, and she, by reason of her timid nature, more ready to keep watch over it; and while he brings in provisions from outside, she keeps safe what lies within.[78]

Some details of this internal ordering are given in *Oeconomica* I.6; I will not discuss them here, for what matters to me is that even in this exercise of disposition, the wife is subordinate to her husband. Acquiring and overseeing the slaves is clearly, in *Oec.* I.5, man's work. If the wife supervises certain activities within the household, it is under the aegis of her husband, who rules her: "the courage of a man is shown in commanding, of a woman in obeying" (*Pol.* I. 13 1260a23f). Hence the household—like the knowing soul—is a "monarchy"; its telos is the leisure of the pater (*Pol.* I.7, 1255b18f; 11273a36f, 1334a18ff, 1337b30f; *EN* 1177b4ff).

Aristotle pursues the analogy between the structure of the household and the proper relation of reason, soul, and body:

> And it is clear that the rule of the soul over the body and of the mind and the rational element over the passionate is natural and expedient. . . . The male is by nature superior and the female inferior; the one rules, and the other is ruled; this principle of necessity extends to all mankind. Where, then, there is such a difference as that between soul and body or between men and animals . . . the lower sort are by nature slave. (*Pol.* I.5 1254b5-18)

The household as portrayed in the *Politics* and *Oeconomica* thus exhibits the hierarchical structure of ousia. Its bounding, dispositive, and initiatory "essence" is located in the father. The wife is analogous to what I call a "relegated" property: just as the rationality of a human being can manifest itself in a specific capacity to perform music, so the wife can order certain events within the household. But just as one is a musician only in virtue of being rational, so the authority in virtue of which she does this is her husband's, not her own. The slaves play the role of "material parts," in that they are necessary to the functioning of the household but "live, for the most part, at random." They are prone to accidental behavior, involving such things as wine and sex, and must be regulated by the master (*Metaph.* XII.10 1075a20-23; *Oec.* I.5). Guests and other temporary visitors are, presumably, wholly accidental, which is perhaps why Aristotle's texts do not discuss them.

We saw that in respect of cognition, biology, and ethics, the parametric use of ousia led to problems. The proper object of cognition had to be reduced to connection and disjunction, while the ousiodic accounts of generation and ethics were in massive disaccord with the facts, condemning most births as "monstrous" and most people as corrupt. The situation is different when we reach the level of domesticity, for the ancient household actually exhibited, in a comparatively straightforward way, the three traits of an Aristotelian ousia.[79] Its *boundaries* were secure, for there were only three ways into a household: by purchase, marriage, or birth. The father was able to establish and secure those boundaries; he not only bought the slaves but had the right to have his children exposed at birth, and later on he approved their marriages. His wife and children, to say nothing of slaves, had to obey his orders and heed his advice as a matter of course; they were at his disposition. And he alone was allowed to leave the house and play an independent role in the larger community: he alone had the initiative to affect things outside the household. Aristotle did not invent these structures; they are crystallized in ancient domestic architecture and in a particularly clear way by the House of Pansa at Pompeii, which is designed quite visibly along the lines of an Aristotelian ousia (see chapter 4).

There is, however, an important constraint on the power of the *pater*—one which will play an enormous role in the emancipatory side of the West. For he has his authority only in virtue of the fact that his actions are governed by his form, reason—i.e., in virtue of his own ousiodic structure. Aristotle proclaims this repeatedly: "we do not allow a *man* to rule, but *logos*"; the husband "rules in accordance with merit"; a master should be "the source of excellence in the slave," and a ruler "ought to have moral virtue in perfection."[80] When the pater's rationality is manifest to the other members of his household, he has their goodwill: they submit to him because it is in their best interest to do so. In this, they have *philia*, or "friendship," toward him.[81] When his actions originate not in reason but in desire, his rulership becomes visibly oppressive and wrong.[82]

Domesticity for Aristotle appears to be both a particularly clear and particularly familiar example of ousiodic structure in the social sphere. As William Booth has argued, for example, Aristotle uses the "natural" hierarchy of the household to overcome the fact that political rule is always contestable:

> The problem for the polis is to approximate, as closely as possible, the abiding sort of rule encountered *in nature* and which, *by nature,* is the principle feature of composites (including the polis)—which order is, among human associations, most clearly visible in the household.[83]

It is in keeping with this that Aristotle occasionally uses analogies to domesticity to explain developments in other, more arcane, areas. Ethically speaking, for example, man is "the begetter of his acts as of his children." In deliberation, desire listens to reason "as one does with one's father," and desire should live according to reason "as the child should live according to the direction of his tutor."[84] In biology the fetus, once its heart begins to beat, is like a grown son who has set up house for himself, "away from the father" (*Gen. An.* 740a7-9). *Metaphysics* XII uses the analogy of a household to explain the cosmic order itself:

> For all [things] are ordered together to one end, but it is as in a house, where the freemen are least at liberty to act at random, but all things or most things are already ordained for them, while the slaves and animals do little for the common good and for the most part live at random. (1075a20-23)

Domesticity thus functions as what I call an *analogical* parameter in the order of knowing: if something can be likened to a family, it can be more readily understood. Analogical functioning can be viewed as a species of the hermeneutical variety mentioned at the beginning of this chapter. In it, the hermeneutical basis is furnished by a concrete and familiar realm rather than by a metaphysical theory. Such analogies thus play an important role in the philosophical movement from what is better known by us (here, the households we grow up in) to what is better known in itself (ousiodic structure as instanced in less familiar ways). Aristotle's philosophy is shot through with such analogies; like philosophy in general, it does not have an exclusively argumentative structure.

STATE

We can now better understand why ousia was capable of withstanding the massive disaccord with the facts that it encountered in the cognitive, biological, and ethical realms, as well as the massive and intractable problems with its metaphysical articulation. For if Aristotle were to abandon his hylomorphism in the face of these problems, he would have no way to codify the domestic hierarchies that he found around him in Athens and elsewhere.[85] I suggest that the practices which actually existed in the ancient household not only exemplify, on a social level, the domination of form over matter; they help hold together Aristotle's theories of cognition, generation, and the good life. That can be seen not only on the level of the individual organism in cognition, biology, and ethics but also in Aristotle's account of the polis or state. Once again I restrict my discussion to the traits of boundary, disposition, and initiative; it can hardly claim to be even a brief summary of his political thought as a whole.

The state, to begin with, has definite boundaries. They are in the first instance territorial. Ideally the ground the state covers should be viewable at one glance, for that makes it easy to defend. It should also be difficult for an enemy to get inside it and easy for its own people to get out. The center, for purposes of both defense and interior trade, should be the city. As the center of motion (commerce) within the state and the place where its form, the magistracies, are to be found, the city occupies a position analogous to that of the heart in an animal.[86] As with the household's possessions, there is also a limit to the number of inhabitants the state can contain: "a great city is not to be confounded with a populous one," especially when the population consists largely of slaves and artisans. For such a population cannot be orderly; the disposition of the rulers will be impaired (*Pol.* VII.4 1326a17–40).

A state, then, is more than a boundary; you could put a wall around the Peloponnesus and it would not be a state (*Pol.* III.3 1276a26f). The need for the state to have an internal structure of rule and domination is argued on the following principle:

> In all things which are composed out of several other things and which come to be some single common thing, whether continuous or discrete, in all of them there turns out to be a distinction between that which rules and that which is ruled; and this holds for all ensouled things by virtue of the whole of nature. . . . (*Pol.* I.4 1254a28–32)

The global nature of this claim shows once again the breadth of ousia in Aristotle's thought: it applies to *all* composites, including *all* ensouled beings, in virtue of the *whole* of nature. The state is itself a composite entity, and the way to get at its nature, Aristotle says, is by way of its telos.[87] And this leads back to the duality of form and matter. For as Curtis Johnson notes, Aristotle's characterization of the telos of the state is twofold: it is to be "self-sufficing" and "for the sake of the good life." The former refers, as Johnson puts it, to "the ability to provide for . . . material requirements without dependency on outside sources"; the good life is life in accordance with virtue and hence a matter of form.[88]

The basic framework which pursues and realizes this double end is the "constitution" (*politeia*) of the state, which Aristotle defines as "the arrange-ment . . . for the distribution of offices of power and for the determination of the sovereign and the end at which the community aims."[89] It is in the constitution rather than in the aggregate of its inhabitants that the identity of the state lies—as the identity of an animal is provided by its soul, not the matter in its body.[90] The most basic element in the constitution is the delib-erative body, which in a sense *is* the constitution (recalling the metaphysical claim that a thing *is* its essence).[91] This body, which Aristotle calls the "sov-ereign" (*to kurion*), consists, as R. G. Mulgan puts it, of "the sovereign group acting in its sovereign function, namely, the deliberative body."[92] This body is responsible for making war and peace and forming and ending alliances; for making and interpreting the laws, which are the rules by which the magistrates operate (*Pol.* IV.1, 1289a18-20); for administering the more severe penalties (e.g., death and confiscation of property); and for dealing with the selection of magistrates. Though Aristotle also recognizes judicial and executive functions in any constitution (*Pol.* IV.14), the sovereign is supreme. As Mulgan notes,

> it limits the initiative and autonomy of the other two elements, the mag-istrates and the courts, by controlling the laws which regulate their func-tions and by retaining the power to decide the most important "executive" and "judicial" functions.[93]

As the most basic principle in the state, the constitution constitutes its "essence."[94] Embodied in the sovereign, it orders not only the various of-fices of the state but also the "citizens" who man them. For citizenship is defined as "sharing in the administration of justice and offices" (*Pol.* III.1 1275a23), and the activities of the citizen are defined by the offices he holds. Such an office would thus function as a specific manifestation of the rationality embedded in the state, somewhat as being-a-musician is a spe-cific manifestation of Mozart's human rationality, and similarly for the citizen who fills such an office: he would function analogously to what I call a "relegated property" of the state as a whole. The difference, as the opening words of the *Politics* remind us, is that the state for Aristotle is not an ousia but a community; and the individual, rather than merely a prop-erty, is the ontological bedrock. The state thus exhibits the ousiodic traits of disposition, boundary, and initiative in attenuated forms.[95]

Any natural being, for Aristotle, has some parts because of its essence and others which are necessary or beneficial to it without belonging to or following from its essence.[96] Similarly, the state needs certain things done that are not conducive to the good life; those who do them, the slaves and artisans, are only hypothetically necessary for the state (*Pol.* VII.8, VII.9 1328b23-1329a2). Slaves are "living but separated" parts of their master's body. Like the rest of the household, as we saw, they are means to—but do not share in—their master's leisure, which allows him to take on civic office

(*Pol.* III.5 1278a10-12). Artisans, for their part, are servants of the whole society, a class of "further separated" slaves who do not live with those they serve.[97]

As John M. Cooper has pointed out, hypothetical necessity is the requirement for a certain sort of matter; the human eye must be made of fluid and must therefore be covered with a surface that resists penetration.[98] All the individuals who live in the state are ordered by it and hence constitute its "matter" (*Pol.* III.1 11274b39f). But, as in the household, some are more material than others.[99] Slaves and artisans are to the state what eyelids are to the human being: necessary material parts.[100] Beneath them would presumably be the "accidental" people in the state—visitors, exiles from other states, and perhaps resident aliens (cf. *Pol.* III.1 1275a8-21). And beneath everything is the "matter" of the state, the living human materiality shared by all its inhabitants.[101]

Sovereign power, then, is the political version of what I call disposition. It orders the magistrates—the active citizens—in that it sets forth the limits of their offices and how they are to act. Each of them in turn is not only, as a citizen, a specific manifestation of the constitution but is also the head of a household and so disposes of the necessary people within that household.[102]

Initiative in the state is (as always) troublesome. Aristotle discusses the state's relations to the world outside its borders under the two rubrics of war and foreign trade. War, for its part, is clearly a bad thing.[103] A war of conquest is an attempt to gain despotic power over others, and even defensive war is at best a necessary means to the desired end, i.e., peace. Indeed, external relations in general are accidental to the city as such: a wholly isolated city, if well governed, would be as happy as one with neighbors (*Pol.* VII.2 1324b25, 1325a1-7). Foreign trade is thus unnecessary to the state; it should presumably be for the ornaments of life, not for its necessities.[104] Foreign goods will enter by sea, and the harbor should not be in the city but at some remove from it so that it will not be swamped by an influx of commercially minded foreigners (*Pol.* VII.6 1327a29-39).

The state thus incorporates, to varying degrees, the three traits of boundary, disposition, and initiative.[105] As such, it forms another link in the chains of mutually supporting arguments and analogies by which Aristotelian discourse is structured. Aristotle himself notes this in *De Motu Animalium:*

> We should consider the organization of an animal to resemble that of a city governed through good laws. For once order is established in a city, there is no need of a separate monarch to preside over everything that happens; each does his own work as assigned, and one thing follows another through habit. In animals this same thing comes about through nature, i.e., because each part of them, since they are so ordered, is naturally disposed to do its own work. There is no need, then, of soul in each part; it is in some governing origin of the body, and other parts live

because they are naturally attached and do their work through nature. (703a28-b2)

Or, in the famous closing words of *Metaphysics* XII—themselves quoted from an even more ancient authority, Homer—"the rule of many is not good; one ruler let there be."[106]

Functioning to cue and structure other parts of Aristotelian discourse, the parameter of ousia in effect carries out an equation of Being itself with domination. Within any complex entity that *is* and insofar as it can be said to *be,* there is a structure in virtue of which one aspect—the form—establishes the thing's boundaries, orders and/or generates its parts, and affects the outside world. Human individuals, as well as households and states, exhibit various degrees and forms of such domination, which renders each—and especially, I argue, the household—a source of analogies for understanding the others. The Aristotelian cosmos can thus be considered as a set of nested ousiai: the individual human soul, itself a complex nest of ousiodic structures, is further nested within a household, within a polis, and finally within the cosmos itself.[107]

Ousia has a complex history in what follows. In Aquinas, ousiodic structure is *consolidated* in that it is underwritten not by "the whole of nature" but by an all-powerful, all-good God; to contest it in the human realm is to sin. With the rise of modern science, ousia begins to encounter vicissitudes. For science discovers that nature does not contain ousiai but is a domain merely of bodies in motion; science *evicts* ousia from nature. That jeopardizes ousia's right to structure the human world of communities and individuals. Some philosophers—those usually called "Rationalists"—attempt to relocate ousia even more decisively to the divine realm, from which it can continue to structure the human world. Others, the "Empiricists," are more radical. Rejecting all knowledge of a divine realm, they leave ousia no existence at all outside the human world and no justification for any kind of absolute status within that world. It continues to operate nonetheless, unjustified and unseen, structuring such modern political inventions as Hobbes's sovereign state, Locke's theory of property, and Hume's theory of the understanding. That is the situation challenged, most radically, by Heidegger.

3

THE DOCILITY OF MATTER IN
THOMAS AQUINAS

The interweaving of argumentative and analogical structuring in Aristotle's philosophy shows the two sides of what I call "codification." On one side, ethical, household, and political practices already under way in Athens (as elsewhere) are *defined* by Aristotle as ousiodically structured, which means that they can be understood in terms of the domination of matter by form. On the other, practices thus defined are *legitimated* by their place in what Aristotle, arguing on the basis of his metaphysics of ousia, calls "the whole of nature," or simply "nature."[1] Such definition and legitimation are not separate phases in a two step method of codification but are mutually entangled throughout Aristotle's philosophy. Thus the concept of ousia, which did not apply straightforwardly to phenomena of ethics or reproduction, is (as I argued following Booth) importantly legitimated by its success in codifying the practices of the household. Such phenomena as cognition and its excellence, truth, are defined in ways that allow them to be legitimated by the "natural" schema of matter and form which they, in turn, flesh out.

Aristotle's codification of ousia was followed by a long period of consolidation, comprising much of what is usually called "medieval" philosophy. In general, of course, the medieval period stabilized and prolonged many structures of the ancient world—the hierarchical structure of the Roman Empire, for instance, clearly lived on in the medieval papacy. In philosophy, however, the "tension and commotion"[2] of Aristotle's cosmos was subdued by the arrival of the all-powerful Christian creator God. The attribution of ousiodic traits to this God is beautifully carried off by St. Augustine at the beginning of his *Confessions,* where God is addressed as *ex quo omnia, per quem omnia, in quo omnia:* all things are "out of" God (via the divine initiative, or creation of the Father); "through" him (via his disposition, or providence through Christ's sacrifice); and "in" him (particularly within the boundaries of the religious community, or the Holy Spirit).[3]

But ousia, like some other parameters, operates most freely in the dark; its medieval consolidation is partly a hiding of its threefold structure of domination. Not that the structure in question was ever very clear; if it had been, the two preceding chapters would have been unnecessary, or at least much shorter. But Aristotle's worthy, if baffled and baffling, effort to codify ousia was followed not by further efforts but by its occlusion—by a return, on the part of philosophers, to a concern with substance. A key step in this occlusion, one carried out by Thomas Aquinas, is the rendering docile of matter. Matter is seen as passively receiving form rather than actively seeking to realize its own elemental nature, and form's dominance over it ceases to be a struggle. In addition to this "docilization" of matter, the obscuring of ousia and its structure of domination has at least five other strands:

A. Aristotle's own account, in the *Categories,* of substance as a passive substrate. In chapter 1 I contrasted this "substance ontology" with Aristotle's later hylomorphism. Since the *Categories* was more accessible than the *Metaphysics* (which was lost from Europe for hundreds of years) and since medieval commentators did not recognize any evolution in Aristotle's views, this account was assumed to cohere with the later ousiodic one. Hence the structure of domination inherent in the later conception of ousia was more easily overlooked.

B. The Stoic reduction of matter to *apoios ousia,* ousia without qualities, an unformed substrate whose only role was to be passive.[4] With this, the tense, commotional Aristotelian cosmos, whose highest human achievement was the active use of reason in the governance of one's life, was converted into an unchallengeable universal order to which the individual could only acquiesce. The Roman Empire, like later political (and intellectual) institutions, aspired to be just such an unchallengeable universal order.

C. What Jean-François Courtine calls "l'approche spécifiquement romaine de l'être comme substantialité, corporeité, substrat matériel."[5]

D. Augustine's appropriation of unformed matter to show that God created matter *ex nihil: tu enim, domine, fecisti mundum de materia informi, quam fecisti de nulla re paene nullam rem. . . .* [6] That God could create matter is not as unintelligible as the Greeks would have thought, because matter is "almost nothing."

E. The Christian doctrine of the Incarnation: when *ho logos sarx egéneto* (John I.14), flesh could hardly be of a nature to resist. And though the divine nature is far from an ordinary form, it could not help but serve ontologically as a model (just as Christ, though divine, was a moral exemplar for humanity). What resists form cannot any longer be "natural." Resistance to form is, when possible at all,[7] no longer natural but sinful.

DESIGNATION AND DOCILITY IN AQUINAS'S CONCEPTION OF SUBSTANCE

Aquinas inherited this tradition of occlusion along with the newly re-Europeanized texts of Aristotle on which he based much of his philosophy. This dual heritage, along with his own greatness as a thinker, makes him an apt representative of what I call the "consolidation" of ousia. My discussion here is restricted to this aspect of his work, and so remains highly selective. After discussing the relation of matter and form in the material thing, I adduce a couple of illustrations of how this structures aspects of the human realm.

At the beginning of his short and early but crucial and, in crucial respects, representative *De ente et essentia*, Aquinas tells us that "being" is said in two main ways.[8] In one sense, anything has being if a true proposition can be formulated about it, and this includes anything that may be thought or imagined: any determinate quality. It is true, for example, that the Golden Mountain does not exist—from which it follows that the Golden Mountain has "being," in at least this sense. Because propositions can stand alone in the mind—i.e., do not need to be asserted as parts of larger chains[9]—anything which can be the object of a proposition must itself be capable of standing alone, i.e., of being cognized without reference to its context. Hence, in fidelity to Jacques Derrida's characterization of "presence" as the capacity to be "summed up (*résumée*) in some absolute simultaneity or instantaneity,"[10] I refer to this kind of being as "presence." The other sense, more robust, "posits something in reality" (*in re ponit*, as Aquinas puts it). To assert this kind of being is to assert that something actually exists, and in this sense the Golden Mountain has no being.

These two senses of "being" are not mutually indifferent. One is prior, and it is the second of the two: the sense in which to say that something exists is to posit it in reality. For this sense, as Averroës had put it, "signifies the substance of the thing." In it, being is said absolutely, while in the other sense it is said only in a certain respect and secondarily (*EE* p. 19/27; translation altered). The two senses thus relate to each other as absolute and relative, primary and secondary, and stand as a classic example of what Derrida will come to call a metaphysical binary. But such binaries, we are perhaps beginning to see, are merely new versions of the ancient structures of ousiodic domination. If so, the general structure of Aristotelian ousia appears to be in place, from the first page of the first chapter of *De ente et essentia.*[11]

And yet there has been a change. For though Aquinas attributes his two main senses of being to Aristotle, the specific text he cites—*Metaphysics* V.7—actually gives four. In addition to those mentioned by Aquinas, which are the first two, Aristotle goes on to list being as truth and being as either potential or actual.[12] In other words, the binary relation in which the first two senses stand has been manufactured by Aquinas by the simple stratagem of ignoring (or perhaps conflating) two of the four senses of Being that Aristotle actually considers. The result of this is that where for Aristotle (as I argued in chapter 2) truth was one of many effects of ousia, for Aquinas the possibility of truth is distinctive enough to found a second type of "being."[13]

The primary sense of being, which gives rise to the term *essentia* (*EE* p. 17/27), also has two senses. The linguistic indication of this is that the essence of an individual thing, such as Socrates, can be referred to either as "humanity" or as "human being."[14] "Humanity" as designating the essence of Socrates refers to a certain form (*forma quaedam*). But humanity-as-essence is not *simply* the form humanity, which can be abstracted from all matter and considered simply as a concept. Rather it is form considered *as* the form of a material object: as form in some sort of matter. In this sort of predication, form is intended as embracing both itself and matter. Thus in referring to the essence of Socrates as "humanity," we use the form humanity to designate the whole human being. In a sort of metaphysical synecdoche, it is the "form which is the whole," *forma quae est totum.*[15]

As with Aristotle, then, the form of a thing is "equivalent" to the thing itself. But there is a difference. For Aristotle, to say that the form "is" the whole meant that the form of a thing, as essence, was exercising its threefold domination over its matter. It was in this sense that we saw Aristotle maintain that the reason of a moral agent "is" the man himself. For Aquinas, I argue, the nature of such domination has changed.

What enables us to subsume the whole of a composite substance into its form in this sort of synecdoche is the kind of matter in which that form is considered to inhere. In the case of humanity-as-essence, it is what Aquinas calls "nondesignated" matter (*materia non signata*): matter which is qualitatively, but not locally, distinct from other matter. Matter which is distinct from other matter in location is *materia signata,* designated matter or matter considered as bounded in (three) determinate dimensions, *quae sub determinatis dimensionibus consideratur* (*EE,* p. 25/32). When we refer to the essence of

Socrates as "humanity," then, we are indicating the form of human being as present in matter which has the qualities of human flesh, bones, and so on, but not as present in any particular packet of such material.

When we say that Socrates is "a human being," we are indicating his form as present in designated matter. In this case, we consider the form as individuated in *some* discrete packet of matter but without characterizing that packet itself. This sense of "essence" thus includes the matter as determinately but "implicitly and indistinctly" extended (*EE*, p. 39/38). In other words, it includes the idea that the form is realized in some quantity and shape of matter but leaves just which quantity and shape vague and indeterminate. We cannot, by contrast, say "Socrates is a humanity," because when we use the term "humanity" we are not thinking of his matter as an individual packet at all. Hence, since (as will be seen) designated matter individuates, there is only one humanity but many human beings. When, finally, I think of the human form as residing in Socrates's own body, with all the unique features which constitute that body as different from other human bodies, I am no longer thinking of the essence of Socrates but of Socrates himself.

There are thus, for Aquinas here, three ways in which matter may be considered. The least determinate of them is "prime matter," matter without any form whatsoever (*EE*, p. 35/36). Wholly indeterminate, prime matter is the same for all things and is without nature or properties of its own. It is also without actuality, for (as with Aristotle) it is form which gives existence to matter (*forma dat esse materiae; EE*, p. 55/44). Prime matter is thus pure potentiality to be actualized by form, which is the *actus materiae* (*EE*, p. 23/31). But unlike Aristotle, for whom prime matter was probably at best a sheer intellectual construct,[16] Aquinas can be said to regard prime matter not only as existing—presumably in the sense that true propositions can be formulated of it—but even (as Averroës had argued) to be one; since it is the only thing with no form at all, it is entirely indistinguishable from itself.[17] More determinate is "nondesignated" matter, which has the qualities which fit it to receive a certain essence but which cannot do so because it is not spatially distinct from other matter.

Most determinate is matter as designated: qualitatively distinct and spatially extended. Such designated matter is Aquinas's principle of individuation. Socrates is not Phaedo, not because their form is different or because their human matter is qualitatively distinct but because their common human form has been "received" in two different packets of matter (*EE*, p. 55/45). Such a packet of designated matter, conceived with its determinate extension but without regard to any further form which it may have or come to have is what Aquinas calls a "body" (*EE*, p. 29/34). The body of Socrates is thus a determinate, discrete parcel of human matter.

For Aristotle, matter was bounded, made into a "this-something" and so individuated, by the action of form. Similarly for Aquinas: the designation of matter into an individual "packet" is the action of the form of the thing. Because of Aquinas's doctrine of the "unicity" of substantial form, this action is accomplished by the thing's substantial form, or essence, itself; my body is individuated by my complete human form, not by a form of corporeality which it has prior to the reception of that essence.[18]

But the way in which essence brings about boundaries differs in the two thinkers. For Aquinas, geometrical attributes (i.e., shape and location) are inherently individual; that is why designated matter, which has such attributes via the action of its substantial form, can individuate that form.[19] Strictly speaking, then, the principle of individuation for Aquinas is not sheer materiality but determinate extension. For Aristotle, the boundaries of a body also result from the activity of its form. But (I suggested in chapter 1) it is that activity itself, rather than the body it produces, which individuates; the form of a composite is individuated by holding together the elements which compose its material side and which would otherwise fly apart. This activity is not a gaining of geometrical attributes by the form but the replacement of whatever boundaries those elements already have in the surrounding environment with the boundaries set by the form. Determinate extension, rather than being the principle of individuation, is a result of this individuating activity.

Had Aquinas made a similar move it would have saved him from a problem pointed out by J. Christopher Maloney.[20] The determinate extension of a composite is accidental to it; and so if matter individuates through its extension, then composite things are individuated by their accidents. But this means that Phaedo differs from Socrates only accidentally, which for Aquinas is strange talk indeed; would it be "accidental" for Phaedo to be saved and Socrates to be damned? To put this more generally: Aquinas seems to have made matter into something which is merely accidental to the forms it individuates rather than naturally opposed to them. Where the bounding activity of form for Aristotle consists in a struggle against elemental natures whose nature is to oppose the form, for Aquinas it apparently comes about through something which is merely indifferent to form: the individuated geometrical attributes the thing comes to have. And yet this indifferent accidentality is essential to the individual it constitutes, for *essentia comprehendit materiam et formam (EE, p. 21/30)*.

How can matter be both accidental and essential to form? We can sharpen this question by noting that Aristotle's language of domination is replaced in Aquinas by a vocabulary of "signum," stamp or impression. This metaphor, which characterizes the primary relation between form and the matter in which it comes to be, is a revealing one. One thing it suggests is that for Aquinas, form does not gradually come to control its own matter. It does not "give it existence" in the way that Aristotle thought, by gradually transforming matter which already exists under other forms into its own material parts. Rather extension and indeed form in general are simply "impressed" upon matter (*EE*, pp. 51f/44). The gradual attainment of dominance by the form, so important to Aristotle's view of disposition, is thus downplayed in favor of the instantaneousness of an impression.

The metaphor of the *signum*, or the stamp, seems singularly inept—indeed, it seems to reproduce metaphorically both sides of the dilemma Maloney poses. For if matter is given being through form and yet form is "stamped" upon matter, Aquinas seems to say that what is stamped exists only through the stamp upon it. How can this be so? The shape of the ring is merely accidental to the wax which receives it—which is why the wax could be there to receive it in the first place. How can something be "stamped" with what first gives it being? Must matter not preexist the impress of form? How can we make sense of something which comes to exist only by virtue of something else being stamped upon it?

The dilemma, for Aquinas, is a false one. For it presumes, as Aristotle did, that the matter of a thing preexists that thing in actuality. If it does, then it must have a nature of its own—one which is either opposed to the form of that thing, like an Aristotelian element, or indifferent to it like designated matter. But for Aquinas, matter which has not yet received the form of a thing is potential—indeed, potentially that very thing. It is simply as such potentiality that matter preexists the impress of form. The determinate extension which matter receives from the form is thus not a mere accident of that matter; matter is defined by its capacity to receive determinate extension. Form is to matter neither an accident nor an opposite but a potential actuality. As Etienne Gilson puts it,

> Matter is only a potency determinable by the form. But the form itself is the act by which the matter is made to be such or such a determined substance. The proper role of the form is, therefore, to constitute substance *as substance*.[21]

The words sound Aristotelian but are not. What exists prior to the impress of form is not matter in elemental states but sheer potentiality: indeterminate potentiality for prime matter (which can be anything), determinate potentiality for designated matter (Socrates's body cannot be anybody else's body). Such potentiality, even in its purest form—that of prime matter—exists because it has been created by God. This is what Gilson views as Aquinas's key insight:

> Now, the Pre-socratics had justified the existence of individuals as such. Plato and Aristotle had justified the existence of substances as such. But not one of these seemed ever to have dreamed that there was any occasion to explain the existence of matter.[22]

But why does Aquinas need to explain matter's existence? Is he merely a better dreamer than Aristotle, Plato, and the Presocratics? Or is matter somehow in greater need of explanation for him than for them?

Part of the answer, surely, is the role of determinate extension in Aquinas's philosophy. For Aristotle, who of course had no creator God, there were many things which could not be explained; matter was one of them, an inexplicable principle of explanation. But even for Augustine, who did have a creator God, matter was in no great need of explanation because, as my previous quote from him shows, it was almost nothing: the creation of matter is merely the creation from nothing of almost nothing. But for Aquinas, matter is inherently richer than this. It is capable, in virtue of its own nature, of being determinately extended or designated; and that clearly calls for explanation. The explanatory factor, of course, is God. In order for God's creative gift, the *actus essendi*, to bring matter and form together, the two must also in some way be clearly apart, or "external" to one another. Their mutual externality is achieved by what we saw to be Aquinas's troublesome gesture of making matter at once the principle of individuation (and so intrinsic to the individual thing) and—potentially—spatially extended.

As sheer potentiality, matter does not have its own elemental nature, as it did in Aristotle. Designated by God to receive form, it is incapable of resisting the imposition of form—or at least such resistance must be accidental, for it cannot follow from the basic nature of matter itself. Hence, where for Aristotle the elements resisted form on behalf of their own natures, for Aquinas they do not. Instead, they "operate only according to the exigencies . . . which prepare matter to receive form" (*EE*, p. 63/49).

It is noteworthy that in my quote from Gilson on the relation of form and matter, matter absents itself in a strange way: substance is constituted as substance "properly," as the quote has it, through form alone: "the proper role of the form is, therefore, to constitute substance *as substance.*" This locution seems strange, for it is of course not only form which constitutes composite substances. That, for Aquinas, is the doing of matter as well, and apart from matter, the form of a composite is not substance. It is just form.[23] The strangeness vanishes when we see that matter is indeed necessary to composite substance—but only because, and insofar as, *matter effaces itself in its reception of form.* Which it can do, because *actually* it is nothing anyway. The entire role that matter plays on Aquinas's ontological stage is thus to step aside, allowing substance to be constituted as substance. Matter is so docile in this destiny of effacement that it can go entirely unnoticed, even by so astute a scholar as Gilson, for whom only form has a "proper role" in constituting substance as substance.[24]

The docility of matter is thus part of Aquinas's account of the radical createdness of beings. This account has no room for Aristotle's conception of the relation between matter and form as a struggle for domination. Matter, like everything else, is created by God; and since matter is potentiality, this means that the basic possibilities of anything are what God has created them to be. The docility of matter is thus explained and guaranteed by the irresistible power (though Aquinas does not use that term here) of God, "whose bidding alone matter obeys, as its own proper cause."[25]

OUSIODIC STRUCTURE AND THOMISTIC SUBSTANCE

The three traits of Aristotelian ousiodic domination are to be found, with modifications, in the Thomistic conception of substance. As we saw, the only role of matter in this conception is to allow substance to constitute itself as substance; essence has unresisted disposition over what happens within its boundaries. In contrast to Aristotle, however, disposition is not brought about by the intrinsic nature of form but requires the power of God, which creates both matter and the form which shapes it. Thus shaped, a substance has for Aquinas definite boundaries, signaled by the *materia signata* which makes it up (*EE*, p. 71/54).

Within a substance, only the form is intelligible and can exercise the initiative associated with cognition: "nothing is intelligible except through its definition and essence" (*EE*, p. 18/28; also see p. 21/30). Matter belongs to the definitions of material things (as opposed to mathematical things); hence matter is part of the thing. But, as for Aristotle, it is not an intelligible part. That is why separate substances, such as angels, which must be wholly and transparently intelligible, cannot be in any way material—indeed, are "in every way immune from matter" (*omnimodo immunitas a materia; EE*, pp. 19f/29, 51/43f).

Initiative is possessed in plenary form by God, for he is what Aristotle would have called the "moving cause" of the universe. In this, God is wholly unlike the Prime Mover, who had no initiative:

> Aristotle's pure actuality was confined to itself, unable to know anything else or to have interest in anything outside itself. It could only be a final cause, and not an efficient cause, a radically different kind of being from the actuality inferred by Aquinas.[26]

In Aristotle's view of initiative, the ousiodic form of a thing moves from cause to caused. For Aquinas, beings other than God receive from him what he is—existence itself (*EE*, pp. 53-59/44-47). This poses obvious questions, which would take us, and only first, to the heart of Aquinas's mysterious and compelling doctrine of analogy between creator and created.[27]

Angels, being pure minds, affect one another cognitively—in such a way, the *Summa Theologiae* tells us, that their communication is not a transgression of their boundaries: the "interior word" of one angel is revealed to the interiority of another without passing through any sort of exteriority (*ST* I.107.1).[28] Material beings occupy lower places in the hierarchy of the Thomistic universe, so for one being to affect another through its matter is, in *De ente et essentia*, a sign of lowly ontological status (*EE*, p. 63/49). Hence, though Aquinas does not discuss the issue here, any good or intelligible effect that one composite substance may have on others must be by way of its essence. As he puts it in the *Summa Theologiae,* "the active qualities in nature act by virtue of substantial forms" (*ST* I.45.8). If the (accidentally) hot water in a pot heats the stone placed into it, that is only in virtue of some (essentially) hot fire heating the water.

Aquinas's concept of divine power as constitutive of substance enables him to replace the gradualistic Aristotelian account with an instantaneous one and gives purchase to the metaphor of "impression" of form upon matter. Among the many things that are reconceived on the basis of this replacement are the concepts of truth and of body, as well as what I call the empirical purchase of ousia.

My point concerning truth is extremely general. As I argued in chapter 2, truth for Aristotle was a complicated effect of ousia; cognition conceived as the reception into the soul of an unchanging form meant that accuracy to the object was the sole excellence of cognition. For Aquinas, as I noted at the outset of this chapter, truth is detached from substance to the extent of being placed into binary opposition to it. That paves the way for important developments later in the long story I am telling, in which truth eventually detaches itself wholly from substance (and ousia). We see the beginnings of this detachment, which Hume carries through, in Aquinas's view that anything which is the object of a true proposition has a sort of being other than substantial being (within the binary that, we saw, encompasses them both).

Aquinas's concept of body has a place within a larger narrative which also leads to modernity. For Aristotle, as Montgomery Furth puts it in a passage I quoted in chapter 1, "the existence of material individuals is . . . 'given' only in the sense of a datum requiring explanation . . . and not as something that can be regarded as assumed as part of the primitive basis of the theory."[29] The reason Furth emphasizes this point is that for moderns (including ourselves), material bodies are such obvious "givens" that it is hard to conceive of them otherwise. Aquinas's account is, so to speak, midway between the two.

An earlier phase was represented by Averroës, who did not accept the unicity of substantial form and for whom matter was dimensional prior to receiving such form; otherwise it would not be capable of receiving some forms into some parts of itself and other forms into other parts, and there would only be one thing in the universe.[30] My body is *a* body, ontologically speaking, before being a *human* body. This, then, is what Aquinas denies because of his doctrine of the unicity of substantial form. But his denial led to a further problem: while Christ's body was in the tomb, between the crucifixion and the resurrection, it was apart from his soul or substantial form. Hence it was not really his body at all, and in particular could not have been divine. The idea that Christ's body could lose and then regain its divinity was repugnant enough to Christian sensibilities to have motivated some aspects of the church's condemnation of Aquinas's writings in 1277.[31] The way was then clear for the modern conception, taken for granted by Hobbes, that matter simply comes in discrete packets called "bodies"—a conception that, like almost all philosophical concepts, has a long, difficult, and clearly theological provenance. In particular, Aquinas's account is a forerunner of what Hobbes and Descartes, who do not accept Aristotelian essences, call "body" and "extended thing" respectively.[32]

Finally, the problem of the empirical purchase of ousia—of demarcating those features of our experience which indicate ousiodic structures—has now lost its Aristotelian solution. For Aristotle, I argued in chapter 2, we need to observe something over time and then string our observations together into a story of gradual growth and purposive movement in order to know that it is an ousia. For Aquinas, the creative act of God is immediate and extends to everything; the old tests no longer apply, and divine power has rendered narrative unnecessary. Indeed, there is no need to discriminate substances from non-substances: everything sensible is created as form in matter. Because it applies to everything in our experience, the concept of substance, unlike that of ousia, has no empirical utility. Nor is it intended to; it is formulated by Aquinas as part of a metaphysical, indeed theological, account of creation. When modern philosophers abandon Thomistic metaphysics, the concept has no metaphysical work to do. When they ask themselves what empirical work it does, there is no answer. Substance then seems to mean no more than "being" in the weak sense and is abandoned.

PARAMETRIC FUNCTIONS OF OUSIA IN AQUINAS: TWO ILLUSTRATIONS

In spite of the ways in which Aquinas's metaphysics of substance innovates upon Aristotle's *concept* of ousia, the *parameter* of ousia continues to function in his thought. Space prevents a detailed account of these functions here; I offer only a couple of illustrations, from Aquinas's ethics and politics.

Aquinas's well-known doctrine that all human acts are moral acts directly connects morality with the human essence. For what makes acts distinctively human can only be human nature itself:

> Human beings differ from irrational creatures in this, that they have *dominion* over their actions. That is why only those actions over which a human being has *dominion* are called human. But it is thanks to reason and will that human beings have *dominion* over their acts: free will is said to be the faculty of reason and will.[33]

The "dominion" of a human over her acts follows upon her "dominion" over her desires, which unlike sensation are morally relevant because they are internal to her:

> The senses require for their acts exterior sensible things . . . whose presence does not lie in the power of reason. But the interior powers, both appetitive and apprehensive, do not require exterior things. Therefore they are subject to the *command* of reason, which can not only incite or modify the affections of the appetitive power, but can also form the phantasms of the imagination. (*ST* I.81.3, "Reply to Objection 3"; emphasis added)

The Thomistic moral agent thus has definite boundaries. Within them, the will is the disposing factor.[34] For, as the "superior appetite," it decides which of the lower desires are to be acted upon at any moment:

> For wherever there is order among a number of motive powers, the second moves only by virtue of the first; and so the lower appetite is not sufficient to cause movement, unless the higher appetite intervenes. (*ST* I.81.3).

As the highest "motive power," i.e., the highest power capable of changing the outside world through movement, the will exercises initiative in the moral agent. It also orders the moral faculties in general, because its object—"the good and the end in general"—is the most universal (as versus, for example, color and truth, which are the specific objects of vision and intellect respectively):

> Therefore the will as an agent moves all the powers of the soul to their respective acts, except the natural powers of the vegetative part, which are not subject to our choice. (*ST* I.82.4; cf. I.II.1.1; I.II.17.1)

The control of reason over the mind is so important to Aquinas that the peculiar shame of even married sex is that the genitals, unlike other external members, do not obey reason in their motions (*ST* II.II.151 Art. 4)—a violation of what I call disposition. But his overall ethical theory is subject to a complex interplay between Aristotelian prudence, which aims at human happiness in this life, and Christian love, which aims at union with God. A similar interplay takes place in Aquinas's view of the household. Even if Adam and Eve had not sinned, writes Aquinas, the social world would contain masters and subordinates. Among the latter are women. Explicitly following Aristotle, he considers women to be genetic anomalies. The sole relation between them and men is instrumental—and the sole function for which women are fit instruments is the bearing and educating of children in the home (*ST* I.90.1; II.II.177. 2). But the situation is complicated for Aquinas because some women have the gift of prophecy, and women were among the closest associates of Jesus himself (*ST* II.II.177.2; III.55.1).

Ethics and political philosophy constitute a whole for Aquinas (as for Aristotle), and he often makes analogies from one to the other. *Summa Theologiae* I.81.3, while discussing the will as "higher appetite," also mentions Aristotle's claim that the soul has despotic power over the body but kingly power over the desires (*Pol.* I.2 1254b2). The passage just quoted concerning the will's role in ordering the powers of the soul is even more wide ranging:

> wherever we have order among a number of active powers, that power which is related to the universal end moves the powers which refer to particular ends. And we may observe this both in nature and in political things. For the heaven, which aims at the universal preservation of things subject to generation and corruption, moves all inferior bodies, each of which aims at the preservation of the species or of the individual. So, too, a king, who aims at the common good of the whole kingdom, by his rule moves all the governors of cities, each of whom rules over his own particular city. (*ST* I.82.4)

This argumentative deployment of the parameter of ousia is couched in terms of final causes and ends rather than in terms of form and matter. Given the complete submission of form to matter in Aquinas's ontology, a degree of submission rarely found in the human realm, this is perhaps not surprising.

Aquinas's political philosophy, as outlined for example in *De regimine principium* of 1265–1267, contains an argumentative application of ousiodic structures which makes specific reference to the rule of form (rationality) over matter. It is more straightforward than Aristotle's political deployment of ousia, for Aristotle at times conceived of the state as a "network of friendships" rather than in terms of his politics of natural domination.[35] Aquinas's parametric application of ousia is more consistent:

> in everything that is ordered to a single end, one thing is found that rules the rest. In the physical universe, by the intention of divine providence all the other bodies are ruled by the first or heavenly body, as divine providence directs, and all material bodies are ruled by rational creatures. In each man the soul rules the body, and within the soul reason rules over passion and desire. Likewise among the parts of the body there is one ruling part, either the heart or the head, that rules all the others. So in every group there must be something that rules.[36]

This passage virtually paraphrases *Politics* I.2 1254a28–33.[37] Like that passage, it appeals to the totality of nature and human life to justify rulership. It uses the standard Aristotelian concept of *telos*, comporting the notion of actuality as control of matter by form. The final sentence highlights the trait of boundary: "in every group"—*all* groups, it appears, have insides and outsides. And it proclaims the need for rulership, disposition.

But the political sphere itself has a very different context for Aquinas. For Aristotle, man is a "political animal" because the state is the only social structure which can provide more than subsistence or even commodity. In the state alone can we achieve the good life and the full development of human nature; our possession of language, which binds our minds more tightly together than even bees and ants are bound, is a sign of that (*Pol.* I.2). Aquinas's arguments for our political nature are by contrast instrumental:

we are deficient in certain ways which require us to live in groups (for one thing, "we" need women to reproduce). Unlike other animals, we have no natural weapons, and we do not have specific instincts regarding what to pursue or avoid. And, most important, we need guidance:

> If men were intended to live alone as do many animals, there would be no need for anyone to direct him towards his end, since every man would be his own king under God, the highest king, and the light of reason given to him on high would enable him to act on his own. But man is by nature a political and social animal. (KG, p. 14f)

The state—indeed, as we have seen, "all groups"—is not for Aquinas what it is for Aristotle, a community which fulfills and expresses our nature. It is a necessity for us in virtue of certain weaknesses to which our nature is prey. Were it not for these weaknesses, the perfect human community would consist of the individual and God. Because it is founded on human weakness, the political community (like all others) is a matter less of the free use of reason than of direction. The individual must be directed toward his own best end, and that is the business of the government:

> it is the duty of the king to promote the good life of the community so that it leads to happiness in heaven—so that he should command the things that lead to heavenly bliss and as far as possible forbid their opposite. (KG, p. 28)

For Aquinas, legislating morality is not only legitimate; it is the very essence of governance. And within the framework of this overall goal, governance consists in boundary, disposition, and initiative: for the government must establish and improve the good life of the community, as well as defend it against outside enemies (KG, p. 28).

Finally, the government is, at best, a monarchy. For a state is not a heap; it must exist as a unified being, and the more unified the better:

> the more effective a government is in promoting unity in peace, the more useful it will be. . . . But it is evident that that which is itself one can promote unity better than that which is a plurality, just as the most effective cause of heat is that which is in itself hot. Therefore government by one person is better than by many. (KG, p. 17)

In spite of Aquinas's innovations on Aristotelian ousia, then, the parametric functioning of ousia remains in place on the political level.[38]

Aquinas's philosophy, of course, springs from and deals with—codifies—a world which is radically different from Aristotle's. Such notions as createdness in metaphysics and Christian love in ethics were not merely un-Aristotelian but unthinkable for Aristotle. But the matter-form binary is in place, and Aquinas's main innovation upon Aristotle with respect to it is what I call the "docilization" of matter. Matter no longer exists as elements whose nature is to resist form; it is now mere potentiality whose entire nature is to receive form. Resistance to the domination of form is now not merely un-wise but unnatural or sinful. Ousiodic domination has been consolidated throughout the universe. As Gilson notes,

> precisely because every operation is the realization of an essence, and because every essence is a certain quantity of being and perfection . . . the universe reveals itself to us as a society made up of superiors and inferiors.[39]

Thus ontologically legitimated, the parameter of ousia maintains its stand-ing as the main paradigm of ethics and politics, at least insofar as they are merely human pursuits.

Alas, as part 2 shows, the very completeness of form's victory over matter is the undoing of ousia. For Aristotle, it was easy to see what in our expe-rience had an ousiodic structure and what did not: anything which visibly persisted in its own nature, whether moving or resting, was resisting the subversive pull of its matter and therefore must contain a disposing form. When Aquinas makes matter entirely receptive of form, form loses this function, so that there is literally nothing left for it to do except undergird Thomistic metaphysics and its derivative discourses. What is traditionally called "substantial form" loses its empirical purchase and in modernity becomes a target not of critique but of ridicule—as in Locke:

> Those, therefore who have been taught that the several species of sub-stances had their distinct internal *substantial forms,* and that it was those *forms* which made the distinction of substances into their true species and genera, were led yet farther out of the way by having their minds set upon fruitless inquiries after "substantial forms"; wholly unintelligi-ble and whereof we have scarce so much as any obscure or confused conception in general.[40]

Before pursuing, in part 2, the modern "eviction" of ousia from nature, chapter 4 briefly adduces some examples of how ousiodic structure func-tioned in the ancient and medieval worlds, in household and empire, cloister and castle keep.

TWO ANCIENT ENGINES OF OPPRESSION

I argued in chapter 1 that Being itself for Aristotle is the domination of matter by form and that this domination can be defined along three axes: boundary, disposition, and initiative. I suggested in chapter 2 that this metaphysical doctrine, abstract and general, became specified and concretized in two stages of parametric structuring. First, it hermeneutically structured other Aristotelian discourses, such as biology, psychology, ethics, and politics; it told the Aristotelian investigator how the objects of these respective discourses are to be understood. Second, these discourses themselves became normative at certain points. The norms they yielded organized in turn a broad variety of cognitive, social, and ethical practices. These practices, finally, had the overall task of bringing sometimes recalcitrant realities into line with the ousiodic norm. Deviations from this norm came to be stigmatized—as monstrosities, women, incontinent and unhindered men, badly organized states, and the like. Because the social relations these discourses define and legitimate are always relations of domination in which one set of people is reduced to the status of matter while another set is allowed the privileges of form, I call them "oppressive." So construed, oppression has four dimensions. To be "oppressed" is then

1. to be *bounded,* cut off from relation to those outside the boundaries within which one exists;

2. to be *disposed,* i.e., to be permitted to relate to others within the boundaries that contain one only as prescribed and allowed by those in control;

3. to be deprived of *initiative,* i.e., of any opportunity to affect the world outside the boundaries;

4. to be regarded as *unintelligible,* as a mere mass of chaotic, conflicting, contingent drives, perhaps obstreperous but always "irrational."

Such an account of oppression is not without contemporary resonances. Marilyn Frye, for example, traces the term back to its root, "press," and isolates three main aspects of oppression: molding, reduction, and immobilization.[1] To be molded means, in the first instance, to be caught in a mold: to be confined within boundaries. In this aspect, oppression "is the experience of being caged in: all avenues, in every direction, are blocked or booby trapped."[2] The reduction, in turn, is to nature: "it has to do with your membership in some category understood as a 'natural' or 'physical' category."[3] Biology thus becomes destiny; being a merely physical or natural entity, the oppressed person is unable to think for herself and consequently is at the disposal of those who can. Finally, the immobilization of oppressed persons renders them unable to affect the world beyond the barriers which enclose them.[4] Frye's account of oppression thus, to a degree, accords with the three axes of ousiodic domination.

These three aspects of oppression are obviously to be found the world over. The fourth, which Frye does not mention, concerns the complicity of metaphysics in such oppression and appears to be the specific contribution of the philosophical heritage of the West, for it is the only heritage which proclaims the intelligibility of being. This maxim, more familiar to us as the "unity of being and thought" first formulated by Parmenides, means that the oppressed person is unintelligible. She is reduced to nature, not as cosmos but as chaos, to the kind of massed drives and needs that, in Aristotle's view, constitute the "unhindered" man. On the other hand, it also turns out to mean that one who is in a position of domination ought to conduct herself in ways that are intelligible to others; otherwise there would be no sense to Aristotle's whole enterprise in his ethical writings, which are based on the presupposition that to be good is to be rational. Hence rule which exhibits the human forms of contingency—whimsy and arbitrariness—is incomprehensible and evil. The intelligibility of the ruler's conduct must be evident first and foremost to his peers; it is they who are the appropriate judges of whether his actions stem from reason or whimsy. When the ruler's actions are not rationally explicable by his peers, he is liable to their censure and bad opinion of him.

87

But not to actual intervention, as Euthyphro discovers in Plato's dialogue of that name. The man whom Euthyphro wants to prosecute for causing the deaths of some of his own slaves is not merely a fellow citizen but Euthyphro's own father. At dialogue's end, Euthyphro decides not to carry out his plan. The implication is clear (and is driven home by the *Lysis*): the conduct of men in the home can be judged, if not by outsiders, at least by their own sons, against whom they do not want to use brute force, and perhaps by others over whom they must rule without using raw coercion. Seen in this perspective, the main problem of rule is to find a way to get people to acquiesce in their own oppression. Philosophy's contribution is to define rule metaphysically and thence, as we saw, to legitimate it as rational. It thus demonstrates to slaves, children, women, or ordinary citizens that they are less rational than their rulers, to the point of being unable to care for themselves. This can be because their desires are dominant within them or (if they are mature citizens) because they do not have adequate information.[5]

Philosophy, at least in its metaphysical dispensation, thus comes to include discourses which, like Aristotelian ethics and political philosophy, have the effect of proving to people belonging to various categories that because of this adherence they are inferior and need to be oppressed (and to those not belonging to such categories that they are superior and entitled to oppress others). Such discourses go far beyond their ancient origins, having had a long and honorable history in the West; Plato's Noble Lie, for example,[6] has been taken up in modern theories of innate intelligence. The phenomenon of Church Latin, inability to master which relegated one to serfdom or servitude, has proliferated into a dazzling array of professional jargons, each of which lets outsiders know that they are unequipped to participate in the discourse. And Aristotle's own philosophy has remained profoundly influential.

A discourse such as the Noble Lie is not only oppressive in itself but also defines and legitimates a broad variety of other oppressive practices. It is a veritable "engine of oppression," an organizer of more specific oppressive practices. There are many such engines of oppression, in the West as elsewhere. Some of them, like the lie, are discursive; others, like the domestic architecture I shall discuss here, show rather than say their legitimation of ousiodic structure. A complete inventory of them, indeed, even a full discussion of those few that I adduce here and in later chapters, would require entire books or even libraries. If my examples are well chosen and do show what I claim they show, they will serve at most to adumbrate possible future case studies and to indicate the extent and prevalence of ousiodic structure.

As my first example I advance figure 1, the House of Pansa at Pompeii. This private dwelling (obviously of a very rich man) appears to be constructed, however unknowingly, to realize the structure of Aristotelian ousia. It has, to begin with, very definite boundaries. On the ground floor, which

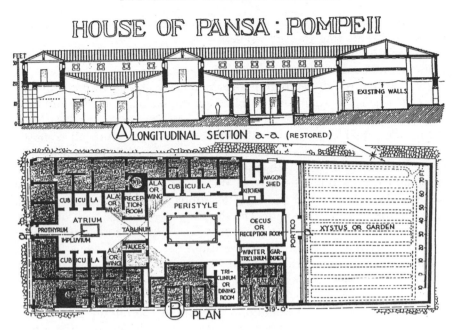

FIGURE 1. The House of Pansa, Pompeii. From Banister Fletcher, *A History of Architecture,* ed. Dan Cruickshank (Oxford: Architectural Press, 1996).

is the main floor, there are no external windows at all; the rooms open onto two interior courtyards. There are only three entrances from the outside, all of them long and complex.

External influences are thus reduced to a minimum, and this is no accident. Surrounding the house are other dwellings and shops, which are rented out by the house's owner. Historically speaking, these were once parts of the house; each *cubiculum* was the anteroom to an entire private suite. Over time these exterior rooms have been walled off so that everything in the house opens immediately onto the courtyards, and the entrances are reduced to three. The house thus establishes its boundaries by excluding elements which are of a kind with those it contains and could quite well have belonged to it. That they do not is a case of what I called, in chapter 1, "external" exclusion.[7]

What the house now contains of the apartments is merely their innermost rooms. These have become its sleeping rooms, the *cubicula*. All the *cubicula* open directly onto the two central courtyards, the atrium (the "public" part of the house, into which guests arrive and where sits the *domina,* the mistress of the house)[8] and the peristyle (surrounded by the more private, "familial" quarters devoted to physical needs such as sleeping, eating, and procreating). With the exception of the master suite at upper right, the *cubicula* do not have access to each other; you cannot go

89

from *cubiculum* to *cubiculum* without passing through one of the court-yards—and rendering yourself visible.

The entire house centers on the *tablinum,* the living room (or, in some cases, master study). I have drawn in the sight lines from the *tablinum,* so as to show that the doors to all the *cubicula* are visible from the center of the *tablinum.* Those rooms not visible from the *tablinum* are *alae* and have no front walls at all; they are entirely unprivate. The center of the *tablinum* is thus the center of the house, the single place from which all domestic activities—who comes in and out of the house, who visits whom within it, who does what and to or with whom—can be noted and organized. The vision which does this—the gaze of the master—thus sets up a distance between the *tablinum* and the other locations in the house; it is central, and they are merely peripheral. The instating of this distance is an exclusion of everything and everyone not the master from the center; it is what I called, in chapter 1, "immanent" exclusion.[9]

Even the wife, in the atrium, receives sanction for her activities from the gaze of her husband. She may be rational, as Aristotle said, but only derivatively so: the authority visibly in force is really his. His gaze gives her the authority to operate as he would do within the home but does not authorize her to function in the world beyond the household. Her authority is thus a specific form of his, as, on the ontological level, "musical" is a specific way of being "rational." *Domina* collaborates with *dominus* as a "relegated" property, in chapter 1, collaborated with the essence itself.

In the security of its boundaries, the existence of an organizing center, and the immediate openness of everything in the house to that center, we have the basic structures of boundary and disposition. What I call initiative is also built into the house: the *pater familias* is the only person who can enter and leave at will. Women and children should be accompanied by slaves, and slaves cannot in principle go out without the master's permission. Only *pater* is strictly free, then, to come and go as he pleases.

The contrast of this sort of dwelling with earlier ones is marked. Consider the following description, which I quote at length, of the non-ousiodic domestic architecture of ancient Crete:

> The first impression received by a visitor to the site of a Minoan palace is one of disorder, confusion, and a jumble of multiple elements unrestrained by any formal discipline. The impression comes from the agglomerative system of construction and the absence of a unified façade. . . . The living quarters and workshop blocks simply cluster together, forming setbacks and salients. . . .
>
> There are no right angles or continuous straight lines; instead there is a sinuous movement of projections and recessions. . . . In fact, the location and role of the central courtyard provide the only unifying principles of the composition, but this unity is purely functional and makes no

concessions to any demand of symmetry or axiality. It is based on the relations and lines of communication which unite the various quarters of the palace; it is physically realized in the long corridors into which the visitor to the palace is immediately plunged.

One last feature of these compositions has particular appeal for the modern student of architecture: linked with movement and currents of circulation, it is never closed in upon itself. At every instant it opens upon the outdoors by a knowing use of porticos and loggias disclosing neatly framed glimpses of the countryside.[10]

The Minoan palace, then, violates the canons of ousiodic domination. It has no encircling wall but is open to the outside at a variety of points; it has no unifying center from which the whole can be grasped and understood but consists of chance agglomerations of disparate rooms joined by corridors that move from part to part of the palace without passing through a true center. The kind of domination afforded to Pansa would be simply impossible for the "master" of such a palace.

I have chosen the House of Pansa not only because it is a particularly good example of the structures of ousia realized architecturally but also because the house in classical times was the greatest engine of oppression, the place of confinement of women and slaves. But the same structures can be found operating on other levels of the ancient world. The "Roman Oration" of Aelius Aristides, delivered in 143 C.E., provides an example on a particularly grand scale. In it, the Greek Aristides seeks to gain the favor of his Roman audience (which included the Emperor himself) by praising Rome in the right way, by appealing to values both Greeks and Romans hold dear. Though like any idealized portrayal this one is at some remove from actual practice,[11] it stands today as an expression of the common ideals of Greek and Roman at the time—as, in the words of one scholar, a "summation of Roman themes that had been treated by Greek writers for the last three hundred years" and, in those of another, as "the greatest literary expression of what the Golden Age could mean to the world of Hadrian and the Antonines."[12]

Aristides conceives of the Roman Empire as a giant artifact, achieved by applying Roman statecraft to the materials (*hylais*) furnished by Roman power. The imperial "formed matter" thus constituted exhibits the three axes of ousiodic domination I have isolated from Aristotle's thought, and they are discussed by Aristides at length—though not, of course, under the names I have given them.

The borders of the Empire, first, are very definite—enforced by a "wall of men," the Roman army stationed around the periphery of the civilized world (78-84). As in the case of an ousia, boundaries are determined from within, by Rome itself: "you do not reign within assigned boundaries, nor does an other dictate to what point it is permitted for you to dominate" (*krateîn*, 10). In regard to its boundaries, the Empire is explicitly compared to a house. It is gathered around the Italian peninsula, which divides the Mediterranean (as the *tablinum* of Pansa separates the atrium from the peristyle). The farthest geographical features of the earth—the Red Sea, the cataracts of the Nile, and Lake Maeotis—are no more than the Empire's "courtyard walls" (28). Within these walls, Roman rule is continuous; no city, tribe, harbor, or fortress holds out against it except "possibly some that you have condemned as worthless" (28).

To be part of this wondrous artifact is thus an honor; only the "worthless" remain independent. The various cities and regions which make up the Empire stand to one another in relations of harmonious attunement (*akribeia*). The Emperor plays his domain, indeed, as if it were a stringed instrument which emits from the diversity of its components, somewhat paradoxically, a single, pure, flutelike note (29-31).

The seat and source of this attunement, the beating heart of the Empire, is the city of Rome, the *archê* and *teleutê* of all goods and the site of all knowing as well: "whatever one does not see there [at Rome] neither did nor does come into being" (13). In this, Rome is the city of cities:

> What another city is to its own boundaries and territory, this city is to the boundaries and territory of the entire civilized world, as if the latter were a country district and she had been appointed common town. (61)

The Empire is thus not merely like a house but like a city. Secure within his capital, the Emperor has no need to wander about his possessions or make himself visible to provincials; his letters, which arrive as if "carried by winged messengers," suffice to convey his orders, which are obeyed (again somewhat paradoxically, given earlier metaphors) in silence: the only hand plucking the strings is his (33, 89).

The result of this arrangement for the individual cities and regions of the Empire is peace. There are no internal pockets of resistance to Rome, and the various cities and satraps do not fight one another (29). There is no envy among the states which the empire comprises, no disputing for rule and primacy, for all rule and all primacy belong to Rome (65, 69). This absence of strife, for Aristides, fully characterizes the relations of the parts of the Empire to one another. Even in his concluding panegyrics (92-109) there is no mention of positive relations among the regions of the Empire, such as trade with one another rather than with Rome—though we know that it existed and was a major benefit of the empire.[13] Each part of the Empire is thus presented as related to Rome alone and as abjuring relations (which apparently could only be hostile) with its neighbors. The disposition of Rome over its Empire is absolute.

The cities and regions which the Empire comprises also have no initiative, no capacity to affect what lies beyond the boundaries of the Empire. The only trade mentioned, again, is with Rome (12f); the cities send their tributes to Rome with more pleasure than they would receive equal tributes from someone else (67b). The power to affect what lies beyond the boundaries of the Empire is exercised solely by Rome itself, through its army.

The army does not exist, in the view of Aristides, to maintain an internal order which no one could, or would, breach; there are no garrisons in the towns (64, 67a). Nor does the army exist to expand the Empire, which already embraces the entire known world—Aristides claims to be unsure whether anyone outside Roman hegemony even exists (99). Certainly Rome has no external enemy of its own type to threaten it, as the Greeks had the Persians. Like Aristotle's Prime Mover, Rome is a *singulum singularum,* an altogether unique and unassailable plenum, and has no need to concern itself with anything but itself. But walls are necessary, in spite of the lack of anyone to wall out. The soldiers stationed on the peripheries of the Empire constitute a "wall of men," "altogether unbreachable and indestructible." Their function is apparently only to solidify the existing boundaries, which thus appear as ends in themselves (78-84).

It is the army which most clearly reveals what Aristides considers the primary innovation of Roman statecraft, as important as all its other principles put together. This is the division of political sway in the Empire into two groups: those who lead and those who are led (59). The former—composed of most of the world's talent, courage, and leadership—are by decree citizens of Rome, no matter what their origins and no matter where they live (59). The Empire thus divides everywhere into Romans and non-Romans (63), leaders and led, those exercising the formative powers of statecraft and those upon whom it is exercised. On the civil side, this means that "the men of greatest standing and influence in every city guard their own fatherlands for you. And you have a double hold upon the cities, both from [Rome] and from your fellow citizens in each" (64). On the military side, Rome has selected those best fitted for service and then

> when you found them you released them from the fatherland and gave them your own city. . . . Those performing military service would none the less be citizens, who on the day of their enrollment in the army had lost their own cities but from that very day had become your fellow citizens and defenders. (75)

Disposition and initiative are both in the hands of the "formal parts" of the Empire, its citizens—under the aegis, of course, of the Emperor, from whom their power (analogously to that of the *domina* in the household) derives. That in turn is the key to the Empire's attunement, its *akribeia.* For it means that Rome alone, of all the imperial powers in history, rules over men who are free. When Rome sends out governors to the cities (31, 36), it is in cooperation with the Roman citizens who are natives of each (64). The cities themselves are free to administer their own internal affairs, subject only to the jurisdiction of Rome ("Caria has not been given to Tissaphernes, nor

Phrygia to Pharnabazus," 36). And the citizens of each city are free because they can appeal decisions of the local authorities to Rome itself (37–39). Thus, where previous rulers had reigned, so to speak, over "naked bodies belonging to various tribes" (92) or over open country and strongholds, the Romans rule over genuine cities (93) containing free men.

The three axes of ousiodic domination are thus the key to Aristides' presentation of the ideal Roman Empire. In his discourse, the Empire is defined and legitimated as a giant "engine of oppression," though Aristides would never call it that. Its structures are analogous to those of the House of Pansa; the analogy to the household, we saw, is explicitly made at paragraph 28 and again at 102: "you organized the whole civilized world [*oikouménê*] as if into one household [*oikon*]."

Unlike the House of Pansa, however, the Empire has many levels, and they exhibit a "nesting" structure of ousias within ousias. The Empire, the world-ousia, contains, as relatively autonomous sub-ousias, cities and regions whose structures it shares: each has its own boundaries (unviolated, thanks to Rome), and each contains its own distinction between rulers (local citizens of Rome) and ruled. Within the cities, in turn, are individual households, to which the Empire is also compared. Each household contains its own ruler and ruled. Finally, the individual citizens of Rome are shown as, though not explicitly said to be, moral agents, able to control themselves and their desires.

The nesting structure thus outlined extends even beyond the human sphere, to the divine order itself, as this is conveyed by the poets. Under the rule of Zeus, order has been brought into a divine world formerly torn by "strife, confusion, and disorder" (103). Just so, the Empire has brought universal freedom from fear to the civilized world. It not only mirrors the divine harmony but actually completes it, by giving to each god his or her due and making them all happy with mortals (104f).

We thus find ousiodic domination on every level of social organization within the Empire. Because of this domination, no single ousia (except perhaps the one constituted by the gods) is absolute or self-legitimating. The individual citizen, for example, can appeal decisions of the local authorities to Rome, so the disposition of the local rulers over him is limited. Failure to appeal indicates assent, so that "one might say that the men of today are ruled by the governors who are sent out, only insofar as they are content to be ruled" (37). The ultimate legitimation of the structures of ousiodic domination comes from their recurrence on every level, lying in the overall harmonious cooperation (*ákribeia*) of each level with the others. The primary example of harmonious cooperation for Aristides is that between the levels of individual city and world empire. But *akribeia* originates on the divine level, whose pantheon is a paradigm of harmony (as the single God of modernity constitutes a paradigm of power).

The nested ousiai of the ancient world thus tend to replicate themselves internally, so that each component of a social ousia comes to exemplify in its own sphere the structure of ousiodic domination without any change in its boundaries (which, in the account of Aristides, are definitively fixed by Rome). That is true even on the level of domestic architecture: Vitruvius, for example, calls *ordinatio* the principle that each component of an ousia should itself be well-ordered and contrasts it with *dispositio* or *diathesis,* which is the "fit assemblage" (*apta conlocatio*) of the parts of a whole building.[14]

This nesting, in which each part comes to exhibit the structure of the whole, inevitably leads to a set of social organisms increasingly differentiated internally, as in the proliferating bureaucracies of the Roman Empire (and other bureaucracies since). In such bureaucracies, each official exercises the traditional forms of ousiodic domination over his subordinates. His job, the boundaries of his mandate (Latin: *provincia*),[15] are clear; he is permitted to hire and fire at will; his subordinates are at his disposition to carry out his orders, and their acts count as his own, so that he alone has initiative. Application of the same ousiodic model to these subordinates gives them subordinates of their own, over whom they exercise such domination in turn; and so on down the bureaucratic line.

The ancient world—like later worlds—is thus structured along what are usually called hierarchical lines. But this term, connoting only order as to merit, does not convey the domination each level exercises over those directly below, and it does not account for the internal proliferation of bureaucratic posts. A bishop or a duke is "better" than I am, is higher in the sacred governance or hierarchy. But *my* bishop and *my* duke govern me, and that is a matter not of "hierarchy" but of ousia. I can approach their status, without overthrowing them, by finding others to dominate as they dominate me.

These structures of domination functioned long after the Roman Empire. The ancient peristyle, for example, evolved into the most private of spaces and, in the Dark Ages, the most important: the medieval cloister.[16] In the castle, the walls would become as high and unbreachable as possible, and the *tablinum* would evolve into the donjon or (in a revealing name) the "keep." The medieval church can be read as a monotheistic translation of the House of Pansa. The atrium develops into the nave, which receives the faithful; the peristyle becomes the apse in which God's domestics, the clergy, have their prayer stalls. The *alae* are lengthened into transepts, and the *cubicula* become side altars. The whole is surveyable from the high altar, which thus constitutes a sort of *tablinum* inhabited by the greatest master of all—God himself, in the form of consecrated hosts.

But only on official occasions. Most of the time the hosts are not kept on the high altar, and for a striking reason: the convenience of the domestics. Whenever one passes before the repository of the hosts, various obeisances have to be performed—bows and/or genuflections. That proves to be cumbersome for those who must work in the church, maintaining its sacred equipment or just sweeping the floor. And so God himself is "deposed," relocated to one of the side altars, where his presence is indicated by a red lamp. The deposition is not an overthrow, however. For the Christian God, unlike the ancient master (or even the Emperor), is not of this world and is not relegated to occupying any single place within it; his center, as the saying has it, is everywhere and his circumference nowhere. His majesty is thus unaffected by being "sidelined." And this humble practice has significant metaphysical implications, for it is only possible if the source of being has withdrawn from the world to the extent that it can no longer be located within it. The world, correspondingly, is losing the internal differentiations which once made it a cosmos. It is on the way to becoming homogeneous space-time, here implicitly defined by the single property of being incapable of holding God.

But the House of Pansa finds its most startling realizations not in stone and stucco but in modern theories of the human order. To sketch this briefly: if we hang a curtain at the back of the *tablinum* (through the letter "M"), do we not have a model of Freud's famous depiction of the human mind as a room with a curtain hanging down the middle?[17] The peristyle and associated rooms (dining rooms, kitchen, etc.) would correspond to the unconscious, from which an occasional desire (slave, woman) would escape through the *tablinum*, where Ego resides and censors, into the atrium, the entrance onto the public world. Similarly, when Marx, at the end of part two of *Capital*, takes us from the marketplace to the factory, is he not in effect taking us from the public realm of the atrium, the market (on which previous economists had focused exclusively), back into the garden and kitchen, where the productive (and reproductive) forces reside?[18]

Like the House of Pansa, the human domains treated by Freud and Marx—and many after them—are threefold. There is in every case a public realm, characterized respectively as the superego and the market. Behind this, supporting it and a necessary condition of its existence, is a productive or creative domain which does not find its way into acceptable public speech: the id or the factory. And there is a third factor, consciousness or ideology, which controls access from the unspoken domain to the spoken, thereby maintaining a repressive control over the private, creative forces. The oppression and repression diagnosed by Freud and Marx turn out, it seems, to be realizations of the ancient structures of ousia.

APPENDIX TO PART ONE: PLATO AS PREHISTORY

Plato, I have suggested, belongs to the prehistory of ousia—and, if metaphysics is the history of ousia, to the prehistory of metaphysics as well. This view is unusual if not unpopular, for Plato is generally revered or excoriated as the founder of metaphysics. This view begins, perhaps, with Nietzsche, who wrote: "My philosophy is reversed Platonism. The farther from that which truly is, so much the better, purer, more beautiful. Living in appearance as the goal."[1] But it hardly ends there. Heidegger states the matter with dogmatic strength: "Plato's thinking, in transmuted forms, remains determinative for the entire history of philosophy. Metaphysics is Platonism."[2] Gilles Deleuze, while admitting that "with Platonism the issue is still in doubt," also claims that "Platonism . . . founds the entire domain that philosophy will recognize as its own."[3] For Jacques Derrida, the epoch of presence that defines philosophy "began in Platonism."[4] In the words of Jürgen Habermas, "Metaphysics believes it can trace everything back to one. Since Plato, it has presented itself in its definitive form as the doctrine of universal unity."[5] For Richard Rorty, Plato is "the man who dreamed up the whole idea of Western philosophy."[6] Even Daniel Graham, who comes from a very different philosophical tradition than the above thinkers, takes the Aristotelian preeminence of form over matter to be an unfortunate Platonic relic.[7]

If metaphysics is importantly the story of ousia, then all these illustrious thinkers are importantly wrong. An anecdote, as far as I know wholly apocryphal, shows the innovative nature of Aristotle's account of ousia in contrast with Plato. Someone once claimed, in Plato's later years or even after his death, to have sneaked into the Academy. He said he found Plato's pupils, the first academics, standing around a grapefruit, trying to tell what it was. "It is yellow," said one. "It is spherical," said another. "It is grapefruit," said a third. (They were helped by the fact that the Greek language lacks an indefinite article.) "It is bitter," said a fourth, and so on. The debate about the "what" of the grapefruit continued, with no one able to persuade the others, until our stealthy hero slipped away.

Whatever the anecdote's provenance, its point is a valid one: for Plato, all a thing's properties are on a par. That the object under investigation was *primarily* a grapefruit and only subsequently anything else is simply not part of his world.[8] There, then, are no ousiodic forms for Plato, no immanent basic units that are responsible for whatever other properties a thing may have. And no ordinary Platonic thing can have a dispositive center. Sensibles cannot, because all their properties are equally imitations of Forms. And Forms cannot because, being wholly simple, they have nothing to center or dispose.

Hence, in Plato's world of becoming, there are not necessarily sharp insides and outsides; a particular Form can come to be instantiated anywhere within space,[9] and its instantiation may well be fuzzy at the edges. Sensible beings may even blend and interpenetrate, as humans do, for example, in eros. That can be seen from the *Phaedo* and, even better, from the *Timaeus*. At *Phaedo* 100e–102e, Socrates distinguishes among three levels of ontology: the Form (say, the Large), the "largeness in us," and "us" ourselves. The first two levels receive a good deal of discussion in the course of the dialogue. But what sort of thing are "we"? The *Phaedo*'s answer, fittingly, is on the moral plane: we are our souls, which are not sensible things at all but akin to the Forms. But what about non-human or inanimate sensible things? What, in other words, about the thing in general?

The question is not answered in the *Phaedo*. The *Timaeus*'s answer, by contrast, is fairly clear, if puzzling in many details. There are the Forms, eternal and nonsensible units; there are the qualities that participate in them; and, instead of "us," there is the "receptacle" in which those qualities come to be (*Timaeus* 49a seqq.). The receptacle, since it is able to receive any Form whatever, has no qualities of its own; it is, we may say, dynamically homogeneous in its constant self-othering. Because it is an intrinsically featureless and unstable expanse in every direction, the Receptacle can provide no grounds at all for any particular Form to be instantiated at one point in it rather than at any other. As far as the *Timaeus* is concerned, then, the empirical world could exhibit colors foaming through the Receptacle like snow on a television set. Or the whiteness of a sugar cube might be next to its sweetness, rather than having the sweetness "in" it. Bodies themselves are merely gatherings of elements and are in constant flux; their sameness itself is dynamic, "circulating" (*peripheromenon, Timaeus* 49e) within them. A phenomenon such as sensation is physically described not as the progressive inwardization of a sensible form toward a rational center but as a mixing in which "parts communicate with each other" (*Timaeus* 64b). In principle, no stable boundaries can be drawn among entities, and where there is no boundary there can be neither disposition over what is inside nor initiative toward the world outside.

That Plato actually envisages the sensible world as thus disordered is further indicated by the fact that he adopts a variety of strategies for explaining the observable order of nature. In the *Timaeus,* he invokes both the world-soul and the divine craftsman, or Demiurge, to explain how order comes to be in a receptacle which is of itself wholly chaotic (*Timaeus* 29 seqq). When he reduces physical things to gatherings or agglomerations of basic elements, he specifies that each of these, at least, has a purely geometrical—and hence definitely bounded—shape (*Timaeus* 53b). In the *Phaedo,* he attempts to account for order over time—causality—by arguing that some Forms, when they "come to" a thing, necessarily bring other Forms to it, as fire always brings heat (*Phaedo* 103c-104c).

Neither of these strategies, however, suffices to bring forth physical entities with definite boundaries, to say nothing of entities with single immanent sources of their own unity and activity. As agglomerations of elemental shapes, sensible objects would still be just what Aristotle insists they are not—heaps. The Demiurge and the world soul, for their parts, are not infinite creators. They can bring some order to the cosmos, but not all that much. Similarly for the Forms themselves, which are realized in the sensible world only through the limited activity of the Demiurge and the world soul. Plato's accounts of sensible order remain consistent with a world like that portrayed in the *Phaedo*'s concluding myth of the True Earth, a world in which entities, like colors in this myth, run into and out of one another, never attaining any stable demarcations. It is a world in which nothing *is* and everything at most *becomes* (see *Phaedo* 108e-114d, *Timaeus* 49d-50b, *Theaetetus* 157a). Plato's empirical world is thus, to say the least, loosely organized and continually other than itself. Difference is given, and unity must be explained.

The non-ousiodic nature of Plato's account of physical objects continues into his accounts of cognition and ethics. It is only consistent with his view of the fuzziness of empirical reality, for example, that sensation for Plato is, as I mentioned, not the transgression of a boundary in which a form comes "into" the soul. According to the theory advanced in the *Theaetetus,* it is a mutual insemination by thing and (sense) organ (*Theaetetus* 156a seqq); this view is restated, without the sexual imagery, at *Timaeus* 45c and is expanded upon at *Timaeus* 67c seqq.

That Plato was not interested in establishing stably bounded entities in his moral philosophy is evident in his account of eros in the *Symposium,* in which (as Aristophanes has it) the lovers blend into a single larger organism. In the *Phaedrus,* the "true" human society is not the *polis,* which Socrates and Phaedrus leave in their quest for philosophy, but what I have elsewhere called the social environment of the loving couple, in which (because neither Socrates nor Phaedrus knows the Forms) both lovers are equal. Neither can function, then, as an Aristotelian master.

The political implications of this way of thinking are massive. No human is in possession of the human essence, which resides in the world of Forms; we are all radically defective. Hence, in Plato's loosely organized world, a woman may well be as intelligent as any man, and such a woman should be allowed to share in the government of the ideal state—two possibilities which Aristotle never even mentions (*Republic* V 454d seq., 466c seq.). In spite of the dictatorial features of Plato's ideal state, one of its basic premises is that no human has the right to dominate any other unless he or she can do so by reason, as do the Guardians in the *Republic.* In this, as we saw in chapter 2, Plato prefigures Aristotle, as well as much that is good in the West. But in the case of Plato the rational basis of the Guardians' rule is left in doubt. For they are said to use as their guide the knowledge of the Good itself—and the Good, of course, has no knowable nature. It is *epekeina tês ousîas,* beyond determinate being. It can no more be known than the sun can be gazed at (*Republic* VI 509a seqq). Plato's sensible universe is thus given an accounting which, except for being complemented by another, Formal world, is in its undeterminability and constant self-differentiation somewhat akin to contemporary postmodern views.

It is, of course, Plato's repeated encomia to that Formal world—his near constant evocations of its purity, its stability, its perfect intelligibility, and the like—which have obtained for him the dubious distinction of being the founder of metaphysics. But it must not be forgotten that for Plato the Forms are far away, in another world, and unavailable to us; we cannot know them in this life. Plato's accounts of such knowledge as we can have of them are notably problematic. In the *Symposium,* for example, it is suggested that we can know the Forms by a kind of intellectual vision (*Symposium* 211a-e). But if such is the case, why is Plato, throughout the dialogues, trying to *define* various Forms? Why does Aristotle count it as a criticism that Platonists have been unable to agree on the nature of specific forms (*Metaph.* I.9 933a3-7)? It is, in fact, not entirely sure whether Plato actually thought we can even know that the Forms exist.[10] What is clear is that they are displaced from our human world by an unfathomable gap that we cannot, in this life anyway, ever traverse. This distance, the "separation" of Forms and sensibles decried by Aristotle in *Metaphysics* I.9, is an ever-changing gap filled only by the meaningless word "participation."[11] Unmeasurable but active in the way it defines our human situation, the gap between Forms and sensibles is perhaps the first explicit *diakenon* in philosophy—and certainly the last until Heidegger.[12]

The Forms, foundations for all our knowledge, are thus unknowable by us. This enormously important fact about them is never mentioned by those who (mis)credit Plato with founding metaphysics. The major accounts of Plato by Derrida, Heidegger, Nietzsche, and Deleuze never discuss in any detail the immateriality of the Forms, their unavailability for us.[13] Occasionally, in fact, they deny it: "The true world," Nietzsche writes, "[is] reachable by the wise man, the pious and virtuous—he lives in it, *he is it*. . . . Transcription of the assertion, 'I, Plato, am the truth.'"[14] Derrida claims that for Plato, "in the anamnesic movement of truth, what is repeated must present itself as such, as what it is, in repetition. . . . The true is the presence of the *eidos* signified."[15] And Rorty says that "a Platonic Form is merely a property considered in isolation and considered as capable of sustaining causal relations"—just, Rorty adds, like a Lockean idea.[16]

Everything these writers say would hold if the Forms were, like the standard meter, somehow gathered in an earthly depository where we could go and look at them. In practice, they deny what Plato so laboriously sought to codify, the diakenic separation between Forms and sensibles. When this separation is ignored, the man they call Plato becomes—of course—Aristotle.[17]

As Plato's Seventh *Letter* warns us,[18] no doctrine should be attributed to Plato without utmost care. In particular, as I have argued here, it is not accurate to tax Plato with being the first metaphysician. It is only when the Formal world is relocated to the sensory realm—when Aristotle denies the separation between things and sensibles—that metaphysics begins to function in earnest as codifying the deep and inescapable (because "natural") structures of our lives. In valorizing the purity and stability of form, Plato undoubtedly prepared this move and hence belongs to the "prehistory" of ousia. But because he located this purity and stability in a realm unbridgeably distant from our own, Plato does not himself belong to this history. He is at most a John the Baptist preparing its way, or a Moses who led Westerners to the Kingdom of Metaphysics—but took good care to die before entering it himself.

THE MODERN EVICTION OF OUSIA (DESCARTES, HOBBES, LOCKE, HUME)

INTRODUCTION TO PART TWO

The development narrated in this section is complex.

On one side, modern thinkers mount a drumbeat of attacks on the idea that ousiai, as Aristotle conceived them, exist in nature.[1] Since they don't, what I call the "concept" of ousia ceases to do any descriptive or explanatory work, at least with regard to nature. The philosophers I discuss here—especially Descartes and Hobbes—replace it with the older concept of substance, the passive substrate. The hylomorphic Aristotelian cosmos becomes merely bodies in motion.

As I noted in chapter 3, this replacement of ousia by substance had been long prepared. The Stoics had already returned to the idea of the passive substrate in explaining the unity of material things. A further step was the thought of Thomas Aquinas, for whom matter was docilized by the divine will. Without the subversive, decomposing tendencies of Aristotelian matter, a physical thing for Aquinas no longer had to maintain its unity against its own material substrate, as it did for Aristotle. To be sure, Aquinas continued to maintain the existence of ousiodic or substantial form. But it is no longer *needed,* in Aquinas's philosophy, to describe or explain anything.

For one thing, there is no way to discriminate empirically those things which have ousiodic forms from those which do not. Since God has created everything, the designation of matter *should* apply to everything material. But for a concept to have either descriptive or explanatory value, it must divide the reference: there must be some things it does not describe or explain. When everything material comes to have ousiodic form, that notion no longer has serious work to do.

Moreover, the designation of matter by God himself can be viewed as producing a discrete body which only then received its substantial form. This view deprives ousiodic form of the main function which distinguished it from other properties of a thing: that it actively shapes the thing. It was not clearly formulated or accepted by Aquinas, I argued in chapter 3, because of his doctrine of the unicity of substantial form. It gains the day, however, in the Condemnation of 1277. Traces of it jostle with other views in Descartes's nobly incoherent account of the individuation of matter; and Hobbes puts an end to the confusion by simply presupposing that matter comes packaged in discrete "bodies," or individuated passive substrates.

But the replacement of the concept ousia with that of the passive substrate runs into mounting difficulties. Already for Descartes, the passive substrate cannot be experienced empirically. But it can be be clearly conceived, through its essential attribute (extension), to exist outside us. Descartes's attempts to explain how this clearly conceived extended thing is related to individual bodies in the empirical world, however, runs into a complex knot of problems explored in chapter 5. The knot is cut away by Hobbes, who salvages descriptive powers for the concept of substance by simply assuming that individual material substances contain attributes which we perceive. The question is reawakened by Locke, who attacks certain ambiguities in Hobbes's account, arriving at the view that we do not know substances, even indirectly through their attributes. Reduced to the famous "x I know not what," substance for Locke loses its descriptive efficacy for natural objects; but he retains it because of its explanatory value. Hume, finally, dispenses with substrates altogether, leaving philosophy with a "nature" that is both insubstantial and non-ousiodic.

The other main side of the story narrated here concerns what I call the *parameter* of ousia. In marked contrast to their rejection of the concept of natural ousia, modern philosophers, like earlier thinkers, retain ousia as a parameter structuring the human realm. This enterprise, however, is now much more problematic. For Aristotle, I have noted, ousia's parametric status as the norm for ethics and politics derived from its existence in nature. Everything natural exhibits the structures of ousiodic domination; human beings, households, and *poleis* are natural, so they exhibit these structures. The more they exhibit them, the more perfect they are. Similarly for Aquinas: the complete domination of matter over form, together with the loss of empirical purchase, means that everything—up to and including the universe as a whole—is an exhibition of ousiodic domination, now consolidated by the creator God.

With ousia evicted from nature, ousiodic domination in societies and communities becomes more difficult to justify. Modernity here presents a decisive break with previous philosophy. Its central, unspoken problem can be stated as follows: given that ousiodic structures of domination are not validated by nature itself, what entitles them to remain in normative force, ethically and politically?

Modern philosophers handle this issue in two basic ways, which differentiate what have traditionally been called "Rationalism" and "Empiricism." The Rationalists (chapter 5 discusses Descartes, leaving Spinoza and Leibniz to the subsequent appendix) react to the eviction of ousia from nature by *relocating* it to a supersensible or divine world. Though deprived of any descriptive role within nature, ousiodic structures apply to God himself and to his relation to the world. From this position, they can be appealed to by the Rationalists as basic moral norms structuring self and society. For the Empiricists (Hobbes, Locke, and Hume, to be discussed in subsequent chapters), the pathway through the divine realm is an impossible detour, and their rejection of the concept of ousia is complete. But this does not mean that they abandon ousia altogether. Instead, they simply *reinstate* it parametrically as an ethical and social paradigm, without arguing for this or, apparently, even noticing it.

The standard, epistemological way of contrasting the Rationalists and the Empiricists is thus misleadingly incomplete. It is not enough to say that the Rationalists thought we could have knowledge of a realm independent of our senses, while the Empiricists denied the possibility of such knowledge. Also crucial to the philosophical undertakings of each group was the *nature* of the supersensible objects of which knowledge was, respectively, asserted and denied. These objects, I argue in part 2, include various versions of Aristotelian ousia, exhibiting various versions of boundary, disposition, and initiative. Because the Rationalists retained such entities on a divine level even more authoritative than that of Aristotle's nature, they were able to produce theories of the human individual and society which cohered with their ontology and metaphysics. The Empiricist rejection of knowledge of such beings led to an incoherence within philosophy which Hume celebrates in his famous refusal to deduce "ought" from "is."[2]

As Kant recognized, the Empiricists were right on the epistemological issue: we do not in fact have knowledge of supersensible ousiai. In terms of the present narrative, they are more radical than the Rationalists, because they have rejected ousia not only as part of nature but also as applicable to the divine realm. But if the Empiricists are more radical than the Rationalists in their critique of the concept of ousia, they do not, I argue, apply their critique to the parameter of ousia, which remains in place in their theories of the human individual and society.

The Empiricists and the Rationalists, in spite of their differences, thus work within the same basic ontological framework. Its centerpiece is the modern "subject," an intellectual being which exhibits, as the ensuing pages show, the structures of domination proper to an Aristotelian ousia. Unlike their Aristotelian ancestors, modern subjects exist in a non-ousiodic nature, in a universe of mere "objects" or bodies. And this means that modernity, insofar as it can be defined through these thinkers, is a sort of halfway state in which ousia has been evicted from nature but continues to shape the human world. In this section's concluding chapter on modern engines of oppression, I suggest that the effects of this incomplete eviction can be seen in such projects as colonialism, American slavery, and modern marriage. It is Heidegger's fate not to "critique" these formations in any Kantian or dialectical sense but to "challenge" them by showing that their metaphysical underpinnings are unjustified.

THE CARTESIAN RELOCATION OF OUSIA

THE REPLACEMENT OF NATURAL OUSIA
WITH MATERIAL SUBSTANCE

Descartes, in his letter to Mersenne of January 28, 1641, says that his Meditations will "destroy the principles of Aristotle."[1] Such vehemence is unusual for Descartes, who is usually concerned not to provoke antagonism.[2] But the destruction of Aristotle is in fact a basic aim of his entire philosophy and in particular of his *Principles of Philosophy,* with the first part of which I am primarily concerned here.[3] In this work, ousia is absent from the empirical world. Its functions have been assumed by extended matter:

> if [philosophers] distinguish substance from extension and size, then either they mean nothing by the word substance, or they merely form in their soul a confused idea of immaterial substance, which they apply to material substance, and assign to extension the true idea of material substance, which they call an "accident," so improperly that it is easy to recognize that their words have nothing in common with their thoughts.[4]

Anything which is assigned to corporeal substance (*substantia*) over and above its extension is merely "a confused idea of immaterial substance." Such illegitimate assignation is not merely the work of philosophers:

> The earliest judgments which we made in our childhood, and the common [Scholastic] philosophy later, have accustomed us to attribute to the body many things which belong only to the soul, and to attribute to the soul many things which belong only to the body. So people commonly mingle the two ideas of body and soul when they construct the ideas of real qualities and substantial forms, which I think should be altogether rejected.[5]

The "substantial forms" Descartes attacks here are, he tells us in another letter, substances which (a) are joined to matter so as to make up a single, merely corporeal whole, and (b) themselves remain more "substantial" than the matter to which they are joined.[6] This characterization is true to one important trait of the traditional concept of ousia: the *pars pro toto* aspect that I noted in Aquinas and Aristotle. For in Descartes's view of substantial form, such a form is both part of a corporeal thing and what is truly substantial in it. Substantial forms, he goes on to maintain, are useless; they are incomprehensible ("occult") in themselves and so cannot be used to explain anything else.

With this, ousia can neither describe nor explain anything in our experiences of natural objects. It is quickly and definitively evicted from nature. But for the moment, it should be noted that while something very close to the traditional concept of ousia is being denied of natural objects, the denial does not extend to the immaterial or thinking substances from which the concept of substantial form is drawn. Those who are evicted from their domiciles must, of course, find shelter elsewhere.

Indistinguishable from its extension in three dimensions, material substance for Descartes is without other qualities; it is quantitatively determinate matter, not form. It is a necessary condition for other physical properties, which it underlies but does not actively help bring into being. Like substance in Aristotle's *Categories,* then, the Cartesian substrate is passive, a sort of spatial outline to be filled in by other properties. In virtue of its extension, however, it is not an entirely featureless, unknowable receptivity like Aquinas's prime matter. Because it is determinately bounded, it is more like his *materia signata.*

While it is difficult to find ousiodic forms within our experience, it is easy to find bodies. It would therefore seem that this replacement of ousia by substance gives empirical purchase to the notion of the ultimate substrate. In fact, however, Descartes has major problems in explaining how we can know corporeal substance, existing outside us; what individuates the bodies that we perceive; and how such bodies (which we experience) are related to such substances (which we know). These problems, I suggest, do not arise separately from one another but constitute a single philosophical knot. They begin with the view that because substance is an ultimate substrate, it is—like the ultimate substrates of earlier thinkers—unknowable.[7] For Aristotle and Aquinas, there was a distinction in an ousia between that in it which can be known (form, essence) and that which cannot (matter). For Descartes, that in a physical thing which cannot be known is precisely its substance—the ultimate substrate in which its attributes inhere and which gives it existence independently of us.[8]

That substances exist independently of us (and indeed, as will be seen, of all else) constitutes the *Principles of Philosophy*'s strictest definition of the term: substance is "whatever we can conceive to be something which has need only of itself in order to exist." In this sense, of course, only God is a substance; everything else needs his "concurrence" to exist. But some things need *only* his concurrence, i.e., have no need of other finite things to exist; and these, Descartes says, are also substances.[9] The ultimate substrate is unknowable, but not because it is featureless or because, as Aristotle would have it, it is other than the categories. It is unknowable because of its very independence of us:

> Substance cannot first be discovered merely from the fact that it is a thing that exists, for that fact alone is not observed by us. We may, however, easily discover it by means of any one of its attributes because it is a common notion that nothing is possessed of no attributes, properties, or qualities. For this reason, when we perceive any attribute, we therefore conclude that some existing thing or substance, to which it may be attributed, is necessarily present. (*PP* I.42)

All we can know of a thing, including its genus and species, are attributes which we take to inhere in it. Species and genera—traditional substantial forms in general—are, therefore, known, but as "ideas" in us, not as properties in the thing. We "attribute" them to substances outside us, but they could, in fact, be produced in us by quite other things—such as our own overworked imagination or an evil demon. As Descartes argues in *Principles* II.1—and as becomes crucial for him when he writes the *Meditations*—we cannot know for sure, without appeal to the veracity of God, whether that in which attributes inhere really is the individual object it appears to be.

But why is it that what is independent of us cannot be known by us? Certainly Aristotle never doubted that natural things were independent of us; but they could be known, as we saw, when their forms entered our souls. Descartes's association of independence and unknowability is, as Etienne Gilson points out, a result of his more basic position concerning matter and form. Form, as intelligible determinacy, is for Descartes entirely on the side of the intellect; it is the property of "ideas" which reside within the mind. As such, it cannot be located in matter. The form-in-matter, to say nothing of such form as exercising disposition and initiative over matter, is now inconceivable.[10] We see here an example of how Descartes at once rejects and depends upon the Aristotelian tradition: what is knowable in things must be their form, as for Aristotle; but form is now solely within the mind. But if all form is in the mind, then what is outside the mind must be featureless, a kind of undifferentiated substrate. This has predictable consequences for nature. As R. S. Woolhouse puts it,

> Secondary substances (such as the species man, horse, oak) fade away, and what were individual substances of those kinds become merely differently modified pieces of corporeal substance.[11]

This "fading away" is what I call a loss of empirical purchase; everything we experience, if anything, now seems to inhere in the undifferentiated substrate that is "corporeal substance" in general. It is not possible, as it was for Aristotle, to distinguish empirically substances (and their attributes) from nonsubstances (and theirs).

Given that substance has lost the kind of empirical purchase that ousia had for Aristotle, Descartes must show what sort of purchase it can have: how we can know the corporeal substrate(s). He takes two tacks. One is to argue that we can make such determination through the powers of our minds alone. Substance then has a sort of "conceptual" purchase. Descartes gives an account of how our minds can form an idea of material substance; because God is truthful, we know that such substance actually exists. The other kind of purchase is empirical; it tells us how the bodies we experience with our senses are individuals.[12]

The concept of substance gains its conceptual purchase through the notion of the attribute: while we cannot "discover" substances outside us, we can "perceive" their attributes within our minds. The relation between external substance and mental attribute, however, is unclear. Descartes begins to explicate it with the view that all attributes are not equal:

> Although any one attribute is sufficient to give us a knowledge of substance, there is always one principle property of substance which constitutes its nature or essence, and on which all the others depend. Thus extension in length, breadth, and depth constitutes the nature of corporeal substance; and thought constitutes the nature of thinking substance. (*PP* I.43)

For any substance existing unknowably outside us, then, there is one basic attribute which exists in us and which is the essence of that substance. But how can ideas in our minds be the essences of things which exist outside them? Our knowledge that such is the case is grounded from two sides, which together constitute what I call the "conceptual purchase" of Descartes's concept of substance. One side of this grounding is through the operations of our mind:

> Thus, for example, we cannot conceive figure but as an extended thing, nor movement but as in an extended space. . . . But, on the other hand, we can conceive extension without figure or action. . . . (*PP* I.43)

That the attribute of extension must be the essence of material things is thus shown by the fact that we cannot conceive of the two other main components of natural objects, figure and movement, without it; but we can easily conceive of it without them. True to Aristotle, as I noted in chapter 1, the "essence" of a thing is that which is basic and knowable in it. But in the present case this leads to problems. First, to know that the essence of things outside us must be extension is not to know that such things really exist; it is simply to know what their nature would have to be *if* they exist.

Descartes's answer to this problem can only be understood after we have seen him treat the second problem: that the above quotes maintain that the essence of any extended thing is not its own determinate shape or "figure" but simply extension in general. God's creative activity, in the "Synopsis" of the *Meditations,* extends only to the creation of material substance in general, to "body taken in the general sense" (*in genere sumptum*). Individual bodies are merely arrangements of this infinitely divisible, extended stuff. Even the logical operations of my mind cannot teach me that individual corporeal substances exist outside me with the specific sizes and shapes which I attribute to them. All they can teach me about material things is the existence outside me of extension in general, i.e., of "body taken in the general sense." And so, for Descartes, the entire physical universe proves to be a single giant material substance. As Woolhouse puts it, just as a galenic deposit contains not "leads" but "pieces of lead," so bodies are *sensu strictu* pieces of body.[13]

At least we can know that this single substance exists, because of the veracity of God. That solves the first problem I mentioned:

> if God immediately and of Himself presented to our mind the idea of this extended matter, or merely permitted it to be caused in us by some other object which possessed no extension, figure, or motion, there would be nothing to prevent Him from being regarded as a deceiver. (*PP* II.1)

In sum, the operations of our minds tell us that the most basic feature of body is extension in general, and the veracity of God tells us that such extended substance must exist. But the passage just quoted concerns individual things: "*this* extended matter." Must not each such thing have an independent substrate of its own?

This problem arises, of course, only because our mind contains not only the idea of extended matter in general but also separate ideas of individual parcels of extended matter. The veracity of God underwrites both:

> we can be certain that . . . each and every part [of such a substance], as delimited by us in our thought, is really distinct from the other parts of the same substance. (*PP* I. 60)

My mind can tell me, then, that individual bodies exist as "parts" (or, as Descartes calls them at *PP* I. 65 and elsewhere, "modes") of extended substance in general. We now seem to have a distinction between substance and its parts, and the concept of substance has a chance to do some real work: some things are substances, i.e., substrates independent of everything but God, and other things are parts of such substrates. But the chance slips away. For it is based on what I can distinctly conceive, and I can distinctly conceive not only individual bodies as separate parts of matter but parts of such bodies. I can conceive, for example, of the left half of the surface of my desk without thinking of the right half. Is the left half of my desk then a substance separate from the right half? God could have made the one half without the other, just as he could make a mountain without a valley. Each half of the desk depends only on him for its existence, and so by *Principles of Philosophy* I.51 is a substance. Descartes's answer, then, has to be yes; any extension which I can conceive separately on its own account is a substance in its own right. As his letter to Gibieuf makes clear, any part of a thing which can be conceived as distinct from other parts counts as an independent substance:

> For, from the sole fact that I consider the two halves of a part of matter, however small it may be, as two complete substances . . . I conclude with certainty that they are really divisible.[14]

The conceptual purchase of the concept of substance is now threatened from a second direction. On the one hand, my intellect tells me that things outside me are merely parts of extended substance in general, so that nature is actually a sort of single giant corporeal substance; and this knowledge of the outside world is underwritten by the divine veracity. But since God guarantees that whatever I can think clearly and distinctly actually exists, any "piece" of extension which I can conceive independently of other things is also a substance in its own right. And since matter for Descartes is infinitely divisible (*PP* II.34, 35), anything which I can conceive clearly will have parts which, my mind tells me, are conceivable distinctly from one another. So substance is not only coextensive with the entire universe, but also infinitely divisible: the smallest part of matter I can conceive is a substance in its own right. So are its parts—for even if I cannot conceive them myself, I know that they *can* be conceived separately from all else by God. Descartes's attempt to give the concept of substance conceptual purchase thus ends in aporia: my intellect tells me that substance is both infinitely small and as large as the universe.

What I actually experience, of course, is not substances of either sort but physical bodies. If Descartes can show that the bodies I experience as distinct are in fact distinct individuals outside me, he would make a start at salvaging empirical purchase for the concept of substance, for he could then identify such bodies as privileged cases of "independent" beings. This problem is no longer conceptual, but one of physics: Descartes needs to show how portions of extended matter in general, each of which has an infinite number of really distinct parts, can cohere enough to be experienced as individual bodies.

The individuation of body in *PP* seems to be accomplished in a way broadly similar to the way Aristotle gave empirical purchase to the concept of ousia:

> By *one body* or by a *part of matter* I understand all that which is transported together, though it may be composed of many parts which in themselves have other motions.[15]

As with Aristotle, unified motion (and rest)[16] is what individuates a parcel of matter into a body. Such unity does not require an ousiodic form as its principle, because a Cartesian body is not pulled apart by its own matter; its parts could, for example, cohere with each other rather than fly apart—a key point, of course, in gravitational theories. But Descartes does not get very far with this argument because just before the above quote he has defined the concepts of body and motion in reverse order. Motion is

> the transference of one part of matter or one body from the vicinity of those bodies that are in immediate contact with it, and which we regard as in repose, into the vicinity of others. (*PP* II. 25)

We now have, instead of an explanation, a circle: body is individuated because it is moved as a unit and motion is the transference of an individual body. In fact, Descartes's insistence that matter is merely extended renders him unable to give an account of what individuates a body. As Daniel Garber puts it,

> Since at any given time there are no intrinsic properties to differentiate one portion of the homogeneous whole ["matter in general"] from any other, there are no possible grounds for saying that *this* hunk of matter is now in one place with respect to that hunk and at a later time, *this same hunk* is in a different place.[17]

In order to allow for such reidentification, Descartes would have to posit in matter something over and above extension—at a minimum, duration. As it stands, individual corporeal bodies are not only not "designated" by God; they are not substrates of change, for in and of themselves they do not have duration. The concept of the individual body becomes very slippery indeed; any set of things which move together constitute a body, and, as Garber puts it,

> any arbitrary collection of particles can be constituted into a system, with its own center of gravity and its own common motion. As a consequence, every arbitrary collection of particles would seem to be a Cartesian body.[18]

There is then no clear way to distinguish a heap from a body; a pile of grain in a moving cart would be an individual body. The two sides of the conceptual knot I discussed above thus reemerge in Descartes's physics, as body is either an indistinguishable part of matter in general or a contingent congeries of particles.

Descartes's concept of material substance thus falls victim to a whole knot of problems. We cannot know merely from the operations of our mind what individual substances exist, because while extension in general is the essence of matter, any part of an extended substance can be conceived as a distinct substance in its own right. Material substance is agglomerated upward to the size of the entire universe and infinitely divided downward. Empirically, any chance connection of bodies can become a single larger body; natural bodies are indeterminately agglomerated upward. The boundaries of individual material things thus become inherently unstable. Though Descartes habitually speaks as if it were obvious that the universe contains individual bodies and substances, he cannot show how it comes about. Corporeal individuals cannot be stably distinguished from each other. Substance has neither empirical nor conceptual purchase.

GOD

What, then, is a Cartesian substance? I have noted that *PP*'s strictest definition of "substance" says that it is "whatever we can conceive to be something which has need only of itself in order to exist" (*PP* I.51). That is why whatever we can conceive of separately from anything else can count as a substance, even the tiniest conceivable part of a body. Two differences from Aquinas and Aristotle are immediately apparent. First, instead of talking about what "is said" of a thing or what "is predicated" of something else, Descartes is concerned with what is "conceived" regarding it and things in general. The proper activity of the mind has changed, for reasons I mention at the end of this chapter, from speech and dialogue into an internal mental process. Descartes makes this change in the service of rigor; he seeks to replace the relatively relaxed and flexible standards of speech and conversation with an emphasis on the (presumptive) rigor and clarity of ideas and conceptions.

It perhaps follows from this concern for exactitude that a substance is not, as an ousia was for Aristotle and Aquinas, merely more or less independent of other things. Rather a true Cartesian substance must be *wholly* independent of other substances, able to exist if the rest of the universe fell away. In this sense, there can exist, as Descartes immediately points out, only one substance, God. Problematic in the empirical realm, located behind it as an unknowable and unstable substrate, substance now reappears on the spiritual level, as God himself, the "infinite" substance.

With it reappears, unstated, a Cartesian version of ousia with its three characteristic traits. In the first place, God, wholly distinct from his creatures, has very definite boundaries indeed. We cannot know them or what resides within them. What we can know of God is his perfection, for that—

plus the knowledge that existence is a perfection—is what enables us to know that he necessarily exists as a "true and immutable nature."[19]

Thus unknowable, God has no knowable disposition over his own "contents." But he does retain a version of initiative which is so strong as almost to amount to dispositive power. For he both generates (creates) and orders the physical universe. Indeed, if the substrate of a corporeal thing, its extended body, does not have any internal disposing form, it is because of God. For all power belongs directly to him. A finite thing cannot even sustain itself in being from moment to moment; only God can conserve it for the space of even a second (*PP* I.21). Similarly, all motive power is, directly or ultimately, God's. As Descartes puts it in a letter to Henry More,

> The power of causing motion may be the power of God Himself conserving the same amount of translation in matter as He put in it in the first moment of creation; or it may be the power of a created substance, like our soul, or of any other thing to which He gave the power to move a body. . . . I did not want to discuss [this] in my writings. I was afraid of seeming inclined to favor the view of those who consider God as a world-soul united to matter.[20]

It is the first of these alternatives which is underwritten in the letter's next paragraph:

> I consider matter, left to itself, and not receiving any impulse from elsewhere, to be perfectly at rest. And it is pushed by God who conserves in it as much movement or transport as he put in it at the beginning. . . . [21]

God thus moves and orders the universe via the law of conservation of motion; he sees to it that the interactions of matter preserve the "amount of motion" he put into the universe when he created it.[22] While God is not a world-soul, then—he and the universe do not constitute a single composite entity—he comes, as Descartes recognizes here, close to looking like one. For his power over material objects and their interactions entails a sort of immanence of them in him: "It is certain that God's essence must be everywhere for His power to be able to manifest itself everywhere."[23] The way in which God creates and sustains the universe[24] is similar to the paradigm of dispositive power in Aristotle's biology—to the way in which a finite soul has disposition over its own body:

> I confess that the only idea I can find in my mind to represent the way in which God or an angel can move matter is the one which shows me the way in which I am conscious that I can move my own body by my own thought.[25]

This way of putting things, however, has difficulties. In the first place, it seems to be obtained improperly, for the proper order of knowledge is from God to finite things. As Descartes puts it in a letter to Clerselier,

> I say that the only notion I have of the infinite is in me before that of the finite because, by the mere fact that I conceive being or that which is, without thinking whether it is finite or infinite, what I conceive is infinite being; but in order to conceive a finite being, I have to take away something from this general notion of being.[26]

We should not analogize from ourselves to God, but in the reverse order. And indeed, we have already seen Descartes object to the procedure of conceiving material objects on analogy to immaterial substances; why should conceiving of an infinite substance on analogy to a finite one be any less objectionable?

The reason, as Garber points out, lies in the genesis of this view of God's relation to motion. The view that all natural motion is directly caused by God follows from Descartes's rejection of substantial forms conceived on the analogy of souls. Garber writes:

> Descartes rejects the tiny souls of the schools only to replace them with one great soul, God, an incorporeal substance who, to our limited understanding, manipulates the bodies of the inanimate world as we manipulate ours.[27]

The substantial forms of traditional philosophy were conceived on analogy to immaterial substances, and in thus conceiving them we attribute to material objects a sort of soul: the form in matter is an illegitimate generalization of the soul in the body.[28] The rejection of such substantial forms leads to the view that the universe is, as it were, a single giant body, which God moves as if it were his own. Descartes may be uncomfortable with this view,[29] but he is led toward it, first by his inability to account for the individuation of bodies and second by his inability to conceive any other way in which God could order the universe.

One difference between the way we move our bodies and the way God moves the universe, however, is treated by Descartes at length. We move our bodies in accordance with our purposes and intentions, and these vary from moment to moment. God, who is immutable, moves the universe in immutable ways: the laws of physical motion are all derived by Descartes from the immutability of God, who always conserves the same amount of motion in the universe.[30]

We are now in a position to understand the complex development which I call "eviction" and which, in different forms, is carried through by other modern philosophers. In Descartes, appearances to the contrary, it is anything but a simple rejection of ousia; Aristotelian essence, with its three traits of boundary, disposition, and initiative, is not simply dispensed with. Rather the many different natural ousiai to be found in the Aristotelian cosmos are replaced by one enormous spiritual ousia: God himself.

In the first step in this eviction, the material world is reconceived on an analogy to an underlying substrate, "body taken in the general sense." The fixed and inviolable boundaries proper to ousiai are not to be found within the corporeal universe; though infinite in extent, in a sense material nature is like a single body. It is as if the boundaries of corporeal ousiai had, rather like the boundaries of Aristides' Rome, been expanded to encompass the entire physical world, demarcating it from the world of immaterial substances.[31]

Descartes has not, therefore, abandoned form entirely. Matter is, in itself, wholly docile: it gains its being and motion directly from God. The "essence of God" is present in every part of the world, creating and ordering it through God's power. The power of God, as manifestation of his essence, operates like ousiodic disposition: it both generates and orders everything that happens within the boundaries of material world. In this it exercises the two sides of a virtually dispositive power which Descartes calls "very absolute and very free" (PP I. 38).

The extreme of such cosmic disposition would be the kind of occasionalism advocated by Malebranche and (as will be seen) Leibniz and flirted with by Locke,[32] in which no two things interact but all changes are produced directly by God; the fire does not make the water hot but provides the occasion for God to do so. If Descartes does not clearly embrace this kind of occasionalism, his view that God's immutable will orders all changes and that all power is ultimately his is a long way from a contemporary view like that of Niklas Luhmann, for whom a "system" is a bounded field whose different members transform each other.[33] For Descartes, all change and motion and all causal activity come from a single source outside the system of material beings: from God.

God, we saw, is not for Descartes a world-soul; he and the matter over which he exercises power do not constitute a single composite being. So it is, strictly, wrong to call his power dispositive. His absolute creative power, then, is to be regarded as his divine initiative. To put it slightly differently: the divine ousia, located on a radically different ontological level, manifests itself in our empirical world as initiative which has achieved the irresistible intensity of disposition.

As initiative—as God's capacity to affect what is radically other than he—the divine power will be troublesome, for finite souls must, in Descartes's view, remain able to act on their own. They must be able to cause changes in the bodies to which they are attached[34] (and attached in such a way as to constitute single composite beings). They do this, as the quote from the letter to More tells us, in virtue of the power God somehow loans to them. But this must not (and here is the problem) make God responsible for the sins and errors of his creatures (PP I.23, 29). Causal power, then, is the manifestation of divine reality in the natural universe; it is the remnant of *ousia abscondita*. And because ousia has been evicted from nature, power in general is also beginning to be detached from ousia; it is not the effect of essences we experience in the world, as active potency was for Aristotle, but the manifestation of one very special being, God himself.

Like power, truth is also conceived as an effect of the one infinite substance. God underwrites truth for us in two ways. First, he has set up the laws of nature so that each thing seeks simply to continue in its present state rather than to attain perfection or "actuality" (*PP* II. 43). The aim thus is stasis. There can be no revealing story about how a form gradually comes if not to dominance at least to manifestness in a thing. For what a thing is at any given time really depends not on what it was previously— even a moment before—but on the creative power of God. God's power, in other words, guarantees that things can be completely known without recourse to the retrospective and tentative reconstruction of narratives of development that we saw were part of Aristotelian *epagôgê*. The full perfection of knowledge is cognition of the *present* state of things. Truth not only is securely located within the domain of the present but is guaranteed adequate to knowledge.

Second, this all-sufficing truth as presence is underwritten by God in individual cases. To know a thing is, as we saw, to have an idea of its attribute "in us." And it was not certain that the ideas of things we have in us are really caused by things outside us which correspond to those ideas. Into this breach stepped God's veracity, which guarantees that the ideas in us—when clear and distinct—correspond to the things outside us of which they are ideas.[35] Just as one thing can affect another only through powers which are ultimately God's, so one being can know another only through the mediation of God's truthfulness. As in Aristotle, then, truth and power are effects of ousia—but of the single, unique, divine ousia rather than of individual ousiai among which we act and which we know. The relocation of ousia to the divine level distances it from "empirical" phenomena such as truth and power. From that distance, the divine ousia can be appealed to for explanations: it shows why things exist and how they can move, and underwrites our knowledge of them. When Hobbes refuses all such explanatory appeals, power becomes further detached from ousia.

ETHICS AND THE MIND

There is a second reappearance of ousia in Descartes. The human intellect is a substance, though in a "finite" sense radically different from God's infinite substantiality.[36] It too exhibits the ousiodic traits of boundary, disposition, and initiative.

As a finite substance, the mind is "independent" of other things in that it is epistemically primary; though it needs God to exist, it can be conceived without respect to him or to any other thing. From the

> mere fact that each of us . . . is capable, in thought, of excluding from

himself every other substance . . . it is certain that each of us . . . is really distinct from every other thinking substance.[37]

Indeed, as Descartes's concern with the divine veracity in the *Meditations* attests, the mind's boundaries are so secure that without the truthfulness of God it is impossible to see beyond them, either into the nature of external things or into other minds.

Descartes's solution to the problem of how we can know ourselves to be intellectual substances is thus similar to and on his own terms more successful than his explanation of how we can know corporeal substances outside us. The answer there—one of them, anyway—was that any thing which can be conceived to exist independently of other things actually does, and this answer ran into problems because of the infinite divisibility and what I called the "agglomerativity" of matter. The mind, however, is not infinitely divisible or agglomerable; the cogito provides it with an unassailable unity.

The very instability of the boundaries of material objects highlights the inviolability of the boundaries of the intellect. Descartes would have no problem explaining empirical knowledge if the mind's boundaries were any less secure than they are. He could view it, for example, as a temporary merging of subject and object, in which both share for a time the same trajectory.[38] That Descartes does not take any such tack is no testimony to the inviolability of the boundaries of material objects (a problem which I argued arose in Aristotle's account of cognition), for material objects do not for him have inviolable boundaries. It is strictly, then, because of the unbreachability of the mind.

In addition to boundaries, the mind also has a sort of active form.[39] We saw that form in general was for Descartes strictly on the side of the mind. But the mind also exhibits dispositive power over itself, and in two ways: it orders both its own faculties and its own ideas. I will momentarily postpone discussing the latter sort of power, for understanding it requires a brief discussion of Descartes's view of science, which is the means by which ideas are properly ordered.

The Cartesian mind has two fundamental faculties, understanding and willing. To arrive at judgments about reality, we need both (*PP* I.32, I.34). Understanding gives us content; it gives us clear and distinct ideas. But for a judgment, the mind must not only *have* such ideas. It must also *affirm* or *deny* them, which is an action of the will. That is because, on the one hand, the reality represented by any idea at all (except my idea of my own existence) can be doubted, and many of them should be. Conversely, any idea, however dubious, can in principle be affirmed as the idea of something that actually exists. Thus, while only some of our ideas are clear and distinct—and thus guaranteed true by the veracity of God—any idea at all can be assented to or denied. But we should assent only to ideas that are clear and distinct, for difficulties arise when we affirm or deny ideas whose relation to reality is not entirely certain. So our will—our faculty of assenting to or dissenting from ideas—must neither outstrip our understanding nor lag behind. If it outstrips, we fall into error. If it lags, it is because we have not taken the trouble to make our ideas clear and distinct. In short, we need the proper balance between the understanding and will if our mind is to function correctly in cognition, if it is to achieve its proper goal of knowing the world accurately. This balance, attained by an act of will, is "freedom" in the most basic sense.[40]

In order to be truly free, then, the will for Descartes needs to gain control over its own capacities and those of the understanding. It needs to make the ideas of the understanding clear and distinct, and it must then limit assent to only those ideas. Cognition is not simply a matter of happening to have a correct idea about reality but of the will's establishment of the right order of the faculties, of its instillation into them of the proper balance, or form, and in short of its disposition over (in the sense of ordering, though not of generating) the whole of the mind. Such disposition is a normative goal for the mind, and its achievement is the aim of philosophy.[41]

Philosophy thus has an *ethical* function for Descartes: it is to achieve the proper ordering by the mind of its own faculties. One who achieves the proper philosophical balance of the faculties will obtain all other virtues:

> For whoever forms a firm and constant resolve always to make use of reason to the best of his power, and in all his actions to do what he believes to be best, is truly wise . . . and by this alone he is just, courageous, moderate, and possesses all the other virtues.[42]

In philosophy the will does not generate its faculties; but it orders and arranges them, and in this exercises a degree of dispositive power over its own contents. The mind thus has unbreachable boundary and achieves a form of disposition. Its initiative—how the will can actually affect beings outside the mind—is (as it was for Aristotle) a problem. For the mind, as I have noted, is completely self-enclosed; like the thinking activity of the Prime Mover, it cannot even be known by other entities (at least not by other finite ones), but only from within. As to the mind's capacity to affect other beings in more substantive ways, Descartes has a famous problem: since mind is entirely self-enclosed, it has nothing in common with body and therefore cannot affect it. It cannot be understood how what happens in the mind can transgress the mind's boundaries and affect the world outside. Hence Descartes's desperate appeal to the pineal gland as the point of connection between mind and body.[43]

And hence also, perhaps, the third maxim of his "provisional morality":

> to try always to master myself rather than fortune, and to change my desires rather than the order of the world. . . . Nothing lies entirely within our power except our thoughts, so that after doing our best in dealing

with matters external to us, whatever we fail to achieve is absolutely impossible so far as we are concerned."[44]

The appeal to ousiodic structure is unmistakable: the ethical agent has boundaries, within which are thoughts and desires—the former controllable, the latter to some degree changeable. Outside is an uncontrollable world for which we cannot be held responsible. Initiative is thus problematic; ethics is properly concerned with the mind's disposition over its own contents.

Descartes thus has, appearances to the contrary, an ethics: his science, a "firm and permanent" foundation for knowledge, also has ethical import. It is what we may call an ethics of disposition, a study of how to instill the right order within the soul. What Descartes does not have, by contrast, is what may be called an ethics of initiative, an account of how the human being ought to affect things in the outside world. This point, of course, is the crux of ethics today, and the lack of it can make it seem that Descartes has no ethical theory whatever. But its omission is understandable, for we have now seen two problems with such initiative. One of them was the problem of showing how the human mind could affect even its proximate outside object, the human body; the other was showing how the mind could be morally responsible for its actions in the world, given that all motion derives ultimately from God.[45]

The concept of ousia, evicted from nature, is thus held (though not under that name) to apply to two other sorts of entity: God and the human mind. Once relocated to these supersensible realms, it has, as ousia had for Aristotle, parametric, normative functions: the good life consists in the mind's gaining disposition over its own faculties and ideas. The normative status of ousia for our minds, moreover, is gained through the attribution of ousiodic properties to God: our "freedom" in attaining the right order of our faculties is a finite version of his "very absolute and very free" power to order the entire universe. That can be seen in two ways, one general and one more specific.

In general, God is defined as the most perfect being (a definition from which his necessary existence follows; *PP* I.14). All perfections, including those of our souls, are pre-eminently in God:

> As we know that we are subject to many imperfections, and that we do not possess those extreme [divine] perfections of which we have the idea, we should conclude from this that they exist in some nature which is different from ours and in sum very perfect, that is to say which is God; or at least that they are previously in this thing. . . . (*PP* I.18; cf. I.17, 20)

Not only analogies, as I noted, but conception itself must proceed from God to creature; Descartes holds that anything finite can be conceived only on the basis of our knowledge of infinitude. Our minds can be understood, then, only in terms of their deviation from God's.[46] So also, it would follow, for their excellence: the purpose of our existence can only be to attain the greatest perfection possible for our nature, and this means to become more like God. We can do this because we, like everything else, are as God has created us. Our power to order our own minds is ultimately his, which he has "loaned" to us. If God's freedom in his relation to us exhibits the traits of boundary, disposition, and initiative, then we in turn can and should exhibit our versions of these traits in the domain proper to us, our own minds.

This general view that we ought to make our minds as like to God's as we can is carried through in Descartes's plan for science, in which the second sort of dispositive power he attributes to the mind becomes clear. In the Author's Letter prefixed to the French version of *PP*, Descartes locates his own originality in the recognition that the basic truths "are principles from which may be derived a knowledge of all things that are in the world."[47] But though he is the first to employ the principles in this way, he is not their discoverer; they "have been known from all time, and by all men."[48] They are not only certain but, like God himself, immutable, for they constitute the "firm and secure foundation" for all other knowledge. The need for such immutability for the principles of science is clearly expressed in the opening words of Meditation I:

> It is some years since I detected how many were the false beliefs I had from my earliest youth admitted as true, and how doubtful was everything I had constructed on this basis; and from that time I was convinced that I must once for all seriously undertake to rid myself of all the opinions which I had formerly accepted, and commence to build anew from the foundations, if I wanted to establish any firm and permanent structure in the sciences.[49]

Philosophical doubt is then preceded by the ordinary experience of having ordinary beliefs turn out to be false—of having our beliefs be mutable. As against this, the principles of philosophy must be immutable. And in this they are akin to the laws of motion, which as we saw are derived from the immutability of God. When we order our minds by philosophical principles, then, our disposition over our ideas comes to resemble that of God over material nature: both are ordered by immutable principles. The traits of boundary, disposition, and initiative, attributed tacitly to God, thus serve as standards for human perfection. Cartesian science inculcates such perfection by first securing the boundaries of the mind through doubt and then ordering what remains on immutable principles.

In sum, there are two ways in which the power of God manifests itself in the sensible universe. It manifests itself universally in motion in general, but it also has an occasional and limited sort of manifestation. For it is the power of God which allows and requires human beings to make themselves into ousiai, to operate with intellectual will power borrowed from God and give their minds a "firm and certain resolve" to exercise disposition over their own contents: their faculties and ideas.

POLITICS

Descartes does not invoke the normative status of ousia in political philosophy, for he has no political philosophy. Among the moderns, certainly, it is only Berkeley who so completely avoids writing on political subjects. But Descartes did write one text on politics, in response to Queen Elizabeth of Sweden, who had sent him Machiavelli's *Prince* and asked for his views on it. After a number of comments, some confused and others less so,[50] Descartes closes with what might be a statement of his reasons for avoiding political matters:

> the principle motives of the actions of princes are often circumstances so unique [*particulières*] that, if one is not oneself a prince, or has not been privy to their secrets for a very long time, one would not know how to imagine them.[51]

Political philosophy, then, has to do with the purposes of princes and would have to be teleological in its approach; and that makes it unfit for philosophy. For such purposes and the actions which (somehow) are produced by them do not come under general laws and are unknowable anyway. Descartes thus seems to abjure political philosophy altogether. But, like his general views on ousia, his refusal to discuss the minds of princes is less of a rejection of the project of political philosophy than it appears. It is, in fact, a restatement of one of the central views of Western political philosophy since Aristotle—the view that political rulership is akin to the divine rulership which God exercises over the world. For Descartes has, in the *Principles of Philosophy*, made exactly the same point about attributing final causes to nature:

> We will not pause here to examine the purposes which God had in creating the world, and we will exclude entirely from our philosophy inquiry into final causes: for we should not think so highly of ourselves as to believe that God has made us privy to his plans. . . . (*PP* I. 28)

The reduction of politics to the chance intentions of princes—wholly foreign to the steady pursuit of the good life that characterized the Aristotelian polis—reveals another trait of Descartes's treatment of ousia, one which extends to other modern philosophers: the absence of the "nesting" characteristic of the ancient and medieval worlds. For Aristotle and for Aristides and Aquinas,[52] among others, certain ousiai, if they were not discrete physical bodies but rather ousiodic unifications of such bodies, could contain other ousiai within them. Thus the human being, as an ousia, was nested within a household, which resided within a city, which in turn occupied a region either directly of the earth itself and thence of the cosmos or first of the empire and subsequently of the earth and cosmos.

For Descartes, such nesting has been eliminated by the power of God. Finite substances, we saw, are each of them dependent solely upon this single power—such independence is their defining quality. It follows that no two of them can be nested within each other or within anything exhibiting the traits of an ousia, because then each would have need of the larger "nest" to exist at all: a human would, as for Aristotle, be unable to exist outside the polis. Nesting remains problematic for other modern thinkers, with the result that ousia is wholly absent from nature and fully evident only on one level of the human world.

It is, in particular, the independence of the individual mind from anything but God which motivates the turn I have noted from the Aristotelian "said of" and the Thomistic "predicated of" to the Cartesian "we can conceive of." Language, so far from being the key to ontology, becomes for Descartes what I have elsewhere characterized as "a sort of subrepository into which drip cognitive evils, themselves several times distilled."[53] Cognition now requires an escape from language, which relates us to others in random and prejudicial ways.[54] The escape is made to ideas, which remain within the boundaries of the self and are given to it—as with angelic illumination for Aquinas, without passage through exteriority—by a veracious God. This escape to ideas, as Descartes's grounding of truth in the divine veracity shows, is an escape to a situation in which the individual mind is dependent for its knowledge strictly on God alone, and so is (in Descartes's sense) truly "substantial." This freedom from the conditioning factors of culture and history, so beguiling to philosophers even today, is possible for Descartes only because it is theologically sanctioned.

With Descartes, philosophy as I narrate it here arrives at the view of the human mind as an inviolably closed system. It is independent of any cosmic order, capable of knowing only its own contents, and governed by the immanent activity of its will. This is the "modern subject" which Heidegger and others excoriate. I hope to have shown that it is not the result of any Heideggerean "gift of Being" or unfathomable convolution of history but is simply an ousia existing in a material nature from which ousia has been evicted. Outside it is not a cosmos of other ousiai but merely matter in motion—matter which is, like the matter of Aquinas, docile and unresisting, because its existence and motion are due to the immutable will and the power of God. The combination of the eviction of ousia from nature and the absence of ousiodic nesting in the human world has manifold consequences. I mention here two very general ones, to be taken up in what follows.

First, since the nesting of one ousia in others has become problematic, ousiodic structure in its plenitude can be located on only one level of the human world. Two conflicting political discourses are thus prepared. One, like that of Hobbes, locates ousia on the level of the state and does not tolerate independent action by individuals and groups. The other, like that of Locke, locates it on the level of the individual and seeks to weaken the independent action of the state.

Both these discourses, for all their conflict, unite on one fatal point. Anything which is not a human ousia—a state or an individual—is mere matter, lacking both inviolable boundaries and a disposing form of its own. Whether the human ousia is the state or the individual, outside its domain there can only be matter awaiting the implantation of ousiodic form. In both discourses, then, the task of the political ousia is to grow horizontally, extending itself across the earth, rather than articulating itself internally. Ousia becomes absolute, and Nature—including not only "raw material" but, in practice, other lands and peoples—lies before modern man with her legs spread.

6

OUSIA AND SOVEREIGNTY IN HOBBES

If not proclaiming, like Descartes, intentions to "destroy" Aristotle, Hobbes is modern enough (in thought, if not orthography) to have a low opinion of the father of ousia:

> And I belieeve that scarce any thing can be more absurdly said in naturall Philosophy, than that which is now called *Aristotle's Meta-physiques;* nor more repugnant to Government, than much of what hee hath said in his *Politiques;* nor more ignorantly, than a great part of his *Ethiques.*[1]

Aristotle thus contributes nothing, it would appear, to Hobbes's philosophy: not to his physics, his ethics, or his politics. But the appearance is belied by the very subtitle to *Leviathan:* "the Matter, Forme, & Power of a Common-Wealth Ecclesiasticall and Civill." What does Hobbes mean by "matter," "form," and "power"? Answering this question means tracing Hobbes's social philosophy back to his physics (which, because of his materialism, is the focus of his "first philosophy").[2]

PHYSICS

Like Descartes, Hobbes has rejected the concept of ousia before his physics begins; the fundamental corporeal reality is substance, the passive and relatively indeterminate substrate. Substance for Hobbes is far from exhibiting the complex structure of domination that ousia had for Aristotle. It is, as for Descartes, simply extended matter, or body.

> The word "Body" in the most general acceptation, signifieth, that which filleth, or occupyeth some certain room, or imagined place, and dependeth not on the imagination, but is a reall part of what we call the Universe. For the Universe, being the Aggregate of all Bodies, there is no reall part thereof that is not also Body. . . . And according to this acceptation of the word, *Ousia* and *Body* signify the same thing. (*Lev*, p. 207)

Body occupies "a *certain* room"; it has determinate dimension. In addition to configuration, it exhibits as well the major defining characteristic of Cartesian substance, that it subsists of itself as a "reall part of . . . the universe." Independence and configuration are summed up in another way in which Hobbes defines body: "that, which having no dependence upon our thought, is coincident or coextended with some part of space."[3]

In the present perspective, it is his views on configuration which set Hobbes apart from Descartes and previous thinkers. For Descartes, to be extended was not to have a "figure" of one's own; how to individuate bodies was, we saw, a problem for him. Hobbes is so certain that matter is of itself not only extended but configured—that extension *is* configuration—that he assigns configuration to *materia prima* (thereby obliterating any distinction between prime and designated matter); "prime matter" is

> a mere name; yet a name which is not of vain use; for it signifies a conception of body without the consideration of any form or other accident except only magnitude or extension, and aptness to receive form and other accident. (*De Corp.* VIII.24, p. 68)

If extension is magnitude, it is always determinate or configured, especially if extension is defined as the extension of a body, i.e., of something itself which has already been defined as occupying "some certain room." In making extension thus basic to material beings, Hobbes shows that the concept of ousia has been evicted from nature; Aristotelian substantial forms are denied, and what remains is merely "body," i.e., an updated version of Aristotelian substance.

In this, Hobbes agrees with Descartes. But there are three important differences. First, the designated matter of Aquinas is not only made independent of essence (in line with the Condemnation of 1277 discussed in chapter 3) but is elevated to the status of an ontological absolute. Its "real existence" does not need to be explained, even by the creative power of God (which cannot explain anything anyway because, as will be seen, it is itself incomprehensible). Because matter, even prime matter, is nothing other than what is real and configured, docility is intrinsic to it in a new way; like configuration, it is not a property that has to be accounted for—not by Aristotelian ousiodic form, not by Thomistic designation, not by Cartesian creation, nor in any other way. It is simply presupposed as basic.

Second, as will be seen throughout this section, substance (and, with it, ousia) is not relocated by Hobbes to the divine realm. God, in Hobbes's view, is strictly "incomprehensible; and his greatnesse, and power are unconceivable."[4] While for Descartes we could know God's perfections, for Hobbes he is wholly unknowable—and so philosophically useless. As a concept, then, ousia fails completely; there is no thing, either in nature or in heaven, that can be known to be an *Aristotelian* ousia. Ousia is body, and God is incomprehensible.

The third salient difference between Descartes and Hobbes concerns the status of accidents. An "accident," like a Cartesian "attribute," is that through which a body is conceived. A Cartesian attribute, we saw, was located entirely within the knowing subject and required the veracity of God to give us knowledge of things outside ourselves. Hobbesian accidents, by contrast, have ambiguous ontological status. On the one hand, an accident is "the manner of our conception of body" (*De Corp.* VIII. 2, p. 54). This makes an accident something subjective, because our conceptions of bodies, for Hobbes, are conditioned by the "phantasm" of space; the place that a body occupies is actually a product of our imagination. Hence, Hobbes writes, body "is called the *subject*, because it is so placed in and *subjected* to imaginary space, that it may be understood by reason, as well as perceived by sense."[5] Similarly with all the accidents of things that we perceive as spatial: "magnitude, motions, sounds, colours . . . order and parts."[6]

So far, Hobbes remains broadly with Descartes: accidents belong to the subject, and the substances in which they inhere are, correspondingly, epistemically unavailable. On the other hand, immediately after the above definition and "all one" with it, we find that an accident is "that faculty of any body, by which it works in us a conception of itself."[7] According to this definition, an accident is not merely our manner of conceiving of a thing but the external cause of our conception. It seems clearly to lie in the thing itself, independently of our apprehension of it. Accidents are thus for Hobbes assigned both to things outside us, as their power to make us cognize them, and to the manner of our cognition.[8] That makes substance epistemically elusive. When I know a body, do I know something that is extended outside me? Or is extension, being defined in terms of space, merely part of my imaginative "manner" of cognizing the thing?

It is not so much that Hobbes is confused here—such a confusion would be gross indeed—as that he does not want to locate all accidents on one or the other side of the subject-object divide. As he puts it in *De Corpore* VII.3, for example,

> Whether these very accidents are not also certain motions either of the mind of the perceiver, or of the bodies themselves which are perceived; for the search of this, a great part of natural philosophy consists.[9]

That accidents as such have an unclear ontological status, then, does not mean that cases of specific accidents cannot be sorted out eventually. In the meantime, the fact that accidents can be on either side of the subject-object divide has the merit of obviating another of Descartes's important appeals to God. For Descartes, accidents were clearly in the mind, and God was needed to guarantee that the attributes we know correspond to things outside us. For Hobbes, accidents may be in the mind or in the things, and this indeterminacy keeps Descartes's general problem from arising. Hume, following Berkeley, later attacks this ambiguity in order to maintain, as Descartes would, that "the manner of our conception" of body does not in itself imply that the bodies thus conceived actually exist. Hobbes, for his part, seems to see no problem. He constructs his philosophy—and, as will be seen, his account of cognition itself—on the basis of the real existence, independently of ourselves, of extended substances or bodies.[10]

The problems Descartes ran into as to how corporeal substances and bodies are individuated and known thus do not arise for Hobbes. He cuts the Cartesian snarl I investigated in the preceding chapter by simply taking the individual body of our everyday experience to be ontologically basic. And two of Descartes's important explanatory appeals to God—as individuator (because creator) of bodies and as guarantor of truth—are circumvented.

Hobbes's main concern here is not to pinpoint the exact location and ontological status of accidents but rather to underline the point that accidents are not strictly speaking "in" their bodies at all, for a body can contain only other bodies. The relationship of accident to substance is not spatial but temporal. Accidents, to begin with, are dependent upon the bodies which underlie them: "An accident is in its subject, not as any part thereof, but so as that it may be away, the subject still remaining" (*De Corp.* VIII.3, p. 55). Because accidents depend on substance, it must be more permanent then they; accidents are "accidental" precisely in that they can come and go, while the bodies of which they are accidents endure.[11]

Those bodies, docile and configured, are more basic to Hobbes than any form. Consider humanity, which for Aristotle was a form of a very special kind—a substantial form, prior to the individual human body to such a degree that without it the body was not *a* body. For Hobbes, humanity is just another accident; a body can become or cease to be human just as it can gain or lose any other accident (*De Corp.* VIII.20, p. 66). The essence of a thing is just the accident from which we give a name to some body, i.e., it is the accident which "denominates" its subject: "the privileged status of the essence is with respect to us, not in the thing itself" (*De Corp.* VIII.23, p. 67). Thus for Hobbes, extension is not something in our minds which gives us privileged knowledge of what is outside them but merely a fact about bodies which we seize upon in thinking about them.

Not being "contained in" their bodies but causally dependent on them, accidents do not migrate (*migrare*) from one body to another:

> When the hand, being moved, moves the pen, motion does not go out of the hand into the pen; . . . but a new motion is generated in the pen, and is the pen's motion. (*De Corp.* VIII. 21, p. 67)

The docility of matter—its inert residence within determinate boundaries— is thus absolutized: nothing transgresses or opposes these boundaries.

Other terms from the metaphysical tradition are, as we would expect, redefined by Hobbes in terms of the basic status of body (*De Corp.* VIII. 23, p. 67). Thus essence, as we saw, is just the "denominating" accident. Form is the essence inasmuch as it is generated.[12] The subject, or substrate, is body in respect of any accident which it might receive; matter is body in respect of form. There are, finally two kinds of bodies, natural bodies and bodies made by the will and agreement of men: commonwealths.[13]

If essence is merely the set of properties which lead us to give a distinct name to a thing, it does not have the active shaping capacities of the Aristotelian form. What I call "disposition" is gone, for bodies are simply inert within their boundaries. Those boundaries, by contrast—and in contrast to Descartes—are unproblematically absolute. To lose them is to lose everything, and Hobbes in fact argues, in puzzling ways, that they cannot be lost: "that magnitude for which we give to anything the name of body is neither generated nor destroyed" (*De Corp.* VIII. 20, p. 66).

What Aristotle called "actualization," the immanent shaping of a thing by its substantial form, is thus absent from Hobbesian nature, and only motion remains:

> Universal things (accidents common to all bodies) . . . have all but one universal cause, which is motion . . . and motion cannot be understood to have any other cause besides motion. (*De Corp.* VI.5, p. 22)

It is in terms of motion and of the concept of causation which is defined in terms of it that Hobbes undertakes to account for what I call initiative.

Motion itself is variously defined as "the privation of one space, and the acquisition of another," "the leaving of one place and the acquiring of another, continually," and "a continual relinquishing of one place, and acquiring of another" (*De Corp.* VI.6 and 13, VIII.10; pp. 22f, 32, 59). In addition to being caused only by motion, motion produces only motion, and motion in general thus constitutes a closed domain of transformation; all mutation is motion, if not of the whole then of its parts (*De Corp.* VI.5, p. 22; *Lev.*, p. 3).

Causation is to be explained in terms of motion: "A body is said to work upon or *act*, that is to say, *do* something to another body, when it either generates or destroys some accident in it . . . " (*De Corp.* IX.1, p. 69f). Such generation or destruction cannot, as we saw, consist in the migration of a sensible quality or form from one body to another. It must be reducible to a motion or change in place. Causality is thus the "invasion" (*incursus*) of one body by another, i.e., the displacement of one body when another body intrudes into the place it occupies (*De Corp.* VI.6, VIII.19, IX.5; pp. 23, 65, 72). The body which suffers this displacement, i.e., the body "in" which a new accident is generated, is the "patient"; the body which attempts the invasion is the "agent." The cause itself is the aggregate of those accidents in *both* the agent and the patient which "concur to the producing of the effect." When all these accidents are brought together so that the cause is "complete," the effect is produced instantaneously and necessarily. Indeed, it cannot be conceived not to be produced; causal necessity is rational necessity (*De Corp.* VI.10, IX.1; pp. 28, 69f).

This view of causality enables Hobbes to eliminate two of Aristotle's four causes, the formal and final causes. The aggregate of relevant accidents in the causal agent is the "efficient" cause of the effect; the aggregate of such accidents in the patient is the "material" cause (*De Corp.* IX.4, p. 71). The formal cause of a thing is simply that thing itself, since the form, as we have seen, is nothing other than the (generated) accident by which we denominate that thing.[14] The final cause reduces to the efficient cause, for, as Hobbes argues in his account of deliberation in *Leviathan*, purpose is merely a type of efficient causality (*Lev.*, p. 28).

"Where there is no effect, there can be no cause": efficient and material causes—"causes" in general—exist only once the effect has actually been produced.[15] Before the effect has been produced, i.e., before agent and patient have actually been brought together, the aggregate of accidents which would suffice to produce an effect is the "power" to produce this effect. The distinction between cause and power is thus, like that between substance and accident, temporal: cause has to do with the past and power with the future (*De Corp.* VIII.24, p. 76). If causality is a category of memory (for the past exists in memory), power is a type of fiction. For the future exists only as a fiction of the mind, "applying the sequels of actions Past, to actions that are Present" (*Lev.*, p. 10). Power has the same bifurcation into active and passive that causality has. Those accidents in the agent which, *if* it is brought together with a patient, will produce an effect constitute the "active power" of producing this effect; the accidents in the patient are the "passive power" to produce the effect. The entirety of these accidents, in both the agent and the patient, is called the "plenary power" to produce the effect. The effect thus comes into being and the powers become causes the moment the power is plenary (*De Corp.* X.1-3, p. 76f).

This account of power obviates a third of Descartes's appeals to God; the power of natural bodies to move other natural bodies is not for Hobbes to be attributed, even indirectly, to God. For though God is the first cause (see n. 6), his power, we saw, is unknowable by us. Knowable power for Hobbes seems to reside in the individual things themselves, and in this respect he seems to return to a pre-Cartesian view of it as an effect of material beings—with the proviso, of course, that it is the effect of accidents of these beings rather than of their ousiodic essences. If power for Descartes was the relict of *ousia abscondita,* the manifestation of God in a world which is radically other than he, for Hobbes power is a manifestation of *substantia abscondita:* it is not substances which cause things but their accidents.

Knowledge, in turn, is an effect of power. It is strictly representational: every thought of man, taken singly, is "a *Representation,* or *Apparence,* of some quality or other accident, of a body without us" (*Lev.,* p. 13). But it proceeds not by similarity (as we saw to be the case with Aristotle) but by efficient causality. In Hobbes's account, pressure is communicated inward from our sensory organs to the brain or heart, where it excites a counter-pressure or "endeavour, of the heart, to deliver itself." This outward movement constitutes the "phantasm" of things existing outside our minds (*Lev.,* p. 13). What we know, then, is such phantasms; even the annihilation of the world would, in this respect at least, have no consequences for our knowledge (*De Corp.* VII., p. 43f).

Hence, as for Descartes, what we can know is not, strictly speaking, things outside us. We do not even, in contrast to Descartes, know our own ideas or phantasms. What we really know are the patterns of the interactions of things outside us, as conveyed to us through their phantasms.[16] Thus what we ultimately can know are causes and powers—the temporal regularities of motion. And we know them because what affects us in cognition are the causal powers of objects outside us: "the *effects* and the *appearances* of things to sense, are faculties or powers of bodies, which make us distinguish them from one another" (*De Corp.* I.4., p. 9). Hobbes is thus something of a precursor of Foucault: knowledge is of powers, is generated by power—and is also for the sake of power (*propter potentiam*).[17]

It follows that truth is also a matter of power, of the power of the object to be known. It is confined for Hobbes to propositions, which in his view consist of two names, which we today would call subject and predicate. In a proposition, both of these are asserted (or, in a negative proposition, denied) to name the same object. In the proposition "The grass is green," then, both "the grass" and "green" are names of one and the same body, which through its causal power generates these two representations in us.[18] Thus to be the possible object of a true proposition it is necessary and sufficient to have more than one name. Names themselves come from the will of human beings, for it is we who "denominate." But they are imposed in accordance with similarities and differences found in nature.[19] Thus to have more than one name is to be similar to or different from other things in more than one respect. That holds not merely for bodies but even for dream images, which, though they do not "exist," have names.[20] Truth is thus not the manifestation of ousiodic form in a knowing soul but the apprehension by the soul of a concatenation of accidents.

While Hobbes is in agreement with Descartes that the most basic aspect of the material world is not a thing exhibiting the structure of ousiodic domination but simply an extended body, we see that he recurrently avoids Descartes's philosophical appeals to God. God does not sustain objects in existence or give them determinate configurations. He is not directly responsible for the motion of bodies, and the causal power of one body over others is not directly his. He does not underwrite truth. The eviction of ousia from nature, in short, is not followed by any relocation of it to the divine realm. The questions which Descartes used such relocation to answer—why things continue in existence and affect one another, for one—are not asked by Hobbes. Also unasked are questions which Descartes does not answer, such as that of how bodies can be individuated. The result of all this is that the natural world is not conceived as any sort of single, giant ousia, generated and ordered through the disposition and/or initiative of a single (divine) source, but as a field of bodies in motion.

THE MIND AND ETHICS

But if Hobbes thus carries through the eviction of ousia more radically than Descartes—refusing to relocate it to the divine realm—ousia more than holds its own as a parameter for him. For, true to what I am suggesting is the general configuration of modernity, he makes ample use of it to structure his accounts of the human mind and of society.

For Descartes, the inviolable boundaries of the mind contrasted with the unstable boundaries of individual bodies. For Hobbes, who views configuration as basic to bodies in a way Descartes did not, the same result has the opposite ground: just because it *is* a body, the mind has determinate boundaries. Hence, as we have already seen, the knowing mind is for Hobbes securely bounded. It knows only the transformations of its own phantasms, which are (somehow) its own reactions to the actions of various outside efficient causes. The mind exhibits disposition as well, in the case of the order or "trayne" of thoughts. This disposition, however, can be of two types, and that results in two very different kinds of unity being attributed to the mind.

As with Descartes, the order of thoughts can be unregulated (Hobbes's examples are dreams or careless reveries) or regulated. Regulation is provided by "desire and designe":

> From Desire, ariseth the Thought of some means we have seen to produce the like of what we aime at; and from the thought of that, the thought of means to that means; and so continually, till we come to something beginning within our own power. And because the End, by the greatnesse of the impression, comes often to mind, in case our thoughts begin to wander, they are quickly again reduced into the way. . . . *Respice finem;* that is to say, in all your actions, look often upon what you would have, as the thing that directs all your thoughts in the way to attain it. (*Lev.,* p 9)

This regulated pattern of thought, which as far as it goes is a near paraphase of Aristotle's account of deliberation in *Nicomachean Ethics* II.2-4, is intended by Hobbes to apply far beyond the moral realm, even widely defined; it is the basis for science as well. For our knowledge, always conditional and never absolute, is simply this sort of means-end thinking:

> In summe, the Discourse of the Mind, when it is governed by designe, is nothing but a *seeking* . . . a hunting out of the causes, of some effect, present or past; or of the effects of some present or past cause. (*Lev.,* p8f)

Our thought is thus regulated by our aims and ends. The distinction between regulated and unregulated thought, which Hobbes shares with Descartes, is now formulated in terms that we saw Descartes carefully abjure: those of purpose, i.e., of final causality. *On one level,* the purposes for Hobbes are specific. That is in contrast to earlier thinkers. Cartesian science is too great an enterprise to be harnessed to any specific purpose; it provides, most basically, wisdom itself. Aristotelian deliberation, which Hobbes so carefully parodies, aims at the overall goal of happiness (*eudaimonia*). Hobbesian purposes, by contrast, come and go as accidents. They regulate our thought in that our intention—our image of the desired state of affairs— excludes wayward thoughts, thus determining the boundaries of the "trayne"; and it orders what remains into the succession of ends and means we have just seen described. The mind for Hobbes is thus shaped by two kinds of exclusion. Externally excluded are things outside us, for we know only the interactions of our own phantasms; internally excluded, like Cartesian prejudices, are wayward thoughts.

The mind thus has, in addition to its boundaries, the capacity to order itself into the disciplined investigation of how to go about getting what it desires. When the deliberative process issues in action, the mind exercises what I call initiative; it affects the outside world. In this, the mind functions as will. Hobbes views willing as a case of efficient, not final, causality. The desire for a future good is present as an accident in the mind, and in what Hobbes calls deliberation alternates with its alternatives until finally one wins out: "The last appetite or aversion, before acting or not, is WILL"[21] The will is thus desire regulating not merely the thoughts of the Hobbesian subject but its actions as well. Moral actions are to be conceived as cases of efficient causality; accidents within the agent cause it to "invade" the universe and change it so as to conform to its own intentions.

The mind's activities of regulating (disposing) its own thoughts and acting (initiating) externally are both grounded in desire; the active "form" of the mind is not, for Hobbes, reason but desire.[22] And true to his general account of form as generated accident, desire is for Hobbes nothing but a set of accidents within the mind:

> For there is no such *Finis ultimus* . . . as is spoken of in the books of the old Morall Philosophers. . . . Felicity is a continual progress of the desire, from one object to another; the attaining of the former, being still but the way to the latter. (*Lev.*, p. 47)

Thus life itself is "but motion," and its objects and activities vary over time:

> And because a man's body is in continuall mutation; it is impossible that all the same things should always cause in him the same Appetites and Aversions: much lesse can all men consent, in the Desire of almost any one and the same Object. (*Lev.*, pp. 24, 29)

There is, apparently, no desire that will remain with us for life. When the mind orders the train of its thoughts into the pursuit of its desires, it is not structured by a single disposing form, as it is when it orders itself into Cartesian cognition and science. It is rather a sort of field (Hume calls it a "theater") in which desires, themselves "accidents" of our bodies, come and go. The only overarching need that can be formulated for the body, i.e., for "the man," is the need, having achieved one object, to achieve others.

That leads, however, to a reinstatement of ousiodic structure within the mind. For the general means, the currency, to satisfy our various desires is what we saw Hobbes call power: the present ability to acquire future good. As a general means, power becomes an object of desire on its own account. Indeed, power is the most overarching and universal object of desire: "I put for a general inclination of all men, a perpetual and restlesse desire of Power after power, that ceaseth only in death."[23] The human mind is not, then, *merely* a field in which specific desires come and go. In addition to adventitious desires, the mind possesses one overriding desire: the desire for power, for the capacity to achieve the objects of its adventitious desires. As the universal goal, power has the same sort of capacity to structure our train of thought as the objects of adventitious desires have: it functions as an ordering or disposing form in the mind. For unlike other desires, it is not an accident which comes and goes but a general,[24] abiding dispositive form; whatever else I may pursue, I can ask myself whether my pursuit of it will enhance or diminish my power to obtain other objects.

While on one level the mind for Hobbes is a field in which various desires come and go, on a deeper level we see that it has a single, overarching desire that orders all its activities and is its basic goal: the desire for power. This desire then plays the role of dispositive form in the Hobbesian view of the mind. To put it another way: for Aristotle power was the manifestation of an ousia in its presence, its capacity to cause changes in other things. For Aquinas and Descartes, it was the manifestation of ousia in its absence; it was allocated, either directly or ultimately, to God. In all three cases, power was an effect of ousia, either *praesens* or *abscondita*. When, for Hobbes, ousia disappears from both God and nature, power is no longer the effect of anything and is thus absolutized—into the basic goal of ousia itself.[25]

This supplementation of desires for objects with the general desire for power, the conversion of the universal means to satisfying desires into a universal object of desire on its own account, is important here for two main reasons. First, objects—bodies—come in configured packets; when I desire a body, I desire a particular extended thing, and when I "achieve" it, my desire is assuaged—at least for a time. Power, as a general and undifferentiated goal, is not like that: the acquisition of some specific power is merely an instance of the acquisition of power as such, and hence my desire need not rest, even momentarily. Second, I cannot acquire all human power; some of it inevitably resides in other people. This means that there is always more power to be not only desired but also feared. Because of their power, which unfortunately is not mine, others threaten me. I need to increase my power in order to fend them off. Thus the Hobbesian individual "cannot assure the power and means to live well, which he hath present, without the acquisition of more" (*Lev.*, p. 47). Power is thus unlike other objects of desire: acquiring it not only does not permanently quench the desire, it immediately augments it. The Hobbesian subject thus finds itself needing to acquire all the power in the world—which is of course impossible.

Hobbes, in summary, has what amounts to a two-level theory of the mind. On one level, the Hobbesian desiring mind does not have a single formative center but a variety of them; its "substantial form" is actually a set of forms, i.e., of desires which do not reduce to one another and may even compete with one another. The unity given the mind through these desires is thus a series of accidental "sub-unities." To the extent that the self's cognitive and practical unity is a function of the succession within it of radically different objects of desire, the self is not a unified knowing or acting agent.

On the second level, unity is restored to the self by the fact that there is a universal means to satisfying particular desires. This means is power. Hence the subject seeks to acquire enough power to enable it to acquire the other objects it desires. But that brings the individual into conflict, real and potential, with others. For power always inheres in others as well as in me, so that I cannot obtain all of it. And since power is a universal means, others can use their power just as I can—to acquire goods, perhaps the same ones that I desire and even, perhaps, the very ones that I have already acquired. Thus, on this second level, the mind experiences an increasing need to acquire more and more power. Where the Aristotelian *phronimos* and the Cartesian subject could "coincide" with themselves so that their primary concern was to remain secure within their established boundaries, the Hobbesian subject is afflicted with a constant desire to invade others— and with the constant fear of being invaded by them.

POLITICAL PHILOSOPHY

Aristotelian ousia has thus not disappeared entirely from Hobbes's universe. Power, though not a *finis ultimis* in the sense that it can ever be sufficiently reached, is an overriding goal for Hobbesian man, one that shapes his life and actions. And at least one kind of body does come about via final causes: the body politic, the commonwealth (*Lev.*, p. 85). It is brought into being for a reason, and this reason is, in a word, *invasion*.

"Invasion" (*incursus*), we saw, was how *De Corpore* characterized causality; it is the displacement of a body or of its parts by another body, which thereby generates new accidents in the first body. People are bodies and are able to "invade" one another, to "dispossesse, and deprive [others], not only of the fruit of [their] labour, but also of [their] life, or liberty" (*Lev.*, p. 61f). Indeed, since the only way one body can affect another for Hobbes is via efficient causality, or invasion of some sort, it is hard for Hobbes to see how people could relate to each other in any other way than that. How people come to try to displace one another forcibly is relatively easy for him to explain, for it is in accord with his general model of causality. How people can love each other, nurture each other, and care for each other is for him a more difficult matter. Thus in chapter XIII of *Leviathan,* war is natural to man; peace is what, in the chapter's final paragraph, needs to be explained. The burden of proof for Hobbes lies not in showing that "natural man" is in a state of war with all other such men—a task which he speedily discharges—but how any other type of human relations could arise without contrivance.

Invasion, being just a form of causality, is recurrent in human affairs. Hobbes's solution to the problem of recurrent invasion, which as I noted arises through the *substantia abscondita* manifested in causal power, is nothing other than *ousia recrudescens:*

> The only way to erect such a Common Power, as may be able to defend
> them from the invasion of Forraigners, and the injuries of one another,
> and thereby to secure them in such sort, [that] they may nourish them-
> selves and live contentedly; is, to conferre all their power and strength
> upon one Man, or upon one Assembly of men, that may reduce all their
> Wills, by plurality of voices, unto one Will. . . . This is more than Con-
> sent, or Concord; it is a real Unitie of them all, in one and the same
> Person, made by Covenant. . . . By this Authoritie, given him by every
> particular man in the Common-Wealth, he hath the use of so much
> Power and Strength conferred in him, that by terror thereof, he is

> inabled to conforme the wills of them all, to Peace at home, and mutuall Ayd against their enemies abroad. *And in him consisteth the Essence of the Common-Wealth.* (*Lev.*, p. 87f; emphasis added)

A commonwealth, we see, must have determinate boundaries, to distinguish its inhabitants from "forraigners." Within these boundaries a single authority, the sovereign, exercises a power so absolute as to be able to "conform" the wills of everyone else to peace (i.e., the sovereign exercises disposition over his subjects) and mutual aid in war (the sovereign exercises initiative). Hobbes does not shrink from referring to the sovereign, here, as the "essence" of the commonwealth, in a sense radically other—and radically older—than that of "denominating form" which he himself had defined in *De Corpore*.

The weak sort of unity Hobbes attributes, on one level, to the individual—a set of temporary unities achieved by and for specific aims and intentions—is expressly denied to the commonwealth. For, he argues, once any such provisional purpose is achieved, the people will fall back to their natural state of war unless there is sovereign power to hold them in check (*Lev.*, p. 86). The unity of the commonwealth, unlike that of the individual subject, must be permanent—and so must the power of the sovereign.

With this, the parameter of ousia is fully reinstated: the commonwealth has boundaries, as well as a dispositive and initiating power. The discussion of sovereign power in chapter XVIII of *Leviathan*, in fact, is largely an expansion upon these ousiodic structures, in a total of twelve points. According to the first two of them, the people cannot overthrow their sovereign and get a new one; nor can he relinquish his position and allow them to do that, because he *is* their unity, and without him they are not "a people" but merely a "multitude."[26] Sovereign power can end only when the sovereign no longer has the power to fulfill his part of the covenant, and that is phrased in terms of an analogy to the ousiodic structure of the human individual:

> The Obligation of Subjects to the Sovereign, is understood to last as long, and no longer, than the power lasteth, by which he is able to protect them. . . . *The Soveraignty is the Soule of the Common-Wealth;* which once departed from the body, the members do no more receive their motion from it. (*Lev.*, p. 114; emphasis added)

Boundary, already implicit in the fear and identifiability of foreigners, is further determined and consolidated (in point 3) by what I call an immanent exclusion (see chapter 1). For anyone who protests against an act of the sovereign excludes himself from the commonwealth:

> he must either submit to their decrees, or be left in the condition of warre he was in before; wherein he might without injustice be destroyed by any man whatsoever. (*Lev.*, p 90)

The sovereign's dispositive power is great indeed. Though power is given him for the sake of preserving the peace and has to be exercised to that end, he has the right to decide what conduces to peace and war and (in a leap of generalization) what can be taught (point 6). He sets up the regulations which govern the apportionment of property (7),[27] of office (10), of rewards and punishments (11), and of honors (12). His dispositive power over his subjects is so extensive that he cannot injure them, or vice versa; there are no standards for the right exercise of his power other than those he himself sets (points 4, 5). He determines the lawfulness of smaller groups which may form within the society, which Hobbes calls "systems subject" (*Lev.*, pp. 115-123). Finally, the sovereign alone exercises initiative, in the form of the right to make war on outside forces (point 9). Sovereignty, in short, is "power unlimited" (*Lev.*, p. 115), and the relation of subjects to sovereign has a familiar air of ancient domesticity:

> As in the presence of the Master, the Servants are equall, and without any honor at all; So are the Subjects, in the presence of the Soveraign. And though they shine, some more, some lesse, when they are out of his sight; yet in his presence, they shine no more than the Starres in presence of the Sun. (*Lev.*, p. 93)

When we confine our gaze to Aristotle's and Hobbes's strictly political doctrines, the polis and the commonwealth look very different. Curtis Johnson has summed their differences up as follows: For Aristotle, the state exists by nature, and man is by nature political; the aim of the state is the good life. For Hobbes, man is by nature inimical to man; the state exists by convention, and its aim is security.[28] But when we look to the metaphysical bones which underlie these very different bodies politic, we find them both to be versions of ousiodic structure, exhibiting the three traits of boundary, disposition, and initiative. To answer, finally, the questions with which I began this chapter: the form of the Hobbesian commonwealth is the sovereign, exercising both dispositive and initiatory power. Its inhabitants are the matter.

Though Hobbes's political structure thus has the classical features of an Aristotelian ousia, the justification for them is different indeed. It is not for Hobbes, as for Aristotle, written in all of nature that for any community there must be a single *archê*. Nor does he attempt, as did Descartes, to argue that substantial structures have normative force in society because of their preeminent existence in the divine realm. Ousia has neither natural nor supernatural warrant—and seems, in fact, to break out here with no warrant at all.

The sudden outbreak of absolutism in Hobbes's political thought—what Baumgold calls the "Hobbesian paradox"—is the main problem which has exercised students of it from Hobbes's day to ours.[29] Scholarly attempts to state or reconstruct valid philosophical arguments for it have left it unpersuasive.[30] A variety of other warrants—usually in terms of the tumult of Hobbes's times—have been suggested.[31] The literature on these issues is vast, and the problem comprises numerous separate issues. I will briefly discuss two.

The first is that of why Hobbes takes such a dim view of human nature. It may be that if humans are as aggressively egoistic as Hobbes presents them, an absolute sovereign is the only thing that can keep them away from one another's throats. But why should we accept Hobbes's account of human nature as an egoistic quest for power? Why does he ignore the massive sociability of human beings, their delight in their families and friends, their willingness to help each other in time of need? Why does he attribute to his own species a selfishness so sordid and irremediable that only a totalitarian regime can save it?

Philosophical justifications being hard to find, other explanations multiply. It may be, as David Gauthier has written, that Hobbes's account of sovereignty is a thought experiment, an "attempt to construct a political order on the least favorable assumptions."[32] It may be, as I noted, that Hobbes's view of human nature results from his observation of the strife and tumult in the England of his times, in which society seemed indeed to be a sort of war of "each against all." It may be that his views are religious in inspiration, amounting to a reworking of the Biblical story of the fall of man.[33] It may be that his materialistic biology leads to it.[34] Or it may be, as I suggested earlier, that he is operating in terms of his physics, so that the pursuit of power occupies a place in explaining human behavior similar to that of inertia in explaining the behavior of natural objects, leading in both cases to "invasions." None of these explanations, however, counterweights the obvious facts of human sociability.

The second issue follows on this one: even if we grant such a dim view of human nature, is Hobbes's totalitarianism justified?[35] If so, the need for the commonwealth is actually a pragmatic one: only by subjecting themselves to such a single authority can humans lead decent lives. But why people wishing to lead decent lives would subject themselves to "power unlimited" is not immediately clear—especially if the selfish nature that has already been attributed to them has any effect on what they consider "decent."[36] Why should people give *all* their power to the sovereign? Why not just give him enough to defend the country and keep the peace? Why not institute some checks and balances? As Locke puts it, does Hobbes "think that men are so foolish that they take care to avoid what mischief may be done to them by *Pole-Cats*, or *Foxes*, but are content, nay think it safety, to be eaten by *Lions*?"[37]

Attempts either to read Hobbes as more charitable and liberal than he seems to be or to rescue what are considered to be his valid insights from the disfigurement of absolute sovereignty are many and ingenious.[38] The explanations, justifications, and modifications advanced in this enterprise have varying degrees of validity. The religious explanation of Hobbes's views on human nature, for example, is supported by the many scriptural quotes which he adduces in presenting them; but it is weakened by the fact that Hobbes is unafraid, throughout his philosophy, to operate with conceptions and ideas that are at odds with established religion; he is, after all, a materialist. In general, the very existence of this scholarly industry shows that the sordid selfishness of human nature, as sell as the totalitarian structures of the commonwealth, is not adequately legitimated by Hobbes himself.

I do not wish here to sort out the many explanations and arguments but to supplement them by pointing out that the dim view of human nature and the totalitarian character of sovereign power break out in Hobbes's political theory just as suddenly and surprisingly as what I called the discourse of domination does in Aristotle's biology. The outbreak is, I suggest, the same: the parametric functioning of ousia to structure discourse about the human world.

Thus Hobbes's *explicit* arguments for the irremediable selfishness of the individual are quite loose and empirical; he merely notes that men are in constant competition for honor, like to compare themselves with other men and hence seek preeminence over them, continually criticize each other, and so on.[39] That Hobbes argues for his view of human nature only loosely and empirically accords with that part of his view of the mind which says it is a field of accidental desires; for if the individual self is unified merely by a succession of adventitious objects of desire, there is no way such a self "has" to behave and we cannot generalize about people except empirically. But empirical generalization cannot rule it out that humans— even the general run of humans—may at times be very different from that. Indeed, if "a man's body is in continuall mutation" and his desires as well, then there is no way to proclaim all humans to be either irremediably selfish or intrinsically altruistic; which character they assume at any given time is an accident.

As my earlier presentation suggested, it is on the second, deeper level of Hobbes's view of the mind—when he instates power as the universal object of desire—that his pessimistic view of human nature begins to show through, for only then does "invasion" (*incursus*), the general nature of causality, become the constant motif of human interaction. The introduction of ousiodic structure to the mind thus provides a bridge between Hobbes's physics and his social philosophy;[40] his view of human nature becomes unempirically dim just when the desire for power becomes a universal determinant of human action, exercising as a single, dispositive form the regulative functions that Hobbes elsewhere allocates to adventitious goals. Hobbes attributes ousiodic structure to the human mind in such a way, moreover, that no human mind can fully realize it. For no such mind can attain its telos, which is the possession of all power. This inability amounts, more generally, to an inability to realize the structures of ousia

143

in their plenary form; the mind for Hobbes cannot achieve what Aristotle would call "actuality." From then on, conflict is not a contingent failure of harmony but the fundamental character of human relations.

Similarly, the totalitarian character of sovereign power is, as I have shown, a detailed invocation of the traditional structure of ousiodic domination, modified by modern problems with nesting. The problematic nature of nesting for Hobbes means that when the state is conceived as the plenary realization of ousia in the human world, ousiodic structure can be present on other levels only in weakened or deficient form. The irremediable inadequacy of the individual mind's ousiodic structure, its inability to capture all power, requires that it be replaced as the director of its own actions by the power of the sovereign—itself conceived as an ousiodic form operating in all possible plenitude.

Understood in terms of the parameter of ousia, Hobbes's dim view of human nature and the totalitarian character of his state have philosophical explanations, though not philosophical justifications. Into the gaps between empirical generalization and the attribution to the mind of irremediable selfishness and those between the need for social regulation and totalitarian control come the ancient structures of ousia, functioning unrecognized to structure Hobbes's account of the human world.

In sum, the concept of ousia has neither descriptive nor explanatory value for Hobbes. The structures of ousiodic domination have been evicted not merely from nature but from the divine realm as well. Such phenomena as motion, truth, and power do not manifest the action of even a divinely relocated ousia; Hobbes is able to give thoroughly non-ousiodic accounts of the material world which avoid the appeals to an ousiodic God that I have noted in Descartes. But his refusal to employ ousia as a *concept* does not mean that he abandons it as a *parameter*. Rather it means that when ousiodic structures break forth in the individual human mind and the state, they do so without argument or justification. They are simply reinstated, perhaps because on some level Hobbes sees no alternative to them. The unargued and unnoticed nature of Hobbes's reinstatement of ousia helps render it absolute, for the ousiodic structures of the state, legitimated by nothing further, can only legitimate themselves. As self-legitimating political structures, they provide not only political norms but also final norms; there is nothing to moderate them. Hence the unrestrained, even pristine character of the sovereign's disposition over his subjects. We see such unnoticed radicality also, in different ways and on different levels of the human world, in the cases of Locke and Hume.

7

OUSIA AND PROPERTY RIGHTS IN LOCKE

John Locke seeks employment, in his famous phrase, "as an under-la-borer in clearing the ground a little, and removing some of the rubbish which lies in the way to knowledge." The "rubbish" he has in mind is Scholastic Aristotelianism, including most particularly its doctrine of substantial form:

> Those . . . who have been taught that the several species of substances had their distinct internal *substantial forms,* and that it was those *forms* which made the distinction of substances into their true species and genera, were led yet farther out of the way by having their minds set upon fruitless inquiries after "substantial forms"; wholly unintelligible and whereof we have scarce so much as any obscure or confusd conception in general.[1]

In Locke (and Hume), the concept of ousia thus remains evicted from nature, while that of substance continues increasingly to lose empirical purchase. For Locke, substances are completely unknowable but remain indispensable presuppositions of our knowledge, while for Hume they can be dispensed with altogether. But throughout this critique of substance, the parameter of ousia remains in effect in the human world. It plays the key role in structuring the way Locke and Hume think about how human individuals should be and the associations they should form. In this unargued use of ousia to structure the human world, Locke and Hume follow Hobbes. In contrast to him, however, they locate ousiodic structure predominantly on the level of the individual human being. True to the modern suspicions of nesting, communities and states exhibit such structure only in attenuated and derivative form.

The kinds of ousiodic individual with which Locke and Hume are concerned, however, are quite different. The Lockean individual has the structures of ousia in and through his ownership of property, and higher levels of community are justified primarily in terms of their ability to protect property rights. The Humean individual possesses the structures of ousia immanently to the mind, as was the case with Descartes. In contrast to Hobbes and Locke, neither state sovereignty nor individual property is ultimate for Hume: both must be justified in terms of the immanent ordering principles of the mind, those of the "association of ideas."

SUBSTANCE

For Hobbes, substance was body and was cognitively elusive; bodies (by definition) were extended, and the space in which they extended was our phantasm. Yet somehow we knew that extended bodies subsisted independently of us—independently, then, of the very phantasm in terms of which they were supposed to be defined. Attributes, the vehicles of such knowledge, were for their part ambiguously located: they were variously ideas in our mind and the capacities of things outside us to cause these ideas. Both attributes and space itself, in other words, were without clear ontological locus in Hobbes. He was unable to say, or to say clearly and consistently, whether they belong to objects or subjects.

For Locke, extension is not uniquely basic to body; "body" comports, in addition to extension, solidity and the power of communicating motion by impulse (*Essay* II.xiii.11-17). A body is thus composed of solid and powerful parts. Their unification into a single extension is not basic, as it was for Hobbes, but requires explanation, as it did for Descartes. None, Locke thinks, is possible: "a solid extended substance is as hard to be conceived as a thinking, immaterial one" (*Essay* II.xxiii.27). Body as extended, which for Hobbes was an *explanans,* is thus for Locke an *explanandum* that cannot itself be understood, much less explained. And yet we do have concepts of extended substance, and with them the concept of body:

> Sensation convinces us that there are solid extended substances; and reflection, that there are thinking ones: experience assures us of the existence of such beings, and that the one hath a power to move body by impulse, the other by thought; this we cannot doubt of. Experience, I say, furnishes us with the clear ideas of both the one and the other. But beyond

these ideas, as received from their proper sources, our faculties will not reach. If we could inquire further into their nature, causes, and manner, we perceive not the nature of extension clearer than we do of thinking. . . . From whence it seems probable to me, that *the simple ideas we receive from sensation and reflection are the boundaries of our thoughts;* beyond which the mind, whatever efforts it would make, is not able to advance one jot; nor can it make any discoveries, when it would pry into the nature and hidden causes of those ideas. (*Essay* II.xxiii.29; emphasis added)

Extension, along with solidity, is no longer (problematically) assigned both to objects and the subject but is located on the subjective side as a "clear idea." Though the causes of such ideas are substances outside us—in the case of sensation, atoms[2]—we do not know what such substances are like or how they are possible. Substance is now even more elusive—or perhaps we should say it is more *clearly* elusive—than it was for Hobbes.

Hobbes, I noted in the preceding chapter, simply takes the existence of bodies as basic. Locke takes over a version of atomic theory from Boyle, and attempts to vindicate it philosophically; it is a theory to which he is committed rather than a primary *explanans*.[3] Hence his views on substance—particularly the negative ones—are independent of corpuscularian theory; we do not know how substance exists and operates. But we do know where the ideas of substances can be found: in our faculties of sensation and reflection, which are their "proper source." Where for Hobbes accidents are both ideas in us and the external causes of these ideas, substances for Locke are causes but not objects of our cognition. In this Locke carries the Empiricist critique of substance a decisive step beyond the unclarities with which Hobbes had left it.[4]

Substances are, then, unknowable in themselves. Any features we can attribute to an individual substance—those in its definition, for example—must be derived from our experience. For Locke, the idea of a particular substance[5] is definable because it is complex; it "contains" a number of simpler ideas, which are conjoined in the definition of that substance. These simpler ideas themselves, if our definition of a particular substance is to be a good one, will be given in experience. The warrant for conjoining them in a definition is that they are ideas which are experienced as occurring and recurring in concatenation. Such concatenation requires an explanation; and we are prone to explain it by assuming a substratum, outside ourselves, in which those ideas inhere together (*Essay* II.xxiii.1f, III.vi.29).

Considered generally, this substratum is "substance" in the singular, or "pure substance in general." Locke has no use for it, subjecting it (at *Essay* II.xiii.19) to what Berkeley calls "banter."[6] Considered as the individual substrate in which a concatenation of ideas is said to inhere, substance is (in Locke's opinion) an indispensable but unscientific adumbration of a thing's atomic structure.

The members of such concatenations of sensory ideas vary—not merely with the substance in question, but according to the nature of our experience, our care and industry in seeing just what ideas are recurring when and where, and so on. Hence the definition of a substance does not give its real essence—what characteristics really constitute its nature—but only what appears to someone to be such (*Essay* II.xxiii.1f, II.vi.9, II.vi.21). What we know for Locke is our own ideas, which we take to be the appearances of something else—substance—behind them. Substance is thus presupposed by but not found in experience: it has explanatory but not descriptive purchase: "of substance, we have no *Idea* of what it is, but only a confused obscure one of what it does" (*Essay* II.xiii.19). As the substrates of concatenated ideas, substances explain their concatenation. But substance is not itself one of these ideas or even the set of them together. It is a featureless "x I know not what," from which observed sets of attributes are held to be derived.[7]

Though unknowable, substances are not for Locke passive. That is because, to begin with, appearances appear to affect one another: fire burns, a magnet draws iron. That leads us to form ideas of the *capacities* of some substances to affect others. That turns out to be only a complicated version of the more basic procedure by which we form our ideas of the capacities of substances to affect us, which in turn is the way we form our ideas of substances themselves. For example, we see fire burn things, and in this way we can form a complex idea of its power to burn. But fire can burn us as well; whatever it is that resides outside us, in the substance itself, must be a capacity—or, as Locke calls it, a "power"—to burn: "we immediately by our sense perceive in fire its heat and colour; which are, if rightly considered, nothing but power in it to produce those ideas in *us*. . . . " (*Essay* II.vi.7). The ideas that are concatenated in our experience and lead us to view them as inhering in a substance are thus viewed as the effects of "powers" which are outside us and are held to reside in this substance, which is the "unknown cause of their union" (*Essay* II. xxiii. 6). Substance, for its part, is not merely an inert substrate in which various qualities inhere; it causes the union of various powers, which we then perceive as a set of concatenated ideas. Hence the most that can be attributed to a substance is the power to produce a particular set of ideas in us.

Power thus originates in something unknown;[8] it is the effect not of an ousia which is present to what it affects (us) but of a substance which is absent from it. Truth, too, is dissociated from substance. Instead of being explained by a causal process (as in Aristotle, Aquinas, and Hobbes) or by God himself (as in Descartes), it is simply given; it is the "joining or separating of signs in conformity with things signified."[9] How this comes about, other than through the mind's own powers to join and separate ideas, is not a topic for discussion; there is no talk, for example, of substantial forms migrating from known objects to knowers. This dissociation of truth and power from substance is clearer in Hume, and I defer discussion of it until the next chapter.

Locke's account of our idea of substance is clearer than Hobbes's, which not only contained ambiguities but depended crucially on them. It also avoids Descartes's appeals to the creative power of God.[10] But it is problematic nonetheless, for it means that in addition to the concatenated ideas which are the objects of our knowledge there is one more idea, and an inherently obscure one at that: the idea of their substrate. Ontologically, all the concept of substance does is provide an explanation for the observed fact that certain ideas are always found together with certain others. But is it the only possible explanation? Why cannot such concatenation be explained by appeal to God himself (as Berkeley does do) or taken for a brute datum (as Hume does do)?

Locke wavers on this issue. At one point, he characterizes the attribution of an explanatory substrate to be a matter of "custom" and "supposition," which suggests that the idea of substance could be entirely dispensed with — an attractive move, in view of the epistemological problems it would put to rest (*Essay* II. xxiii.1f). But when challenged on this ground by Stillingfleet, who thought that Locke was making substance an optional concept, Locke responded that any other explanation for the subsistence of concatenated ideas is "inconceivable."[11] It is Berkeley who establishes definitively that the idea of an unknown material substratum for the concatenated ideas we actually perceive is untenable—a main thesis of his "subjective idealism."[12]

OUSIA AND THE MIND

Substance for Locke is, we see, merely an explanatory concept; it describes nothing in our experience. At *Essay* II.27, Locke argues at length that it cannot explain the unity of the human self, which therefore is not a substance.[13] What makes Socrates one person and Plato another is not the different substrates which support their thoughts but simply their consciousness of themselves as unified over time. Personal identity consists "not in the identity of substance, but in the identity of consciousness." It does not depend upon something unknowable like a substrate[14] but upon one's consciousness of one's present and one's memory of one's past.[15] Hence in Locke's own sense of substance, the self is not a substance: it is not an unknown underlying "x."

But the denial of substantial status to the human mind does not entail the denial, to that mind, of ousiodic structure. For living things in general, like human beings in particular, are not unified by their substrates:

> In the state of living creatures, their identity depends not on a mass of the same particles, but on something else. For in them the variation of great parcels of matter alters not the identity: an oak growing from a plant to a great tree, and then lopped, is still the same oak; and a colt grown up to a horse, sometimes fat, sometimes lean, is all the while the same horse:

> though, in both these cases, there may be a manifest change of the parts; so that truly they are not either of them the same masses of matter. . . . [A plant] continues to be the same plant as long as it partakes of the same life, though that life be communicated to new particles of matter vitally united to the living plant, in a like continued organization conformable to that sort of plants. . . . The case is not so much different in *brutes*. . . . This also shows wherein the identity of the same *man* consists. . . . (*Essay* II. xxvii.4-7)

Locke seems to be a sort of vitalist.[16] But the emphasis is not on a life-force but on a dynamic principle of organization. The identity of a man can be placed in nothing other than

> in one fitly organized body, taken in any one instant, and thus contin-ued, under one organization of life, in several successively fleeting parti-cles of matter united to it. . . . For the identity of *soul alone* makes the same *man*. . . . (*Essay* II.xvii.7)

Both the argument and its conclusion are broadly Aristotelian; as Harold Noonan has put it,

> Although Locke's notions of substance and matter are so manifestly un-aristotelian, something like Aristotle's *substantial form* holds a prominent place in his thought, at least with respect to living creatures.[17]

Denying that the human mind is united by a passive substrate thus makes room for the possibility that it is unified by a kind of ousiodic form. And if we look at Locke's account not of human minds but of simple ideas, we uncover a rather familiar situation. Simple ideas, we saw, are the "bound-aries" of our thought; in virtue of the unknowability of external substance, simple ideas in general are the closest the mind can approach to anything outside itself (*Essay* II. xxiii.29). As with all the moderns, then, what the mind immediately apprehends is "ideas," a set of cognitive objects which are ultimately within itself; its boundaries are unbreachable.[18] But simple ideas are more than simply limits to the mind. Residing within it, they are the "materials" of its operation, materials which are not generated by the mind but can be ordered by it:

> For the materials in both [the intellectual and material worlds] being such that [man] has no power over, either to make or destroy, all that man can do is either to unite them together, or to set them by one another, or wholly separate them. (*Essay* II.xii.1)

Lockean mind thus has both inviolable boundaries and a restricted immanent ordering power over its own "materials," a form of disposition. Such restricted power is also exhibited in memory, which is "the power to revive in our minds those ideas which, after imprinting, have disappeared or as it were have been laid out of sight" (*Essay* I.x.2). Lockean person-hood—and thus moral responsibility—is an effect of this dispositional power of the mind, which, Locke notes, is sometimes active and sometimes passive; memories

> very often are roused and tumbled out of their dark cells into open daylight, by turbulent and tempestuous passions; our affections bringing ideas to our memory, which had otherwise lain quiet and unregarded. (*Essay* I.x.7)

The definitive assignment of moral responsibility, in the Great Day, thus depends upon the plenary exercise of the restricted dispositional activity of memory, on the "not unreasonable" fact that the soul will remember and acknowledge everything which it has done.

The mind also exhibits a type of initiative, for we find upon reflection that it contains

> a power to begin, or forbear, or continue to end several [thoughts or actions] of our minds and motions of our bodies. . . . This power which the mind has thus to order the consideration of any idea, or the forbearing to consider it; or to prefer the motion of any part of the body to its rest; we call the *Will*.[19]

As is usual with philosophical accounts of initiative, Locke's views on the will are particularly tortured, and he changed his mind radically.[20] What is clear is that it is only in virtue of willing that a human can act upon the world outside. Hence the mind has both a passive component, the ideas it receives from the external world, and an active one. The active side of the mind both orders the original simple ideas to produce complex ones and determines the individual to act or not to act. Exhibiting these traits, the mind itself is, if not a thinking substance, what we might call an ousiodic consciousness, structured by the three traits of boundary, disposition, and initiative.

STATE AND FAMILY

The parameter of ousia plays a variety of roles in Locke's social philosophy. On the levels of state and family, it appears in distinctively weakened forms, with which he undertook to combat absolutists such as Robert Filmer (and Hobbes).[21] It is these weakenings which, as I outline them, are seen to account in large part for the ongoing fruitfulness of Locke's thought for subsequent political philosophy. And it is their limit—the point at which the parameter of ousia breaks through in full force—which accounts for some of the problems which beset such thought today. This point, I argue in the next section, is the ownership of property.

I have noted that substance, for Locke as for other moderns, is the underlying principle of power; and substance, for him, is unknown. Power thus cannot be traced back to any single source or indeed to any known source whatever. In Locke's social philosophy, its nature is distinctly pluralized, taking such radically different forms as paternal power, husbandly power, and political power. All these forms of power, for all their differences, share three things: "ends, tyes, and bounds" (*T2* ¶ 77). Any relation exhibiting social power can be characterized in terms of the purposes it serves, the people whom it connects, and its own proper limits. It thus has final, material, and formal principles of explanation. It also has a moving cause, which differs with the type of power relation involved. The moving cause of paternal power is nature; that of husbandly and political power is the agreement of those related (*T2* ¶¶ 78, 173).

The structures of ousia find their plenary realization in Locke on the level of the property-owning individual, and there only. Communities exhibit them only in derivative and weakened forms. These weakenings in my account take five different types. First and foremost, the legitimation of power relation is what I call "inverted." In previous views, power was legitimated from above—by the superior rationality of free citizens, for Aristotle; by God himself, for Aquinas and Descartes; or by the unargued status of ousia, for Hobbes. For Locke, by contrast, the authority of government derives from the consent of the governed and that of marriage from the consent of the spouses.

For someone like Aristotle, Locke's view would not be merely false but ontologically false; it would amount to saying that form derives its dispositive and initiatory capacities from matter. In arguing that government derives not merely its existence but its structures and limits from the consent of the governed, Locke begins a gesture—of action as well as of thought—which I call "inversion," in which matter "usurps" the ancient prerogatives of form.

The structures of ousia are weakened in a second way in that a community can be porous, weakening boundary; individuals are relatively free to enter and to leave it. Moreover, the ordering power deployed over the community can be (thirdly) restricted and/or (fourthly) dispersed. I call power "restricted" if it can govern some kinds of act and not others and "dispersed" if it is exercised not by a single source but by a plurality of competing ones, which must reach agreement on what to do. Both of these weaken disposition. Finally, the power relation can be intrinsically temporary, which weakens boundary, disposition, and initiative.

Not all of these types of weakening appear in every case for Locke, and they are not all new with him. But he is the first in my narrative to deploy them systematically. One reason he does so lies in the absence, characteristic to modernity, of ousiodic nesting. The traditional structures of ousia can exist in full form only on one level of Locke's human world, which is that of the individual property owner. They are found on higher levels only to the extent that they are legitimated by the lower level, only to the extent that they further and safeguard the ownership of property. In this way,

Locke begins to emerge as a sort of counter image to Hobbes. For Hobbes, the presence of ousiodic structure on the level of the state meant that the individual had to be viewed as a deficient exhibition of such structure, as the ceaseless attempt of power to acquire power, an unending motion that could not reach its telos and therefore threatened others. For Locke, the state and family exhibit ousiodic structures, but in forms which are weakened in the interest of the underlying and legitimating type of ousia, the individual property owner.

An explicit move in this direction, of course, comes in Locke's view that government derives its powers from the consent of the governed, who are preeminently property owners.[22] But on the highest level, that of the state, Lockean political society retains structures of boundary, disposition, and initiative. It has determinate boundaries in that

> it is easie to discern who are, and who are not, in *Political Society* together. Those who are united into one Body, and have a common establish'd Law and Judicature to appeal to . . . *are in Civil Society* with one another. (*T2* ¶ 87)

This version of ousiodic boundary is weakened, in one respect, by the view that governmental power reposes on the consent of the governed. That means that such power is not merely a matter of control over territory: a foreigner can reside in a commonwealth and be protected by its laws without being a member of that commonwealth. Such a resident is free to go elsewhere (*T2* ¶¶ 120 ff). Only those who explicitly consent to the commonwealth become members of it (*T2* ¶ 119). Such consent, however, is irrevocable:

> he that has once, by actual Agreement, and any *express* Declaration, given his *Consent* to be of any Commonwealth, is perpetually and indispensably obliged to be and remain unalterably a Subject to it. . . . (*T2* ¶ 121)

The commonwealth, then, is not temporary, and its citizens are not free to leave it to the extent of withdrawing the allegiance they have explicitly given it. Hence the boundaries of an ousia, porous for those who have not consented to the government, are inviolable for the citizens by virtue of their original consent.

The commonwealth also has some power to order the behavior of its subjects and to regulate their affairs with outsiders:

> And thus the Commonwealth comes by a Power to set down, what punishment shall belong to the several transgressions they think worthy of it, committed amongst the Members of that Society (which is the *power of making laws*) as well as it has the power to punish any injury done unto any of its Members, by anyone which is not of it (which is the *power of War and Peace*. (*T2* ¶ 88)

This ordering power of the commonwealth is weakened in three ways.

First, it is restricted to negative rather than positive listing—it defines and punishes transgressions, rather than establishing and enforcing positive norms. Second, it is dispersed, in that it takes the three forms of legislative, executive, and "federative" powers which are distinguished from one another (*T2* ¶¶ 143-145). The first two powers concern making and enforcing laws and are in my terms dispositive; the third concerns all relations with foreign powers and is initiatory. The executive and federative powers need to be in the same hands, for they both require "the force of the society for their exercise." Conflicting claims on this force would lead to "disorder and ruine" (*T2* ¶ 148). The executive and legislative powers may or may not be vested in the same set of people; they differ in that the executive power is permanently in place, while the legislature meets only intermittently (*T2* ¶ 143).

The degree to which ousiodic structures, though weakened, are still in place for Locke can be clarified by looking more closely at the most basic governmental body, the legislative (or legislature). The legislative exercises the fundamental power to order society by making laws and is characterized by Locke in tellingly traditional terms which I quote in full:

> 'tis in their *Legislative,* that the Members of a Commonwealth are united and combined together into one coherent living body. *This is the Soul that gives Form, Life, and Unity* to the Commonwealth. From hence the several Memberes have their mutual Influence, Sympathy, and Connexion. . . . For the *Essence and Union of the Society* consisting in having one will, the Legislative, when once established by the Majoritie, has the declaring and, as it were, the keeping of that will. The *Constitution of the Legislative* is the first and fundamental Act of Society, whereby provision is made for the Continuation of their Union, under the Direction of Persons, and Bonds of Laws made by persons authorized thereunto, by the Consent and Appointment of the People. . . . (*T2* ¶ 212; emphasis in original)

The legislative, we see, is the commonwealth's "soul," giving it "form, life, and unity," and is the effective existence (or actualization) of the commonwealth's "essence and union." It thus plays the role of ousiodic form in the society. Locke (at *T2* ¶ 89) even refers to it as "all one" with society: *pars quae totum est,* as Aquinas would have said.[23]

But again, the dispositive power exercised by the legislative is weakened. First, the legislative is intermittent; it need not always be in session (*T2* ¶ 143). That makes it porous, for it means that legislators spend part of their lives living as ordinary citizens.[24] Second, legislative power is not a fully dispositive power to order *tout court* but is defined as a "limited fiduciary Power to act for certain ends" (*T2* ¶ 149), according to the overall principle of *salus populi suprema lex* (*T2* ¶ 150; chap. 15), which—tellingly, as will be seen—is centered on the preservation of property (*T2* ¶¶ 135, 222).

Consent of the governed, restriction and dispersion of powers, temporary membership in government: these features of Locke's thought, taken up for example into the United States constitution, are so many gestures at weakening the ancient paradigm of ousia while leaving it basically in place.

The legislative is thus the limited dispositive power within the commonwealth, holding the position (but not all the prerogatives) of ousiodic form. Quite traditionally, it can come to be only in a body politic which is ready to receive it. The constitution of the legislative is the "first and fundamental act of society"; but prior even to it is the constituting of society itself, so that society can act at all. That, like government in general, is brought about by the consent of those involved. It consists in the creation not of a government but of what I call the primordial community. In such a community, there is as yet no constituted government; everything is decided by majority rule.[25] So the primordial consent which establishes community is the consent to be governed by majority rule, under which the "consent of the majority" is regarded as "the act of the whole," and this for pragmatic reasons; for the only other alternative to ungoverned chaos is consensus, which "is next to impossible ever to be had" (T2 ¶ 98).

The originary *pars quae est totum* is thus not the legislative but the majority in the primordial community, and here structures of ousiodic domination are yet weaker. The power of the majority is bound to the same restrictions and purposes as is the power of the legislative—i.e., the wellbeing of the people through the protection of property. And the majority is, at least in principle, wholly porous; if majority rules, any member of the community who votes with the majority is a "ruler." Who the rulers are can change with every vote taken and is a function of the issue debated. It follows that while majority rule is adopted with a view to permanence—a community run by consensus would not "outlast the day it was born in" (T2 ¶ 98)—any given majority is temporary. This primordial community is not only, then, a participatory democracy; in Locke's view it does not exhibit ousiodic structures at all:

> For that which acts any Community, being only the consent of the individuals of it, and it being necessary to that which is one body to move one way; it is necessary that the Body should move that way whither the greater force carries it, which is the *consent of the majority*. . . . (T2 ¶ 96)

The primordial community is thus, to take this quote at face value, a body composed—in good corpuscularian fashion—of independently moving individuals. When these individuals constitute themselves as a primordial community, they acquire a body's capacity to move as a unit, the kind of unity Descartes attributed to body as that which is "transported together, though it may be composed of many parts which in themselves have other motions."[26] And that reveals a very traditional metaphysical basis for Locke's concept of the consent of the governed: such consent is what accomplishes what Aquinas would have called the "designation" of the body politic. When they agree to be governed by majority rule, individuals become a single community fit to receive the "form" of government. The difference with Aquinas, however, is clear: designation is not accomplished by God (or, as with Descartes, by natural coalescence); it is accomplished by the will of the "parts" themselves: in traditional terms, it is as if body parts gathered themselves, of their own accord, into a body.

It is out of this sort of body politic that the commonwealth constitutes itself. We thus have a sequence in which a group of individuals initially constitute themselves as a community under majority rule and then, in their "first and fundamental act" as a community, establish a legislative. In doing this they establish a relatively stable distinction between government and citizen, with the former exercising weakened forms of substantial domination over the latter. The sequence is thus a passage from less to more ousiodic structure. Why?

It is clear why the community constitutes itself to be governed by majority rule: consensus, we saw, is too unstable. But it is not clear why the legislative power does not remain coextensive with the entire community, so that all issues continue to be decided by majority rule—a state Locke refers to as "perfect democracy."[27] Indeed, just when is the legislative power born—when the majority starts making laws? Or when legislation comes to be exercised by a distinct group of representatives? As might be expected from someone who thinks that the legislative is "all one" with society, Locke does not focus on the question. *T2* ¶ 132 refers to the majority of the community as exercising legislative power; but ¶ 135 defines this power as "given up to that Person or Assembly who is Legislator," and throughout Locke refers to the legislative as a distinct group of representatives.[28] Similarly, as Peter Laslett notes in his introduction to the *Two Treatises,* Locke has trouble focusing on the termination of legislative power, on the distinction between the dissolution of the government and that of society.[29]

The transition from community to commonwealth remains in this respect obscure, then, even to Locke himself. The answer he actually gives as to how governments come about is historical—and paradoxical. At first, he explains, governments were not in fact what I call primordial communities but were each under the administration of one man. The arbitrary willfulness of such rulers eventually led to the vesting of powers in groups of men, such as parliaments and senates (*T2* ¶¶ 94, 110–112). But that, of course, does not explain why it *should* be that way or how legislative power comes to be defined as representative in character.[30] It also suggests that the trend of history, if we are to follow it, may be toward increasing diffusion of legislative power, so that "perfect democracy" might *follow* on the commonwealth—reversing Locke's actual sequence.

At *T2* ¶ 105, Locke refers to the election as monarch of a society of that person "whom they judged the ablest, and most likely to rule well over them." If unfolded into an actual argument for the later stage of representative government, this allusion to natural superiority would repeat the kind of argument we see Locke give in favor of the domestic dominance of husbands and parents: the representatives are more able to govern than the majority, who are "naturally" weaker.

But formulating this argument on the political level would pose some problems for Locke.[31] Does he mean that mature adults are incapable of governing themselves, as are Aristotelian slaves by nature? If so, what can be the justification for the community's original majority rule? If not, in what does the partial incapacity of the subjects consist? Are they less quick? More venal? In either case, what would become of wives and children? They submit to the husband/father, as will shortly be seen, solely because he is "abler and stronger" than they are. But if the representatives are significantly abler and stronger than the typical husband/father, does not Locke's argument suggest that all wives and children be allocated to them? The argument from natural superiority is, here on the level of the state, perhaps wisely left in embryonic form.

But none other takes its place. My point is not that Locke does not, at times, show he is aware of considerations that mitigate in favor of representative government, and still less that the needed arguments cannot be supplied by other thinkers in his wake. It is that he does not recognize the question explicitly as a problem. That the normative development should represent an increase in ousiodic structure while the actual historical development shows the reverse is presumably in Locke's view too obvious to need much or careful argument. In this, his thought exhibits what I take to be a defining characteristic of Empiricism: the traits of ousiodic domination, banished from nature, break forth without explicit justification in the human world.

Weakened ousiodic structures are also to be found, I have noted, within the household. The nature of parental power is to "inform the Mind, and govern the Actions" of the child (*T2* ¶ 58). Both the forming of (or disposition over) the child and the initiative for her actions thus belong to the parent. But these traditional traits of substantial domination are weakened in three of the four ways I mentioned. The family is not, of course, a notably porous group; except for cases of adoption, one is born into it and remains the child of one's parents. But the very fact of adoption, Locke argues, means that paternal power is not grounded on "the bare *act of begetting.*" It is not the "course of nature" in reproduction that grounds such power but rather the nature of the human child. For it is the undeveloped character of a child's reason that requires her to be placed under the jurisdiction of the parent (*T2* ¶ 55f). Adoption is thus not an exceptional way of becoming a parent but inheres in every case; all children, natural or not, must in a sense be "adopted" by their parents. The jurisdiction the parents acquire, moreover, is (1) restricted: it reaches no further, than by such a Discipline as he finds most effectual to give such strength and health to their Bodies, such vigor and rectitude to their Minds, as may best fit his Children to be most useful to themselves and others. (*T2* ¶ 64)

It also is (2) dispersed: paternal power must be shared with the mother, to such an extent that "strictly speaking, there is no such thing as 'paternal' power, but only 'parental' power" (*T22* ¶ 58). And it is (3) temporary: it ends when the child is able to take care of herself, i.e. reaches maturity (*T2* ¶ 52). It will shortly become evident why, if power over children is "parental" rather than "paternal," Locke uses the masculine singular to refer to its bearer. For the moment, we can see that marriage, for its part, also exhibits a weakened sort of ousiodic structure. Like political society and the primordial community, it results from a voluntary compact and goes together with community of interest (*T2* ¶ 78). Here again the ousiodic structure is only weakened, not abolished, for the community is not one of equals:

> But the Husband and Wife, though they have but one common Concern, yet having different understandings, will unavoidably sometimes have different wills too; it therefore being necessary that the last Determination, i.e. the Rule, should be placed somewhere, it naturally falls to the man's share, as the abler and stronger. (*T2* ¶ 82)[32]

Just why the "last Determination" must be placed "somewhere" is not explained. In any case, will for Locke is the determination to act (*Essay* II.xxi.5, 28), and so in exercising final determination, or disposition, over his wife's opinions, the husband retains as well initiative for her acts; he must have consented to all of them, either explicitly (when there is disagreement) or implicitly. He has this prerogative in virtue of what Locke regards as the natural superiority of the male to the female, in virtue, then, of the same kind of nature that placed the child into the care of the parents—and, for Aristotle, placed the slave by nature into the household of her master. Since the common concern of husband and wife for Locke is the raising of children, the earlier dispersion of parental power is now to some degree undone; if husband and wife disagree about the children, the husband is to prevail.

Nonetheless, as with parental power, the substantial domination of the husband over the wife is weakened. The wife is not mere matter but a consenting party; she "designates" herself as ready to receive the disposing form of the marriage. The union is temporary, in that divorce is possible once the children have been raised.[33] And the power of the husband is restricted to those matters which are of common concern to the two spouses. Otherwise, it "leaves the Wife in the full and free possession of what by Contract is her peculiar Right, and gives the Husband no more power over her Life, than she has over his" (*T2* ¶ 82). Locke's view of the natural superiority of the male renders the last clause, perhaps, disingenuous—unless we are to say that the wife's "life" begins where her shared concerns with her husband leave off. In any case, Locke's intent—to weaken but not destroy the dominance of the husband—is clear.

In both parenthood and marriage, then, weakened forms of ousiodic domination are instituted because of the natural weakness of one of the parties, the child or the woman. The argument is as old as Aristotle's justification of slavery as "by nature." What is new are Locke's emphasis on the consent of the wife and his concern to limit the domination of the father/husband to just those aspects of the power relation where it is required by the purpose of the relation and the weakness of the child/wife, It is as if, in Thomistic terms, the designation of matter not only allowed the matter to receive a certain form but actually defined the nature of that form itself.

PROPERTY

The defining purpose of Lockean government, I have noted, is the preservation of property. It is this purpose which legitimates the actions of government, for it is with this end in view that the governed consent to be governed. In Locke's concept of ownership, the traits of ousiodic domination are once again present. But the weakenings that we have seen in his accounts of state and family—the dispersions and inversions, the rendering of relationships temporary and boundaries porous—are absent; ousiodic domination breaks out in full force.

Consider, first, how Locke sets the whole issue up in chapter 5 of the *Second Treatise*. Both reason and revelation, he writes, tell us that nature has been given "to Mankind in common," and that makes the explanation and justification of private property difficult indeed (*T2* ¶ 25). Locke's own explanation begins with the claim that God gave the world to humans, not e.g., as an object of aesthetic contemplation but in order that it be used "for the Support and Comfort of their being"; not as a beautiful world but as a useful one. And the use of nature, for Locke, is individualistic. Consider his prime example, at *T2* § 26, of natural appropriation:

> The Fruit, or Venison, which nourishes the wild *Indian* . . . must be his, and so his, i.e. a part of him, that another can no longer have any right to it, before it can do him any good for the support of his Life. (*T2* ¶ 26)

This example is suspect on several grounds. It not only shows classic European contempt for Native Americans—a contempt which Hume, tellingly, does not share—but it instates eating as the primary example of the use of nature; we "use" nature primarily, it suggests, in that we incorporate it into our bodies. The larger point that it exemplifies is that property, for Locke, first comes about through the establishment of boundaries; nature that was originally ours is apportioned into mine and yours. This boundary, we see from the quote, is inviolable; if something is mine, others have no right to it at all, and it cannot be taken from me.[34] In the example which is perhaps chosen for this reason, the inviolability is guaranteed by the boundary of my body; what I ingest becomes part of me, and what nourishes me can nourish no one else. The ground of private ownership is thus the individuality of the user's body. For my body and its activity—labor—are what is primordially and fundamentally mine. Though human bodies are natural objects, they are not part of the nature which is common to all but rather are that to which such nature is given (*T1* ¶¶ 40-43).

The boundary between mine and ours and thence between mine and yours has a single source: the owner himself. Hence ownership is not established by the explicit consent of others; it is not as if it consisted in the recognition by my fellows of my right to use an object (*T2* ¶¶ 28-30). Rather it is conceived strictly as a binary relation between the owner and the owned. The relation is established by labor; we gain title to something by laboring on it. As Locke puts it (taking as example acorns gathered by someone), it is

> labour [that] put a distinction between them and common. That added something to them more than Nature, the common Mother of all, had done; and so they became his private right. (*T2* ¶ 28)

Similarly for land: its tiller "by his Labour does, as it were, inclose it from the Common."[35]

Political society is legitimated by private ownership, which preexists it. Private ownership, in turn, is grounded in labor.[36] And labor, as Locke understands it, is for its part quite traditionally a migration of form. When I use my body's activity to alter natural things, these things become mine; the "mineness" which unquestionably belongs to my body is added to the beings of nature on which my body works:

> The *Labour* of his Body, and the *Work* of his Hands, we may say, are properly his. Whatsoever then he removes out of the State that Nature hath provided, and left it in, he hath mixed his *Labour* with, and joyned to it something that is his own, and thereby makes it his *Property.* (*T2* ¶ 27)

For Locke, to labor is, as it is for Marx, to reshape natural materials.[37] And it is the fact that a natural object has been reshaped—in the case of land, for example, "tilled, planted, improved, and cultivated"—that for Locke makes it mine. Thus labor consists in the extension of ownership from the boundaries of the body to include everything which that body's activity reshapes; the initiative of the working body, the way it affects nature outside it, becomes dispositive power once this nature is owned. Even after that, the owner retains initiative toward the world that still remains outside; he is free to use the fruits of his labor himself or to barter or give them away (*T2* ¶ 46). The great infringement of ownership, for Locke, in fact consists in the failure to exercise such disposition/initiative by allowing some of what one owns to rot: "the *exceeding of the bounds of . . . just Property* lying not in the largeness of his Possession, but the perishing of anything uselessly in it." Willmore Kendall calls Locke's statement of this view at *T2* § 37 an example of society's right to interfere with a person's private use of his property. But it is not; what the passage invokes is society's right to interfere with the *nonuse* of property, i.e., with a failure to exercise what I call dispositive power over the property.[38] Ousiodic structure, in other words, is an imperative of ownership.

There is thus for Locke a natural limit to property, and this limit is again defined on Aristotelian principles—by the power of the formative force. A man is entitled to just as much as he can shape and use (or allow others to use) and no more.[39] That means that all ownership of perishables is temporary, lasting only until they spoil.[40]

For Aristotle there was another way in which limits were imposed on the amount of matter a particular form could dominate. That was through the cosmic order, into which the individual thing had to fit and which set bounds for it that it could not exceed. For Locke, the social sphere has some constraints on how much property we obtain and how we use it; but nature itself confronts us not as a set of ousiai like ourselves but merely as matter to be worked on and transformed—in other words, as matter receptive to the form of "mineness" that our labor imposes on it. What renders matter thus receptive of form is not any action of the matter itself; it is not even the consent of other people in a community. Rather, for Locke's political philosophy as for Aquinas's metaphysics, it is God. For it is God who gave the earth to man:

> And hence, subduing or cultivating the Earth, and having Dominion, we see are joyned together. The one gives Title to the other. So that God, by commanding to subdue, gives Authority so far to *appropriate*. And the Condition of Humane Life, which requires Labour and Materials to work on, necessarily introduces *private possession*. (*T2* ¶ 35)

It is, once again, God who gives human ousiai—here owners of property—the power to constitute themselves as such. It is as such an ousia that the Lockean owner has total disposition and initiative over what lies within the inviolable bounds of his property. Such ownership, like Hobbesian sovereignty, is structured in terms of the threefold domination characteristic of ousia.

Locke's account of ownership has, like Hobbes's view of sovereignty, been understood in many ways and can be questioned on many grounds. As Kant might ask, why is the world given to us as an object of use rather than one of beauty? As Hume will ask, why does the power to reshape give the right of ownership? As Marx might ask, why is labor for Locke always viewed as, like consumption, the activity of a solitary individual? The last question is particularly telling, for in fact Locke is quite well aware of the communal nature of labor:

> For 'tis not barely the Plough-man's Pains, the Reaper's and Thresher's Toil, and the Baker's Sweat, is to be counted into the *Bread* we eat; the Labour of those who broke the Oxen, who digged and wrought the Iron and Stones, who felled and framed the Timber employed about the Plough, Mill. Oven, or any other Utensils which are a vast number. . . .
> (*T2* ¶¶ 41, 43)

Do all these others have no share in the bread? Why not? Is it because the transfer of form is not immediate enough?

Locke does not answer these questions about his explanation of ownership; he does not even pose them.[41] One thing which would explain both these problems and Locke's failure to notice them is something we have already seen in Hobbes and Descartes: tacit reliance on the parameter of ousia. This parameter suggests that labor and consumption, as formative activities, must be carried out by individual units; that labor as a reshaping of nature imparts the form of the laborer to natural materials; that boundaries are inviolable; and that nature cannot be an aesthetic object without rendering the entire parameter unemployable in this way. As with Hobbes, so with Locke, but on a different level: the structures of ousia burst forth in the human realm, unargued and unspoken, and so absolutized beyond anything the ancient world would recognize.

THE TRIUMPH OF THE INDIVIDUAL IN HUME

"The opinions of the antient philosophers, their fictions of substance and accident, and their reasonings concerning substantial forms and occult qualities," David Hume writes, "are like the spectres in the dark, and are derived from principles, which, however common, are neither universal nor unavoidable in human nature."[1] Hume thus rejects, no less vividly than did Descartes, Hobbes, and Locke, what he takes to be Aristotelianism. In my account, he begins by taking up and following through more radically the Lockean critique of substance (relying on elements of Berkeley's critique of Locke's view).[2] The result is that when Hume turns to the human world he retains Locke's location of ousiodic structure on the level of the individual mind. But he delimits these structures more narrowly than Locke; they do not concern the individual's relation to nature as actual or potential property but remain, as with Descartes, entirely immanent to the individual mind. Hume's ontology is thus radically anti-substantialist and his philosophy of the human world restrictedly ousiodic. From this position, he formulates critiques of the absolutist deployments of ousia in both Hobbes and Locke while trading on yet another such deployment.

The Humean answer to where in the "objective" world ousiodic structure is manifested is thus "nowhere." That is in contrast to Locke and Hobbes, who believed that such structure could be found, if not in nature, in the human or social world but who disagreed on where in this world. For Hobbes, property was distributed by the sovereign; for Locke, it was a natural right. For Locke, sovereignty was limited to what was necessary to protect property; for Hobbes, it was absolute. The ousiodic state (*homo politicus*) thus meets the ousiodic individual (*homo economicus*). Neither survives the encounter; ousia, for Hume, I argue, does not "manifest" itself other than within the subject.

HUME'S RADICALIZATION OF LOCKE'S
CRITIQUE OF SUBSTANCE

For Locke, substances were the unknown external origins of (some of) our ideas. They are needed (though, as I pointed out in the preceding chapter, Locke wavers on this) in order to explain the recurrent concatenations of the ideas we do know. For Hume, whatever external origins our ideas may have are likewise unknown, and explaining their concatenation is not a problem, except for those who falsely believe they can do so. That is evident from the first two chapters of Hume's *Treatise of Human Nature*, which argue that complex ideas are derived from simple ones and that simple ideas correspond to simple impressions of sense. These latter, then, are what Locke would call the "limits of our mind"; they, if anything, would show their origin in an external cause. But they do not. What distinguishes impressions of sense from mere ideas, simple or complex, is not anything we can know about their causes but simply the "vivacity" or force with which they "enter" the mind (*Tr*, p. 1). Hence there is no reason to postulate the existence of substances outside us:

> By what argument can it be proved, that the perceptions of the mind must be caused by external objects, entirely different from them, though resembling them (if that be possible) and could not arise either from the energy of the mind itself, or from the suggestion of some invisible and unknown spirit, or from some other cause still more unknown to us? It is acknowledged that, in fact, many of these perceptions arise not from any thing external, as in dreams, madness, and other diseases. And nothing can be more inexplicable than the manner, in which body should so operate upon mind as ever to convey an image of itself to a substance, supposed so different, and even contrary a nature.

The argument cannot be found because for Hume, as for other modern philosophers, what we know are our ideas—most basically, for Hume, simple impressions of sense. But impressions of sense (and ideas generally) do not have or exhibit causal efficacy. It follows that we cannot know of any such thing as causal power.

> Nothing is more evident, than that the human mind cannot form such an idea of two objects, as to conceive any connexion betwixt them, or comprehend distinctly that power or efficacy, by which they are united. Such a connexion wou'd amount to a demonstration, and wou'd imply the absolute impossibility for the one object not to follow, or to be conceiv'd not to follow, upon the other. . . . Since we can never distinctly conceive how any particular power can possibly reside in any particular object, we deceive ourselves in imagining that we can form any such general idea. (*Tr*, p. 161f)

What Hobbes thought was obviously the case—that effects follow necessarily from their causes—is for Hume inconceivable. What Locke thought we obviously experience—the causal effects objects have on one another and on us—is for Hume invisible. And so, Hume concludes, we have no legitimate idea of causal power at all. Ideas, unable to produce one another, are related only in that they resemble one another, occur in the same place, or succeed one another in time.[3] These three principles of association (which Hume respectively calls resemblance, contiguity, and succession) lead our mind from one idea to another; but the movement is in the mind, not in the ideas themselves. Hence what we might call Hume's ideational atomism:

> Every quality being a distinct thing from another, may be conceived to exist apart, and may exist apart, not only from every other quality, but from that unintelligible chimera of a substance. (*Tr*, p. 222)

From the fact that we have no experience of causal powers it follows that we not only do not experience ideas as produced by one another; we also do not experience them as produced in us by things outside us. Locke's claim that "sensation convinces us" of this is, then, simply wrong. All ideas are philosophically grounded solely in the mind whose ideas they are. They have no causal relations, certainly none that we can ever know, to each other or to any reality independent of ourselves. And that means that they have no need of an "unknown x" to serve as their substrate, or the principle of their connection. Substance is not a necessary presupposition but just an "unintelligible chimera." Hume, in maintaining this, goes ahead where Locke, challenged by Stillingfleet, drew back: substances are indeed mere matters of "custom" and "supposition."

And misguided ones at that. In the *Treatise*'s chapter "The Antient Philosophy," Hume formulates a radical and devastating critique of the very idea of substance.[4] It is, he claims, inherently contradictory, for a substance is supposed to be at once simple and complex over time and identical and distinct at the same time, in both cases a one and a many. According to Hume's ideational atomism, we do not "fall into such evident contradictions" because reality actually presents itself as such unities-of-diversities, or complex units. In fact, reality presents itself to us as a set of distinct qualities—as simple ideas.[5] We "feign" to ourselves the idea of substance because of certain misleading tendencies in the way our minds work—notably, failures of attention.

We think of substances as unities of diverse components over time because when we perceive a thing the successive ideas we have of it may differ only minimally from one another. If I simply stare at something, for example, I have a succession of ideas of it that may be very nearly identical with one another. When I do this inattentively, these minimal differences go unnoticed and I seem to myself to have had only one idea. It is only later, when I compare my successive awareness of the thing, that I discover that my experience of it was in fact composed of a series of quite distinct ideas, ideas that, as distinct, can be perfectly well conceived as existing independently of one another. When I try to reconcile these two contradictory ways of experiencing a succession of ideas, I tend to do so by assuming that there was some single underlying substrate,

> something unknown and invisible, which [the mind] supposes to continue the same under all these variations; and this unintelligible thing it calls a *substance, or original and first matter.* (*Tr,* p. 220)

Similarly for the attribution of substantial identity to a set of properties coexisting at the same time. When I perceive, for example, the color, taste, shape, and so on of a peach and do so without overmuch attention, I fail to notice how distinct these ideas really are from one another. When I subsequently reflect upon this perception and do notice the diversity, I am confronted with a situation very similar to the previous one. I resolve it the same way: I

> feign an unknown something, or *original* substance and matter, as a principle of union or cohesion among these qualities, and as what may give the compound object a title to be call'd one thing, notwithstanding its diversity and composition.[6]

The other traditional criterion of substance—most forcefully deployed by Descartes (see chapter 5)—is independence from other things. The problem with this criterion is not that it applies to nothing in our experience but that (again because of Hume's ideational atomism) it applies to everything:

> My conclusion is, that since all our perceptions are different from each other, and from every thing else in the universe, they are also distinct and separable, and may be consider'd as separately existent, and may exist separately, and have no need of anything else to support their existence. They are, therefore, substances, as far as this definition explains substance. (*Tr,* p. 233)

Hence the concept of substance has no legitimacy whatsoever. Defined as independent existence, substance applies to everything and informs us of nothing. Defined as the substrate of change, it does not describe or explain our experience but is "feigned," contradictory in itself.

For Hobbes, substances—bodies—were presumed to cause our ideas via their accidents, which were, I noted, confusingly indistinct from the ideas they caused in us. It was unclear for Hobbes, then, whether and to what degree we actually perceive substances. For Locke, it is quite clear that we do not; the concept of substance has no descriptive but only an explanatory purchase on our experience. For Hume, it does not even have that; the explanatory role of the concept of substance is taken over by that of the movements of our mind.[7] When conducted according to the principles of the association of ideas, these movements lead us to attribute similarity to sets of ideas. When conducted inattentively, they lead us to "feign" an underlying substrate for such sets.

Hume's denial of causal power amounts, in terms of the present account, to a radical dissociation of power from ousia (as well as from everything else except the movement of our mind); power is not the effect of ousia, either in its presence or its absence, because power does not exist. This move is complemented by a dissociation of truth from ousia. Truth, for traditional philosophers, was generally characterized as the agreement of our ideas of things with the things themselves. But this agreement was, up to now, viewed as the result of a process: for Aristotle and Aquinas, of the migration of a form from the known object to the knowing soul; for Hobbes, of the inward communication of pressure to the mind (*Lev.*, p. 3). For Descartes, truth was the result of a veracious process of divine instruction. For Hume, as for Locke, all such accounts of the genesis of truth would involve appeals to power, and hence all are illegitimate. Truth is the necessary result of nothing whatever. It is merely the agreement of "ideas, considered as copies, with those objects, which they represent" (*Tr*, p. 415). Though all our ideas are in fact copies—or images—of other things, as the first quote in this section shows, it is we who consider them as such and we who note their agreement or disagreement with the originals. The originals, moreover, are ultimately simple ideas, and so truth has a very restricted role to play in Hume's philosophy. One of the important lessons of his skepticism, indeed, is not merely that fundamental truth is unattainable but that it is not needed. As he puts it in the introduction to the *Treatise,*

> For nothing is more certain, than that despair has almost the same effect upon us with enjoyment, and that we are no sooner acquainted with the impossibility of satisfying any desire, than the desire itself vanishes. . . . And as this impossibility of making any farther progress is satisfying to the reader, so the writer may derive a more delicate satisfaction from the free confession of his ignorance. . . . When this mutual contentment and

satisfaction can be obtained betwixt the master and scholar, I know not what more we can require of our philosophy. (*Tr*, p. xxii)

SOCIAL PHILOSOPHY:
HUME AGAINST HOBBES AND LOCKE

Hume makes full use of the principles of the association of ideas in his accounts of government and property. Instead of absolutist, unargued appeals to ousiodic structure, these accounts relativize both government and property to other, more fundamental concerns. By doing this, Hume produces an important critique of Locke and an implicit critique of Hobbes (whom he rarely mentions). But he does so, as will be seen, on the basis of yet another unargued and unspoken reinstatement of ousiodic structure, one which locates it in the individual mind itself. Before discussing this reinstatement, I will present brief sketches of Hume's critique of Locke on property and of his alternative to Hobbes on sovereignty.

Property, to begin with, is for Hume what he calls "constant possession" and is

> a relation between a person and an object [which] permits him, but forbids any other, the free use and possession of it, without violating the laws of justice and moral equity. . . . Property may be look'd upon as a particular species of *causation:* whether we consider the liberty it gives to the proprietor to operate as he pleases upon the object, or the advantage, which he reaps from it. (*Tr*, p. 310; cf. p. 491)

Ownership thus exhibits, for Hume as for Locke, the ousiodic traits of boundary (objects I own can be used by no one else), disposition (my liberty to operate on the object), and initiative (the advantage it gives me). But it is not absolute; it is, as will be seen in more detail shortly, a concomitant of justice and moral equity. For the moment, the fact of ownership, as opposed to its legitimacy as a social institution, is grounded in causality, i.e., in one type of association of ideas:

> This in the meantime seems certain, that the mention of the property naturally carries our thought to the proprietor, and of the proprietor to the property, which being a proof of a perfect relation of ideas is all that is requisite to the present purpose. (*Tr*, p. 310)

Hume's "present purpose" in this passage is to explain pride in possessions. Those who think well of what I own tend to think well of me, and the passage of the mind from the idea of my possession to the idea of me is a case of constant conjunction, or causality.

Hume reduces ownership to the association of ideas in other ways. For one thing, the primary form of possession is, Hume says, contiguity, another basic principle of the association of ideas; we possess something when we immediately touch it. He then extends this relationship to what in fact are merely particular forms of touching: our capacity to "use, move, alter, or destroy [an object], according to our present pleasure or advantage" (*Tr*, p. 506). Such immediate possession is converted into property by being made permanent, or customary, so that "everyone continue to enjoy what he is at present master of"—a move Hume labors, in a footnote, to explain via the principle of resemblance (*Tr*, pp. 503, 504 n. 1).

All property cannot remain permanently, however, in the possession of its current owner; there must be ways to transfer property from one person to another. Hence the rule that possession must be stable is merely the first step in constituting society. It must be supplemented by ways of transferring property, which Hume once again reduces to principles of the association of ideas. The first of these is "occupation," which is simply possession as recognized by society and is, as such, "a species of cause and effect"—and so of the association of ideas.[8] When the possession of an object is interrupted by its occupation by another person, as may happen over long periods of time, doubts arise as to who owns what; these doubts can be settled by the principle of "long possession or *prescription*." If I have used what was originally the property of another for a long period, I have title to it, a point which is an "effect of the sentiments" and so (once again) reducible to movements of the mind (*Tr*, pp. 507-509). My possession of the thing has become customary enough to counterbalance the title of the original owner.

Similarly for "accession," or what we might call mediated possession, our title in things we do not touch, such as "the fruits of our garden, the offspring of our cattle, and the work of our slaves" (*Tr*, p. 509). It is explained by the association of ideas in that the objects in question (fruit, offspring, work) are associated by the imagination with objects we already possess (gardens, cattle, slaves), and hence are viewed as ours. The same goes for "succession," the rights of inheritance, in which our mind passes from the idea of the owner to that of his children (*Tr*, pp. 511-513).

Occupation, prescription, accession, and succession are all basic ways in which property is obtained in society (*Tr*, p. 505); and all, for Hume, are at bottom ways of associating ideas. The final case, the transference of property by consent, is not for him so grounded; no natural passage of the mind leads from the idea of the horse's present owner to that of the stranger who buys it. But even there, the principles of the association of ideas are operative; we tend to view such cases in terms of such similarity as we can imagine or symbolize (*Tr*, pp. 514-516).

While ownership thus preserves for Hume the ousiodic structure accorded it by Locke, this structure is not invoked absolutely or without argument. It is grounded, as facts of our lives, in the basic principles by which the human mind associates ideas. Moreover, as Hume's critique of the idea of substance shows, our minds do not always have to work the way that they usually do. Hence property for him is not *merely* a fact and still less one which is intrinsically capable of legitimating other social facts and practices. It is, rather, something which needs to be legitimated on an ongoing basis. For the preservation of property is not the basic motive for founding society but a means for avoiding discord. It does not legitimate society but is legitimated by it as such a means:

> 'Tis very preposterous, therefore, to imagine that we can have any idea of property, without fully comprehending the nature of justice, and show- ing its origin in the artifice and contrivance of man. (*Tr,* p. 491)

The need to preserve property is specifically grounded in our capacity to lose it. The "internal satisfaction of our minds," one of three basic types of human good, cannot be taken a way from us by anyone. The second type, the "external advantages of our body," can be taken away, but not in such manner as to profit the taker; someone who cuts my arm off cannot use it himself. Hence there is small incentive for hurting others physically. The only kind of good I can possess which can be taken from me in such a way as to benefit the taker of it is property. The reason for instituting the permanence of possession is to see that such discord does not arise (*Tr,* p. 487).

Property is thus grounded not only factually, in a set of propensities for associating ideas—those of the owner and of his property—but normatively as well, as a means for avoiding discord. Thus grounded by society, property does not preexist it, a point Hume argues against Locke. Property is not grounded "ontologically" in the transference of form via labor, for "we cannot be said to join our labor to anything but in a figurative sense" (*Tr,* p. 505 n. 1). Nor does it exist in the state of nature. Ownership of property, in sum, is legitimated by the agreement of others to allow me to continue in possession of it.

Hume's critique of Locke's account of property, then, has stripped prop- erty of its absolute status, much as Locke had weakened the ousiodic struc- tures of the Hobbesian state. Locke undertook this weakening, of course, because he located ousiodic structure on another level of the human world, on that of the individual property owner. The same, as will be seen, holds for Hume.

To understand Hume's alternative to Hobbes's account of sovereignty, I begin with his attack on the idea of the state of nature, which is basic to both Hobbes and Locke.[9] Hume criticizes it on the most basic grounds his philosophy will allow: it is untrue to our experience. As an account of how humans are, it exaggerates our conflictive side—under the metaphysical constraints, I argued, of Hobbes's view of causality as incursion and his assignment of the pursuit of power as the general "form" of human action. As against this, Hume asks us to

> consult common experience: Do you not see, that tho' the whole experi- ence of the family be generally under the direction of the master of it,

yet there are few that do not bestow the largest part of their fortunes on the pleasures of their wives, and the education of their children, reserving the smallest portion for their own proper use and entertainment.[10]

The idea of the state of nature is counterfactual in another way. It is formed by considering humans, who are rational, as possessed merely of emotions or "affections" (*Tr,* p. 493). But reasoning together is every bit as natural to us as invasion of one another's possessions; our nature itself provides us "a remedy in the judgment or understanding, for what is irregular and incommodious in the affections" (*Tr,* p. 489). The miseries of the state of nature are, like the idea of substance itself, fruitless fictions. In this connection, Hume writes approvingly, for example, of what we saw Locke call the "wild *Indian*":

> This we find verified in the *American* tribes, where men live in concord and amity among themselves without any establish'd government; and never pay submission to any of their fellows, except in time of war, when their captain enjoys a shadow of authority, which he loses after their return from the field, and the establishment of peace with the neighbouring tribes. (*Tr,* p. 540)

Like Locke, Hume here explicitly opposes his account of the origin of government to the patriarchal explanation. The original "sovereign," for Hume, has powers which are both restricted and temporary; his sole brief is to fend off external enemies. That eventually leads, however, to permanent government:

> society without government is one of the most natural states of men, and must subsist with the conjunction of many families, and long after the first generation. Nothing but an increase of riches and possessions cou'd oblige men to quit it. . . . But when men have observ'd, that tho' their rules of justice be sufficient to maintain any society, yet 'tis impossible for them, of themselves, to observe those rules, in large and polish'd societies; they establish government, as a new invention to attain their ends, and preserve the old, or procure new advantages, by a more strict execution of justice. (*Tr,* pp. 541–543)

Even such permanent government is a mere means, and is restricted in its powers; only when injustice occurs does it become relevant. Hence the unity of society is not derived from a single overarching power (as for Hobbes the sovereign constitutes the unity of the people) but emerges from below, via many small interactions among the members of the society. That is shown by Hume's comparison of the human mind to

> a republic or commonwealth, in which the several members are united by the reciprocal ties of government and subordination, and give rise to other persons, who propagate the same republic in the incessant changes of its parts. And as the same individual republic may not only change its members, but also its laws and constitutions; in like manner the same

person may vary his character and disposition, as well as his impressions and ideas, without losing his identity.[11]

From this perspective, as Hume writes in one of his rare mentions of Hobbes, Hobbes's account of the sovereign state is "fitted only to promote tyranny."[12] The paradigm of political power in the *Treatise* is not the sovereign but the magistrate, the individual empowered to settle disputes (and of whom the king is merely the highest). That is because the resolution of disputes requires disinterested distance from them, and is best vested in

> civil magistrates, kings and their ministers, our governments and rulers, who being indifferent persons to the greatest part of the state, have no interest, or but a remote one, in any act of injustice; and being satisfied with their present condition, and with their part in society, have an immediate interest in every execution of justice, which is so necesary to the upholding of society. Here, then, is the origin of civil government and society. (*Tr*, p. 537)

The central political phenomenon is the magistracy,[13] and the main problem for political philosophy is a narrow one, that of deciding how magistracies are to be allocated. The key to solving this, for Hume, is to recognize that "right to authority is nothing but the constant possession of authority" (*Tr*, p. 557). Because authority is thus (*contra* Locke) a form of property, political power is legitimated by society in the interests of avoiding discord, and is to be passed along by the same principles as property in general (*Tr*, p. 555). It is therefore, also like property, grounded in the principles of the association of ideas.[14]

Hume has now formulated important critiques of Hobbes and Locke. That of Locke, though not directed against Locke only, is advanced as a criticism of the absolute status Locke had accorded to property. Property for Hume is not an "ontological" phenomenon whose legitimacy is secured by appeal to divine bestowal, but a human contrivance. It clearly follows that if my possession of something leads to social discord, I can justly be deprived of it. That of Hobbes is less direct, taking the form of an alternative account of the state. The commonwealth is not unified from above by a sovereign who is its "essence" and "soul" but is a network of customary interactions overseen by disinterested magistrates whose power derives from their authority to resolve local disputes. In both cases, Hume's criticisms are directed against the absolute status of ousiodic structure. Both property and the state are explained and justified by something other than they: by the principles of the association of ideas. These principles are the proper modes of operation of the individual human mind.

HUME'S OUSIODIC IMAGINATION

Rarely has a view so influential as Hume's account of personal identity been so unsatisfactory to its author.[15] My treatment of it will be restricted to arguing that, like Hobbes and Locke, Hume has a two-level account of the human mind. On the first, descriptive level of this account, an underlying substrate is denied to the mind; the mind is a field in which various things—similarly to Hobbesian desires—come and go. The second level, where the overriding goal of power became operative for Hobbes, is for Hume normative: the mind gains, or ought to gain, unity by being structured according to ousiodic norms.

It follows from Hume's critique of substance that the mind will not be unified by an unchanging substrate in which various mental events (such as thoughts and passions) come and go. Indeed, according to the first level of Hume's account, the human mind, like a commonwealth, has no single underlying source of its unity but is "nothing but a *heap* or collection of different impressions united together by certain relations, and suppos'd, tho' falsely, to be endow'd with a perfect simplicity and identity" (*Tr*, p. 207; emphasis added). On this level, the canonical level of Hume's account, we see a radical denial of substantiality to the mind; even the *question* concerning the substantiality of the soul is, Hume writes, "absolutely unintelligible" (*Tr*, p. 250). Together with the loss of substantiality goes a loss of ousiodic structure; for, on this level, the mind for Hume is merely a train of ideas or "bundle of perceptions" that are related to each other in many small ways—by their various mutual resemblances, by contiguities, and especially by the recurrent patterns of their succession—rather than by any single unifying form.

It is then all the more astonishing to find Hume, immediately after his critique of substance in "Of the Antient Philosophy," applying to the mind the very categories of unity and diversity that he has denied to external things.

> I must distinguish in the imagination betwixt the principles which are permanent, irresistible, and universal . . . and the principles, which are changeable, weak, and irregular. . . . The former are the foundation of all our thoughts and actions, so that upon their removal human nature must immediately perish and go to ruin. The latter are neither unavoidable to mankind, nor necessary, or so much as useful in the conduct of life; but on the contrary are observ'd only to take place in weak minds. . . .
> (*Tr*, p. 225)

The imagination, then, has its fixed and enduring (or, we might say, "essential") principles and its changeable (or, we might say, "accidental") operations.[16] It is the former which constitute the stable relations of our ideas. On this level, the mind for Hume is not *merely* a heap, as his canonical account suggests. The many small interconnections of ideas out of which its unity emerges must themselves be produced by the operation of just a few "fixed and enduring" principles: those of the association of ideas with respect to resemblance, contiguity, and conjunction. Otherwise, human nature "must immediately perish and go to ruin." How could it not? It is, after all, these very principles which (after a good deal of labor) Hume has established as the ground of property, of its preservation, and so of social order generally.

The mind is not as much like a commonwealth as my earlier quote from Hume suggested. While a commonwealth could lose even its "laws and constitutions" without changing its identity, when an individual fails to use the principles of the association of ideas she destroys her very humanity. These principles thus have a double status for Hume. On the one hand, they are the "permanent, irresistible, and universal" foundations of the mind. On the other—and *because* they are foundational—they are the indispensable norms of its behavior. Hume, then, is doing here what he elsewhere claims cannot be done: deducing an "ought" from an "is."[17] The blatancy of this deduction suggests that Hume simply does not see what he himself is up to, that what we have here is a case of what I call the "reinstatement" of ousiodic structure to the mind.

Certainly the mind exhibits, on this second, normative level, the ousiodic traits of boundary and disposition. The imagination, to begin with, is at once drastically bounded and utterly unlimited. It cannot of itself produce any original idea, being able only to combine and dissociate ideas derived from sensory impressions (*Tr*, p. 1), and so its boundaries are given by these impressions themselves; we can know nothing that does not "enter" our mind. But once impressions have entered the mind, its power of combining and dissociating them is absolute. Because "inseparable connexion" is excluded from the imagination (*Tr*, p. 9f), any two ideas can be disconnected from one another; and, correspondingly, any two can be combined (though not, to be sure, always in accordance with the principles of association of ideas). Hence, though the mind does not have disposition in the sense that it *generates* its ideas, it has full *ordering* power over them; it "has the command over all its ideas, and can separate, unite, mix, and vary them, as it pleases" (Tr, p. 623f). All relations among ideas, except for the original succession in which they enter our minds, are thus at the disposition of the imagination.

Moreover, the fixed and enduring principles of an individual mind, including presumably those by which the imagination is to operate, are nothing less than the character of the agent, which is responsible for all her acts. They thus exercise the mind's initiative with respect to the outside world:

> If any *action* be either virtuous or vicious, 'tis only as a sign of some quality or character. It must depend upon durable principles of the mind, which extend over the whole conduct, and enter into the personal character. (*Tr*, p. 575)

The "character" of a moral agent is thus what John Bricke has called a set of "dispositional properties" in the mind, which (like water's tendency to freeze) can be empirically manifested in the regular behavior they cause.[18]

In contrast to Descartes (and later to Kant), Hume thus denies moral primacy to the will. Since we have no idea of power, we can have none of will power; "will" is just the name for the feeling we have "when we knowingly give rise to any new motion of our body" (*Tr*, p. 399f). Hume also denies the Aristotelian account of the moral agency of reason, and in fact inverts it. The fixed and enduring principles of association from which moral action springs are not principles of reason but of passion:

> Reason has no power whatever to move us; only passion can do that, and reason is, and ought to be, the slave of the passions, and can never pretend to any other office than to serve and obey them.[19]

The passions are many and particular; the will is one, and traditionally pursues one universal good.[20] Hume's account of initiative is thus an exercise in supple good sense; but it is still one which allows us to praise or blame an individual on the basis of a subset of her causal properties, those constituting her character: "For these alone are *durable* enough to affect our sentiments concerning the person" (*Tr*, p. 575): *pars quae totum est.*

We have seen that people must act in terms of the principles of the association of ideas if they are to recognize property rights and establish an ordered society generally. But action requires passion, and the dominant passion in constituting society is sympathy, the fact that associating with other human beings leads me to think and, especially, to feel as they do.[21] Sympathy for Hume is thus not merely a feeling but a process in which, from learning that another person has a particular feeling, I come myself to share, actually to feel, the same thing. When, for example, anger that I perceive in someone else makes me feel anger at whatever provoked it in her, I am in sympathy with this person.

Sympathy is thus a "change of the idea into an impression,"[22] and that poses a problem for Hume. At the very beginning of the *Treatise*, he presents an account of the mind in which the strongest of our ideas, impressions of sense, *lose* "vivacity and force" when they enter the mind, becoming mere "ideas" (*Tr*, p. 107). Since the mind has only the power of ordering our ideas by associating them with and dissociating them from one another, the question arises of how the mind is able to give ideas greater vivacity than they already have, let alone actually converting them into impressions.

The middle term which lends force to ideas of the feelings of others is, once again, grounded in the principles of the association of ideas; it is the resemblance of these others to myself (*Tr*, pp. 317-320). When I perceive another person who resembles me—i.e., another human being—to be feeling anything, the resemblance of this person to my concrete idea of myself leads me, by the association of ideas, to associate this feeling with my idea of myself. And since I have a very strong awareness of my concrete self at a given moment, when I imagine myself having a particular feeling the idea of this feeling becomes intensified to the point where I can actually feel it.

Thus sympathy itself, though a feeling, reposes on the operation of my imagination in accordance with its "fixed and enduring principles"; it reposes on the ousiodic view of the mind as having a dispositive form for its activities.

It is important to note that Hume's reinstatement of ousiodic structure to the imagination comes *immediately* after his own severe critique of substantial forms with respect to "the Antient Philosophy." Hume never attempts to bring the two together; but he might have done so. The final paragraphs of his considerations on "the Antient Philosophy" list several traditional philosophical ideas, such as those of natural sympathies, antipathies, and nature's "horrors of a vacuum," which Hume says are simply projections of qualities of the mind onto nature. Attributing such human qualities to nature is similar to children beating the stones which hurt them and to poets personifying nonhuman things. Absent from the list, though discussed elsewhere in the section, are substantial forms. The same *could have been* argued for them, as Descartes did (cf. chapter 5). Hume could have attempted to show that we are aware of our own mind as possessing both fixed and enduring principles, without which the mind cannot function and which in this sense are its true nature, together with various adventitious associations which come and go. To form the idea of a substance would then be to project these two specific features onto things. That Hume does not argue this way suggests, I take it, that he is unaware that he has just attributed to the imagination the kind of unity he has elsewhere denied to external things generally, and indeed to the mind itself.

Hume's philosophy presents what can be called the "triumph of the individual." For the human individual has been freed from all dependence on the outside world. Ontologically, it has no demonstrable need of God to sustain it in existence or to guarantee the truth of its ideas. Politically, it has no inherent need of the sovereign state and no inherent need to own property. For property and government are mere contrivances to give the mind what it really needs: tranquillity and concord with others. As such, they can be modified or dispensed with at will and piecemeal. In this they differ from the principles of the association of ideas, which cannot be abandoned without causing human nature itself to "perish." As I have argued, the principles of the association of ideas constitute the bedrock of Hume's social philosophy in that they legitimate such basic structures of the human world as property and political authority. The triumph of the individual, then, is the instatement of the human mind as the only place in the universe where ousiodic structure is to be found.

In terms of my narrative, Hume presents in final form the ousiodic structures I have located in other modern philosophers. For him, as for Descartes, Hobbes, and Locke, the structures of Aristotelian ousia are absent from nature. What for Aristotle was an ordered cosmos of nested ousiai became for Descartes and Hobbes a set of bodies. For Hume, as for Locke, it is not even that: nature is given us only as ideas. And with Hume, its need for material substrates, suspect for Locke, is gone.

But the characteristic traits of Aristotelian ousia remain in force in the human realm; they provide the basic norms which these modern philosophers think should structure our minds and societies. For Hobbes, they were present in the sovereign structures of Leviathan, the totalitarian state which is the centerpiece of his political philosophy. For Locke, they structured the individual ownership of property, which is for him the ultimate legitimating factor in the social order. For Hume, the ousiodic structures of boundary, disposition, and initiative are properties of the internal order our minds should maintain.

The themes discussed in this section can be ordered into a variety of stories. Natural objects, for example, go from being substances supported directly by God in Descartes to being bodies which, for Hobbes, simply are as they are. In Locke they are then volatilized into ideas, and in Hume their substrates are finally dispensed with. At the same time, on the side of the subject, the individual mind is gradually freed from dependence on outside realities. Hobbes frees it from its Cartesian dependence on God and Locke from its Hobbesian dependence on the sovereign state. Hume, finally, frees it from its last vestige of dependence on the outside world: the requirement that it own something. The state, for its part, goes from being an absolute foundation in Hobbes to being a mere means legitimated, in Locke, by quite a different absolute foundation: the individual and his property. For Hume, even ownership is not ultimate and must be grounded by the principles of the association of ideas, i.e., immanently to the individual mind.

Modernity's final stage—the detailed articulation of the infinite sovereignty of the subject in Kant and Fichte and its dialectical overthrow in Hegel—is now at hand. I will not go into it here, for it actually belongs better in a different story—the story of the capture of *logos*, of thought and speech, by time. For present purposes, it is enough to see that modernity—the epoch philosophically articulated from Descartes through Fichte—must be thought of rather differently than hitherto. What Heidegger calls the "modern subject" is nothing new.[23] Rather it is something very old—an Aristotelian ousia—which has come to be in a new kind of place, in a nature devoid of ousiai, a universe which is at most nothing more than matter in motion and at least a set of ideas.

Such a universe can provide no moral norms, and the modern mind turns elsewhere for them. In Descartes and other "rationalists," it turns to God, who both makes possible and legitimates the efforts of human beings to constitute themselves and their communities in terms of ousiodic structure. In Hobbes, Locke, and Hume, such appeal to God is barred by the constraints of their empiricism; God, whether ousia or not, is unknowable.

In the Empiricists, however, ousiodic structures break forth unargued as legitimating norms. Because they are unargued, they are ultimate; and as the ultimate sources of legitimation, they are absolute. Hence the absolute nature of the sovereign for Hobbes, of property rights for Locke, and of the principles of the association of ideas for Hume.

These ousiodic discourses are still much with us. The Hobbesian vision of the totalitarian state has gone from history, but only in the past decade; the absolutism of property rights, in much cruder versions than Locke's, still afflicts us. Modernity is thus, as Habermas also points out,[24] an incomplete project. But its completion, we can now see, will not be achieved by a yet fuller account of rational sovereignty, whether in terms of the individual or of the dialogical community. The most basic way to complete modernity would rather be to extend its banishment of ousiodic structure into the human world itself, to conceive of our selves and societies in non-ousiodic ways.

The questions that immediately arise, however—and which lie behind almost all the myriad critiques of postmodernity—are these: How will such a "completion" of modernity, banishing ousiodic form from the human world, avoid turning ourselves and our communities into mere matter in motion, mere heaps? Is contemporary "antihumanism" anything more than the valorization of formless matter? Are the studied meaninglessnesses that have become postmodern clichés—difference and power, as well as such familiar motifs as Deleuze's body without organs and Lyotard's differend—anything more than invocations of the drifting heap? Those are questions which, however important, are not yet ready to be asked, much less answered. For until modernity is understood, postmodernity cannot be understood; and if my account here is correct, modernity cannot be understood until it is seen as a manifold set of attempts to relocate and reinstate ousia after it has been evicted from nature.

Essential to any adequate understanding of modernity is the role played in its constitution by the Empiricists. It is a startling fact—or would be if we thought about it at all—that three centuries after its inception, Empiricism has still not been integrated into the history of philosophy. The great historical philosophers—Hegel, Nietzsche, Heidegger, and recently Derrida and Foucault—have left the Empiricists out of account. Empiricist philosophers, for their part, are notoriously blind to their own status as the outcome of history.

An historically informed account of the present situation which included serious attention to the Empiricists could not fail to note two major achievements of Hume's philosophy. One is the detachment of truth, or presence, from ousia. We saw that, for Aquinas, "being" had two significations. One designated the capacity of a thing to be the object of a true proposition; the other "posited something in reality" and was, I argued, bound up with substance and ousia. In Hume, the former of these senses is retained, but the latter disappears, except for the ousiodic structure he attributes to the individual human mind. The dissociation of truth from ousia is with that nearly complete and stands as a possible resource for a truly postmodern (that is, post-ousiodic) philosophy.

The second acquisition lies in Hume's account of the atomicity of ideas. This doctrine comprises several promising insights. First, it holds that any idea, except one which is absolutely simple (if there be any such) can be resolved into simpler ideas. Second, it holds that no idea needs to be in any particular connection to any others; once ideas have entered the mind, the mind has the power to connect them with each other in any way it chooses. Because the ultimate ideas are simple, truth has ultimately a very restricted role to play for Hume; it consists, on its most basic level, of correctly "pronouncing one thing not to be another."[25] Any connection of ideas beyond that can be accomplished by the human mind and need not "represent" anything in the ideas themselves.

The view that connection may be nonrepresentational is, of course, not new; fears of illegitimately concocting complex entities that do not exist are endemic to modernity (though not, oddly enough, to Aristotle, whose *De Anima* does not deal with the possibility). But philosophical exploitation of the fact is new. It is basic to Kant's view of the human mind as accomplishing, in all its varied operations, some form of synthesis. It is also, as I have argued elsewhere, the key to Hegel's philosophical method.[26] As I will argue in a subsequent work, it eventually plays a key role in resolving the current crisis of modernity, of becoming non-ousiodic without reducing the human world to a mere heap of heaps. For the connection and separation of ideas, suitably temporalized, turns out to be what I call the situating activities of narrative and demarcation.[27] And a situation, as I admittedly have yet to show, is neither an ousia nor mere matter in motion.

9

CRITICAL ACCOUNTS OF OPPRESSION IN MUDIMBE, DOUGLASS, AND BEAUVOIR

Driven from nature, where it never existed in the first place, ousia in modernity continues its ancient work of structuring the human world. But it does so behind the backs of the philosophers; in spite of all their tortured discussions of "substance" as the inert material substrate, none of the thinkers I have discussed here ever notices that he is leaving the ancient structures of Aristotelian Being in their traditional role with regard to humans and their communities. Such relocations and reinstatements of ousia in modernity are only to be expected; for if modernity carries out the eviction of form from the universe, it is incompletely. Indeed, the modern project, as understood here, is not only incomplete but inherently incompletable.

We can see this by noting that in one sense, all the modern philosophers I have discussed are "materialists," for none of them thinks that there is anything more to nature than matter in motion.[1] So understood, materialism is basic to modernity. But, like Christianity, it has never really been tried. However piously scientific the materialist cant and however sincere the materialist belief that reality is nothing more than matter in motion, no one has ever succeeded in carrying the insight consistently into practice. For we cannot, it seems, help treating some matter as qualitatively, indeed generically, distinct from all other matter: the matter in our own bodies. One has never been able to regard so much as one's own toe—to say nothing of one's nose, or breast, or penis—as "mere matter" like the rest of nature.

When it is a question of one's own body, matter signifies: it acquires meaning through another, through the subject to which it is attached. To signify in this way is my body's very nature. Unrelated to my self, it would have no more meaning for me than does other mere matter; it would not be "my" body at all.[2] Nor am I free to bestow significance on my body; its meaning for me resides not only in what I *can* do with it but in what I *must* do with it. I *can* use it, as I use the matter in other bodies, for work or enjoyment. I *must* use it for living and for manifesting my thoughts and feelings to others. I *must* suffer its pains and feel its pleasures. Modern materialism was never carried through consistently because our own bodies always remain matter for the formative power of our minds. There is always, in other words, at least one ousia in the modern universe: Me.

A similar exception can also be made on the political level. Those with whom I join in the shared activities of a commonwealth cannot be mere matter because, simply in order to associate with them, I must recognize them as human beings; they must be more than their bodies. But they also cannot be ousiai in their own right. For if our society is to be anything more than a Humean heap of customary interactions, it must have a form of its own. Given the absence of nesting in modernity, if form resides in the individual, then the community is wholly formless. So form comes to be exclusively vested in something over and above individuals, in a sovereign government. When others join with me to constitute an ousiodic commonwealth, as we saw with Hobbes, they in effect relinquish their own formative powers to the state. There is always, then, at least one ousia in the political universe: Us.

We saw that when matter was docilized in Thomas Aquinas, the concept of ousia began to lose empirical purchase. In modernity it was replaced by substance, which also gradually lost such purchase. Increasingly and in various ways, it became difficult to tell what in our experience is an ousia (or a substance) and what is not. But on another level of modernity, the line was very clear: the domain of application of the concept of ousia was the ethical and social world, while that region to which the concept of ousia did not apply was nature. With this, the problem of empirical purchase became largely practical. It is not a question of what in the natural world is an ousia but of who has or will be allowed the capacity to constitute themselves as either political or ethical ousiai. On both the ethical and the political levels, everything outside the boundaries of the individual or her community became mere matter for them to inform. Modernity gave birth to its ideal twins, *homo economicus* and *homo politicus*.

Homo economicus, the Lockean ousiodic individual, confronts, as we

181

saw, a nature of mere matter. Its primary relation to this nature is one of ownership. To be sure, as such an individual I am surrounded by other human beings, whom I recognize as more than merely natural bodies. But I am not *forced* to make an exception for their matter as I do for my own. Though I may think it evil to refuse to view others as equally human with me, to refuse such recognition to them is not senseless or impossible— merely, perhaps, evil and foolish. I can, if I wish, assert my status as the only ousia in the universe by seeking to own everything, expanding my wealth without limit. Or, in the extreme, by converting other people into my property.

That takes a straightforward form in slavery, one example of which I discuss shortly. It takes a less obvious form, I suggest here, in monopoly capitalism. For such a capitalist in a sense owns not merely his goods but also those who must buy them from him. This reduction of the consumer to a sort of property of the producer is achieved by transforming the ancient structure of the market in two ways. The first step is to give the market fixed boundaries, which individual consumers cannot transgress: to prohibit or impede them, by a variety of means, from going and buying the goods they need elsewhere. The second step is to make sure that, within these boundaries, there is just one supplier, who "orders" consumers in that he makes them into his customers. The development of monopoly presents itself historically, to be sure, as a transformation of the older structure of the market, which traditionally (e.g., in Athens) was free of entry and a place of competition among sellers. But it is a transformation apparently as obvious and natural to many moderns as the change of the state of nature into Leviathan was to Hobbes.

For *homo politicus* has also been born. To be sure, the commonwealth to which I belong exists as one among many—or, in the early days of modernity, among several. But we moderns recurrently seem to find that our state is really—or should be—the only one. Consider, for example, the incessant wars by which Europeans, inventors of the ousiodic state, have from its inceptions sought to establish theirs as the only genuine state in Europe. Consider the repeated quests for continental hegemony which resulted: Napoleon, Hitler, Stalin. Consider that the ending of these quests in the formation of the European Community was accompanied by a growth of regionalism within the individual states, i.e., with the loss of the dispositive powers of central governments.

The modern reduction of outside societies to mere matter was more clearly evident, however, with respect to areas of the globe which were not themselves already constituted as states: America, Africa, and parts of Asia. According to papal bulls of the fifteenth century, land not belonging to Westerners was *terra nullius,* no one's land; it was free for the taking.[3] With these bulls the adventure began. Where the ancient world tended to expand ousiai internally, so that a polis (and later the Roman Empire) could populate a given domain with more and more sub-ousiai without changing its external boundaries, in modernity ousia tends to develop by expanding its boundaries; *homo politicus,* dressed out as Europe, swallows the world.

This chapter briefly adduces three critical discussions of modern oppression: V. Y. Mudimbe's characterization of colonialism, Frederick Douglass's account of his experience of slavery, and Simone de Beauvoir's analysis of modern marriage. I argue that all three view the objects of their criticism as ousiodic structures in the human world.

That does not mean, of course, that the simple and abstract structures of ousia can of themselves explain such complex phenomena as colonialism, slavery, and marriage, to say nothing of the other manifold structures of oppression and violence which have beset the Western world. Nor do I claim that ousia somehow generated these structures. Or that it underlies them as a substrate. Or that it is the genus of which they are species. Rather, ousia seems to function generally as a kind of recipe; it suggests how people should deal with the world. And it has plausibility as such a recipe for at least two reasons. First, the very fact that it is abstract and simple means that it can be readily understood and carried into practice via a complex variety of engines. The other reason is that people engage these engines, to some extent, independently of ousia's codification in the texts of Aristotle. Ousia does not create practices of oppression but clarifies and legitimates them *to their practitioners.* And it has done so, paradoxically, without its own functioning being either clarified or legitimated. It has guided us from behind our backs, and all the more surely for that.

THE "INVENTION OF AFRICA"

The manifold engines of colonialism, the full Augustan panoply of *capitanias* and *encomiendas* and *latifundias* and patroonships and proprietary colonies and seigneuries, cannot easily be reduced to the structures of ousia. But according to V. Y. Mudimbe, the West's enormous project of ingesting the peoples of Africa—the "colonizing project"—operated in three ways. It sought, and to some degree achieved, "the domination of physical space; the reformation of *natives'* minds, and the integration of local economic history into the Western perspective."[4] The three traits of ousiodic domination could not be clearer: the colonialist imperative is to delimit the territory of Africa into controllable regions, to reform or dispose the minds of those who dwelled within them, and to appropriate the fruits of their labors, i.e., take over the economic initiative. This imperative was not purely political or economic; as I have noted, it received papal sanction early on, and the Protestants would follow. In 1820, an English missionary quoted by Mudimbe could write:

> Let us thus go forth in the name and under the blessing of God, gradually
> to extend the moral influence . . . and the territorial boundary also of
> our colony, until it shall become an Empire.[5]

The moral influence of Christianity will play (so hopes the missionary) the dispositive role in structuring the colony; its initiative will be displayed not in the transmission of form beyond its boundaries but in the expansion of these boundaries themselves. Colonialism so understood amounts to the implantation of ousiodic political structures in non-European territory. The empire itself stands as a global ousia. Its boundaries are the territories of its colonies. Its disposition is exercised by what the British call the mother country and the French, no less perspicuously, the *métropole*. This center disposes, as Mudimbe indicates, of the minds of the natives. It appropriates the fruits of their labor: if all roads no longer lead to Rome, all seas lead to London or Paris.

The "imperial" project, it is clear, took more than its name (and the names of its engines) from ancient Rome. But modern empires, of course, differed from the ancient one in many ways. In particular, they conceived both their spatiality and their temporality differently than someone like Aristides conceived Rome's, and the contrasts highlight certain distinctively modern features of the modern empires. First, they are not spatially contiguous like Rome but dispersed across the globe; the colonies are geographically distant from one another and, even more important, from the mother country. Second, the modern empire is impermanent, as Rome proved to be; but unlike Rome the colony was, in the minds of many, actually *proclaimed* to be temporary. Some (distant) day, the White Man would lay down his burden and each colony would "become an Empire" on its own. The mother country is maternal not least in that one day her children will leave her.

This pious hope, however bad its faith, is for several reasons a strange one. It amounts, for one thing, to the colonist disowning his own condition of possibility—the colonial structure itself. Moreover, it is in startling contrast to the attitude of Europeans to the different regions of their own countries. Despite some obstreperous contestation even then, the general view was (and is) that Wales was and would remain a part of Britain and Provence a part of France. Not so for Ghana and the Congo; as colonies, they were destined someday for self-rule. This pious hope is in notable conflict with standard colonialist racism; it amounts to nothing less than the view that the "savages" of Africa will one day achieve, through their tutelage to Europeans, a degree of autonomy and self-rule to be forever denied to the Welsh and Provençals. This difference in fate between the colonies of the mother country and its regions is not merely a stark and unexplained contrast. It testifies to a distinct lack of comfort on the part of the European mind with the imperial structure itself. If my argumentation to this point is correct, the discomfort has metaphysical antecedents: the colony, a well-bounded ministate implanted among "savages," should not be nested within a larger entity. It should rather eventually be freed to become an empire in its own right.

That, again, is presumably due to the spatial dispersion of modern empires. It is as a discrete bounded unit that the colony is a potential ousia on its own rather than a permanent part of a larger political entity. Distance from the mother country is thus essential to the colony: Cameroun and the Ivory Coast, both French, can border on each other; the one country they can never, as colonies, border on is France. And so the improvements in transportation and communication in the mid–twentieth century did not mitigate against the dissolution of the colonial empires but hastened it; it was just at the moment when colonial power could become speedy and efficient that it also became intolerable to the colonies themselves.

It is thus necessary to the colony that, as Northrop Frye has said concerning the Canadian colonial experience, "the head office is elsewhere."[6] The geographic distance of the mother country guarantees its cultural remoteness as well and renders it incomprehensible. Specific projects and policies are best left to the local authorities; the power of the mother country serves less to institute detailed operations on the spot than to enable and legitimate these authorities to constitute themselves along ousiodic lines. The mother country functions as did the God of Descartes, which enabled individual minds to gain control of their own ideas. Its power over the colony is thus manifested in the absence, from the colony, of its own governing center; imperial power is *ousia abscondita*.

Colonialism, though a distinctively modern phenomenon, is thus in some respects the continuation of ancient structures. In spite of the differences, what the colonists were doing in Africa was at bottom, as Mudimbe points out, only what they had already done to themselves—though with a brutality and at a distance now magnified by more advanced technology. With regard to the seventeenth-century Italian missionary to the Congo Giovanni Francesco Romano, Mudimbe writes:

> It struck me that . . . he could have accomplished the same type of work with St. Boniface in Germany. He boasts of the number of people converted, masses celebrated, sacraments given, churches erected. . . .[7]

Colonialism was in all its guises a giant exercise in assimilation which "tended to organize and transform non-European areas into fundamentally European constructs."[8] One such construct, the goal toward which the colonies were assumed to be working, is evident in figure 2, a map of the railroads in France. The map extends the disposing power of the capital, Paris, almost all the way to the six boundaries of the hexagon (three on land, three on water). All railroads, at least at the time the map was drawn (1957), lead to and from the

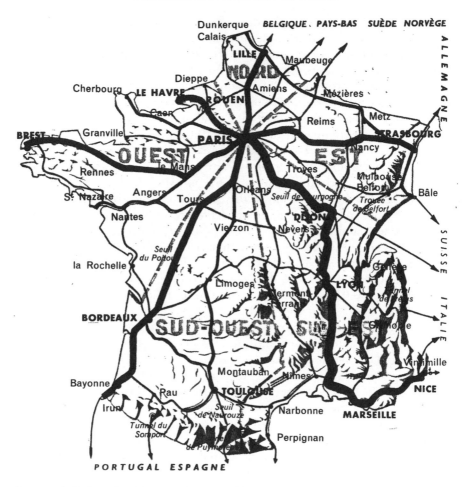

FIGURE 2. Railroads of France. From V. Chagny and J. Forez, *Géographie de la France* (Paris: Armand Colin, 1957).

capital; they do not connect provincial cities with one another except inciden-tally. Since such railroads are primarily vehicles of commerce, they enable—indeed, require—what Mudimbe, as I noted, called the "integration of local economic history into the [Parisian] perspective."

For all its newness, then, there was nothing fundamentally new about colonialism. It was a new way of instituting ousiodic structure, an inevitable consequence of the stabilization of the mother country around a disposi-tive center, enabled by the new technologies of transportation and warfare and legitimated by the reduction of the non-European world to mere *terra nullius,* to bodies in motion.

THE PLANTATION OF COLONEL LLOYD

In Empiricist discourse, we saw ousiodic structures break forth to structure two different phenomena of the social realm. Humans are related to humans by the Hobbesian model of unrestrained sovereignty. They are related to nature by ownership, in accordance with the equally absolute character of Lockean private property. We tend to view these two parametric operations of ousia as deeply opposed to one another, thanks in large part to the Cold War, which divided the world into a battle between private property and the totalitarian state.[9] But long before the Cold War, at least two modern engines of oppression combined ownership with totalitarian sovereignty. Because of the modern world's rejection of nesting, however, the combination was uneasy.

This uneasiness was discovered by the twelve-year old Frederick Douglass when he arrived at the Maryland plantation of Edward Lloyd:

> It was a little nation unto itself, having its own language, its own rules, regulations and customs. The troubles and controversies arising here were not settled by the civil powers of the State. The overseer was the important dignitary. He was generally accuser, judge, jury, advocate, and executioner. The criminal was always dumb, and no slave was allowed to testify other than against his brother slave. . . . There were, of course, no conflicting rights of property, for all of the people were the property of one man, and they could themselves own no property.[10]

The plantation thus wears a double visage: structured at once by sovereignty and ownership, it is a human "community" whose sovereign is an owner and whose citizens—in faithfulness to the modern absence of ousiodic nesting—own nothing. Its boundaries are virtually Aristotelian in their immobility, reinforced as they are by the boundaries of other plantations. Egress, and with it initiative, is well controlled:

> every leaf and grain of the products of this plantation . . . [was] transported to Baltimore in [Lloyd's] own vessels. . . . In return everything brought to the plantation came through by the same channel. To make the isolation more apparent, it may be stated that the estates adjoining Col. Lloyd's were owned and occupied by friends of his, who were as deeply interested as himself in maintaining the slave system in all its rigor. (*LT*, p. 486)

The boundaries of the plantation are thus fortified by being as well the boundaries of kindred plantations. The plantations are gathered together into a cosmos guaranteed by the power of the government. The government itself is, as Douglass points out, hardly evident within the plantation; like the global empire, its role is merely to allow the local authority to constitute itself as such and in this it functions as *ousia abscondita*. Within the plantation, social order is imposed by the rarely seen Colonel Lloyd through his overseers. Once again the traits of ousiodic domination are evident:

> separated from the rest of the world, . . . the whole place was stamped with its own peculiar iron-like individuality, and . . . crimes, high-handed and atrocious, could be committed there with strange and shocking impunity . . . Each farm was under the management of an overseer, whose word was law. (*LT*, pp. 487–489)

The order, though not the owner, was visibly manifest:

> [In addition to slave quarters] there were barns, stables, storehouses, tobacco-houses, blacksmith shops, wheelwright shops, cooper shops; but above all there stood the grandest building my eyes had ever beheld, called by everyone in the plantation the *great* house. . . . It was a treat to my young eyes to behold this elaborate exhibition of wealth, power, and beauty (*LT*, p. 488)

The great house thus functions as did the *tablinum* in the house of Pansa, with the exception that the master himself is invisible: *ousia abscondita*. Like the colonial mother country, like the government of Maryland itself, Colonel Lloyd is outside the monstrous world of the plantation. He manifests himself within it in the power he gives to his overseers to constitute themselves as little masters. Douglass, like Mudimbe, is careful to note the European antecedents of the plantation: "It resembled, in some respects, descriptions I have since heard of the old baronial domains of Europe" (*LT*, p. 487).

The aim of the display, of course, is to "reform the minds" of the slaves, reducing them *in their own eyes* to their proper status, that of owned animal matter. It is thus what I call an "engine of manipulation." When the manipulation fails to achieve its intended effect with young Douglass, overt coercion is called for. He is sent to Edward Covey, a "Negro breaker" who does to slaves what is also done to horses and other animals:

> I saw in my own situation several points of similarity with that of the oxen. They were property; so was I. Covey was to break me; I was to break them. Break and be broken was the order. (*LT*, p. 567)

Even before he arrives at Covey's, Douglass begins to admit to himself the truth of his situation in almost Foucaldian terms: "'I am,' thought I, 'but the sport of a power which makes no account of my welfare or happiness' "(*LT*, p. 563). And the treatment eventually, though temporarily, has the desired effect:

> My natural elasticity was crushed; my intellect languished; the disposition to read departed, the cheerful spark that lingered about my eye died out; the dark night of slavery closed in upon me, and behold a man transformed into a brute! (*LT*, p. 572)

The failure of slavery as an efficient economic system lies in this final cruelty, that Douglass knows that he has been brutalized. And together with that, of course, knows that he is *not* a brute, and somehow must escape. This truth is conveyed to him by the labor he performs (cf. the quote about Covey); he is not merely a broken animal, but a breaker of animals as well. To put this in the vocabulary of my account of metaphysics: the labor structure of the plantation is nested in a way missing from its ownership structure. Slaves own nothing and are, within the human order, dependent on their master for their subsistence in a way reminiscent of the way in which a Cartesian thing is dependent upon God. But they retain a certain independence in the performance of their work, and that keeps the human spark alive in their hearts, if not cheerful in their eyes.

The Lloyd plantation thus exhibits a complex mix of what I call ancient and modern structures of ousia. Its boundaries are secure, while disposition and initiative are ultimately in the hands of the owner. It coexists peaceably with kindred plantations, and its boundaries are reinforced by theirs. The whole populace of plantations is made possible and legitimated by an absent power, the government of the state. This hierarchy—overseer, owner, state government—is a sort of modern version of the ancient nesting of ousiai. But it is different, because the higher levels are not manifest; they rule, not in the plenitude of the ancient form, but through their very absence.

Within the plantation, parallel structures of domination trace the outlines of both *homo economicus* and *homo politicus*. Ownership is entirely in the hands of Colonel Lloyd, who is represented by his most singular possession: the great house. A wretched sovereignty—"break and be broken"—is visibly exercised by the overseer and is made possible and legitimated by the absent owner. The union of political and economic oppression, of sovereignty and ownership, is as we might expect a discordant one. Ownership is not nested; the owned slaves own nothing in turn. But sovereignty is; the slaves direct their own work as they are directed to do, and so do the overseers. The result, we saw, is one of the many sources of the slaves' knowledge of their own brutalization. One way to harmonize the two lines of domination would be to allow the slaves to own things, to pay them in scrip which they could then spend only in the plantation stores. But that would move the plantation from slavery to an extreme form of what I have called monopoly capitalism.

MARRIAGE

This uneasy interlocking of oppressions—a community among humans which is nonetheless a relationship of the subject to matter—can also be found in Simone de Beauvoir's seminal analysis of woman as other in *The Second Sex*. On the one hand, as Beauvoir puts it, woman is reduced to matter, on the principle that *tota mulier est in utero*. As in Aquinas's doctrine of the equivocity of essence, the part is here equal to the whole. In the case of woman, the part in question is not a substantial form but a material organ—so that, as Beauvoir also puts it, woman "thinks with her glands."[11]

On the other hand, man cannot help but stumble occasionally—or be tripped, as Beauvoir trips Lévinas and as Douglass would trip Covey—over the fact that woman is not purely matter or evicted nature but a conscious being.[12] Though shrews can to various degrees be tamed, a woman cannot be broken as thoroughly as can a slave, and the reason has to do with visibility. While Colonel Lloyd only rarely saw any of his slaves (except for the few who were privileged to work in the great house), Lévinas, like other married men, had to live with his wife; she had to be his companion as well as his servant. So woman wears a double visage: "Man seeks in woman the other as nature and as his fellow being" (*SS*, p. 152). If woman is "matter, passivity, immanence . . . the flesh" she is also "nature elevated to the transparency of consciousness" (*SS*, pp. 152, 149). Like Hegel's bondsman, she is not exactly nature but "the wished-for intermediary between nature, the stranger to man, and the fellow being who is too closely identical."[13]

This double visage is presumably responsible for Beauvoir's famous misreading, or tacit rewriting, of Hegel's account of the "battle of the opposed self-consciousnesses" in the *Phenomenology of Spirit*.[14] There, Hegel presents two living things, not yet human, engaged in mortal combat. The outcome will decide who is lord and who is bondsman. Beauvoir wishes to appropriate this account; both the problem she sees with woman as other and its solution are Hegelian.[15] But she cannot use it as it stands. For the battle, as Hegel presents it, is between individuals who are (almost) equal,[16] and that is not the case in the battle of the sexes. Hegel's model, as Beauvoir sees it, would apply more directly to anti-Semitism than to patriarchy:

> to the anti-Semite [as to Hegel's battling consciousnesses] the Jew is not so much an inferior as he is an enemy for whom there is to be granted no place on earth, for whom annihilation is the fate desired. (*SS*, p. xlviii)

Woman's situation, Beauvoir continues, is by contrast more similar to that of the "Negro."

The battle of the opposed self-consciousnesses—Hegel's reworking of the Hobbesian state of nature—leads to a sort of Hobbesian total sovereignty of one over the other. Wishing to amalgamate this with the other sort of oppression—that of the dominance over nature presented by Locke in terms of ownership—Beauvoir tacitly amends Hegel's account. Instead of risking his life combating another human being, the man risks it fighting wild animals; instead of self-affirmation in the eyes of the other, the goal is food (*SS*, p. 67f).

Beauvoir's analysis of the married woman locates the three axes of ousiodic domination in a strikingly double way: woman at once submits to and reinforces all of them, thus becoming the agent of her own oppression—her own overseer. The boundaries of her married life are physical ones, and have

> taken material form in the house, whether cottage or castle; it stands for permanence and separation from the world. Within its walls the family is established as a cell or unit group, and maintains its identity as generations come and go. . . . (SS, p. 471f)

But, in an effort to establish herself as a "conscious being," the woman takes over care for the boundary: "When a living being enters her house, her eyes gleam with a wicked light: 'Wipe your feet' . . . " (SS p. 475).

Similarly for disposition, which operates under another name: "That 'obedience' is legally no longer one of her duties in no way changes her situation; for this depends not on the will of the couple but on the very structure of the conjugal group" (SS, p. 480). The structure in question is the "mentorship" of the husband, in which he undertakes, like a colonizer, to "reform" his wife's mind in accordance with his superior logic and insight. Beauvoir cites, as an extreme example of this, a widow who, after her husband's death, "still tried to determine what he would have thought in each case" (SS, p. 487f). The husband's dispositive power can operate, here, even in the case of his final and definitive absconsion.

Deprived of disposition over her own mind, the wife seeks to exercise it over the material contents of the house, once again reinforcing her own oppression:

> she is the one who has chosen, made, hunted out furnishings and knick-knacks, who has arranged them in accordance with an aesthetic principle. . . . Because she *does* nothing she seeks self-realization in what she *has*. (SS, p. 474)

Finally, initiative too is denied the woman: as conscious,

> woman, too, must envisage purposes that transcend the peaceful life of the home; but it is man who will act as intermediary between his wife as an individuality and the universe. (SS, p. 471)

The man does this, of course, because he goes out into the world, into the public domain, to earn money and take his role in public affairs. And this means that he, too, like Colonel Lloyd, is *ousia abscondita:* he is absent from the home for most of the day. That is what enables the wife to constitute herself as an accomplice in her own oppression: left in the house, she furnishes and cleans it; her husband, like everyone else, must wipe his feet when he enters. But though he is absent, it is her husband who gives her a house to furnish; without him she would not have the power to acquire even a doormat. Once again, power is an effect of ousia in its absence.

It is evident from this brief rehearsal of some modern discussions of oppression that modernity has become increasingly unhappy with its reinstatements of ousia in the human world. Slavery and colonialism have largely had their day, though their vestiges continue to plague us; the domination of women within marriage is under attack. But ousiodic structures remain with us—in other places, under other names, and not always in a pure and obvious way. One example of the disguised operation of ousiodic structure can be derived from my discussion of Descartes in chapter 5. When ousia has been evicted from nature, the idea may remain, as it did for Descartes, of a single disposing form continuing to operate on all of nature from some metaphysical location outside, as did Descartes's God. The entire natural universe can then be conceived to be within the boundaries of this single giant ousia, as I argued it was for Descartes. Its single (divine) disposing center, withdrawn from nature, can be experienced as a variety of external powers, independent of and even conflicting with one another, with the oppressed person at the mercy of each in turn.

Thus a contemporary Western woman is (usually) not confined within the walls of her home; she may in fact have won the right to a career of her own. But when she goes to work she may find herself in an office dominated by a single man or a group of men acting in concert. They oversee her labors, fire her at will, and take the credit for her achievements. She may return home to cook and do the housework in the most traditional of ways, and on Sundays she may go to church and hear men in the guise of God tell her what to do with the inmost parts of her own body. She has no single master, no clearly identifiable oppressor; she moves among several different spheres. And yet, in each sphere, ousiai rise up to enclose and dominate her. What manifests itself in such cases, I take it, is nothing other than the ancient oppressive power of ousia, now evident as the recurrent condensation, from what appear to be forces of nature, of various ousiai which the oppressed person encounters in turn, as God's power, for Descartes, enabled the human soul to form itself into an ousia.

Ousiodic oppression, if not oppression's only form, is thus more widespread than might first appear; my effort in the present discussion is to provide not an exhaustive account of its modern guises but only a couple of examples to suggest the need for further investigation. My final example of a modern engine of oppression, one of many I could have chosen, will be directly known by most of my readers, though—like other ousiodic engines—it has recently come under various sorts of challenge. It is the university classroom.

A classroom is highly specialized, in fact usually serviceable for one thing: to enable one person to speak to a group of people. It has secure boundaries. Unless very large, lecture rooms have only one door, to keep students (and others) from wandering in or out at will. Windows are problematic: a classroom with a beautiful view will be unpopular with professors; most have as few windows as possible, to keep the students' minds from wandering. If a classroom has many windows on one side, students are usually seated facing the opposite wall; that wall is usually filled not by a view but by the unprepossessing presence of a blackboard, which is a mere backdrop and tool for the professor. What happens within the room, the class itself, has boundaries that are secured by the professor's ability to throw anyone out or to make enrollment conditional upon her permission. While in class, students are not permitted to speak with one another; they must attend to the lecturer, not to each other. If they have anything to say, they must say it to her—after she gives them permission. The professor, then, is the ordering center for the behavior of the students, who can relate to each other only as she permits. She disposes their minds by re-forming, or perhaps in-forming, them. She, in short, is form; they are matter.

We have seen that initiative is always troublesome. In an engine of oppression as perfectly realized (in the other two respects) as the university classroom, it is particularly vexing. For it is not the professor who goes off to affect the world outside, it seems, but the students. True, their minds will have been molded and formed in accordance with the knowledge possessed by the professor; but so were the minds of the slaves and children of an ancient household. The *pater familias,* however, could hardly be said to exist for the sake of rendering his domestics capable of functioning in the outside world. Nor did Colonel Lloyd exist for the sake of his slaves. But the professor seems to exist for the sake of her students; it is they, if anyone, who will carry her wisdom to the outside world, they who have initiative. If only there were a way for the professor's knowledge to move directly into that world outside, without needing the mediation of the students.

Fortunately, of course, there is a way: by publishing. For in publication the professor presents her knowledge directly to the outside scholarly world in a traditional exercise of ousiodic initiative. It is by publishing, then, rather than by teaching, that she can fully satisfy the ancient paradigm, attaining a sort of initiative, a capacity to affect the outside world which her students do not share. The privileging of research over teaching is itself of ousiodic origin; "publish or perish" is an ancient imperative indeed.

APPENDIX TO PART TWO: OUSIODIC STRUCTURES IN SPINOZA AND LEIBNIZ

The post-Cartesian "rationalists" lie off the path of the current narrative, and I will not discuss even their most illustrious representatives, Spinoza and Leibniz, in detail. It may be useful, however, briefly to point out in them traits of the relocation of ousia that I have found in Descartes. For both Spinoza and Leibniz, while denying that the entities that we live among and experience sensibly are ousiai, also maintain that these entities are not what is most truly real; they are not what I call "ontological bedrock." This bedrock consists of what Spinoza and Leibniz, following Descartes, call "substance": God for Spinoza and the monads for Leibniz. Both Spinoza's God and Leibniz's monads, however, turn out to exhibit two of the essential traits of ousia: they have inviolable boundaries and dispositive power over what is within these boundaries. And because both thinkers, again like Descartes, associate ousiodic structure with freedom, ousia turns out to help structure the Spinozistic and Leibnizian discourses on ethics and politics.

SPINOZA'S ETHICS

Arriving at his own thought via a critical confrontation with Descartes, Spinoza continues the modern rejection of substantial forms: they are

194

"clearly absurd," "childish and frivolous."[1] The result is that he takes his basic category to be not ousia but substance. His deployment of this concept in his *Ethics* is unique in philosophical history, both in the rigor of its monism and the method of its presentation; its details are obscure. In its general outlines, however, the deployment begins in the first axiom of the *Ethics*: "Whatever is, is either in itself or in another."[2] Substance is that which is in itself and[3] is conceived through itself. As with Descartes, then, it is defined in terms of independence: a substance is both ontologically and epistemologically independent or *zelfstandig*.

But Spinoza goes decisively beyond Descartes here. The independence which a substance exhibits is for Spinoza always unqualified; to be a substance, a thing must be *wholly* unconditioned by anything else, and as Proposition 14 finally proves, only God is like that. It is not that, as with Descartes, God is the only true substance. It is that he is the only substance at all: finite substances cannot even be conceived (*Ethics*, Part I Prop. 8). Every other thing that exists, whether thinking or extended, somehow inheres in this single divine substance, either as an attribute or as a mode. The boundaries of the physical universe are figurative for Spinoza, since it is of infinite extension; but that does not keep him from saying that it and all the things which it contains are "in" God as in another (*Ethics*, Part I Prop. 15).

Spinoza's God has in fact the securest of boundaries, that between being and non-being: everything that is is within those boundaries. What was threatened in Descartes, then, is affirmed by Spinoza; the entire universe is included within a single giant ousia. And not merely the extended universe, for in denying finite substances, Spinoza is taking issue with Descartes's view that individual minds are, though to a lesser degree than God, substantial in nature.[4] The extended and intellectual universes are thus ontologically parallel for Spinoza.

Both show a radical absence of nesting: no ousia is contained within another ousia. Leaving attributes aside, a "mode" is defined as the opposite of a substance; it is what is and is conceived through another (*Ethics*, Part I Def. 5). All the things we normally encounter are modes:

> Particular things are nothing but affections of Gods attributes, or modes by which God's attributes are expressed in a certain and determinate way.
> (*Ethics*, Part I Prop. 25 Scholium)

In particular, we ourselves are very clearly identified, in Book II of the *Ethics*, as modes: "The being of substance does not pertain to man, or substance does not constitute the form of man" (*Ethics*, Part II Prop. 10). There are, then, no ousiai within the divine ousia, but only modes. Ousia has vanished from our level of reality completely.

Ousia (iterum) abscondita manifests itself on our level of things as divine power. We, like other modes, are wholly dependent upon God; God is the efficient cause of all things and is so "immanently" rather than "transitively" (*Ethics*, Part I Propp. 17, 18). The details of such immanent efficient causality are unclear; for Aristotle, efficient (or moving) causality was the paradigm of "transitivity" as Spinoza understands it, the movement of a form from one thing to something else. But it is clear that God, for Spinoza, operates on modes "within" himself, and so his causal power, in my terms, is dispositive rather than initiatory.

That is so even though modes must also be caused by other modes. For nothing can act upon anything except as the divine power ordains; individual modes do not affect each other directly but only through the infinite power of God, who in this way not only generates modes but orders them, exercising perfect disposition over the universe (*Ethics*, Part I Prop. 28 Scholium, Propp. 26, 29). This disposition manifests itself as the total determination of the individual thing by other individual things—by causal chains stretching throughout the infinity of space and time. The divine disposition of the divine ousia over its own parts finds its achievement, then, in Spinoza's determinism (*Ethics*, Part I Propp. 26, 28).

Substance, defined in terms of independence, thus turns out to have the ousiodic characteristics of inviolable boundary and disposition, and the Spinozistic universe is a single perfect ousia. Its boundaries are unbreachable, since beyond them there is only nonbeing. Because there is nothing beyond on which to act, God has no initiative. But he has perfect disposition over what is "within" his boundaries. Thus where Descartes's God had initiative but no knowable disposition, Spinoza's God, identical with the totality of finite things, has disposition but not initiative.

In spite of the variance of their views on the relation of God to the finite cosmos and on the existence of finite substances, Descartes and Spinoza agree in that they both relocate ousia to another realm of reality, but in such a way that it remains at work in us. Once again, and not for the first or last time, power is called upon to guarantee and explain docility—here, the docility of the mode.

Thus relocated to the divine, supersensible level, ousia is in a position to structure the human world. As did Descartes, Spinoza has defined substance in terms of independence; and this means that, as with Descartes, substance for Spinoza is associated with freedom: to be free is to be able to act from one's own nature alone (*Ethics*, Part I Def. 7). To be able to do this, it helps to have a certain kind of nature: that, precisely, of a substance. For unless my nature is to be independent of other things, I will be unable to act from it alone; my action, like my existence itself, will require the concurrence of those other things. Only God "acts from his nature alone" (*Ethics*, Part I Prop. 17).

Freedom, thus understood as originally a characteristic of God, is for Spinoza the fundamental human virtue. The final part of the *Ethics*, "Of Human Freedom," is devoted to showing how the human mind can assimilate itself to God's by becoming free. That turns out to mean, as the preface to Part Four tells us, controlling the affects. Spinoza has here just told us that emotion is merely confused thought (*Ethics,* Part II, p. 204f; English translation, p. 542f), and it is thought, not emotion, which is an attribute of God. We control our affects by converting them from emotions into thoughts, from confused ideas into clear and distinct or even "adequate" ideas (*Ethics,* Part V Prop. 3). Achieving such adequacy means seeing individual things, the objects of our ideas, in their full causal context, which is ultimately that of all creation. The vision of a thing in the context of all creation is, ultimately, God's vision. As our finite mind approximates this, it undergoes a sort of *homoiosis* in which our mind, gaining ever more adequate cognition, becomes more like God's mind—*in* which it already is (*Ethics,* Part V Prop. 36). Thereby, finally, it approximates the inviolable boundaries and perfect disposition of the divine ousia.

Ousiodic structure finds its way not only into Spinoza's ethical account of the mind's rise to God but into the political philosophy of the *Tractatus politicus* as well. Anything which exists can only exist by the power of God. That holds for the state as for the individual. and so the state, like the individual, has a divine right to exist and to act:[5]

> It is clear . . . that the right of the state or sovereign is nothing but the right of nature itself, and as such determined by power; not however by the power of a single individual, but by that of a people which is guided as if by one mind. In other words, it is clear that what is true of each man in the state of nature is true likewise of the body and mind of the whole state—it has as much right as it has power and strength. Hence the more the commonwealth exceeds a citizen or subject in power, the less right he has . . . and consequently a citizen does nothing and possesses nothing by right unless he can defend it by the common decree of the commonwealth. (*Tractatus politicus* III.2)

Because the sovereign is the "mind" of the state and because—true to the connection already noted between ousia and freedom—the man who is guided by reason is free, the sovereign alone has the power/right to regulate the conduct of individual citizens and to provide for the defense of the state from outside forces; he alone has political disposition and initiative (*Tractatus politicus* IV.2). The former power/right—that of disposition—is extensive indeed:

> If a commonwealth gives anyone the right to live as his own judgment dictates, and consequently the power to do so . . . it thereby surrenders its own right, and vests it in the man to whom it gives such power. If it gives this right to two men or more, and allows each of them to live in accordance with his own judgment, it thereby divides the sovereignty; and if, finally, it gives this same power to each of its citizens, it thereby destroys itself; it ceases to be a commonwealth, and everything reverts to the state of nature. (*Tractatus politicus* III.3)

The individual in the state is then an authorized instance of the power of the state, just as a mode, for Spinoza, is an instance of the power of God. Like the control of the individual over her affects, the dispositive power of the state is grounded in the ousiodic nature of the divine realm—a nature which Spinoza never identifies as such.

LEIBNIZ

Still another set of strategies for relocating substance to the divine realm is presented by Leibniz, who reinstates ousiodic structure in what he calls "monads." As the first of the "Principles of Nature and of Grace" tells us,

> Substance is a being capable of action. It is simple or compound. *Simple substance* is that which has no parts. *Compound substance* is a collection of simple substances, or *monads*. Compounds, or bodies, are pluralities, and simple substances—lives, souls, and spirits—are unities. There must of necessity be simple substances everywhere, for without simple substances there would be no compounds. As a result, the whole of nature is full of life.[6]

For Leibniz, substance is defined not in terms of independence, as with Descartes and Spinoza, but in terms of activity. The move from substance to ousia will thus be shorter than it is for the other two "rationalists," for it begins from a conception of substance not as a passive substrate but as that which is capable of action.

The quote suggests that the main distinction to be made among substances is not whether they are finite or infinite, as for Descartes, but whether they are simple or compound. The former are more basic, and Leibnizs ontological bedrock is the "monad," a simple substance, i.e., one without parts. Being without parts, it has no place to receive anything from outside and is "windowless": "accidents cannot be detached from substances and march about outside of substances, as the sensible species of the Scholastics once did."[7] A monad thus has inviolable boundaries.

An Aristotelian ousia is characterized by a duality; it contains both matter and form, with the latter exercising what I call dispositive power. A Leibnizian monad, however, is simple; it would seem that such duality, and with it ousiodic disposition, cannot be ascribed to it. But the kind of simplicity which Leibniz attributes to monads is a subtle matter. For one thing, a monad, while simple, is not so simple that nothing at all can be predicated of it. If that were the case then all monads would be identical, and by Leibniz's principle of the identity of indiscernibles there would be only one of them ("Monadologie" ¶ 9). Monads are therefore different from each other, while being alike in that they are monads; so their simplicity, somehow, does not exclude all variety. Moreover, all created monads—i.e., all monads other than God—are constantly changing. They change in that they contain "details," which turn out to be a multiplicity of perceptions, a manifold which (it is stated) does not constitute a set of "parts." Thus a monad, for all its simplicity, contains a plurality of mutually distinct perceptions. What, then, makes it "simple"?

Responding to Bayle, who asked how a simple being could change, Leibniz writes that a monad changes its perceptions moment by moment via an internal principle of order ("Monadologie" ¶¶ 12-17). A monad can be simple without always being the same because it "follows perpetually the same law of order or of succession."[8] The simplicity of the monad consists in the fact that all its changes are generated, as it were, by such a single mathematical formula. As Jacques Jalabert has put it, nothing in the monad derives from matter; everything in it is due to its quasi-mathematical form.[9] This form, then, both generates and orders—or, better, generates in order—the multiplicity in the monad. It is the multiplicity which, though immaterial, plays the subordinate role of matter within the closed boundaries of the monad; the monad's internal principle is thus its dispositive form.

To say that the perceptions of a monad are not "parts" of it, Leibniz says, is just to say that they do not arrive in it from outside, as classical substantial forms were thought to do, but are logically implicit in it from the beginning.[10] The simplicity of the monad is thus accounted for on two levels. On one, it is underwritten by the absoluteness of the monad's boundaries. These boundaries are absolutely unbreachable; nothing whatsoever can move beyond the monad in which it inheres, and so (as we saw) a monad has no "parts." On the other level, the monad's simplicity consists in the immanent and logical nature of its development over time, in that the particular multiplicity in any given monad follows, like a series of theorems, from its basic nature. These two sides go together. Because everything in any monad follows from its own basic law or nature, nothing in it can come from other monads.

Two traditional traits of ousia clearly apply to Leibniz's monads. First, in their windowlessness, they have inviolable boundaries. Second, within these boundaries, the "form," or the formula which constitutes the law by which the various perceptions of a monad follow each other, has absolute disposition over these perceptions; they not only come from within but do so in a way univocally specified by the formula. Matter not only causes no trouble; it causes nothing at all.

This docility is, once again, explained and guaranteed by divine power. For the most basic of the simple monads is God himself. As *Monadology* ¶ 47 has it,

> only God is the primary unity or the simple original substance of which all the created or derivative monad are products, and from whom they are born, so to speak, by continual fulgurations of the divinity from moment to moment, but limited by the receptivity of the created thing, for whom it is essential to have limits.

199

God, for Leibniz, is the supreme monad, the one who produces the rest and is responsible for all perfection, i.e., everything positive, in other things ("Monadologie" ¶¶ 38–41). As Christianity teaches under the heading of "God the Father," the power of God is "the source of everything."[11]

As with Cartesian relative substances, a monad has need only of God in order to exist. What God thus bestows upon it, however, is not a free will, which then struggles to balance various faculties and to order a plethora of ideas, but, as with Spinoza, every single perception that it ever has, the full range of its "mental contents."[12] It is thus God who enables the internal principle of the monad to generate and order its complexity.

Once again, ousiodic structures have been relocated; they are not to be found in our experience. The bodies we see around us are not substances or monads but what I call "quasi-ousiai," aggregates of monads which, if organized, are ruled by one of their number:

> Hence we see that each living body has a dominant entelechy which is the soul in the case of an animal; but the members of this living body are full of other living beings, plants, and animals, each one of which also has its dominant entelechy or soul. ("Monadologie" ¶ 66)

The things we perceive are actually sets of nested quasi-ousiai. Each part or organ is made up of a (vast) number of entelechies, all "dominated" by a single one of their number, and these are in turned dominated by higher ones, until we reach the single entelechy which dominates the whole: the soul. A body is thus a complex structure of domination which is only an incomplete version of the ousiodic structure of the simple substance or monads. Monads are known to us intellectually, not through the senses; ousia is what our mind tells us reality must be like rather than how we actually perceive it.

Like Descartes and Spinoza, Leibniz associates substantiality with freedom, for freedom is "spontaneity with reason" and

> we see . . . that every substance has a perfect spontaneity, which becomes freedom in the intelligent substances, that everything which happens to it is the result of its idea or its being, and that nothing determines it save God alone.[13]

Thus, contraposed to nature, which is a "realm of power," is the realm of substantial spontaneity, which is a rational domain of its own. In words that prefigure Kant, Leibniz writes:

> It must be maintained in general that all existent facts can be explained in two ways—through a kingdom of *power* or *efficient causes* and through a kingdom of *wisdom* or *final causes;* that God regulates bodies as machines in an architectural manner according to laws of *magnitude* or of *mathematics* but does so for the benefit of souls and that he rules over souls, on the other hand, which are capable of wisdom, in the manner of a prince or, indeed, of a father, ruling to his own glory according to the *laws of good-*

ness or *of morality.* Thus these two kingdoms everywhere permeate each other, yet their laws are never confused and never disturbed, so that the maximum in the kingdom of power, and the best in the kingdom of wisdom, take place together.[14]

Substance is, then, not only the inner nature of reality but also the model of governance itself. This model is most clearly called in toward the end of the "Monadology":

> 84. . . . spirits [are] capable of entering into a kind of society with God and . . . he is with respect to them not merely what an inventor is with respect to his machine (as he is with regard to other creatures) but also what a prince is to his subjects and even a father to his children.
> 85. Whence it is easy to conclude that the assembly of all spirits must compose the city of God, that is to say the most perfect state under the most perfect of monarchs.
> 86. This city of God, this truly universal monarchy, is a moral world within the natural world and is the most lofty and divine of the works of God, and it is in it that that the glory of God really consists, for there would be no glory if the greatness of God were not known and admired by spirits. It is also in relation to this divine city that he has goodness, while his wisdom and power are shown everywhere.

Taken strictly as a model for earthly societies, this perfect state would mean that an earthly sovereign is "like a little divinity within its own sphere" ("Monadologie" ¶ 83). A state would then have a single unifying essence (its monarch) and determinate boundaries (enclosing those "spirits" which belong to it). All power would belong to the sovereign, who would hold his kingdom and its provinces together as the soul unifies the body and its members.

We are braced for a repetition, then, of Spinoza's political philosophy. But Leibniz's rehabilitation of finite substances, along with the relocation of even these substances on a level of reality removed from our ordinary experience, allows him a good deal of leeway in construing the phenomena of such experience; they do not have to show the ousiodic structures evident in the "kingdom of wisdom." Hence Leibniz can write to Arnauld that the state is not a true unity, "any more than would be the water of a pond with all the fish it holds, even though all the water and the fish were frozen together."[15] In general, the Leibnizian state is not viewed in terms of the imposition of form upon (hopefully) docile matter but as the result of a complex and enormous number of individual negotiations for rights and privileges.[16] It is for Leibniz a society of unequals, in which dominance ideally accompanies merit. The political order thus for him resembles a body; it is not a monad but an aggregate of monads, with one (the "soul") governing the others, each of which is dominant in its own sphere, much as were the German princes of Leibniz's day.

Like Descartes, Spinoza and Leibniz thus conceive of the supersensible realm as the repository of Aristotelian ousia, which the rise of science has banished from nature. Located on this ideal, indeed divine, level, ousia has a home which enables it to retain its parametric functions. These functions are exercised, in the first instance, over the discourses of the philosophers themselves, and on the most general level. For in spite of the differences among the three philosophers, it is the parameter of ousia which enables them to bring their ontologies together with their Ethics, and social theories: to be like ontological bedrock is to be free, and freedom is the prime ethical and political excellence. The parameter of ousia itself thus functions as the unifying form of philosophy, a unifying form which the Empiricists contest by reinstating ousiodic structures in the human world without argument.

Philosophy, thus unified around its central parameter of ousia, is then able to justify ousiodic structures in the individual (for Descartes, the proper balance of the faculties under the disposition of the will), in the state (the power of the Spinozistic sovereign), and in society in general (when suitably weakened, as in Leibniz). These structures, as with the ancients, are grounded outside themselves—not in nature, but in the divine or supersensible realm. So construed, the "Rationalists" are a sort of rear-guard action to maintain an ontological justification for the ousiodic structures of the human realm. It is the Empiricists, who dispense with such justification altogether, who are the more radically "modern" of the modern philosophers.

PART THREE

HEIDEGGER'S CHALLENGE TO OUSIA

10

HEIDEGGER'S PRESENTATIONS OF DIAKENA IN
BEING AND TIME

And so, at last, to Heidegger. In terms of the present narrative, he is the inheritor of a long history and of a complex situation. For with the rise of modernity, the parameter of ousia, the basic structure of Western Being, began to encounter difficulties. First, we saw, it was evicted from nature but was retained as the basic structuring principle of the human realm. This retention was philosophically problematic because it required either the suspicious *relocation* of ousia to a supersensible realm or an unjustified, indeed unnoticed, *reinstatement* of it in the human realm. It was humanly problematic because of the sordidness of the phenomena founded upon modernity's relegation of everything outside the individual or society to the status of mere unformed matter. Modern colonialism and slavery, both notably more oppressive than their ancient counterparts, were, for example, philosophically legitimated by the view that non-Europeans were mere matter; similarly, though perhaps somewhat more benignly, for modern marriage.

For present purposes, *Being and Time* stands as the beginning of the final confrontation of the history of metaphysics—of the parameter of ousia—with the thick and thin of our lives. That the battle is staged at all is a victory for metaphysics, which Empiricism had comfortably dismissed as a compendium of errors. This dismissal merely covered over and so helped absolutize ousia's parametric functioning. Heidegger's phenomenological reawakening of the question of Being shows his refusal to accept such comfort, for it amounts to asking after the (parametric) role that metaphysics plays in what Husserl called our life-world. But if staging the battle is a victory for metaphysics, its outcome is a defeat. For *Being and Time* shows—sometimes wittingly, sometimes not—that ousia, with its three axes of domination, is inadequate as a descriptive framework for the fabric of our lives. In showing that, Heidegger accomplishes for the human world something akin to what the Empiricists had accomplished with respect to nature; he provides a philosophical articulation of the inapplicability of the concept of ousia to the human world, as they had articulated its incapacity to apply to nature. In his later writings, this articulation takes the form of a challenge to ousia's status as parametrically structuring discourse.

But this challenge has remained inexplicit and subterranean, in part because, like Hegel, Heidegger has usually been read in ousiodic terms.[1] More fatefully, as I argue at the end of this chapter, Heidegger himself misunderstood its object and its import. What he would later call the decisive "flash of genius" (*Geistesblitz*) that determined his entire career was, he tells us, the insight that the Greeks had defined *ousia* as constant presence. The Greek error—the error that founded the West—was thus to allow the notion of presence to dominate that of Being.[2]

If my argumentation in this book is correct, Heidegger's "flash of genius" was, like most such flashes, drastically misleading. The meaning of *ousia* for the first philosopher to make it a basic technical term—Aristotle—was not presence but domination. To be a being, for Aristotle, was to contain a structure in which one part dominates the whole, via the three axes of boundary, disposition, and initiative. Equating such structure with Being itself meant writing domination into the basic nature of the universe, and that has in Modernity been seen to be in complicity with a variety of evils: with patriarchy, colonialism, and slavery; with absolute status for private property and for state sovereignty; with the melancholy "triumph" of the individual.

When Heidegger focuses on presence rather than ousia, he confuses his targets. On the one hand, on his own understanding he questions presence itself. On the other, he also challenges the ways in which presence achieves its baneful effects—through its dominance over metaphysical discourse. There is thus in Heidegger's writings a fundamental lack of clarity over whether the problem with the "dominance of presence" lies with the presence or with the dominance.

This lack of clarity has several results. One is that the challenges to presence and to ousia are never adequately separated so as to be adequately articulated on their own account. Instead, Heidegger's questioning of presence, in places, turns almost magically into a challenge to the way in which the theme of constant presence has dominated metaphysical discourse, thereby skewing the basic conceptual apparatus of the West: into a critique of ousia. Perhaps the most unfortunate effect of Heidegger's failure to separate presence from ousiodic domination, however, is (as I argue at the end of this chapter) that the questioning of presence itself inevitably turns into a challenge to truth. Presence and truth have been, we saw, explicitly associated with each other at least since Aquinas. When the questioning of presence becomes a challenge to truth, it faces the problem of making itself intelligible without appeal to that which it is challenging, a problem which neither Heidegger nor anyone else has been able to solve. My intention in this book, among other things, is to *dis*solve that problem: to show that when we redirect our critique against ousia rather than presence, truth can take its rightful place as a nondominating value of discourse.

Heidegger, I have written, "questions" presence and "challenges" ousia. Though I briefly discuss the role of the question in Heidegger's views on knowledge in this chapter, my focus is on his challenge to ousia. The key to understanding the nature of Heideggerean challenge is to see that for Aristotle, not everything that existed was an ousia; he was quite willing to accept that his model of being was not universal. But there was no alternative to ousia as a model for interpreting the (natural or human) world. Where it did not apply, therefore, it should be made to. Heidegger's "challenge" to this view is simply to show that there is an alternative. He shows that certain things which cannot be described by ousiodic structures can be captured in another way, in terms of what I call the *diakena,* the gaps which grow and gather. *Being and Time* abounds in examples of such diakena. But because Heidegger does not see ousia as the object of his critique, *Being and Time* does not discuss or even admit what it so often and profoundly exemplifies: the diakenic structures of phenomena. These structures are not part of what the book *says* so much as of what it *shows.*[3]

EXAMPLES OF DIAKENA IN *BEING AND TIME*

I begin by discussing seven of *Being and Time*'s many examples of diakena. The discussion is meant to be introductory and provisional, for two reasons. First, it is only on the basis of a preliminary acquaintance with some examples of diakena can we begin to understand the "nature" of diakenicity itself, insofar as it has one. Second, as I have noted, *Being and Time* itself never goes beyond exemplifying diakena to discuss them for their own sake.

Example 1. Dasein, the being that we are, does not have at its core a unified essence or form (as did both the ancient soul and the modern subject). Rather it has three "equiprimordially" constitutive moments: understanding, discourse, and state-of-mind. These three moments of Dasein are never found apart:

> A state-of-mind always has its understanding, even if it keeps it suppressed. Understanding always has its state-of-mind. . . . The understandability of Being-in-the world, an understandability which goes with a state-of-mind, expresses itself as discourse.[4]

None of the three, then, can be what it is without its relation to the others; a state-of-mind, for example, is clarified and sharpened by the understanding that plays against it, and the clarifying and sharpening themselves are accomplished in discourse. But none can be reduced to the others, either, and there is no yet more basic unity to bring them together; in Heidegger's term, they are *gleichursprünglich,* equiprimordial. Heidegger himself is aware of the untraditional nature of this claim:

> The phenomenon of the *equiprimordiality* of constitutive moments has often been overlooked (*misachtet*) in ontology, because of a methodologically unbridled tendency towards tracing the derivation of anything and everything out of a simple "Urgrund." (*SZ,* p.131)

That Heidegger should mistake one of the basic gestures of metaphysics for a mere "methodological tendency" has its reasons, which I will bring out later. For the moment, one thing is clear: at the center of ourselves we find not a single unifying form but a space in which there play three mutually irreducible factors. Heidegger's name for this interplay is "care" (*Sorge*), and Dasein has no unity over and above the specific configurations which care assumes from time to time.[5]

The configuration which at any moment "unifies" an individual Dasein must be understood in terms of the three factors that constitute it—and each of these factors is to be understood in terms of the more general economy or configuration of which it is part, i.e., in terms of the other two. In this situation, understanding, state-of-mind, and discourse confront each other in a play which defines them all without subordinating any to the others or subjecting all of them to some higher or more general principle of unity. Each is what it is because of its *gap* with the others. The space of such gapping is the defining emptiness, or what I call the diakenon, at the core of Dasein.

Such an emptiness, simply because it is empty, cannot itself be made into a "phenomenon." But we see here that it can show itself indirectly, when three criteria are met: when a number of phenomena, (e.g. the three constitutive moments of Dasein) are related such that

A. none is adequately understood apart from the others;

B. none is the ground of the others, i.e., explains them;

C. no yet more basic phenomenon can ground, i.e., explain, all of them together.

These criteria are of course very general and indeed vague. (Also vague is the degree to which Heidegger's thought can and should fill them in on a general level or leave them to be determined in concrete situations). I refer to them respectively as the demands for "no indifference" of any to the others, "no reduction" of any to the others, and "no sublation" of them into a higher unity.

Example 2. Dasein can exist in two basic ways: authenticity and inauthenticity. These constitute a second diakenon. To begin with, there is no third possibility, and so all Dasein must be either authentic or inauthentic: "Dasein is mine to be in one [of these ways] or the other."[6] That these two basic ways for Dasein to be meet criterion A of diakenicity is clear. For authenticity and inauthenticity are not mutually indifferent; the very fact that they exhaust the possibilities for Dasein means that neither can be understood on its own terms alone. If we try to understand inauthenticity without regard to authenticity, we will conclude that there is no alternative to inauthenticity and thereby will fail to see that "inauthenticity is based on the possibility of authenticity" (SZ, p. 259). If we try to understand authenticity without regard to inauthenticity, we cannot see how it is really an alternative to or indeed (as Heidegger also says) a "modification" of inauthenticity (SZ, pp. 129, 131, 179).

But criteria B and C are not so clear. That authenticity is a "modification" of authenticity, which in turn is "based upon" the possibility of inauthenticity, certainly makes it sound as if the two stood in a complicated relationship of mutual grounding. And when Heidegger says that both inauthenticity and authenticity are "grounded" in Jemeinigkeit, mineness—that they are the two ways in which "Dasein is mine to be" (SZ, pp. 42f)—it seems as if he is invoking a more basic unity which grounds them both.

There is, however, more to "grounding," as the criteria above conceive it, than a simple causal relation. Indeed, criterion A, that diakenically unified phenomena are not mutually indifferent, itself suggests that they can be subjected to Humean versions of causality as a brute "constant conjunction" of ideas. Phenomena which are diakenically related, in other words, go together; the question is whether this co-occurrence can be explained. In order to show that one "grounds" the other, we must show that their connection is intelligible. Heidegger indicates this necessity in his association of "ground" with logos and when he writes that "a ground becomes accessible only as meaning, even if it is itself the abyss of meaninglessness" (SZ, pp. 32, 152). Are authenticity, inauthenticity, and mineness related to each other in ways that can be understood?

Mineness, for its part, is merely a characteristic of Dasein, the fact that it is always a human individual; it is not a way of Being, of encountering things and itself, for the individual (SZ, p. 41). Authenticity and inauthenticity are thus much richer conceptions than mineness, and it does not follow from the nature of mineness alone that Dasein can accept itself either authentically or inauthentically. Mineness therefore cannot provide an explanation of how Dasein comes to be authentic or inauthentic.[7] It thus seems as if criterion C holds: mineness does not qualify as a higher unity which can explain both authenticity and inauthenticity or into which they can be sublated. And it is *Being and Time*'s only candidate for such a higher unity.

What about criterion B? Can the relation of authenticity to inauthenticity be understood by making either basic to the other?

This question can be sharpened in two stages. In order to establish a "ground" as a meaningful connection among other things, we must first be able to say what those other things are. Thus *Being and Time* could show that authenticity grounds inauthenticity or vice-versa only if there were some standpoint from which both could be articulated. But authenticity and inauthenticity themselves, as the two basic ways in which Dasein encounters itself and other things, are the only possibilities for such a standpoint. The question of whether authenticity and inauthenticity can be intelligibly grounded in one another thus becomes the question of whether either standpoint offers the resources to understand the other for what it is. If so, then grounding in the sense of criterion B is at least possible; if not, then not.

This question can be sharpened again. *Being and Time* is itself the first and so far the most sustained attempt to state phenomenologically what authenticity and inauthenticity are. It must itself be written from either an authentic or an inauthentic standpoint. From which?

In the introduction to this book, I discussed the difficulties Heidegger has with bringing his later versions of authenticity and inauthenticity together in his later writings, where there is no difference between what the texts are about and how they operate. But *Being and Time* proceeds in a more traditionally descriptive (or interpretive) way. So the Augustinian solution I mentioned in the introduction ought to be open to Heidegger here: he could "remember forgetting," i.e., inauthenticity, if a sign of forgetting, rather than the reality of it, is "in" his description. And such would surely be the case; the words in Heidegger's phenomenological accounts of authenticity and inauthenticity are presumably mere signs of the thing itself. But if the relation of the two is diakenic, I have just argued, it will comport a measure of incommensurability and there will not be any such thing as a "sign" which could represent one way of being to someone who is "in" the other. I maintain that such is the case and that a unified account of Dasein is impossible.

Being and Time clearly cannot be written from the standpoint of inauthenticity, because inauthenticity is defined as the loss (forgetting) of that of which authenticity is the recovery (Being towards death; *SZ*, pp. 44, 62, 129f, and 339 and ¶ 57.). Authenticity, then, cannot be understood by inauthentic Dasein without such Dasein recovering what it has forgotten and ceasing to be inauthentic. That, I take it, is one reason why the "call of conscience" which summons inauthentic Dasein to authenticity can have no content; if Dasein understood the call clearly and concretely, as applying for example to Dasein's own circumstances at the moment, it would already be authentic.[8] The same goes for *Being and Time* itself: if it has the terms with which to describe authenticity, then it must be written from an authentic standpoint. Indeed, Heidegger says, inauthentic Dasein will deny that the descriptions he gives of its own nature, to say (perhaps) nothing of authentic Dasein's, are valid (*SZ*, p. 175).

But *Being and Time* cannot be written from an authentic standpoint either, though Heidegger seems to have tried. For authentic Dasein knows too much—or thinks it knows too much—to be able to take inauthenticity on its own terms. That is what happens in *Being and Time*'s portrayal of inauthenticity in ¶¶ 27 and 35-38. This "description" proceeds in strongly pejorative terms instead of the laudatory language with which inauthentic Dasein refers to itself throughout the section—to such an extent, as I have noted, that Heidegger says that inauthentic Dasein would not accept this portrayal of itself. This pejorative language is in spite of Heidegger's warning that his interpretation "has a purely ontological intention, and is far removed from a moralizing critique of everyday Dasein"—a warning which is repeated no fewer than six times.[9]

Heidegger's warning, intended perhaps for himself most of all, is surely appropriate, for he has just noted that what he is describing is not a set of sinful lapses or an otherwise defective condition of Dasein but an "essential tendency of Being of everydayness" (*SZ*, pp. 16). The pejorative language in which *Being and Time* treats inauthenticity is not only not what inauthenticity would say about itself; it is also not the kind of neutral description a phenomenological investigation, oriented to "the things themselves," would adopt, especially as regards an "essential tendency of Being." Given the existence of these warnings, it is also clear that the use of such language is not a mere lapse of Heidegger's due to lack of awareness or attention. It is instead, I suggest, inherent in the nature of authenticity itself; having recovered Being, it cannot but look down upon Dasein, which has not done so. Thus, when we attempt to find words that would describe inauthenticity from an authentic standpoint in a nonpejorative way, we find ourselves at a loss, just as Heidegger apparently did.

The outbreak of pejorative language in *Being and Time* indicates, I suggest, a failed attempt to write the book from an authentic perspective. Authenticity inescapably looks down upon inauthentic Dasein and distorts its nature: *Being and Time* describes how inauthenticity looks not to itself but to authentic Dasein. The description fails because, using value-laden language, it distorts the inauthenticity it purports to describe. It renders it almost impossible not to perceive inauthenticity as a moral failing, which in fact it is not. On the other hand, inauthenticity, having "forgotten" being, has for its part no resources to understand Dasein which has made this recovery.

Authenticity and inauthenticity are thus mutually incomprehensible. It is unsurprising, then, that the nature of the "modification" by which inauthenticity is converted into authenticity should remain in some ways highly mysterious. The transformation of Dasein from inauthentic to authentic and back is not, for example, the intelligible result of a process of growth or education; nor is it the result of a moral resolution. It is portrayed as a sudden and unpredictable transformation at the heart of Dasein itself, in which Dasein passes from one to the other in the "blink of an eye" (SZ, pp. 297f, 328, 371, and esp. p. 338). Dasein, in other words, appears to oscillate between two basically different ways of Being, one of which—inauthenticity—is usual and standard and the other of which "overcomes" it at times. Neither is derived from the other, and no higher unity is possible; but both, like the interplay of understanding, state-of-mind, and discourse, define each other and Dasein itself. In all this, the relation between authenticity and inauthenticity shows itself as what I call a diakenic relation.[10]

Example 3. A third diakenon, connected with the first two, is between temporality and what I call "relative atemporality." The most basic organizational move of the published portion of Being and Time is to present the structures of Dasein twice, first in terms of everydayness or inauthenticity, which sees them under the domination of the present and hence as relatively static or atemporal, and then in terms of the three "ecstasies" of time authentically understood (SZ, p. 234f). The two halves of the book fall apart so radically that it is quite possible to read the second part ("Division II") on its own if one is given explanations of the terms of art introduced in the first part ("Division I"). And the first part is so independent of the second that an important English-language commentary restricts itself to just the first part.[11] The connection between the two divisions, in other words, is so loose as to seem—in spite of Heidegger's own protestations—to violate criterion A of diakenicity: they seem to be indifferent to one another. Yet they are not. The relative atemporality of the first presentation cannot be understood except as preparatory to the subsequent presentation. Again, there is no higher standpoint, somehow at once static and truly temporal, which can present both. While it is possible that Heidegger, had he had time, would have articulated such a standpoint, as matters stand Divisions I and II are thus themselves in a diakenic interplay.[12]

And this interplay itself relates diakenically to the other two diakena. The distinction between authenticity and inauthenticity (2) cannot, to begin with, be understood separately from that between authentic temporality and relative atemporality (3). For to be "inauthentic" is, at bottom, to deny one's own temporality, to deny that one not merely has but is a past and a future and that one's future contains, as its final event, death (SZ, pp. 233f). The flight from future death is the flight into a present inauthentically assumed to be eternal and hence into a relatively atemporal view of one's own Being. But the relation of dependence here is unclear; it does not follow from the nature of time that there should be a being, Dasein, which can deny its past and future in favor of its present. Nor can we deduce Dasein's authentic temporality directly from its structure, for if that were possible the inauthentic account of this structure in Division I would be unnecessary.

Diakenon (1) also cannot be understood without taking into account the nature of time. For Heidegger, time's ecstasies—past, present, and future— are *generically* distinct, and none can be reduced to the others. Understanding, showing us possibilities, is geared to the future, state-of-mind, revealing "how things [already] stand with us," to the past. Discourse is geared to the present (*SZ*, ¶ 68). To find a "simple *Urgrund*" at the core of Dasein would be to violate the nature of time itself. But there is nothing about the nature of time that dictates that it should have these three ecstasies and no others and nothing about any or all of them which dictates that there should be a being which contains basic factors geared to each.

To say that these three diakena themselves stand in diakenic relationships is to say that while they clearly go together, no clear derivation of any from the others or from any higher principle can be given. But it is not to deny that some are more basic than others. Dasein's three core moments are responses to time, which in turn becomes manifest through them. Time and Dasein are thus irreducible to one another, even as they condition and reveal one another: two more "equiprimordials." Inauthenticity is likewise a way of responding to time, one which denies the mutual irreducibility of its three ecstasies. Authenticity allows this diakenic nature of time to be experienced.[13]

Example 4. Time itself is thus for Heidegger the overarching diakenon in this series. The nature of time for Heidegger, and of our response to it, is a matter too large to discuss in detail here.[14] Suffice it that, as I noted, past, present, and future are from his point of view generically distinct from one another. The future is not simply a present which has not yet come to be, any more than the past is a present which has already been. Rather the future (*Zukunft*), which is basic, is the unknowable domain out of which possibilities—including Dasein's ownmost potentiality, that for death—encounter it: "It is the coming (*Kunft*) in which Dasein, in its ownmost potentiality for Being, comes towards itself" (*SZ*, p. 325). The phenomenologically accessible past is that toward which such possibilities come:

> As authentically futural, Dasein is authentically as *having been*. Anticipation of one's uttermost and ownmost possibility is coming back understandingly to one's ownmost "been." (*SZ*, p. 326)

And the present authentically understood is the resultant state of affairs, the outcome of the past understood in light of the future:

> The character of having-been arises from the future, and in such a way that the future which "has been" (or, better, which "is in the process of having been") is the present. (*SZ*, p. 326)

It is to the three "ecstasies" of Heideggerean time that the constitutive moments of Dasein are diakenically geared: understanding reveals futural possibilities in things and in the environment (SZ, ¶ 31); state-of-mind is a cognitively significant type of mood and shows Dasein how its past is conditioning its current state, i.e. "how things are with us" (SZ, ¶ 29); and discourse articulates the other two into a horizon of current significance. And it is this diakenic structure of time which is either authentically accepted or inauthentically forgotten.

This brief characterization of time and its fundamental nature for Heidegger allows us at least to glimpse the measure of his assault upon metaphysics. For Aristotle had designated time as an "enemy" of ousia, not just in the sense that the passage of time in itself seems to destroy ousia but in that time does not seem to "participate" in ousia, cannot be captured or understood in ousiodic categories.[15] By rendering time basic to Dasein and to Being itself (a move implicit in *Being and Time*'s very title) and by giving time the character not of a domain structured by a single basic principle (the present) but of a diakenic interplay, Heidegger has set himself radically against Aristotle and against the whole development of metaphysics that I have narrated in this book. When Heidegger presents beings in accordance with his version of temporality, according to which they are shaped by an unknown future, he cannot help presenting them diakenically. Though that does not account for all the instances of diakena which I discuss in this chapter and the next, diakenic presentation is a long way from the questioning of presence (to which I return at the end of this chapter).

The introduction of time as an overarching diakenon leads to a further set of diakena, which have a different structure from the ones I have previously adduced. The diakena discussed so far have a temporal structure of dynamic synchronicity. In them, two or more irreducible incommensurables confront each other in a play which defines both without subjecting them to any higher principle of unity, so that each becomes what it is through its gap from the others. The incommensurables do not simply coexist in a mutually indifferent stasis, but neither has a temporal priority. Thus Dasein passes from inauthenticity to authenticity *and back* in the "blink of an eye." At times, Dasein's response to time is an *Ergreifen*, a resolute grasping of possibilities (so that the initiative comes from Dasein); at other times, it is a mere "waiting" so that the initiative is with time itself and what it delivers or withholds (SZ, pp. 261f, 243, 337). And from one moment to the next, Dasein can be invested primarily in its understanding, its state-of-mind, or its discourse, though the others are still there (if as "suppressed"; cf. SZ, p. 142f; ¶¶ 29–32).

But the basic nature of time for Heidegger means that any entity has a concrete past and future as well as a determinate present. Another kind of diakenon in *Being and Time* operates in terms of this nature and so has a diachronic character; one side precedes the other in time, so that the two appear as incommensurable phases of a single development. Because the development is a single one, the two phases are not mutually indifferent. But neither of them is basic to the other, and there is no third characteristic which is basic to both phases in such a way as to "underlie" the development. While we can say *that* there is a development from one phase to the other, we cannot say in what it consists. As Heidegger puts it in *The Question of Being*, "It rests in a play which, the more richly it unfolds itself, remains the more strictly bound to a *hidden* rule."[16]

Example 5. Such diachronicity is to some extent true of discourse, which—though it is one factor among the three and can, at any given moment, be or not be primary for Dasein—is always directed upon the specific features of understanding and state-of-mind which it articulates and which must, therefore, already be given to it (*SZ*, p. 133; ¶ 31). Discourse thus belongs in a temporal sequence in which, though (as I noted in discussing diakena 1) it is never developed out of understanding and state-of-mind in an intelligible way, it somehow always follows on them.

Example 6. Another example of a diachronic diakenon is what Heidegger calls the "assertion." Its basic structure is indicated by the word "as" (*SZ*, p. 154). The "as-structure" of an assertion means that I do not, for example, "assert" that the grass is green; rather, I affirm the grass *as* green. We can clarify this point by seeing how it differs from other, more traditional accounts of predication. In Hobbesian terms, as I noted in chapter 6, the subject and predicate of a true sentence name the same thing: greenness "coincides" with the grass in that both are accidents of the same body. In more up-to-date terms, we might say that both "greenness" and "grassiness" are satisfied by the same object or sequence. In a Heideggerean assertion, by contrast, they are not; to affirm the grass *as* green is to recognize that, in some respects, it is not green but, say, largely yellow or even brown. The properties of being grass and being green are not, then, "united" in the object. Rather the assertion only partially connects greenness with grassiness. The as-structure thus holds apart, opens a gap between, what conventional grammar calls the subject and predicate of a sentence. What I *assert* is not "the grass is green" but something much more complicated, along the lines of "I, right now, for purposes of the moment, am taking the grass as green (even though, upon examination or in other contexts, it is not strictly green)." As Heidegger puts it,

> The pointing-out which assertion does is performed on the basis of what has already been disclosed in understanding, or discovered circumspectively. Assertion is not a free-floating kind of behavior which, in its own right, might be capable of disclosing beings in general in a primary way; on the contrary, it always maintains itself on the basis of Being-in-the-world. (*SZ*, p. 154)

While predication traditionally conceived is a matter of yes and no, Heideggerean assertion is thus a matter of more and less. The predicate is not stated to apply exactly to the subject but only to a degree. This degree cannot usually be specified, certainly not by the assertion itself. How can I possibly list the manifold ways in which this lawn is not quite green? It is this unspecifiable degree of difference which places subject and predicate into a diakenic relationship, holding them apart in such a way as to characterize both.

In Tarski's famous example of a true sentence, "snow is white,"[17] there occur two universal terms: "snow" and "white." If Tarski had instead given a sentence more closely related to actual observation, such as "that patch of snow over there is white," he would have introduced a whole series of problems concerning the exact color of that patch. For any patch of snow is, like any patch of grass, in fact of myriad colors, as light and surrounding objects play upon it. This suggests that our reports of observations are more like Heidegger's "assertions" than like Tarski's "sentences." Except in rare and highly artificial cases which, Heidegger claims, have no right to be paradigmatic of all utterances, our statements are really assertions, in which the predicate does not exactly describe the subject (which itself may not exactly be described by the word used to designate it). Subject and predicate are connected for Heidegger not merely in virtue of properties actually exhibited by the objects they refer to but by a whole network of concerns and contexts which lead to my making the assertion and to the particular predicate I use being (perhaps) the best available.

The assertion so conceived has a specific kind of temporality. On the one hand, I make an assertion only on the basis of what I *already* know about the world—of what cognitive psychologists and others call "background information." The "already known" here includes as well the entity which the assertion is about, for I cannot, with my assertion, give something a definite character unless it has already been disclosed to me independently of this character having been made definite:

> In accordance with this [as-] structure, something is understood with respect to something—it is taken together with it, yet in such a way that this *understanding* confrontation *interpretatively* articulates it, and takes apart what has been taken together.

In order for my assertion to throw an x up against a y, to take it *as* y, whatever it is that I designate as "x" must be given in advance of my making the assertion and also in advance of what I designate as "y." Hence the "x as y" formula for the Heideggerean assertion designates a temporal process. "That grass over there is green" and "That green over there is grass" are then two different assertions. In one, I have perceived the grass and take it as green, so that the movement is

$$\text{grassiness} \rightarrow \text{greenness} \rightarrow \text{assertion.}$$

In the other, I have perceived the green and take it as grass, so that the movement is greenness → grassiness → assertion.

In both cases, the relation between the first two stages and the third is what I call diakenic; it is not possible to explain how it is that the perception of greenness and grassiness leads me to make the assertion that I make without spelling out the whole set of contexts and purposes that constitute my concrete Being-in-the-world at the moment I make the assertion—which is impossible. Similarly, the relation between the greenness and grassiness that I attribute to part of my environment and the actual properties that it has is intrinsically unspecifiable.

One important result of this kind of diakenon being intrinsic to (much) speech is that the true proposition is no longer the paradigm of cognition. Rather, knowing becomes the experiencing of gaps; its paradigm is not the answer, but the question. Thus in spite of *Being and Time*'s optimistic talk about answering the question of Being (*SZ*, pp. 11, 39), the book's actual aim—at least in its published portion—is not to answer this question but to "pose" it and "work it out."[18] Correspondingly, the "level" of any science is not indicated by the number of truths it has established but by the degree to which it is capable of undergoing a crisis in its basic concepts (*SZ*, p. 9). Similarly with speech: its paradigm is not merely the utterance but a plurality of phenomena which include hearing (which precedes speaking) and keeping silent (which opens gaps within a conversation; cf. *SZ*, p. 163f).

Example 7. Another diachronic diakenon is provided by the phenomenon of truth. Rejecting traditional attempts, from Aristotle on, to see truth as residing in the simultaneity of sentence and fact, Heidegger presents it in ¶ 44 of *Being and Time* as a temporal development. He explicitly identifies it with confirmation and identifies confirmation as the two-stage presentation of a single entity. Thus when someone with her back to a wall hears that the picture she is standing next to is askew and believes it, her belief is about the picture—not, for example, about a mental image which she forms as a result of hearing the statement. The statement and the belief are for Heidegger just two ways of presenting the picture itself—as askew. When she turns around and sees that the picture really is hanging crookedly, the statement and belief are confirmed.

But the confirmation occurs across a gap, one derived from the structure of the assertion. The sentence "the picture is hanging askew" gives us a more-and-less, but one which is much less exact than what we see with our own eyes. In order to have our vision confirm the utterance (or belief), we must make the same kind of leap the original utterer did; we must agree that the predicate "askew" is sufficiently applicable to the picture that the utterance is confirmed. A fraction of an inch the other way and the utterance would be disconfirmed; we would say that the picture is hanging straight. But, again, we would not be able to specify exactly why; it would be a matter of feel, of linguistic know-how. For here again the gap between "concept" and "reality"—or between what Heidegger calls two different presentations of the same entity—cannot be measured with exactitude and must simply be leaped across. Or, to put it another way: sometimes we can say *that* an assertion has been confirmed without being able to say exactly *why*.

The idea that a single development or process can have multiply discontinuous stages in its presentation while remaining somehow unified will be seen in the next chapter to be central to Heidegger's later work.[19] That which resides in the interstices, bringing the different phases of a phenomenon together without itself being anything over and above them, is what I call a gathering emptiness or diakenon. Unifying the phenomenon from within its interstices, it is an immanent principle like Aristotelian form. But it cannot be identified with any single phase or property of the thing and, as empty, cannot be distinguished from other emptinesses; so it is also external. Perhaps it is Being itself, for the Being of a being, Heidegger tells us, is not itself a being (*SZ*, p. 6).

In sum, then, *Being and Time* puts forward a number of examples of what I call diakena. We still do not understand very well, of course, what these examples really signify. And *Being and Time* will not tell us. For even as Heidegger uncovers one diakenon after another, he is hedging bets, wavering, and encountering problems and unclarities. Thus, though understanding, state-of-mind, and discourse are supposed to be equiprimordial, discourse seems to have a certain priority over the other two—precisely because it can articulate them.[20] Similarly, given the pejorative language in which inauthenticity is articulated, it is tempting (and Derrida has succumbed)[21] to see authenticity as the plenitude of Dasein, with inauthenticity as a sort of privation. Similarly again for the verifying gaze at the picture itself, which stands as the telos of the process of confirmation (or of truth) and which seems to smack more than a bit of the "full presence" appealed to by Husserl's "Principle of Principles."[22] And, finally, the view that the predicates of assertions never fully coincide with their subjects (in their objects) seems to run against an ancient paradox: How can we know that the grass is not *exactly* green unless we know, with some exactitude, what green really is? Must not some sort of presence be presupposed even by the assertion?

It is not my purpose here to answer these objections, though I believe that answers are possible. What is important is that Heidegger's attack on ousia, we see, is radical. But its radicality is not evident in *Being and Time*. Heidegger's treatment there is not only problematic but is accompanied by an ambivalence about ousia—an ambivalence which he cannot even articulate. To see this ambivalence in a developed form and show why Heidegger cannot clarify his own attitude or even make it consistent, I turn to *Being and Time*'s account of "world."

WORLD

Heidegger's critique of Cartesian subjectivity is famous indeed, lauded by Hubert Dreyfus, Richard Rorty, and many others.[23] It is noteworthy, then, that the main treatment of Descartes in *Being and Time* (¶¶ 19-21) should be directed not against *res cogitans* but against *res extensa*, not against the self-enclosed Cartesian subject but against extended substance. For Descartes, Heidegger says, "Extension in length, breadth, and depth constitutes the authentic Being of that corporeal substance which we call 'world'" (*SZ*, p. 90). It is this Cartesian conception of world as *res extensa* which Heidegger wants to distinguish from his own and criticize. As he reconstructs Descartes's argument, all other physical properties—e.g., *divisio, figura, motus,* and the like—are to be thought of as inhering in matter as extended; but matter's extension cannot be thought of as inhering in them. Extension is thus the most permanent property of a material thing, the one that must remain the same while all others can change:

> That in the corporeal thing which suffices for its remaining constant [*ständigen Verbleib*] is the authentic Being in it, to such a degree that the substantiality of the substance is characterized through it. (*SZ*, p. 92)

In contrast to his extended treatment and critique of this view, Heidegger's explicit critique of Descartes's view of the subject is merely a terse corollary of the critique of *res extensa*. It amounts to the view that Descartes "takes the Being of 'Dasein' . . . in the very same way he takes the Being of the *res extensa*—namely, as substance" (*SZ*, p. 98). While Descartes investigates the *cogito* of *cogito ergo sum,* he leaves the *sum* unexamined, simply equating it with presence-to-hand and thus with remaining constant (*SZ*, pp. 24, 46, 203f, 211).

The view that Being is definable as remaining constant leads Descartes, in Heidegger's view, to various other problems. Most central to Heidegger's critique is that, as he points out, to characterize substance as that in a thing which is "sufficient to its remaining constant" amounts to defining substance in terms of self-sufficiency. And only one substance, God, is truly self-sufficient. All others must be produced by him and are "finite," while he alone is "infinite" (*SZ*, p. 92f). "Substance" is thus for Descartes a systematically ambiguous term; it means one thing when applied to God and something radically different when applied to anything else. Descartes makes no attempt to bring these two meanings into any kind of connection (remaining in this respect, Heidegger observes, far behind the Scholastic doctrines of analogy). Indeed, Heidegger points out, Descartes goes so far as to deny that substance can even be known; all that can be known of it are its "attributes" (*SZ*, p. 94). Because of this, substance is understood in terms of that in it which encounters us—and not just any attributes, but those which are most adapted to the previously assumed vision of Being as permanence. "Being," then, is not only ambiguous; its various meanings have no discernible relation to each other at all, and no unitary account of it is possible.

It is not accidental that Heidegger's critique is directed against *res extensa*. The designation of material objects as extended things was for him Descartes's first *overt* wrong move and was motivated by Descartes's covert view that remaining constant is the defining characteristic of Being. With this act of submission to the dominance of presence, Descartes introduced self-sufficiency as the defining criterion of substance and opened the way for Being to fall apart into many beings that were finite and one that was infinite. And he also rendered Being necessarily unknowable, for what we can know of a thing are only the ways in which it affects us, and those are always transitory.

Heidegger, then, is criticizing the notion that beings have extension before they have any other properties. In terms of the current narrative, his attack is directed not only against Descartes but also against both the Hobbesian and the Thomistic conceptions of body. But these conceptions, we saw, were part and parcel of the docilization of matter. For to be docile was simply to have boundaries and nothing else. Otherwise, as with Aristotle, form will have to establish boundaries which are foreign to and hence possibly resistible by matter.

We are thus entitled to ask: If Heidegger's critique of the Cartesian conception of world is really directed against the post-Aristotelian concept of docilized matter, might it not be conducted in the service of something resembling Aristotelian ousia? In other words, if the Heideggerean world does not exhibit the docile permanence of post-Aristotelian ousia, does it exhibit features of the original Aristotelian conception? If so, Heidegger's attitude toward ousia will be ambivalent; he will dislike it in certain cases (those in which he introduces the diakena), but in other cases (e.g., that of world) he will accept it. It will then be hopeless to look in *Being and Time* for a coherent critique of Aristotelian ousia itself—or for any coherent account of the diakena, the engines of this critique.

Does the Heideggerean world exhibit the structures of an Aristotelian ousia? At first, it seems unlikely. Heidegger further accuses Descartes of what seem to be other Aristotelian sins: of taking a part and mistaking it for the whole (as when Aristotle, though with more awareness than Heidegger attributes to Descartes, reduces the moral agent to his reason; cf. *SZ*, p. 97). In this respect, Descartes is said to "dictate" and "prescribe" to the world what its Being must be (*SZ*, p. 96). In Heidegger's view, it seems, Descartes conceives of a world whose dominating form is permanence itself. That, for Heidegger, is why mathematics is Descartes's paradigm of knowing—not just because, as a great mathematician, he loved and admired the discipline (*SZ*, p. 97).

So far, what Heidegger seems to be criticizing in Descartes are parametric activities of ousia, the ways in which it functions to structure Descartes's ontological discourse, indeed to make that discourse possible at all. Heidegger's own account of world, we might expect, will not attribute to it a dominant form—or, at least, not *this* sort of dominant form. Has it any other?

World for Heidegger is encountered through "equipment," the things we use and the more or less organized structures which permit us to use them; any tool is "essentially something for the sake of" something else. The objects and arrangements within which and for which a tool can be used constitute its "context of involvement." And these contexts themselves are useful for wider contexts and more distant purposes. My pen is useful for putting ink on paper, which can become a postcard to be sent by airplane across the world to an absent friend. The pen only works well indoors, out of wind and rain; my house is in turn a "tool for dwelling," a *Wohnzeug* (*SZ*, p. 68f). And all this teleology, like Aristotle's, comes to a final end: the different tools I use, and the contexts of involvement through which I move, eventually arrive at a point beyond which there is no further purpose or involvement, no wider "for the sake of." This ultimate point is Dasein itself, going about its Being (*SZ*, p. 84). The various contexts of use and involvement thus constitute an overarching unity, which Heidegger calls "world": "The context of the tool lights up . . . as a whole which has already been [unthematically] envisioned. With this, world announces itself" (*SZ*, p. 75). World thus has an explicitly teleological structure. Its most basic components—individual tools—also have their various kinds of materiality: "Hammer, tongs, and needle of themselves refer to—are constituted of—steel, iron, mineral, stone, wood" (*SZ*, p. 70). Having matter in this way, tools also have form, in virtue of which the natural components become serviceable to Dasein. The Heideggerean world, like the Aristotelian cosmos, is thus a whole of material beings brought together, through their forms, for the realization of a single telos.

Since what counts as serviceable or not is determined by the overall criterion of usefulness to Dasein, this criterion serves as a general, if relatively empty, form for the Heideggerean world. Moreover, world so structured disposes of its parts: the tools and contexts which make it up are shaped and determined by their usefulness to Dasein. World does this so well that these tools and contexts are unnoticed—as long as they function properly. It is only when a tool fails—when there is a *Bruch* in the ongoing project of using things—that our circumspection "comes up against nothingness" and we become aware of the contexts that together constitute our world (*SZ*, pp. 73-75).

World is thus known, for Heidegger, not through the plenitude of forms it presents but through the breaks and emptinesses which occasionally intervene in its smooth functioning. But these breaks and emptinesses are not like the diakena that we saw before. They are not gathering forces which themselves shape world but simply checks, privations of function which occasion the wider awareness of involvement. The involvement they reveal is not gathered and shaped by them but is already there. To reiterate a passage previously quoted in part:

> The context of equipment is lit up, not as something never seen before, but as a totality constantly sighted beforehand in circumspection. With this totality, however, the world announces itself. (*SZ*, p. 75)

Equipmental breakdowns not only do not impeach the overall disposition of world but serve to reinforce it. For defective equipment, of course, does not lead only to ruminations on what would have happened if it functioned properly; it does more than merely illuminate preexisting contexts of involvement. It also presents itself as a problem in need of solution, a defect in need of repair. And when repairs are effected and the problem is solved, these contexts of involvement are reinstated. The situation is similar, in fact, to that with the Aristotelian household. As we saw, household slaves are not noticed as long as they carry out their orders faithfully. When one fails to do so—when his servile rationality reveals itself as deficient—he draws the baneful attention of his master, and the situation is rectified: the structures of the household are reinforced. In the present case, the checks and failures of equipment, though "nothingnesses," are not *creative* nothingnesses; they do not shape world but merely provide occasions to reveal and reinforce it.

In addition to this version of dispositive power, world has as well strict, though unclear, limits. In ¶ 17, Heidegger argues that contexts of involvement are contexts of significance: to "understand" something is to know what it can be used for and what is used for it. Language itself, as a vehicle of understanding, is thus an inner-worldly phenomenon (*SZ*, ¶¶ 32, 34; p. 87), and to go beyond world would take Dasein beyond its language; in Wittgenstein's famous phrase, "the limits of my language are the limits of my world."[24] That is why Dasein, leaving world behind in authenticity, cannot go anywhere else and is simply restored—though now "authentically" committed—to its previous world. For there is, in *Being and Time*, no escape from world:

> The world is . . . something in which Dasein as a being already *was*, and whenever it in any way explicitly comes away from something, it can never do anything more than come back to the world. (*SZ*, p. 76; cf. p. 118)

This quote shows, finally, that world, again like an Aristotelian *ti ên einai*, is essentially related to the past. As such, world is what Heidegger calls an "a priori perfect," something which structures our lives because it has already been in place all along (*SZ*, p. 85). It follows that Dasein's inherence in its world is knowledge of the past, given in state-of-mind (*SZ*, p. 139). And it follows that inherence in world is a denial of the future; it is a consigning of oneself to structures derived from the past and is ineluctably inauthentic. Inauthentic Dasein is thus Dasein which understands itself in terms of its world alone (*SZ*, pp. 144, 146).

Thus, even as Heidegger instates world as exemplifying the bounded and disposing structures of an Aristotelian ousia, he is preparing a critique of it—or of Dasein's allowing itself to be determined by it. Since world itself is of the past, the vehicle of this critique will be the future, and here we see one crucial respect in which Heideggerean world differs from an Aristotelian ousia. Both are teleologically structured. But an ousia, we have seen, is structured by its form, by a determinate and intelligible nature. World is structured by Dasein's concern for its own possibilities. But Dasein's possibilities are not, ultimately, the Aristotelian plenitude of the life of reason. For Dasein's ultimate end is death, its "ownmost, unrelational, and inescapable possibility" (*SZ*, p. 250; the whole of pp. 248–250 is relevant here). And death is entirely indeterminate; it is only the "possibility of the total impossibility of Dasein."[25]

That frees Dasein from the dominance of world without taking it out of world altogether. For the awareness of death enables Dasein to get a view of its world and of the possibilities its world offers as something approaching (though never reaching) a whole. In the awareness of death as its own immanent (but unknown) telos, Dasein no longer takes up its possibilities piecemeal as its world offers them but does so in the light of its own conscious freedom (*SZ*, p. 263f). Being authentic is thus being toward death.

In spite of the Aristotelian structures of Heideggerean world, then, at bottom Heidegger's conception turns out to be something quite different. For the telos which shapes world and renders it authentically accessible is the unfathomable mystery of death. Like the various checks and failures of equipment, death as a phenomenon makes the structures of world accessible to Dasein; but it is also responsible for these structures, for it is the final possibility which gathers and accounts for all the rest. It is then a nothing which gathers, a diakenon.

But this valorization of the diakenic basis of world remains below the surface of *Being and Time*. World, as I have argued elsewhere, is problematic for Heidegger—it is the "non-object to which we are ever subject" and will, in "The Origin of the Work of Art," be deposed in favor of earth and sky.[26] But the critique of world in *Being and Time* remains covered over by the even more searching, and perhaps more urgent, critique of the present-at-hand, of the being viewed merely as something which "remains constant." Indeed, when Heidegger maintains, as he does throughout *Being and Time*, that the readiness-to-hand of the tool is an ontologically more primary way of encountering things than the theoretical perspective of presence-at-hand, it certainly sounds as if he thought highly of world. Ousiodic structure in itself, in other words, is not an explicit problem in *Being and Time*; the problem is remaining constant, presence-at-hand, or just simply presence.

THE QUESTIONING OF PRESENCE

Heidegger's treatment of world in *Being and Time* is related to what I have called his questioning of presence, and in ways that make problems for Heidegger, both as a philosopher and as a person. I have argued that, in *Being and Time,* Heidegger fails to articulate clearly the negative side of world, the fact that, in spite of its diakenic telos, it is a bounded and disposing unit. Heidegger thus does not see that what he is in fact challenging are structures of ousia. The suspicion arises that ousia, as far as Heidegger is aware, is not the problem. This suspicion is enhanced when we note that Heidegger speaks highly of the Aristotelian *analogia entis* (the doctrine that what resides in plenitude in a fully formed "actual existent" is approximated by other beings, whose nature is defined by the approximation), as well as of its Scholastic descendants (*SZ*, pp. 3, 93).[27] For the *analogia entis* clearly goes together with Aristotle's hylomorphism, according to which some beings can possess a form in plenary fashion (e. g., as mature free males possessed the human form; see chap. 1), while others are intrinsically deficient (e.g., as I noted in the same chapter, women, children, and slaves).

Suspicions multiply when we look at Heidegger's critique of the Aristotelian immanence of form in matter in "On the Essence and Concept of Physis in Aristotle's *Physics* B.1," written in 1939.[28] Heidegger there criticizes the conception of such immanence, not because it is an imposition of the one on the other (and still less because what it imposes is a relation of domination) but because it allows matter to be an independent principle at all. Heidegger phenomenalizes ousia to such an extent that Aristotelian beings actually lose their materiality (as Thomistic ones did; see chapter 3). The coming-to-be of an Aristotelian ousia, thus phenomenalized, is the self-showing of a form. And with that, "*morphê* is not merely more *physis* than *hylê* but solely and completely [*physis*]."[29] Another way to put it is that, for Heidegger, *physis*—or emergence into unconcealment—is to explain not merely the essence of the thing but its existence as well.[30] Hence, he claims, *physis* as *eidos*—as form—is all there is to a thing. Matter is not an independent principle but merely form still "setting itself into" the opening of disclosure.

At the other (temporal) extreme of metaphysics, consider this passage from Heidegger's *Nietzsche,* which refers to

> the reserve [*Bestand*] of present beings which is immediately disposable for the will (*ousia* in the everyday meaning of the word among the Greeks). What is reserved [*das Beständige*] is however stabilized [*wird jedoch zu einem Ständigen*], i.e., rendered something which constantly stands at [one's] disposal, in that it is brought to a stand through a positing. . . .[31]

Though there is here a passing reference to ousia (property) as "disposable" for the will of the owner, the emphasis slides quickly to being "stabilized." Stability is, of course, explained by the substance-ontology of Aristotle's *Categories;* indeed, the *Categories'* avoidance of issues concerning affection and change suggest that it can account for little else. But there is more to ownership than stability. What I own is not merely ready for me but is something that I can order and arrange (disposition) and whose fruits I enjoy (initiative). Heidegger does not seem to see the importance of these other two traits or that his famous questioning of presence is, on at least one of its many levels, a challenge to what I call ousia.

But the most fateful evidence that Heidegger in *Being and Time* fails to understand the anti-ousiodic bent of his own thought is the book's own conflation of the Greek words *ousia* and *parousia* and its equation of the former with "presence." On page 25, he refers to *"parousia* or *ousia,* which signifies, in ontologico-temporal terms 'presence.'" The singular verb is telling; as the translators MacQuarrie and Robinson note, "Heidegger suggests that *ousia* is to be thought of as synonymous with the derivative noun *parousia,* [which] has a close etymological correspondence with the German *Anwesenheit.*" On the next page, Heidegger goes on to identify *ousia* (not *parousia*) with *Anwesenheit,* further confusing the two terms.

Heideggers essay "The Anaximander Fragment," in spite of its careful dissociation of various Greek and German words for presence, also relentlessly pursues the conflation of ousia and presence, as taken for granted (*offenkündig*); it calls *parousia* (actually, the related form *pareonta*) an "elucidation" (*Verdeutlichung*) of *ousia* but again does not distinguish their meanings—a point at which Jacques Derrida, in "Ousia and Grammê," throws up his hands and simply quotes the entire paragraph.[32]

This equation of ousia with presence is a constant theme with Heidegger.[33] I have noted that, he himself identified it as the "flash of genius" which determined his entire path of thought. As Winfred Franzen has put it,

> The basic thesis of Heideggerean philosophy of history goes like this: "Being, from the early days of the Greek to the recent time of our century means: presence."[34]

In Greek, however, the terms *ousia* and *parousia* have radically distinct meanings. The language, indeed, wears this difference on its face: "presence" (*hê parousia*) is compounded out of *para-,* meaning "by" or "at," and *ousia,* meaning "ousia." Presence is thus something that happens to an ousia, namely that it finds itself "at" or "by" something else. Accordingly, Plato's *ousiai* are the Forms, which alone "are" anything at all. Only they, in his standard parlance, can have "presence" with respect to anything else; *Sophist* 247a specifically remarks that in order to be present, a thing must first wholly be something (*pantôs einai ti*).[35] Aristotle, in contrast to all the discussions of *ousia* in his *Metaphysics*—the word occurs on virtually every page—uses the word *parousia* only twice, both times in the same passage, referring to the helmsman (himself obviously an *ousia*) whose presence guides the ship safely.[36] In chapter 3, finally, I showed how ousia and presence came, for Aquinas, to be the two sides of a binary opposition, with ousia—not presence—as the dominant member and with presence defined as the capacity of a thing to be the object of a true proposition. But Heidegger simply conflates the two. Hence his questioning of presence simply detaches from the most fecund aspect of his own philosophy, its presentation of an alternative to ousiodic structure.

Propositional truth and presence are deeply associated for *Being and Time* as well:

> As far as philosophical theorizing is concerned, the *logos* itself is a being, and in accordance with the orientation of ancient ontology, a being present at hand. Words are proximally present at hand, i.e., we find them before us like things; so is the sequence of words in which the *logos* is uttered. (*SZ*, p. 159)

When such a sequence of words (i.e., a sentence) matches the combinations of things and their properties, this sequence is true; when not, it is false. So propositional truth is derived from presence; it is, in Heidegger's words,

> The conformity of one thing present at hand—the assertions expressed—*to* something else which is present-at-hand: the being which is under discussion. (*SZ*, p. 224)

If the aim of *Being and Time* is to criticize presence (rather than, say, the ousiodic *dominance* of presence), then it would seem that it cannot use propositional discourse to do so. This point is made quite explicitly at the end of Heidegger's "On Time and Being," which some suspect presents a concise version of the argument of the final section of Part One of *Being and Time* (which never appeared but which was announced as having the heading "Time and Being"; *SZ*, p. 39):

> It is imperative to overcome, unceasingly, the hindrances which make such Saying inadequate. One hindrance of this type continues to be the Saying of Appropriation in the manner of a lecture. For the lecture has spoken only in propositional assertions.[37]

The ruefulness could also be applied to *Being and Time* itself, for it, too, seems quite clearly to "move in assertions" which are advanced as true. Even the Heideggerean assertion, we saw, is a displacement of presence rather than an escape from it; to affirm the grass as green is not to deny the presence of the grass or of greenness to the individual who makes the assertion. It is to deny their *complete* coincidence, the view that the grass in its greenness has reached a plenary givenness which can never be improved upon. But to deny that anything is ever fully given in this way, while certainly an important doctrine, is hardly a radical one. Even Plato,

.

to say nothing of many empiricists, would deny that such final presence is possible.

Thus *Being and Time* remains bound to assertional and propositional truth, and thence to presence. Unlike Heidegger's later writings, it operates in terms of a distinction between what is described or interpreted phenomenologically (the structures of Dasein) and the discourse which describes or interprets them. And this distinction means that if *Being and Time* is to make any sense at all, the former must somehow be "present" to the latter. *Being and Time* thus confronts a dilemma: either its questioning of presence is global, in which case it is itself senseless because it itself cannot operate except in terms of some version of truth as presence to discourse, or it merely questions "full presence," presence which is final and cannot be improved upon, in which case the questioning is not radical or distinctive.

Heidegger's treatment of "world" shows another, more specific dimension of this problem. World itself, as a whole, is "not a being in the world" (*SZ*, p. 72) and is thus unthematizable; it cannot be fixed in a description or assertion and therefore resists presence. What *can* be described is on a lower level: individual pieces of equipment and their contexts of involvement. These contexts, we saw, become known when equipment fails to function, so that the ongoing functioning of Dasein in its world is disturbed. But "disturbance," of course, is always relative to Dasein. What is and is not a check or a failure is always determined relative to the purposes and projects of the moment. Thus when Heidegger's disclosure of world describes such checks and failures, what it is describing is not "world" itself or even individual contexts of significance which it contains. What is revealed is world as it is being inhabited, at that moment, by an individual Dasein with its particular projects and purposes. To put it in other words: what is being described is not world itself, as what has been there all along, but certain aspects of Dasein's current inherence in its world.

But that seems to be a transgression of Heidegger's own phenomenological problematic. World itself, as the totality of contexts of involvement, must like them be something that exists "in itself" (*an sich*), not in the presence-at-hand of a Kantian noumenon but as what has been there all along, "constantly sighted beforehand" (*SZ*, p. 74). But it is explicitly revealed only as it from time to time indirectly affects an individual Dasein, only insofar as equipment fails and these contexts of involvement are (partially) revealed. Heidegger seems to have fallen into the trap in which he had placed Descartes: world, like Cartesian substance, is something that cannot be known in itself but only insofar as it affects us.

Heidegger's answer to this trap would presumably be that it is a problem for Descartes because he wants to maintain a radical otherness between self and world—between *res extensa* and *res cogitans*. For it is clearly problematic to maintain both this substance is radically outside the knowing mind and that it can be known through representations within this mind. But world, for Heidegger, is not to be independent of Dasein in that way; Dasein is basically characterized as "Being-in-the-world," and to describe Dasein's inherence in world is an indirect way of rendering world itself cognitively accessible. Dasein and world are not radically outside one another but mutually interdependent.

The only way to articulate this interdependence is to deny any radical otherness, not merely between Dasein and world but also between world itself and those particular contexts of involvement that are revealed by specific checks and failures. These checks and failures, I have suggested, are themselves determined as such only in light of the projects and purposes of Dasein at the time; so by assimilating them to world, we assimilate world to Dasein. This assimilation, however, can be construed in two very different ways.

One way would be to take "world" to be not a bounded totality of contexts of involvement but simply those contexts which are explicitly revealed by particular failures of equipment. Such failures would not reveal contexts of involvement as preexisting structures of something larger called "world" but would constitute them in their present uniqueness as world itself. World would not be something preexisting that is revealed by them but would surge out of them. They would function, in other words, as true diakena; they would gather "world" together for the moment and would be not merely occasions for wider awareness but creative emptinesses. But world, so conceived, would have no unity at all; to find oneself confronted by a new and different breakdown would be to find oneself in a new and different world. Thus deprived of its ousiodic structures, "world" would approximate to what Sartre has called "situation."[38]

The problems with simply substituting "situation" for "world" are evident. Heidegger certainly does not take this route. Instead he denies the otherness of world, not by assimilating world to individual breakdowns in equipment but in the reverse way. He claims, in effect, that these breakdowns are nothing more than features of world itself, for Dasein is nothing over and above the world in which it is: "Dasein, existing, *is* its world" (*SZ*, p. 364). In the present context, this statement means that the projects and purposes of individual Dasein, for their part, are nothing over and above features of its world. The checks and failures of equipment which are relative to these projects and purposes thus do not, in the final analysis, reveal world to Dasein. They reveal world to world.

That makes the inherence of Dasein in world far more radical than it was in my previous account. For now world does not merely, as the basis for language, set the limits of what I *can* understand articulately. It also determines how, on specific occasions, I *will* understand things. Very little leeway is left for Dasein, as the qualifier at the end of the following quote at once disguises and highlights:

> Only *what* [Dasein] at various times uncovers and discloses and in *which* direction, *how far* and *how* it uncovers and discloses, are matters for its freedom—though always within the limits of its thrownness.[39]

Heidegger has with this qualifier salvaged the ousiodic structures of world, but at an enormous ethical cost. This cost is demonstrated by the accuracy of Habermas's charge that Heidegger later used the radical inherence of Dasein in world to excuse his own moral failings in becoming a National Socialist.[40]

If I am right, these problems have grounds which are in part *methodological.* If world cannot become present, if it remains unthematizable, and if our only method of inquiry is bound to presence because it is descriptive, interpretive, or otherwise "assertional," then we must "get at" world by interpreting or describing not world itself but something else. For *Being and Time,* this something else is Dasein's inherence in world, which thus has to be total and unconditional.

This methodological problem traces back, then, to a more fundamental error which Heidegger shares with much of the postmodern thought that follows in the wake of *Being and Time.* On the one hand, presence is the enemy, and the appropriate "reality" for philosophical investigation is something that cannot be present. On the other hand, presence is a necessary condition for any discourse which claims truth, including philosophical discourse. These views, in turn, are conveyed via a conflation of ousia and presence, by the wrongly assumed synonymy of *ousia* and *parousia.* For, I have suggested, at least some of Heidegger's efforts in *Being and Time* are directed against the ousiodic structures which have been inherent in philosophy from ancient times, as when he decries Descartes for allowing a part to dominate a whole, understanding Being only in terms of constant presence. And much of the radical achievement of *Being and Time* relies, as I have also suggested, in its presentation of various diakena—of gaps which bring together and unify entities without possessing any nature of their own. But because Heidegger does not focus on ousia and its structures, he neither perceives the real object of his critique nor gives, in *Being and Time,* any adequate treatment of the diakena. Rather he objects to presence and directs his critique against that—at an enormous intellectual price. The basic gesture of metaphysics—the instating of just part of an entity as its single dominating principle—remains for *Being and Time* a mere "unbridled methodological tendency."

11

DIAKENA AND THING IN THE
LATER HEIDEGGER

Writing to William Richardson in April 1962, Heidegger still equates *ousia* with *Anwesenheit,* with presence rather than with domination.[1] That this is the symptom of a deeper and enduring problem is shown by some of Heidegger's comments about the successor to "world" in his later thought: the idea of an historical "epoch" of Being.

"The Time of the World Picture," written in 1938, opens with the following words:

> In metaphysics, meditation on the essence of beings and a decision concerning the nature of truth are brought to completion. Metaphysics grounds an age in that it gives it the ground of the *form of its essence* via a determinate interpretation of beings and a determinate comprehension of truth. This ground thoroughly *dominates* [*durchherrscht*] all the phenomena that distinguish the age.[2]

Like the earlier concept of world, the "metaphysical age" so depicted clearly bears the three characteristic traits of of ousia. It has a definite set of contents ("phenomena" that "distinguish" it) and to this extent definite (if, like those of world, perhaps unknown) boundaries. Within this historically distinct domain, phenomena are disposed ("dominated") by the "ground" of the epoch, which is the "form of its essence." Indeed, the dispositive dominance is so great that, as Heidegger puts it to Jean Beaufret in his "Letter on Humanism," "The history of Being . . . sustains and defines every *condition et situation humaine*."[3]

From this point of view, which is that of the later Heidegger's project of "history of Being," or *Seinsgeschichte,* everything that happens in the human world happens in *a* human world. Such an historical world, or epoch of Being, is founded upon an understanding of Being that is itself determinate. But because this determinate understanding shares nothing with the founding understandings of other such "worlds," it is radically incommensurable with them.[4]

Because it disposes the actions and projects of those who inhabit it, the ground of world—a determinate understanding of Being—cannot result from those very actions and projects. Rather it results from Being itself, which is what the founding understanding attempts to capture adequately: "The epochal essence of the Mittence of Being, within which is authentic world history, comes from the epochê of Being itself."[5]

Such an "epochê," a withholding bestowal or, as Heidegger also calls it, a "gift" of Being, is inexplicable. Any explanation of what it is would apply to other epochs as well and so would require categories which transcended the specific understanding of Being which has been granted to *this* epoch; and that is impossible. But Being, though its gifts have no explanation, does have henchmen: the metaphysicians who articulate the understanding of what it is to be. Such thinkers, in spite of the austerity of their calling, have an enormous social role to play:

> In the thinking of Being, the freeing of man for Ek-sistence which grounds history comes to word, a word which is not primarily the expression of an opinion, but always the well-preserved articulation of the truth of beings-as-a-whole. How many there are who have an ear for this word does not matter. *Who they are, who can hear, is decisive for man's standpoint in history.*[6]

It is perhaps not too much to say that for Heidegger, historical actors such as Hitler and Napoleon are mere epiphenomena when compared with thinkers such as Descartes and Nietzsche. Historical processes such as modernization, industrialization, and the rise of science are all grounded and determined properties, not the determining form or ground. What is really important to history is, rather, the "freeing of man for Ek-sistence" accomplished by metaphysics; that is what enables the "gift of Being" to take effect in its full dominance over the age.

These theses—the unconditional inherence of individuals in determinate but incommensurable historical epochs, the origin of these epochs in an inexplicable "gift of Being," and the world-historical importance in this of metaphysicians—constitute the basic themes of Heidegger's *Seinsgeschichte.* In them we see residues of *Being and Time*'s concept of world as the ultimate horizon of intelligibility, in which Dasein also unconditionally inheres. But here these residues appear without the diakenic unification performed in *Being and Time* by death, individual Dasein's ultimate end. When the perspective turns from Dasein to history, teleology vanishes.

The historical epoch so viewed clearly exhibits the essential features of ousiodic domination. It has its "matter"—individual Dasein and social processes. These are disposed by the epoch's single "form of essence," which it gets from outside—not from a father, to be sure, but from Being. The matter, at least if it is individual Dasein, is "designated" by being "freed for Eksistenz"; such freeing is abetted by the metaphysicians who render it articulate and who in this play the role of designating agents. And, like the Prime Mover, the historical epoch exercises no initiative; because of its incommensurability with other historical periods, the epoch remains within its own boundaries, closed off from even the understanding of outsiders. While the entire succession of epochs that constitutes *Seinsgeschichte* may exhibit features of diakenic interplay—a point I will not argue here—Heidegger's account of each individual epoch is clearly ousiodic in character.

This ousiodic discourse in the later Heidegger is remarkable on several counts. First, it is so global that one is at a loss to see how it could ever be tested or verified. Second, and in part because of its globality, it is so dogmatic that it seems that it is all to be taken on faith—or, more likely, on the authority of Heidegger himself (who clearly aspires to the kind of world-historical importance he accords to other thinkers). And third, its hierarchical opposition of ground and grounded is so absolute that nothing except the history of metaphysics needs to be discussed at all; the "position of humanity in history" is to be decided by a few philosophers rather than by the kind of economic and social processes that we would normally call historical. *Seinsgeschichte* is thus a self-enclosed and unargued discourse which irrupts into Heidegger's thinking to structure his view of the human world; and this unargued irruption of ousiodic structure marks Heidegger, even in his later phase, as in important respects what I have called a "modern" thinker.

Seinsgeschichte is easily discredited.[7] It is not, for all that, beyond possible rehabilitation. It could be viewed, for example, not as a set of dogmas but as a heuristic device for seeking, *in* the facts of history, relatively stable meanings which are discontinuous with what came before and what went after. So reconceived, *Seinsgeschichte* would redirect historical investigations away from overall narratives of progress or decline and into highly specific and detailed investigations—the kind of thing which is in fact undertaken by Michel Foucault.[8]

Remaining within the thought of Heidegger, I will ask a different question. Given that *Seinsgeschichte* reduces to a bizarre set of ousiodic dogmas, can all of Heidegger's later thought itself be reduced to *Seinsgeschichte*? No. In "The Origin of the Work of Art," for example, which I have discussed at length elsewhere,[9] the structures of *Seinsgeschichte* are violated in dramatic ways. The self-enclosure of world there is not absolute but is punctured by the work of art itself, which "sets up" a new world in the midst of an old one. There it is art, not metaphysics, which grounds history. And art does this not by playing some subsidiary role (as does a metaphysical "henchman") but by actually constituting a primordial giving of Being. As two further examples, more revealing for the moment, of a path of Heidegger's thought which escapes the structures of *Seinsgeschichte,* I will take an essay of 1951, "The Thing," along with the discussion of Hölderlin's poem "Andenken," a discussion dating from 1942.

THE THING

The exemplary "thing" in terms of which Heidegger pursues his thought here is a jug. The jug can be understood in two very familiar ways and one very unfamiliar one. First, it can be understood as an artifact, something produced; it is made from clay and has a particular shape, introduced into the clay by the potter for the purpose of making a container.[10] In addition to this deployment of the Aristotelian four causes, the thing can also be understood in terms of modern science, as a material object (DD, p. 42/169f). Both ways of understanding it, Heidegger says, are correct—as far as they go. His alternative to them begins with the fact that in order to contain fluids such as wine or water, the jug must be hollow. Though physics will always remind us that even an "empty" jug is filled with air, as far as *we* are concerned in our daily use of it a jug which contains only air is empty: "The emptiness is what does the jug's holding. The emptiness, this Nothing in the jug, is what the jug is as a container which contains." From this perspective, the potter does not instill a plenitude of form into clay but "shapes the void" (DD, p. 41/169). The void, then, is what holds the jug together as a thing; its other features—sides, bottom, spout—are then in what I call a diakenic interplay.

The defining emptiness in the jug is specific to it: *its* own void (DD, p. 43/171). And it is dynamic, for it is, in the first instance, a twofold activity of taking in and keeping. These, in turn, are for the sake of—find their essential nature in—pouring-out. Unlike a cistern, for example, the jug has its specific nature as an emptiness which can take in and hold liquids in such a way that they can be poured out again (DD, p. 44f/171f). Pouring-out is thus the function which the jug (with its handles) most specifically accomplishes; in Aristotelian terms, its *ergon.*

That brings us to a second diakenic interplay. What the jug pours out from its interior emptiness may be water. Water comes from the earth—the spring or well—and from the sky as rain. Or the jug may pour forth wine. Wine is made from grapes borne by the earth and nourished by sunshine and rain. When the dynamic emptiness that is the jug pours forth water or wine, it stands in a relationship to earth and sky: "In the essence of the jug linger earth and sky" (DD, p. 44/172).

The jug in its outpouring is related to two further domains. One is that of "mortals," those who use the jug, whose thirst it slakes and whose conviviality it enlivens. The other domain is that of the "immortals." For sometimes the jug is used to pour forth libations to the gods—a connection strong enough, says Heidegger, that the modern German *gießen,* to gush, is derived from an ancient Indo-European root meaning "to sacrifice" (DD, p. 45/173). So mortals and immortals also "linger" in the jug's outpouring.

Earth, sky, mortals, and immortals thus constitute four realms in terms of which the jug can be understood and out of which it can be encountered. Its interpretive projection against these four regions and its emergence out of them are what Heidegger calls a "gathering" (*sammeln*). This manifold gathering is the essential activity of the jug as a "thing": *Dieses vielfältig einfache Sammeln ist das Wesende des Kruges* (DD, p. 46/174).

The gathering of these different regions by the jug does not homogenize them but enhances their mutual disparity; it "brings the four into the light of what is their own."[11] But it does that in such a way as to "entrust them to one another."[12] We begin to suspect that earth, sky, mortals, and immortals are in a diakenic play with one another, a suspicion confirmed by Heidegger's more general discussion a few pages further on:

> Each of the four mirrors backs in its own way the essence of the others. Each, in this, mirrors itself in its own way back into its own, within the unity of the four. This mirroring is no presentation of an image. The mirroring appropriates, as it lights each of the four, its own essence into simple authenticating [*vereignung*] of one another. (DD, p. 52/179)

As an interplay of four mobile mirrors, this *Spiegel-Spiel* brings each of the players (mirrors) into a peculiar clarity of essence. Hence none of the four can be understood independently of the others:

> None of the four makes itself obdurate in its separate particularity. Each of the four, within their mutual authentication, is expropriated into its own. This expropriating-authenticating is the mirror-play of the Fourfold. (DD, p. 52/179)

To be "expropriated into one's own" is to leave one's "own," one's stable nature, behind and to be given a new one; it is to be fundamentally transformed. Hence the mobility of the mirrors—and hence the fact that the moves of each mirror are in response to the other three:

> The unifying four are already stifled in their essence if we merely regard them as individual real things, which are supposed to be grounded through one another and explained out of one another. (DD, p. 52/180)

The configurations and deployments of earth, sky, mortals, and immortals that come about (*sich ereignen*) in the course of this *Spiegel-Spiel* constitute nothing less than world itself: "The thing allows the Fourfold to linger. The thing things world" (DD, p. 52/181).

"The Thing" has now presented us with two different examples of diakenic interplay, each of which enriches our conception of such interplay itself. In the first—the diakenon presented by the gathering and gushing emptiness at the core of the jug—we see such interplay functioning to unite not a set of phenomena or the stages of a development but an individual thing. In this respect, Heidegger's jug is a clear alternative and challenge to Aristotle's original concept of ousia. For the model of a thing as unified by a determinate plenitude whose function is to establish its boundaries and control what goes on within them is replaced by a model which presents a thing as unified by an emptiness whose function is to take in and give out. The breadth of applicability of this model and its usefulness in general and in specific circumstances remain unexplored.

The interplay in the second diakenon is evidenced not merely by the fact that the elements unified can only be understood in terms of their difference from one another but also by the fact that they change together, that the transformation of any of them is a response to and is responded to by transformations in the others. These transformations are simultaneous, and—if they are true to the uniqueness of each member of the fourfold—have no common characteristic.[13] Caught up in such responsive transformations, Heidegger's Fourfold sounds something like a jazz quartet, concentrating itself around—but never actually quite playing—a song.

The contrasts with *Being and Time* are as important as they are obvious, for world is now deprived of the ousiodic structures it retained both there and in *Seinsgeschichte.* It is not dominated by a single gift of Being and the formulations of metaphysicians but is set into play by a humble jug. Thus capable of being set into play by every single "thing" that exists *as* a thing (the nature of the "as" here remains to be examined), world is inexhaustibly pluralized. And if every "thing" brings world about differently, world itself is not unified enough even to be punctured by an artwork. It is radically non-ousiodic. Heidegger has taken the path he avoided in *Being and Time:* seeing world not as revealed by the checks against which Dasein runs in its daily circumspection but as surging up through nothingness. Such nothingness, as creative, is not merely the check or failure of an ongoing project; it is the active "essence" of a thing.

It is important to note here that, as the previous quotes attest, Heidegger has presented two different ways of misconstruing the mirror-play of the four regions. One is to allow each of the four to be "obdurate in its separate particularity," to investigate it independently of the others. The other is to "stifle" the play by grounding its four players in one another in any way. The first misconstrual amounts to seeing each of the regions as a stable and separate being, one about which true propositions could be uttered: construing it, then, as a present being, indifferent to the others. The second amounts to taking one of the four as basic and understanding the others in terms of it: seeing the fourfold as exhibiting a hierarchy of ousiodic domination in which one grounds the others.

Each misconstrual thus violates one of the criteria of diakenic interplay advanced in the preceding chapter. The first sees its components as indifferent to one another (criterion A of diakenicity), while the second grounds them in one of their number (criterion B). But there is more to Heidegger's discussion of these misconstruals than that. For implicit in the very distinction between these two types of misconstrual is an unstated separation of presence from ousia. When we misconstrue the diakenic interplay of the Fourfold by seeing its components as indifferent to one another, we are operating with an uncritical conception of presence. When we attempt to ground them all in one of their number, we are seeing this one as generating the others—as akin to an ousiodic form.

Both types of misconstrual, to be sure, are objects of Heidegger's criticism; both presence and ousia, when taken as our sole interpretive cues, fail to grasp the nature of the jug as a "thing." The important point, however, is that the two moves are here the objects of *separate* criticisms. And when these criticisms are separated, something else becomes apparent: that the criticism of presence is in fact quite old. It amounts, here, to saying that none of the four can be understood independently of its relation to the other three. But the idea that things, even things as evanescent as "plays," cannot be understood independently of their relations to other things goes back to Plato's account of the "bastard logos" in the *Timaeus* and the view of the *Meno* that "all nature is akin."[14] It is highlighted, of course, by holistic thinkers such as Spinoza and Hegel, as well as by the more reflective versions of Empiricism. Also clear, from the histories of both Platonism and Empiricism (especially, as I noted in chapter 8, in the thought of Hume), is that the critique of presence leaves truth in place—but as something localized and approximated, if not inscrutable. Hence it is unsurprising that Heidegger should write that the "claims (*Angaben*) of physics [with respect to the jug as a material object] are correct" (DD, p. 42/170). They just do not reach the dimension of the jug as a "thing," a dimension which we have yet to understand fully. They are "correct" in the sense proper to physics, a sense which we should not mistake for the only possible one.

It is a different matter with the criticism of ousia, which is new with Heidegger. For this criticism amounts to the idea that a "thing" is to be understood with respect to a plurality of dimensions which play against each other in ways that define them, without the interplay itself being established either by any one of these things or reducible to some further unifying principle over and above them. It amounts, in other words, to a reaffirmation of what *Being and Time* called "equiprimordiality"—here viewed not as merely a property of that highly unusual being called Dasein but as basic to any "thing."

The Heideggerean Fourfold, normally the source of much perplexity for readers, can thus be seen as part of a critique of ousia. That brings us to a third diakenon presented, though not stated, by the essay.

Consider the jug's material, which Heidegger does not simply call "clay" (*Ton*) but lengthily characterizes as "specially chosen and prepared earth" (DD, p. 39/167). Seen in these terms, the Heideggerean jug stands in a twofold relation to earth; it relates not merely to the prepared and designated matter out of which it is itself formed but to the earth from which gushed its water or which bore and nourished the grapes from which came its wine. These two earths—one the Aristotelian material cause, the other a Heideggerean region—stand in an *indeterminate* relationship to one another. The relation of the jug to the earth from which its water or wine came is essentially indeterminate, even if it can be determined precisely by chemical analysis or measured exactly in miles, feet, and inches. For we would not understand the jug as a "thing" any better if we knew the exact distance between its present location and the source of the water it contains or the differences in chemical composition between the earth of which it is made and the earth from which its liquids come. The earth of the spring or field and the matter of the jug thus stand in a relation that is indeterminable but essential—and whose indeterminability is essential to it. This essential indeterminability is *part* of what Heidegger means by "lingering" (*weilen*). Established by an indefinable gap yet definitive of the thing itself, such lingering is what I call a diakenic interplay.

No less diakenic, it follows, is the relation between the two sets of "categories" that articulate each kind of earth. In order to specify the relation between Aristotle's material cause and Heidegger's earth, thereby aligning them on some overarching conceptual continuum, we would have to undertake such investigations as determining their respective spatial locations, comparing their chemical constituents and reconstructing the causal and productive chains that led to the water's presence in the jug. We could certainly undertake these investigations. But we would complete them only to find that we had lost the essential indeterminacy of the jug as Heidegger presents it. The same holds for the other components of the jug as a "thing." The space intrinsic to the jug, deploying its shape in the dynamism of outpouring, has no clear relation to the "form" imposed on the clay by the potter. Mortals, the sometime recipients of the liquid as drink, and immortals, the sometime recipients of the liquid as sacrifice, are not clearly assimilable to the Aristotelian telos—though the jug's pouring-out is for their sakes and its taking in and retaining are for the sake of pouring-out.

The two sets of categories thus stand in no clear relationship. But they cannot be understood except in terms of one another. We cannot, I suggest, understand the Heideggerean Fourfold, which seems so arbitrary and willful, except as a diakenic displacement of the Aristotelian *aitiai*.[15] Nor can we understand these *aitiai* for what they are unless we accept this same diakenic displacement. For the diakena are an *alternative* to ousia. Unless we know that there is such an alternative, we will view ousiodic structures as the only way in which to understand the jug or any other artifact; we will be compelled to see it as something that was shaped by someone for a purpose.

Heidegger's Fourfold is thus not a conceptual apparatus with which he seeks to replace or even ground the causal factors of Aristotle. Heidegger's four regions are *alternatives* to Aristotle *which can never be anything more than that*. Thus, while in "The Thing" Heidegger tries in various ways to explain the four regions, what they are and how they mean, he never tries to justify them; he never tries to argue that they *have* to be adopted or that they capture the way things *really* are. They are what "The Origin of the Work of Art" would call a "polemical" check on the traditional, Aristotelian categorial system; they enter into a strife with it, a *polemos* which sets up not a further mediation but merely an emptiness (UKW, p. 37f/49f). This emptiness, again, defines *both* sides of the conflict. For if the Fourfold can never be more than an alternative to Aristotle's four causes, the same is true of these causes: they are an alternative to the Fourfold. Both sets of "categories" are thus defined by their indeterminate distance from one another.

In spite of this diakenic distance between Heidegger's Fourfold and Aristotle's categories, there is one theme that they share. That is the notion of gathering or coming together. For Aristotle, we saw, Being was the coming-together of form and matter under the dominating aegis of form. For Heidegger, the jug's gathering of the Fourfold is under the aegis of the emptiness which enables it to gush. This "Nothing in the jug" establishes the mutual interrelations of its sides and bottoms, the essential nature of which is to surround it. The Nothing *in* the jug, then, establishes the boundaries *of* the jug. Containing the water or wine, the emptiness disposes over their preservation. Dispensing them in its outpouring, the Nothingness exercises initiative in the jug and enables it to serve its purpose, which is to give out liquids.

But the boundaries thus established are essentially open, because they are established through a nothingness, a hollow which allows matter in and out. It is because of this that the jug is related not just to its own material but also to the earth of the source, earth at an indeterminate remove. The Nothing's disposition over the contents of the jug is likewise not final but open; the containing is achieved by the sides and bottom, which are not merely passive components but dynamically cooperate to give forth a certain amount and speed of outflow. And the disposition is of a very unconstraining kind; because the liquids contained are homogeneous, the wine in the jug mixes indiscriminately with wine, and water with water, and both with each other. The jug's emptiness does not direct their different members or parts into their proper places (the way an Aristotelian *pater familias* establishes order in his household). Finally, the jug's initiative is not a troublesome transgression of its boundaries but manifests and completes its very nature as emptiness, as a passageway through which liquids can pour. We cannot, then, understand the jug in terms of its form alone — or even in terms of its form plus the matter it contains. Rather it must be understood in terms of regions at indeterminate removes from it: earth, sky, mortal, immortals.

I have argued that Heidegger rightly leaves his Fourfold at an indeterminate remove from Aristotle's categorial structure of causes. The same is not exactly true, however, when it comes to the relation between the Fourfold and the categories of modern physics. Heidegger in fact indicates a quite determinate difference between these categories and the Fourfold:

> It is said that the knowledge of the sciences is constraining (*zwingend*). Of course. But in what does its constraining power consist? In our present case, in the constraint which requires us to relinquish the wine-filled jug, and to posit in its place an empty space in which liquid diffuses. (DD, p. 42/170)

"Science" for Heidegger, here as so often, means physics. And as far as physics is concerned, any liquid can be contained and poured out by the jug: wine, water, motor oil, mercury, molten wax. For Heidegger, the jug contains, *as a thing,* water or wine: drink for mortals. It is a thing, then, through the way in which it affects mortals; to see it *as* a thing is to see it in its relation to mortals. That, indeed, is why the "immortals" are an essential part of the Fourfold. As Heidegger notes, a jug is only *sometimes* used to pour a libation. But the relation of mortals to what they take, because of their mortality, to be "above" them — religion in the very broadest sense, encompassing our awe before such *things* as the quantum theory and the civil rights struggle — is always essential to mortals.

Heidegger expands this view via a series of etymological ruminations. In them he seeks to establish that historically the word "thing" (*pragma, res, causa*) designates not just any being in the cosmos but only things which have to do with us, with mortals. He seeks to refocus attention from entities of which it is logically possible that someone *might* speak (the entities with which physics and natural science generally deal) to things of which we *actually do* speak — because they are sufficiently important and, perhaps, sufficiently problematical. That serves to demarcate his own thinking from the investigations of modern science, which then amounts to the effort to understand what reality is like when we are not around.

Though we do not create things on some sort of idealistic model, we mortals are therefore necessary to the Being of a thing. The jug will be there when we are not present; so will the earth and sky. But the gathering of the Fourfold and the thinging of world cannot come to completion unless we allow them to. And we do that only when we get outside the frameworks of Aristotle and of modern science, which seek in their different ways to explain beings in terms of other beings. Only when we allow ourselves to encounter beings as the interplays of various sorts of diakena can these diakena exhibit their gathering interplay. So we do not in Heideggers view create the diakena; as nothings they cannot be "created" or produced. But we can allow them to be (DD, p. 54/181). Thus the "lingering" of earth and sky in the water and wine of the jug—the fact that the water and wine are there across an indeterminate distance from their "origins"—is not independent of our encounter with the jug and its contents. We are perfectly free to ignore it and to understand the jug in more traditional ways.

Because diakena exist fully only in our encounters with them, they cannot simply be described, as if they existed independently of the description. Rather, discourse on diakena must itself set them into play: they must be enabled and cultivated rather than covered over with determinate explanations. Heidegger's standard name for this mode of discursive comportment, not used here, is *Seinlassen,* "letting-be."[16]

"The Thing" has now presented us with no fewer than four separate diakenic interplays. The first is the interplay which occurs within and constitutes the jug itself. It is the "fact" that what gives the jug Being, what enables it to encounter us, is the dynamic action of its own proper emptiness as it holds and gives forth water and wine. The second is the interplay between the jug and four wider regions: the earth and sky, which provide what the jug essentially gives forth and are thus conditions for its existence as a jug, i.e., as a thing, and the mortals and immortals for which this interplay occurs. The third is the mirror-play of these regions among themselves. And the fourth is the distance between these four regions, viewed as conditions of the thing, and Aristotle's four constitutive principles or causes. Of these four interplays, I have suggested, the first two are for present purposes the most important. For the first shows diakenic interplay brought into the core of an individual being and so constitutes Heidegger's most decisive challenge to the Aristotelian model of ousia. The second shows that a diakenon is an interplay among things which have their own histories—histories which ousiodic structure, viewing them as entirely determined by their unifying form, suppresses.

ANDENKEN

Diakenic structures can occur, for Heidegger, not merely in and through physical objects but—and perhaps more important—in and through language. As an example of how Heidegger, in his later works, uses words not merely to describe but to allow and enable diakena—to "let them be"—I will take his discussion of Hölderlin's poem "Andenken." Poetry, of course, is an art; and the essence of art, according to "The Origin of the Work of

Art," is "the setting into the work of truth" (UKW, p. 25, 64/36, 77). As the beginning of this essay argues, we cannot understand this essence without understanding the individual work of art. But "work of art," again, is not a universal essence which could be understood apart from encounters with individual works of art; for each such work is unique, and its uniqueness is essential to its character as an artwork (UKW, p. 50, 54/62, 65f).

These theses merely apply to poetry, the most primordial (because linguistic) art, what Heidegger says elsewhere about philosophy. There is for him no common essence of philosophy over and above its history which would be accessible to someone who has not encountered this history.[17] Philosophy *is* nothing more than the sayings of philosophers; to have any sort of understanding of it is to encounter such saying:

> When do we philosophize? Only, obviously, when we enter into dialogue with the philosophers. To this belongs that we talk through them that of which they speak. This talking-through with one another of that which always anew uniquely concerns philosophers as the Same is speaking, *legein* in the sense of *dialegesthai,* speaking as dialogue.[18]

When Heidegger calls for understanding philosophy together with understanding poetry,[19] then, this can only mean that his thinking assigns itself a double dialogue: with philosophers and with poets. The essay "Andenken" carries this dialogue forward via an interpretation of Hölderlin's poem of the same name.[20] Heidegger begins by discussing the circumstances of the poem's origin, not in the sense of treating happenings in the life of the poet, its producer or moving cause, but by discussing the Rhine and the Danube. These are the two rivers which flow through Hölderlin's native Swabia, nourishing it and relating it to the rest of the world (Adk, p. 75). The "origin" of the poem is thus not the individual human being whose quill first inscribed its words on paper but two rivers at an indeterminate remove from *any* text of the poem (even from Hölderlin's original transcription, which could have been written inside or outside Swabia).

Heidegger then presents the full text of the poem itself (Adk, pp. 76-78). The first circumstance in it to which he draws attention is the riddlesomeness of its title. *Andenken* means remembrance or souvenir. But the poem, in its crucial center (the first line of the third stanza), asks a question, one about where the poet's friends are now (*Wo aber sind die Freunde?*). This question cannot be answered by memory, for it is asking about a current state of affairs. In addition, Heidegger notes, the last line of the poem refers to poets as "founding" something, an act which clearly bears an essential reference to the future rather than directly to the past. The "remembrance" of the title seems somehow then to be a "remembrance" of something that is not in the past but (perhaps) in the future; the rest of the poem, Heidegger says, expands on the meanings of such remembrance (Adk, pp. 78-80).

The title of the poem is thus ambiguous. Taken in one sense, which for Heidegger is the more profound, *Andenken* turns out to mean, roughly, a retrieval of past experiences, an experience which leads back beyond these retrieved experiences to their inexhaustible and thus in some way still futural source and a "founding" of this futural source (Adk, p. 142). Taken in the ordinary German sense, however, *andenken* means merely to reminisce. Once again, we see a diakenic play at work. The ordinary and profound meanings cannot be placed into a clear relationship to one another, if only because the "object" of the more profound sense of *Andenken* turns out to be not a being at all, past, present, or future, but Being itself. Yet they do not wholly fall apart, either; both are necessary to understanding the poem. Orienting ourselves only to the ordinary sense of the term, for example, leads us to consider the content of the poem—the memories which Hölderlin, recently returned from Bordeaux, had of it; and it leads as well to an investigation of the lyric form in which this content is arranged (Adk, p. 78). It leads, then, to all the things which conventional literary criticism has to say about the poem. But it cannot, in Heidegger's view, give the only possible account of the poem; for it cannot explain the poem's concluding reference to "founding" or its central question. Pursued exclusively, it is not a basis for understanding the poem but rather one for misunderstanding it.

As for dispensing with the ordinary understanding and attempting to interpret "Andenken" without regard to what its title normally means in German—that is simply impossible. Heidegger insists, so bluntly and often that we must regard it as the major impetus to his interpretations of Hölderlin, that Hölderlin has not been understood by the German people, his primary audience, in spite of all the scholarly efforts spent on him.[21] Thus the ordinary understanding of "Andenken" is not merely a mistake which Heidegger must clear out of the way; Heidegger's own efforts begin from the failed dialogue of Hölderlin with the German people, a failure brought about by this very understanding. This failed dialogue is the historical condition for Heidegger's own "dialogue" with Hölderlin. Thus both meanings to *Andenken* are necessary to Heidegger's project, which is concerned to open up the gap between them.

The overwhelming bulk of Heidegger's essay presents a close reading of the poem. The closeness of the reading is essential to it: "Even the most inconspicuous word and every 'image' which seems fit only for poetic decoration," Heidegger declares, "is an [essentially disclosing] word . . ." (Adk, p. 95f; also p. 101). In the course of his essay, as Emil Staiger notes with some wonderment, Heidegger actually does explicate every single word of Hölderlin's fifty-nine-line poem.[22]

As Heidegger views it, the basic path of the poem is the following. The first five lines introduce the basic relationship between Hölderlin, Being (the "Northeaster" which blows), and the "future poets of Germania," the "seafarers" (Adk, pp. 80–82). The rest of the first stanza and the second stanza describe the poet's trip to a foreign land, which in the poem is France but which, according to Heidegger, is in truth Greece (Adk, p. 78f). The third stanza shows the poet back in his native land, engaged in dialogue with others there; the fourth begins to poetize his solitude in his native country and does so by showing how his dwelling in his native land is a nearness to "the Source" (which, presumably, is Being; Adk, p. 130). The fifth and final stanza continues these themes, restating the necessity for travel to foreign lands and the nature of the voyage, culminating in two different visions of "Andenken." One of them, a wandering over the sea, is a constant running-towards-the-foreign which awakens, and consistently forgets again, what is one's own (Adk, p. 134). The other is the steady loving gaze backward to the Source (Adk, p. 135f).

Neither vision, however, appears to be the primordial type of "Andenken" for Heidegger, the one because it does not mount to the Source, not having arrived in the native land, and the other because it does not see itself as founding all human existence (Adk, p. 136). There is thus a third type of "Andenken," the truest form of remembrance for Heidegger, which in dwelling by the Source does not simply leave the sea-voyage behind but rather makes it into its own authentically disclosed object:

> Andenken thinks of the landscape of the place of the Source in its thinking of the wandership of the wandering through the foreign. Andenken thinks of the Source out of the thinking of the sea which has been traversed, into which the Source previously had flowed out. (Adk, p. 141)

Following the course of the poem in this way gives Heidegger opportunity to discuss a number of ancillary points. Among them are the relationship of the Germans to the Greeks, part of Hölderlin's Brot und Wein, the nature of the poet, and the need for experience of the broad world, the "sea" which the poet must traverse in order to return to the Source at all.[23]

Through all of this explication, Heidegger's basic procedure is simple. He takes each word or phrase of the poem and thinks it through in terms of its significance to poetry as Andenken in its three senses. The seafarers thus become the poets themselves. The "braune Frauen" of Bordeaux become participants at the "marriage of mortals and immortals" that gives birth to poetry (Adk, pp. 96–102). The "dark light" of the wine glass becomes the mortal thoughts through which is expressed what the poet has seen, and so on (Adk, p. 112f). If, as Heidegger says in Being and Time, "apophansis" is both "synthesis," putting-together, and "diairêsis," taking-apart,[24] then we can say that Heidegger conducts an apophansis of the poem: he splits it up into individual words and phrases and considers each of these separately, yet unifies them all by thinking each back into the one primordial (and primordially ambiguous) word, Andenken. The poem thus is read as unified not by a determinate theme or "message" but by the equiprimordial interplay of the different meanings of the word *Andenken.*

These meanings, again, have no clear relationship to one another: wandering and retrieval, leading back to a source, and founding something still futural cannot be derived either from one of their number or from some more general concept. Heidegger's main gesture in this essay is thus to highlight irreducible ambiguities in the meanings of this and its other terms and to show such ambiguity as itself the basic unifying force in the poem. That confronts the ordinary way of understanding the poem with its own limits. For if we are going to approach words in the usual Western way, as sensible signs of supersensible meanings, each single word should have a unique meaning. Heidegger can shatter this usual understanding by pointing out that the meanings of some of the words employed by Hölderlin, or another poet or philosopher, have, rather than a single general meaning, an irreducible plurality of specific ones.

That such irreducible ambiguity is itself a type of diakenic interplay can be shown by singling out the word which, for Heidegger, is most susceptible to such vagueness and ambiguity: "Being." The semantic field of this term as ordinarily used (*Seiendes*) is so wide that Heidegger, in *Was Heißt Denken?*, suggests that the chaos of the modern world may be rooted in it. Yet stranger, he says, is the fact that we all nonetheless understand one another—that the ambiguity of the term can be ignored in everyday life.[25] This ambiguity, when examined, proves to be of a peculiar type:

> It remains difficult, perhaps even impossible . . . to bring out a common meaning as a universal generic concept under which the . . . types of "is" could be ordered as species. Yet a unitarily-determined strain runs through all of them. It refers the understanding of "Being" to a determinate horizon, out of which the understanding fulfills itself. The delimitation of the meaning of "Being" holds itself within the circuit of presence and being present, of constitution and duration, of abiding and occurring.[26]

An "irreducible" ambiguity thus appears, from this passage, to be one in which the different meanings of a term can neither be reduced to a single basic one (as can the different meanings of "bear" in reference, say, to children and to water jugs) nor completely dissociated from one another (as in the case of the meanings of "bear" and the noun denoting the animal). "Irreducible" ambiguity is thus one form of what I call diakenic interplay.

Heidegger attempts to point out such linguistic diakena on many occasions. At the beginning of *Was Heisst Denken?*, for example, the question itself proves to be ambiguous, but in a way which "points toward" a single, determinative meaning (*WHD*, p. 130). Much of the early part of "On Nietzsche's Word 'God is Dead'" is devoted to bringing out the different yet connected meanings Nietzsche attaches to "nihilism."[27] In *Was Heißt Denken?*, the Greek participle is argued to be of such a type as well (*WHD*, pp. 134f, 148). Here the title "Andenken," we have seen, turns out to be ambiguous in that it can be taken either in its ordinary German sense or in the unique one that Hölderlin gives it, one which as I have noted has several mutually irreducible meanings of its own.

In *The Question of Being*, Heidegger explicitly identifies the Saying of language with an ambiguity which is neither merely coincidental nor reducible to universal rules:

> It always traverses the essential ambiguity of the word and its uses. The ambiguity of Saying in no way consists in a mere collection of meanings which turn up arbitrarily. It rests in a play which, the more richly it unfolds itself, remains the more rigorously bound by a concealed rule. . . . Therefore, Saying remains bound by the highest law.[28]

Moving through such irreducible ambiguities, Heideggerean thinking will not be an inference from premises to conclusion, a fugue of such inferences (like Plato's *Phaedo,* Spinoza's *Ethics,* or Quine's *Word and Object*), or a "dialectical" progression in Hegelian or Marxian fashion. The essay "Andenken," in fact, progresses by *not* establishing and moving along syntactic or semantic connections among the poem's terms. It interprets the poem's movement as one of "jerk" and contrasts.[29] Thus Heidegger's final statement on Hölderlin's poem is that it is a "single articulated structure, articulated in itself, of 'however'" (Adk, p. 142f). The German *aber,* which in Heidegger's analysis is the key on which the poem is structured, serves grammatically to indicate not a smooth development of what has gone before and still less a logical inference but precisely the introduction of something new and unexpected. And indeed, in Heidegger's treatment of the poem, both the poem itself and his own discussion of it contain abrupt changes of theme and perspective—changes which are unified, in both cases, by the irreducible ambiguity of the poem's title.

Heidegger remains faithful to such abrupt changes by focusing on individual words, which he meditates *seriatim.* The different meditations through which his essay moves are not "grounded" in what comes before or in what comes after them, any more than the words meditated are considered to be; they do not constitute lemmas of a larger argument or phases in a larger dialectical development. In this sense, we may say that the movement of Heideggerean reading is one of "wandering," of stopping and questioning on what Heidegger calls *Holzwege.*[30] In this it is like poetizing itself, which, as what Hölderlin called "Andenken," is said to require the future poets to "wander" over the sea (Adk, pp. 123-126). The state of mind of someone who wanders, of course, is that she does not know where she is going and continually expects to be surprised by what she finds; she is, then, questioning as she progresses. We can sum up these two characteristics of progress by contrast and wandering by characterizing Heideggerean thinking as a continual stopping and questioning rather than a smooth progression from premises to conclusions.[31]

But this absence of smooth and intelligible transitions does not mean that the poem or Heidegger's reading of it is without unity. The individual words meditated are what Heidegger calls "hints"; and this means that they direct the thinker into new paths of thought.[32] No individual meditation thus follows from a previous one or provides grounds for a later one in any logically rigorous way, and no word meditated is connected to others by a logically oriented syntax. But each word and each meditation upon it are suggested by and hint at earlier and later words. This suggestiveness, then, provides a "reference" from one word to others which, if it cannot be made transparent to reason, nonetheless gives a certain sort of unity to Heidegger's treatment of the poem, a unity which is seen to "unfold itself" in the series of hints which constitute the basic progression of the reading. This progression, it now appears, is itself a diakenic one: the different phases of the poem, its different words, are seen as stages to be unified by a series of dynamic gaps.

Given the looseness of the poem's structure in Heidegger's interpretation, it would seem that a true "end," an arrival *somewhere* of the way of an individual poem or pathway of thinking, does not exist. That is, however, not the case:

> Such ways do not end in that they just break off. The ways end in that they rest—and this because they gather themselves in the singing of completion. The singing, however, lingers in a continual wandering and traveling, which continuously measures its stops in the metre of the versification, in the measure of poetic Saying. (Adk, pp. 133f, 141f)

A poem or a Heideggerean discussion of a poem does, then, have an ending; it is an ending which "gathers" up its entire progress but does not disturb its ongoing movement through words. In order not to disturb the progress, the "end" of the poem must be the kind of thing that belongs *in* the progress; it must itself be a word. The "riddle of thinking," Heidegger says in "Andenken," demands that its simple unity comes clearly to word. This it does in the poem itself, which in Heidegger's interpretation of it "names the word of the riddle" (Adk, pp. 133f, 141f) after an experience of the ambiguities of its own title. Thinking for Heidegger is thus a "calling into word" in the sense of the bestowal of an authentic name on something which is already "speaking" in language but which has not been recognized. According to Heidegger, such "speaking" is also a "gathering"; and what is gathered in this must exist, prior to the gathering, in some sort of dispersed form in language—like the principle of sufficient reason before Leibniz's formulation of it.[33]

If the thinking bestowal of an authentic name is for Heidegger a gathering, it is not a gathering which means that the activity of gathering can stop; for, as he puts it, "every originary and authentic naming says the Unspoken, and indeed does so in such a way that it remains unspoken"

(*WHD*, p. 119/196). It seems, then, that, though Heideggerean reading as such will never be completed, it has "sub-completions" which are the arrival of a way of thought in a name. These individual "ways to language" always, however, leave more to be thought and said.[34]

The meaning of "Andenken," for example, is not finally established in Hölderlin's poem or in Heidegger's interpretation of it. There is always new meaning to be brought forth, and the word is taken up again in "From a Dialogue on Language," where Heidegger remembers (*denkt an*) his departed friend Count Kuki (AGS, p. 85, 102/1, 14). The context is illuminating. Heidegger does not simply take the final formulation of "Andenken" from the earlier essay and apply it to a new situation. Rather the new situation is itself a continuation of the context of emergence of the name in Hölderlin's poem. Hölderlin there "remembers" his younger friends, the future poets of Germany, who in the last stanza are said to have departed for India (Adk, p. 133f, 81). Heidegger thinks of his younger friend and pupil Count Kuki, who has departed for Japan. The two major aspects of the new use of *Andenken* which do not seem to extend the old context of its emergence are that Hölderlin and the coming poets share nationality, which Heidegger and Kuki do not, and that Hölderlin, presumably, expects the young poets to return from India, while Kuki is buried in Japan. It is precisely these departures from the previously established context, however, which give "From a Dialogue on Language" its poetic power as a memorial to Count Kuki—as an *Andenken*. For the former departure works out to a reaffirmation of Heidegger's and Kuki's common homeland, their mutual "dwelling in the claim of the Two-fold"; and the latter affirms that the true concern of Kuki's life, the nature of the essence of Japanese art, is inexhaustible (cf. AGS, pp. 85f, 126/1f, 33).

The explication of the authentic name *Andenken* in the essay of that name thus achieves completion when the term is fully exposed in its progressive emergence in Hölderlin's poem; but that does not mean that the term can then be set down in dictionaries and used as if its meaning were firmly established in the fashion of our ordinary understanding of meaning. The term can always take on new meanings in new contexts which transform and enrich the old.

We can view these contexts in general, I think, as exhibiting linguistically the noema-noeton structure which Graeme Nicholson finds in Heideggerean thinking as presented in "Andenken." What I have called the "final" or "essential" word of the poem and of Heidegger's reading of it corresponds to the "noeton," which gathers other noeta and which, in Nicholson's interpretation of "Andenken," is symbolized there by the Garonne (and the Rhine). The "hints" are then the multiplicity of noeta which are gathered into a unity-in-dislocation through this essential noeton; and the metaphysical language of the poem, posited (unlike the "noeta") by the subject but "aimed" at something beyond it, would be the "noematic material" with which thinking approaches and handles its object, or noeton.[35]

Heideggerean thinking can thus be understood as a passage from "hint" to "name" in the qualified sense just outlined. That enables us to see what Heidegger means when he says that his later writings are not "about" language but are, rather, "from" language (AGS, p. 147ff/49). They do not state and discuss the primordial disclosure affected in and by language but instance it; Heideggerean thinking does not describe but *is* the emergence of an authentic name. This emergence takes place in the course of the essay; what seems to be a series of unconnected discussions of individual words turns out to have been, as Heidegger puts it in *What Is Called Thinking?*, an "ever-narrowing spiralling in" on what is to be said (*WHD*, p. 166/171). The "spiral" begins with the hints dispersed through language or through a poem and gathers them into a final name; this gathering takes the form, as we have seen, of a progressive experiencing of different meanings of the name which can be neither reduced to a single generic meaning nor dissociated completely from one another.

Heidegger's treatment of "Andenken" can thus be viewed as a letting-be of the linguistic diakena which constitute it and therefore as an extended polemic against construing the text exclusively along ousiodic lines. The poem originates, for example, not with an author as its moving and shaping cause but with two topographies—those of Swabia and Bordeaux. These topographies are, in the poem, at indeterminate removes from each other. They are also indeterminately removed from the poem itself, which in Heidegger's reading is not really about them at all. The reason it is not about them is that its unifying "element"—the basic word *Andenken*—receives in the poem a meaning which is in no clarifiable relation to what the word means in ordinary German; Hölderlin is not—or not only—writing in Swabia about his memories of Bordeaux but doing something altogether different.

Just as the unifying element of the poem is not a determinate form or nature but an interplay of disparate meanings, so the components of the poem—the words it contains—are not mere matter to be shaped and disposed by this unifying element. As "hints" they relate to each other in a variety of ways, each directing the reader (at least if the reader is Heidegger) into a variety of meditations upon what each such word suggests and highlights about the other words in the poem, as well as about ancillary topics. In all this, the individual words—each of which relates in a unique way to the basic word, *Andenken*, as well as to the other words in the poem—gradually reveal the diakenic interplay through which this basic word unifies them. This interplay, again, is the play of a set of mutually irreducible meanings; and it is that which, in being gradually revealed by the words the poem contains, exercises such "disposition" of them as obtains.

Where an Aristotelian ousia is to be understood in terms of its form alone, a Heideggerean poem must, we saw, be approached through each word it contains individually. This emphasis on individual words makes the boundaries of the poem suspect and porous. Individual words migrate into the poem, we might say, from the German language as it existed at the time of writing. In this immigration, they are transformed—sometimes, as with *Andenken* itself, radically. But their ordinary German meanings form the crucial background for Heidegger's own reading. They bring their individual histories with them, in other words, and are never transformed so radically that they can be understood independently of these histories— as if they had never existed outside the poem (the way my hands and arms never existed outside of my body).

The poem's words also continue their histories beyond the poem, for, as we have seen, they wander out of it again as well, in something akin to ousiodic "initiative." It is a type of initiative, however, which is exercised not merely by the poem's basic word but by all the words it contains and transforms. Such polymorphous initiative is guaranteed by the fact that all endings, in Heideggerean thinking, are merely provisional. If the words in which a poem is written are transformed by their sojourn within that poem, these transformations are such as to render them able to migrate from the poem into yet other contexts, in which they further transform themselves.

The poem, like the jug, is thus a gathering; words are brought into it, dynamically contained for a time by it, then leave it again. Heidegger's reading of the poem establishes this gathering through focusing on the individual words rather than on some overall structure or "message," seeing these words in relation not to a unifying theme but to the empty space of an interplay, and highlighting the transformations of words as they enter and leave the poem. Heidegger thus does not allow the poem to remain with the inviolate boundary, disposition, and initiative of an ousia. Nor does he merely describe non-ousiodic or diakenic features which the poem already has—for, in the standard understanding of it, it does not have these features at all. Rather his reading operates performatively; it does not describe the diakena but allows them to play.

But Heidegger does not, in all this, abandon description altogether. He must, for example, faithfully reproduce the text of the poem (or philosophical text) he meditates. Thus if the version of "Andenken" which is given at the outset of Heidegger's essay were not Hölderlin's established text but contained distortions introduced by Heidegger himself, his discussion of the poem would obviously be worthless. Similarly if the text were a falsification, if it had not been written by Hölderlin but, say, by a high school German teacher in Wisconsin a hundred years after Hölderlin's death. And the individual meanings that words like *Andenken* inherit from the German language of Hölderlin's day, as well as the new meanings that they take on in his poem and subsequently, must also be accurately conveyed and even (as Heidegger does throughout the essay) argued for.

It is not the individual words and their specific meanings to which Heidegger's reading does "violence," then, but the *connections* in terms of which they are understood. For when Heidegger is through, the poem can no longer be viewed solely in ousiodic terms, as the continuous development, through the formative artistry of its author, of a single meaning or message which is to pass unchanged into the mind of the reader. It is instead to be construed as a diakenic interplay. On this level, it is not presence—the ability of the poem and the words it contains to be, on some levels, the stable objects of true propositions—that is contested by Heidegger's interpretation. Rather Heidegger's reading is directed against viewing the poem in terms of the threefold domination of ousia. Heidegger's reading of "Andenken" thus "de-ousiodicizes" it into a diakenic interplay. It is this interplay which the reading does not describe but allows to take place.

With this, Heidegger's account of diakenic interplay is complete for current purposes. In general, what it shows (but does not say) is that a diakenon is, as form was for Aristotle, a unifying principle. What it unifies can be either a single thing, a series of phases, or a set of phenomena. In all cases, the unifying factor has no determinate nature of its own and is an emptiness—a nothing, rendered accessible solely through what it unifies. In such unification the unified elements, as we saw in the previous chapter, are

A. not mutually indifferent to one another: they must be encountered together in order to be understood;

B. not susceptible of being explained through any one of them;

C. incapable of explanation by any higher or more basic phenomenon.

That leads to major reconceptualizations of the three traits of ousiodic domination. First, emptiness, as empty, cannot be distinguished from other emptinesses; a Heideggerean thing is not self-contained but has at its core a radical openness to what is outside it. Its constitutive principles are not immanent to it, as the four causes are for Aristotle, but in a sense radically external to it; they are basic regions in terms of which it should be encountered, regions which themselves change dynamically as they "mirror" one another. The thing's boundaries, then, are porous. Because its very core opens to what is outside, the phenomena it unifies do not have their existence strictly as parts of it but have their own histories; they migrate into and out of the thing, as do the words of Hölderlin's poem.

The disposition exhibited by the thing is correspondingly empty. What it unifies are beings engaged in their own specific histories and processes of transformation. The positions they take up within the thing are determined not merely by the unifying form of the thing but also by these histories, as *Andenken* brings to the poem its own history in the form of the ordinary German understanding of the word.

Finally, the capacity of the thing to affect the world outside is directly exercised not by its unifying emptiness (which is already "outside") but by the beings it contains themselves, through the transformations they undergo while "within" the thing—as the word *Andenken*, transformed by Hölderlin's poem, plays its role, as I noted, in Heidegger's own later writings.

A thing is not an ousia but a place of transformative tarrying.

12

CONCLUSION

Heidegger provides no "theory of diakena." Nor is one possible. The diakena, to begin with, do not admit of a typology, demonstrating the possible species that their genus can admit or the possible modifications they can undergo while still remaining diakena. Nor do they admit of an etiology, showing their causes and conditions. They are not matters of fact; they are "nothings" and so on one level are all alike: nothing "in" one, no attribute or property, distinguishes it from any other. Indeed, we can, if we wish to invoke Leibniz's principle of the identity of indiscernibles, quite as well amalgamate them as distinguish them, so that they "are" one "thing"—*the* nothing which resides at the core of so many other "things": *das Nichts nichtet.*

But we cannot do so without quotation marks. For being nothings *which gather,* the diakena are also all different. What each gathers is a unique individual thing (in Heidegger's sense) which has no determinate form to share with other things and so cannot (except, like the jug, trivially) be seen as an instance of any species or class. In this respect, the diakena are multiply different and can be quite as well dispersed as distinguished—dispersed into a dissemination which underlies and escapes all classification and for which Heidegger's preferred name, perhaps, is *Differenz.*

What is possible and what Heidegger does provide (perhaps unknowingly) is minimal. It consists, first, in three general and empty criteria of what diakenicity consists in. A being is diakenically unified if it exhibits aspects or components which

A. cannot be understood independently of one another;

B. cannot be grounded in or explained by any one of their number;

C. cannot be grounded in or explained by any higher principle.

No indifference, no reduction, no sublation.

Heidegger provides two small enrichments of this empty scheme. The first is that the lack of indifference (criterion A) can be a matter, to use Humean terms, of either contiguity or succession. The different aspects or components of a diakenically unified "thing" may be given synchronically, so that we are free to move from each back to the others as we will, or diachronically, in a succession which we must respect. The second enrichment is that when the diakenon is a synchronous one, its components or aspects may themselves be either static or dynamic; they may be simply found together, like the walls and bottom of Heidegger's jug, or they may change in tune with one another, as in the mirror play of Heidegger's Fourfold.

Beyond these thin theoretical observations, which probably cannot be fleshed out much further, we find in Heidegger a practice: the practice of putting diakena into play. That is a discursive enterprise which remains faithful to the three principles just listed. It does not take up the aspects and components of a thing as independent objects in their own right, indifferent to one another, but allows recognition of whatever togetherness they may exhibit. It does not rush to explain this togetherness by attempting to derive all the participants in it from one of their number or to invent or discover some higher principle for it.

Putting-into-play remains content, then, with the nothingness that shows its own principled incapacities. It can operate via a vigilantly self-aware description, as with Heidegger's account of the jug, or it may actually copy into itself the words of the thing it treats, if this thing is a discourse or a poem such as Hölderlin's "Andenken." By attention to its incapacities, by not slipping into the limitless expanses of reduction or sublation, putting-into-play encounters active nothingness at work in the thing; or, better, it allows such nothingness to encounter us and to work in us. It thus transforms the things it is "about," allowing the diakena in them to play freely in our encounter with them. Traditional philosophical enterprises, such as description and inference, and traditional philosophical goals, such as truth, are for Heidegger subordinate parts of this enterprise: media not messages.

Diakena are then primarily features of our encounter with things: of things as phenomena. The universe when we are not around—the universe which science seeks to uncover—presumably contains no diakena at all. But when we *are* around they come into play, and that is because we are finite. For our finitude means, as *Being and Time* showed over and over again, that we cannot fully or finally know anything. There is always a residuum, a gap in our knowledge. This gap, in its specificity, helps define the things we encounter, as our death helps define our life. Putting diakena into play is thus a recognition of our own finitude; it is a *moral* sensitivity to the provisional truth of our existence.

It is because diakena are preeminently aspects of our encounter with things, not of things themselves, that the proper approach to them is to put them into play rather than to describe, classify, and explain them. This aspect of his thought places Heidegger at the end of a very ancient story, one he neither told nor heard: the story of ousia. For the diakena, we have seen, are challenges to ousia—to the idea that the unifying force in a thing can never be an emptiness but must always be the plenitude of a determinate form. Heidegger's view that our encounters with things are, because of our finitude, often unavoidably diakenic means that the human world is open to diakenic unity and can no longer be seen as structured on exclusively ousiodic lines. The long history of Western attempts to construe individuals and construct communities exclusively as bounded and disposed units is over.[1]

The fact that the end of the history of ousia is reached via a discussion of the abstract and arcane topic of Being—an ontological enterprise if ever there was one—means that Heidegger's challenge is double. First, it challenges standard versions of the history of philosophy. It sees that Aristotle helped to codify and Aquinas to consolidate ousia as the basic principle of the cosmos itself. It sees Descartes and the Empiricists as conducting rearguard attempts to maintain ousia as parametrically structuring the human realm once modern science had evicted it from nature. For it shows Descartes relocating ousia to the divine realm and the Empiricists simply reinstating it as a parameter without argument. After Heidegger, all codifications and consolidations, relocations and reinstatements, are over. *Ousia can henceforth be advanced as a parametric model only consciously, piecemeal, and with good reason.*

Heidegger himself, of course, explicitly construed his thought as a challenge to the history of metaphysics. But, I have argued, he misconstrued what he was challenging: he saw the primary problem with metaphysics as presence, not the ousiodic domination of presence. Since presence is an abstract and global characteristic which anything must have if it is to be the object of a true proposition, that left Heidegger's understanding of his enterprise abstract, empty, and arcane. His attempts to apply his thought to concrete social issues were correspondingly vacuous, vicious—and silly.

When we see the object of Heidegger's challenge to metaphysics as ousia, his thought becomes challenging in ways more fecund than he ever dared dream, and that is his second challenge to us. This challenge asks us to see human communities, some of them anyway, as diakenic, as porous, contingent, ungoverned, purposeless, unfathomable—and yet as communities nonetheless. It bids us turn away, if only temporarily, from the paradigms of domestic patriarchy and toward such things as the baffled stare of lovers into one another's eyes. It calls us to see the *agon* of parent with child, of sibling with sibling, as a strife which produces no victor but eases each into her own. It invites us to look away from the boundaries, dispositions, and initiatives of governments and toward the multifarious ferment of concrete social actions. It urges us to recognize the fragility of our identities and communities. And it presses us to accept the mortality of absolutely everything we love.

Social arrangements which exhibit forms of diakenic interplay would be Heideggerean "engines of liberation." Such engines are rarely to be found, at least in the West; nondiscursive diakenic structures are in social play only there in very marginal ways, in practices whose recalcitrance to philosophical

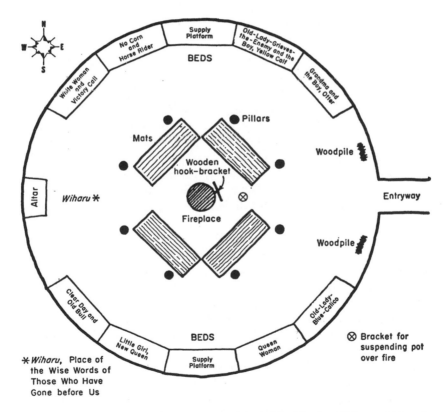

FIGURE 3. Pawnee earth lodge. From Gene Weltfish, *The Lost Universe: Life and Culture* (Lincoln: University of Nebraska Press, 1977).

255

discussion is all too easily explained. But I will briefly consider one: Gene Weltfish's classic description of the Pawnee earth lodge (figure 3).[2]

Like the House of Pansa, to which it forms a decisive antithesis, such a lodge has very definite boundaries—here required by the climate, since the lodge is to provide shelter against winters on the high prairies. But the outside world is constantly present, because the lodge is a "microcosm of the universe":

> As one was at home inside, one was also at home in the outside world. For the dome of the sky was the high-arching roof of the universe, and the horizon all around was the circular wall of the cosmic house. Through the roof of the house the star gods poured down their strength from their appropriate directions in a constant stream. In the west was the Evening Star, a beautiful woman, Goddess of Night and Germination, and in her garden the corn and buffalo were constantly being renewed so that the people could eat; and in the western part of the house the sacred buffalo skull and the bundle with its ears of corn symbolized this power. In the eastern sky was the Morning Star—god of light, of fire, and of war. As he rose every morning he sent his beam into the long entryway of the house and lit the fire in an act of cosmic procreation. . . . (LU, p. 78)

As the act of "procreation" which begins each day suggests, the house is also structured, not as the domain of a man but as the womb of a woman. The most female body parts, then, are in this culture not mere matter but structuring principles. Beds are assigned to women and their partners. Household activities represent woman's reproductive powers, which means that the young women are to the west, away from the inseminating power of the entering sun, while the old women are to the east, near the entrance and "on their way out" (LU, p. 78f).

Like the House of Pansa, the lodge has a spatial center. But unlike the *tablinum*, it is not a center which anyone can occupy, for a fire burns in it. Above the fire is a smoke hole, through which the smoke escapes—and through which the lodge is open to the sky, which sends in light, rain and snow, and wind. The lodge is thus, like Jeremy Bentham's "panopticon" which Foucault discusses in *Discipline and Punish*,[3] spatially centered on a vertical axis—but one which is permanently empty. Also in contrast to Bentham's panoptic prison, the earth lodge does not open out onto a larger society but stretches its empty vertical axis from the fire, the inner source of light and warmth, to the top of the sky. Stretches, that is, to the farthest, highest part of the outside world—and into a constantly changing interplay of fire and heaven.

There is another center to the house, the *wi-haru*, "the place where the wise words of those who have gone before us are resting." This center is a temporal one; it locates the repository of ancient wisdom and orients the house to its own traditions. Like the spatial center, the *wi-haru* is empty; indeed, it is invisible. And no one can occupy it; rather than step over it, people moving from the north or south half of the house to the other half always circle around by way of the east.

The household so structured is impermanent and porous in membership:

> Twice a year when the tribe set out on its semiannual buffalo hunts, the household work group fragmented itself into many smaller groupings, which reassorted themselves so that an able hunter became the nucleus of each new composite grouping. When they returned to the village the households did not necessarily reassemble with the same personnel as before. This was entirely optional, and there were many reasons why people might decide to join a different household group than the one they had been with before leaving. . . .
>
> The three duplicate stations on the north and south sides of the lodge . . . [were] a frame into which any individual woman could fit herself in whatever household she entered with little loss of efficiency, since her duties were so clearly defined once she selected the category to which she belonged. And a child with a grandmother to care for it could fit in anywhere. Young men led a more transient existence. They were likely to congregate at different times in one lodge or another. . . .
>
> Old men also moved about rather freely, staying over-night in various households whenever they were detained late of an evening telling stories or participating in a ceremony. As for the mature man, his "married-in" household was not considered his "true" home. There he was an outsider with formal obligations, which sometimes tended to weigh rather heavily on him. Then he would go where his home really was—that of his sisters and his mother. . . . When this happened, his wife understood, and she knew he would be back after a few days. (LU, p. 23f)

The earth lodge is thus a home in which no one "belongs" in an ousiodic sense; all are, like the lodge itself, transient.

The furnishings of the house are symmetrical ("three duplicate stations") because in fact it is inhabited by two groups of people, one along the north wall and one along the south. The two groups share household tasks equally, but not according to any preconceived plan: each group sees and does what needs to be done at any particular time.

> From our [Western] point of view a plan would be made and the people fitted into it—from the Pawnee view, the plan emerged from the feelings of the people. This difference of approach is so basic I feel impelled to stress it particularly. . . . In a sense the rhythm of Pawnee work life was like a ballet, whereas ours is like a prison lockstep: "You must, you must, you must get to work!" (LU, p. 18f)

Weltfish's account of the Pawnee earth lodge gives the paradigm of a way of life, indeed of a domesticity, which is not ousiodically structured. It is a nondiscursive engine of liberation from ousiodic structure.

Discursive engines of liberation exist. They are to be found, still unheard, in the discourses of what I call the Great Demarcation, in the thought of philosophers who follow Heidegger both in challenging ousiodic structures and in not recognizing that they are doing so. I make this point rise in a companion work, *Philosophy and Freedom,* which treats of Derrida, Foucault, Habermas, and Rorty, the key thinkers of a Great Demarcation originally envisaged, if only darkly, by Nietzsche.

To raise the Great Demarcation out of the darkness, we must identify—as I have not yet done—the final modern redoubt of ousiodic structure. In chapter 8, I argued that for Hume, the domain of such structure had been reduced to the individual human mind (after Descartes had located it in God, Hobbes in the state, and Locke in property ownership). But its residence even there is dubious, because the human mind does not, for Hume, unproblematically exhibit ousiodic structure. Only when the imagination is disciplined—dispositively ordered—by the principles of the association of ideas can it have it; and only such discipline, we saw, allows human nature to survive. In spite of Hume's recurrent dismissals of philosophy as either mere amusement or "melancholy and delirium,"[4] philosophy has an important role to play in instilling ousiodic structure into the individual mind. For it is philosophy, of course—Hume's philosophy—which discovers these principles and discerns their influence on the mind. Similarly, if the reader will recall, for the other modern philosophers, for Descartes, Hobbes and Locke—as well as for Spinoza and Leibniz—philosophy itself (or "science") is the right ordering of ideas and hence the right ordering of the mind. The final unchallenged redoubt of ousiodic form in the West is therefore philosophy itself. And that is where Derrida, Foucault, Habermas, and Rorty come in: they all contest ousiodic structure in philosophy itself, though in varying ways and never with full success. And so it is they who can point us toward the future of philosophy, toward what I call "situating reason."

What philosophy will be like once it has passed through the Great Demarcation is beyond the scope of this book. But a clue emerges from consideration of another group of Native Americans. The Tewa of New Mexico, one of the most ancient Native American groups, have been amply studied by anthropologists. One problem that has attracted attention concerns the dual organization of the pueblo. The problem was that the two moieties of the Tewa pueblo did not seem to stand in any stable relationship to one another. Neither was dominant over the other, as with the helots and Spartans of ancient Greece or the free men and slaves of the American South. Nor were they co-equals, either. At some times and in some respects, one moiety would dominate; at other times and in other respects, the other. But there was no identifiable mechanism for allocating these exchanges of dominance.

This situation (which has obvious analogues among the Pawnee and throughout the "primitive" world) confounded anthropologists. All attempts to find a single, governing center to the Tewa pueblo failed. Lévi-Strauss finally argued that such dual organizations do not really exist, that the two moieties in what appears to be a closed system are really determined by their shared opposition to some third thing (such as the outside world or nature) which is then the hidden factor determining the status of the other two. Sometimes this third factor was even "confused" with one of the two, reducing what was really a triadic (or even more complex) organization to an appearance of duality. Lévi-Strauss's conclusion was that

> the study of so-called dual organizations discloses so many anomalies and contradictions in relation to extant theory that we should be well advised to reject the theory and to treat the apparent manifestations of dualism as superficial distortions of structures whose real nature is quite different and vastly more complex.[5]

The complexity is required, ultimately, by Lévi-Strauss's tacit adherence to the structure of ousiodic domination. That requires there to be, at the core of any organization, an identifiable dominating factor, either something over and above the members of the organization themselves, like the Cartesian God, or something in the possession of one of the two sides of the organization, as rational form for Aristotle was enacted by the master and not the slave.

The problem remained until a Tewa, Alphonso Ortiz, became an anthropologist and studied his own people. He found, first, that there is not merely a single mediating link but a number of them—"people of the middle" who on specified occasions are detached from their own moieties and oversee ceremonies, *Towa é* who have certain responsibilities for the whole, and so on.[6]

But who mediates the mediators? How are specific mediating functions determined and allocated among the various mediating groups? It emerges from Ortiz's recounting of the various occasions on which mediation occurs and of the ways it is achieved that "the entire cycle is tied to nature's basic rhythm and to the Tewa's attempts to influence that rhythm for his well-being."[7] Or, to put this differently, and to reveal my second clue:

> We have a persuasive answer to the question of how the moieties can be in a reciprocal relationship and in a relationship of hierarchical superordination. . . . The answer the Tewa present is, in a word, *time*. The asymmetrical relationship which obtains *at any given time* between the moieties becomes symmetrical over a period of a year or two years. . . . How can the society be united and divided at the same time? The answer here is simply that since there is temporal overlap, no clear and consistent lines of division can emerge; the moieties can never really be uniformly divided on a major structural issue.[8]

This answer is suggested by the very names of the moieties: the Summer People and the Winter People.

What if time were the single phenomenon, familiar and inescapable, which can "unite" the antithetical sides of situating reason? The possibility is tempting, and not only in view of Heidegger's claim, in the Preamble to *Being and Time,* that the provisional aim of the book is "the interpretation of *time* as the possible horizon of any understanding of Being whatever." Weltfish's account of the Pawnee joins with Ortiz's account of the Tewa in that both see the social order at any given moment as governed not by individuals or by laws but by time itself—manifest among the Tewa in the movements of heavenly bodies and among the Pawnee in interplay of the feelings and domestic requirements of the moment. The clue which these accounts of Native American life furnish to reconciling the thoroughly temporal nature of the Great Demarcation with philosophical cognition is thus that we should view such cognition not merely as itself a temporal process but as a *response* to time; time not only characterizes our cognition and our lives but governs them.

Following up this clue is a matter for future work, and I can only make some suggestions here. Conceiving of philosophy as a temporal response to time rather than as a temporal push toward eternity will mean reshaping, once again, our understanding of time itself. We must see it not as a concept or a natural phenomenon but as a parameter, something which tells us how to treat things. Understood in such terms, past and future would become not tenses but rubrics. The past, for example, could be the space of possible convergences and of connections under way, for nothing can converge with other beings unless it already exists, no matter how much its convergence with these beings transforms it. Connections, then, are not given in a sort of timeless present—for in truly temporalized thought there are no timeless structures—but are always connectings, processes. Even causality, as we experience it, is such a dynamic encounter with the past. For we do not see that A causes B until we have seen both A and B; only then can we relate them. Causality *as we experience* it thus arranges itself, not in the form

$$A \rightarrow B$$

(where → denotes causal connection) but in the form:

$$A\ B \rightarrow .$$

In the human sphere, we can be connected with one another only through the past, through our acceptance of ourselves and others as products of a common history, if only the history that has produced the language in which we share ourselves as *zôa logon éxonta,* animals with speech. These histories are conveyed via narratives of various sorts, through which we are suspended and centrated.

The future, by contrast, might be reconceived as the parametric space of necessary disconnection—of rupture and incommensuration. It would not be the smooth or catastrophe-ridden perpetuation of the present, but—as for Heidegger—something wholly unknowable (and hence incommensurable) which structures all our cognition. For in the human world, otherness arrives from the future; someone is "other" than me if she retains the capacity to surprise me. Or, as Levinas puts it, "The other is the future."[9]

Ousia, we see, is structured in such a way as to discipline time itself. The emergence of a being on the ousiodic model is not the emergence of anything new; it is not even, at bottom, the emergence of anything at all but simply the continuous progression of an unchanging, atemporal form from one "packet" of matter to another. The future of the thing, its initiative, is the other side of this idea, the passage of the form of a thing beyond its boundaries. The disciplining force, of course, is presence, the unchanging nature of form. But it is not the lack of change in itself which is problematic; there are many things which change only slowly and so are stably present. It is not presence itself but the use of presence as a disciplining force which is the difficulty.

And so situating reason, codifying the slow emancipation of the West from ousia, comes to see beings as radically temporal, as gathered around their pasts and riven by their futures. Time, which Aristotle hoped to capture with the structures of Being, turns out to capture them back—in suspension, incommensuration, centration, and rupturing. The path to post-ousiodic thought must (like all responsible philosophy) begin historically—in this case, with a codifying reflection on the capture of time.[10]

Our time is a time of crisis, and the crisis is often identified as the "end of metaphysics." The identification, if my argumentation in the present book is persuasive, is correct; metaphysics, as the legitimation and deployment of ousia in thought, is over. The resulting situation, if I am right, is dangerous but far from hopeless. It arises from the final collapse of *one* great parameter, that of ousia. But, as Hume could teach us, it does not extend to reason, language, intelligibility, or moral action, except insofar as these have been conceived in ousiodic terms. That is a large exception, to be sure; it is only to be expected that it should occasion a vast tumult of confusion and lament, both within and outside of philosophy. It is unavoidable in such a situation that many quiet and challenging voices go unheard and that the most important insights of major thinkers go unappreciated. But because the crisis is ontological, these quiet voices, as well as the arcane insights that they proffer, are momentous.

As quiet and momentous, Janka, as your letters were to me.

NOTES

INTRODUCTION

1. Victor Farias, *Heidegger et le nazisme,* trans. Myriam Bennaroch and Jean-Baptiste Grasset (Lagrasse: Editions Verdier, 1987).

2. Joseph Kockelmans, *On the Truth of Being* (Bloomington: Indiana University Press, 1984), p. 264f.

3. A single example of Farias's unfairness: after the war, Heidegger attempted to find a job in Germany for several of his students, among them Karl Löwith, who had spent the war years in Italy and then Japan. Farias recounts this with the single goal of showing that Heidegger, at a time when he was under *Berufsverbot* and was forbidden to exercise any of the functions of a university professor, was still trying to be a power in German academic politics (Farias, *Heidegger et le nazisme,* p. 286). That Heidegger might have had humanitarian concerns or a high regard for Löwith's work, which was certainly of the highest quality, is not mentioned. Neither is the fact that Löwith was Jewish by birth.

4. Jean-François Lyotard, *Heidegger and "the Jews,"* trans. David Carroll (Minneapolis: University of Minnesota Press, 1990), p. 53f.

5. See Hans Sluga, *Heidegger's Crisis* (Cambridge, Mass: Harvard University Press, 1993), for an investigation of the overwhelming complicity of the German philosophical establishment in the Nazi project.

6. Among the most important of these are Jacques Derrida, *Of Spirit: Heidegger and the Question,* trans. Geoffrey Bennington and Rachel Bowlby (Chicago: University of Chicago Press, 1989); Philippe Lacoue-Labarthe, *Heidegger, Art and Politics,* trans. Chris Turner (Oxford: Basil Blackwell, 1990); and Reiner Schürmann, *Heidegger on Being and Acting: From Principles to Anarchy* (Bloomington: Indiana University Press), 1987.

7. Lyotard, *Heidegger and "the Jews,"* p. 71f.

8. Derrida, *Of Spirit,* p. 32.

9. Lacoue-Labarthe, *Heidegger, Art and Politics,* pp. 97f, 1102f.

10. The main writings are Jürgen Habermas, "Zur Veröffentlichung von

Vorlesungen aus dem Jahre 1936," and "Die große Workung," *Philosophisch-politische Profile*, 3rd ed. (Frankfurt: Suhrkamp, 1981), pp. 65-81; chap. 6, *Der philosophische Diskurs der Moderne*, 2nd ed. (Frankfurt: Suhrkamp, 1985), pp. 158-190; hereinafter *PDM* (English translation, *The Philosophical Discourse of Modernity*, trans. Frederick Lawrence [Cambridge, Mass.: MIT Press, 1987]); and "Work and Weltanschauung: The Heidegger Controversy from a German Perspective," trans. John McCumber, *Critical Inquiry* 15 (1989), pp. 431-456.

11. In my *Poetic Interaction* (Chicago: University of Chicago Press, 1989), pp. 124-142.

12. This is not the whole or even the brunt of Habermas's critique of Heidegger. Another major focus of his attack is Heidegger's enterprise of *Seinsgeschichte*, the uncovering of epochal transformations in Being which somehow lie wholly beyond, yet govern, everything else that happens: *PDM*, p. 183/154; "Work and Weltanschauung," pp. 437, 438f. I discuss this topic in chaps. 9 and 10. For the moment, I wonder if reducing Heidegger's later thought to *Seinsgeschichte* can do justice to Schürmann's point that even in Heidegger's writings on *Seinsgeschichte*, "it is still one entity [rather than Being itself] that institutes a world"; Schürmann, *Heidegger on Being and Acting*, p. 144.

13. Guido Schneeburger, *Nachlese zu Heidegger* (Bern, 1962).

14. Heidegger did not himself publish *Hölderlins Hymne*, which appeared after his death as vol. 53 of *Gesamtausgabe* (Frankfurt: Klostermann, 1984).

15. Habermas, "Work and Weltanschauung," p. 440.

16. See my "Language and Appropriation: The Nature of Heideggerean Dialogue," *Personalist* 60 (1979), pp 384-396, and *Poetic Interaction*, pp. 143-161.

17. The "meaning" of a thing for Heidegger at this stage of his career is, briefly, the way it encounters us as something that we already understand—the way it enters into and, if "poetic," radically transforms previously existing cultural and linguistic frameworks. See Martin Heidegger, "Der Ursprung des Kunstwerkes," *Holzwege*, 4th ed. (Frankfurt: Klostermann, 1963), p. 60f (English translation, "The Origin of the Work of Art," *Poetry, Language, Thought*, trans. Albert Hofstadter [New York: Harper & Row, 1971], p. 73f).

18. Martin Heidegger, "Aus einem Gespräch von der Sprache," *Unterwegs zur Sprache*, 4th ed. (Pfullingen: Neske, 1971) (English translation, "From a Dialogue on Language," *On the Way to Language*, trans. Albert Hofstadter [New York: Harper & Row, 1971], p. 123/30).

19. Martin Heidegger, "Hölderlin und das Wesen der Dichtung," *Erläuterungen zu Hölderlins Dichtung* (Frankfurt: Klostermann, 1951), p. 36f.

20. Martin Heidegger, "Andenken," *Erläuterungen zu Hölderlins Dichtung*, p. 95f. I discuss this essay further in chap. 11. In the course of "Andenken," as Emil Staiger notes with some wonderment, Heidegger really does discuss every single word of Hölderlin's fifty-nine-line poem; Emil Staiger, "Hölderlin-Forschung Während des Krieges," *Trivium* 4 (1946), p. 215. Cf. Beda Alleman, *Hölderlin et Heidegger*, trans. François Fedier (Paris: Presses Universitaires de France, 1959), pp. 151-155.

21. As I put it elsewhere, "Hölderlin's poem is not robbed of its poetic truth if no oak ever grew above the Garonne at Bordeaux, and van Gogh's painting of peasant shoes is not 'false' if no peasant ever wore the models. But if no Greek ever uttered the words in Parmenides' fragment B.6, *Was Heißt Denken? is* false, from the start of part II." See McCumber, "Language and Appropriation," p. 393.

22. Heidegger's fullest, though still cryptically brief, discussion of hints is in "From a Dialogue on Language," pp. 114-117/24-26.

23. Martin Heidegger, "Hölderlins Erde und Himmel," *Erläuterungen zu Hölderlins Dichtung*, p. 164. This essay is not contained in the earlier edition of *Erläuterungen zu Hölderlins Dichtung*, to which reference is made elsewhere in this chapter.

24. I discuss this aspect of Heidegger's writings in more detail later in this introduction and in chap. 10.

25. McCumber, "Language and Appropriation," p. 393.

26. Martin Heidegger, "Der Weg zur Sprache," *Unterwegs zur Sprache*, p. 261 (English translation, "The Way to Language," *On the Way to Language*, trans. Peter D. Herz [New York: Harper & Row, 1971], p. 130).

27. For the earlier concept of "phenomenon," see Martin Heidegger, *Sein und Zeit* (Tübingen: Niemeyer, 1967), p. 32 (page numbers to the German edition of *Being and Time* are given marginally in Heidegger, *Being and Time*, trans. John MacQuarrie and Edward Robinson [New York: Harper & Row, 1962]). Heideigger's later concept of "way" must be reconstructed from examples given in a number of his texts; for such a reconstruction, see my *Poetic Interaction*, p. 145ff.

28. And so (presumably) "irrational" if it cannot; cf. Jürgen Habermas, *Theorie des kommunikativen Handelns*, vol. 1 (Frankfurt: Suhrkamp, 1981), p. 25ff (English translation, *Theory of Communicative Action*, vol. 1, trans. Thomas McCarthy [Boston: Beacon Press, 1984] p. 8ff).

29. Habermas, *Der philosophische Diskurs der Moderne*, p. 181/153.

30. Martin Heidegger, "Bauen Wohnen Denken" and "Dichterisch wohnet der Mensch," *Vorträge und Aufsätze*, vol. 2 (Pfullingen: Neske, 1967), pp. 19-36 and 61-78 respectively. The two essays frame a third, "Das Ding," which I discuss at length in chap. 10. The three clearly form a unit; none is mentioned by Habermas. Also Heidegger, "Der Ursprung des Kunstwerkes," *Holzwege*, pp. 7-68 (English translation, "The Origin of the Work of Art," *Poetry, Language, Thought*, pp. 15-88).

31. See the discussion of "world disclosure" and the general account of the life-world in Habermas, *Theorie des kommunikativen Handelns*, vol. 2, pp. 182-228 (English translation, *The Theory of Communicative Action*, vol. 2, pp. 119-152).

32. I have argued for a view of *Being and Time* which is in substantial agreement with Habermas's, in "Communication and Authenticity in *Being and Time*," *Tulane Studies in Philosophy* 32 (1984), pp. 45-52. The *Rektoratsrede* and other speeches from the Nazi period speak for themselves. Also see Habermas, "Work and Weltanschauung," p. 437f.

33. Cf. Habermas, "Work and Weltanschauung," pp. 445f and 453 for examples.

34. Martin Heidegger, *Einführung in die Metaphysik* (Tübingen: Niemeyer, 1966), p. 28f (English translation, *Introduction to Metaphysics*, trans. Ralph Manheim [New Haven, Conn.: Yale University Press, 1959], p. 37).

35. The lecture in which Heidegger makes this claim has never been published. For discussions of the issue of Heidegger and the Holocaust, cf. Habermas, "Work and Weltanschauung," pp. 447-453, as well as Robert Bernasconi, *Heidegger in Question* (Atlantic Highlands, N.J.: Humanities Press, 1993), p. viii and n. 4; Philippe Lacoue-Labarthe, *Heidegger, Art, and Politics*, trans. Chris Turner (Oxford: Basil Blackwell, 1990), p. 34f; and the essays in Alan Milchman and Alan Rosenberg, eds., *Martin Heidegger and the Holocaust* (Atlantic Highlands, N.J.: Humanities Press, 1996).

36. See on this Stephen Toulmin, *Cosmopolis* (New York: Free Press, 1990).

37. See Martin Heidegger, *Basic Problems of Phenomenology,* trans. Albert Hofstadter (Bloomington: Indiana University Press, 1982), pp. 4-12; *Beiträge zur Philosophie* (Frankfurt: Klostermann, 1989), p. 25.

38. This is the general topic of the section of Augustine's *Confessions* which Heidegger quotes, selectively, in *Sein und Zeit,* p. 43f: *factus sum mihi terra difficultatis et sudoris nimii;* St. Augustine, *Confessions,* X.16.

39. Reginald Lilly, "Toward the Hermeneutic of *Der Satz vom Grund,*" in J. Sallis, G. Moneta, and J. Taminiaux, eds., *The Collegium Phaenomenologicum* (Dordrecht: Kluwer, 1988), p. 208.

40. Heidegger, "Brief über den Humanismus," *Wegmarken* (Frankfurt: Klostermann 1967), p. 187 (English translation, "Letter on Humanism," *Basic Writings,* ed. and trans. David Farrell Krell [New York: Harper & Row, 1977], p. 235). With regard to the unclarity of referential language, I am thinking of such things as the ongoing controversy about the role of causality in reference, with the ensuing uncertainty as to whether reference is, in Alfred Tarski's sense, a "semantic" concept at all; see the essays in Stephen P. Schwartz, ed., *Naming, Necessity, and Natural Kinds* (Ithaca, N.Y.: Cornell University Press, 1977); Alfred Tarski, "The Semantic Conception of Truth and the Foundations of Semantics," *Philosophy and Phenomenological Research* 4 (1944), pp. 341-376. Also see the brilliant "undoing" of the concept of truth in Arthur Fine, *The Shaky Game: Einstein, Realism, and the Quantum Theory* (Chicago: University of Chicago Press, 1986).

41. Hence, as Heidegger says, the issue for him is one of getting people to see what is right before their eyes; "Vom Wesen und Begriff der *Physis.* Aristotles' Physik B, 1," *Wegmarken,* p. 333.

42. Martin Heidegger, "Vom Wesen der Wahrheit," *Wegmarken,* pp. 73-98 (English translation, "On the Essence of Truth," *Basic Writings,* pp. 113-142).

43. Martin Heidegger, "Die Frage nach der Technik," *Vorträge und Aufsätze,* p. 19.

44. Cf. on this Schürmann's treatment of the unity of the "originary origin" in *Heidegger on Being and Acting,* p. 144ff.

45. For this term of art, see the general introduction to my *Poetic Interaction.*

46. Whether emptiness can gather emptiness is an arcane point, perhaps related to the possibility of the "keeping silent about silence" (*Schweigen über das Schweigen*) to which Heidegger briefly refers near the end of "From a Dialogue on Language"; see Martin Heidegger, "Aus einem Gespräch von der Sprache," *Unterwegs zur Sprache,* p. 152 (English translation, "From a Dialogue on Language," *On the Way to Language,* p. 52).

47. In a work entitled *(Up)ending Metaphysics: Nineteenth-Century Challenges to Ousia,* forthcoming.

48. J. L. Ackrill, *Aristotle the Philosopher* (Oxford: Oxford University Press, 1981), p. 24.

49. For a discussion of the sense in which I use this term, see my *Company of Words* (Evanston, Ill.: Northwestern University Press, 1993), pp. 112-118.

1. ARISTOTLE'S CONCEPT OF OUSIA

1. For the key philosophical antecedent of Aristotle's conception of ousia, see the appendix to part 1 of this book, "Plato as Prehistory"; for an account of ousiodic structure as early as the Homeric household, see. William James Booth, *Households:*

On the Moral Architecture of the Economy (Ithaca, N.Y.: Cornell University Press, 1993), pp. 17-93.

2. Hence I do not use "disposition" in the sense of *Cats.* 8b28f, 36ff, in which—as in *Metaph.*—it refers to a temporary quality of a thing, as opposed to "habit" (*hexis*), the more permanent possession by a thing of some quality.

3. Montgomery Furth, *Substance, Form, and Psyche: An Aristotelian Metaphysics* (Cambridge: Cambridge University Press, 1988), p. 2.

4. Terence Irwin, *Aristotle's First Principles* (Oxford: Clarendon Press, 1988), p. 471; among the examples given by Irwin there are Bonitz, Eucken, and Leblond.

5. Hermann Bonitz, *Aristotelis Metaphysica*, vol. 1 (Bonn, 1848), p. 29; quoted in Irwin, *Aristotle's First Principles*, p. 640 n. 4.

6. Furth, *Substance, Form, and Psyche*, pp. 5f, 67f.

7. Terence Irwin, in a way, comes close to this view; he believes that Aristotle's "first principles" need to be understood as the basis for his more concrete investigations. The main contrast between us, in addition to the much more selective nature of my treatment and the different specific issues it focuses on, is that Irwin works from the Aristotelian ideal of demonstrative science and so tends to view Aristotle's principles not as merely a hermeneutical basis for subsequent understanding but as, at least ideally, a set of premises which are true in themselves (being established by what Irwin calls "strong dialectic") and can be built upon in a logically rigorous way; see Irwin, *Aristotle's First Principles*, pp. 122-133, and Irwin's example of Aristotle's use of form in his psychology, pp. 288-290. Irwin recognizes throughout his book, however, that this ideal is often not attained or even very relevant; see p. 15. I dispense with it altogether, working only with the looser notion of a "hermeneutical base." Furth also approaches the view I hold, regarding Aristotle's metaphysics not as an independently validated foundational theory but as a "methodology . . . for the biological sciences" (Furth, *Substance, Form, and Psyche*, p. 8). True—but not only. As I show in chap. 3 Aristotle's metaphysics provides a parametric (again, not deductive) basis for ethics, politics, and household management as well as for biology and psychology.

8. Anyone who has read my *Poetic Interaction* (Chicago: University of Chicago Press, 1989) will not be surprised at the idea that philosophical texts can and should function in this way.

9. See in particular Joseph Owens, *The Doctrine of Being in the Aristotelian Metaphysics*, 2d ed. (Toronto: Pontifical Institute of Medieval Studies, 1963).

10. Furth suggests that it is *Metaph.* V; Furth, *Substance, Form, and Psyche*, p. 227.

11. J. L. Ackrill, *Aristotle's Categories and De Interpretatione* (Oxford: Clarendon Press, 1963), pp. 74f.

12. G. E. L. Owen, "Inherence," *Phronesis* 10 (1965), pp. 97-105.

13. And hence I tend to side with Furth, *Substance, Form, and Psyche*, pp. 16, 20, 41-47. For the other side of the controversy, see Daniel Graham, *Aristotle's Two Systems* (Oxford: Clarendon Press, 1987), pp. 27-29.

14. Montgomery Furth, "Transtemporal Stability in Aristotelian Substances," *Journal of Philosophy* 75 (1978), p. 628. It is immaterial to my purpose whether Aristotle's avoidance of these matters in *Cat.* is intentional, as Furth thinks, or not ("intention" is a slippery category for philosophers). That the failure to account for how one thing can cause changes in another is part of the failure—or refusal—of the ontology of *Cats.* to provide an account of change in general is argued by Graham, *Aristotle's Two*

Systems, pp. 104f, 120-123. Also cf. Irwin's account of the issue in the *Physics,* a text which on this matter is notably more developed than the *Cat.;* Irwin, *Aristotle's First Principles,* p. 223f. Aristotle's use, in defining inherence, of *eggignesthai* rather than, for example, *eneinai* suggests that *Cats.* massively presupposes, rather than accounts for, change.

15. Furth, "Transtemporal Stability," p. 628; *Substance, Form, and Psyche,* p. 34f.

16. The distinction between these two ontologies is pursued at length in Graham, *Aristotle's Two Systems.* The reason for my terminology here is given in Ellen Stone Haring, "Substantial Form in Aristotle's *Metaphysics* Z I," *Review of Metaphysics* 10 (1956-1957), p. 308f: "'Substance' suggests something standing under something else. Therefore it is nearest in meaning to the Greek *hypokeimenon,* not to the much more inclusive *ousia.*"

17. Also cf. Irwin, *Aristotle's First Principles,* p. 199f. The two criteria, as Irwin notes (p.206), are divergent: "The essence-criterion seems to lead to the universal . . . but the subject-criterion seems to lead to the particular." For Irwin, Aristotle solves the problem of divergence with his argument in Z.3 that form itself—and so essence, and so the universal—is in a sense the most basic substrate, for which see Irwin, pp. 211-217, as well as the treatment in Graham, *Aristotle's Two Systems,* pp. 230, 263-289. I present a different view in this chapter. The persistence of substance-ontology in the later metaphysics is perhaps part of what Furth had in mind in a passage deleted from my earlier quotation of his *cri de coeur:* "the views in question not only are ones which Aristotle arrived at in stages, and perhaps never fully disentangled from their superseded antecedents in earlier thought of his."

18. Graham locates the transition to the new account in Aristotle, *Physics* I, esp. I.7; see Graham, *Aristotle's Two Systems,* pp. 123-152. A clear account of at least some of Aristotle's probable motives in following this trajectory is given in Edwin Hartman, "Aristotle on the Identity of Substance and Essence," *Philosophical Review* 85 (1976), pp. 545-561, esp. pp. 545-549. My interpretation of Aristotle's hylomorphism in this and the next chapter owes much to Mary Louise Gill, *Aristotle on Substance: The Paradox of Unity* (Princeton, N.J.: Princeton University Press, 1989).

19. Cf. *Metaph.* V.22 11022a3-36; also cf. Haring, "Substantial Form in Aristotle's *Metaphysics* Z, I," p. 311. In contrast to recent scholarly practice, I use Roman numerals for the books of the *Metaphysics.* Bostock's arguments against this usage simply do not convince me; David Bostock, *Aristotle: Metaphysics Books Z and H* (Oxford: Clarendon Press, 1994), p. ix.

20. In *Cats.,* no substance is more truly substance than any other; *Cats.* 5 2b26-28. Cf. Graham, *Aristotle's Two Systems,* p. 102f.: "the man is *prior in substance* to the boy. Surely the boy is a substance according to Aristotle. But he does not have the complete form of the man, and so he is not fully a substance. In fact, though Aristotle does not use the word, the boy is less of a man than the adult." Also cf. Irwin, *Aristotle's First Principles,* p. 205, and Furth, "Transtemporal Stability," p. 645.

21. Separability and self-accordance are related in Aristotle's philosophical lexicon, at *Metaph.* V.18: it can in one sense be said that any property a thing has when it is considered as existing by itself, separately from other things, it has "according to itself."

22. Indeed, even if we just talk about "walking" or "to walk," it is understood that such action is the action of an ousia, indefinite though the reference may be—just as Descartes, two millennia later, would assume that by referring to the act of thinking he was referring to a thinker: *I* think, therefore *I* am.

23. At *Metaph.* VII.12, 1039a214, Aristotle argues that one ousia cannot be "present in" another. I will not expatiate on the meaning of or the reasons for Aristotle's recurrence to his earlier vocabulary. The claim that ousiai are independent of one another seems clear.

24. As *Metaph.* VII.1 1028a33-36 puts it, "for of all the categories none is separable, but only ousia." Part of the problem here, I take it, is the fine line between "actually separate" and merely "separable." Aristotle's text crosses this line at will: properties cannot be separated from substances and hence are said to be not "separable" from them; but substances are not merely "separable" from properties but actually "separate." The relation between separation of properties from substances, on the one hand, and separation of substances from each other, on the other, is explored in more detail than I can go into in exchanges between Gail Fine and Donald Morrison in *Oxford Studies in Ancient Philosophy* 2 (1984), pp. 31-87, and 3 (1985), pp. 125-157, 159-165, and 167-173. My view is that of Fine, vol. 3, pp. 159-165, except that I stress that the inseparability of properties from ousiai implies the separability of ousiai from each other. Neither of these authors considers "separation" in conjunction with *Generation of Animals* II.1, 732a4-8, where males are said to be "separate" from females because, as Form, they are better and more divine. See also chap. 2, n. 53.

25. For an excellent brief account of the propulsion, see Michael Frede, "Substance in Aristotle's Metaphysics," in Alan Gotthelf, ed., *Aristotle on Nature and Living Things* (Pittsburgh: Mathesis Press, 1985), pp. 17-26.

26. *Metaph.* VII.1 1028a 37-1028b2. The list given in the Oxford Classical Text of Aristotle mentions priority in "*logos,* cognition, and time." Irwin prefers the listing of Asclepius: ousia is prior "in nature and logos and time and knowledge" (Irwin, *Aristotle's First Principles,* p. 553 fn. 8); but since *logos* and cognition are on both lists, the point does not affect my account here. The list and the senses of "priority" on which it trades have been the subjects of a rather extensive literature; in addition to Irwin, see Michael Frede and Günther Patzig, *Aristoteles. Metaphysik,* vol. 2 (Munich: C. H. Beck, 1988), p. 21; W. D. Ross, *Aristotle's Metaphysics: A Revised Text with Introduction and Commentary* (Oxford: Clarendon Press, 1924); John J. Cleary, *Aristotle on the Many Senses of Priority* (Carbondale: Southern Illinois University Press, 1988), pp. 65-69.

27. As Donald Morrison (*Studies in Ancient Philosophy III* [1985], p. 141) succinctly puts what I call the ousiodic traits of disposition and initiative, "For Aristotle the form of something is, among other things, its principle of organization and the source of its characteristic behavior."

28. *Metaph.* VII.12 unpacks this unity in terms of the hierarchy of genera and species, which we need not go into here.

29. *Metaph.* VII. 4 1031a12-14. Michael Loux has argued that non-ousiai also have essences, so that for Aristotle there is a whole hierarchy of essences, with those of ousiai being primary; Loux, *Primary Ousia: An Essay on Aristotle's Metaphysics Z and H* (Ithaca, N.Y.: Cornell University Press, 1991), pp. 80-84 and passim. Cf.

Furth, *Substance, Form, and Psyche,* pp. 234, 239f. For my purposes, the issue is a semantic one; for simplicity, I speak of ousiai alone as having essences, leaving the reader to append "in the strict sense" at will.

30. Graham, *Aristotle's Two Systems,* p. 67. Cf. Aristotle, *Topics* I. 4 101b2, II.5 passim.

31. Aristotle makes the point for "white surface" and "smooth surface" at *Metaph.* VII.4 1029b20-22.

32. To which he alludes in *Metaph.* VII.6 and discusses most completely at *Metaph.* I.9.

33. For a recent summary of the controversy, see Loux, *Primary Ousia,* p. 94f. I agree with Loux's conclusion—yet another *cri de coeur*—on p. 95: "So there is no settled view on Z 6. Indeed, the myriad interpretations to which the text has given rise bear on so many issues and take us in so many different directions that it is unlikely we can find in the existing debates much common ground for understanding Aristotle's aims in Z 6."

34. The essence, as we saw, is not a passive substrate.

35. *EN* IX.8 1168b31-1169a1; also *Metaph.* VII.6 1031a15-1032a12.

36. *Metaph.* VII.10 1035a23ff. As *Metaph.* VII.11 admits, it is sometimes difficult to distinguish between formal parts, which belong to the essence, and material parts, which do not. If every sphere ever made had been made from bronze, for example, it would be very hard to keep "bronze" out of our formulas for the essence of spheres. But it would be possible, and must be done, because "bronze" denotes matter.

37. *De An.* II. 12 424a12f. Irwin notes that this broad sense is not Aristotle's usual understanding of form (Irwin, *Aristotle's First Principles,* pp. 225, 588 n. 13) but does not go on there to discuss why "form" is polysemic for Aristotle. Furth does so for "essence" in *Substance, Form, and Psyche,* pp. 234, 239f; on sensible and intelligible parts, cf. *Substance, Form, and Psyche,* p. 244f. David Balme uses the notion of form as any determinate quality to distinguish between form and essence; Balme, "Aristotle's Biology Was Not Essentialist," *Archiv für Geschichte der Philosophie* 62 (1980), pp. 1-12, esp. p. 4. But that won't work; for why, then, does Aristotle use "form" to refer to the substantial form of a thing at all? Why not just call it the "essence" and any nonessential property a "form"?

38. *Metaph.* VII. 3 1029a33; G. E. M. Anscombe and Peter Geach, *Three Philosophers* (Oxford: Basil Blackwell, 1961), p. 75. On the multiple ambiguities of "form" in Aristotle, see also Irwin, *Aristotle's First Principles,* pp. 101, 246, 248-250.

39. David Bostock's recent judgment must read like a confession of defeat to those still convinced that if we only work a little longer and think a little harder, Aristotle's *Metaph.* will come into rigorous focus: "If we make the assumption that in every passage we are dealing with a finished work, then there will be a strong pressure to find ingenious lines of interpretation which minimize conflicts between one passage and another, and such conflicts as remain must simply be put down to inadvertence on Aristotle's part. But if we assume instead that what we are dealing with is more like a record of 'work in progress,' then it will not be too surprising if we find Aristotle pursuing a line of thought in one place that does not harmonize very well with a different line pursued elsewhere, or if what has been clearly asserted at one stage seems later to be superseded by a fresh approach. In my opinion . . .

the conflicts that are to be found in our text demand something more like the second assumption. But even so there are many serious problems of interpretation that remain"; Bostock, *Aristotle: Metaphysics Books Z and H,* p. x. Just so; except that Aristotle left things in a state of "work in progress" because it was more appropriate to do so than to turn them into something as lucid as *Word and Object.*

40. For examples of such identification, sometimes quite casual, see Bostock, *Aristotle's Metaphysics Books Z and H,* p. 173 (where he recognizes that it is a problem for Aristotle); Gill, *Aristotle on Substance,* pp. 116-120, esp. 119 n. 17; Haring, "Substantial Form in *Metaphysics* VII, I," p. 332; Hartman, "Aristotle on the Identity of Substance and Essence; Irwin, *Aristotle's First Principles,* pp. 239f, 245f, 377; Loux, *Primary Ousia,* p. 168ff; Owens, *The Doctrine of Being in the Aristotelian Metaphysics,* p. 180; Lynne Spellman, *Substance and Separation in Aristotle* (Cambridge: Cambridge University Press, 1995), p. 45; Charlotte Witt, *Substance and Essence in Aristotle* (Ithaca, N.Y.: Cornell University Press, 1989), p. 101, chap. 5.

41. Various suggestions have been advanced and have encountered as many problems. Owens and Schwegler, for example, view the matter developmentally: *Metaph.* VII.7-9, where form is introduced via a sudden discussion of generation, shows (so Owens) "no smooth connection with the foregoing discussion, such as the previous chapters of VII have exhibited among themselves." In a footnote, Owens suggests that chaps. 7-9 were written before other chapters and incorporated into the book before completion; Owens, *The Doctrine of Being in the Aristotelian Metaphysics,* p. 358 and n. 45. But Owens's answer is a nonanswer; to say that VII.7-9 was composed early and then redacted into the manuscript does not even attempt to answer the question of the relation of the two different locutions. Schwegler notes the main discrepancy to be precisely this terminological one: "Mit den früheren Capiteln hängt unser Cap. dadurch zusammen, daß es fortführt, das *ti ên einai* zu erörtern. Nur tritt jetzt an die Stelle dieses Begriffs der Begriff des *eidos*"; A. Schwegler, *Die Metaphysik des Aristoteles,* vol. 4 (Tübingen: L. F. Fues, 1847-1848), p. 74. Again, calling attention to the change does not explain it. Daniel Graham has suggested that the two locutions come from different language games: the essence vocabulary comes from Aristotle's consideration of definitions, while the form/matter vocabulary derives from a consideration of artifacts; Graham, *Aristotle's Two Systems,* pp. 241-244. Graham then goes on to admit, however, that Aristotle "combines the notions of form and essence into a single concept" (p. 243) and that Aristotle did not seem to notice that he was doing this (p. 244). It is always better, of course, to find conscientious philosophizing instead of inattention and mistake, and that is what I will try to do here. Bostock suggests that *Metaph.* VII.4-6 belongs to the logical works, not strictly to the *Metaphy.* itself; Bostock, *Aristotle: Metaphysics Books Z and H,* p. 116. But plenty of other terms continue from the logical to the metaphysical works, often with changed meanings; why not *to ti ên einai?* Finally, Michael Loux argues that VII.4-7 is intended to be theory-neutral, exploring the structure of any theory of ousia; Loux, *Primary Ousia,* pp. 7f, 96. Loux's most telling point, taken from Russell Dancy, is that the view that a thing must be identical with its essence also applies to Platonic metaphysics; Loux, *Primary Ousia,* p. 95f; Russell Dancy, *Sense and Contradiction: A Study in Aristotle* (Dordrecht: Reidel, 1975), p. 100. The problem with this solution is that Platonic and Aristotelian metaphysics do not exhaust the field; also possible is an ontology

such as I mentioned in the opening paragraph of my discussion of ousia, which views beings as merely heaps or clumps of matter, without any internal or external "standard" to which they conform. That Aristotle is here concerned to capture common ground with Plato is beyond dispute; but for this purpose, use of the term *eidos*, which he shares with Plato, would be more effective.

42. Cf. *Metaph.* VII.4 1303a3: *hoper gar tode ti esti to ti ên einai.*

43. As a small but proximate example of this kind of anxiety, consider the following couplet ascribed by Diogenes Laertius to Aristotle's great teacher:

> While kissing Agathon, my soul leapt to my lips
> As if fain, alas! to pass over to him.

From Diogenes Laertius, *Lives of Eminent Philosophers,* vol. 1 trans. R. D. Hicks (Cambridge, Mass.: Harvard University Press, Loeb), 1925 I 304 (III.32: "Plato").

44. In *De An.,* sensory perception (*aisthêsis*) is defined as the reception of the sensible form of a thing into a sensory organ without its matter; *De An.* II. 12 424a12f. Cf. *De An.* II.5–12: When I perceive Callias on this account, his color somehow comes to be in my eye. When I perceive him to be a human being, humanity—his essence, the ultimate thing that makes him what he is—somehow comes to be in my soul. Similarly for reproduction: the ousiodic form of the species is passed on from the father to the offspring. As A. R. Lacey puts it, "One obviously relevant feature of natural objects [as vs. artifacts] is that they are self-reproductive, so that the form is not confined to any instance it may be in but can be passed on to another . . ."; Lacey, "*Ousia* and Form in Aristotle," *Phronesis* 10 (1965), p. 65. I discuss both examples again in chap. 2.

45. Furth, *Substance, Form, and Psyche,* p. 13.

46. Another way of putting this paradox comes from L. A. Kosman. Granted that Aristotle gained philosophical independence from Plato by insisting upon the "inseparability" of form from matter, it is notably odd that for Aristotle, as Kosman puts it, "the activities of life are activities which depend upon the separability of form from matter. Thus the reproductive faculty is the ability to recreate the form of the animal in another individual. . . . Similarly, the activities of consciousness are activities of taking on form; thus the aisthetic faculty is said to be the power of receiving selectively form without substratum"; Kosman, "What Does the Maker Mind Make?" in Martha Nussbaum and Amélie Oksenberg Rorty, eds., *Essays on Aristotle's de Anima* (Oxford: Clarendon Press, 1992), p. 357.

47. It is, then, appropriate for Aristotle to speak of our "knowing the essence" of a thing (cf. 1031b5–7, 20f). As the medievals would put it, we do not know the form in our sensory organ, but by means of it we know the form in the thing, or the essence.

48. At least it cannot be shown to do this within the scope of the present book. The many passages in which Aristotle equates form and essence are not counter-examples to my view, since in my view form and essence *are* the same. Nor would a few inconsistencies be fatal: which locution Aristotle uses depends upon the point of view he happens to have in mind, and that can vary. Two passages where Aristotle talks of "form" remaining within the thing whose form it is actually support my view, precisely because Aristotle finds it necessary to specify just this fact: the form "as present in the sensible thing" (*Metaph.* VII.8 1033b5) and the "in-dwelling form" of *Metaph.* VII.11, 1037a29. *Metaph.* VII.17, which calls the form

"that by reason of which the matter is some definite thing" seems a clearer coun-terexample, though the whole discussion of the universality of substance in VII.17 is, of course, a counterexample to *every* theory of what Aristotle means. Hence the plausibility of R. D. Sykes's argument that Aristotle simply, and irreparably, contra-dicts himself there; Sykes, "Form in Aristotle," *Philosophy* 50 (1975), pp. 311-331. For a more favorable, genetic conjecture, see Bostock, *Aristotle's Metaphysics Books Z and H*, p. 205f. D. W. Hamlyn's point that form, unlike essence, is correlative to matter does not tell against my suggestion as long as we remember that both form and matter continually, so to speak, slide past each other into new relationships. Indeed, this correlation cannot be expressed in terms of essence, which resides not in matter but "in the thing." See Hamlyn, "Aristotle on Form," in Gotthelf, ed., *Aristotle on Nature and Living Things*, pp. 55-65.

49. Hermann Bonitz, *Index aristotelicus* (Graz: Akademische Druck- und Ver-lagsanstalt, 1955; rep. Berlin, 1870), pp. 217-219. *Eidos* as visible shape trades upon the notion of form as passing from a body to its beholder (as when someone "delights in the form of another": *EN* IX.5 1162a5; the example is Bonitz's). *Eidos* as formal cause obviously trades on the context of generation; and *eidos* as species refers to the result of a series of such transitions, which will be a form shared by a plurality of individuals. None of these contexts is in the least suggested by the discussion of essence in *Metaph.* VII.4-6, which deals with the true identity of a thing with regard to its immanent logos. Our expressions conform to this logos, but without regard to its transmissability, shareability, or knowability (something can be "predicable" of something without being known to be so).

50. Bostock, *Aristotle's Metaphysics Books Z and H*, p. 72.

51. Irwin, *Aristotle's First Principles*, p. 253, gives the following list: *Metaph.* XII.5 1071a20-22, 27-29; *Generation of Animals* 767b29-35. *On Generation and Corruption* 321b25-28 shows that growth—the accretion of matter by a form—is a case of this as well.

52. Aristotle, *Metaph.* VII.15 1039b27-30. Accounts of material things, to be sure, may have to make at least indirect reference to their matter, for the material parts of a material thing, those into which it resolves, are in a way constituent principles of its existence—we cannot, for example, make a saw out of wool or a human being except of flesh, bones, etc.; *Metaph.* VII.11, 1036b5f, VIII.4 1044a27. But what these accounts actually contain, as definitions of a thing's essence, is a set of predicates which refer to formal parts.

53. Frede and Patzig have argued vigorously that this cannot have been Aris-totle's view; see their *Aristoteles. Metaphysik*, vol. 1, pp. 48-57. The question can probably never be definitively settled; in any case, as Graham argues (see next note) there are at least good circumstantial reasons for thinking that form is universal for Aristotle.

54. Graham, *Aristotle's Two Systems*, p. 250f. Graham traces this through to a final aporia: Aristotle "fails to tell us how substance can be both universal and not universal. . . . Form proves to be particular and non-particular, universal and non-universal, and by extension substantial and non-substantial," p. 261. For the view that Aristotle's investigation ends ingloriously, also see Sykes, "Form in Aris-totle," and Bostock, *Aristotle's Metaphysics Books Z and H*, p. 185f.

55. See, e.g., *Metaph.* VII.111 1036bb23; for the soul as form, see *De An.* II.1, 2, and *Metaph.* 1037a5-7. On this issue cf. Rogers Albritton, "Forms of Particular

Substances in Aristotle's *Metaphysics*," *Journal of Philosophy* 54 (1957), pp. 699-708; Bostock, *Aristotle's Metaphysics Books Z and H*, pp. 186-189; Michael Frede, "Substance in Aristotle's Metaphysics," *Essays in Ancient Philosophy* (Minneapolis: University Minnesota Press, 1987), p. 77; Furth, *Substance, Form, and Psyche*, p. 193f; Irwin, *Aristotle's First Principles*, pp. 248-261; Wilfrid Sellars, "Substance and Form in Aristotle," *Journal of Philosophy* 54 (1957), pp. 688-699; and Sykes, "Form in Aristotle." A good summary of the literature can be found in Edward D. Harter, "Aristotle on Primary *Ousia*," *Archiv für Geschichte der Philosophie* 57 (1975), p. 11. For a helpful summary and provocative discussion, see Edward Halper, "Aristotle's Solution to the Problem of Sensible Substances," *Journal of Philosophy* 84 (1987), pp. 666-672.

56. Irwin's argument is that Aristotle's remark about health shows that potential instantiation is not enough to give existence to a universal; only actual existence is relevant. But if a universal were instantiated only once while being "such as" to exist in many cases, then all its instances but one would be merely potential, and this would not suffice. If *possibly* being instantiated more than once were enough, then *possibly* being instantiated once would also be enough; Irwin, *Aristotle's First Principles*, pp. 80, 513 nn. 16, 17. For a contrary view, see Bostock, *Aristotle's Metaphysics Books Z and H*, pp. 190, 192; but *pephyke* at *Cats.* 17a38-b1 will not support the weight Bostock needs to give it; he does not deal with Irwin's argument at all; and one of his examples (*Parts of Animals* 644a27f) is of unclear relevance.

57. Aristotle, *On the Heavens*, I.9, 278a15. Together with the thesis that universals have necessarily plural instantiations, this amounts to saying, "any shape or form is, or may be, a universal." This could be taken, of course, as denying that universals necessarily have plural instances; but that is Aristotle's general view, and it is unlikely that he would simply deny it in so offhand a way.

58. To spell out a bit more my view of the relation of universality and particularity within form: Michael Frede has suggested that what distinguishes one particular form from another form of the same species is their histories. There is no characteristic that makes humanity-in-me different from humanity-in-you other than that humanity-in-me came from my father and has been in me since my conception, while humanity-in-you came from your father and has been in you since your conception; Frede, "Individuals in Aristotle," pp. 49-71. To that I would add that the history in question is one of the active bounding and disposing of matter by form. As Furth puts it (not using those terms), "The particular form . . . is the specific form, Man, seen as molding a matter into a specifically-formed parcel (a *man*) and an individual unitary this (a man)"; Furth, *Substance, Form, and Psyche*, p. 231; cf. pp. 168, 194f. To put it in my terms: bounding and disposing *individuate* form; initiative *universalizes* it—which is just another way of saying that initiative is in tension with the other two. The activities of bounding and disposing, of course, are not merely extrinsic to form; they are its very nature, which is just another way of saying that for Aristotle there is no "separation" between forms and material things. So a better way to put it would be: form individuating itself is bounding and disposition; form universalizing itself is initiative. Matter thus, as Furth points out *contra* an ancient interpretive tradition, does not individuate form (*Substance, Form, and Psyche*, pp. 179-181); it is too passive for such an important role. But it is not wholly irrelevant to individuation either. It provides, let us say, the matrix in which, and into which, form individuates itself.

59. As Irwin points out, Aristotle gives no reason why the human form has

always had a plurality of instances; he simply assumes that the species is everlasting (Irwin, *Aristotle's First Principles*, p. 524 n. 25), from which it would follow—since human reproduction requires it—that there have always been at least one male and one female human.

60. Ellen Stone Haring, "Substantial Form in *Metaphysics* Z, II," *Review of Metaphysics* 10 (1956-1957), p. 495.

61. Form is thus "the responsible factor (*aition*) by which matter comes to be a this"; *Metaph.* VII.17 1041b7f. Furth has argued that form provides the "diachronic individuation" of the composite, i.e., the continuity of its history—a point further developed, as noted, by Frede—while matter individuates it synchronically; Furth, "Transtemporal Stability," p. 644, and Frede, "Individuals in Aristotle," p. 68f. Jennifer Whiting has argued that form provides both diachronic and synchronic individuation; Whiting, "Form and Individual in Aristotle," *Journal of the History of Philosophy* 3 (1986), pp. 359-387. I follow Whiting but prefer to use "unification" and "individuation" as complementary names for the same process; when a form unifies a particular domain of matter, it individuates itself by bounding and disposing that matter. Cf. n. 22.

62. This insight is carried through in detail in Aristotle's account of fetation, which is considered in the next chapter. On the crucial role of such internally directed "self-generation" in establishing Aristotle's distinction between natural beings and artifacts, cf. W. Charlton, *Aristotle's Physics: Books I and II* (Oxford: Clarendon Press, 1970), p. 89; also Witt, *Substance and Essence in Aristotle*, p. 72f, arguing against Sarah Waterlow, *Nature, Change, and Agency in Aristotle's Physics* (Oxford: Oxford University Press, 1982), p. 52.

63. *Metaph.* V.25 1023b13-25; cf. Aristotle, *Generation of Animals* II.1 734a30-33, and my discussion of it in the next chapter.

64. *Metaph.* I.3 984a22-26; *Physics* I.7 191a8-12. For the misleading character of these examples, see Furth, "Transtemporal Stability," p. 644f, and *Substance, Form, and Psyche*, pp. 148, 183f; and L. A. Kosman, "Animals and Other Beings in Aristotle," in Allan Gotthelf and James G. Lennox, eds., *Philosophical Issues in Aristotle's Biology* (Cambridge: Cambridge University Press, 1987), pp. 360-391.

65. As Wilfrid Sellars notes, it is difficult to keep clear hold of the fact that the form of a thing is not one of its parts but the activity which unifies the parts. Even Aristotle, Sellars notes, "sometimes seems to think of the form of a materiate substance as a substance which is more truly substance than the substance of which it is the form . . . the soul [of Socrates] seems to be in a *primary* sense a *this*, and Socrates a *this* in a derivative sense, as having a primary *this* within him"; Sellars, "Substance and Form in Aristotle," p. 698f.

66. Haring, "Substantial Form in *Metaphysics* Z, II," p. 498. Cf. Owens, *The Doctrine of Being in the Aristotelian Metaphysics*, p. 356.

67. The explanatory use of the form can be seen in chap. 17, the last chapter of Book VII of the *Metaph.* This chapter takes up a different sort of issue from the rest of the book, and in this sense constitutes a new beginning. It starts from the attempt to say not what a thing is but why it happens. (Events, of course, are contingent; if even they can be explained through forms, then the explanatory power of form is clearly vindicated.) A "why" question such as "why did this happen?" assumes that there are two things—at minimum, one subject and one predicate—and asks why they are attached to one another. Suppose, for example, I ask

why it is thundering. What I am really asking about is the inherence of a predicate in a subject; I am asking why I am justified in asserting or judging that there is, at this moment, noise in the clouds. The connection between clouds and noise is explained by adducing the nature of thunder: thunder is the sound made by the quenching of fire in the heavens. It is thundering right now because fire (resulting from the flash of lightning a moment ago) is currently being quenched in the sky. This answer, like all such answers, has the general trait of pointing out a universal, a form, which shows why a particular attachment of subject to predicate is warranted at the moment. And so in asking "Why" we seek, ultimately, a "What," the universal form which explains why the original subject and predicate are connected when they are rightly connected.

68. In addition to the relationship of ousiodic form to intelligibility, ousia gains parametric status for Aristotle from its status as the nature of being itself; as will be seen in the next chapter, it is the way of nature for him that any being should have full ousiodic structure, and this includes individual moral agents, households, and states. In modernity, the latter justification will ostentatiously drop away while the former persists unnoticed, giving rise to a new and even greater set of problems.

69. Owens, *The Doctrine of Being in the Aristotelian Metaphysics,* p. 356.

70. *Metaph.* VII.3 1029a23-26. As Joseph Owens puts it, "In a word, matter as reached by Aristotle escapes in itself both determinative and negative characterization. It cannot be conceived or described in any direct fashion, either determinatively or negatively. It is not even a 'what' or an 'it' that is capable of being indicated . . . because it cannot be presented directly to our cognition"; Owens, "Matter and Predication in Aristotle," in Ernan McMullin, ed., *The Concept of Matter* (Notre Dame, Ind.: University of Notre Dame Press, 1963), p. 107.

71. For an introduction to the extensive literature on this passage, see Donald Stahl, "Stripped Away," *Phronesis* 26 (1981), pp. 177-180.

72. Another way of putting this would be to say that matter lacking all form is just—nothing. And then the view that Aristotle is combating here—one related to his own earlier formulations in the *Cat.*—would be, as Russell Dancy puts it, that "matter, which is nothing in its own right, is what makes things real"; Dancy, "On Some of Aristotle's Second Thoughts about Substance," *Philosophical Review* 87 (1978), p. 413. If I am right, this ontological road is not taken until Heidegger.

73. *Metaph.* VII.3 1029a23-26. For an extended argument against the view that Aristotle believed in prime matter, see W. Charlton, *Aristotle's Physics I, II* (Oxford: Clarendon Press, 1970), pp. 129-145; for an argument in favor, see Bostock, *Aristotle's Metaphysics Books Z and H,* p. 73f (though even Bostock does not claim that matter can exist independently of *all* form, p. 82); for a summary of the debate, see Sheldon Cohen, "Aristotle's Doctrine of the Material Substrate," *Philosophical Review* 93 (1984), pp. 171-194, esp. pp. 171-173.

74. V. C. Chappell, "Matter," *Journal of Philosophy* 70 (1973), p. 694; emphasis added. I follow Gill rather than Chappell in holding that matter has another tendency than simply to be constituted or compounded by form: its push toward its own elemental nature. It is this push to be itself that is kept "unfree" in Aristotle's conception of matter.

75. *Metaph.* V.12 1019b1-10; IX, esp. IX.7 1049a13-34; VIII.4 1044a28. Cf. n. 54.

76. Aristotle, *On Coming-to-be and Passing-Away* II.1-3.

77. Aristotle, *On the Parts of Animals* I.1 642a7-13.

78. See Gill, *Aristotle on Substance,* pp. 77–82, for an account of the nature and status of the elements. Also cf. the somewhat differing account of Cohen, "Aristotle's Doctrine of the Material Substrate." I follow Gill (p. 45) in agreeing that of itself matter can have no nature, not even that of extension (which in my narrative turns out to be a modern idea requiring the mediation of Christianity for its codification).

79. Gill, *Aristotle on Substance,* p. 166; emphasis added. Cf. Gill, "Aristotle's Doctrine of the Material Substrate," pp. 212–214; Haring: "[The elements] can be taken up into more determinate beings. . . . They become limited, pervaded, and oriented by the nature of the whole containing them . . . within wholes, they are in the *dominion* of something other," "Substantial Form in *Metaphysics* Z, I," p. 310, emphasis added; Witt, *Substance and Essence in Aristotle,* p. 120.

80. Gill, *Aristotle on Substance,* p. 213.

81. That means, for Furth, that the substance-ontology which I took from the *Cat.* is not really Aristotle's; existing individuals are presupposed only on the "surface" of the *Cat.* If we examine certain hints and ask about certain lacunae in the text, we find something like the later hylomorphic analysis waiting (Furth, *Substance, Form, and Psyche,* p. 58f). I leave this matter to itself; Aristotle's public insights are difficult enough without trying to fathom the ones he kept to himself, and the surface is all I need. In terms of the more important ousiodic ontology, I agree with Furth: "The existence of material individuals is for Aristotle 'given' only in the sense of a datum requiring explanation . . . and not as something that can be regarded as assumed as part of the primitive basis of the theory" (*Substance, Form, and Psyche,* p. 59f).

82. Cf. *Metaph.* V.12 1019a15–21, IX.1 1046a10f. Unlike the other topics I have treated, the nature of active potency has received relatively little attention by scholars. In general I follow Gill, *Aristotle on Essence,* pp. 194, 200f; but she does not see the problem that I do, a problem which my later narrative confirms. The difference between active potency and Aristotle's more "metaphysical' sense of potentiality, which is associated with matter and has drawn much more scholarly attention, is discussed in Graham, *Aristotle's Two Systems,* p. 202f.

83. *Metaph.* IX.8 1049b23f. Cf. "heat and the art of building are present, one in that which can produce heat and the other in the man who can build," *Metaph.* IX.1 1046a27f. See also *On the Generation of Animals* II.1 732a4, as well as *De Anima* II.5 430a12.

84. Gill, *Aristotle on Substance,* p. 195.

85. *Metaph.* IX.8 1049b9–13; also IX.1 1046a28seq., IX.7 1049a12–18. Cf. Graham, *Aristotle's Two Systems,* p. 200.

86. The "absence" is minimal: an active cause of change must be touching that which it affects. See the discussion in Gill, pp. 195–198. This is just one of many ways in which Aristotle tries to keep the transgressions of boundaries minimal; I discuss another in my account of cognition in the next chapter. When, as a result of modern science, ousia is evicted from nature, active potency—under the modern name of "power"—becomes, as for Hobbes (and Foucault), the central explanatory category.

87. Aristotle, *Generation of Animals* 768b15; *Physics* II.2 202a3–12.

88. Aristotle, *De An.* II.4 413b3–8. Cf. Aristotle, *On the Generation of Animals* II.11 731b32–732a1: "Since it is impossible for the nature [of living things] to be eternal,

that which comes into being is eternal in the manner which is open to it. For it is incapable of eternality numerically, since the ousia of beings is found in the particular; and if it really were so, then it would be eternal. But in species it is possible. . . . And as the proximate motive cause, to which belongs the logos and the form, is better and more divine in its nature than the matter, it is better also that the superior be separate from the female, since it is something better and more divine. . . ."

89. That is, unless they are certain relations which it has to other things, such as being between them—a set of complications which I will not go into here.

2. OUSIA AS PARAMETER IN ARISTOTLE

1. Montgomery Furth, *Substance, Form, and Psyche: An Aristotelian Metaphysics* (Cambridge: Cambridge University Press, 1988), pp. 54–58, 201–205. As Terence Irwin puts it, "First philosophy shows us how to reach a plausible conception of substance. It does not tell us the answer to some empirical questions we need to answer in order to know what the substances are but tells us which empirical questions are relevant and what we should conclude from the answers to these"; Irwin, *Aristotle's First Principles* (Oxford: Clarendon Press, 1988), p. 21. I discuss Irwin's view of our knowledge of essence later in this chapter.

2. *Metaph.* VII.11, 1036a26-b6. We must see spheres made of many different materials, for example, before we can conclude that sphericity concerns shape alone, that bronze or marble, say, do not belong to the essence of sphere. We find our own human form realized only in flesh, bone, and the like; and, says Aristotle, we are incapable of wholly separating these materials from our conception of the human essence; *Metaph.* VII.1 1036b6f. Cf. Aristotle, *Posterior Analytics* II.13 97b7-26; *Topics* VIII.2 157a21-29; 157b3-8; *Parts of Animals* I.3 643b9-29, 644b1-8.

3. See *Metaph.* I.1 and *Posterior Analytics* II.19 for portrayals of this. Aristotle's accounts are rather cryptic, and I will not discuss them in detail here; see Irwin, *Aristotle's First Principles*, p. 32f, for a brief treatment.

4. Irwin, *Aristotle's First Principles*, p. 121.

5. Cf. Sanford Cashdollar, "Aristotle's Account of Incidental Perception," *Phronesis* 18 (1973), pp. 156–175.

6. Robert Heineman has argued that while we cannot for Aristotle "know" composites because of their matter, which brings change (cf. Aristotle, *Metaph.* VII.15 1039b27-30 and note 49 below), we can know their essential forms. That Callias is a human being is not, for example, a changeable fact about him. See Heinaman, "Knowledge of Substance in Aristotle," *Journal of Hellenic Studies* 101 (1981), pp. 63–77, esp. pp. 71–77.

7. Hence when Christopher Shields writes that Aristotle's account of the relation of soul and body has given rise to "an alarmingly large and diverse literature," he also notes that the problems are inherited from Aristotle's metaphysics: "the obscurities in [his] account of the unity of form and matter carry over into his analysis of soul and body"; Shields, "Body and Soul in Aristotle," in Julian Annas, ed., *Oxford Studies in Ancient Philosophy VI* (Oxford: Clarendon Press, 1988), pp. 103, 105.

8. And not only from me. As Irwin's discussion of the knotty texts concerning soul and intellect indicates, the secondary literature here is much less imposing, being devoted mainly to issues not of what Aristotle meant but of how and whether

he can be updated; Irwin, *Aristotle's First Principles*, pp. 303-328. Cf. the emphasis on Aristotle and functionalism in the articles by Miles Burnyeat, S. Marc Cohen, Martha Nussbaum and Hilary Putnam, Jennifer Whiting, and K. V. Wilkes in Martha Nussbaum and Amélie Oksenberg Rorty, eds., *Essay on Aristotle's De Anima* (Oxford: Clarendon Press, 1992).

9. *De An.* II.1 412a6-21; my translation uses "ousia" etc. instead of the usual "substance." Soul is identified as "primary substance" and the body as matter already at *Metaph.* VII.11 1037a5-7. That the soul is a formal cause is for Irwin the "most important part" of Aristotle's psychological doctrine; Irwin, *Aristotle's First Principles*, p. 295. This passage also presents some difficulties which need not detain us. Why, for example, does Aristotle here (in view of the "stripping-off" argument at *Metaph.* VII.3 which I discussed in the preceding chapter) call body both "subject" and "matter"? How can a natural body have life "potentially" within it and yet be essentially ensouled? I will avoid the former question altogether. I take the latter one, raised in J. L. Ackrill, "Aristotle's Definitions of Psyche," *Proceedings of the Aristotelian Society* 73 (1972-1973), pp. 119-133, to have been resolved by Jennifer Whiting, "Living Bodies," in Nussbaum and Rorty, *Essays on Aristotle's De Anima*, p. 76: "there are two distinct things Aristotle calls the 'matter' (*hylê*) of an animal: the one (the organic body) is essentially ensouled, while the other (the quantity of elements constituting the organic body) is only accidentally ensouled." This solution has obvious affinities with Gill's reading of the relation of form and matter, discussed in chap. 1.

10. *De An.* II.12 424a17-23. Sensation thus differs from nutrition, which is the reception of matter into the living thing. A sensory form, it should be noted, cannot itself be the empirical purchase for the concept of ousia that I earlier suggested was required to incite our reflection, for things which are not ousiai, such as heaps of grain or landscapes, can have forms in Aristotle's broader sense of determinate sensible qualities.

11. That the transmission of form is strictly a physiological process, so that the sense organ actually takes on the sensed quality, is argued by Thomas Slakey, "Aristotle on Sense Perception," *Philosophical Review* 70 (1961), pp. 470-484. Miles Burnyeat, in a highly influential paper, argued the reverse; Burnyeat, "Is an Aristotelian Philosophy of Mind Still Credible?" in Nussbaum and Rorty, *Essays on Aristotle's De Anima*, pp. 15-26. For an exhaustive discussion and adjudication, see Stephen Everson, *Aristotle on Perception* (Oxford: Oxford University Press, 1997). Alan Code and Julius Moravcsik maintain that the notion of "reception of form" is left undefined by Aristotle, as by later theorists of representational mind; Code and Moravcsik, "Explaining Various Forms of Living," in Nussbaum and Rorty, *Essays on Aristotle's De Anima*, p. 137. Their view that it points toward contemporary notions of information also points them toward Furth's view of the storage of form in the semen, which I discuss later in this chapter.

12. D. W. Hamlyn obliquely recognizes boundary in his note to *De An.* 417a2: "The reference to 'external objects' is especially noteworthy; it indicates that the idea of a world external to ourselves or our body . . . with the implication that we are somehow *inside*, is to be met with as early as Aristotle. The idea, erroneous and misleading as it is, has persisted throughout most of Western philosophy, but it is not altogether clear what motivates it in Aristotle himself; he pays very little attention to those aspects of the privacy of experience which have generally led to it"; Hamlyn,

Aristotle's de Anima Book II, III (Oxford: Clarendon Press, 1968), p. 99. What motivates the view, I suggest, is ousia itself, which was exhibited on many levels of Aristotle's world and provided the key for much of his philosophy; the privacy of experience is, as I argue in part 2, a modern *effect* of ousia rather than a motivation for it.

13. Though many commentators have discussed the role of "motions" in sense perception, the relation of motions to form is unnoticed by those I have cited here, as is the fact that this relation also plays an important role in Aristotle's theory of reproduction. One of the signal defects of the English language literature on Aristotle is that it only rarely focuses on interdiscursive strategies and gestures such as I am trying to highlight here.

14. *De An.* II.9 4221b9, II.11 423a 15-17. See Slakey, "Aristotle on Sense-Perception," for an interpretation of *kinêseis* as physiological changes.

15. Furth, *Substance, Form, and Psyche*, pp. 117-120.

16. Furth, *Substance, Form, and Psyche*, p. 119.

17. The question of how form can resolve itself into *kinêsis* and then reconstitute itself poses a number of crucial problems for the history of philosophy, for which see John D. Caputo, *Radical Hermeneutics* (Bloomington: Indiana University Press, 1987).

18. The problems with Aristotle's discussion of the imagination in *De An.* III.4, sketchy even for him, are many. For an important account of the discussion and the difficulties it contains, see Malcolm Schofield, "Aristotle on the Imagination," in G. E. R. Lloyd and G. E. L. Owen, *Aristotle on Mind and the Senses* (Cambridge: Cambridge University Press, 1978), pp. 99-130.

19. *De An.* III.3 427b18-22; the translation is from Hamlyn, *Aristotle's De Anima Books II, III*, p. 53.

20. "*Phantasia* . . . does not happen without sense-perception but comes to be as the result of the activity of sense-perception and is *like* the perception"; *De An.* III.3 428b11-115, as rendered by Dorothea Frede, "The Cognitive Role of *Phantasia* in Aristotle," in Nussbaum and Rorty, *Essays on Aristotle's De Anima*, p. 281.

21. Even that prerogative is then, as Frede notes, partially retracted, for we cannot call up dreams when and as we wish; Frede, "The Cognitive Role of Imagination in Aristotle," p. 281.

22. *De An.* III.4 429a24-26. Problems with this view are discussed in Edwin Hartman, *Substance, Body and Soul* (Princeton, N.J.: Princeton University Press, 1977), pp. 251-256. Hartman's account of its motivation is, as it stands, unpersuasive. The facts that we can think many things which we have not sensed and that sensation and *phantasmata* are the only kinds of cognition that are physiological for Aristotle beg the question of whether the latter claim has to be the case. Was it inconceivable to Aristotle that we could put *phantasmata* together into images that we have never sensed, *à la* Hume?

23. "Everything is a possible object of thought . . . the co-presence [within the intellect] of what is alien is a hindrance and a block"; *De An.* III.4 429a18-21. There are two arguments here which I wish to keep separate. One, alluded to here before the ellipsis, is that the intellect is a unique kind of thing, which is, I suggest, required by the claim that since everything must be capable of "entering" it, it can have no ordinary boundaries. The other, after the dots, is that its uniqueness consists in having no nature at all, so that nothing will be contrary to its own nature and hence unthinkable.

24. *De An.* III.4 429a27-29. For better or worse, Aristotle thus accepts Anaxagoras's account of intellect as "simple, impassable, and [having] nothing in common with anything else"; *De An.* III.4 429b24f.

25. As is suggested by Aristotle's cryptic remark and indecipherable analogy to a writing tablet at *De An.* III.4 429b29-430a2.

26. Deborah Modrak, "Aristotle on Thinking," in John J. Cleary, ed., *Proceedings of the Boston Area Colloquium in Ancient Philosophy II* (Lanham, Md.: University Press of America, 1987), p. 224f. For an account of abstraction which relies heavily on the *Analytics*, see Hartman, *Substance, Body and Soul*, pp. 232-247.

27. *De An.* III.4 429b5. Cf. Modrak, "Aristotle on Thinking," p. 224f. Unlike an image in the imagination, an intellectual universal thus exists within the intellect independently of the specific sensations which originally entered the soul and from which it is abstracted. The set of human beings from which my concept of humanity has been abstracted, for example, is wholly different from the set which led to Aristotle's; yet the two concepts are (in Aristotle's view) the same.

28. See Aristotle, *Posterior Analytics* II. 13, for an account of this.

29. Hence, as *Metaph.* VII.10 1034a30ff has it, "as in syllogisms, ousia is the start of everything." Cf. *Posterior Analytics* 90b31. For equations of ousia with logos itself, see *Metaph.* VII.10 1035b27f, VII.14 1039b20f. Though Aristotle does not explicitly carry out his concrete analyses in syllogistic form, hylomorphism does structure his treatments of concrete matters; see Daniel Graham, *Aristotle's Two Systems* (Oxford: Clarendon Press, 1987), pp. 319-323.

30. Modrak, "Aristotle on Thinking," p. 217. Cf. Charles Kahn, "Aristotle on Thinking," in Nussbaum and Rorty, *Essays on Aristotle's De Anima*, pp. 359-379, esp. pp. 361-367.

31. Modrak, "Aristotle on Thinking," p. 215

32. *De An.* III.8 432a2; Kathleen V. Wilkes, "The Good Man and the Good for Man," in Amélie Oksenberg Rorty, ed., *Essays on Aristotle's Ethics* (Berkeley: University of California Press, 1980), p. 345. On the dispositive role of reason in cognition, see Takatura Ando, *Aristotle's Theory of Practical Cognition*, 2nd ed. (The Hague: Nijhoff, 1965), pp. 58-62.

33. Cf. Robert Heinaman, "Knowledge of Substance in Aristotle," pp. 71-77; also Modrak, "Aristotle on Thinking," p. 213.

34. Cf. a passage quoted chap. 1: "True knowledge can be only of things which have no matter . . . there is neither definition nor demonstration about sensible individual ousiai, because they have matter whose nature is such that they are capable of being or not being"; *Metaph.* VII.15 1039b27-30.

35. *De An.* II.7 418a33seq and, more generally, III.2, 425b225-426a1, 416a6-11. Cf. Aristotle, *On Dreams* 459a27-460a32. On the origins of this view in Aristotle's account of form in matter, see Hartman, *Substance, Body and Soul*, pp. 175-180. The place of the form's arrival seems to be what differentiates sensation from other sorts of active power. When my hand is heated by a warm stone, the form of heat is received into the matter of the hand and informs it. When I perceive that the stone is hot, the same form is received, without the matter, in my soul. Or, as Everson puts it, it is received into the perceptual system as a whole; Everson, *Aristotle on Perception*, p. 139f.

36. *De An.* II.6, 418a12; III.3 427b11-18. Irwin, who regards this claim as motivated by a desire to refute the sceptic, is puzzled by its strength in this regard: "If

this is the only anti-sceptical strategy, then first philosophy is incoherent"; Irwin, *Aristotle's First Principles,* p. 314f. Without denying the incoherence in which this lands Aristotle's epistemology (via a "subjectivizing" of perceived qualities), it is only too coherent with his metaphysical view that sensation is the transmission of an unchangeable form. Irving Block argues that the truth of proper sensibles follows from their being perceived only by a single sense, which was made by nature for that purpose: "Normal senses must perceive their proper sensibles accurately, else Nature would have made an imperfection in the case of a fully and completely developed organ"; Block, "Truth and Error in Aristotle's Theory of Sense Perception," *Philosophical Quarterly* 11 (1961), p. 6. That makes Aristotle's account of sensory perception follow what Michael Wedin calls the "faculty/function/object" condition: that faculties should be defined in terms of their functions and ultimately their objects; Wedin, *Mind and Imagination in Aristotle* (New Haven, Conn.: Yale University Press, 1988), p. 13. But this requirement itself, I suggest, makes sense only if the function of the sensory organs has previously been defined as the reception of unchangeable forms. That parallels a point that arises explicitly in the context of reproduction. Because the animal cannot exist forever, i.e., because its form cannot remain forever in its own matter, it attempts to instill this identical form into other matter, preserving identity in species if not individual identity.

37. *Metaph.* IV.5 1010b1–29; cf. Aristotle, *On Dreams* 460b3–16, 461a30-b11.

38. Cf. *De An.* II.12 424a22ff: "the sense is affected by what is colored or flavored or sounding, but it is indifferent what in each case the ousia is; what alone matters is what [sensible] quality it has. . . ."

39. Aristotle, *De Interpretatione* 1 16a11; *Metaph.* IX.9 1051b2f. For problems with the picture theory of truth in Aristotle, see Hartman, *Substance, Body and Mind,* p. 248f. My point here is that Aristotle adopted the theory, in spite of its problems, for metaphysical reasons.

40. For a discussion of this conflation of truth and the goal of cognition in recent philosophy, see my *Company of Words* (Evanston, Ill.: Northwestern University Press, 1993), pp. 70–90.

41. *De An.* III.4 429a14–17. It is because the objects of reason do not come directly from without that reason is a "higher" activity than sense; cf. *De An.* II.5 417b19–25.

42. For a general account of metaphysical themes in Aristotle's biology, see L. A. Kosman, "Animals and Other Beings in Aristotle," in Alan Gotthelf and James G. Lennox, eds., *Philosophical Issues in Aristotle's Biology* (Cambridge: Cambridge University Press, 1987), pp. 360–391. Kosman overdraws the difference between artifacts, whose matter is only accidentally unified with their form, and living things, whose matter (according to Kosman) is on all levels essentially related to their form. The result of this exaggeration is that "Aristotle sees the entire range of being as naturally constituted for the sake of the complex modes of animal activity" (p. 389). As my discussion of Whiting in n. 10 and of Gill in the preceding chapter shows, this problem can be avoided by adopting Gill's view that elemental matter is always only accidentally related to that which is composed from it. On the relation of *De An.* to the biological writings, see G. E. R. LLoyd, "Aspects of the Relationship between Aristotle's Psychology and His Zoology," in Nussbaum and Rorty, *Essays on Aristotle's De Anima,* pp. 147–167.

43. Furth, *Substance, Form, and Psyche,* pp. 110–120.

44. *Gen. An.* II.1 734a30-33; cf. *Metaph.* V.25 1023b13-25, which I discussed in chap. 1.

45. *Gen. An.* II.1 734b13-15, 735a12f. The whole context from 735b24 to the end of II.1 concerns, tellingly, whether that which first generates the living thing is internal or external to it. Cf. Furth, *Substance, Form, and Psyche*, p. 112.

46. Aristotle, *History of Animals* III.11 518a2-5; *Parts of Animals* II.13 657a31-657b1. Even the eyes, for Aristotle, are covered with a form of skin, usually taken to be the eyelids; *Gen. An.* V.2 781a20f. Eyelids do not, however, *usually* cover the eyes. Aristotle is either referring to something else or implying, presumably for the sake of boundary, that the "natural" state of eyes is to be closed—in which case vision is not "natural" to them!

47. Aristotle, *Progression of Animals* 6, *Movement of Animals* 9, 10. The attribution of ousiodic structure to the animal body requires that an animal actually manifest a single central source of movement. This is presumably the reason why Aristotle devotes so much attention to this "central source," which, as Martha Nussbaum notes, is not required by the rest of the investigation here; Nussbaum, *Aristotle's De Motu Animalium* (Princeton, N.J.: Princeton University Press, 1978), p. 372f.

48. *Gen. An.* IV.3, 767b8-768a9, italics added; the entire chapter is relevant here.

49. As Furth notes, the sexism has an important *philosophical* source. For a form to unify a living thing, it must itself be unitary. Since unity cannot come from plurality, for a form to be one in the offspring it must have been one in the parent—which means it could not have been received from both parents. Either the father or the mother must have it, and it goes to the father; Furth, *Substance, Form, and Psyche*, p. 140. This is an early reliance on one of the chief axioms of European culture, *unum ex uno.* The momentous American rejection of this axiom is on the Great Seal of the United States (and every dollar bill): *e pluribus unum.* Aristotle's sexism, though grounded in his philosophy, is strong enough to override it on occasion. In the discussion at *Gen. An.* II.1, he who called Plato to task for "separating" forms and sensibles not only accepts but calls for the separation of form from matter: "Again, as . . . the definition and the form . . . is better and more divine than the material on which it works, it is better that the superior principle should be separated from the inferior. Therefore, whenever it is possible and so far as it is possible, the male is separated from the female"; *Gen. An.* II.1 732a3-7.

50. Though they are "necessary" in the sense that they are inevitable, given the prevalence of accident on the sublunary world; *Gen. An.* IV.3 767b13-15.

51. *De An.* II.4 216a6-8 As Gill puts it, "The Aristotelian cosmos is a world of tension and commotion—ordered and preserved by form, disordered by matter"; Mary Louise Gill, *Aristotle on Substance: The Paradox of Unity* (Princeton, N.J.: Princeton University Press, 1989), p. 242.

52. Nor need such insults be specific: time itself is inimical to ousia, notes Aristotle, for it is "by nature the cause of decay." Though time provides the dimension for both coming to be and passing away, it is more intimately related to passing away; Aristotle, *Physics* IV.12 220a30-b2.

53. Aristotle, *Physics* II.1 192b13-23. Each natural thing is said to be a substance at 192a33seq; the form or nature of a thing is said to be "exhibited" in its process of growth at 193b13seqq. My formulation is designed to capture the fact that we

can tell that a thing at rest is so in virtue of an immanent principle—rather than merely as an undisturbed heap—is that it holds itself together. This may have bearing on the cryptic imperfect tense in Aristotle's own phrase for essence: *to ti ên einai*, "that which it was-being to be": an ousia must have been maintaining itself over time in order to have an essence. Kosman argues for what seems to be a different kind of empirical purchase: the matter of a natural thing cannot exist apart from that thing (Kosman, "Animals and Other Beings in Aristotle," pp. 367-371). Empirically, this cashes out to the terminal stage of the criterion I propose: we know that a thing's (proximate) matter cannot exist apart from that thing only because when the thing dies, its matter decomposes, i.e., resolves to more elemental natures.

54. *EN* I.3; X.8 1179a18-20, b18ff. Thus when he comes in *EN* to discuss the ethical nature of the soul, Aristotle is quick to point out that "some things are said about it adequately . . . even in the discussions outside our school"; *EN* I.13 1102a26f. In the earlier *Eudemian Ethics*, this constraint is not carried through as consistently as in *EN*, and Aristotle's own philosophical vocabulary is more in evidence. There we read that, "all ousiai are by nature first principles (*archai*) of some kind." As ethical ousiai, human beings are first principles of things that may or may not happen. They have this characteristic, moreover, in virtue of their capacity to receive opposites—what Aristotle will later call their matter; Aristotle, *Eudemian Ethics* II.6, 1222b16ff, 42. The *Eudemian Ethics* seems to have been written before Aristotle settled on the vocabulary for his hylomorphism; he is still using the terms of the *Categories*. The relationship between the *Eudemian Ethics* and *EN* is explored in detail in Anthony Kenny, *The Aristotelian Ethics* (Oxford: Clarendon Press, 1978).

55. Daniel Graham and Terence Irwin, for example, have to some degree noticed it; see Graham, *Aristotle's Two Systems*, p. 190; Irwin, *Aristotle's First Principles*, pp. 344-346, and "The Metaphysical and Psychological Basis of Aristotle's Ethics," in Rorty, ed., *Essays on Aristotle's Ethics*, pp. 35-53.

56. *EN* I.7 1097b25. The word *ergon* is, of course, at least etymologically related to *energeia*, "actuality"; see Graham, *Aristotle's Two Systems*, p. 190.

57. *EN* I.7 1098a3-18. The literature on just how "inclusive" this exercise is supposed to be is enormous; for instructive treatments, see John M. Cooper, *Reason and Human Good in Aristotle* (Cambridge, Mass.: Harvard University Press, 1975), and "The Role of *Eudaimonia* in Aristotle's Ethics," in Rorty, ed., *Essays on Aristotle's Ethics*, pp. 359-376; Irwin, "The Metaphysical and Psychological Basis of Aristotle's Ethics," p. 49; and Richard Kraut, *Aristotle on the Human Good* (Princeton, N.J.: Princeton University Press, 1989), pp. 237-241, 267-311.

58. *EN* I.7 1098a3-5; the point is expanded upon in *EN* I.13, which I discuss shortly.

59. For discussion of the doctrines and difficulties, see Sarah Broadie, *Ethics with Aristotle* (Oxford: Oxford University Press, 1991), pp. 266-312, and the references there; W. F. R. Hardie, *Aristotle's Ethical Theory*, 2nd ed. (Oxford: Clarendon Press, 1980, pp. 258-293; Richard Robinson, "Aristotle on Akrasia," in Barnes et al., eds., *Articles on Aristotle* II, pp. 79-91; James Walsh, *Aristotle's Conception of Moral Weakness* (New York: Columbia University Press, 1960).

60. "As one does one's father"; *EN* I.13 1103a3. Desire is thus the "passive" part of the rational principle.

61. "Whoever pursues excessive pleasure not by choice (*prohairesis*) but against

choice and reason (*dianoia*) is said to be incontinent"; *EN* 1148a6-11; cf. 1147a34f. For a more perspicuous treatment, see *De An.* III.9-10, esp. 433b27-31.

62. Desire, as Jonathan Lear points out, is always for something which the desiring being lacks; Lear, *Aristotle: The Desire to Understand* (Cambridge: Cambridge University Press, 1988), p. 142. The desire for one's own well-being is then the desire of the one part of the soul—the desiring faculty itself—for the well-being of active reason. Cf. Marcia Homiak, "Virtue and Self-Love in Aristotle's Ethics," *Canadian Journal of Philosophy* 11 (1981), pp. 633-652.

63. Lear, *Aristotle: The Desire to Understand*, pp. 160-170. I will not tarry to discuss how this organization is achieved; for valuable reflections, see J. A. Stewart, *Notes on the Nicomachean Ethics of Aristotle*, vol. 1 (Oxford: Clarendon Press, 1892), pp. 202-209. For virtue as the middle "form" of the "material" tendencies of excess and defect, see p. 209; this has obvious but unexplored affinities for the view that matter tends to fly apart unless restrained by form, as evidenced at *De An.* II.4 216a6-8, quoted earlier in this chapter and in the preceding one: excess and defect, like the elements of a living body, tend to travel in contrary directions; if there is no counteracting force, they will be "torn asunder."

64. *EN* 1139b4f; IX.4 1166a14-20; cf. Irwin, *Aristotle's First Principles*, pp. 379-383, and Homiak, "Virtue and Self-Love in Aristotle's Ethics."

65. It is no accident that the *Nicomachean Ethics*' main example of moral deliberation concerns whether or not to eat "dry food" (bread) rather than "wet" (porridge); *EN* VII.3 1147a5ff.

66. For a pathbreaking introduction to this controversy, see M. I. Finley, "Aristotle and Economic Analysis," *Past and Present* 47 (1970), pp. 3-25, along with the more recent discussion in Scott Meikle, *Aristotle's Economic Thought* (Oxford: Clarendon Press, 1995), pp. 147-179.

67. See *EN* VIII.12 1162a16-18: "Man is by nature a wedded being even more than a political one, since the household is earlier and more necessary than the city."

68. This de-emphasis of household administration is perhaps due to the fact that, as Kurt Singer notes, "the office of an *oikonomos* was in the eyes of an old style Athenian tainted by its association with women and with slaves or hirelings"; Singer, "Oikonomia: An Inquiry into the Beginnings of Economic Thought and Language," *Kyklos* 11 (1958), p. 44. Though Aristotle was not an Athenian, there is only too much evidence that he was "old style" in this sense.

69. It seems clear that Book I of *Oeconomica*, if not actually written by Aristotle, was written by someone of his time who had a clear and detailed understanding of his thought; see Jean Tricot, Introduction to Aristotle, *Les économiques*, ed. J. Tricot, (Paris: Jean Vrin, 1983), pp. 7-9; G. Cyril Armstrong, "Introduction" to Aristotle, *Oeconomica*, in Aristotle, *Metaphysics X-XIV, Oeconomica, Magna Moralia* (Cambridge, Mass.: Harvard University Press [Loeb], p. 323. Further citation will be to the latter edition, abbreviated "*Oec.*"

70. *Pol.* I.4 1253b29-1254a17. *EN* at one point applies this to children; V.7 1134b10-12.

71. *Pol.* I.13 1260a13-15. W. W. Fortenbaugh has argued that the lack of "authority" (*kyrios*) Aristotle imputes to woman's reason resides first in its inability to control her own emotions—in my terms, to dispose of the ethical matter of her life; Fortenbaugh, "Aristotle on Slaves and Women," in Jonathan Barnes, Malcolm Schofield, and Richard Sorabji, eds., *Articles on Aristotle*, vol. 4 (London: Duckworth,

1977), pp. 135-139. It is this which deprives her of independent authority within the household, for which see below. It is not necessary, perhaps, to go so far afield. The *Eudemian Ethics* identifies a *kyrios* agent as one from which changes first arise (Aristotle, *Eudemian Ethics* II. 6 1222b20ff). A woman, merely carrying out the instructions of her husband, would not be *kyrios* in this sense.

72. An especially troublesome one, since nature, which would like (*bouletai*) to make slaves look different from free men, allows them for no discernible reason to resemble one another; *Pol.* I.5 1254b25-1255a1. Booth argues that this means that political hierarchies—even this most basic—are intrinsically suspect for Aristotle, who recurs to family structures to justify them; William James Booth, "Politics and the Household: A Commentary on Aristotle's *Politics* Book One," *History of Political Thought* 2 (1981), pp. 203-226.

73. Or (in the case of boys) cannot acquire it soon. Young, freeborn males are in a slightly different situation than the others, because they will one day be mature moral agents; but that will come about only after decades of maturation and instruction.

74. See *Pol.* I.13 1260a23f for such community of interest between husband and wives; I.2, 1252a32-b1 for that between master and slave; and I.12 1259b10-16 for that between father and children, especially sons.

75. Booth, "Politics and the Household," pp. 222, 224.

76. *Pol.* I.9 1257a29-35, 1257b11-6; I.10 1258b1. *Xenikôteras* at 1257a31 should probably be rendered as "more foreign" rather than "from another country," as Jowett does; Aristotle, *Politics*, trans. Benjamin Jowett, in Richard McKeon, ed., *The Basic Works of Aristotle* (New York: Random House, 1941), p. 1138.

77. As Booth notes; William James Booth, *Households: On the Moral Architecture of the Economy* (Ithaca, N.Y.: Cornell University Press, 1993), p. 49.

78. *Oeconomica* I.3 1343b30-1344a3. As Stephen G. Salkever points out, this is a long way from claiming that women "are mere matter needing to be ruled entirely by male form"; Salkever, "Women, Soldiers, Citizens: Plato and Aristotle on the Politics of Virility," in Carnes Lord and David K. O'Connor, eds., *Essays on the Foundations of Aristotelian Political Science* (Berkeley: University of California Press, 1991). True indeed; they are not *merely* that. Cf. Everson, "Aristotle on the Foundations of the State," p. 97.

79. Cf. the general discussion of ancient households in Booth, *Households*, pp. 17-93.

80. *EN* V.6 1134a35f, VIII.10 1160b33-39; *Pol.* I. 12 1260a17-19, b3-5.

81. On *philia* in the household, see *EN* VIII.12 1162a4-9 (children toward their parents); 1162a16-29 (wife and husband); and VIII.11 1161b2-8 (master and slave; ambivalently, as is usual in Aristotle's discussions of slavery). Cf. A. C. Bradley, "Aristotle's Conception of the State," in David Keyt and Fred D. Miller, Jr., eds., *A Companion to Aristotle's Politics* (Oxford: Basil Blackwell, 1991), p. 17.

82. I.e., "oligarchic"; *EN* VIII.10 1160b11-15, 36-39.

83. Booth, "Politics and the Household," p. 225.

84. *EN* III.5 1113b18; I.13 1103a3; III.12 1119b11-14. That the individual body, not the household, is Aristotle's great example of ousia is argued by Wolfgang Kullmann, "Man as a Political Animal in Aristotle," in Keyt and Miller, eds., *A Companion to Aristotle's Politics*, p. 110, and their argument is certainly true. But analogies run in many directions, and the role of the household in rendering

ousiodic structures comprehensible is both important and based on an acute insight: that the child understands its familial household better than its own body.

85. That presumably is why Aristotle cannot take the route that Graham thinks he should have: making form and matter coequal "aspects" of the composite. The domination of form is essential if Aristotle's metaphysics is to justify his social philosophy. Graham, *Aristotle's Two Systems*, pp. 263–289. The attempt to instate co-equality between matter and form assumes major importance in modernity, for which see my forthcoming book *(Up)Ending Metaphysics: Nineteenth-Century Challenges to Ousia*.

86. *Pol.* VII.5 1326b41, 1327a5–10; VII.7 1330b36–1331a18. For Aristotle's views on the heart, see Theodore Tracy, S.J., "Heart and Soul in Aristotle," in John P. Anton and Anthony Preus, eds., *Essays in Ancient Greek Philosophy*, vol. 2 (Albany: State University of New York Press, 1983), pp. 321–339.

87. "The nature of a thing is its end"; *Pol.* I. 21252b32–34. For the identity of final and formal cause in the state, see *Pol.* I.2 1252b30–1253a1, and Bradley, "Aristotle's Conception of the State," p. 25. For a helpful list of the places where Aristotle speaks of the state as being a composite, see Curtis N. Johnson, *Aristotle's Political Theory* (London: Macmillan, 1990), p. 63 n. 13. On form and matter in the state, see also Maurice Defourney, "The Aim of the State: Peace," in Barnes et al., *Articles on Aristotle* II, p. 195.

88. Johnson, *Aristotle's Theory of the State*, p. 48f. For this statement of the end of the state, see *Pol.* I.2 1252b28ff; for the "material" side, see *Pol.* III.6 1278b28–30. For more on "self-sufficiency," see Stephen Everson, "Aristotle on the Foundations of the State," *Political Studies* 36 (1988), p. 93f.

89. *Pol.* IV.1 1289a15–18. For the constitution as the arrangement of magistracies in a state, see *Pol.* III.6 1278b10.

90. For the constitution as providing the identity of the state, see *Pol.* III.1 1276b11–14. *Pol.* III.1, 1274b37–40 refers to the constitution as the arrangement of the inhabitants, not of offices.

91. For an account of the constitution and its sovereign body, see R. G. Mulgan, *Aristotle's Political Theory* (Oxford: Oxford University Press, 1977), pp. 56–60. For the sense in which the constitution, as the set of specifically political institutions, *is* for Aristotle the state as a whole, see Mulgan, *Aristotle's Political Theory*, p. 26.

92. R. G. Mulgan, "Aristotle's Sovereign," *Political Studies* 18 (1970), p. 519.

93. Mulgan, *Aristotle's Political Theory*, p. 58.

94. *Pol.* IV.4, 12911a24–28; the likeness is stated again at II.4 11277a5–10. Though Aristotle does not use the term "essence" here, he does at least twice liken the state to a living thing with body and soul; and the "soul" of the state is its higher parts: the administrators of justice and the deliberative body, as well as the warriors. The constitution would then correspond to a formula for the proper relations among the parts of the individual soul; the sovereign body would be analogous to the intellect. On the constitution as the essence of the state, see Andreas Kamp, *Die politische Philosophie des Aristoteles und ihre metaphysischen Grundlagen* (Munich: Karl Alber, 1985), pp. 132–151. My account here is much indebted to Kamp's exhaustive investigation of the metaphysical concepts and doctrines at work in Aristotle's political thought. Also see the pathbreaking essay by Manfred Riedel, "Politik und Metaphysik bei Aristoteles," *Metaphysik und Politik* (Frankfurt/am Main: Suhrkamp, 1975), pp. 63–86.

95. All the citizens are parts of the state's telos or form, because the end (*telos*) of the state is the same as the end of the individual, though "finer and more godlike"; *EN* 1.2 1094b5-10; *Pol.* VII.1. As Kamp puts the relation of the individual citizen to the constitution, "Als *taxis tôn archôn* ist die Politeia mit anderen Worten im allgemeinen die Ausgliederung der Amtsträger aus der Gesamtheit der Polis-Bewohner, im besonderen aber und in ihrer wesentlichen Hinsicht die immanente Ordnung der Bürgerschaft bezüglich der politischen Befügnisse und Tätigkeiten ihrer Mitglieder (*Die politische Philosophie des Aristoteles*, p. 146). For the attenuated unity of the state, see *Pol.* II.2 1261a17-b15.

96. For this distinction, see Aristotle, *Parts of Animals* I.1 640a33-b4

97. For the slave as a "living but separated part" of the master, cf. *Politics* I.6 1255b12f; for the artisan as a "separate" slave, see *Politics* I.13, 1260a39-b1.

98. Cooper, "Hypothetical Necessity and Natural Teleology," p. 255.

99. Women have no independent political voice: "silence is a woman's glory"; *Pol.* I.13 1260a12-b18. For Aristotle's invocation of the household to justify political hierarchy, see Booth, "Politics and Household."

100. *Pol.* III.5 1278a1-14 and VII.8 1328a22-37 make the analogy to organic parts. John M. Cooper chooses the example of eyes as an example of the hypothetically necessary; Cooper, "Hypothetical Necessity and Natural Teleology," in Gotthelf and Lennox, eds., *Philosophical Issues in Aristotle's Biology*, p. 244.

101. *Pol.* VII.4 1326a3. Schuetrumpf's view that citizens only are the matter of the state is not supported by this passage; E. Schuetrumpf, "Kritische Überlegungen zur Ontologie und Terminologie der aristotelischen 'Politik," *Allgemeine Zeitschrift für Philosophie* 6 (1981), p. 29ff. On the "matter" of the state, see further Kamp, *Die politische Philosophie des Aristoteles*, pp. 163-173. Kamp assumes that the living capacities of the inhabitants of the state do not persist as its matter once the state has come into being—they are matter for the potential state, not the actual one. I do not see why they cannot be both.

102. Hence the household remains the primary engine of domination in the Aristotelian social world; cf. Booth, "Politics and the Household." My own characterization of the hierarchical structure of ousia, traced at the end of chap. 1, applies quite well to the state. At its top we find its constitution, which—in terms I there used of essence—consists in "a complex but unified activity whose different aspects—the being's formal parts (magistracies)—are always found together." One step down are the individual citizens, who, like relegated properties, "have secondary status because they are specifications of the primary ones, as 'musician' is a specification of 'rational animal.' Another step brings us to the "necessary people," material parts which "because they can only be formed from certain sorts of matter, are not parts of the essence and, since they contain matter, are only incompletely knowable; yet are, like heart and lungs, necessary for the maintenance and welfare of the being itself." A fourth step down are the wholly accidental residents, who "do not derive from the essence and do not normally contribute to the welfare or maintenance of the thing." All the quotes are from chap. 1.

103. See Defourney, "The Aim of the State: Peace."

104. Foreign trade, like retail trade on the level of the household, makes the state dependent on other states and so is in tension with Aristotle's claim that the telos of the state is to be self-sufficient or very nearly so. The need for self-sufficiency is used as a guideline in determining such matters as the state's degree of unity and

the size of its population and territory. *Pol.* I.2 1252b28; II. 2 1261b14f; VII.4 1326b2-5; VII.5 1326b29.

105. Cf. the summation by Stephen R. L. Clark of Aristotle's political philosophy: "Government and the state are institutions which permit some people to *impose* their will upon all those within the *boundaries* fixed by historical accident to mark the limit of one state's *power* over against another's"; Clark, "Slaves and Citizens," *Philosophy* 60 (1985), p. 46, emphasis added. Though Clark does not use the term, ousiodic structure is very near the surface here.

106. *Metaph.* XII. 10 1076a4; quoted from Homer, *Iliad* II.204.

107. See *Metaph.* XII.10 1075a20-23, quoted earlier, for the cosmic order, which I do not have space to discuss here.

3. THE DOCILITY OF MATTER IN THOMAS AQUINAS

1. For example, at *De An.* III.5 430a10-14 and *Pol.* I.2 11254a28-32, both discussed in the previous chapter. To recap: in the Aristotelian texts I have treated, definition tends to be analogical (for example, moral deliberation is said to be similar to listening to one's father, an analogy which helps define it for the reader). Legitimation, by contrast, tends to proceed argumentatively. The general pattern is: all things are ousiai; the present object of investigation is a class of thing; therefore we will find in it characteristics of ousiai, especially matter and form. This way of arguing legitimates the practice or institution in question by showing that it is necessary (and, for Aristotle, that it is good).

2. For which see Mary Louise Gill, *Aristotle on Substance: The Paradox of Unity* (Princeton, N.J.: Princeton University Press, 1989), p. 242, and the previous two chapters of this book.

3. So constituted, God as ousia "is" the human situation: *"an potius non essem, si non essem in te?";* Augustine, *Confessions* I.II.

4. See Johannes von Arnim, ed., *Fragmenta stoicorum vetorum,* vol. 1 (New York: Irvington, 1986), p. 24.

5. Jean-François Courtine, "Note complémentaire pour l'histoire du vocabulaire de l'être: les traductions latines d'*ousia* et la compréhension romano-stoiciennc dc l'être," in Pierre Aubenque, ed., *Concepts et catégories dans la pensée antique* (Paris: Jean Vrin, 1980), p. 61; also see pp. 33-87, esp. p. 72.

6. Augustine, *Confessions* XII.VIII.

7. In the strict sense, for Aquinas, nothing can resist the divine governance; Thomas Aquinas, *ST* I.103.1. Where possible, the *Summa Theologiae* will be cited after Anton C. Pegis, ed., 2 vols. (New York: Random House, 1945). Other citations will be conventional.

8. Thomas Aquinas, *De ente et essentia, L'être et l'essence,* Latin text with trans. and notes by Catherine Capelle (Paris: Jean Vrin, 1965), p. 17 (hereinafter: *EE*) (English translation, *On Being and Essence,* trans. Armand Maurer [Toronto: Pontifical Institute of Medieval Studies, 1949], p. 26f). For the representative character of this text for Aquinas's views on composite substances, see the introduction to Maurer's translation, p. 13. For a concise account of the status of *De ente et essentia* in Aquinas's corpus, see James A. Weisheipl, *Friar Thomas d'Aquino: His Life, Thought, and Works* (Garden City, N.Y.: Doubleday, 1974), p. 78f.

9. See Scott MacDonald, "Theory of Knowledge," in Norman Kretzmann and

Eleonore Stump, eds., *The Cambridge Companion to Aquinas* (Cambridge: Cambridge University Press, 1993), pp. 168-172.

10. Jacques Derrida, "Force et signification, *L'écriture et la différence* (Paris: Éditions du Seuil, 1967), p. 26.

11. *De ente et essentia* has been dated to 1254-1256, almost 1,600 years after Aristotle; *EE,* Introduction, p. 6; also see Maurer, Translator's Introduction to Aquinas, *On Being and Essence,* p. 7. For a brief listing of what Aquinas's metaphysics has taken over from Aristotle, see Leo J. Elders, *Die Metaphysik des Thomas von Aquin in historischer Perspektive* (Salzburg: Anton Pustet, 1985), pp. 193-196.

12. Cf. Jean Tricot's note in Aristotle, *La métaphysique* 2 vols. ed. Tricot (Paris: J. Vrin, 1981). W. D. Ross points out, also *ad loc.,* that these four are also given, and in a different order, at *Metaphysics* VI.1 1026a33-b2; Aristotle, *Metaphysics,* ed. Ross, 2 vols. (Oxford: Clarendon Press, 1924). The variation in order suggests that the four senses have no particular relationship among themselves, in Aristotle's view. Aquinas recognizes the other two senses in his *Commentary on the Metaphysics of Aristotle,* trans. John P. Rowan, vol. 1 (Chicago: Regnery, 1961), p. 346f.

13. The association of presence with the possibility of truth, which I suggest here is implicit in Aquinas, will be made very clear in the seventeenth century by Antoine Arnauld, arguing against Malebranche; Arnauld, *On True and False Ideas,* trans. Stephen Gaukroger (Manchester: Manchester University Press, 1990), p. 58f. The middle term assimilating the two is vision: to be present is to be the object of either the body's or the mind's eye. The association of presence with truth and its dissociation from the ousiodic structures exhibited in the other, "primary" sense of being make problems for postmodernists who wish to contest presence without contesting truth altogether; but neither the association nor the problems it causes are my topics here. For an exploration, see my *Philosophy and Freedom,* forthcoming.

14. These two terms enter into different games of predication, for we can say that Socrates is a human being but not that he is a humanity; Aquinas, *EE,* p. 39/37f.

15. Ibid. I will prescind for the moment from Aquinas's main difference with Aristotle, which can be expressed as follows: for Aristotle, essence is form *in* matter; for Aquinas, it is form *and* matter which are united by the un-Aristotelian "act of existing," *actus essendi.* In *De ente et essentia,* this distinction is introduced to preserve the createdness of separate substances other than God. For Aristotle, these essences were immaterial forms and hence existed from eternity; they were not created by the Prime Mover. For Aquinas they still require, in addition to their form, the act of being which they receive from God, who is the only being that exists necessarily (cf. Aquinas, *EE,* p. 58/47). Aquinas's espousal of this, we will see, changes but in no way impeaches the priority of form over matter in composite substances.

16. For this controversy, see the references in chap. 1, note 85.

17. *EE,* p. 35/36. As I noted in chap. 1, for Aristotle none of the categories can be either asserted or denied of matter as such; it would not have being even in Aquinas's secondary sense. Note Aquinas's subtle treatment, in his *Commentary on the Metaphysics of Aristotle,* of the "stripping-away" argument of *Metaph.* VII.3, which I discussed briefly in chap. 1. As Aristotle says, writes Aquinas, matter is not separable or a this because it "cannot exist by itself without a form by means of which it is an actual being, since of itself it is only potential." But "dimensive quality seems to

belong immediately to matter, since matter is divided in such a way as to receive different forms in its different parts, only by means of this kind of quality"; Aquinas, *Commentary on the Metaphysics of Aristotle*, vol. 2, pp. 499, 501.

18. *EE*, p. 29/33f. See also Norman Kretzmann, "Philosophy of Mind," in Kretzmann and Stump, *The Cambridge Companion to Aquinas*, p. 131; G. E. M. Anscombe and Peter Geach, *Three Philosophers* (Oxford: Basil Blackwell, 1961), p. 83.

19. See Anscombe and Geach, *Three Philosophers*, p. 74f.

20. J. Christopher Maloney, "Esse in the Thought of Thomas Aquinas," *New Scholasticism* 55 (1981), p. 159–177, esp. p. 164f.

21. Etienne Gilson, *The Christian Philosophy of St. Thomas Aquinas*, trans. L. K. Shook (New York: Random House, 1956), p. 32.

22. Gilson, *The Christian Philosophy of St. Thomas Aquinas*, p. 131.

23. As Gilson says elsewhere; Gilson, *The Christian Philosophy of St. Thomas Aquinas*, p. 88.

24. Maloney takes a similar tack: Aquinas should have defined designated matter not as extended in three dimensions but simply as that which form forms in an individual; Maloney, "Esse in the Thought of Thomas Aquinas," p. 165. My point here is not that Gilson and Maloney are right (or wrong) but that the plausibility of their interpretations shows how far Aquinas's text goes in the direction of making matter wholly subservient to form. It is a tack which Heidegger follows in "On the Essence and Concept of *Physis* in Aristotle." I discuss this essay briefly in chap. 10.

25. Aquinas, *ST* Ia 65.4 The text also says that subsequently, things have their corporeal forms from God, but in some cases through the mediation of angelic intelligences which God creates. Cf. Aquinas, *EE*, p. 59/47.

26. Joseph Owens, "Aristotle and Aquinas," in Kretzmann and Stump, eds., *The Cambridge Companion to Aquinas*, p. 51f.

27. For a brief discussion and references, see John F. Wippel, "Metaphysics," in Kretzmann and Stump, eds., *The Cambridge Companion to Aquinas*, pp. 89–93.

28. Cited after Anton Pegis, ed. and trans., *Basic Writings of Saint Thomas Aquinas*, vol. 1 (New York: Random House, 1945), p. 989.

29. Furth, *Substance, Form, and Psyche*, p. 59f.

30. For Averroës, then, as Sertillanges puts it, "A la forme de définir la quantité; a la matière d'en fournir come l'étoffe"; A. D. Sertillanges, *Thomas d'Aquin*, vol. 2 (Paris: Alcan, 1925), p. 12. The "form" in question is the form of corporeity, which a body has for Averroës prior to receiving its own essence.

31. See Weisheipl, *Friar Thomas d'Aquino*, pp. 335–338.

32. Under its Cartesian appellation, that is the object of Heidegger's critique in sections 19–21 of *Being and Time*. This critique then goes beyond its stated target of Descartes, even beyond Heidegger's modern colleague Hobbes, to hit Aquinas himself.

33. *ST* IIaIae. 1.1.; quoted by Ralph McInerny, "Ethics," in Kretzmann and Stump, eds., *The Cambridge Companion to Aquinas*, p. 197; emphasis added. For the sense of "dominion" here, see Alan Donagan, "Thomas Aquinas on Human Action," in Norman Kretzmann, Anthony Kenny, and Jan Pinboig, eds., *The Cambridge History of Later Medieval Philosophy* Cambridge: (Cambridge University Press, 1982), pp. 649–651.

34. The will operates as subordinate to reason, which must tell it what to will, i.e., what is good; see Donagan, "Thomas Aquinas on Human Action," pp. 652–654.

35. *Poetic Interaction* pp. 232f, 239-241

36. Thomas Aquinas, "On Kingship or the Governance of Rulers," *Saint Thomas Aquinas on Politics and Ethics,* ed. and trans. Paul E. Sigmund (New York: Norton, 1988), p. 14 (hereinafter: KG).

37. A passage which Aquinas explicitly cites at *ST* I.96.4.

38. This survival of ousiodic domination in the medieval human world goes far beyond Aquinas. Consider the twelfth-century thinker John of Salisbury: "Wherefore deservedly there is conferred in [the sovereign], and gathered together in his hands, the power of all his subjects, to the end that he may be sufficient unto himself, in seeking and bringing about the advantage of each individually, and of all, and to the end that the state of the human commonwealth may be ordered in the best possible manner. . . . Wherein we indeed but follow nature, the best guide of life; for nature has gathered together all the senses of her microcosm or little world, which is man, into the head, and has subjected all the members in obedience to it in such wise, that they will all function properly so long as they follow the guidance of the head. . . . Therefore, according to the usual definition, the prince is the public power, and a kind of likeness on earth of the divine majesty"; John of Salisbury, *Policraticus,* Book IV, chap. I (in Julius Kirschner and Karl F. Monson, eds., *University of Chicago Readings in Western Civilization IV: Medieval Civilization* [Chicago: University of Chicago Press, 1986], p. 180).

39. Etienne Gilson, *The Christian Philosophy of St. Thomas Aquinas,* p. 361.

40. John Locke, *An Essay concerning Human Understanding,* ed. Alexander Campbell Fraser, 2 vols. (New York: Dover, 1959), III.6.10.

4. TWO ANCIENT ENGINES OF OPPRESSION

1. Marilyn Frye, "Oppression," *The Politics of Reality* (Trumansburg, N.Y.: Crossing Press, 1983), pp. 1-16; see p. 2 for this point.

2. Frye, "Oppression," p. 4.

3. Frye, "Oppression," p. 7f.

4. Cf. Frye, "Oppression," p. 11.

5. Cf. the account of responsibility for one's acts in *Nicomachean Ethics* III.1-5, as well as in my *Poetic Interaction,* pp. 220-222.

6. Plato, *Republic* III 414b-415c.

7. Cf. my discussion of "extraneous" and "immanent" externalization in Hegel in my *Poetic Interaction,* p. 70f.

8. Cf. on this Simone de Beauvoir, *The Second Sex,* ed. and trans. H. M. Parshley (New York: Knopf, 1952), pp. 98, 472.

9. The difference between "immanent" and "external" exclusion is then a practical realization of the Aristotelian distinction between an accidental property of a thing—i.e., a quality within its boundaries but excluded from its identity—and a property of some other thing.

10. Roland Martin, *Greek Architecture* (New York: Rizzoli, 1988), pp. 23-25.

11. See Andrew Lintott, *Imperium Romanum* (London: Routledge, 1990), for detailed accounts of the actual chaos and flexibility within the Empire.

12. The quotes are respectively from Betty Forte, *Rome and the Romans as the Greeks Saw Them* (Rome: Proceedings and Monographs of the American Academy in Rome 24, 1972), p. 406, and James H. Oliver, *The Ruling Power* (Philadelphia:

Transactions of the American Philosophical Society, NS 43, pt. 4, (1953), p. 874f. The Oration's text is given at pp. 982-991 of this work, and an English translation on pp. 895-907. References in the text are to paragraphs of Oliver's edition and translation; translations included here are slightly altered.

13. Cf. P. Garnsey, K, Hopkins, and C. R. Whittaker, *Trade in the Ancient Economy* (Berkeley: University of California Press, 1983), pp. 145-162.

14. Vitruvius, *De architectura*, Book I, chap. II.

15. See Lintott, *Imperium Romanum*, pp. 22-32.

16. See Frank Granger's note in Vitruvius, *De architectura*, trans. Granger vol. 2 (Cambridge, Mass.: Harvard University Press(Loeb), 1934), p. 29 n. 2.

17. Sigmund Freud, *A General Introduction to* Psychoanalysis, trans. Joan Rivière (New York: Washington Square Books, 1960), p. 306.

18. Karl Marx, *Capital*, trans. Samuel Morse and Edward Aveling (New York: Modern Library, 1906), p. 195.

APPENDIX TO PART ONE

1. Friedrich Nietzsche, *Der Philosoph*, para. 79, *Gesammelte Schriften*, vol. 10, ed. Alfred Bäumler (Stuttgart: Kroner, 1965), p. 38.

2. Martin Heidegger, "Das Ende der Philosophie und die Aufgabe des Denkens," *Zur Sache des Denkens* (Tübingen: Niemeyer, 1969), p. 63 (English translation, "The End of Philosophy and the Task of Thinking," *On Time and Being*, trans. Joan Stambaugh [New York: Harper & Row, 1972], p. 67).

3. Gilles Deleuze, *Différence et répétition* (Paris: P.U.F., 1968), p. 83 (English translation, *Difference and Repetition*, trans. Paul Patton [New York: Columbia University Press, 1994], p. 59); "Platon et le simulacre," *Logique du sens* (Paris: Minuit, 1969), p. 298 (English translation, *The Logic of Sense*, trans. Mark Lester [New York: Columbia University Press, 1990], p. 259).

4. Jacques Derrida, *De la grammatologie* (Paris: Minuit, 1967), p. 104 (English translation, *Of Grammatology*, trans. Gayatri Chakravorty Spivak [Baltimore: Johns Hopkins University Press, 1974], p. 71).

5. Jürgen Habermas, "Die Einheit der Vernunft in der Vielfalt ihrer Stimmen," *Nachmetaphysisches Denken* (Frankfurt: Suhrkamp, 1988), p. 153 (English translation, "The Unity of Reason in the Diversity of its Voices," *Postmetaphysical Thinking*, trans. William Mark Hohengarten [Cambridge, Mass.: MIT Press, 1992], p. 115).

6. Richard Rorty, *Philosophy and the Mirror of Nature* (Princeton, N.J.: Princeton University Press, 1979), p. 369 n. 15; see also pp. 155-160 for further discussion.

7. Daniel Graham, *Aristotle's Two Systems* (Oxford: Oxford University Press, 1987), pp. 268-275; see also my comment in chap. 2, n. 76.

8. For Aristotle, as Graham puts it, "Form must attach directly to matter. The accidents attach . . . to the form"; Graham, *Aristotle's Two Systems*, p. 64. See in general the account of participation at *Timaeus* 49d seqq., which I discuss in this appendix.

9. That this was a problem for Plato, because it suggests that sensory experience is entirely chaotic, is shown by *Phaedo* 103c seqq.

10. See, for example, the hedging in Plato, *Phaedo* 107b, *Symposium* 211e, *Timaeus* 29b seq.

11. The gap is "ever-changing" because things may come to resemble the Forms more or less closely.

12. For the meaninglessness, see Aristotle, *Metaph.* I.9 991a20-22, 992a27f. I am indebted to Karen Feldman for this point.

13. For Deleuze and Heidegger, see Deleuze, "Platon et le simulacre," *Logique du Sens,* pp. 292-307/263-266; Heidegger, "Platons Lehre von der Wahrheit," *Wegmarken* (Frankfurtam Main: Klostermann, 1967), pp. 109-144.

14. Nietzsche, *Götzen-Dämmerung, Gesammelte Werke,* vol. 8, p. 99 (English translation, *Twilight of the Idols,* trans. R. J. Hollingdale [London: Penguin, 1990], p. 50).

15. Jacques Derrida, "La pharmacie der Platon, *La dissémination,* p. 127 (English translation, "Plato's Pharmacy," *Dissemination,* p. 110); cf. pp. 155/135, 192/166.

16. I swear I am not making this up; see Rorty, *Philosophy and the Mirror of Nature,* p. 32.

17. On the word of Aristotle himself, who at *Metaph.* I.9 makes the denial of the separation of Forms and sensibles into his single main criticism of Plato.

18. Plato, *Seventh Letter* 341b-d, 344c.

INTRODUCTION TO PART TWO

1. The eviction of ousia from nature was largely, of course, the work of the founders of modern science. This story, though without explicit reference to ousia, is magisterially told in E. J. Dijksterhuis, *The Mechanization of the World Picture,* trans. C. Dirkshoorn (Oxford: Clarendon Press, 1961).

2. Cf. David Hume, *A Treatise of Human Nature,* ed. L. A. Selby-Bigge (Oxford: Clarendon Press, 1896), p. 469f.

5. THE CARTESIAN RELOCATION OF OUSIA

1. Descartes, letter to Mersenne, January 28, 1641, in Charles Adam and Paul Tannery, *Oeuvres de Descartes,* 13 vols. (Paris: Cerf, 1896-1913 (hereinafter: AT)) (English translation in Descartes, *Philosophical Letters,* ed. and trans. Anthony Kenny (Oxford: Clarendon Press, 1970), p. 94.

2. See the advice in his letter to Regius of January 1642, AT III 491/126f.

3. For the genesis and status of the *Principles of Philosophy* (*PP*) in Descartes's *oeuvre,* see Daniel Garber, "Descartes' Physics," in John Cottingham, ed., *The Cambridge Companion to Descartes* (Cambridge: Cambridge University Press, 1992), p. 291f.

4. *PP* II.9. Roman numerals refer to parts of this work in the Adam and Tannery edition, while Arabic numerals refer to individual principles. These numbers are valid also for the English translation in Elizabeth Haldane and G. R. T. Ross, trans., *The Philosophical Works of Descartes,* vol. 1 (Cambridge: Cambridge University Press, 1931), pp. 201-312.

5. Descartes, letter to de Launay, July 22, 1641, AT III 419/109.

6. Because, it is said, they are actual, while the matter is merely potential; Descartes, letter to Regius, January 16, 1642, AT III 491f/128.

7. This view is also clear from a very general definition of substance which Descartes gives in his "Reply to the Sixth Set of Objections" to the *Meditations:* "Anything in which there inheres immediately, as in a subject, or through which there exists something which we perceive, that is some property, or quality, or attribute, of whose reality there is an idea in us, is called substance. . . . Neither do we have any other idea of substance itself, precisely taken, than that it is a thing

in which this something that we perceive . . . exists formally or objectively; AT VII 161/Haldane and Ross II 53.

8. *PP* I.52. Even extension itself can be viewed as an attribute of a deeper and hence unknowable substance; *PP* I.64.

9. *PP* I.51. Descartes's views on substance have attracted little attention; see Peter Markie's pathbreaking "Descartes' Conceptions of Substance," in John Cottingham, ed., *Reason, Will, and Sensation: Studies in Descartes' Metaphysics* (Oxford: Clarendon Press, 1994), pp. 63–87.

10. Etienne Gilson, *Etudes sur la rôle de la pensée médiévale dans la formation du système cartésien* (Paris: Jean Vrin, 1930), pp. 143–184; cf. Jean-Luc Marion, "Cartesian Metaphysics and the Role of the Simple Natures," in Cottingham, ed., *The Cambridge Companion to Descartes*, p. 115: "The 'nature' is a 'knowable object' in the sense of 'object in so far as it can be known by us'; it thus deposes traditional *ousia* or essence, and banishes it once and for all from modern metaphysics."

11. R. S. Woolhouse, *Descartes, Spinoza, Leibniz: The Concept of Substance in Seventeenth-Century Metaphysics* (London: Routledge, 1993), p. 24.

12. Cf. the account of these two different kinds of purchase, with respect to the idea of motion, given at Amélie Oksenberg Rorty, "Descartes on Thinking with the Body," in Cottingham, ed., *The Cambridge Companion to Descartes*, p. 374f.

13. Descartes, *Meditationes de prima philosophia*, AT VII.14/Haldane and Ross I 141; cf. *PP* II.1; Woolhouse, *Descartes Spinoza Leibniz*, p. 24; John Cottingham, *Descartes* (Oxford: Basil Blackwell, 1986), p. 84f.

14. Descartes, letter to Gibieuf, January 19, 1642, AT III 477/142f.

15. *PP* II. 25; cf. Cottingham, *Descartes*, pp. 86–88.

16. For the relativity of motion and rest in Descartes's physics, see *PP* II.25–30 and Garber, "Descartes' Physics," pp. 305–307.

17. Daniel Garber, *Descartes' Metaphysical Physics* (Chicago: University of Chicago Press, 1992), p. 180f.

18. Garber, *Descartes' Metaphysical Physics*, p. 178.

19. *PP* I.19, I.15; "in God any variableness is incomprehensible," *PP* I.46.

20. Descartes, letter to More, August 1649, AT V 401/257. Cf. *PP* II. 36.

21. Ibid.; cf. Gary C. Hatfield, "Force (God) in Descartes' Physics," *Studies in History and Philosophy of Science* 10 (1979), p. 131.

22. This theological dimension to Descartes's physics is explored in Margaret J. Osler, "Eternal Truths and the Laws of Nature: The Theological Foundations of Descartes's Philosophy of Nature," *Journal of the History of Ideas* 46 (1986), pp. 349–362.

23. Descartes, letter to More, August 1649, AT V 401/257.

24. I.e., as efficient cause; that God is an efficient cause of created things, as Aquinas held, is suggested in Descartes, *First Replies*, AT VII 109/Haldane and Ross II 14.

25. Descartes, letter to Henry More, April 15, 1649, AT V 340/252.

26. Descartes, letter to Clerselier, April 23, 1649, AT V 352/254.

27. Garber, *Descartes' Metaphysical Physics*, p. 116.

28. Descartes, letter to Mersenne, April 26, 1643, AT III 648/135. The relevance of this passage, which mentions not substantial forms but "real qualities," is argued by Garber, *Descartes' Metaphysical Physics*, p. 353 n. 9.

29. The reasons for his discomfort are perhaps well stated in Martial Guéroult's

summary of the strange status of force in Descartes: "owing to their ambiguous situation with respect to creator and created, the forces which are in the world— the force of rest and moving force—have a complicated status: insofar as they are identical with the divine conserving force, they are *causes;* insofar as they appear in the conserved world, they are *effects;* insofar as they participate at one and the same time in cause and effect they are *second causes.* . . . In short, their position between creator and created condemns them to bring together contraries in themselves": Guéroult, "The Metaphysics and Physics of Force in Descartes," in Stephen Gaukroger, ed., *Descartes: Philosophy, Mathematics, Physics* (Totowa, N.J.: Barnes and Noble, 1980), p. 198f. The problem of the "ambiguous situation between creator and created" is, in my terms, the problem of whether God's power over the universe is a case of disposition or initiative. Gary Hatfield, pointing out that "second causes" for Descartes are laws of motion rather than moving things, shows that they derive from the principle of inertia, i.e., God's "concurrence" in their continued being; Hatfield, "Force (God) in Descartes' Physics," p. 123.

30. *PP* II. 36; the derivation is presented in detail in Garber, *Descartes' Metaphysical Physics,* pp. 280–293. Cf. Osler, "Eternal Truths and the Laws of Nature," p. 353f.

31. And even there they are not spatial, because Descartes's physical universe is infinite in extent.

32. See R. M. Mattern, "Locke on Active Power and the Obscure Idea of Active Power from Bodies," *Studies in the History and Philosophy of Science* 11 (1980), pp. 39–77. For the view that the later thinkers are "merely extending what was already implicit in [Descartes's] treatment of matter," see also Hatfield, "Force (God) in Descartes' Physics," p. 136 and n. 87.

33. See Niklas Luhmann, *Soziale Systeme* (Frankfurt: Suhrkamp, 1984), pp. 40, 52. The problem with this view, which Luhmann does not discuss, is this: Given that the unity of the system consists in the fact that its members transform each other, what is to keep them from also transforming things outside the system? And what then happens to the boundaries of the system?

34. Descartes, letter to Henry More, February 6, 1649, AT V 267/239.

35. For a discussion of clarity and distinctness in Descartes, see my *Company of Words* (Evanston, Ill.: Northwestern University Press, 1989), pp. 100–102.

36. *PP* I.52. This view of human nature is of course at play in the famous inference in the first *Meditation,* from the existence of thought to the existence of a thinking thing. It is also at play in the fact that, as Garber puts it, "Descartes saw the Aristotelian substantial forms as impositions of mind onto matter"; Garber, "Descartes' Physics," p. 302.

37. Descartes, *PP* I.60; also see *PP* I.8 and *Meditationes* III. For the contrast with material substance, see Markie, "Descartes' Concepts of Substance," pp. 81–87.

38. A view which sounds suspiciously, as will be seen, like that of Hobbes.

39. Woolhouse sketches the mind's Aristotelian origins as follows: "As for Cartesian minds, they do in effect fulfill the function served by the specifically 'rational' part of that form which [for Aristotle] is the human soul"; Woolhouse, *Descartes Spinoza Leibniz,* p. 25.

40. *PP* I.6, I. 37. Cf. the paean to what Amélie O. Rorty calls the "imperial will" of Descartes in his letter to Queen Christina, November 20, 1647: "Now free will is in itself the noblest thing we can have, since it makes us in a way equal to God and seems to exempt us from being his subjects . . . indeed there is nothing that

is more our own or matters more to us" (AT V 85/326); Rorty, "Descartes on Thinking with the Body," p. 372.

41. Descartes, *Principle of Philosophy* I.1, 43-50, 70-75. On the primacy of the will, cf. also Peter Schouls, "Human Nature, Reason, and Will" in Cottingham (ed.) *Reason, Will, and Sensation: Studies in Descartes' Metaphysics* pp. 159-176, pp. 172-176.

42. Descartes, Dedication, *PP,* AT VIIIA 3/217. For the ethics implicit in the later *Passions de l'âme,* see Cottingham, *Descartes,* pp. 152-156.

43. Descartes, *Les passions de l'âme,* AT XI 351-370 (English translation, Haldane asnd Ross I, p. 345-350); cf. Descartes, letter to Meysonnier, January 29, 1640, AT III 18/69f.

44. Descartes, *Discours de méthode* III AT VI 25 (English translation, Haldane and Ross I pp. 96f; my translation).

45. These two types of volition are clearly distinguished in *Les passions de l'âme,* AT 343/340. I am not claiming that Descartes could not have solved these problems, only that their intractability may explain why he did not try to write an ethics of initiative.

46. *PP* I.24. The whole approach of Meditation IV to the question of error moves from a consideration of God's nature to one of our own; see Descartes, *Meditationes,* AT VII 54/172f.

47. Descartes, Author's Letter, in *PP,* AT IXB 10f/209.

48. Ibid.

49. Descartes, *Meditationes,* AT VII 17/144.

50. For a concise statement of some of the infelicities, see Pierre Guenancia, *Descartes et l'ordre politique* (Paris: Presses Universitaires de France, 1983), pp. 224-227.

51. Letter to Elizabeth, September 1646, AT IV 485ff/199ff.

52. See Thomas Aquinas, *Summa Theologiae* I Qn 104a2, a1c, a2 ad 1.

53. See my *Company of Words,* p. 278.

54. "The more . . . science is regarded as the scattered possession of a community, the more each individual in the community possesses it vicariously, without making it his own. . . . At best, members of the community enable [original thinkers like] Aristotle or Aquinas to speak through them . . . to see Cartesian science as a kind of anti-erudition is to see it as a self-consciously modern intellectual production, not necessarily free of all traces of the past, but insistent on the need to conduct inquiry with the influence of the past firmly under control"; Tom Sorell, "Descartes' Modernity," in Cottingham, ed., *Reason, Will, and Sensation,* p. 40.

6. OUSIA AND SOVEREIGNTY IN HOBBES

1. Thomas Hobbes, *Leviathan, or the Matter, Forme, & Power of a Common-Wealth Ecclesiastical and Civill,* edition of 1651, reprinted in Hobbes, *Leviathan,* ed. Richard Tuck (Cambridge: Cambridge University Press, 1991). My pagination is to the original edition. For a general summary of Hobbes's reduction of Aristotle's cosmos to the "rigid unity of geometrical science," see Jean Bernhardt, "L'Aristotelisme et la pensée de Hobbes," in Martin Bertman and Michel Malherbe, eds., *Thomas Hobbes: De la métaphysique a la politique* (Paris: Jean Vrin, 1989), pp. 9-15.

2. This procedure is not uncongenial to Hobbes himself. Defending himself in the third person in his *Dialogus physicus,* he could write: "content with Hobbesian physics, I will observe the nature and variety of motion. I will also use the same

Hobbesian rules of politics and ethics for living"; Hobbes, *Opera omnia quae latine scripsit,* vol. 4, ed. William Molesworth, (London: John Bohn), p. 287; English translation in Steven Shapin and Simon Schaffer, *Leviathan and the Air-Pump: Hobbes, Boyle, and the Experimental Life* (Princeton, N.J.: Princeton University Press, 1985), p. 391. But just what makes the "rules" in question the "same" is a subject of intricate scholarly dispute. R. Peters takes a strict approach to the unity of Hobbes's system; R. Peters, *Hobbes* (London, 1956). Tom Sorell has defended a more relaxed view of the unity of Hobbes's thought; Sorell, *Hobbes* (London: Routledge and Kegan Paul, 1986), pp. 7-14. Gérard Boss has carefully sorted out some of the major deductive gaps; Boss, "Système et rupture chez Hobbes," *Dialogue* 27 (1988), pp. 215-223. A somewhat different set is summarized nicely in Howard Warrender, *The Political Philosophy of Hobbes* (Oxford: Clarendon Press, 1957), p. 1. Parametric structuring of the type I am examining here seeks connections which are weaker and thus less easily ruptured than the deductive terms in which the question is usually couched. It is closely related to W. K Greenleaf's "discrete systematization," which is merely "the application to different areas or topics of a given style of analysis and discussion without attempting to relate the conclusions achieved in each case into a whole"; Greenleaf, "Hobbes: The Problem of Interpretation," in Maurice Cranston and Richard S. Peters, eds., *Hobbes and Rousseau: A Collection of Critical Essays* (Garden City, N.Y.: Doubleday Anchor, 1972), p. 31.

3. Thomas Hobbes, *De Corpore* VII.1, reprinted in part in M. W. Calkins ed., *The Metaphysical System of Thomas Hobbes* (LaSalle, Ill.: Open Court, 1963), p. 53; future page references will be to the English edition; section references hold for English and Latin.

4. *Lev.,* p. 11. Cf. the epistemologically rigorous way Hobbes puts it at the outset of *De Corp.* Philosophy there excludes "*Theology,* I mean the doctrine of God, eternal, ingenerable, incomprehensible, and in whom there is nothing neither to divide nor compound, nor any generation to be conceived"; *De Corp.* I.7, p. 13. On Hobbes's problems in continuing to accept scriptural authority in the face of this skepticism concerning knowledge of God, see Ronald Hepburn, "Hobbes on the Knowledge of God," in Cranston and Peters, eds., *Hobbes and Rousseau,* pp. 85-108. Yves Charles Zarka points to one philosophical function of the deity; as the first cause of everything, God provides the unity of all causal chains and thus makes possible the concatenation of causes that, as will be seen, constitute the Hobbesian "complete cause"; Zarka, "First Philosophy and the Foundation of Knowledge," in Tom Sorell, ed., *The Cambridge Companion to Hobbes* (Cambridge: Cambridge University Press, 1996), p. 78f: "if there were no first cause, there would be an infinite regress of causes, and therefore no possibility of making sense of a given effect."

5. Ibid. Also see *De Corp.* VII.2, p. 45.

6. Hobbes's argument is that even if we imagine the external world to be annihilated, these things will remain; hence they must be in us, not in the world; *De Corp.* VII.1, p. 44.

7. As Hobbes also puts it in the *Short Tract on First Principles,* "Accident is that which hath being in another so as, without that other, it could not be. As Colour cannot be, but in somewhat coloured"; quoted by Jan Prins, "Hobbes on Light and Vision," in Sorell, ed., *The Cambridge Companion to Hobbes,* p. 149 n. 5. (I should note that Richard Tuck has cast doubt on the authorship of this work; Tuck, "Hobbes and Descartes," in G. A. J Roger and Alan Ryan, eds., *Perspective on Thomas*

Hobbes [Oxford: Clarendon Press, 1988], p. 17f.) M. M. Goldsmith attempts to harmonize the two definitions of "accident" by saying that each describes a causal relation between a body and a percipient; Goldsmith, *Hobbes' Science of Politics* (New York: Columbia University Press, 1966), p. 21. But this attempt is inadequate, because they clearly refer to different aspects of the relation, the first to the relation itself, the second to its external cause.

8. Zarka suggests that Hobbes *may* be invoking the standard distinction between primary and secondary qualities here—the former residing in bodies, the latter in us; Zarka, "First Philosophy and the Foundation of Knowledge," p. 66. But the list quoted includes what *De Corp.* VIII.3, p. 55, comes fairly close to suggesting are primary qualities:

> And as for the opinion that some may have, that all other accidents are not in their bodies in the same manner that extension, motion, rest, or figure are in the same; for example, that colour, heat, odour, virtue, vice, and the like, are otherwise in them, and, as they say, *inherent;* I desire that they would suspend their judgment for the present, and expect a little, till it be found out by ratiocination, Whether these very accidents are not also certain motions either of the mind of the perceiver, or of the bodies themselves which are perceived; for the search of this, a great part of natural philosophy consists.

This, I take it, is a clear statement that the ontological status of attributes is, in itself, unclear.

9. Sorell states that all qualities which reason holds are necessary for the production of phantasms are for Hobbes objective; Sorell, *Hobbes*, p. 79. But there are difficulties with this, because reason teaches us that in order to produce effects, objects must be (spatially) outside us and must (temporally) precede their effects, making them subject to the phantasms of space and time. In Sorell's words, "Hobbes' distinction between phantasms in the sentient and accidents of bodies, is no less unstable than his distinction between matter that is animate and matter that is not"; p. 75.

10. As Tuck puts it, "Hobbes was untroubled [by Cartesian doubt] because . . . he stuck in a clear-headed fashion to the argument that whatever we experience, whether in sleep or waking, or at the hands of a malicious demon, has been caused by some material object or objects impinging upon us"; Tuck, "Hobbes and Descartes," p. 39f.

11. Exceptions to this notion are the accidents of extension and figure, which are common to all bodies and without which no body can be; ibid.

12. Hobbes, *De Corp.* VIII 23, p. 67. Hobbes also refers to form as merely "the aggregate of all accidents together, for which we give the body a new name"; Hobbes, "An Answer to Bishop Bramhall," *The English Works of Thomas Hobbes*, vol. 4, ed. William Molesworth (London: John Bohn, 1840), p. 309.

13. Hobbes, *De Corp.* I.9, p. 14. These two types of body are very different, for if the one is merely matter, the other is, as will be seen, ousiodic. Zarka notes the difference, but not in these terms; Zarka, "First Philosophy and the Foundation of Knowledge," p. 76. Also see Sorell, *Hobbes*, p. 14f.

14. Hobbes, *De Corp.* X.7, p. 80. If, for Aristotle, the formal cause was that in a thing which could be known, for Hobbes this cognitive role of the form also

reduces to efficient causality; for cognition, as we will see, is a type of efficient causality.

15. Hobbes, *De Corp.* IX.4, p. 71. For Hobbes's conception of natural power, see S. I. Benn, "Hobbesian Power," in Cranston and Peters, eds., *Hobbes and Rousseau*, pp. 184–212, esp. pp. 184–195.

16. As Hobbes puts it, our knowledge is always conditional, not "P" or "Q" but "If P, then Q"; *Lev.*, p. 30.

17. *De Corp.* I.3., p. 8. That does not mean, for either Foucault or Hobbes, that knowledge is *reduced* to power. As Foucault put it, "Those who say that for me knowledge is the mask of power don't seem to have the capacity to understand. There's hardly any point in responding to them"; Michel Foucault, "Le souci de la verité" (interview with François Ewald), *Dits et écrits*, vol. 4, ed. Daniel Defert and François Ewald, (Paris: Gallimard), p. 676 (English translation in Foucault, *Interviews*, ed. Sylvere Lotringer, trans. John Johnson [New York: Semiotext(e), 1989] p. 304f).

18. Hobbes, *De Corp.* III.7, *Computatio Sive Logica*, ed. ashot trans. Aloysius Martinich et al. (New York: Abaris Books, 1981), p. 233.

19. Hobbes, *De Corp.* II.7, V.1, *Computatio Sive Logica*, pp. 233, 271.

20. Hobbes, *De Corp.* II.6, *Computatio Sive Logica*, p. 201; cf. *Lev.*, p. 16.

21. *Lev.*, p. 28. Martine Pecherman relates this statement to Hobbes's general account of complete causality; Pecherman, "Philosophie première et théorie de l'action," in Charles Zarka and Jean Bernhardt, eds., *Thomas Hobbes: Philosophie première, théorie de la science, et politique* (Paris, 1990), pp. 47–66, esp. pp. 47–59.

22. That makes Hobbes, in a sense, a forerunner of Hume in the view that "reason is, and ought to be, the slave of the passions," which I discuss in the next chapter. See Jean Hampton, *Hobbes and the Social Contract Tradition* (Cambridge: Cambridge University Press, 1986), pp. 35–42.

23. *Lev.*, pp. 29, 41, 47. This desire for power includes, then, that for self-preservation, on which cf. Hampton, *Hobbes and the Social Contract Tradition*, p. 14f. Bernard Gert, "Hobbes' Account of Reason and the Passions," in Bertman and Malherbe, eds., *Thomas Hobbes*, pp. 82–92, actually sees reason as a type of passion: "Reason differs from the passions in that, since it is concerned with the life-long, long-term attainment of its goals, it considers not merely immediate consequences but also the long-term consequences of an action. The passions consider only the immediate consequences," p. 85. In Gert's view, then, the passions are—as the philosophical tradition in general maintains—"subservient" to reason (p. 84f). But reason is itself a passion, one stable enough to last an entire life—much as the desire for power (and self-preservation).

24. Indeed, as M. M. Goldsmith points out, it is empty: "power" for Hobbes is a generic term covering anything that could be used as a means to an end; Goldsmith, *Hobbes's Science of Politics*, p. 66f. As noted, power for Hobbes is, after all, a collection of accidents. But it is not the object of the desire for power that is the unified active form I am locating here but the desire itself, which is the "form" of the mind for Hobbes. Cf. Hampton (who, as noted, argues in terms of self-preservation), *Hobbes and the Social Contract Tradition*, pp. 17–19.

25. Even liberty is defined, implicitly, in terms of power. It is not the ability to exist as an ousia or as one's own final cause but simply unopposed power, exercised according to judgment and reason:

By LIBERTY is understood, according to the proper signification of the word, the absence of externall Impediments: which Impediments, may oft take away part of a man's power to do what hee would; but cannot hinder him from using the power left him, according as his judgment and reason shall dictate to him. (*Lev.*, p. 64)

26. See the helpful comments on this by Tuck in his introduction to Hobbes, *Leviathan*, p. xix.

27. In crucial contrast to Locke, for Hobbes there is no right to private property.

28. Curtis Johnson, "The Hobbesian Conception of Sovereignty and Aristotle's Politics," *Journal of the History of Ideas* 46 (1985), pp. 327-347.

29. D. Baumgold, *Hobbes's Political Theory* (Cambridge: Cambridge University Press, 1988), p. 133f. For some examples of early reactions, see Hampton, *Hobbes and the Social Contract Tradition*, pp. 189f, 192f.

30. An excellent recent example of such critical reconstruction is Hampton, *Hobbes and the Social Contract Tradition*, pp. 97-207.

31. Cf. the appeal to historical circumstances—one of many which could be cited—in Quentin Skinner, "The Context of Hobbes's Theory of Political Obligation," in Cranston and Peters, *Hobbes and Rousseau*, pp. 109-142.

32. David Gauthier, *The Logic of Leviathan* (Oxford: Clarendon Press, 1969), p. vi.

33. Cf. Goldsmith, *Hobbes' Science of Politics*, p. 177: "It might even be argued that *Leviathan* describes the political organization necessary for peace among fallen men." Also cf. F. C. Hood, *The Divine Politics of Thomas Hobbes* (Oxford: Oxford University Press, 1964), pp. 57-67.

34. J. W. N. Watkins has made this argument: because all human bodies are the same and mind is only an accident or type of body, all human minds must work alike; and since the body aims at the increase of "vital motion" in the heart, all humans are egocentric, naturally programmed to increase this motion (and hence to preserve themselves and seek power); Watkins, *Hobbes's System of Ideas* (Oxford: Clarendon Press, 1965), pp. 129-133.

35. Howard Warrender has traced the excesses of Hobbes's absolutism with regard to the question of whether the sovereign is accountable to his subjects; in place after place, Hobbes's argument turns out be stronger than necessary. Warrender does not discuss reasons for the excess. Warrender, *The Political Philosophy of Hobbes*, pp. 129-133.

36. Tom Sorell puts it as follows: if Hobbes is right, "perhaps [people's] nature is so unfortunate that their being left free to kill themselves off in the state of nature would be, from a sufficiently detached point of view, no bad thing. . . . So unattractive do they turn out to be that it is a question why their survival should seem desirable from any point of view but their own, pre-scientific one"; Sorell, *Hobbes*, p. 125f.

37. John Locke, *Second Treatise of Government, Two Treatises of Government*, ed. Peter Laslett (Cambridge: Cambridge University Press, 1960), para. 93.

38. For an excellent example of such rescuing, see Hampton, *Hobbes and the Social Contract Tradition*, pp. 208-255. A recent "liberal" reading of Hobbes is presented by Tuck in his introduction to Hobbes, *Leviathan;* also cf. Tuck, *Hobbes* (Oxford: Oxford University Press, 1989), pp. 69-76. An attempt to keep only the "good" insights of Hobbes can be found in Gregory Kavka, *Hobbesian Moral and Political*

Philosophy (Princeton, N.J.: Princeton University Press, 1986). All three contain references to the wider literature. An apex of such ingenuity is Howard Warrender's conclusion that "what emerges most strongly from [Hobbes's] account is the appalling weakness of the sovereign"; Warrender, *The Political Philosophy of Hobbes*, p. 317. For a critical response to Warrender, see Brian Barry, "Warrender and His Critics," in Cranston and Peters, eds., *Hobbes and Rousseau*, pp. 36–65.

39. Hobbes, *Lev.*, p. 86f; also see *Lev.*, chap. 13.

40. Cf. on this C. B. Macpherson, *The Political Theory of Possessive Individualism* (Oxford: Clarendon Press, 1962), p. 42.

7. OUSIA AND PROPERTY RIGHTS IN LOCKE

1. John Locke, *An Essay concerning Human Understanding*, ed. Alexander Campbell Fraser (New York: Dover, 1959), Epistle to the Reader, vol. 1, p. 14; III.vi.10. (Except for the Epistle, citations to the *Essay* are to part, chapter, and section.) For the identification of the "rubbish," see Edwin McCann, "Locke's Philosophy of Body," in Vere Chappell, ed., *The Cambridge Companion to Locke* (Cambridge: Cambridge University Press, 1994), p. 59.

2. There is, as will be shown, much more to Locke's views on substance than mere existence independent of us. The importance of such independence for Locke's view of substance emerges very clearly, however, from Martha Brandt Bolton's contrast of his views on substances with his views on mixed modes; Bolton, "Substances, Substrata, and Names of Substances in Locke's *Essay*," *Philosophical Review* 85 (1976), pp. 488–513. The externality of substances to us is given them, of course, by their substrata.

3. On the *Essay* and Boyle, cf. McCann, "Locke's Philosophy of Body," in Chappell, ed., *The Cambridge Companion to Locke*, p. 57f. For Locke's corpuscularianism, see the groundbreaking article by Maurice Mandelbaum, "Locke's Realism," in Mandelbaum, *Philosophy, Science, and Sense Perception* (Baltimore: Johns Hopkins University Press, 1964), pp. 1–60. For an extended account, see Peter Alexander, *Ideas, Qualities, and Corpuscles: Locke and Boyle on the External World* (Cambridge: Cambridge University Press, 1985).

4. Not that Locke carries this insight through consistently. As Mandelbaum notes,

> Throughout his discussion of the substrate [Locke] fails to take into account his own distinction between ideas as they exist in the mind and the qualities and powers which are to be attributed to objects. . . . Associated with his failure in this respect there is also a confusion between our belief in the substratum as being that which explains why certain sets of ideas go together and a belief in the substratum as that in which *qualities* inhere. (Mandelbaum, "Locke's Realism," p. 34f)

Also cf. John Yolton, "Locke on Knowledge of Body," *Jowett Papers 1968–69*, ed. B. Y. Khabhai, R. S. Kats, and R. A. Pineau (Oxford: Basil Blackwell, 1971), p. 82f. As Yolton points out, Locke is clearly aware of the ambiguity, and it does not do the kind of work for Locke that it does in Hobbes: Locke does not simply assume that we know that substances exist, in discrete material packets, outside us. For a critical account of Mandelbaum's important article, see Margaret Atherton, "Knowledge of Substance and Knowledge of Essence in Locke's Essay," *History of Philosophy Quarterly* 1 (1984), pp. 413–428. Atherton overstates her claim that "for Mandelbaum's reading to stand . . . there must be reason to believe that Locke regards our ignorance of substances as a temporary matter, or at least something that is in principle curable" (p. 416). If and when our ignorance is cured, for Locke, our knowledge will not be of "substance" but of what he calls "the minute particles of bodies and the real constitution on which their sensible qualities depend" (*Essay* II. xxiii.11).

5. Which he calls an idea of "real essence"; see M. R. Ayers, "The Ideas of Power and Substance in Locke's Philosophy," *Philosophical Quarterly* 25 (1975), pp. 1–27.

6. George Berkeley, *Philosophical Commentaries*, or *Commonplace Book, Berkeley's Philosophical Writings*, ed. David M. Armstrong (New York: Collier, 1965), p. 359. Though Berkeley (and other commentators) do not mention it, all the raillery at *Essay* II.xiii.18–20 is directed against substance in general. On the idea of substance in general versus ideas of particular substances, see Alexander, *Ideas, Qualities, and Corpuscles*, p. 224, and Mandelbaum, "Locke's Realism," p. 31. Francis Pelletier points out that the ideas of particular substances presuppose the idea of substance in general, of which they are considered to be precipitates; Pelletier, "Locke's Doctrine of Substance," in Charles E. Jarrett, John King-Farlow, and Francis J. Pelletier, eds., *New Essays on Rationalism and Empiricism* (*Canadian Journal of Philosophy Supplementary*, vol. 4) (Guelph: Canadian Association for Publishing in Philosophy, 1978), p. 132. The idea of such precipitation of the particular out of the general is also, as will be seen, carried through in Locke's account of property.

7. The featurelessness, then, applies to substance in general; individual substances are really concatenations of atoms. I am not assigning to Locke a doctrine of "bare particulars."

8. For a discussion of Locke's distinction between powers insofar as they are accessible to observation—such as the power of fire to burn—and the powers actually residing in things, which are unknown to us, see Alexander, *Ideas, Qualities, and Corpuscles*, p. 166.

9. Locke, *Essay* IV.5.2, Epistle to the Reader, p. 22ff.

10. As Mandelbaum notes, the indeterminate substrate of a thing stands for "something in the object which makes that object a self-subsisting thing, that is a thing which (in Cartesian language) needs nothing else in order to exist"; Mandelbaum, "Locke's Realism," p. 39. What does this job for a finite thing for Descartes, as I argued in chapter 5, is nothing in the thing but God's conserving creation of it.

11. Locke, *Essay* II. 23.1f. See also the Editor's Note, *Essay* II.23.1 (p. 390 n. 3).

12. See, e.g., George Berkeley, *The Principles of Human Knowledge* in Armstrong, ed., *Berkeley's Philosophical Writings*, pp. 74–96. The qualities we actually sense cannot for Berkeley be shown to be caused by external substances, or at least by a plurality of unintelligent ones; they are all caused directly by God, who is thus once again—as he was for Descartes—the only power; see Berkeley, *The Principles of Human Knowledge* p. 71f.

13. Though Locke agrees that it is probably "annexed to, and the affection of, one individual immaterial substance"; *Essay* II.xxvii.25.

14. William P. Alston and Jonathan Bennett have argued that substance, in the account of personal identity, does not mean substrate but just basic ontological item—a use which they admit is not found in Locke outside this discussion. Their

argument is that Locke does not appeal to the unknowability (or emptiness) of the substrate in arguing against it but to the fact that animals, as we saw, have for Locke unstable substrates in that matter flows through them; Alston and Bennett, "Locke on People and Substances," *Philosophical Review* 97 (1988), pp. 25-46. Whether Locke appeals to substance as substrate in the argument is not my issue here; my point is that knowability is the *motivation* for Locke's claim. That is because personal identity is the ground of moral responsibility, and we cannot be held responsible for acts we do not know we performed:

> in the Great Day, wherein the secrets of all hearts shall be laid open, it may be reasonable to think, no one shall be made to answer for what he knows nothing of; but shall receive his doom, his conscience accusing or excusing him. (*Essay* II.xxvii.22; II.xxvii18-22 is relevant here)

15. Locke, *Essay* II.27.19; cf. in general Henry E. Allison, "Locke on Personal Identity," *Journal of the History of Ideas* 27 (1966), pp. 41-58.

16. Which I take to be the general point of Vere Chappell's account in "Locke on the Ontology of Matter, Living Things, and Substances," *Philosophical Studies* 60 (1990) pp. 24-27.

17. Harold Noonan, "Locke on Personal Identity," *Philosophy* 53 (1978), p. 344. Noonan helpfully distinguishes the notions of "self," "person," and "immaterial substance" which run through Locke's account of personal identity.

18. An idea is defined as "whatsoever is the Object of the Understanding when a Man thinks" (*Essay* I.i.8); as R. S. Woolhouse points out, "thinking" for Locke includes sensing, perceiving, remembering, and imagining; Woolhouse, "Locke's Theory of Knowledge,"in Chappell, ed., *The Cambridge Companion to Locke*, p. 152. Douglas Lewis argues that Locke did not believe that we are aware *only* of ideas; we also have what he calls "knowledge" of things outside us; Lewis, "The Existence of Substances and Locke's Way of Ideas," *Theoria* 35 (1969), pp. 124-146. There is a distinction, however, which needs to be drawn here. As Chappell puts it, Locke characterizes ideas as the "immediate" objects of our thought, through which things outside us can be said to be known; Chappell, "Locke's Theory of Ideas," in Chappell, ed., *The Cambridge Companion to Locke*, p. 29f. John Yolton puts it differently: we "apprehend" ideas in order to "know" objects; Yolton, "Locke on Knowledge of Body," pp. 81, 92. In any case, my point is that simple ideas are, as Locke puts it, the "limits" of our thought. As I would put it, they are the cognitive *boundaries* of our mind.

19. *Essay* II.xxii.5; in the bracketed phrase, "thoughts" occurred in the first edition of the *Essay*, "actions" in the second, an index of Locke's confusion in accounting for this transgression of the mind's boundary.

20. See *Essay* I.xxi.74 and the editor's note to chap. 21, vol. 1, pp. 375-380. Sterling Peter Lamprecht traces Locke's evolution from considering the "spring of action" as pleasure to his later view of it as "unease"; Lamprecht, *The Moral and Political Philosophy of John Locke* (New York: Russell & Russell, 1962), pp. 112-115.

21. Locke summarizes Filmer's views on power in Locke, "First Treatise on Government," *Two Treatises of Government*, ed. Peter Laslett (Cambridge: Cambridge University Press, 1960), ¶ 9. Further references are to paragraph number or chapter number of this edition.

22. Cf. C. B. Macpherson, *The Political Theory of Possessive Individualism* (Oxford: Clarendon Press, 1962), pp. 248-251. Note that Macpherson's point and the quote

from *T* on which it rests do not rest upon MacPherson's argument that Locke denies full rationality to those who do not own property (for which see pp. 232–238). There have been many critical reactions to this argument. Alan Ryan, in particular, has argued that Locke allows rationality to all men and thus the possibility of participation in political life; Ryan, "Locke and the Dictatorship of the Bourgeoisie," *Political Studies* 134 (1965), p, 223. Ryan allows that Macpherson is correct about the economic justice: "Since all men have profited by entering a market economy, there is no case for complaint if some men have done better than others." Macpherson is thus wrong to hold that political oppression is "piled on top" of economic inequality; Ryan, "Locke and the Dictatorship of the Bourgeoisie," p. 228. Isaiah Berlin also holds that Macpherson's differential rationality argument fails, and his argument comes to a conclusion similar to Ryan's:

> Having established by clear and cogent argument Locke's claims to be regarded as the spokesman of unlimited capitalist appropriation, Professor Macpherson falls once again into exaggeration [when he] represents Locke as loading the political scales against the poor. (Berlin, "Hobbes, Locke, and Professor Macpherson," *Political Quarterly* 135 [1964], p. 461)

Joshua Cohen also points out that Macpherson here runs together property and political authority, which as he notes contradicts "one of the two main lines of criticism of Filmer in the First Treatise" (cf. *T1* ¶¶ 41f); but Cohen concludes that the property owner's state is "consistent with Locke's philosophy"; Cohen, "Structure, Choice, and Legitimacy: Locke's Theory of the State," *Philosophy and Public Affairs* 15 (1986), pp. 308f, 323. But Macpherson's point at p. 249f does not rest on the rationality argument but on Locke's wording at *T* 120, where "every Man, when he incorporates himself into an Commonwealth," is said to bring with him his land. This is not a philosophical argument, as Berlin, Cohen, and Ryan point out; but it is not a *mere* slip, either—it is repeated three times at *T* 120–121. In general, Macpherson traces Locke's political theory back to what he calls "possessive individualism," in which "the individual was seen neither as a moral whole, nor as part of a larger social whole, but as an owner of himself" (*The Political Theory of Possessive Individualism*, p. 12). If I am right this view of human beings has philosophical roots which Macpherson does not trace. It is perhaps because he does not see them that he attempts to intrude possessive individualism deeper into Locke's political theory than it belongs.

23. Cf. Locke, "Second Treatise of Government," *T2* ¶¶ 132, 149–150.

24. Locke writes approvingly of electing members for fixed terms, before and after which they would be common citizens; *T2* ¶ 143; also ¶¶ 138, 154)

25. *T2* ¶¶ 96, 99; cf. Dunn, *The Political Thought of John Locke*, p. 128f.

26. Descartes, *Principles of Philosophy*, II.25; see my discussion in chap. 5.

27. *T2* ¶ 132. Dunn's suggestion here is telling: "it simply never occurred to [Locke] that anyone could have reason to espouse such a peculiar theory"; Dunn, *The Political Thought of John Locke*, p. 129. Peculiar, perhaps, because insufficiently ousiodic to seem workable.

28. See the classification at Locke, *T2* ¶ 213.

29. Peter Laslett, Introduction, Locke, *Two Treatises of Government*, p. 116.

30. Locke does not believe that "the Example of what hath been done [should] be the Rule of what ought to be" (*T1* §17).

31. Such formulation is attempted for Locke by Macpherson; see my note 34.

32. Locke, "Second Treatise of Government."

33. *T2* ¶ 80f. In "Atlantis," Locke had even allowed for porosity in the form of "marriages of the left hand," contractual concubinage between a woman and a man who was already married. The case as regards a woman who was already married is left unclear; Locke, *Two Treatises*, p. 321 n. *ad T2* ¶ 82.

34. Cf. Locke, "Second Treatise of Government," *T2* ¶ 35.

35. *T2* ¶ 32. On the general nature of the appropriation of nature by labor and by enclosure, cf. Karl Olivecrona, "Appropriation in the State of Nature: Locke on the Origin of Property," *Journal of the History of Ideas* 35 (1974), pp. 211–230.

36. That is Locke's main argument. He also argues that God wills private property; see Joan A, Simmons, *The Lockean Theory of Rights* (Princeton, N.J.: Princeton University Press, 1992), p. 236ff, for a critical discussion of this argument.

37. Though Locke does not use the term "materials" in the quote just given, he does at *T2* ¶¶ 35, 42, 43. Marx writes that "the bodies of commodities . . . are combinations of two elements—matter and labor. If we take away the labor expended upon them, a material substratum is always left, which is furnished by Nature without the help of man. The latter can work only as Nature does, that is, by changing the form of matter"; Karl Marx, *Capital*, trans. Samuel Morse and Edward Aveling (New York: Modern Library, 1906), p. 50; also see pp. 197–201.

38. *T2* ¶ 46. Willmore Kendall, "John Locke and the Doctrine of Majority Rule," *Illinois Studies in the Social Sciences* 26 (1941), p. 72; cf. James Tully, *A Discourse on Property* (Cambridge: Cambridge University Press, 1980), p. 121f. As Simmons notes, Locke does not discuss limits in use beyond this imperative to exercise disposition, which is the only kind he really understands; the rights of the civil order are given very subordinate and obscure status by Locke; Simmons, *The Lockean Theory of Rights*, pp. 278, 288f; pp. 278–298 are relevant here.

39. *T2* ¶ 32.

40. This view changes, of course, with the invention of money. Not being subject to spoilage, something like gold has no natural limit on its possession. With the introduction of money, then, men have "by a tacit and voluntary consent found out a way, how a man may fairly possess more land than he himself can use the product of, receiving in exchange for the overplus, Gold and Silver, which may be hoarded up without injury to anyone, these metals not spoiling or decaying in the hands of the possessor"; *T2* ¶ 51; cf. Macpherson, *The Political Theory of Possessive Individualism*, pp. 211–214.

41. Ryan suggests that given Locke's (relatively) enlightened views on the family, a man might be expected to use his property to benefit his wife and children, but he gives no reference to Locke's writings for this; Ryan, "Locke and the Dictatorship of the Bourgeoisie," p. 225.

8. THE TRIUMPH OF THE INDIVIDUAL IN HUME

1. David Hume, *A Treatise of Human Nature*, ed. L. A. Selby-Bigge (Oxford: Clarendon Press, 1896), p. 226.

2. A critique which I will not discuss here; see my *Company of Words* (Evanston, Ill.: Northwestern University Press, 1993), p. 288f, for a brief treatment.

3. For the *Treatise*'s account of these, see *Tr*, pp. 10-13.

4. For an excellent summary of Hume's critique of substance, see Daniel E. Flage, *David Hume's Theory of Mind* (New York: Routledge, 1990), pp. 61-82. Cf. Norman Kemp Smith, *The Philosophy of David Hume* (New York: St. Martin's Press, 1966), pp. 497-505.

5. Cf. *Tr*, p. 15f. H. H. Price notes that for Hume there is nothing permanent in our sense perceptions, and hence no enduring "substrate"; Price, *Hume's Theory of the External World* (Oxford: Clarendon Press, 1940), p. 46.

6. *Tr*, p. 221. Cf. on this Price, *Hume's Theory of the External World*, p. 47.

7. Like Locke, Hume is not consistent in his discussion of the status of the qualities we perceive. Sometimes he uses "object" to mean the immediate objects of mental attention, i.e., ideas, and at other times he uses the term to refer to genuinely external objects. See Galen Strawson, *The Secret Connection: Causation, Realism, and David Hume* (Oxford: Clarendon Press, 1989), pp. 47, 65f. But like Locke and unlike Hobbes, Hume gives an account that does not *depend* on this inconsistency for anything.

8. *Tr*, p. 506. For causality and the association of ideas, see, for example, *Tr*, pp. 73-78.

9. For Hume's critique of social contract theories in general, see David Miller, *Philosophy and Ideology in Hume's Political Thought* (Oxford: Clarendon Press, 1981), pp. 78-80.

10. *Tr*, p. 487. In the remarkable withdrawn essay "Of Love and Marriage," Hume goes so far as wish that "everything [between husband and wife] was carried on with perfect equality, as between two equal members of the same body"; Hume, "Of Love and Marriage," *Essays*, ed. Eugene F. Miller (Indianapolis: Liberty Fund, 1985), p. 560. The wish is not carried through into argument or deliberation; Hume seems to think women are the cause of the inequalities of marriage. Cf. Annette Baier, "Good Men's Women: Hume on Chastity and Trust," *Hume Studies* 5 (1979), pp. 1-19.

11. *Tr*, p. 261. The force of this analogy is discussed at length in John Biro, "Hume on Self-Identity and Memory," *Review of Metaphysics* 30 (1976), pp. 19-38.

12. David Hume, *The History of England from the Invasion of Julius Caesar to the Abdication of James the Second*, vol. 5 (Philadelphia: Porter & Coates, 1854), p. 56.

13. As Annette Baier points out, Hume's political philosophy discusses only allegiance to the magistrates, omitting that of servant to master, of wife to husband, and of child to parent; Baier, *A Progress of Sentiments* (Cambridge, Mass.: Harvard University Press, 1991).

14. Hume pursues this grounding at length in *Treatise*, pp. 556-563.

15. As Hume writes in the appendix to the *Treatise*, "upon a more strict review of the section concerning *personal identity*, I find myself involv'd in such a labyrinth, that, I must confess, I neither know how to correct my former opinions, nor how to render them consistent"; *Tr*, p. 633. For an introductory account, see John Biro, "Hume's New Science of the Mind," in David Fate Norton, ed., *The Cambridge Companion to Hume* (Cambridge: Cambridge University Press, 1993), pp. 33-56, esp. pp. 47-56. A discussion of previous literature can be found in Biro, "Hume on Self-Identity and Memory."

16. Hume's "argument" for this general proposition is so brief as to suggest he thought it was simply obvious:

Unless nature had given some original qualities to the mind, it cou'd never have any secondary ones; for in that case it wou'd have no foundation for action, nor wou'd ever begin to exert itself. (*Tr*, p. 280)

17. Alasdair MacIntyre comes at this from a different angle:

Hume clearly affirms that the justification of the rules of justice lies in the fact that their observance is in everyone's long-term interest; that we ought to obey the rules because there is no one who does not gain more than he loses by such obedience. But this is to derive an "ought" from an "is." (MacIntyre, "Hume on 'Is' and 'Ought,'" *Philosophical Review* 68 [1959], p. 456f)

My discussion here adds to this view that the reason such behavior is in everyone's long-term interest is that observing the rules of justice is, at bottom, observing the principles of the association of ideas; and this is in our long-term interest because it accords with the basic nature of our minds. For the undeducibility of ought from is, see *Tr*, p. 469f.

18. John Bricke, "Hume's Conception of Character," *Southwestern Journal of Philosophy* 5 (1974), p. 112. Jane L. McIntyre, less anachronistically, considers the properties which constitute character in terms of Hume's account of human powers; McIntyre, "Character: A Humean Account," *History of Philosophy Quarterly* 7 (1990), pp. 193–206.

19. *Tr*, p. 415. For the equation of character with passion, see McIntyre, "Character: A Humean Account," p. 200f.

20. Cf. Rachel Kydd: "Hume seems to have thought that the passion which prompts us to reason is always a passion for some particular end or happiness"; Kydd, *Reason and Conduct in Hume's Treatise* (Oxford: Clarendon Press, 1946), p. 156f. Kydd draws an instructive contrast with Spinoza's view of the human will as pursuing its own proper "universal" good.

21. On the status of sympathy, see *Tr*, pp. 320, 353, 500, 576, 618f, and McIntyre, "Character: A Humean Account," pp. 202–205.

22. *Tr*, pp. 317, 555–557. On this tendency in the passions in general, cf. *Tr*, p. 344f, Jane L. McIntyre, "Personal Identity and the Passions," *Journal of the History of Philosophy* 27 (1989), pp. 545–557; and Kemp Smith, *The Philosophy of David Hume*, pp. 150–152, 170–174. Kemp Smith observes that "Hume's exposition [here] does not [show] its usual lucidity," p. 171. That may be why Hume abandons this explanation of sympathy in the *Enquiry concerning the Principles of Morals*, in Hume, *Enquiries*, ed. L. A. Selby-Bigge (Oxford: Clarendon Press, 1894), p. 219 n.:

It is needless to push our researches so far as to ask, why we have humanity or a fellow-feeling with others. It is sufficient, that this is observed to be a principle of human nature. We must stop somewhere in our examination of causes.

23. See esp. Martin Heidegger, "Die Zeit des Weltbildes," *Holzwege*, 4th ed. (Frankfurt: Klostermann, 1963), pp. 69–104. Heidegger explicitly connects the modern subject with the ancient *hypokeimenon:*

the essence of man as such is transformed, in that man becomes subject. We must, to be sure, understand this word "subjectum" as the translation of the Greek *hypokeimenon*. . . . When man becomes the first and authentic subject, that then means: man becomes that being, upon which every being in the mode of its Being and its truth is grounded. (P. 81)

The questions I would like to pose are: Why does this development, presented by Heidegger as cognitive and scientific, go together with such distinctively modern enterprises as colonialism and slavery? And why does Heidegger not even mention either of these? My argument in this book is that attention to ousia can answer both questions.

24. Jürgen Habermas, "Modernity: An Incomplete Project?" in H. Foster, ed., *Postmodern Culture* (London: Pluto), pp. 3-15.

25. David Hume *Enquiry concerning Human Understanding, Enquiries*, ed. L. A. Selby-Bigge (Oxford: Clarendon Press, 1894), p. 193.

26. See my *Company of Words*, pp. 33-118.

27. Cf. the general introduction to my *Poetic Interaction* (Chicago: University of (Chicago Press, 1989).

9. CRITICAL ACCOUNTS OF OPPRESSION IN MUDIMBE, DOUGLASS, AND BEAUVOIR

1. Some of them are materialists in the more conventional sense that they think there is nothing more to reality as a whole than matter in motion, but that is not my concern here.

2. For an extended critique of this way of viewing the body, see David Michael Levin, *The Body's Recollection of Being* (London: Routledge & Kegan Paul, 1985), esp. p. 121f.

3. The bulls in question are *Dum Diversas* (1452) and *Romanus Pontifex* (1455); see V. Y. Mudimbe, *The Invention of Africa* (Bloomington: Indiana University Press, 1988), p. 45.

4. Mudimbe, *The Invention of Africa*, p. 2.

5. Quoted in Mudimbe, *The Invention of Africa*, p. 47.

6. Northrop Frye, "Journey without Arrival," videotape, Canadian Broadcasting Corporation, Toronto, 1976; National Film Board of Canada no. 106 C 0176 140.

7. Mudimbe, *The Invention of Africa*, p. 48.

8. Mudimbe, *The Invention of Africa*, p. 1.

9. But as realizations of ousia the parties to the Cold War were deeply complicitous, as Hegel recognized before the fact; see my *Company of Words* (Evanston, Ill.: Northwestern University Press, 1993), pp. 15-18.

10. Frederick Douglass, *Life and Times of Frederick Douglass*, reprinted in Douglass, *Autobiographies*, ed. Henry Louis Gates Jr. (New York: Library of America, 1994), p. 486f (hereinafter: *LT*).

11. Simone de Beauvoir, *The Second Sex*, ed. and trans. H. M. Parshley (New York: Knopf, 1952), p. xxxvi (hereinafter: *SS*).

12. *SS*, p. xl n. 3. Beauvoir carries this through in her entire brilliant analysis of traditional marriage; *SS*, pp. 447-508.

13. *SS*, p. 148; Hegel, *Phenomenology of Spirit*, trans. A. V. Miller (Oxford: Clarendon Press, 1977), pp. 111-115.

14. Hegel, *Phenomenology of Spirit*, pp. 115-119. On Beauvoir's misreading of Hegel, see Tina Chanter, *Ethics of Eros* (New York: Routledge, 1995), pp. 60-79.

15. The basic problem in Beauvoir's view is that all awareness of the other is fundamentally hostile, a view attributed to Hegel at *SS*, p. xli; the solution, also clearly Hegelian, is given on p. 148: "It is possible to rise above this conflict if each individual freely recognizes the other, each regarding himself and the Other simultaneously as object and subject in a reciprocal manner." This recognition of the other as a free being is "obviously man's highest achievement, and through that achievement he is to be found in his true nature" (ibid.).

16. See my *Poetic Interaction* (Chicago: University of Chicago Press, 1989), p. 39f.

APPENDIX TO PART TWO

1. See Benedict Spinoza, Part I of "Appendix concerning Metaphysical Thoughts," *Parts I and II of Descartes' Principles of Philosophy*, in vol. 1, ed. *Opera*, ed. C. Gebhard (Heidelberg: Winter, 1925), p. 249; Spinoza, "Letter to Oldenburg of July 1663," *Opera*, vol. 4, p. 64. The pagination is given marginally in *The Collected Works of Spinoza*, ed. Edwin Curley (Princeton, N.J.: Princeton University Press, 1985).

2. Spinoza, *Opera*, vol. 2, p. 46. Where possible, subsequent references will be to part and proposition.

3. The order of ideas and of things being for Spinoza identical; *Ethics*, Part II Prop. 7.

4. See R. S. Woolhouse, *Descartes, Spinoza, Leibniz: The Concept of Substance in Seventeenth-Century Metaphysics* (London: Routledge, 1993), pp. 35f, 155.

5. Spinoza, *Tractatus politicus* in *Opera*, vol. 3, pp. 269-360 (English translation, *The Political Works*, ed. and trans. A. G. Wernham [Oxford: Clarendon Press, 1958]). Citations will be to chapter and paragraph; here, II.2f.

6. G. W. Leibniz, "Principes de la nature et de la grace, fondés en raison," *Die philosophischen Schriften*, vol. 6, ed. C. J. Gebhardt (Hildesheim: Georg Olms), p. 598 (English translation, Leibniz, "The Principles of Nature and of Grace, Based on Reason," *Philosophical Papers and Letters*, 2nd ed. ed. Leroy Loemker [Dordrecht: Reidel, 1969], p. 636 [hereinafter: Loemker].

7. Leibniz, "Monadologie," *Werke*, vol. 6, pp. 607-623 (English translation, "Monadology," Loemker, pp. 643-652). Citations will be to paragraphs, which are valid for both editions; here, ¶¶ 1, 2, 3, 7.

8. Leibniz, "Eclaircissement des difficultés que Monsieur Bayle a trouvés dans le système nouveau de l'union de l'âme et du corps," *Werke*, vol. 4, p. 522f (English translation, "Clarification of the Difficulties Which Mr. Bayles Has Found in the New System of the Union of Soul and Body," Loemker, p. 495f).

9. Jacques Jalabert, *Théorie leibnizienne de la substance* (Paris: Presses Universitaires de France 1974), p. 76f.

10. Which, since monads do not pass into and out of existence, means from the beginning of time.

11. Leibniz, *Théodicée, Werke*, vol. 6, ¶ 150; paragraph numbers are valid also for the English translation (Leibniz, *Theodicy*, trans. E. M. Huggard [London: Routledge & Kegan Paul, 1952]).

12. Leibniz, "Monadologie" ¶¶ 51-60; Leibniz, "Système nouveau de la nature et de la communication des substances," *Werke*, vol. 4, p. 484f (English translation, Leibniz, "A New System of Nature," Loemker, p. 457f).

13. Leibniz, "Animadversiones in partem generalem Principiorum Cartesianorum," *Werke*, vol. 4, p. 362f (English translation, Leibniz, "Critical Thoughts on the General Part of the Principles of Descartes," Loemker, p. 388f); "Discourse de métaphysique," *Werke*, vol. 4, p. 458 (English translation, Leibniz, "Discourse on Metaphysics," Loemker, p. 324).

14. Leibniz, "Specimen dynamicum," *Mathematische Schriften*, vol. 4, ed. C. I. Gerhart (Berlin and Halle, 1849–1854), p. 244 (English translation, Leibniz, "Specimen dynamicum," Loemker, p. 442); also Leibniz, "Monadologie" ¶¶ 85–90.

15. Leibniz, letter to Arnauld, November 28–December 8, 1686, *Werke*, vol. 2, p. 76 (English translation, *The Political Writings of Leibniz*, ed. and trans. Patrick Riley [Cambridge: Cambridge University Press, 1972], p. 26).

16. Leibniz, *Caesarinus Fürstenerius*, available to me only in the translation in *The Political Writings of Leibniz*, p.116.

10. HEIDEGGER'S PRESENTATIONS OF DIAKENA IN BEING AND TIME

1. Some of the dangers of reading Heidegger, particularly the later Heidegger, as if his work were ousiodically structured are illustrated by Winfred Franzen, who is constantly on the lookout for unified doctrines and clearly defined relations and is constantly disappointed. A few examples:

> Heideggers Bemühungern um die Bestimmung der ontologischen Differenz können kaum als erfolgreich bezeichnet werden. . . . Eine einheitliche Konzeption der Verhältnisses um Sein und Zeit läßt sich im späteren Denken Heideggers nun allerdings kaum ausmachen. . . . Es ist nicht verwunderlich, daß der Begriff des Denkens bei Heidegger inhaltlich relative unbestimmt bleibt. (Winfred Franzen, *Von der Existentialontologie zur Seinsgeschichte* [Meisenheim/Glan: Anton Hain, 1975], pp. 107, 115, 148 respectively)

If my own reading of Heidegger is correct, each of these "failures" is really a success.

2. See Otto Pöggeler, "Zeit und Sein bei Heidegger," in E. W. Orth, ed., *Zeit und Zeitlichkeit bei Husserl und Heidegger,* in *Zeitschrift für phänomenologische Forschung* 14 (1983), pp. 152–191, esp. p. 169.

3. For a more detailed account of this sort of challenge in Heidegger, an exemplary case of which is given in "The Origin of the Work of Art," see my *Poetic Interaction* (Chicago: University of Chicago Press, 1989), pp. 140, 158–161. The term "critique," of course, suggests a practice of holding some social reality up to a set of ideal standards and measuring it against them. Reality and norm must then both be present to the critical mind, and "critique" as generally understood is part and parcel of the dominance of presence. *Being and Time*'s "challenge" to ousia cannot play this metaphysical game, which would allow presence to dominate while arguing against it.

4. Martin Heidegger, *Sein und Zeit,* 11th ed. (Tübingen: Niemeyer, 1967), pp. 142f, 161 (hereinafter: *SZ*). Page numbers to this edition are given marginally in the English translation (Heidegger, *Being and Time,* trans. John MacQuarrie and Edward Robinson [New York: Harper & Row, 1962]).

5. Hence Walter Schulz can locate Heidegger's contributions in *Being and*

Time to the destabilization of the self's boundaries that began with Hegel. Schulz calls it the "desubstantializing" of the self; Schulz, "Über den philosophiegeschichtlichen Ort Martin Heideggers I," *Philosophische Rundschau* 1 (1953-1954), pp. 65-93, esp. p. 70f.

6. Heidegger, *Sein und Zeit,* pp. 42f, 221-223 (where inauthenticity is treated as "falling").

7. Hence it is unsurprising that the project of showing how the connection between inauthenticity and authenticity is "grounded" in mineness is never taken up in *Being and Time.*

8. Heidegger, *SZ,* pp. 272-274, 297f. Inauthentic hearing, of course, understands the call of conscience clearly and concretely—but wrongly, because not in terms of a call to one's ownmost potentiality.

9. Heidegger, *SZ,* p. 167; it is repeated there, again on p. 175, and three times on p. 176, as well as on p. 42. The point is reiterated yet again in Heidegger, "Brief über den Humanismus," *Wegmarken* (Frankfurt am Main: Klostermann, 1967), p. 163.

10. Another diakenon, which I have treated elsewhere and will not discuss in detail here, comes between authenticity, which is individualistic to the point of muteness, and "resoluteness," which is authenticity somehow shared among an entire people—a nasty little dream which led to Heidegger's National Socialistic hybris. See my *Poetic Interaction,* p. 125f.

11. Cf. Hubert L. Dreyfus, *Being in the World* (Cambridge, Mass.: MIT Press, 1991), p. vii: "Almost the only thing which has stayed constant over twenty years of revising has been my decision to limit [it] to Division I of Part One of *Being and Time.*"

12. On the hurried publication of *Being and Time,* see Heidegger, "Mein Weg in die Phänomenologie," *Zur Sache des Denkens* (Tübingen: Niemeyer, 1969), pp. 81-90 (English translation, "My Way to Phenomenology," *On Time and Being,* trans. Joan Stambaugh [New York: Harper & Row, 1972], pp. 74-82).

13. That diakenic ruptures can be "grounded" in other ruptures is uncongenial to much postmodern thought, which is suspicious of all grounds. I have argued elsewhere that elevating such suspicions into a methodological principle—seeing them all, for example, as equally immediate effects of "power" or "différance"—cuts such thinking off from the possibility of its own origin in the "master rupture" of our time, the Holocaust; see my "Possibilities of Postmodernity: Fackenheim and Foucault," in Alan Milchman and Alan Rosenberg, eds., *Postmodernism and the Holocaust* (Amsterdam: Rodopi, 1998), pp. 239-264.

14. As the conclusion to this book indicates, such discussion is absolutely necessary if we are to move beyond the contemporary impasses of ousia. I will undertake it in a future work, *The Capture of Time.*

15. Aristotle, *Physics* IV.12, 221b11; 13, 222b19ff; 10, 218a2f.

16. Martin Heidegger *The Question of Being,* trans. William Kluback and Jean T. Wilde (New Haven, Conn.: Yale University Press, 1958), p. 104; emphasis added.

17. Alfred Tarski, "The Concept of Truth in Formalized Languages," *Logic, Semantics, Metamathematics,* 2nd ed. rev. trans. J. H. Woodger; ed. John Corcoran (Indianapolis: Hackett, 1983), pp. 152-278.

18. Heidegger, *SZ,* ¶ 2. The paradigmatic status of the question is stated very clearly in the *Rektoratsrede,* which shows how, in spite of Heidegger's Nazi zeal, his

thought at certain levels remained resistant to the foul certainties of the Führer; Heidegger, *Die Selbstbehauptung der deutschen Universität* and *Das Rektorat: 1933/34* (Frankfurt: Klostermann, 1983).

19. See Graeme Nicholson, "Heidegger on Thinking," *Journal of the History of Philosophy* 13 (1975), pp. 491-503, for a discussion of these "dislocations" in the phenomenon.

20. John Sallis argues that discourse, as the primordial articulation of understanding and state-of-mind, unifies them without itself being a common root at which they meet. The unification is, rather, similar to how we see the "thing," in Heidegger's essay of that name, unify the Fourfold; Sallis, "Language and Reversal," *Southern Journal of Philosophy* 8 (1970), pp. 381-398.

21. Jacques Derrida, "Les fins de l'homme," *Marges de la philosophie* (Paris: Minuit, 1972), p. 130 (English translation in Derrida, *Margins of Philosophy*, trans. Alan Bass (Chicago: University of Chicago Press, 1982), p. 130.

22. Edmund Husserl, *Ideen zu einer reinen Phänomenologie*, 4th. ed. (Tübingen: Niemeyer 1980), p. 43f.

23. Dreyfus, *Being in the World*, p. 3f; Richard Rorty, "Wittgenstein, Heidegger, and the Reification of Language" *Essays on Heidegger and Others* (Cambridge: Cambridge University Press, 1991), pp. 50-65, esp. p. 60. For further examples, see Robert Brandom, "Heidegger's Categories in *Being and Time*," *Monist* 66 (1983); Charles Guignon, *Heidegger and the Theory of Knowledge* (Indianapolis: Hackett, 1983), chap. 1; Mark Okrent, *Heidegger's Pragmatism* (Ithaca, N.Y.: Cornell University Press, 1988); Charles Taylor, "Language and Human Nature," *Human Agency and Language* (Cambridge: Cambridge University Press, 1985), pp. 215-247, esp. pp. 239-244.

24. Ludwig Wittgenstein *Tractatus Logico-Philosophicus*, trans. D. F. Pears and B. F. McGuinness (London: Routledge & Kegan Paul, 1961), no. 5.62, p. 143.

25. *Sz*, p. 250; see also p. 258 for the indeterminacy of death.

26. See my *Poetic Interaction*, pp. 127-142.

27. Heidegger criticizes this view later, in his "Die Onto-theo-logische Verfassung der Metaphysik," *Identität und Differenz* (Pfullingen: Neske, 1957), pp. 31-67.

28. Martin Heidegger, "Vom Wesen und Begriff der *Physis* Aristotles' Physik B, 1," *Wegmarken* (Frankfurt: Klostermann, 1967), pp. 309-371.

29. Heidegger, "Vom Wesen und Begriff der *Physis* Aristotles' Physik B, 1," p. 360.

30. I am indebted for this point to Chris Leazier. Cf. William J. Richardson, *Heidegger through Phenomenology to Thought* (The Hague: Martinus Nijhoff, 1974), p. 318.

31. Heidegger, "Über Nietzsches Wort: Gott ist Tod," *Holzwege*, 4th ed. (Frankfurt: Klostermann, 1963), p. 221; my translation.

32. Martin Heidegger, "Der Spruch des Anaximander," *Holzwege*, pp. 319f, 324 (English translation, "The Anaximander Fragment," *Early Greek Thinking*, trans. David Farrell Krell and Frank A. Capuzzi [New York: Harper & Row, 1975], pp. 34f, 38); Jacques Derrida, "Ousia et Grammê," *Marges de la philosophie* (Paris: Minuit, 1972), p. 35 n. 2 (English translation, Derrida, *Margins of Philosophy* [Chicago: University of Chicago Press, 1982], p. 33 n. 6).

33. For a sampling, see Heidegger, *Basic Problems of Phenomenology*, trans. Albert Hofstadter (Bloomington: Indiana University Press, 1982), p. 113; *An Introduction to Metaphysics*, trans. Ralph Manheim (New Haven, Conn.: Yale University Press,

1959), the important discussion at p. 194ff, as well as pp. 64 and 206; *The Question of Being* trans. William Kluback and Jean T. Wilde (New Haven, Conn.: Yale University Press, 1958), p. 21; *Wegmarken,* p. 161; and the more extensive listing in Hildegard Feick, *Wortindex zu Heideggers* Sein und Zeit, 4th ed. (Tübingen: Niemeyer, 1991), p. 63.

34. Franzen, *Von der Existenzialontologie zur Seinsgeschichte,* p. 116.

35. Cf. *Gorgias* 497e and *Republic* IV 437d.

36. Aristotle, *Metaph.* 10013b 13ff. Cf. Aristotle, *De motu* 703a32, where the monarch is said to "preside" (*pareinai*) over the polis.

37. Heidegger, "Zeit und Sein," *Zur Sache des Denkens* (Tübingen: Niemeyer, 1969), p. 25 (English translation, Heidegger, "Time and Being," *On Time and Being,* trans. Joan Stambaugh [New York: Harper & Row, 1972], p. 24).

38. Jean-Paul Sartre, *L'être et le néant* (Paris: Gallimard, 1943), pp. 561-638 (English translation, *Being and Nothingness,* trans. Hazel E. Barnes [New York: Citadel Press, 1964], pp. 457-529).

39. I.e., within the limits of its inherence in a preexisting world; Heidegger, *SZ,* p. 366.

40. See Jürgen Habermas, "Work and Weltanschauung," *Critical Inquiry* 15 (1989), pp. 431-456. Also see my discussion of Habermas's views on Heidegger in the introduction to this book.

11. DIAKENA AND THING IN THE LATER HEIDEGGER

1. The letter is printed in William Richardson, *Martin Heidegger: Through Phenomenology to Thought* (The Hague: Martinus Nijhoff, 1974); see p. xii.

2. Martin Heidegger, "Die Zeit des Weltbildes," *Holzwege,* 4th ed. (Frankfurt: Klostermann, 1963), p. 6 (English translation in Heidegger, "The Age of the World Picture," *The Question concerning Technology and Other Essays,* trans. William Lovitt [New York: Harper & Row, 1977], p. 115). Emphasis added.

3. Heidegger, "Letter on Humanism," *Wegmarken,* p. 146 (English translation in Heidegger, *Basic Writings,* ed. David Farrell Krell [New York: Harper & Row, 1977], p. 194).

4. Heidegger's most stringent investigation of such incommensurability is "Aus einem Gespräch von der Sprache," in Heidegger, *Unterwegs zur Sprache,* 4th ed. (Pfullingen: Neske, 1971), pp. 85-156; hereinafter: AGS (English translation, Heidegger, "From a Dialogue on Language," *On the Way to Language,* trans. Albert Hofstadter [New York: Harper & Row, 1971], pp. 1-56).

5. Heidegger, "Der Spruch des Anaximander," *Holzwege,* p. 311.

6. Martin Heidegger, "Vom Wesen der Wahrheit," *Wegmarken,* p. 94 (English translation, Heidegger, *Basic Writings,* p. 138). Emphasis added.

7. As by Winfred Franzen and, following him, Jürgen Habermas: Franzen, *Von der Existentialontologie zur Seinsgeschichte* (Meisenheim/Glan: Anton Hain 1975); Habermas, "Work and Weltanschauung: The Heidegger Controversy from a German Perspective," *Critical Inquiry* 15 (1989), pp. 431-456.

8. I will discuss the Heideggerean background of Foucault's enterprises of archeology and genealogy in my *Philosophy and Freedom,* forthcoming.

9. Cf. Heidegger, "Der Ursprung des Kunstwerkes," *Holzwege,* pp. 29-33; hereinafter: UKW (English translation, Heidegger, "The Origin of the Work of Art,"

Poetry, Language, Thought, trans. Albert Hofstadter [New York: Harper & Row, 1971], pp. 40-44).

10. Heidegger, "Das Ding" at Heidegger," *Vorträge und Aufsätze*, vol. 2 (Pfullingen: Neske, 1967, pp. 38-40; hereinafter, DD (English translation, "The Thing" *Poetry, Language, Thought*, p. 160f).

11. Not, as the English translation has it, into "the light of their mutual belonging" (DD, p. 46/174).

12. They are not, as the translation has it, "betrothed" (ibid).

13. This concept of responsive transformation differentiates diakenic interplay both from Hegelian sublation and from the Saussurian conception of semantic and semiological difference, in which conceptual and phonic differences "issue from the system" but are in themselves fixed and stable, without histories of their own. See Ferdinand de Saussure, *Course in General Linguistics*, trans. Wade Baskin (New York: Philosophical Library, 1959), pp. 11f, 120. Derrida, fatefully, takes his beginnings from Saussure in "La Différance" *Marges de la philosophie* (Paris: Minuit, 1972), p. 11 (English translation, Derrida, "Differance," *Speech and Phenomena*, trans. David B. Allison [Evanston, Ill.: Northwestern University Press, 1973], p. 140).

14. Plato, *Timaeus* 52b; *Meno* 81d.

15. Or of three of them. Here as elsewhere, Heidegger refuses to consider the author as the "moving cause" at all; cf. UKW, pp. 29, 58, 64f/40, 71, 78.

16. See Heidegger, "Vom Wesen der Wahrheit," *Wegmarken*, pp. 83-91.

17. Hence the possibility, mentioned earlier, that the various epochs of *Seinsgeschichte* themselves stand in diakenic relationships.

18. Heidegger, *What is Philosophy?* trans. Jean T. Wilde and William Kluback (New Haven, Conn.: Yale University Press, n.d.), p. 66.

19. Heidegger, *What is Philosophy?* p. 94. I discuss the nature and norms of such dialogue in my "Language and Appropriation: The Nature of Heideggerean Dialogue," *Personalist* 60 (1979), pp. 384-396.

20. Martin Heidegger, "Andenken," *Erläuterungen zu Hölderlins Dichtung*, 1st ed. (Frankfurt: Klostermann, 1951), pp. 75-143; hereinafter: Adk. Page numbers to this edition are given marginally in later editions.

21. See Heidegger, *Erläuterungen zu Hölderlins Dichtung*, esp. p. 21 ("Heimkunft"); cf. pp. 7 ("Vorwort zur 2e Aufl."), 29 ("Heimkunft"), 74 (Adk.), 182 ("das Gedicht"). Also see Heidegger, *Vorträge und Aufsätze*, 2nd ed., vol. 2 (Pfullingen: Neske, 1967) p. 66 ("Dichterisch wohnet der Mensch").

22. Emil Staiger, "Hölderlin-Forschung Während des Krieges," *Trivium* 4 (1946), p. 215. Cf. on this Beda Alleman, *Hölderlin et Heidegger*, trans. François Fedier (Paris: Presses Universitaires de France, 1959), pp. 151-155.

23. These are at Adk., pp. 83f, 85f, 112ff, and 129f respectively.

24. Martin Heidegger *Sein und Zeit*, 11th ed. (Tübingen: Niemeyer, 1967), ¶33 (p. 159). Page numbers to this edition are given marginally in the English translation (Heidegger, *Being and Time*, trans. John MacQuarrie and Edward Robinson [New York: Harper & Row, 1962]).

25. Heidegger, *Was Heißt Denken?* (Tübingen: Max Niemeyer, 1971), p. 130; hereinafter: WHD (English translation, Heidegger, *What is Called Thinking?* (trans. Fred D. Wieck and J. Glenn Gray) [New York: Harper & Row, 1968], p. 216).

26. Heidegger, *Einführung in die Metaphysik* (Tübingen: Niemeyer, 1953), p. 69.

27. Martin Heidegger, "Nietzsches Wort: Gott is Tot," *Holzwege*, pp. 193-247.

28. Martin Heidegger, *The Question of Being*, trans. William Kluback and Jean T. Wilde (New Haven, Conn.: Yale University Press, 1958), p. 104.

29. Such is the case when Heidegger, for example, replaces the "syntactical" translation of Parmenides with a "paratactical" one; for the saying, Heidegger says, "*speaks* there where no words stand, in the spaces between them"; *WHD*, p. 114/186.

30. See the epigraph to Heidegger, *Holzwege*.

31. Cf.*WHD*, pp. 113, 164/185 (where "questioning" [*Fragen*] is mistranslated as "quest," and "questionability" (*Fragwürdigkeit*) is mistranslated as "core"), 168f.

32. For a discussion of Heideggerean "hints," see my *Poetic Interaction* (Chicago: University of Chicago Press, 1989), p. 153.

33. Martin Heidegger, *Der Satz von Grund*, 4th ed. (Pfullingen: Neske, 1971), p. 14f; *Vorträge und Aufsätze*, vol. 3, pp. 5-7, 19 ("Logos"). Cf. Heidegger, "Aus einem Gespräch von der Sprache," *Unterwegs zur Sprache*, 4th ed. (Pfullingen: Neske, 1971), p. 11f; hereinafter: AGS (English translation, Heidegger, "From a Dialogue on Language," *On the Way to Language*, p. 21f; *WHD*, p. 142f/234.

34. Cf. Alleman, *Hölderlin et Heidegger*, p. 151.

35. Graeme Nicholson, "Heidegger on Thinking," *Journal of the History of Philosophy* 13 (1975), pp. 499-501.

12. CONCLUSION

1. To be sure, Heidegger stands at the end of the story together with Hegel, and Hegel's challenges to us are as significant as Heidegger's. But it is only through Heidegger's encounter with the diakena, it seems, that we can understand them fully. Only when we understand Heidegger's challenge to ousia—and understand it better than he did—can we look back and see that Hegel, too, challenged the notion of governing form. Without the interpretative purchase given us by Heidegger, we fall victim to the many ousiodic misreadings of Hegel that I have criticized in *The Company of Words* (Evanston, Ill.: Northwestern University Press, 1993).

2. Except where otherwise noted, my discussion of the Pawnee earth lodge is based on Gene Weltfish, *The Lost Universe* (New York: Ballantine, 1965), pp. 75-79; hereinafter: LU.

3. Michel Foucault, *Surveiller et punir* (Paris: Gallimard, 1975), p. 201ff (English translation, Foucault, *Discipline and Punish*, trans. Alan Sheridan [New York: Vintage, 1979], p. 200ff.

4. For examples of both, see David Hume, "Conclusion of This Book," *A Treatise of Human Nature*, ed. L. A. Selby-Bigge (Oxford: Clarendon Press, 1896), pp. 263-274.

5. Claude Lévi-Strauss, "Do Dual Organizations Exist?" *Structural Anthropology*, trans. Claire Jacobson and Brooke Grundfest Schoepf (New York: Basic Books, 1963), p. 161.

6. Alphonso Ortiz, *The Tewa World* (Chicago: University of Chicago Press, 1969), pp. 61-77, 101.

7. Ortiz, *The Tewa World*, p. 103

8. Ortiz, *The Tewa World*, p. 84

9. Emmanuel Levinas, *Time and the Other*, trans. Richard A. Cohen (Pittsburgh: Duquesne University Press, 1987) p. 77.

10. I expect to carrry this project out in my forthcoming book, *The Capture of Time*.

BIBLIOGRAPHY

Ackrill, J. L. *Aristotle's Categories and De Interpretatione.* Oxford: Clarendon Press, 1963.

———. "Aristotle's Definitions of Psyche." *Proceedings of the Aristotelian Society* 73 (1972-1973): 119-133.

Adorno, Theodor W., and Max Horkheimer. *Dialectic of Enlightenment.* Trans. John Cumming. New York: Continuum, 1993.

Albritton, Rogers. "Forms of Particular Substances in Aristotle's *Metaphysics.*" *Journal of Philosophy* 54 (1957): 699-708.

Alexander, Peter. *Ideas, Qualities, and Corpuscles: Locke and Boyle on the External World.* Cambridge: Cambridge University Press, 1985.

Alleman, Beda. *Hölderlin et Heidegger.* Trans. François Fedier. Paris: Presses Universitaires de France, 1959.

Allison, Henry E. "Locke on Personal Identity." *Journal of the History of Ideas* 27 (1966): 41-58.

Alston, William P., and Jonathan Bennett. "Locke on People and Substances." *Philosophical Review* 97 (1988): 25-46.

Ando, Takatura. *Aristotle's Theory of Practical Cognition.* 2nd ed. The Hague: Nijhoff, 1965.

Anscombe, G. E. M., and Peter Geach. *Three Philosophers.* Oxford: Basil Blackwell, 1961.

Aquinas, Thomas. *Commentary on the Metaphysics of Aristotle.* 2 vols. Trans. John P. Rowan. Chicago: Regnery, 1961.

———. "De Ente et Essentia." *L'Etre et l'essence.* Trans. and ed. Catherine Capelle. Paris: Jean Vrin, 1965. Translated into English as *On Being and Essence.* Trans. Armand Maurer. Toronto: Pontifical Institute of Medieval Studies, 1949.

———. "On Kingship or the Governance of Rulers." In *Saint Thomas Aquinas on Politics and Ethics.* Trans. and ed. Paul E. Sigmund. New York: Norton, 1988.

———. *Philosophical Works.* 2 vols. Ed. Anton C. Pegis. New York: Random House, 1945.

Aristotle. *Works.* Bekker pagination.

Arnauld, Antoine. *On True and False Ideas.* Trans. Stephen Gaukroger. Manchester: Manchester University Press, 1990.

Arnim, Johannes von, ed. *Fragmenta stoicorum vetorum.* 4 vols. New York: Irvington, 1986.

Atherton, Margaret. "Knowledge of Substance and Knowledge of Essence in Locke's Essay." *History of Philosophy Quarterly* 1 (1984): 413-428.

Aubenque Pierre, ed. *Concepts et catégories dans la pensée antique.* Paris: Jean Vrin, 1980.

Ayers, M. R. "The Ideas of Power and Substance in Locke's Philosophy." *Philosophical Quarterly* 25 (1975): 1-27.

Baier, Annette. *A Progress of Sentiments.* Cambridge, Mass.: Harvard University Press, 1991.

————. "Good Men's Women: Hume on Chastity and Trust." *Hume Studies* 5 (1979): 1-19.

Balme, David. "Aristotle's Biology Was Not Essentialist." *Archiv für Geschichte der Philosophie* 62 (1980): 1-12.

Barnes, Jonathan, et al., eds. *Articles on Aristotle.* 4 vols. London: Duckworth, 1977.

Barry, Brian. "Warrender and His Critics." In *Hobbes and Rousseau: A Collection of Critical Essays.* Ed. Maurice Cranston and Richard S. Peters. Garden City, N.Y.: Doubleday, 1972.

Baumgold, D. *Hobbes's Political Theory.* Cambridge: Cambridge University Press, 1988.

De Beauvoir, Simone. *The Second Sex.* Trans. and ed. H. M. Parshley. New York: Knopf, 1952.

Berkeley, George. *Berkeley's Philosophical Writings.* Ed. David M. Armstrong. New York: Collier, 1965.

Bernhardt, Jean. "L'Aristotelisme et la pensée de Hobbes." In *Thomas Hobbes: De la métaphysique a la politique.* Ed. Martin Bertman and Michel Malherbe. Paris: Jean Vrin, 1989.

Bertman, Martin, and Michel Malherbe, eds. *Thomas Hobbes: De la métaphysique a la politique.* Paris: Jean Vrin, 1989.

Biro, John. "Hume on Self-Identity and Memory." *Review of Metaphysics* 30 (1976): 19-38.

————. "Hume's New Science of the Mind." In *The Cambridge Companion to Hume.* Ed. David Fate Norton. Cambridge: Cambridge University Press, 1993.

Block, Irving. "Truth and Error in Aristotle's Theory of Sense Perception." *Philosophical Quarterly* 11 (1961): 1-9.

Bolton, Martha Brandt. "Substances, Substrata, and Names of Substances in Locke's Essay." *Philosophical Review* 85 (1976): 488-513.

Bonitz, Hermann. *Aristotelis metaphysica.* 2 vols. Bonn, 1848.

————. *Index Aristotelicus.* Berlin, 1870. Reprint, Graz: Akademische Druck- und Verlagsanstalt, 1955.

Booth, William James. *Households: On the Moral Architecture of the Economy.* Ithaca, N.Y.: Cornell University Press, 1993.

————. "Politics and the Household: A Commentary on Aristotle's *Politics* Book One." *History of Political Thought* 2 (1981): 203-226.

Boss, Gérard. "Système et rupture chez Hobbes." *Dialogue* 27 (1988): 215-223.

Bostock, David. *Aristotle: Metaphysics Books Z and H.* Oxford: Clarendon Press, 1994.

Bradley, A. C. "Aristotle's Conception of the State." In *A Companion to Aristotle's Politics*. Ed. David Keyt and Fred D. Miller, Jr. Oxford: Basil Blackwell, 1981.

Brandom, Robert. "Heidegger's Categories in *Being and Time*." *Monist* 66 (1983): 387–409.

Bricke, John. "Hume's Conception of Character." *Southwestern Journal of Philosophy* 5 (1974): 107–113.

Broadie, Sarah (Waterlow). *Ethics with Aristotle*. Oxford: Oxford University Press, 1991.

Caputo, John D. *Radical Hermeneutics*. Bloomington: Indiana University Press, 1987.

Cashdollar, Sanford. "Aristotle's Account of Incidental Perception." *Phronesis* 18 (1973): 156–175.

Chanter, Tina. *Ethics of Eros*. New York: Routledge & Kegan Paul, 1993.

Chappell, Vere, ed. *The Cambridge Companion to Locke*. Cambridge: Cambridge University Press, 1994.

———. "Locke on the Ontology of Matter, Living Things, and Substances." *Philosophical Studies* 60 (1990): 19–32.

———. "Matter." *Journal of Philosophy* 70 (1973): 679–696.

Charlton, W. *Aristotle's Physics: Books I and II*. Oxford: Clarendon Press, 1970.

Clark, Stephen R. L. "Slaves and Citizens." *Philosophy* 60 (1985): 27–46.

Cleary, John J. *Aristotle on the Many Senses of Priority*. Carbondale: Southern Illinois University Press, 1988.

———, ed. *Proceedings of the Boston Area Colloquium in Ancient Philosophy II*. Lanham, Md.: University Press of America, 1987.

Cohen, Joshua. "Structure, Choice, and Legitimacy: Locke's Theory of the State." *Philosophy and Public Affairs* 15 (1986): 301–324.

Cohen, Sheldon. "Aristotle's Doctrine of the Material Substrate." *Philosophical Review* 93 (1984): 171–194.

Cooper, John M. *Reason and Human Good in Aristotle*. Cambridge, Mass.: Harvard University Press, 1975.

Cottingham, John, ed. *The Cambridge Companion to Descartes*. Cambridge: Cambridge University Press, 1992.

———, ed. *Reason, Will, and Sensation: Studies in Descartes' Metaphysics*. Oxford: Clarendon Press, 1994.

Courtine, Jean-François. "Note complémentaire pour l'histoire du vocabulaire de l'être: Les traductions latines d'*ousia* et la compréhension romano-stoicienne de l'être." In *Concepts et catégories dans la pensée antique*. Ed. Aubenque Pierre. Paris: Jean Vrin, 1980.

Cranston, Maurice, and Richard S. Peters, eds. *Hobbes and Rousseau: A Collection of Critical Essays*. Garden City, N.Y.: Doubleday, 1972.

Dancy, Russell. "On Some of Aristotle's Second Thoughts about Substance." *Philosophical Review* 87 (1978): 372–413.

Deleuze, Gilles. *Différence et répétition*. Paris: Presses Universitaires de France, 1968. Translated into English as *Difference and Repetition*. Trans. Paul Patton. New York: Columbia University Press, 1994.

———. *Logique du sens*. Paris: Minuit, 1969. Translated into English as *The Logic of Sense*. Trans. Mark Lester. New York: Columbia University Press, 1990.

Derrida, Jacques. *De la grammatologie*. Paris: Minuit, 1967. Translated into English as

Of Grammatology. Trans. Gayatri Chakravorty Spivak. Baltimore: Johns Hopkins University Press, 1974.

———. *La dissémination.* Paris: Editions du Seuil, 1972. Translated into English as *Dissemination.* Trans. Barbara Johnson. Chicago: University of Chicago Press, 1981.

———. *Marges de la philosophie.* Paris: Minuit, 1972. Translated into English as *Margins of Philosophy.* Trans. Alan Bass. Chicago: University of Chicago Press, 1982.

———. *Of Spirit: Heidegger and the Question.* Trans. Geoffrey Bennington and Rachel Bowlby. Chicago: University of Chicago Press, 1989.

Descartes, René. *Oeuvres de Descartes.* 13 vols. Ed. Charles Adam and Paul Tannery. Paris: Cerf, 1896-1913. Translated into English as *The Philosophical Works of Descartes.* 2 vols. Trans. Elizabeth Haldane and G. R. T. Ross. Cambridge: Cambridge University Press, 1931.

———. *Philosophical Letters.* Trans. and ed. Anthony Kenny. Oxford: Clarendon Press, 1970.

Dijksterhuis, E. J. *The Mechanization of the World Picture.* Trans. C. Dirkshoorn. Oxford: Clarendon Press, 1961.

Dodds, E. R. *The Greeks and the Irrational.* Berkeley: University of California Press, 1968.

Donagan, Alan. "Thomas Aquinas on Human Action." In *The Cambridge History of Later Medieval Philosophy.* Ed. Norman Kretzmann, Anthony Kenny, and Jan Pinboig. Cambridge: Cambridge University Press, 1982.

Douglass, Frederick. "Life and Times of Frederick Douglass." *Autobiographies.* Ed. Henry Louis Gates, Jr. New York: Library of America, 1994.

Dreyfus, Hubert L. *Being in the World.* Cambridge, Mass.: MIT Press, 1991.

Dunn, John. *The Political Thought of John Locke.* Cambridge: Cambridge University Press, 1969.

Elders, Leo J. *Die Metaphysik des Thomas von Aquin in historischer Perspektive.* Salzburg: Anton Pustet, 1985.

Everson, Stephen. *Aristotle on Perception.* Oxford: Oxford University Press, 1997.

Fackenheim, Emil. *The Religious Dimension in Hegel's Thought.* Boston: Beacon Press, 1967.

Farias, Victor. *Heidegger et le Nazisme.* Trans. Myriam Bennaroch and Jean-Baptiste Grasset. Lagrasse: Editions Verdier, 1987.

Feick, Hildegard. *Wortindex zu Heideggers* Sein und Zeit. 4th ed. Tübingen: Niemeyer, 1991.

Fine, Arthur. *The Shaky Game: Einstein, Realism, and the Quantum Theory.* Chicago: University of Chicago Press, 1986.

Fine, Gail. "Separation." *Oxford Studies in Ancient Philosophy* 2 (1984): 31-87.

———. "Separation: A Reply to Morrison." *Oxford Studies in Ancient Philosophy* 3 (1985): 159-165.

Finley, M. I. "Aristotle and Economic Analysis." *Past and Present* 47 (1970): 3-25.

Flage, Daniel E. *David Hume's Theory of Mind.* New York: Routledge, 1990.

Forte, Betty. *Rome and the Romans as the Greeks Saw Them.* Rome: American Academy in Rome, 1972. (Proceedings and Monographs 24.)

Fortenbaugh, W. W. "Aristotle on Slaves and Women." In *Articles on Aristotle.* Vol. 2. Ed. Jonathan Barnes et al. London: Duckworth, 1977.

Foucault, Michel. Interview by François Ewald. "Le souci de la verité." In *Dits et écrits.* Ed. Daniel Defert and François Ewald. 4 vols. Paris: Gallimard, 1994. Translated into English as *Interviews.* Trans. John Johnson. Ed. Sylvere Lotringer. New York: Semiotext(e), 1989.

———. *Surveiller et punir.* Paris: Gallimard, 1975. Translated into English as *Discipline and Punish.* Trans. Alan Sheridan. New York: Vintage, 1979.

Franzen, Winfred. *Von der Existentialontologie zur Seinsgeschichte.* Meisenheim/Glan: Anton Hain, 1975.

Frede, Michael. *Essays in Ancient Philosophy.* Minneapolis: University of Minnesota Press, 1987.

———. "Substance in Aristotle's Metaphysics." In *Aristotle on Nature and Living Things.* Ed. Alan Gotthelf. Pittsburgh: Mathesis Press, 1985.

———, and Günther Patzig. *Aristoteles. Metaphysik.* 2 vols. Munich: C. H. Beck, 1988.

Freud, Sigmund. *A General Introduction to Psychoanalysis.* Trans. Joan Rivière. New York: Washington Square Press, 1960.

Frye, Marilyn. *The Politics of Reality.* Trumansburg, N.Y.: Crossing Press, 1983.

Frye, Northrop. *Journey without Arrival.* Toronto: Canadian Broadcasting Corporation, 1976. Videocassette.

Furth, Montgomery. *Substance, Form, and Psyche: An Aristotelian Metaphysics.* Cambridge: Cambridge University Press, 1988.

———. "Trans-temporal Stability in Aristotelian Substances." *Journal of Philosophy* 75 (1978): 627–646.

Garber, Daniel. *Descartes' Metaphysical Physics.* Chicago: University of Chicago Press, 1992.

———. "Descartes' Physics." In *The Cambridge Companion to Descartes.* Ed. John Cottingham. Cambridge: Cambridge University Press, 1992.

Garnsey, K., et al., eds. *Trade in the Ancient Economy.* Berkeley: University of California Press, 1983.

Gaukroger, Stephen, ed. *Descartes: Philosophy, Mathematics, Physics.* Totawa, N.J.: Barnes and Noble, 1980.

Gauthier, David. *The Logic of Leviathan.* Oxford: Clarendon Press, 1969.

Gert, Bernard. "Hobbes' Account of Reason and the Passions." In *Thomas Hobbes: De la métaphysique a la politique.* Ed. Martin Bertman and Michel Malherbe. Paris: Jean Vrin, 1989.

Gill, Mary Louise. *Aristotle on Substance: The Paradox of Unity.* Princeton, N.J.: Princeton University Press, 1989.

Gilson, Etienne. *The Christian Philosophy of St. Thomas Aquinas.* Trans. L. K. Shook. New York: Random House, 1956.

———. *Etudes sur la rôle de la pensée médiévale dans la formation du système cartésien.* Paris: Jean Vrin, 1930.

Goldsmith, M. M. *Hobbes' Science of Politics.* New York: Columbia University Press, 1966.

Gotthelf, Alan, ed. *Aristotle on Nature and Living Things.* Pittsburgh: Mathesis Press, 1985.

Graham, Daniel. *Aristotle's Two Systems.* Oxford: Clarendon Press, 1987.

Greenleaf, W. K. "Hobbes: The Problem of Interpretation." In *Hobbes and Rousseau: A Collection of Critical Essays.* Ed. Maurice Cranston and Richard S. Peters. Garden City, N.Y.: Doubleday, 1972.

Guenancia, Pierre. *Descartes et l'ordre politique.* Paris: Presses Universitaires de France, 1983.

Guéroult, Martial. "The Metaphysics and Physics of Force in Descartes." In *Descartes: Philosophy, Mathematics, Physics.* Ed. Stephen Gaukroger. Totawa, N.J.: Barnes and Noble, 1980.

Guignon, Charles. *Heidegger and the Theory of Knowledge.* Indianapolis: Hackett, 1983.

Habermas, Jürgen. "Die große Workung." *Philosophisch-politische Profile.* 3rd ed. Frankfurt: Suhrkamp, 1981.

———. *Der philosophische Diskurs der Moderne.* 2nd ed. Frankfurt: Suhrkamp, 1985. Translated into English as *The Philosophical Discourse of Modernity.* Trans. Frederick Lawrence. Cambridge, Mass. MIT Press, 1987.

———. "Modernity: An Incomplete Project?" In *Postmodern Culture.* Ed. H. Foster. London: Pluto.

———. *Nachmetaphysisches Denken.* Frankfurt: Suhrkamp, 1988. Translated into English as *Postmetaphysical Thinking.* Trans. William Mark Hohengarten. Cambridge: MIT Press, 1992.

———. *Philosophisch-politische Profile.* 3rd ed. Frankfurt: Suhrkamp, 1981.

———. *Theorie des kommunikativen Handelns.* 2 vols. Frankfurt: Suhrkamp, 1981. Translated into English as *Theory of Communicative Action I.* Trans. Thomas McCarthy. Boston: Beacon Press, 1984.

———. "Work and Weltanschauung: The Heidegger Controversy from a German Perspective." Trans. John McCumber. *Critical Inquiry* 15 (1989): 431-456.

———. "Zur Veröffentlichung von Vorlesungen aus dem Jahre 1936." *Philosophisch-politische Profile.* Frankfurt: Suhrkamp, 1981.

Halper, Edward. "Aristotle's Solution to the Problem of Sensible Substances." *Journal of Philosophy* 84 (1987): 666-672.

Hamlyn, D. W. "Aristotle on Form." In *Aristotle on Nature and Living Things.* Ed. Alan Gotthelf. Pittsburgh: Mathesis Press, 1985.

Hampton, Jean. *Hobbes and the Social Contract Tradition.* Cambridge: Cambridge University Press, 1986.

Hardie, W. F. R. *Aristotle's Ethical Theory.* 2nd ed. Oxford: Clarendon, 1980.

Haring, Ellen Stone. "Substantial Form in Aristotle's *Metaphysics* Z, I." *Review of Metaphysics* 10 (1956-1957): 308-332.

Harter, Edward D. "Aristotle on Primary *Ousia.*" *Archiv für Geschichte der Philosophie* 57 (1975): 1-20.

Hartman, Edwin. "Aristotle on the Identity of Substance and Essence." *Philosophical Review* 85 (1976): 545-561.

Hatfield, Gary C. "Force (God) in Descartes' Physics." *Studies in History and Philosophy of Science* 10 (1979): 130-149.

Hegel, G. W. F. *Werke.* 20 vols. Ed. Eva Moldenhauer and Karl Markus Michel. Frankfurtam Main: Suhrkamp, 1970-71. Translated into English as *Aesthetics.* 2 vols. Trans. T. M. Knox. Oxford: Oxford University Press, 1975; *Hegel's Logic.* Trans. William Wallace. Oxford: Clarendon Press, 1975; *Hegel's Phenomenology of Spirit.* Trans. A. V. Miller. Oxford: Clarendon Press, 1977; *Hegel's Philosophy of Mind.* Trans. A. V. Miller. Oxford: Clarendon Press, 1971; *Philosophy of Nature.* Trans. and ed. M. J. Petry. London: Allen and Unwin, 1970; *Philosophy of Right.* Trans. T. M. Knox. Oxford: Clarendon Press, 1952; and *Science of Logic.* Trans. A. V. Miller. New York: Humanities Press, 1969.

Heidegger, Martin. *Basic Problems of Phenomenology.* Trans. Albert Hofstadter. Bloomington: Indiana University Press, 1982.

———. *Basic Writings.* Trans. and ed. David Farrell Krell. New York: Harper & Row, 1977.

———. *Beiträge zur Philosophie.* Frankfurt: Klostermann, 1989.

———. *Der Satz von Grund.* 4th ed. Pfullingen: Neske, 1971.

———. *Die Selbstbehauptung der deutschen Universität* and *das Rektorat: 1933/34.* Frankfurt: Klostermann, 1983.

———. *Erlaüterungen zu Hölderlins Dichtung.* Frankfurt: Klostermann, 1951.

———. *Hölderlins Hymne,* in *Gesamtausgabe.* Vol. 53. Frankfurt: Klostermann, 1984.

———. *Holzwege.* 4th ed. Frankfurt: Klostermann, 1963.

———. *The Question of Being.* Trans. William Kluback and Jean T. Wilde. New Haven, Conn.: Yale University Press, 1958.

———. *Sein und Zeit.* 11th ed. Tübingen: Niemeyer, 1967. Translated into English as *Being and Time.* Trans. John MacQuarrie and Edward Robinson. New York: Harper & Row, 1962.

———. *Unterwegs zur Sprache.* 4th ed. Pfullingen: Neske, 1971. Translated into English as *On the Way to Language.* Trans. Albert Hofstadter. New York: Harper & Row, 1971.

———. *Vorträge und Aufsätze.* 3 vols. Pfullingen: Neske, 1967.

———. *Was Heißt Denken?* Tübingen: Niemeyer, 1971. Translated into English as *What Is Called Thinking?* Trans. Fred D. Wieck and J. Glenn Gray. New York: Harper, 1968.

———. *Wegmarken.* Frankfurt: Klostermann 1967.

———. *What Is Philosophy?* Trans. Jean T. Wilde and William Kluback. New Haven, Conn.: Yale University Press, n.d.

———. *Zur Sache des Denkens.* Tübingen: Niemeyer, 1969.

Heinaman, Robert. "Knowledge of Substance in Aristotle." *Journal of Hellenic Studies* 101 (1981): 63–77.

Hepburn, Ronald. "Hobbes on the Knowledge of God." In *Hobbes: A Collection of Critical Essays.* Ed. Maurice Cranston and Richard S. Peters. Garden City, N.Y.: Doubleday, 1972.

Hobbes, Thomas. *Computatio Sive Logica.* Trans. and ed. Aloysius Martinich et. al. New York: Abaris Books, 1981.

———. "De Corpore." In *The Metaphysical System of Thomas Hobbes.* Ed. M. W. Calkins. LaSalle, Ill.: Open Court, 1963.

———. *The English Works of Thomas Hobbes.* 11 vols. Ed. William Molesworth. London: John Bohn, 1840.

———. *Leviathan, or the Matter, Forme, & Power of a Common-Wealth Ecclesiastical and Civill,* 1651. Reprinted as *Leviathan.* Ed. Richard Tuck. Cambridge: Cambridge University Press, 1991.

———. *Opera omnia quae latine scripsit.* 5 vols. Ed. William Molesworth. London: John Bohn, 1839–1845.

Homiak, Marcia. "Virtue and Self-Love in Aristotle's Ethics." *Canadian Journal of Philosophy* 11 (1981): 633–652.

Hood, F. C. *The Divine Politics of Thomas Hobbes.* Oxford: Oxford University Press, 1964.

Hume, David. *Enquiries.* Ed. L. A. Selby-Bigge. Oxford: Clarendon Press, 1894.

———. *Essays*. Ed. Eugene F. Miller. Indianapolis: Liberty Fund, 1985.

———. *The History of England from the Invasion of Julius Caesar to the Abdication of James the Second*. 5 vols. Philadelphia: Porter & Coates, 1854.

———. *A Treatise of Human Nature*. Ed. L. A. Selby-Bigge. Oxford: Clarendon Press, 1896.

Husserl, Edmund. *Ideen zu einer reinen Phänomenologie*. 4th ed. Tübingen: Niemeyer, 1980.

Irwin, Terence. *Aristotle's First Principles*. Oxford: Clarendon Press, 1988.

Jalabert, Jacques. *Théorie leibnizienne de la substance*. Paris: Presses Universitaires de France, 1974.

Jarrett, Charles E., et al., eds. *New Essays on Rationalism and Empiricism*. Guelph: Canadian Association for Publishing in Philosophy, 1978. (*Canadian Journal of Philosophy*, supplementary vol. 4).

Johnson, Curtis N. *Aristotle's Political Theory*. London: Macmillan, 1990.

———. "The Hobbesian Conception of Sovereignty and Aristotle's Politics." *Journal of the History of Ideas* 46 (1985): 327-347.

Kamp, Andreas. *Die politische Philosophie des Aristoteles und ihre metaphysischen Grundlagen*. Munich: Karl Alber, 1985.

Kant, Immanuel. *Kants gesmmelte Schriften*. 29 vols. [Berlin]: Akademie-Ausgabe Berlin, 1902- .

Kavka, Gregory. *Hobbesian Moral and Political Philosophy*. Princeton, N.J.: Princeton University Press, 1986.

Kemp Smith, Norman. *The Philosophy of David Hume*. New York: St. Martin's Press, 1966.

Keyt, David, and Fred D. Miller, Jr., eds. *A Companion to Aristotle's Politics*. Oxford: Basil Blackwell, 1981.

Kockelmans, Joseph. *On the Truth of Being*. Bloomington: Indiana University Press, 1984.

Kosman, L. A. "What Does the Maker Mind Make?" In *Essays on Aristotle's de Anima*. Ed. Martha Nussbaum and Amélie Oksenberg Rorty. Oxford: Clarendon Press, 1992.

Kraut, Richard. *Aristotle on the Human Good*. Princeton, N.J.: Princeton University Press, 1989.

Kretzmann, Norman, and Eleonore Stump, eds. *The Cambridge Companion to Aquinas*. Cambridge: Cambridge University Press, 1993.

Kydd, Rachel. *Reason and Conduct in Hume's Treatise*. Oxford: Clarendon Press, 1946.

Lacoue-Labarthe, Philippe. *Heidegger, Art, and Politics*. Trans. Chris Turner. Oxford: Basil Blackwell, 1990.

Lacey, A. R. "*Ousia* and Form in Aristotle." *Phronesis* 10 (1965): 54-69.

Lamprecht, Sterling Peter. *The Moral and Political Philosophy of John Locke*. New York: Russell & Russell, 1962.

Latour, Bruno. *We Have Never Been Modern*. Trans. Catherine Porter. Cambridge, Mass.: Harvard University Press, 1993.

Lear, Jonathan. *Aristotle: The Desire to Understand*. Cambridge: Cambridge University Press, 1988.

Leibniz, G. W. *Mathematische Schriften*. 7 vols. Ed. C. I. Gerhart. [Berlin]: Berlin & Halle, 1849-1854.

———. *Die philosophischen Schriften*. 8 vols. Ed. C. J. Gebhardt. Hildesheim: Georg

Olms, 1966. Translated into English as *Philosophical Papers and Letters*. 2nd ed. Ed. Leroy Loemker. Dordrecht: Reidel, 1969; *The Political Writings of Leibniz*. Trans. and ed. Patrick Riley. Cambridge: Cambridge University Press, 1972; *Theodicy*. Trans. E. M. Huggard. London: Routledge & Kegan Paul, 1952.

Lévi-Strauss, Claude. *Structural Anthropology*. Trans. Claire Jacobson and Brooke Grundfest Schoepf. New York: Basic Books, 1963.

Levin, David Michael. *The Body's Recollection of Being*. London: Routledge & Kegan Paul, 1985.

Levinas, Emmanuel. *Time and the Other*. Trans. Richard A. Cohen. Pittsburgh: Duquesne University Press, 1987.

Lewis, Douglas. "The Existence of Substances and Locke's Way of Ideas." *Theoria* 35 (1969): 124-146.

Lilly, Reginald. "Toward the Hermeneutic of *Der Satz vom Grund*." In *The Collegium Phaenomenologicum*. Ed. J. Sallis, G. Moneta, and J. Taminiaux. Dordrecht: Kluwer, 1988.

Lintott, Andrew. *Imperium Romanum*. London: Routledge, 1990.

Lloyd, G. E. R., and G. E. L. Owen, eds. *Aristotle on Mind and the Senses*. Cambridge: Cambrdge University Press, 1978.

Locke, John. *An Essay Concerning Human Understanding*. 2 vols. Ed. Alexander Campbell Fraser. New York: Dover, 1959.

———. *Two Treatises of Government*. Ed. Peter Laslett. Cambridge: Cambridge University Press, 1960.

Loux, Michael. *Primary Ousia: An Essay on Aristotle's Metaphysics Z and H*. Ithaca, N.Y.: Cornell University Press, 1991.

Löwith, Karl. *Mein Leben in Deutschland vor un nach 1933*. Stuttgart: J. B. Metzler, 1986.

Luhmann, Niklas. *Soziale Systeme*. Frankfurt: Suhrkamp, 1984.

Lyotard, Jean-François. *Heidegger and "the Jews."* Trans. David Carroll. Minneapolis: University of Minnesota Press, 1990.

MacDonald, Scott. "Theory of Knowledge." In *The Cambridge Companion to Aquinas*. Ed. Norman Kretzmann and Eleonore Stump. Cambridge: Cambridge University Press, 1993.

MacIntyre, Alasdair. "Hume on 'Is' and 'Ought.'" *Philosophical Review* 68 (1959): 451-468.

McIntyre, Jane. "Character: A Humean Account." *History of Philosophy Quarterly* 7 (1990): 193-206.

———. "Personal Identity and the Passions." *Journal of the History of Philosophy* 27 (1989): 545-557.

Macpherson, C. B. *The Political Theory of Possessive Individualism*. Oxford: Clarendon, 1962.

Maloney, J. Christopher. "Esse in the Thought of Thomas Aquinas." *New Scholasticism* 55 (1981): 159-177.

Mandelbaum, Maurice. "Locke's Realism." In *Philosophy, Science, and Sense Perception*. Ed. Maurice Mandelbauem. Baltimore: Johns Hopkins University Press, 1964.

Marion, Jean-Luc. "Cartesian Metaphysics and the Role of the Simple Natures." In *The Cambridge Companion to Descartes*. Ed. John Cottingham. Cambridge: Cambridge University Press, 1992.

Martin, Roland. *Greek Architecture*. New York: Rizzoli, 1988.

Marx, Karl. *Capital.* Trans. Samuel Morse and Edward Aveling. New York: Modern Library, 1906.

———. *Early Writings.* Trans. and ed. T. B. Bottomore. New York: McGraw-Hill, 1964.

Mattern, R. M. "Locke on Active Power and the Obscure Idea of Active Power from Bodies." *Studies in the History and Philosophy of Science* 11 (1980): 39-77.

McCann, Edwin. "Locke's Philosophy of Body." In *The Cambridge Companion to Locke.* Ed. Vere Chappell. Cambridge: Cambridge University Press, 1994.

McCumber, John. "Aristotelian Catharsis and the Purgation of Woman" *Diacritics* 18, no. 4 (1988): 53-67.

———. "Communication and Authenticity in *Being and Time.*" *Tulane Studies in Philosophy* 32 (1984): 45-52.

———. *The Company of Words.* Evanston, Ill.: Northwestern University Press, 1993.

———. "Contradiction and Resolution in the State: Hegel's Covert View." *CLIO* 15 (1986): 379-390.

———. "Hegel on Habit." *Owl of Minerva* 21 (1990): 155-165.

———. "Hegel's Anarchistic Utopia: The Politics of His *Aesthetics.*" *Southern Journal of Philosophy* 22 (1984): 203-210.

———. "Language and Appropriation: The Nature of Heideggerean Dialogue." *Personalist* 60 (1979): 384-396.

———. *Poetic Interaction.* Chicago: University of Chicago Press, 1989.

Meikle, Scott. *Aristotle's Economic Thought.* Oxford: Clarendon Press, 1995.

Miller, David. *Philosophy and Ideology in Hume's Political Thought.* Oxford: Clarendon Press, 1981.

Modrak, Deborah. "Aristotle on Thinking." In *Proceedings of the Boston Area Colloquium in Ancient Philosophy II.* Ed. John J. Cleary. Lanham, Md.: University Press of America, 1987.

Morrison, Donald. "Separation in Aristotle's Metaphysics." *Oxford Studies in Ancient Philosophy III* (1985): 125-157.

———. "Separation: A Reply to Fine." *Oxford Studies in Ancient Philosophy III* (1985): 167-173.

Mudimbe, V. Y. *The Invention of Africa.* Bloomington: Indiana University Press, 1988.

Mulgan R. G. *Aristotle's Political Theory.* Oxford: Oxford University Press, 1977.

———. "Aristotle's Sovereign." *Political Studies* 18 (1970): 518-522.

Nicholson, Graeme. "Heidegger on Thinking." *Journal of the History of Philosophy* 13 (1975): 491-503.

Nietzsche, Friedrich. *Gesammelte Schriften.* 11 vols. Ed. Alfred Bäumler. Stuttgart: Kroner 1965.

Noonan, Harold. "Locke on Personal Identity." *Philosophy* 53 (1978): 343-351.

Norton, David Fate, ed. *The Cambridge Companion to Hume.* Cambridge: Cambridge University Press, 1993.

Nussbaum, Martha Craven. *Aristotle's De Motu Animalium.* Princeton, N.J.: Princeton University Press, 1978.

———, and Amélie Oksenberg Rorty, eds. *Essays on Aristotle's De Anima.* Oxford: Clarendon Press, 1992.

Okrent, Mark. *Heidegger's Pragmatism.* Ithaca, N.J.: Cornell University Press, 1988.

Oliver, James H. *The Ruling Power.* Philadelphia: American Philosophical Society, 1953. (Transactions; n.s. 43, pt. 4.)

Olivecrona, Karl. "Appropriation in the State of Nature: Locke on the Origin of Property." *Journal of the History of Ideas* 35 (1974): 211-230.

Ortiz, Alphonso. *The Tewa World.* Chicago: University of Chicago Press, 1969.

Osler, Margaret J. "Eternal Truths and the Laws of Nature: The Theological Foundations of Descartes's Philosophy of Nature." *Journal of the History of Ideas* 46 (1986): 349-362.

Ott, Hugo. *Martin Heidegger: Unterwegs zu seiner Biographie.* Frankfurt: Campus, 1988.

Owens, Joseph. "Aristotle and Aquinas." In *The Cambridge Companion to Aquinas.* Ed. Norman Kretzmann and Eleonore Stump. Cambridge: Cambridge University Press, 1993.

———. *The Doctrine of Being in the Aristotelian Metaphysics.* 2nd ed. Toronto: Pontifical Institute of Medieval Studies, 1963.

———. "Matter and Predication in Aristotle." In *The Concept of Matter.* Ed. Ernan McMullin. Notre Dame: University of Notre Dame Press, 1963.

Pecherman, Martine. "Philosophie première et théorie de l'action." In *Thomas Hobbes: Philosophie première, théorie de la science, et politique.* Ed. Charles Zarka and Jean Bernhardt. Paris: N.p., 1990.

Pelletier, Francis J. "Locke's Doctrine of Substance." In *New Essays on Rationalism and Empiricism.* Ed. Charles E. Jarrett et al. Guelph: Canadian Association for Publishing in Philosophy, 1978. (*Canadian Journal of Philosophy*, Supplementary vol. 4.)

Plato. *Works.* Stephanus pagination.

Pöggeler, Otto. "Zeit und Sein bei Hedegger." In *Zeit und Zeitlichkeit bei Husserl und Heidegger.* Ed. E. W. Orth. *Zeitschrift für phänomenologische Forschung* 14 (1983): 152-191.

Price, H. H. *Hume's Theory of the External World.* Oxford: Clarendon Press, 1940.

Prins, Jan. "Hobbes on Light and Vision." In *The Cambridge Companion to Hobbes.* Ed. Tom Sorell. Cambridge: Cambridge University Press, 1996.

Reich, Wilhelm. *The Sexual Revolution.* Trans. Therese Pol. New York: Farrar, Straus & Giroux, 1974.

Richardson, William. *Martin Heidegger: Through Phenomenology to Thought.* The Hague: Nijhoff, 1974.

Riedel, Manfred. "Politik und Metaphysik bei Aristotles." In *Metaphysik und Politik.* Ed. Manfred Riedel. Frankfurtam Main: Suhrkamp, 1975.

Roger, G. A. J., and Alan Ryan, eds. *Perspective on Thomas Hobbes.* Oxford: Clarendon Press, 1988.

Rorty, Amélie Oksenberg. "Descartes on Thinking with the Body." In *The Cambridge Companion to Descartes.* Ed. John Cottingham. Cambridge: Cambridge University Press, 1992.

Rorty, Richard. *Essays on Heidegger and Others.* Cambridge: Cambridge University Press, 1991.

———. *Philosophy and the Mirror of Nature.* Princeton, N.J.: Princeton University Press, 1979.

Ross, W. D. *Aristotle's Metaphysics: A Revised Text with Introduction and Commentary.* 2 vols. Oxford: Clarendon Press, 1924.

Ryan, Alan. "Locke and the Dictatorship of the Bourgeoisie." *Political Studies* 134 (1965): 219-239.

Salkever, Stephen. "Women, Soldiers, Citizens: Plato and Aristotle on the Politics of Virility." In *Essays on the Foundations of Aristotelian Political Science*. Ed. Carnes Lord and David K. O'Connor. Berkeley: University of California Press, 1991.

Sallis, John. "Language and Reversal." *Southern Journal of Philosophy* 8 (1970): 381–398.

Sartre, Jean-Paul. *L'être et le néant*. Paris: Gallimard, 1943. Translated into English as *Being and Nothingness*. Trans. Hazel E. Barnes. New York: Citadel Press, 1964.

Saussure, Ferdinand de. *Course in General Linguistics*. Trans. Wade Baskin. New York: Philosophical Library, 1959.

Schneeburger, Guido. *Nachlese zu Heidegger*. Bern, 1962.

Schofield, Malcolm. "Aristotle on the Imagination." In *Aristotle on Mind and the Senses*. Ed. G. E. R. Lloyd and G. E. L. Owen. Cambridge: Cambridge University Press, 1978.

Schouls, Peter. "Human Nature, Reason, and Will." In John Cottingham, ed. *Reason, Will, and Sensation: Studies in Descartes' Metaphysics*. Oxford: Clarendon, 1994.

Schuetrumpf, E. "Kritische Überlegungen zur Ontologie und Terminologie der aristotelischen 'Politik." *Allgemeine Zeitschrift für Philosophie* 6 (1981): 26–47.

Schulz, Walter. "Über den philosophiegeschichtlichen Ort Martin Heideggers I." *Philosophische Rundschau* 1 (1953-1954): 65–93.

Schürmann, Reiner. *Le principe d'anarchie*. Paris: Editions du Seuil, 1982.

Schwegler, A. *Die Metaphysik des Aristoteles*. 4 vols. Tübingen: L. F. Fues, 1847-1848.

Sellars, Wilfrid. "Substance and Form in Aristotle." *Journal of Philosophy* 54 (1957): 688–699.

Sertillanges, A. D. *Thomas d'Aquin*. 2 vols. Paris: Alcan, 1925.

Shields, Christopher. "Body and Soul in Aristotle." In *Oxford Studies in Ancient Philosophy VI*. Ed. Julian Annas. Oxford: Clarendon Press, 1988.

Sieg, Ulrich. "Die Verjudung des deutschen Geistes. Ein unbekannter Brief Heideggers." *Die Zeit* (Hamburg). December 29, 1989.

Simmons, Joan A. *The Lockean Theory of Rights*. Princeton, N.J.: Princeton University Press, 1992.

Singer, Kurt. "Oikonomia: An Inquiry into the Beginnings of Economic Thought and Laguage." *Kyklos* 11 (1958): 29-54.

Skinner, Quentin. "The Context of Hobbes's Theory of Political Obligation." In *Hobbes and Rousseau: A Collection of Critical Essays*. Ed. Maurice Cranston and Richard S. Peters. Garden City, N.Y.: Doubleday, 1972.

Slakey, Thomas. "Aristotle on Sense Perception." *Philosophical Review* 70 (1961): 470-484.

Sluga, Hans. *Heidegger's Crisis*. Cambridge: Harvard University Press, 1993.

Sorell, Tom, ed. *The Cambridge Companion to Hobbes*. Cambridge: Cambridge University Press, 1996.

———. "Descartes' Modernity." In *Reason, Will, and Sensation: Studies in Descartes' Metaphysics*. Ed. John Cottingham. Oxford: Clarendon Press, 1994.

———. *Hobbes*. London: Routledge & Kegan Paul, 1986.

Spellman, Lynne. *Substance and Separation in Aristotle*. Cambridge: Cambridge University Press, 1995.

Spinoza, Benedict de. *Opera*. 4 vols. Ed. C. Gebhard. Heidelberg: Winter 1925.

Translated into English as *The Collected Works of Spinoza.* Ed. Edwin Curley. Princeton, N.J.: Princeton University Press, 1985; and *The Political Works.* Trans. and ed. A. G. Wernham. Oxford: Clarendon Press, 1958.

Stahl, Donald. "Stripped Away." *Phronesis* 26 (1981): 177-180.

Stewart, J. A. *Notes on the Nicomachean Ethics of Aristotle.* 2 vols. Oxford: Clarendon Press, 1892.

Strawson, Galen. *The Secret Connection: Causation, Realism, and David Hume.* Oxford: Clarendon Press, 1989.

Sykes, R. D. "Form in Aristotle." *Philosophy* 50 (1975): 311-331.

Tarski, Alfred. "The Concept of Truth in Formalized Languages." In *Logic, Semantics, Metamathematics.* 2nd ed. Trans. J. H. Woodger. Ed. John Corcoran. Indianapolis: Hackett, 1983.

————. "The Semantic Conception of Truth and the Foundations of Semantics." *Philosophy and Phenomenological Research* 4 (1944): 341-376.

Taylor, Charles. *Human Agency and Language.* Cambridge: Cambridge University Press, 1985.

Toulmin, Stephen. *Cosmopolis.* New York: Free Press, 1990.

Tracy, Theodore S. J. "Heart and Soul in Aristotle." In *Essays in Ancient Greek Philosophy II.* Ed. John P. Anton and Anthony Preus. Albany: State University of New York Press, 1983.

Tuck, Richard. "Hobbes and Descartes." In *Perspective on Thomas Hobbes.* Ed. G. A. J. Roger and Alan Ryan. Oxford: Clarendon Press, 1988.

Tully, James. *A Discourse on Property.* Cambridge: Cambridge University Press, 1980.

Vitruvius. *De architecura.* 2 vols. Trans. Frank Granger. Cambridge, Mass.: Loeb Classical Library, 1934.

Von Arnim, Johannes, ed. *Fragmenta stoicorum vetorum.* 4 vols. New York: Irvington, 1986.

Walsh, James. *Aristotle's Conception of Moral Weakness.* New York: Columbia University Press, 1960.

Warrender, Howard. *The Political Philosophy of Hobbes.* Oxford: Clarendon Press, 1957.

Waterlow, Sarah. *Nature, Change, and Agency in Aristotle's Physics.* Oxford: Oxford University Press, 1982.

Watkins, J. W. N. *Hobbes's System of Ideas.* Oxford: Clarendon Press, 1965.

Wedin, Michael. *Mind and Imagination in Aristotle.* New Haven, Conn.: Yale University Press, 1988.

Weisheipl, James A. *Friar Thomas d'Aquino: His Life, Thought, and Works.* Garden City, N.Y.: Doubleday, 1974.

Weltfish, Gene. *The Lost Universe.* New York: Ballantine, 1965.

Whiting, Jennifer. "Form and Individual in Aristotle." *Journal of the History of Philosophy* 3 (1986): 359-387.

Wippel, John F. "Metaphysics." In *The Cambridge Companion to Aquinas.* Ed. Norman Kretzmann and Eleonore Stump. Cambridge: Cambridge University Press, 1993.

Wittgenstein, Ludwig. *Tractatus Logico-Philosophicus.* Trans. D. F. Pears and B. F. McGuinness. London: Routledge & Kegan Paul, 1961.

Woolhouse, R. S. *Descartes, Spinoza, Leibniz: The Concept of Substance in Seventeenth-Century Metaphysics.* London: Routledge, 1993.

329

Yolton, John. "Locke on Knowledge of Body." In *Jowett Papers 1968–69*. Ed. B. Y. Khabhai et al. Oxford: Basil Blackwell, 1971.

Zarka, Charles. "First Philosophy and the Foundation of Knowledge." In *The Cambridge Companion to Hobbes*. Ed. Tom Sorell. Cambridge: Cambridge University Press, 1996.

————, and Jean Bernhardt, eds. *Thomas Hobbes: Philosophie première, théorie de la science, et politique*. Paris: N.p., 1990.

INDEX

difference, 99

differend, 178

Discipline and Punish (Foucault), 256

discourse, 16, 88, 207, 208, 214, 218

disposition, 22, 26, 32, 43, 59, 83, 206, 267n2; architecture and, 90; Cartesian, 123; disappearance of, 132; divine power and, 119; European states and, 182; form over matter, 36-37, 40, 111; Heidegger on, 225; household and, 65; of imagination, 174; initiative and, 33; intellect and, 52; Lockean, 150; marriage and, 191; monads and, 199; property ownership and, 168; reason and, 62; in Roman Empire, 94; sovereign commonwealth and, 197; the state and, 68

domina, 91, 93

domination, 58-59, 72, 230, 259; Aquinas on, 74; architecture and, 91; Being and, 206; language of, 76; ousiodic, 91, 94, 106, 191. *See also* oppression

Douglass, Frederick, 16, 183, 187-89

Dreyfus, Hubert, 219

Economics (Aristotle), 22

ego, 96

eidos (form), 32, 34, 101, 224, 273n49

empirical purchase, 47, 59, 81, 110, 112, 114, 115

Empiricism/empiricism, 187, 236; metaphysics and, 205-206; ousia and, 70, 107, 108, 157, 177, 178, 202, 254; substance and, 147

emptiness, 250, 266n46

Entschlossenheit (resolve), 3

epistemology, 59, 107

eros, 100

essence, 287n94; Aquinas on, 75, 190; Aristotelian, 76, 290n15; Cartesian, 113; commonwealth and, 172; equation with form, 271n41, 272n48; of God, 217; Hobbesian, 131-32; matter and, 129; nothingness and, 235; ousia and, 24-27, 29-31, 33, 35, 45; of the state, 68

ethics, 22, 71, 81, 84, 86, 229; Aristotelian, 106; Cartesian, 120-25; Hobbesian, 135-39; ousia and, 60-62; Plato on, 99; Spinoza's, 194-98; Thomistic, 82

Ethics (Aristotle), 62

Ethics (Spinoza), 195-97, 245

Europe, 182

euteleia, 3

existence, 6

factory, 96

family, 153, 157-59

Farias, Victor, 1-2

females. *See* women

Fichte, Johann Gottlieb, 177

forgetting, 10, 11, 13

form: equation with essence, 271n41, 272n48; migration of, 167; ousia and, 32-38; relation to matter, 58, 59, 71, 72, 76-79, 111, 119, 159, 220; substantial, 32, 176, 194-95; unchanging nature of, 261

Foucault, Michel, 4, 16, 134, 178, 232, 256, 258

France, 184-86, *186,* 243

Franzen, Winfred, 225, 311n1

freedom, 122, 123, 196-97, 200

Freud, Sigmund, 15, 96

Frye, Marilyn, 87

Frye, Northrop, 185

Furth, Montgomery, 23, 26, 33, 46, 50, 56-57, 80

future, 212-13, 222, 241, 260-61

Garber, Daniel, 115, 118

Gauthier, David, 142

Geach, Peter, 32

Geist (spirit), 3

generation, 49-50, 52, 59, 65

Generation of Animals (Aristotle), 56-58

Germans/Germany, 9, 242, 263n5

Gestell (forgetting), 11, 12, 15

Gill, Mary Louise, 40

Gilson, Etienne, 77, 78, 85, 111

God: in Cartesian philosophy, 116-20, 185, 189, 192, 196, 219; incomprehensibility of, 130, 134, 177; Leibniz's, 200; Nietzsche on, 244; sovereign individual and, 176; Spinoza's concept of, 194, 195-98

government, 168, 171, 176, 187. *See also* state, the

Graham, Daniel, 30, 34, 97-98, 271n41

Greece, 91, 243

"grounding," 209, 231, 232, 245

Habermas, Jürgen, 16, 97, 178, 258; critique of Heidegger, 3-6, 9, 10, 12, 13, 229, 264n12

Hegel, G. W. F., 1, 23, 178, 179, 190, 206, 236, 316n1

Heidegger, Martin, 18, 45, 70, 108, 178, 205-207, 230-33; *Andenken* (souvenir, remembrance), 240-51; *diakena* in *Being and Time,* 207-18; "modern subject" and, 126, 177; Nazi involvement of, 1-5, 13, 229,